THE WAY LOVE IS

Felicity reached out and hugged her daughter. "I just want you to be happy, LeeAnn. Don't you know that?"

"I do, Mother. But sometimes I think you only want me to be happy if you approve of the way I get there. I think you're afraid I'm taking after my great-grandmother and running off with a scalawag."

Of course, Felicity thought, she is right. Felicity had seen Anne Lawrence coming to life again in her own daughter, complete with her patterns and fatal mistakes. "Oh, my darling girl," she murmured, "I suppose I'm afraid of exactly that."

LeeAnn took her mother's hand softly. "Edward cherishes me, Mother. And I believe he will forever."

"Forever is such a long, long time," Felicity said. "When you think of how easily we pick a man to spend our lives with, to spend our lives on, it's a wonder any wives are happy at all."

"Lots are," Lee Ann said. "You were. Grandmama was." LeeAnn reached out and touched her hand. "Can't you believe in it for me?"

Felicity smiled, despite the urge to weep, and nodded.

"Thank you, Mother." LeeAnn got up to leave. At the door, she turned, and said, "I hope you find someone to love again someday, Mama. It's too wonderful to miss forever."

PAMELA JEKEL

NATCHEZ

KENSINGTON BOOKS

KENSINGTON PUBLISHING CORP.

KENSINGTON BOOKS are published by

Kensington Publishing Corp.
850 Third Avenue
New York, NY 10022

Kensington and the K logo Reg. U.S. Pat. & TM Off.

First Kensington Hardcover Printing: September, 1995
First Kensington Paperback Printing: April, 1996

Printed in the United States of America

For my brother, Rick Jekel

Smothered and sanctioned by too many girls,
Two older sisters, a mom and grandmom,
Petted too often in short pants and curls,
Fed long and well at the family trough,
At times, dear, we loved you nigh to death
At others, we tried hard to kill you off.

It took you years to find your life
Under our loving, anxious eyes,
But now you're a man, beyond us all,
Cutting your own acres down to size.

I wonder now that we're gone and grown,
Now our affection runs deep and clean,
Do other families try to atone
For sins suffered on the youngest child,
Or does the kinship of blood forgive
A love so cannibal, so ardent and defiled?

This, then, is the lower Mississippi. Under this sun and against these vast fields of white cotton, a hundred thousand whites and three hundred thousand Negroes make themselves a life somehow. "It is a strange and detached fragment thrown off by the whirling comet that is America."

—DAVID L. COHN,
Where I Was Born and Raised

Preface

Down the Big River, the Big Muddy, the Father of Waters, they came, lured by dreams of land, new game trails, freedom, and sometimes even gold. Each people displaced the other as the seasonal tidal floods of the Mississippi displaced its earlier boundaries; each flood of water—or mankind—altered the landscape in some measurable way, often forever.

Few admired the weather, for the air in summer was hot and wet, leaving skin feeling like damp, matted fur with no refreshment for the dampness. The winters were a tedious cycle of rains, colder and somehow more invasive than water should have been so far south. The land, too, at first glance had little to recommend it. Flat and spread out from the river eastward, never rising more than eight hundred feet, and threaded with alluvial swamps and motionless bayous thick with cane, buckvine, and cypress, it harbored deadly fevers, choleric Indians, and swarms of inhospitable insects. The highlands—if these small buttes could be rightly called such by men who had seen the grandeur of the Rockies—were mere red clay hills peopled by the Choctaw, Chickasaw, and Natchez tribes. They were in turn elbowed aside by the Scotch-Irish, a people as irascible, territorial, and insular as the cottonmouths and copperheads they killed as they bullied their lands into submission. To the south were the piney woods, barrens of moss-hung oaks and skinny conifers which gave way to grassy marshes as the Mississippi curved toward the sea.

In many regions of what man would come to call the Natchez Territory, even the birds could scarcely eke a living from the sparse soil and infertile lowlands. In other regions, the prairie soil was so dark and rich that men who planted tobacco and cotton could lay by two harvests in one season and a fortune in three. The difference in geography and soil made for a sectionalism in the Territory which fostered cantankerous neighbors and hotheaded politics—but also—and this became perhaps Mississippi's saving grace—a resilient pride which allowed a man to stand independent of the passing currents of American culture and embrace his land with a love both clannish and tenacious.

Natchez Territory was a place of beguiling sin, more savage than New Orleans, and more headstrong than Charleston. The wellspring of planter culture along the lower Mississippi, it was also the last wilderness outpost for North Carolina loyalists or Mexican War veterans searching for new land and possessed of enough grit to turn a malarial swamp into a fertile cotton field. The Indians, who held it first, built their temples and churches from dirt, just as the whites who came after them would. Their relics, and the remains of the mastodons and great bears who roamed the swamps, still wash out onto Mississippi sandbars when the tides are low. "Mound-builders," the early explorers called the Natchez, the Choctaws, and the Chickasaws, believing them to be all one people. Numbering more than thirty thousand at the beginning of the eighteenth century, the tribes held sway over the land and guarded it as jealously as they did their women.

Prologue

Natchez Territory, 1729

The smoke from the fire in the center of the meeting lodge was harsh in Henri's eyes, mingled as it was with the rancid pipe fumes from the ten braves surrounding him. Each Natchez warrior drew on the calumet, a pipe of peace festooned with swan feathers, and blew the smoke out again as though his bravery might be measured by the fierceness of his expostulation. Henri needed all his concentration to focus on the chief's words, willing his eyes not to water.

"I will not give you leave to mark trees on this side of the river," Chief Tattooed Serpent was saying. "Too many of the *tobohi*, whites, have done so. Now they fence the game trails and steal the corn before our priests can bless it."

The ancient chief had once been scalped, and his red, wrinkled pate almost matched the vermillion of his face paint. His French was immaculate, Henri marveled, most particularly for a minor noble. No doubt he spoke the barbaric English just as well. It was as the Jesuits said, the Natchez tribe, like the Choctaws and the Chickasaws farther upriver, were no longer *naïfs* and innocent of the white ways. *Mais non,* whether the traders be *couriers du bois* or King George's men, the Natchez knew them too well. But he had not come a thousand leagues down the Big River to be thwarted. Land he would have, and on the fertile, eastern side of the Missicipy, too. He frowned, thinking hard on what he might offer as inducement.

The English had flooded the tribes with trade goods, Henri knew, and at better prices than the French could meet. Twenty years ago, the savages used bows and arrows, made their pots from clay, and were adept at curing and dying hides in their favored colors of red, yellow, white, and black. Now, half the warriors had muskets, their women cooked in iron pots, and blue and red trade cloth replaced their deer-skin robes. The lodges were choked with tin cups, blankets, and beads, and silver mirrors were only trinkets for crawling babies. Not even his offer of livres, cash he could ill afford to share, had changed the obdurate set of Chief Tattooed Serpent's jaw. Indeed, the chief made it plain that he was most reluctant to even meet with another *voyageur,* and Henri suspected he did so only to show his warriors that he could still command respect.

"I have come very far," Henri said mildly, hoping to con-vey firmness with his tone.

The chief only shrugged. "Your kind always do," he said.

"I do not mean to be turned away," Henri added. "I come in peace, to live among you as a brother."

"No *tobohi* is a brother to the Natchez!" One warrior spat into the fire with marked disdain. "From the beginning, they have shown no respect!"

Henri was well aware of the past mistakes of earlier ex-plorers. Every Frenchman in the settlement knew that Cadil-lac, two decades before, had declined to smoke the calumet with the Natchez, feeling it beneath him, and Bienville, com-ing a decade later, also refused to smoke, saying he would trade with the Tunica tribe, but not the Natchez.

Both men had made a terrible error, for the Natchez were the largest, most sophisticated, and most powerful of all the tribes in *Louisiane,* though their villages did not give the im-pression of great wealth. Now, the Natchez viewed the French with wariness, no matter how much they might pre-tend alliance.

"Go back to your own lands!" Another warrior spoke up

now, and Henri felt the first prickings of fear along his palms.

The chief held up a hand for silence and was barely able to contain the murmurs around him. This chief will not lead another season, Henri realized. And I pity the man who must *parlez* with his replacement.

"There is no more room," the old chief said resolutely, glancing around the lodge at his braves. "You must go elsewhere. The far side of the river still has room; you can settle there."

Henri saw that even this sentence did not assuage the warriors about him. They muttered angrily among themselves, punctuating their words with hard-edged gestures, and glared at him, despite the tradition of courtesy he knew they should have followed. They scarcely gave their old chief respect, he realized with growing alarm. This ancient's control was tenuous at best.

He hoped there was one thing which might change their minds. Well, and he had little choice, he told himself, his mouth firming to a thin line. He had come too far to settle for worse land than he'd left farther north, and the colonists had already taken the choice pieces within easy distance of Fort Rosalie. "A musket," he said. "But I want land on this side of the river. Good land and much of it."

The warriors bracketing him grinned abruptly, and the buzz of Natchez, a liquid tongue full of clicks and soft vowels, rose just enough to disclose their agitation. They were fully aware of Governor General Perier's recent command from New Orleans: no more muskets traded to the Natchez. They are a clever lot, Henri told himself, make close attention now.

"Two muskets," the old chief said, and a sigh of anticipation circled the lodge.

"*Non,*" Henri answered firmly, his eyes flashing with anger. "One, I break the law; two, they hang me. One musket only."

An elder to the chief's left side spoke low into his ear, and as the old men murmured together, Henri watched the warrior across the fire from him take out his blade and pull it across his thumb slowly. From where he sat, Henri could see the thin line of red well up. The warrior let his blood drop into the dirt at their feet unconcerned. He stared intently at Henri. There was no mistaking the threat. And nothing at all he could do in retort. A passage from the Jesuit Father's writings about the Territory came to Henri then: *Despite their polish, the Natchez are the only tribe who still practice human sacrifice.*

"One musket," he said, keeping his voice level, "and I pay one horse for a Natchez wife." Henri knew that such an offer was rare, for the colonists mostly wed only their own. A horse for a wife was an exorbitant offer. He could likely have had three Natchez wives for one horse, should a man wish for such havoc in his life. He knew that trading for another pony at Fort Rosalie would likely take his last livre, but if he had to start with nary a coin in his pocket, it would be worth it to get the proper piece of land as his own.

But to his dismay, two of the warriors rose in disgust and strode from the lodge, spitting back something insulting over their shoulders. The chief watched them go, the sadness apparent in the lines of his mouth and the slump of his neck. The silence round the circle of remaining braves revealed their shock at the breech of courtesy.

Chief Tattooed Serpent straightened, and his voice held all the dignity of a younger man in full possession of his power. "Done," he said. "The women prepare the feast of corn tonight. You may attend and choose."

Even the dogs knew the interview was over and began to worry and growl over invisible morsels which might have dropped from the men's hands. Henri stood and bowed shortly, quickly leaving the lodge before the old man could change his mind. It was no accident that he was here at the most sacred time of the Natchez calendar, in October, the month of the Old Corn Moon, when the harvest was celebrated for the entire season. If ever the women would be evident, 'twould be now.

He hurried to where he had tethered his horse, mindful that many eyes watched him as he walked. The pack was undisturbed, his musket still hidden carefully under his blanket where he had stowed it before coming into the Natchez village. His horse nickered at him and shoved against his hip eagerly. He'd been standing for an hour or more tormented by clouds of mosquitoes, hearing the Natchez ponies where they were hobbled by the river, and he wanted that water and soft grass. Henri led the roan down to the river, pondering his bargain.

Surely the warriors had other muskets, though he'd seen no evidence of them in camp. They were eager enough to get their hands on another; that much was certain. The new law of *Louisiane* was clear enough: Any man caught selling or trading firearms to the Natchez would be fined and jailed at Fort Rosalie. For gross infractions or multiple sales, the penalty was death by hanging. A recent law which reflected the colonists' growing concern for the Natchez mood, it would doubtless be enforced with relish by the new commandant of the fort.

But he wasn't the first, Henri told himself, nor would he be the last to break the law. The Natchez had muskets already, traded to them eagerly enough by the French, the Spanish, most especially the British, before the most recent tensions. They had them, and they knew how to use them. One more could not make much of a difference.

The alternative was to claim land on the wild side of the river where the swamps were impenetrable or even a long ride home—probably a walk, since his horse would likely be stolen by the trail bandits—over the Natchez Trace, the wilderness path that led from the territory back up to Tennessee. And back to what? Henri asked himself. There was no land left in Saint Louis, little enough in Tennessee, and none for the price of a musket and a horse. Henri sat down in the shade of a gum tree. The Natchez called the little river which coursed through their lands the White Apple, for the trees which lined its banks. His horse grazed contentedly among them, snuffling up rotten fruit and blissfully nickering whenever a mare called from upriver.

It was an achingly beautiful land, he thought as he watched the breeze move through the trees. A bounty of deer, bear, squirrel, fox, rabbit, and alligator thronged the brush. Clouds of doves and mallards blocked the sun, and pigeons roosted low in the grape vines. Wild turkeys clattered and thumped through the woods, calling their young with little fear, and grouse drummed on every open meadow. Peach, plum, walnut, and fig trees were plentiful, honeysuckle, wisteria, wild rose, and magnolia perfumed the air, and the soil was yellow and gray like the earth of France. The ground was flat and wide as a tureen, green from the river, and doubtless fertile as the finest Virginia soil, not a whit of which he would ever afford in his lifetime. After a decade of climbing mountains, chasing after one more pelt, the idea of nothing higher than a small hill pleased him.

He watched as the Natchez children played determinedly with a ball made of deerskin, kicking it back and forth and yelling with abandon. Young men practiced their wrestling holds and jumps under the watchful eye of an ancient, and others sat at the door of the Keeper-of-the-Word, hearing stories of the Natchez past. Under a grove of gum trees, women painted skins and ornamented them with dyed porcupine quills, and the youngest among them laughed softly, vying for their mothers' approval.

He tried to remember all he had heard about the Natchez before coming to their village, much of it from others who had read Father Le Petit's packet on the savages. The Superior of the Jesuits had spent many years trying to convert the tribe, to no avail. The Natchez, he said, unlike the Choctaw and the Chickasaw, had an established worship already in place, and they were loath to accept the Christian God.

Henri had seen their temples readily enough; they dotted the land and sat looming at the convergence of any two roads. Tall and flat at the top like huge earthen ovens, they were more than an arpent in size, with one small door and no windows. Inside the largest Sacred Temple, it was said, a Castillian sword and helmet, gifts from Hernando de Soto, were displayed in a field of woven feathers, alongside a steel hatchet bearing the fleur-de-lys of France, presented by de la Salle. Inside also rested the bones of fallen warriors, arranged carefully in baskets all around the interior—and even more grisly—the bones of *allouez*—the favorites of dead nobility who had been sacrificed to attend their masters in the spirit world. Three carved wooden eagles painted red, white, and black stood guard on the roof of the temple, pointing the way to the Sacred Locust Tree which stood in the middle of the Grand Square. The first *voyageurs* had carved the arms of France in the bark of the locust, the largest tree for a hundred leagues.

The Natchez chiefs told the Jesuits that they had long ago lived in Mexico, for centuries, it seems, until they were driven out by the more warlike Aztecs. They followed the sun from west to east and finally ruled a territory larger than any Aztec chief ever dreamed of possessing. But they could not leave their old gods behind.

Deities they seemed to have aplenty, Henri grimaced to himself, watching for movement from the village. They worshiped the sun, Tai, they called it, and their high chief as a direct descendant of that solar power. A Sun King, like Louis the Fourteenth, Henri grimaced ruefully.

He had seen him twice. The Sacred Imperial Sun of the Natchez had long white hair with a crown of white swan feathers; he wore bear tippets on his shoulders and soft peltries at his feet. Adorned with pearl necklaces and elaborate tattoos, he was borne on a litter garlanded with red and white flowers, served by a host of lesser chiefs and nobles, and when he passed, the lower classes dropped their eyes. At dawn, he rose each day to ascend the mound and converse with his celestial brother, the Sun. After the Sun King saluted the sun each dawn with a long howl, he then waved his hand from east to west, directing what course Tai should travel that day.

Meanwhile, the rest of the savages bowed and scraped to him as though their lives depended on it. As well they might, Henri frowned. At the Fort, they told tales of seeing as many as two thousand stinkards, what the Natchez called the lower classes, ritually strangled whenever a chief died, privileged to accompany him into the Sacred Temple for all eternity.

The Jesuits said that inside the mound was a sacred flame, kept always burning, and that once the Natchez had more than eight hundred Sun Kings over a territory that stretched from the Missicipy to the Wabash. But a keeper of the temple let the fire go out in one of the mounds, a vast sickness swept the tribe, and many of the chiefs died, as punishment, the Natchez said, for their sins. A lot of stranglings, Henri thought doubtfully. No wonder they're down to three kings and little more than a few hundred leagues now.

Twenty warriors in a splendid canoe, five fathoms long, Henri judged, were crossing downstream and rowing toward the Missicipy. No doubt going to trade at Rosalie. He lay down in the shade to rest fitfully. Tonight would likely be one of the most important of his life, he thought soberly. Best be ready.

At the height of the harvest the Natchez gathered from the far reaches of their territory, traveling over the old buffalo trails to the ceremonial mounds to dance the corn dances and receive the priests blessing on their efforts. The earthen mound at White Apple was the largest for a dozen leagues, forty feet high and more than two hundred feet long, but there were more than a thousand mounds in the Natchez Territory, some of them abandoned, some of them still the focus of ceremonies like this one. The men seemed to hold the political power in the tribe, but it was said that the women owned the lodges and the land and the crops. Therefore, this feast would draw more women than any other, Henri reasoned. If there was a wife to be had within those dozen leagues, she would likely be at the village tonight.

Time was, no *tobohi* at all would have witnessed the sacred ceremonies of the Natchez. But gradually, whites had intruded into even these traditions of the tribe—or perhaps the traditions had become somehow less sacred, as the English blankets, socks, hats, and leggings, and the French ironpots, hatchets, scissors, beads, and mirrors littered the lodges. Now as a crowd gathered to watch the dancers, Henri saw a handful of other white faces among the brown shoulders.

He pressed as close as he dared, watching for the telltale signs of maidenhood among the women. Virgins wore their hair loose over their backs, woven with bits of corn silk and feathers. With ebony-black waves of hair to their waist, wearing white skirts and mantles of mulberry linen, they moved with easy grace. Once married, their hair went into long, tight braids, so that signal was clear enough. The last thing he needed was to affront some jealous husband.

About two dozen dancers performed intricate steps at the base of the mound, half men and half women, weaving in and out carrying corn stalks before them like weapons into war. From a high platform on the side of the mound, three priests stood watching them impassively. More dancers sat at the base, beating skin drums and gourd rattles, blowing cane flutes, and the watching crowd moved as one to the music, swaying with the rhythms of the dancers before them.

Henri watched the crowd more than the dancers, for he clearly could not expect to choose a wife from those women performing. Surely they would be considered too valuable to be given to a white man. Other women, though, carried serving vessels to and from the main lodge which sat behind the mound, and they must be, Henri guessed, the daughters of the local tribe. Of those, perhaps only a quarter wore their hair loose over their shoulders. Perhaps twenty from which to choose. More than enough, he told himself, and stood now at the back of the crowd, no longer making any pretense of watching the ceremonies.

The women who served followed along one after another on the path like industrious ants, though each came from a different part of the village. Like ants, too, they often stopped to touch or speak to each other, saying what more was needed, perhaps, and how the preparations were progressing within the lodge. Henri could see as he moved closer that the earthen pots and platters were of elaborate design and carried roasted fish, peanuts, boiled cane, bear oil, grilled fowl, and a score of other delicacies. Others watched the platters and their bearers, and the women were not oblivious to the eyes.

This was like the September rutting of the whitetail, Henri thought, which made the bucks and the does silly with lust and so distracted. Easier to kill. Just as the does postured, so did the Natchez women, smiling and moving their bodies with conscious grace, even giggling loudly to increase the attentions from the young men at the raveled edges of the crowd. These maidens were decidedly unmaidenly, he saw, frowning slightly. But that was clearly the Natchez way.

And then he saw one woman approaching from behind him, a tall, thin girl, likely no more than seventeen or eighteen summers. She had her hair loose in the maiden style, but with no weavings or adornments of any kind. In fact, her light buckskin robe was plain and unflattering, cut too large for her body, making her arms and legs look even more coltish, her gait less graceful. She wore a simple mantle which passed under her left arm and tied at her right shoulder, leaving both of her arms bare. She had no tattoos or piercings, so far as Henri could see. Perhaps her father could not afford the colored cloth of the white man. No eyes followed her, and she did not seem to notice the lack of attention or care. She carried a large basket on her head, moving swiftly along with none of the banter or posturing of the other maidens.

In that instant, one warrior behind Henri called out to a woman passing close by, and the girl turned instinctively and met Henri's gaze. He smiled and bowed his head deferentially, hoping that she did not think his was the voice which had startled her. Instantly, she dropped her eyes and walked on, ignoring his attentions. Somehow, he admired her more for that.

He moved closer to the line of women and watched her carefully. She studiously avoided glancing up again. She was not comely, he saw, but she had a certain dignity, a sureness in the way she placed her steps and handled her basket, a loose and fluid gait despite the length of her arms and legs, which seemed to belong to a woman of more years. He felt his heart shift slightly in his chest, a poignant flutter in his belly, and the other women of the tribe disappeared for him in that moment. This one, he thought. This one I will take to wife. This one and no other.

He felt eyes on him then, and he looked around to see another warrior watching him intently. A tall brave, taller than she was, observing his attentions to her. He froze, stricken at the potential for danger—and also for the loss of her. But the man only sneered disdainfully at him and turned away toward the dancers. Her husband? Surely not, Henri assured himself, for that was not the jealous look of a husband. Her brother, perhaps. And he did not seem to care if he stared at her or not. And so he turned back to the line of the women and did so.

Later that night, he roamed the village and the adjoining campsites restlessly, wondering if she should be his choice. He knew she lived in one of three lodges, and he finally found himself standing in the shadows of the camp, waiting to see if she might come out. Close to four hundred lodges at White Apple, and she might be anywhere in the village, at the corn storage buildings, the long meeting lodge, even in isolated women's huts.

For all the talk about how advanced this tribe was, Henri judged that the Natchez lodges were much like those the Chickasaw and the Choctaw built farther north. They dug a simple shallow circular ditch in the ground and lined it with

poles which stood upright and were bent over and tied at the
top. Even their ceremonial lodge, where he had met briefly
with their minor chief, was only a larger version of their own
homes. He had been in a lodge or two before meeting with
the old chief, endured the martyrdom of the pipes filled with
tobacco and sumac, the only real relief from the mosquitoes.
The women brought the pots of food, and the men ate from
the pots with their hands, shaking the excess grease upon
their bellies and legs and finally, belching with satisfaction,
wiping their hands on the backs of the foraging dogs. Even
after a score of solitary days on the river, Henri did not wish
for more nights with such company.

There was a time, the Jesuits said, when Natchez lands
spread for twelve days' journey east and west and fifteen
days' journey north and south from what was then and now
their largest village, Grand Village on the White Apple
River. What the French called Saint Catherine's Creek. But
now they were down to less than four thousand people. The
Natchez were supposed to have been peaceful enough at the
beginning, Henri had heard, fishermen and hunters who amiably shared the resources of their land with the white colonists. But they were not so peaceful now.

Yet one piece of information he had of them had been
true, after all. Their women were some of the most beautiful
on the river. Taller with fewer tattoos, their speech more mu-
sical than that of the Choctaw, they scarcely looked savage
at all. And one of them was more beautiful to him than any
other.

She had not been present at the corn feast, to his surprise,
although many of the maidens were there, obviously seeking
suitors. The Natchez women were allowed to flaunt themselves rather shamelessly before guests, and there was no
mistaking their gestures of invitation to the warriors present.
Once he saw how the maidens behaved, he was glad to see
her absent. No doubt many of the younger women chose not
to display themselves in that manner. Perhaps, Henri told
himself, it was only those women who had been of marriage-

able age too long who so openly sought attention from visiting males.

The murmurs of the village were dying down now as the darkness became deeper. A rich day of dance and prayer and feasting had tired many, he supposed, and the next day would be full of the same. For six days, they celebrated thus at the end of the final corn harvest, the largest festival of the year. Now the families gathered together and the talk died, like birds roosting, as they told each other over and over of what they had seen and done.

As he stood and watched, a woman came from the farthest lodge and walked quickly toward the river with a vessel, no doubt sent to get the last water of the day. He realized in an instant that it was she. Once again, he told himself as he hurried after her, it is a fine stroke of luck! Surely God had arranged their meeting—

He came up next to her, speaking softly so as not to startle her in the twilight. In the Natchez tongue, he called, "Wait a moment, please, I would speak with you." He could not think of the word for unmarried woman, so he used the word for "girl."

She turned quickly, holding her vessel before her chest as though for protection. But she did not flinch.

"Please pardon me," Henri said courteously, "I am a stranger here."

She dropped her head and did not speak. Neither did she move.

"I saw you today coming and going, bearing the food . . ." Now, he broke into part-French, part-Natchez, for his vocabulary failed him. He prayed that she might understand his tone if she could not comprehend his words. "I wish to tell you this," he finally said, rather lamely. "You are beautiful."

Even at that, she did not raise her head.

Henri faltered to silence now before her mute demeanor. She would not speak, but neither did she flee. What did that mean? Did the Natchez women signal rejection in this way?

Was it a form of interest that she stood her ground? Finally, unable to think of what else he might say and hampered by limited words in her tongue, he reached out slowly for her water pot and, hesitating to touch her without permission, said, "I will carry this for you?" She gave it over easily, as though she had no will of her own, but she did not raise her eyes to his.

At that moment, a woman called behind him, a loud, imploring cry which electrified the girl before him like a whip to a pony. She moved instantly toward the voice, leaving her vessel in his arms, and he turned to see who had called her so imperatively. It was an older woman, likely her mother by the resemblance which was plain enough, even in the shadows. She walked painfully, with the help of a carved stick, and with one hand, she gestured the girl to her as one might call a child.

Henri understood part of what she said in rapid Natchez, something about simply to ignore him, he was of no matter whatsoever, and he almost felt bold enough to confront the old woman and ask for a moment with her daughter. After all, he had offered a musket and a horse, and had the chief's approval to pursue a likely maiden—but then he did not have the courage. The woman so obviously was used to having her way, looking through him so completely, that he could not make himself move. The girl took her mother's arm and helped her back into the lodge, the woman leaning heavily on her. Not once had either of them glanced at him. He might as well have been a rooted apple tree for all the notice they took of his presence.

He put the pot on the ground outside the lodge and stood, wondering what he might do. Well, at least I know where she lives, he told himself in a daze. Although what good that will do me, I scarcely can say if she is deaf and blind to my presence—

And then a man came forth, the same warrior who had seen him watching her at the dance. He came half out of the lodge and stared at Henri, taking a moment to recognize him.

Henri braced himself for a harsh dismissal—perhaps even a fight—perhaps he had trespassed on some tradition, perhaps she was promised to another or too young—

But the warrior only looked him up and down with obvious scorn and laughed softly, shaking his head as though mocking him for showing her attention. Henri stood there for a moment and then turned away into the protection of the darkness.

What did this mean? It was as though she were ugly or deformed in some way that others could see and he could not. Or perhaps she was so inaccessible to a white man, so prized for some reason and therefore not available to such as he, that her brother did not even feel it necessary to confront him.

Whatever the reason, she clearly did not welcome his attentions. Neither did her family, though they must know that he had been given leave to court and also what he had offered for a prospective wife.

Henri walked over to where his horse was tethered. A black mood settled over him, as often did when he felt both thwarted and confused. These Natchez were a surly lot, he told himself, both conniving and obscure. Why would he want a wife from such a tribe? Why court such heartache, after all?

He recalled the accounts of the last time the Natchez made war on the settlers, almost five years before. A chief's son was shot by a sergeant at the fort for not paying his debts, and the savages retaliated by killing some hapless Frenchmen. Bienville swept up from New Orleans with five hundred soldiers and burned three Natchez villages and their crops to the ground. The war did not last a week, they said, and when the Natchez sued for peace, Bienville accepted their surrender on condition they execute one of their chiefs in the Grand Square of their village. They did so, and peace was the result for a while.

Likely, the Natchez had learned their lesson well enough from that defeat, but their manners were scarcely improved.

Well, at least he had the promise of land—that much was
certain—and if nothing else, he could find a wife elsewhere.
Surely a good woman would be eager to join him, once he
had his feet on his own soil.

He yanked the horse's tether and mounted, setting his jaw
in angry determination. Let the Natchez stew in their own
stubborn juices, he told himself as he rode downriver in the
darkness. Not another night would he spend in their heathen
midst.

The Missicipy was faster near the lands of the Natchez,
faster than it had been farther north when Henri started his
journey from Saint Louis and narrower at the banks, almost
as if it knew that the sea was closer and wanted to hasten its
union with that larger water. The sand bars were numerous
and brown in the hot sun, the ones of quicksand revealed by
their luster and moistness in the hottest sun. The tangled jun-
gle and low-lying swamps spread out on both sides in a rumpled coverlet of green, the darker black of the bayous lurking
under the green like wide, fat snakes.

At the base of the bluffs below the village, two whirlpools
lay just under the water, as if guarding the entrance to the
Natchez sacred mounds. Even from horseback at the top of
the cliff, Henri could see their swirling, hidden depths. He
stood a good while and studied them. The water at this juncture was muddy and torpid, moving so deeply that its power
was scarcely apparent. But the Missicipy was master of illu-
sion. When he returned with his raft, he must remember its
tricks. Even with study, the big river could kill him quick
enough.

Henri knew better than to relax when on the Missicipy. He
had managed to bring his raft safely down all these leagues,
but not without incident. Once at a place called Grand Gulf,
known for its boils and eddies, the river threw itself onto a
rocky hill and, being repulsed, formed two large whirlpools
before it resumed its course at an acute angle to its former

direction. Henri had missed the path between the two eddies and was drawn into one of them, jammed onto the rocks on one side and then catapulted off the bank on the other. Finally, he had fetched up on a jam of cypress logs and flotsam which had been similarly trapped. As he fought to regain control, he lost a pack off the raft as a log snagged and then snapped the rope which held it fast. He missed that pack for a hundred miles—his only book, some extra victuals, and his other pair of shoes. But at least none of his livres were lost; those he kept safely sewn inside his trouser legs.

The big river's current was faster than the Ohio's and flooded more often, each time changing its course and its perils so that even the most seasoned *voyageur* might think it a new river altogether. Some of the most treacherous places, however, remained infamous: There was the Grand Chain, ten leagues above the mouth of the Ohio, which ate more than a dozen *bateaux* each season. Devil's Bake Oven, the Grand Tower, Cornice Rocks, Devil's Anvil, Devil's Backbone—all perils built of rocks and snags which had earned their reputation with those who would travel down what the Indians called the Father of Waters.

Even the best boatmen expected to snag several times a day and toil for many hours to work the boat off whatever halted its progress. A few times Henri pushed so long and hard on his pole to escape a tangled snag that he got a nosebleed.

Yet they kept coming and going: the canoes of birch and spruce, bullboats of buffalo hide, dugouts of cypress or cottonwood, and rude *cajeaux,* rafts of cane bound together by stout rawhide, all of them rowed, poled, or sailed the long, weary leagues between the Gulf and the Illinois country.

Of course, the Indians knew the river best. In hollowed-out *pirogues* of cypress, they were able to carry two score men and a whole season's trade goods—usually without incident and with little portage. 'Twas as though the Missicipy gave them leave and withheld it from all other trespassers.

And they usually picked their village sites well. Normally,

bends in the river were the most difficult to navigate, because the current naturally tried to run a straight course and, in doing so, made a force strong enough to undermine the bank, pulling trees and boulders into the bend. In most places, the deflected current carried the sediment downstream in a diagonal path across the channel of the river and side currents built up sand bars, banks, and finally rich bottom land. At the site of the Natchez village, countercurrents ran so fortuitously that Henri could cross the river without being carried too far downstream—in fact, it took great skill not to be carried back *up*river.

Three leagues south of the Natchez village along a packed, indented buffalo trail, the French fort lay well back from the floodplain. Built by the Natchez for Bienville in 1716, Fort Rosalie was the most southerly outpost on the river, the last effort at civilization, whatever that might be in the Natchez Territory. Henri had seen it only once, when he left his raft there, bought a horse, and turned it north once more to White Apple Village. Crowded by Natchez, Choctaw, and Chickasaw traders, Rosalie was not a place which made Henri feel safe. The Commander, Chopart, was so haughty and prideful that even the settlers murmured against him behind his back. The two dozen soldiers paid scant attention to the needs of the settlers, about two hundred Frenchmen, eighty wives, a hundred and fifty children, and nearly three hundred black slaves. Too many for a family and too few for a colony, Henri thought. Best to strike out on his own. Besides the fleas within its walls were worse than in any stable.

He had come so far, he mused as he maneuvered his horse round deep trail ruts, far in leagues and far in life. He had left his parents' farm in Sault Saint Marie when his mother died, for his father took a new wife and there seemed suddenly less room for four brothers at the table. He and his eldest *frère*, Gaston, took off across the land to the west, headed for Saint Paul. But there was no more land to be had there than farther north, so they built a flatboat and headed down the

Missicipy to Saint Louis. There Gaston met and courted a widow with two small children and thirty arpents of fertile cornfields. Henri left him regretfully, and set out alone once more. It was told in Saint Louis that *Louisiane* was the place for a man with little but determination. Land, they said, was still there for the taking and only the Indians to take it from. Henri set his course for the South.

It had been nearly a decade since he'd seen his father and two brothers; a year since he'd left Gaston in Saint Louis. Nothing was as easy as he had hoped or been led to believe. But perhaps that was the way life always was, Henri told himself as he followed the worn road from the village to the fort, giving his horse his head. Nothing was as easy, and nothing lasted long enough to embrace.

Every people eventually got supplanted, even as the cottonwoods replaced the willows at the water's edge. Once, the Indians said, the mammoths ruled this land. Huge, powerful beasts which killed lions with ease. The hunters drove them across the great river to the west, and they eventually disappeared altogether.

Those hunters were the giants, which the Choctaw called *Nahullo,* a race of men who were taller and larger than those who came after and who ate the flesh of other men after victory in battle. The Choctaw legend said the men were *tobohi,* and the Jesuits said they were the ancient Norsemen of Viking myth. But for all their power, they were unable to resist the newcomers, the Natchez with their superior knowledge of crops and their intricate caste system which allowed them to feed many with the work of few. And so the Natchez ruled the lower Missicipy, taking over the mounds of those who had ruled before them.

And now the French would drive out the Natchez; Henri could see it coming as plainly as autumn winds. Perhaps he, too, would be supplanted before he could even take root.

And yet . . . and yet, he could not help but believe that his fate—indeed, his fortune—was coming to him as slowly but steadily as the great river moved over the land. A vision of the Natchez girl floated up again in his mind, and he quelled it firmly, as he had the last ten times she had appeared in his thoughts. What mattered was the land, he repeated like a prayer. Without the land, all else would be ashes in his mouth.

Fort Rosalie sat back from the river atop a levee, four fathoms higher than the level of the water. The earthen dam had been deposited by the Missicipy over the years with each seasonal flood, and at this particular spot on the river, a small bluff distinguished itself from the flat land all around it. The fort was nothing more than a square stockade, four bastions with a *place d'armes* enclosing a space about twenty-five fathoms long by fifteen fathoms wide. A trading house, the chaplain's quarters, a cluster of wooden cabins, a guard house with a torn, faded banner of fleur-de-lys flapping limply, a powder magazine, a few cannons set on logs, barracks for the soldiers, a stable, a small chapel, all sat at the terminus of the well-worn buffalo trail, a morass in winter rains. Crops were laid out in a haphazard fashion around the stockade walls, and livestock wandered at will.

The settlers had built small cabins upon the surrounding lands, crowding together and making their simple houses as identical as possible. They were plain, uniform boxes of logs with sawed-out doors and windows, each surrounded by an enclosure of picket fence. The windows were covered with paper smeared with bear grease, and deerhides hung down from the doorways. The men walked about in cowhide clogs, and the women and children went barefoot, though the October wind was beginning to chill.

Henri tethered his horse within the walls and kicked away a pesky chicken who scratched and squawked at his moccasin. Even the hen looked careworn and frazzled.

To his alarm, there seemed to be more Indians in the fort than usual, few of them working, most merely sprawled about in poses of abandonment. None met his eyes as he walked past. He went into the trade post, which was nothing more than a lean-to shading a three-board counter, with stacks of dusty goods in a corner.

"*Bonjour,*" he called to the proprietor, "I'll be needing supplies for—"

"And what do you pay with?" the man asked brusquely, leaning over the counter with an air of aggression. His French was unlearned; his beard filthy with yesterday's supper.

Henri felt something in him go cold and angry. It seemed to him in that moment that he had not had a polite word since he'd arrived in the Territory. He knew better, however, than to display his silver in such a rathole. He glared at the man and took a single coin from his purse, slamming it on the counter.

"That's well enough," the man guffawed suddenly, "for your good name won't buy much in these parts, stranger. You're in *Louisiane* now."

Henri gave the man his order, matching his brusqueness for brevity, allowing himself a visible sneer when the proprietor had less than half of the goods required. While the man assembled the shot, an iron hoe, two knives, a pickaxe, powder, salt, towlines, and other things Henri needed, he leaned against the wall and watched the inhabitants of Fort Rosalie.

Saint Louis was a bustling city compared to this outpost in the wilderness. Henri sighed as he remembered it, the narrow streets crowded with every kind and color of people and bastard combinations of copper skins, white skins burned raw by the sun and wind, and the ebony skins of slaves. Indians from the Delaware, Sioux from the North, the Knisteneaux from the Great Slave Lake, Mandans from the upper Missouri, Shoshoni and Nez Perce, the tall, dark Seminoles, the native Illinois warriors, and strays from a dozen distant tribes. All of them converged on Saint Louis with their furs.

And to buy the pelts came the whites: Creoles from New Orleans; Spanish from Cuba, Mexico, and Pensacola; French from Canada; *emigrés* from France and England; and then the half-breeds, quarter-breeds, fur traders, and *voya-*

geurs, some of them wild as the Pawnees with the mark of solitary wilderness still on their grave, closed faces. Saint Louis was a nation unto itself, now that he recalled it from a distance. Fort Rosalie, on the other hand, was a desperate, pathetic sumphole in the swamp, a shanty boat bearing a precarious load of the shiftless, the drifters, and the exiles.

The women among them looked stolid and resigned in their shapeless cloaks, half pelt, half worn woolens. Like draft mares used to hard loads, they kept their heads down, mostly, and their backs bent to their hoes. No wonder the Natchez were sick to death of this lot.

"That comes to one hundred livres, silver," the man said, gesturing proudly to the few parcels he'd rustled together on the counter. "Excellent merchandise, *monsieur,*" he added. "Nothing like it south of Memphis."

"And that is the only reason," Henri said dryly, "you are able to keep in business at all." He surveyed the goods carefully, frowning as he did so. " 'Tis a good thing you have less than half of my order, with these prices. And these towlines are rotten; they won't last a league downriver."

The man shrugged. "They're the last I got, *vraiment.*"

"Sixty livres," Henri said, adding two more silver coins to the lone original one on the counter.

"Done," said the proprietor, sweeping them toward him.

Henri had expected an argument, at the very least a display of heartfelt pleas from the man, and so he hesitated for an instant. "You mean to send your scum out to rob me the minute I'm outside the gates?" he asked.

The man's eyes narrowed, but his grin was unwavering. "Naturally," he joked. "That's the only way I can recoup my losses."

Henri snorted. It would not do to take this arrogant pig too seriously. "Losses? For this sort of offal, you might well pay your customers to take it off your hands."

The man grinned. "Plenty are willing to pay. *You* were willing enough, *n'est-ce pas?*"

Henri shook his head in scorn. "I will be back here in a week or more. I will need another mount."

"A horse? I have plenty of excellent horses," the man gestured expansively, "with the finest bloodlines from Spanish ponies—"

"I will be satisfied if the beast lives out the month." Henri sighed hopelessly. "Have one ready for me in a fortnight."

"You trade yours?"

Henri shook his head, reluctant to give any more information than necessary.

"You are leaving the Territory, then? Taking the trace northwards? You know the Natchez are leaving within the month; the commandant has ordered it. Their village will soon be open for settlement, some of the best lands this side of the river—"

"What do you say?" Henri asked, startled.

"Thirty days he gave them to clear off and take their heathen gods with them, or the soldiers will burn them out."

"And they have agreed?"

The man shrugged disdainfully. "They have no choice, yes? Last time they dared open rebellion, they were cut down like grasshoppers before the scythe."

"Where will they go?"

"*Noco,*" the man shrugged, using the Natchez for "who knows?" with ill-disguised irony. "Likely crowd the lodges of the Choctaw or the Chickasaw, or cross the river like the buffalo, who gives a damn? But go they must, and soon. So perhaps you'll not need another mount, eh? No need to leave, with new lands open. Perhaps you need a mule, instead."

"I'll need a horse," Henri said shortly. Without giving the man space to respond with another question, Henri walked away.

He could not get from the fort fast enough to suit him. Perhaps with luck, his visits there would be few: once to get a horse, another to be married in the sight of God. As he

walked from the stockade to where he'd tied his horse, he
slapped at his chest. Finally, he had to put down his supplies
and tear open his shirt. Red welts were beginning up his ribcage, running under his armpits. He pinched a large flea between thumb and forefinger, and a dozen more hopped off
his skin. He hurried to his raft, lashed his goods securely,
and stripped down to nakedness. The water of the Missicipy
had never felt so welcoming.

It took Henri a full day more to reach a place where he felt
he was far enough away from the fort and still within reach
of lands which the Natchez had the right to trade. He rode
inland to the east, pleased to note that the swamps had not
encroached on this area as heavily as to the west. He traipsed
the wooded fields for most of another day, digging in the soil
with his stick, noting carefully the movement of the game
over the land, putting his hand on selected trees, and even
kneeling to taste the dirt with his tongue.

The land was covered with magnolia, walnut, yellow poplar, oak, sassafras, and mulberry, and trellised with grape
vines. Four leagues, he judged, south of Fort Rosalie and a
league east of the river, he stopped and made camp for the
night.

In all, he guessed he had covered more than two leagues,
and by the end of the third day, Henri was certain in his soul
that this piece of land was meant to belong to him. In his
mind, it seemed that the trees almost whispered a welcome;
the grasses reached up to caress him. At the end of his exploration, he sat within the embrace of the roots of an ancient
live oak shrouded with the moss called "Spanish beard,"
and pictured the house he would build on the small rise
before him.

For the first time in more than a decade, he felt he had
come home. His thoughts turned again and again to the Natchez girl, and now he did not try to discipline his mind away
from her. She would grace the land like the wildflowers
which grew in the fields, strengthen it like the tree roots
themselves.

No other piece of land would satisfy him, he knew, and no other woman would possess his heart as she had. Therefore, he told himself, rising with new conviction, he had no choice. He must go back to the tribe and lay his claim to both the land and the woman.

He went back to the river and marked on a flat piece of wood in French the words that "Henri Dablon, in this month of November, the year 1729, claims the land from this point on the river east to the large live oak, north to the edge of the swamp, and south to the red creek, by the Grace of Our Lord." He lashed the board to a post and sank it deeply in the bank, high so that it might be seen from a distance. Then he sat down and cut off his beard, finally shaving himself closely. The Natchez, like most of the tribes, were hairless except on their heads, at least if they were full-blood. He had seen them bathing often enough; even the women had no hair between their legs or under their arms. He felt he would be more appealing to his bride if he matched the men she knew.

The effort did not tire him but only inspired him to new energy and hope. He mounted again, turning the horse upriver to where he had hidden his raft north of the fort. This time, he would pole it through the shallow currents near the shore and leave the roan behind at Rosalie, for he would need to bring not only his woman but her goods along with him. As he rode, it seemed to him that the river murmured now a welcome instead of a rebuke.

It took him twice as long to pole upriver as it had taken him to float down, and by the time he arrived back at the Natchez camp, it seemed as though more than a month had passed. The mood in the village had changed markedly, and Henri felt alarm as soon as he walked among the lodges, even though he cradled his musket openly in his arms.

Not a single set of eyes greeted him with welcome. The women did not glance his way and smile, and the children did not follow after him for what they might find in his pockets. Every face seemed set and hard, closed and secret, and he knew that only his previous agreement with Tattooed Serpent allowed him passage there at all. He had the feeling that after he passed, groups of warriors glared after him, muttering among themselves and fingering their killing knives. He remembered then what the word *Natchez* translated to: "men who run to war." Nothing but the promise of his land and his woman could have kept his feet moving toward the chief's lodge.

And when he found the old man, he was scarcely reassured. The chief looked to have aged five years in ten days. His anxiety had been replaced by bitterness, and he showed little patience for the ritual courtesies which before would have taken up half the morning.

Henri placed the musket and a small sack of powder and shot before him on the chief's mat. "I have chosen my land," he said. "I lay claim to it now, as we agreed."

The chief stared at the musket a long while, and Henri could feel the sadness in him. "We should never have let the first one of you among us," he murmured, half to himself. "The first one, we should have killed instantly and left his head on a spike at the river to warn the rest of you away."

Henri tried to keep the rebuke from his voice. "Soldiers would have come to punish you," he said. "Your people would have been scourged from the river." His words sounded less convincing, weaker in French than in the Natchez gutturals.

"And so we shall be, after all," the chief replied. "It has not mattered. Our crops, our game, our lands, even our women. We have shared all this, and it has not mattered." He picked up the musket and handled it lovingly. "When the summer comes around once more, we shall be gone from the river like the geese. Most of us will be dead."

Henri nodded to the weapon. "That may make a difference."

The old man laughed, but there was no mirth in his voice.

"I told you, Frenchman, nothing will make a difference. Nothing has, and nothing will." He put the musket behind him with finality and clasped his hands. "What need did we have of the French?" the chief asked, almost of himself. "Do we live better today, that they came among us? We used our bows and arrows to provide our lodges with food; now we use their muskets and we give them our corn. We had skins which were warmer than their thin, red cloth. Before the French, we were men. Now we are slaves." The ancient gazed at the ground. "We granted them land, saying it was good for the same sun to shine on us both. That we could walk as friends in the same path, that we should share as brothers. But you French . . . you quarrel and fight among yourselves. We live peacefully. You are envious. You slander your brothers. You are thieves and deceivers. You are not generous." The old man made as if to rise.

Henri saw that the interview was over, and he rushed to make his second trade. "I have chosen a wife," he said. "I will bring the horse up from the fort in less than a week, if she is willing."

The chief said nothing. His tired sadness began to seep over Henri like a cold cloak, and he fought to keep his spirits optimistic, his voice hopeful. "She is young, perhaps," Henri went on, "but not too young. She lives with her mother, I think, and her brother, in the lodge with the two red hands on the side."

The chief made a grimace and stood up painfully. "Choose another, Frenchman. You have chosen badly."

Henri reached out and grabbed the old man's arm, in itself a breach of courtesy, he knew, but he was suddenly desperate. "What do you mean? I have chosen my wife. What is wrong with her?"

"You speak of the girl who does not lift her head to any man? The one with legs like a deer?"

Henri nodded, speechless before the old man's telling description.

The chief pushed off his hand with disgust. "She can be

wife to no man; you should know as much. She is the youngest of her sisters. She must stay unmarried and care for her mother. That is our way, Frenchman, and if you had learned anything at all about our people, you would have known this was so.''

"She will *never* marry?'' Henri asked, his voice hollow.

"Not until her mother dies, and that will likely be ten snows or more.''

"But—that is barbaric,'' Henri said, unthinkingly. ''To enslave her simply because she was born the youngest—''

The chief smiled thinly. ''That is the tradition of our people. We do not find it barbaric at all.'' He turned to walk from the lodge.

"But has she no say in her fate?''

"She wants none. Choose another!'' the old man shouted back at him, and he strode away, his spine straighter and taller than when he first came into the lodge.

Henri sat for a moment, stunned. She would never marry. She might as well be dead to him—to any man—for as much good she could share. All of her life, she would be yoked to an old woman, doing for her what her husband might have done for her if he were alive, simply because she had the misfortune to be born last. The sense of loss he felt was keen and sharp, but the sadness he felt for her was even greater. What a terrible waste of youth!

In fact, it was not surprising, now that he pondered it. The lower castes of the Natchez did the will of the nobility without apparent resentment, seemingly without thought, following them even into death with a mild and unresisting temper. Why should the daughters not show the same blind obedience to their mothers? Such fealty might well mean the destruction of the Natchez, ultimately, but at least it was a sure enslavement.

A barbaric entombment, he thought. Buried alive in her mother's embrace until she would be too old ever to enjoy a man's embrace.

The sadness began to retreat then, and anger flared in him,

almost as if she were his child rather than his intended wife.
He knew, as deeply as he knew that the land he had chosen
was the only place on earth which would fulfill his dreams,
that the woman he had chosen was also the only one for him.
He was determined to have both, for he realized that one
without the other was like food without drink. Both were
necessary to sustain his heart's life.

He recalled, then, how his brother Gaston had reprimanded him for his illusions. "You are more romantic than
a girl," Gaston had laughed at him years ago. "You believe
that there is only one woman who can make a man happy?"
He had grinned, gesturing about the tavern where they sat
then to the half-dozen wenches in attendance. "If a man's in
the mood to be made happy, almost any *femme* will do."

Henri had laughed along with his brother then, but he
thought of those words often as he made his way into the
wilderness. Somewhere, he knew, there was the place for
him, the woman for him, too. And he had always believed
that once he saw her, he would know her. Now he had seen
her, and she was not available to him, not to any man.

He stood abruptly, fired with new firmness. By Christ, it
would not be. He could not bear it. He *would* not let it be.

Henri went from the lodge, ignoring the covert glares
around him. Let them look, he thought, or not look as it
pleases them. For all their fine names—Grand Sun, Tattooed
Serpent, Little Sun—and all their manners, they were nothing more than animals.

Henri waited at the fringe of the camp, sheltered in a
grove of low magnolias, thinking and watching. He could
see, from a distance, the warriors coming and going, to and
from their ponies, from lodge to lodge, from river to camp,
and after hours of watching, their movements began to take
on a pattern. Like watching ants move to and from a discovered source of food, it was possible to discern a communica-
tion, a goal, even a group movement which was somehow
larger than the individual movements of the men.

The men kept circling the Sacred Locust in the middle of

the Grand Square. They filed by the tree, shaking their gourd rattles, gesturing with their painted clubs, and digging their hatchets into the base of the huge roots which broke the surface of the hard-packed earth.

The Natchez were preparing for war. He had not been able to see it clearly when he was among them; perhaps they were not to that stage during his last visit. It was the more alarming since he knew that the tribes never warred in the winter, saving those months for the hunt.

But now, it was obvious to him, especially from a slight distance. There was a controlled frenzy to their movements, with much conversation and gestures which could only be interpreted as aggressive.

Yes, the plan was for war. The sureness of it sent a coldness through him, for what it would mean to his life. War with the tribes meant a large killing and many deaths, for however desperate and pathetic the settlers at Fort Rosalie might appear, they would defend themselves fiercely. Last time, it meant destruction for the Natchez; the time before that, in 1722, they'd nearly wiped out the small settlement, but then smallpox hit the tribe and cut them down in their turn. No matter which way it went, war would mean devastation to every dream he had.

His only choice—indeed, his only hope—was to take his woman and secure his land and stay as far removed from the fighting as he could. His woman. He realized that he now thought of her that way: his woman. His wife. He needed only to make it so.

When dark came, Henri moved closer to the village. The movements of the warriors had slowed but not ceased. Whatever their plans, they would likely implement them soon. Shields had been freshly painted and were hanging up to cure; strips of jerky hung over all the fires in preparation, perhaps, for a time when there would be no time for cooking, no safety for fires. Even the dogs were quiet.

He crept closer to the woman's lodge, glad now that it was set back from its neighbors slightly, in a sheltering grove of trees. He waited silently in the darkness, willing his heart to be calm, his breath to be easy. For what seemed hours, he sat, feeling himself as invisible to the tribe and those he watched as a hidden owl in thick branches who watched a family of field mice.

He thought of the last war the Choctaws had made on the Chickasaw, at the behest of the *Louisiane* governor, who promised them trade goods in payment. *Mercenaires,* they became, and then war was no longer sacred and honorable. Ironically enough, a storm later destroyed much of New Orleans, rushed upriver and flattened the corn crops at Natchez, sank ships at anchor, and made it impossible to get trade goods to the Choctaw after all, despite four hundred Chickasaws scalped and a hundred taken as slaves. Now the Choctaw might well spoil for war again, and this time against the French, who could not keep their promises.

What if, even now, they were allied with the Natchez against every white man in the Territory?

He thought of the dangers he had faced on his journey— the storms which turned the Ohio to ice in hours, the winds which swirled the water so high that he had to hold on to a tree with one hand and bail with the other. The earthquakes which moved the rapids and made islands appear and disappear. The fevers and ague which plagued a man when he spent too many nights on the river, the snakes which fell on him out of the trees as he tied his boat for the night—he had survived them all. Was he now to die under a Natchez tomahawk?

Suddenly, she came from the lodge, hurrying with her head down. There was no time to plan, no time to choose a better space or chance. He rose from the shadows, came behind her, and pulled her back behind the trees, holding her tightly to him, one hand over her mouth. "I will not hurt you," he said in rapid Natchez, keeping his hands from places on her body which might make her fear his intentions. "I will not hurt you, make no sound."

She struggled, but not wildly, as though she had a lesser

force of life in her than he had expected. Or perhaps she had somehow sensed his coming. He pulled her away from the village quickly, still keeping his hand over her mouth. To his surprise, it was almost easy to take her, requiring far less strength than he would have supposed. It made him feel powerful and determined, and as they left the village, he took his hand away from her mouth cautiously, seeing that she was not going to try to sound an alarm.

"I will not hurt you," he said again to her, letting her loose and standing close without touching. "They say you will never marry. But I mean to have you, no matter what they say." He spoke mostly in French, a little in Natchez, and he doubted she understood a third of what he said. "If you try to run, I will hobble you like a pony," he said then, pointing to his rope. "Will you try to run?"

She said nothing; neither did she raise her eyes from the ground. He could only assume that her silence meant assent. He took her hand and led her to his hidden raft, still half-stunned by what he had done.

She fell into an exhausted sleep as soon as he had her bundled aboard the raft. He almost tied her hands, but was afraid to risk her hatred by such treatment. Better that she escape than that she despise him. Fear seemed to come off her like a sheen of sweat. He watched her closely, and she did not stir. Almost as if she sought refuge in sleep, she stayed determinedly still, her eyes shut fast, for what seemed hours as he poled away, farther and farther south.

Henri believed, and more with every dip and push of his pole, that if he could only get the Natchez girl to his land, could only walk her over the soil, let her touch the trees, put her bare feet in the creek, she would love it as he did. She would want to stay with him. She would sense his commitment to it and to her. She would be his wife, bear him children, and tend him lovingly into his dotage. His mind told him that his belief made no sense, but his mind did not mitigate his emotions that night. She was so beautiful, even as she slept, huddled on the middle of the raft, her blanket pulled about her though the river air was warm and damp. So lovely in her silence. Once she was his, all men would envy him his good fortune. The best land on the river; the best wife in the Territory. He mused thus, as he slid downriver, his thoughts a whirling jumble of eddies and confused currents of hope.

When he started from White Apple, the moon was high, so bright on the water that he was able to see to navigate a route he had already taken once. But as the night wore on, the moon slipped lower, and he began to fear for the raft in the eddies and shallows of the great river. He finally pulled to the edge of a sandbar and secured the raft, leaving it in the water lest the river fall in depth and strand it in the night.

The instant the raft stopped moving, she opened her eyes warily, and he saw then that she had not been asleep at all. He bowed shortly to her, watching her carefully. "Please do not be afraid," he said to her in French, wondering if she understood a word.

"Do you mean to kill me?" she asked then, her French comprehensible if badly accented.

He was startled not only by her question but by her ability with his language. *"Mais non!"* he assured her, sitting down beside her at some distance. He hoped by appearing shorter, he would seem less of a threat. "You speak French?"

She was silent.

"I speak some of your tongue," he tried, haltingly, with his few words of Natchez and gestures. "What is your name?" he asked her in her own language.

She was still mute and only watched him carefully, her dark eyes gleaming in the moonlight like those of a cautious doe moving out of shadow and into the open.

"My name," he said, gesturing to himself, "is Henri Dablon. I come from"—and here, he hesitated, not knowing how to tell her how far he had come, so very long ago—"from far to the north. What are you called?"

She murmured something he could scarcely hear, so he moved closer to catch her words. She started when he moved closer. He stopped and put out a hand in a calming gesture. "Please say again. What are you called?"

"Oka Kapassa," she said clearly.

"Cold water," he repeated back to her in French. "Your name means 'cold water,' yes? Oka Kapassa."

She nodded slightly.

He was filled with triumph. She had told him her name and it was as beautiful as she was. "I will call you Oka," he said proudly. "You will call me Henri?"

She said nothing. She glanced away at the river. "You take me to the *tobohi* village?" she asked then, her voice soft and sad.

She asked the question in Natchez, and he was not certain he had understood her. "Say it again, please?"

Her voice rose then, almost a hint of impatience. "You take me for slave? *Tobohi* slave?" As though she were in a hurry to hear the worst.

He was shocked. It had never occurred to him that she would not understand what he wanted her for. And then he remembered that the Natchez women sometimes committed suicide to preserve their honor. "Never for slave," he said. "For wife. I want you for wife. I have land," he rushed to reassure her. "I have many lands, fine lands," he fumbled with the unfamiliar Natchez words. "I need wife. Children." He pantomimed an embrace. "Family. *Famille,*" he added for emphasis.

She began to weep, very quietly, almost too softly to hear.

"Please do not cry," he said sadly. "If you cannot bear me, I will return you to your mother. But I had hoped you might grow to care for me. I want you for my wife, Oka. Over all other women, I want only you." He felt naked before her as he said the words in French, realizing hopelessly that she likely did not understand half of them. "I did not want to steal you," he said in confusion. "I wanted to trade for you with honor. I offered a horse! But the chief said you would never marry." He saw that she was still weeping, and his heart was broken. "I had hoped"—his voice thickened with sadness—"I had hoped that you might accept me. But if you cannot, I will return you. Your mother can keep the horse."

She moved to one side, and the blanket fell away from her slightly. With one hand, she reached to retrieve it; with the other, she reached out and touched his hand. "You want me for wife?" she asked haltingly.

He grasped her hand quickly. "Yes. Before God, I do."

She looked down at her hand enclosed within his, gazing at it as though she had never seen that part of her body before. But she did not remove it. She sighed and closed her eyes for an instant. Then she said, "Oka be wife." She looked up at him timidly. "Wife to Henri."

His heart thudded unexpectedly as he saw the truth. She was not afraid, nor angry at having been abducted. Not even disgusted with him for his clumsiness. She was grateful! He could not fathom his good fortune. Somehow in the midst of chaos, they had found each other. They would rescue each other. They were, in fact, each other's best chance.

He reached over and awkwardly embraced her, pulling her close to him, feeling the strong tide of tenderness rush over him as she hesitantly nestled closer, and he gently kissed the top of her head. Together they sat thus for a long while, listening to the lap of the water on the sides of the raft. And sometime in the early dawn, as the cries of the waterbirds rose over the river, Henri Dablon pulled his Natchez woman closer still and consummated the desire he had felt for her since the first time she passed him by.

With the dawn, they were moving again downriver, her voice low and melodious, answering his questions. They found that if they spoke the Chickasaw trade language, they could understand each other more than if they attempted either Natchez or French. At first, he asked her questions simply to get her to speak, for he so enjoyed watching her, listening to her. She told him stories of her people, how the

Great Spirit had fashioned the first Natchez man out of clay and then, pleased with his invention, had breathed life into him. The first man sneezed and out of his nose hopped the first woman.

Henri smiled at that, and yet he had to admit it was no more impossible to believe than that Adam had donated a rib to Eve's creation.

She also told him that after man had grown in numbers, a great flood came and destroyed all the tribes, but a few escaped to high ground and it was those Natchez who had repeopled the earth. Once again, he could see little to question in her legend. After all, it was not so different from the Christian tradition. And so, he finally asked her, "Could you accept my God, then, Oka?"

She thought for a long moment. And then she nodded mutely.

"It may not be easy," he told her reluctantly. "There are many *tobohi* who will not accept you, even if you accept their ways and their God. We will both need courage, if we are to succeed together."

She lifted her head proudly and gazed at him. "I am young, but I am not a child. I have proven myself in the tests of womanhood."

"And what are those?" he asked, almost amused.

She ignored his amusement. "Many tests, for the young men and for the young women also. I stood longest at the wasp's nest of all my sisters."

"What did you do there?"

"You must stand in the middle of their attack and swing your stick at them, doing battle. You must war as long as you can endure their stings. I stood longer than anyone else."

He was impressed and let her see it. "And did you kill very many of them?"

She smiled. "The wasps always win the war. Only honor in battle matters."

He nodded, understanding. "Then you will do well dealing with the *tobohi* you will meet."

By midday they reached the fort; Henri beached the raft upriver and told her to wait there until he had found someone to marry them. He was anxious to have the ceremony performed as quickly as possible by someone with the authority to do so. Oka did not need to be told to keep low and quiet. She had the knack of becoming very small, he noticed, and almost as invisible as a fawn hidden in bracken. How many times in her girlhood had she used that talent, he wondered, when her mother had called?

When he reached Fort Rosalie, his sense of impending danger bloomed into strong fear. It seemed to him that the numbers of Indians inside the fort had doubled. They lounged everywhere, moving to and fro with an easy grace and a sense of purpose. What if her brother was among them? If he were recognized, surely they would blame him for her abduction. When he asked at the gate, he was told that the Natchez had come to borrow muskets for a big deer hunt. The guard supposed that likely the Natchez would need more provisions than usual, since they were preparing for their move to the north, away from their ancestral village.

"And they've been given the weapons?" Henri asked.

The guard shrugged. "Why not? There was a rumor of war, but the commandant says there's nothing to fear. They dare not try that again. But you should have seen them dance! They sang the old songs and pranced and twirled, blowing on their conch shells and beating on their drums. All painted and cavorting—my boy will never forget the sight of it. Are you going to sign for land? If you want to make a claim, you best do it now, their land is already being portioned out."

Henri thanked him quickly and headed for the chapel.

He found Father Poisson kneeling in the back of the altar, his face lined and half-hidden by his cowl. His black robes were in need of a good brushing, and his hair was unkempt.

"Father, I have a woman, can you come at once? We wish to be married."

"Bring her then," the man muttered. He did not rise from his knees.

"I—I cannot," Henri faltered.

Father Poisson turned to him then and struggled to rise. Henri put out his hand and helped the old man to his feet. "Why not?"

"She—she is ill. I brought her downriver, and she waits at the raft, but I dare not bring her here. I have a horse."

"Is it the smallpox?" Father Poisson hissed in a fearful whisper.

"Ah no, likely just the ague, but—"

The cleric pinned Henri with a hard gaze. "She is heathen?"

Henri gave up and nodded his head. "Please, Father," he murmured.

"Fall to your knees, my son," he said, "and pray to the Holy Father to forgive your sins." He took Henri's arm with strength beyond his years. "Come. I will hear your confession."

"There's no time for that, Father," Henri insisted. "The Natchez mean to make war, I'm sure of it. No one will believe they would dare, but they're on their way here now."

"Nonsense," the priest said, almost kindly. "I have heard the rumors also. They are certainly false. And even if they were true, your sins woud be that much more in need of confession. No time? No time for God? Not on this side of eternity, my son. Now, come." And he took Henri's arm again to pull him toward the confessional.

"Father," Henri said, yanking his arm away. "I have taken a woman." He faltered then, hesitant to say the words in this holy place. "I have—known her. We must be married at once."

The priest frowned at him. "And what woman is this?"

Henri paused, reluctant to tell this priest the worst truth. Yet he would surely discover it sooner or later. "A daughter of the Natchez. I want her for my wife." He tried to help the priest toward the door. "She is innocent of her people's sins,

Father, and we wish to be married in the eyes of God. She will accept the faith—"

"A Natchez woman? You want me to marry you to a savage even as you tell me they will rise against us once more?" The priest's eyes cleared for a moment, and Henri could see on his face the man he once was, before the Territory had pulled the strength out of his soul. "You need more than confession, my son, you need chastisement!" He pushed Henri violently away from him. "Get out! Get out of my sight!"

Henri blanched and stumbled back, stricken by the awfulness of the priest's words. "Holy Father!" he pleaded. "Do not forsake me now!"

"*God* will forsake you!" the priest shouted as he ran from the church, "your own people will forsake you, and she will cut out your heart while you sleep!"

Henri ran across the courtyard, avoiding the Natchez around him, took his horse from the stable, and hurried out the gates, slowing to a trot only as he put the fort well behind him. By the time he reached the river, he was resolved. I will go no more around priests, he told himself. They are made mad by their trials in the wilderness, and they lose sight of God. No God of mine would forsake me as His priest has! We will be married in the sight of God, if I have to say the words myself.

Henri realized that he was thinking heresy, certainly against Mother Church if not against God Himself. But he had no time to wonder if he would be forsaken further, for he heard then the sounds of canoes, many of them by the splashes, and paddled by warring Indians, by the furtiveness of the noise. Another traveler might have not heard them at all, but Henri had spent too long on the river not to know the slip and shush sounds of Indian canoes.

He dismounted, slid behind some tangled cottonwoods, and waited. His jaw stiffened in shock when he saw not a few canoes but eight, each one holding twenty Natchez warriors. The men were painted for massacre, their faces half-red, half-black. Not a quarter-hour from the landing which would take them to Fort Rosalie.

Henri had to make a swift decision. He could race back to the fort ahead of them and warn the people there, possibly saving some lives. Yes, they had been warned, but now war was on them for certain. Perhaps even a few moments' head start might let some of them escape.

But so many Natchez were among them already.

If he went back to the fort, he risked being taken himself, but that was not the worst of it. He also risked losing Oka. The war party might find her, a fleeing colonist could discover her, or she might simply change her mind and leave him of her own accord. And what if he were wounded? Alive but unable to make it back to her for help? She might think him caught and killed and so abandon herself to whatever fate might bring. Or even hasten her own fate in despair and shame.

There was no real choice, he knew then, as his mind catalogued for him all the horrors which she might endure. If he saved a dozen lives and lost Oka in the trade, it were no bargain at all. He could not risk it. He would not warn his own people if it meant losing his wife.

Henri realized that he had crossed a line in his heart, knew, too, that God saw him and likely hated his choice. He mounted noiselessly and turned away, keeping the brush between him and the river, in the opposite direction that the war party paddled.

He soon found the raft. Oka had pulled it into a tangled mass of tall grasses. Clearly, she had heard the war party coming in time to move it from its beached position, and he was thankful she had the sense to do so. But where was she? With mounting concern, he tied his horse and searched the sandy beach and the grasses, looking for prints or matted areas which would reveal her trail. He dared not call out, nor could they stay long so close to the fort. At any moment, they might be discovered. Surely she would not go far from the raft—if, in fact, she were still waiting for him.

Once the thought struck him, that perhaps she had abandoned him after all, his concern turned to despair. He was on the verge of calling out to her, heedless of who else might hear, when she suddenly appeared at his side, startling him.

She had emerged from the reeds like a sleek water creature, covered with waterweeds and drenched to the skin.

"You were hiding under the water?" he asked her, hurrying her to the raft.

She nodded, beginning now to shiver, even though the air was warm. "I saw the warriors," she said.

"They mean massacre," he said. "There must be fifty of them inside the walls already." As he spoke, he was readying the raft for continuing downriver.

"War," she murmured, her eyes horrified. "The chief could not stop them, then."

He turned and stared at her. "You knew it was coming?"

She dropped her eyes. "I hoped it would not."

"And still, you would marry me?"

She lifted her head and gazed at him, and he was struck by how incongruous was her loveliness in that moment, when they could be facing death at any time, alone or together. "Mayhaps"—she faltered—"mayhaps you save my life, Henri Dablon."

He embraced her quickly. "Well, I could not get the priest to come, he is too busy at this time—"

"And he will not marry you to a Natchez woman anyway," she added softly in her own tongue.

"Later, we will marry properly," he promised her. "Now we will go to where neither my people nor yours are likely to hunt us. I will take the raft, you will take the horse, and we will keep each other in sight, moving as quickly downriver as we can. Can you ride him?" he asked, boosting her up on the horse's back even as he asked.

She took the reins in her hands and kicked the horse firmly with her moccasined feet. "I will keep you in sight."

"If we get separated," he called to her as he pushed the raft out into the moving shallows, "look for my claim marker. Two days' ride, before you cross a shallow creek—''

"We will not be separated," she called back in French.

He stopped as the thought struck him, calling back across the water, "Why did they call you by that name, woman?"

She smiled shyly. "As a child, I liked to sit in water."

"Sit in it? That's all?"

"In any season."

He laughed ruefully, and then turned his attention to the swifter current as he poled the raft to the middle of the river.

They had not traveled far when heavy musket fire and war screams cut the air like too-close thunder. Henri could hear them across the water clearly; he knew that Oka must hear them as well. He moved as quickly as he could, poling with all his strength, and he could see that Oka heeled the horse, keeping to the trees, her head forward and her shoulders hunched in determination. The smell of smoke came to him then; the Natchez were firing on the fort, and he feared the horse would shy, possibly buck, but he could not see her for the trees, and he sent a prayer to God that she would not be halted by the mount, the terrain, or worse. He hated that she had to know what was behind her but he was grateful that she did not have to see it. Guilt panged at his heart for what he might have been able to do for his countrymen and had not—but he pushed it firmly away with every strong push of his pole.

Downriver, he hit a bend and the water became rough, tipping the raft this way and that way raucously as if in thoughtless play. Henri felt desperate fear for the first time on the river, for though he knew he could hang on to the raft no matter what happened and eventually fetch up safe on dry land, he might lose Oka somehow as she rode away from him. But he told himself over and over as he paddled hard that soon they would be on their own land; soon they would be safe. Those beliefs kept his arms strong, and as he rounded the bend and came closer to shore, he caught a glimpse of her. She had halted the horse, facing the river. She was waiting patiently for the water to set him free again. He lifted his arm in a wave; she waved back and turned the horse south once more.

With dusk, he beached the raft, she dismounted, and the two of them pulled it under dense cover, hiding the horse in brush and themselves far from both raft and horse. They were still too near to the fort for true safety, and if the massacre involved all the Natchez, which Henri believed it would, tribes from the south may well come upon them.

They could see little of the river, crouched low in an indentation in the earth, an old channel which was ringed by grasses and small brush. But they could hear, now that the water was quieter here, and what they could hear was bad enough. A terrible silence, as though the river and the land, too, held collective breath. Once, they heard distant sounds of cannon, and then the awful silence once more, filled with the sense that great evil was done not far away, a near-shimmering on the air of lost hopes, blood, and death.

She made a nest for them in the brush, and she lay down, pillowing her head on his belly. He dozed fitfully, hearing every noise on the river, every creak of branch, every restless stretch and groan of the very earth beneath him. It was still dark when she woke and rose from the brush slowly, looking all about her before she stood up completely. "I want to get from here," she said softly.

"We should wait for light," he murmured.

"Now I want to go," she said. "We are close to death here."

He looked at her in the shadows of their hiding place. She had never shown any stubbornness before—but then she had never lived through what she had before, either. Had never even been from her own village, likely. Perhaps she was right. It might be as dangerous to wait as it was to travel. "If only the moon were full, I'd feel safer moving on," he said, rising and pulling his musket to him. "If I knew for sure what to do, I would do it . . ." He faltered.

"We go now," she said firmly, and she stepped cautiously out of cover. All was silent on that part of the river, and though they could still smell smoke from the fort's fire, they heard no sounds of war. They uncovered the raft and pulled it out to deeper water. She went to the horse, quieted him, and mounted quickly. Neither of them looked back once.

Finally, finally they reached Henri Dablon's claim, and he saw with immense satisfaction that his marker was still standing. Leaning, actually, but still upright. He beached the raft properly this time for he did not expect to have to move it for a while. Oka dismounted wearily, stiffly, as though her limbs had aged overnight. "This is our land," he said to her formally, with a short bow. "It is mine, by claim and proper payment to your people." He took her hand. "So long as you are mine, it is yours also, Oka."

"The land belongs to the woman," she said firmly. "It is the tradition of my people."

He opened his eyes a little wider. "Is that true?"

She nodded. "The men make war and speak to the gods, but the women own the lodges, the crops, and the land." She smiled at him. "It is a wise way, yes?" This last was in French.

He thought for a long moment. "It is a wise way," he finally agreed.

She straightened her shoulders and walked up the small beach like a queen taking dominion. In that moment, he knew that he had made two of the best decisions of his life: the land and the woman. And the two would be wedded forever in his heart as one.

The massacre at Fort Rosalie changed Louisiana forevermore. On November 29, 1729, the Natchez killed two hundred and fifty French settlers, taking more than two hundred women and children hostage. Only twelve Natchez were killed. Commander Chopart was dragged from his garden where he was hiding and clubbed to death by lesser warriors, for the elite fighters of the Natchez would not dirty their hands with his death. Four women had their abdomens cut open and their unborn children slaughtered before their eyes.

The Natchez had believed that the Chickasaw and Choctaw would join them and had, in fact, agreed on a day when a joint attack would take place over all the Territory. A quiver of sticks went to each tribe. One was to be withdrawn and broken each morning. On the morning when the last of the twenty arrows had been broken, the uprising would begin.

The quiver of the Natchez was deposited in the Temple of the Sun, and each day, the priest burned an arrow in the Sacred Fire. But a woman of the nobility who loved a French lieutenant stole two of the arrows and sent a warning to Fort Rosalie. The warning was not heeded, but the Natchez attack came so early that the Choctaws and Chickasaw disavowed their involvement.

When news of the massacre reached New Orleans, Governor Perier savagely retaliated with a force of two thousand, half of the soldiers recruited Choctaw warriors. Within three years, the Natchez people were destroyed, disappearing from both sides of the Big Water as completely as the mammoths once had before them.

PART ONE
1775–1798

And there are three that bear witness on earth:
the spirit and the water and the blood;
and these three are one.

I John 5:8

Stonington, Connecticut, 1775

Josiah Fleming pulled his worn woolen cape closer about his collar and bent into the cold November wind, telling himself that very soon, he would be warm at last. The road from the Stonington harbor to his rock-scrabble farm was nine miles of ruts and frozen mud this time of year, but he was too excited to wait five hours for Isaac Bree, his neighbor, to finish his marketing and hie him home. After his long journey, nine miles seemed trifling indeed.

As he walked, he took deep satisfaction in his strength, noting with gratitude the difference in the length and vigor of his stride now compared with when he walked this road the last time, more than six months before. It had seemed, for most of the previous year, that he was ill more than he was well. When Dr. Goodrick advised an ocean voyage to restore his health, however, Abigail set up such a hue and cry that he decided a wasting death by consumption was preferable to enduring her protests. Until he heard of Natchez.

He recalled that the very word *Natchez* had set off a secret thrill in his chest. A name at once foreign and accessible, exotic and succinct, Natchez was more masculine than the opulent debauchery of "New Orleans" and "Baton Rouge." A man could say "Natchez" at least, without sounding like a popish rake.

The governor of the Louisiana Territory, the advertisement said, guaranteed fertile land with ample water, ten acres for every man, ten more for each additional mouth to feed including slaves. Fifty acres for a man and wife and three children! Simply for the claiming of it.

And so despite Abigail's fears, he had taken a step no one in his family had considered, boarding a trader from Stonington to Norfolk and then another round the Gulf to New Orleans. There he joined a like-minded party of colonists rafting upriver to Natchez and staked his claim to five hundred, not fifty, acres of land which made his Stonington fields look like the wasteland outside the gates of Eden. Once more, as he had a hundred times in as many days, Josiah stopped and clasped his hands together in prayer. "Thank Ye, Almighty God," he said aloud and fervently, "for all the many blessings Ye have bestowed upon me. I shall praise Your name all of my days."

After a moment's thought, he added, "And Dr. Goodrick's as well."

Josiah was not the sort of man to praise lightly; his wife would attest to that. But he liked to believe that once he found a thing worthy of praise, he did not stint. He would need all that praise to budge Abigail out of Stonington, though she would be the first to say his land was not worth a tenth of her own father's fields and hardly returned the sweat they'd poured into it for these seven long years. But it was familiar.

Abigail was the sort of woman, he knew, who preferred a known evil to a fearsome unknown. Natchez was a huge unknown, but he could no longer endure the cold winters and the hard struggle to make his land produce more than a goodly crop of rocks to his plow each year.

He stopped within sight of his farmhouse, on a stony berm which afforded a view of the stable, the fowl yard, and the sty. It looked smaller and meaner to him now, after the lushness of Natchez and the largeness of the Mississippi. Well, no matter. He'd not tarry another winter in this place. At near thirty, a man should start making his life count for something. Thoughts of his children crowded his mind now, and he hurried to the door, already grinning with anticipation.

"Papa!" his eldest daughter's shriek of delight greeted him the instant his head cleared the gloom into the light of the fire-lit kitchen. "Papa's home!" A bustle of feet and squeals, and Lamon, his son, and Jane, his second daughter, rounded the corner of the room, throwing themselves into his embrace. Right behind them hurried their mother.

"Thank the good Lord," Abigail murmured, tucking under one of his arms. The three children all crowded for space under the other one. Josiah was instantly alarmed to see how wan and frail Abigail looked, though her girth had not diminished one whit in his absence. Since their third, she had always looked as though she expected confinement daily, yet she suffered from the same ills he had before he left, despite the doctor's repeated bleedings, poultices, and other simples. She was only a year elder to him, and she looked older. Also more poorly than he had remembered.

But the children's voices would be answered; time enough for his concerns later. "Papa, did you see Indians and buffalos and wolves? Did you, Papa?" asked Lamon, climbing up on his back and pummeling his shoulders for good measure.

"I told them you'd be home this week, didn't I?" Ruth asked her mother, nestling to her father's chest.

Nearly as tall as her mother, Josiah noted with a painful pride. "And how did you guess that, my miss?" he asked, squeezing her hard. "And who's this mite tugging at my leggings now?" Five-year-old Jane was hugging his legs and laughing the while, her pert face gazing up at him with delight. "Papa!" she called again and again. "Papa! Papa! Papa!"

Eventually Josiah untangled himself, took the hot mug of tea Ruth offered him, and pulled his chair closer to the fire so that there was room on both sides of his legs for his family. Abigail started to pull up a chair for herself, but Lamon leaped to do it for her, a new habit he had formed since Josiah left. Abigail sat down heavily with an audible sigh.

"Tell about the wilderness, Papa!" Lamon begged quickly, for at seven, he wanted only tales of bears and savages and wolves and roaring rapids to be happy.

"Is it as fine as they say?" asked Ruth.

"Is it as fertile?" This from Abigail.

"Papa! Papa! Papa!" crowed Jane, contenting herself with patting and kissing his knee.

" 'Tis just as fine and twice as fertile," Josiah said, laughing down at all of them and embracing each in turn, "and the Fleming family has laid claim to five hundred acres of it, by the grace of God!"

"My Lord," breathed Abigail, "five hundred! But you said fifty, Josiah. How will we ever work such lands?"

" 'Tis a—a plantation," Ruth murmured, her eyes wide with awe.

"Shall we be very rich?" clamored Lamon. "Did you see monstrous bears, Papa?"

Josiah answered all their questions in between hearing their various tales of how they had struggled and triumphed and missed him, each with a hundred details to share with him, and only Abigail sat patiently, quietly, waiting for the children to get their fill of their father, at least for this night. When they were finally packed off to their beds, crowded together in the sleeping loft for comfort and small warmth, he sat once more beside the fire and took Abigail's hand in his.

"I think you would have been as powerfully taken with the place as I was," Josiah said. "I know five hundred acres sounds like a lot of land—"

" 'Tis more land than my father and your father together ever dreamed of," she answered quickly. "And it's one thing to lay claim to it; it's quite another to put it to the plow. We cannot manage such a—such a kingdom!"

"Many do and more," he assured her with a gentle smile. "I know it seems impossible, but I saw men claim two thousand acres, Abby, with no fear at all of making their fortune faster than a Connecticut farmer can clear a single field. I tell you, it's different out there, and a man can feel the difference as soon as he sets foot on the soil. Everything is possible, and even the weather is more harmonious with a man's dreams.''

"Dreams," she said with a weary shrug. "I am sick nigh unto death with dreams, Josiah."

He was instantly saddened, as though a leaden weight had settled on his heart. It was often so, these days, when Abigail spoke to him. He could feel the disillusionment in her flesh like an ague. Indeed, he sometimes wondered if her disappointment was at the root of her constant sicknesses, her female complaints, her lassitude and bilious stomach. But he could also see and touch, rare times, the girl she was before he took her off her father's prosperous farm and set her down on his own paltry acres. By the grace of God, she would not have to work so hard for much longer. "Abby," he said, taking her other hand in his, "I know you've been patient with me for these long years, and our lives have not been as I'd hoped, but Natchez is a new paradise, and we have a piece of it to call our own. This is one dream which is real!''

"But it's so far," she moaned. "Halfway across the continent, they say, and I'll never see my father and mother again. Never see my sister and her children . . .''

"You'll see them again, I swear it," he said earnestly. "Perhaps they will be so persuaded by our success that they'll follow us to Natchez as well!''

"That's surely one dream which will never come true," she said dryly.

"How do you know?" he asked. "How can you say so surely what will and will not happen? For that matter, how do you know they'll live so long in these cold winters, working themselves to death? I tell you, Abby, Mississippi is a paradise next to this rockpile—''

"A paradise! 'Tis a wilderness, Josiah, with scarcely

enough people in it to keep back the wolves and the savages! I told you when you went there that I did not wish you to go, but you went—now you expect me to bundle up the children and follow you to the edge of the earth—and all for a dream!''

He sat back and crossed his arms, watching her carefully for a long moment. ''Are you saying that you will not go? Now that I have claimed five hundred acres for us?''

She turned away. ''Ah my Lord,'' she murmured. '' 'Tis always thus, for women. The men do the dreaming, and we do the packing.''

He waited, silently.

''I wish I had the courage to tell you to go, Josiah,'' she said, her voice low and vibrant with resentment. ''Just go and leave us be. We could scrape by, no doubt, with my father's help.''

He reached out and took her hand.

She sighed. ''But I don't have the courage nor the will to refuse you.''

He moved over next to her and put an arm round her shoulders. ''Look, Abby, I've been sick too long and poor too long; I'll not stomach another year of it. I feel stronger and more sure than I've felt in my life. We're going to Natchez in the spring,'' he said, squeezing her hands for emphasis, ''and God will be with us each step of the way.''

She bowed her head before the sheer persuasiveness of his spirit. ''My father always said you were a dreamer,'' she sighed. ''I suppose this will surprise no one.''

''Sometimes a dreamer finds rare fortune simply because he refuses to give up,'' Josiah said. ''Don't give up on me, Abby.''

She began to weep softly, shaking her head. ''What choice do I have, truly, Josiah?'' She wiped her eyes with the back of her hand, a hard gesture he had not seen before. In that gesture, he saw her fear and her weariness. ''I am too tired to be alone at my age.''

He held her silently, feeling a great tenderness for her in that moment.

She smiled up at him through her tears, a ghost of her girlhood smile. "Well, the children will never let you out of their sight again, so I guess I have no choice but to go along. I suppose we'll have to buy slaves, and another team, and I don't know what I'll do with my laying hens . . ."

Abigail's Rhode Island Reds were her pride and joy, after her children. "We'll carry them to Natchez," Josiah reassured her, "and whatever else we need, we'll purchase when we get there. What we get for the farm will provision us amply, since the land costs us next to nothing. But tell me, dear, of your health since my absence. Are you no better than when I left?"

"I have good days and bad days," she said tiredly. "The doctor says even the leeches are tired from my blood, so weak is it. But I am happy to see *you* looking so well, husband."

"The doctor was right," he said heartily. "The voyage strengthened me, and the salt air cleared my lungs. It will have the same effect on you, I'm certain." He leaned forward and kissed her on both cheeks happily. "In May," he said, laughing, "you'll be my rosy-cheeked lass again, I vow. The sailors will think Ruth your sister, 'stead of your eldest."

"In May," she murmured in reluctant agreement. To Josiah, it sounded like a wedding vow all over again.

In May of 1776, the trader *Providence* took on passengers and provisions in Stonington, after selling off some of her cargo of English furniture, tea, and Brussels lace. She made the round trip from Liverpool to Boston three times a year, stopping in New Bedford, Stonington, Hampton, Savannah, Saint Augustine, and finally in New Orleans, depending on the captain's whims and the price of pelts. A small, unassuming ship, her captain picked ports where she could sell her goods easily with little competition. Not for him the bustle and chaos of Norfolk, Charleston, and Mobile.

But the less bustle the better, Josiah believed. It was hard enough to slip by the British ships these days, and rumors flew in and out of port that the larger the prize, the more zealous the King's pursuit. In fact, Josiah knew that fewer and fewer ships would anchor in Stonington now, for the English were doing their best to cork the Sound. He wished he had more choices as to conveyance, but he dared not wait another season.

And so, on the first Thursday in May, he led his family down to the harbor where the *Providence* lay waiting at anchor. Abigail's father's wagon would barely hold all their belongings, and so she had to say her tearful goodbye to her mother and sisters at her father's front door. Josiah's own wagon and team had been sold, along with Abby's hens, the farm, and whatever else they could not carry along to Natchez, and so he had had to endure his father-in-law's stoic disapproval the long nine miles to where they now stood. His disapproval was all the more severe since he knew his daughter was pregnant again. Josiah had promised Abigail that he would have her to their new land before she was expecting confinement, yet even to make the voyage with a six-month belly seemed much to ask.

But Abigail's father also believed in the story of Ruth, and so he told her she must go with her husband. A dour Episcopalian who believed that a man should root where he was planted, he embraced his weeping daughter once and then turned his team for home. The children watched, pale and wide-eyed, as their mother tried to compose herself and her father departed.

"Won't we ever see Grandfather again?" Lamon asked dolefully. "Not in our whole lives, ever?"

"Of course we will," Josiah said cheerfully, bundling them toward the waiting ship, "we can come back and visit them, and they can sail to see us in Natchez! Won't that be something to show Grandfather? Your own pony and perhaps even an Indian!''

Ruth said soberly, ''Grandfather's too old to go so far. So is Grandmother.'' But then she saw the stricken look on Lamon's face. ''But you can come and see them yourself, Lamon. Perhaps you will even own your own ship one day.''

Dazzled, Lamon turned his full attention to the *Providence* now, pulling Jane along from where she had crouched to examine at nose level a stinking scrod, half-eaten by gulls.

From the docks, the ship looked tall and lean, with surprisingly small deck space and a low hull sheathed in copper. A slaver once, the *Providence* was schooner-rigged for speed and pierced for a dozen guns. But less than half of those were visible now, three on each side, their snouts pointed out to sea. Her slave days were over. ''Not that ye can't make more money in slaves than in pelts and sideboards,'' Captain Barker had confided to Josiah the morning he booked passage, ''but a man's got to rest right with God, when all's said and done. And I'm finished with slaving for good.''

Josiah had enjoyed sharing that story with Abigail, as though somehow the *Providence* was now a better ship for her captain's conversion.

''And yet,'' she had said then, ''we shall have to have slaves of our own to manage so many acres. Where shall we get them?''

''Perhaps we might hire Indians,'' Josiah said, ''or lease out part of the ground to latecomers, or hire a neighbor's laborers. At least if we buy slaves of our own, we shall treat them as creatures of God.'' Of that much, he was certain.

The compartment they were to occupy for the two-month voyage was smaller than the kitchen of their old home, and they were to share it with the Hanovers from Bradford, a man and wife and two tall sons, both boys as likely as colts to endure a cramped stall without kicking.

Three other families were crowded into a similar space on the other side of the ship, and every other square inch of

room onboard was taken with boxes of English furniture
bound for plantations at Charleston, Savannah, and the Cape
of Fear. When Abigail eyed the coffin-like shelf she was to
sleep in for two months or more, she gazed wistfully at one
of the larger packing boxes which blocked the aisle.
"Likely," she said, "there's a bed there somewhere.
Wouldn't you think we could borrow it just for the voyage?"

"Better it should be powder and balls," Mr. Hanover
called to her from across the short passage which divided the
tiny cabin into two compartments, "and we'll wish it such
soon enough if the King's men catch us in open seas!" He
said it cheerfully, as though he almost relished the adventure. He had eyed Abigail's rounded belly under her volumi-
nous skirts most carefully when he first met her, and then
turned his eyes away in some embarrassment when she met
his gaze. "Your pardon, mistress," he had said then with a
short bow. "I wondered only if you would be comfortable
on this journey in your condition."

"Please do not trouble yourself about my condition, Mr.
Hanover," Abigail had said coolly. "It shall not trouble
me."

"More reason to hope that the British warships keep off
our bow," Mrs. Hanover murmured politely.

Josiah frowned at Mr. Hanover's last comment about the
British threat and pulled his wife away toward the stairs
leading to the open deck.

"Mr. Hanover seems to believe the British will put us in
peril," Abigail said uncertainly.

"Nonsense," Josiah said cheerfully. "The captain has
promised me that the King's men have plenty to do without
worrying a small trader which will scarcely be out of sight of
land for the whole voyage."

Seamen were crowding past them now down the stairs to
the passenger compartment, making ready to lash their small
trunks side by side in the middle of the passageway. They
were to be allowed one trunk per family only for the voyage,

and Captain had already warned them not to beg or plead for access to their other goods once under way. "Just tell yourself whatever's not in your trunk is on another ship altogether until New Orleans. That way, you won't be tempted. But tempted or not, you'll not see a trunk until you set foot on land for good."

"Come and wave farewell to old Stonington, Abigail. Let's look forward to the future!" He pulled her to the rail and the children gathered close on either side of them.

High atop the mainmast, just above the morning fog, an English Jack flew in the light breeze. Below it flew the colonial flag of Massachusetts, for Boston, the home port of the *Providence* and her final destination at season's end.

"Let us pray," Josiah said to his family, and they bowed their heads and clasped their hands in unison. "Almighty God, we beseech Thee to see us safely to our new home in Natchez and to keep us in Thy bosom all the while. We know that You dwell even in the wilderness, even as You dwell in our hearts. And we promise Thee, O Lord, that when we arrive safely in Natchez, we will erect a chapel on our lands to the glory of Your name. Amen."

"Amen," the children and Abigail murmured automatically, each one looking up at him curiously.

"A chapel?" Abigail asked quietly. "You had not spoken of this before, Josiah."

"No, I had not," he said, putting a hand on her shoulder and another on Jane's. "I only thought of it last night. But I believe that it's fitting, don't you? When we clear the land, we'll lay a foundation for a chapel for the Lord. We can surely spare Him the space, and I can think of nothing more fitting to celebrate our new beginning."

Abigail smiled then, her first genuine show of pleasure since they had boarded. "That will be something to look forward to," she murmured. "A church in the wilderness. Perhaps my father might come to see such a thing, after all."

A call came then from somewhere aft, a foresail was loosed, and the sails began to unfurl as men clambered like monkeys up the taut ropes to the sky. Barefoot, with strong, brown hands and bare arms, they swung high above the deck amid a flurry of cording and sheet. The canvas cracked and filled and the *Providence* wallowed away from the dock as her anchor was catted and fished up. The harbor at Stonington slowly disappeared as they moved out into the gray open waters to the Sound to round the tip of Long Island to the south.

It was a week at sea before Abigail got over her initial dreadful seasickness. The children grew used to the rolling motion of the *Providence* within the first day, but Abigail stayed in her cramped and fetid bunk for five full days, groaning and weeping with fatigue and nausea. Josiah felt his own equilibrium less than content, but he pushed himself to walk the rail morning and night, keeping his constitution as strong as he could. Mrs. Hanover, also, was prey to the *mal-de-mer,* as the seamen called it, and together the two women made the air of the small compartment rank with their dyspepsia and vomiting.

But finally, on the seventh day, Abigail rose from her bed, wrapped herself in her black woolen shawl, and attempted to cling to the rail for an hour or more. She was too weak to walk, but she did manage to take Josiah's arm to watch the ocean move by them in long troughs of gray-green sea.

Jane and Lamon had already claimed much of the ship as their own. They discovered every hidey-hole and fascinating corner which held untold treasures of salt-rotted cording and tarred timbers, and the seamen no longer cursed them away but seemed to resign themselves to working with children ever underfoot. For her part, Ruth and the two Hanover boys studiously ignored each other for a week, then fell into uneasy comradeship, with occasional bouts of clamor between the boys as to which Ruth might favor.

Once again, Josiah was amazed to see how much like a small village a moving ship could be. The boatswain checked the sea stores each morning, the ropes, the sails, the flags, cables, and anchors; the cooper kept watch over the water casks; the steward counted and tended the candles; the quartermaster and captain consulted their maps and soundings and agreed upon a course; and the rest of the seamen did their rounds of endless labor.

The winds whistled across the tops of the mainyards as they moved south, blowing warmer with each passing day. The *Providence* rolled from one tack to another, men working always at the chain pump, spilling bilge water out over the deck. Constantly awash, Josiah learned to ignore wet shoes and leggings, and the children no longer shrieked with delight to watch the water falling overboard through the scupper holes like miniature rivers as the *Providence* plowed the ocean.

Lamon told him that the sailors were crowded into much less of a space than they shared with the Hanovers. " 'Tis dark and stinks,'' he grimaced confidentially to his father. ''They got a little window, but they have to keep it closed else the water comes in all the time. They smoke their pipes down there, and the air is nasty.''

Josiah told him to pray for the men, for they would help to keep them all safe at sea. But he could plainly see that many of the men knew as little about the workings of the *Providence* as he did, and they learned what they had to know as they had to know it. They washed down the decks with vinegar and sand, but as the weather grew warmer and the bilge water began to stink where it collected on the ship, they burned pitch between decks to try to sweeten the air. And day and night, the great pump groaned and squealed as they lumbered down the coastline of the continent.

There was much talk of war onboard, for there was little for the few passengers to do save speak to each other. Mr. Hanover had a copy of Thomas Paine's *Pennsylvania Magazine,* and it was eagerly circulated. Opinion was divided among the passengers whether it was a cry for freedom or sedition, but no man lacked an opinion.

"The King has no right to forbid us to trade with any country save England," Mr. Hanover said staunchly, ignoring the frowns of Mr. Henderson, a Loyalist on his way to New Orleans. "He just wants to punish us for refusing to buy English goods, a right I have same as any other free man! By God, when the time comes that we cannot buy and sell as our purses dictate, we might as well sell ourselves on the block at Haiti."

" 'Tis a losing battle," Mr. Henderson said firmly. "Even now, General Howe is massing to take New York. When he does so, those traitors who have fought against their King will be punished to the full extent of the law— their purses notwithstanding."

"General Washington may have something to say about that," Josiah said mildly. But at Abigail's glance of rebuke, he quieted. She was quite right, he told himself later. Politics was a volatile topic of conversation these days, and they needed no passion in such close quarters. Let the others wrangle their views; he would pray for a swift resolution to whatever conflict came and that those close to him be spared any danger.

That night, he embraced Abigail warmly before retiring. "Thank you for saving me from Hanover's tongue," he said, smiling down at her.

"I thought we should have to call him Patrick Henry, perhaps, for the rest of the voyage," she quipped ruefully. She turned her cheek up to him and then rolled on her side to face the ship's ribs. "I will praise God when we reach Natchez," she murmured tiredly. "Or even when we simply see land again."

"You are so brave to come with me," he whispered to her, "especially with child. I am very grateful to you, Abby."

"Whither thou goest," she whispered back.

He patted her softly and turned to the children to wish them good night.

"Papa," whispered Lamon loudly, "when we get to Charleston, will we buy us a nigger?"

Josiah turned in annoyance to his son, his frown deepening. "Where did you hear such talk?" he asked Lamon quietly. "I don't want to hear you say that word again."

Lamon glanced at his older sister, subdued now. "Rob Hanover said it," he murmured. "He said the—the black folks are cheaper there than in New Orleans, and if we got to get them, that's the place to do it. We do, don't we, Papa?"

"That remains to be seen," Josiah said. "But if we do, we shall purchase them at a fair price and treat them with dignity and kindness. They are the Lord's creatures, and we must never forget that."

"What should we call them, Papa?" Ruth asked solemnly. "I've never even seen a black man."

"You could call them 'sir,' " Jane piped up helpfully. "Mama says to call all the gentlemens that."

Jane's comment was greeted by ribald snorting giggles from the other side of the passageway, for of course the Hanover boys had heard every word, though each family usually pretended not to listen.

"You will call them negroes," Josiah said patiently, "until you learn their individual names. But perhaps you shan't need to call them anything at all. We may decide to work the land without them altogether."

"It's time to sleep now, children," Abigail interrupted him then. "Enough talk, Josiah."

He looked up at her back, which still faced him. "Yes. Well, your mother's right. Let me hear your prayers."

As he had every night since their birth, at least when he was with them, he listened to his three children say their "Our Father's," kissed each head, and turned to his own bunk with a growing sense of loneliness which he could not explain to himself.

* * *

The *Providence* rolled on south down the Atlantic coast, flirting with the sight of land, sometimes so far out to sea that it seemed they were on the other side of the world altogether. They saw other ships, but always at a great distance, and Captain certainly preferred it so.

But round the coast of Wilmington, their luck ran out. All ships stayed well outside the infamous Hatteras shoals unless their destination was the Cape Fear inlet, for more ships were lost on those narrows than on any other up and down the coastline. Captain meant to anchor at New Brunswick, on the opposite side of the river, but it meant braving the Frying Pan Shoals, a challenge for the most experienced mariner. Just inside the inlet, a British man-o'-war pulled alongside the *Providence* so quickly that they were unable to evade it. Firing a cannon barrage off the port side, the English ship forced the *Providence* to heave to in the water. Captain had no choice but to allow his ship to be taken, and as he protested, they were boarded and lashed to the side of a huge British warship, helpless as a flounder caught in a net.

All passengers were quickly mustered to the forecastle, where the British officer demanded to know their identities, their destinations, and their loyalties. The children stood back with their mothers, wide-eyed and frightened. Josiah was pulled forward with the rest of the men; not a grown male was allowed to avoid the inquisition. The British officers barked questions as though they suspected the *Providence* of carrying powder and arms to the rebels in Boston, but whenever he was addressed directly, Josiah said simply, "I am a farmer. I have nothing but a small claim in Natchez, where I hope to take my family for a new start. My loyalties are to God and my family, in that order."

"You a Quaker?" one officer asked him brusquely.

"No, sir," Josiah said calmly. "My father was Protestant, and I am as well."

"I did not ask your lineage, sir," the officer replied derisively. "We avoid such embarrassment with Americans."

Robert Hanover stiffened at that but his wife shot him a

look of warning, and he remained silent. Meanwhile, another officer came up from the hold and reported that, indeed, the *Providence* carried no armaments of any kind.

"My landing papers are in order," Captain said again angrily, "and you can see I trade only with the colonies. I make no trade with enemies of the King."

"Sir," the officer said silkily, "some of you colonists are the King's *greatest* enemies in these bloody days," and he did not look up from his careful examination of the ship's log and her inventories.

But finally, finally, the British captain gave the orders to relinquish them, the English tars retreated, and the *Providence* was free to get under way again, setting her course once more for the south.

They spent another five days at sea, weathering the rains off the coast of the Carolinas, squalls which come up so suddenly that a man could get drenched before he could get below. The fresh water was beginning to stink of green algae, and each man got an extra ration of beer. Fleas were so thick in the passengers' compartments that the bites kept the children awake at night, and Abigail's temper grew snappish.

Her belly grew larger and larger, though her face and hands and neck seemed to be wasting away before Josiah's eyes. She could eat little when the sea was so rough, and the beer made her bilious, though it did help her sleep. He worried about the child within her, but he said little, for he knew that she must be worried as well. Whatever food he was given, he saved the best morsels for her, trying to tempt her and tease her into eating as he once did the children when they were ill. Sometimes she would eat for him; other times she simply turned her head and ordered him away.

But finally the call "Land ho!" came, and Charleston shimmered at the edge of the horizon like a heat mirage. Captain had not wanted to stop in Charleston, but with provisions and water low, they had little choice. They slid past Hog Island and Johnson's Fort up to the Battery to anchor in the still, fetid waters of the Cooper River, and Charleston lay at their feet. All passengers got off briefly to see and smell land again, if only for a day. "I wish I never had to see that ship again," Abigail said peevishly when she disembarked the *Providence*. "And we've still half the voyage to go."

Lamon fairly skipped as he went down the gangplank to the Charleston loading dock. "We have completed the hardest part of the journey," Josiah reassured her. "From here on, we'll be in warmer waters, no King's men to plague us, and we'll rarely be out of sight of land."

"Tell me again," Abigail sighed, leaning against him, her arms cradling her stomach, "tell me again how beautiful our land is. Maybe then I can force myself to get back aboard."

"Mother!" Ruth called just then, "Lamon left the boat! I told him to wait but—"

"Lord, let him go," Abigail said to her. "We'll be right behind him."

The Flemings disembarked on a Charleston loading dock piled high with bales of cotton, hogsheads of sugar, rice, and tobacco, and thronging with black stevedores. They boarded a small landing skiff with the rest of the passengers, and once on land at Gadsden's Wharf, Abigail pulled her children close to her and murmured, "At all times, I want you either holding on to your father or to me, do you understand?"

Even Lamon nodded, wide-eyed and obedient.

Passengers were embarking and disembarking, the traffic clogged around them, and Josiah was again exhilarated by the energy of so many more varied faces than he had known in Stonington.

Swarthy men who could be Caribbean pirates in green satin and brocaded coats, Europeans with formal dress or simple aprons, slaves fresh off the boat from Africa, freedmen who wore white men's clothes and tawny-skinned women with brilliantly colored turbans, Charleston ladies with wide, fashionable skirts and gay ribbons and parasols, all mingled together like so much flotsam in the Charleston harbor.

Black coachmen in buttoned coats and full wigs pulled up in shiny carriages, offering transport into town, and Josiah decided that this was an investment which could well return itself tenfold. He helped Abigail into the carriage, despite her protests that it was surely too dear for all of them to ride, and away the Flemings swept into the main streets of Charleston like the grandest gentlemen and ladies.

Ruth was smitten with the fine houses facing the river, gazing at them and pointing out this detail of iron fretwork and that vine-entwined porch. Many of them sat behind high-walled gardens, like elegant matrons turning a cold shoulder to the roughness of the world. The air smelled of ripe fruit and overripe flowers.

They dined that afternoon at the Three Sisters, an inn known for its sumptuous Creole food, and they walked the streets admiring the contents of the shop windows and the shadowed, secret passageways into the walled gardens. By dusk, they made their way reluctantly back to the *Providence* and boarded once more, for she would leave Charleston with the early tide.

As Josiah tucked his children into bed that night, the refrain was the same from each. Would Natchez be as wonderful as Charleston by the sea? Yes, he reassured them with nary a twinge of guilt: Natchez would be as wonderful. Different, surely, and perhaps not so crowded and elegant, but every bit as wonderful, for it would be their home—*theirs,* he emphasized, to have and to make prosper. He had no doubt, he told Lamon, Ruth, and Jane, that Natchez would make them happy. And because of his words, each child went to sleep that night smiling.

As he climbed into his upper bunk, he dropped one hand down to Abigail to hold hers. "You are very certain of yourself," she murmured in the darkness.

"No," he said softly. "I am very certain of God's plan for us all."

"I wish I could share your faith," she said quietly.

It was the starkest declaration of doubt he had heard from her in their many years of marriage, and it struck him to silence. But then he told himself that any woman so far along in her pregnancy, in these conditions, must surely ask herself if God was watching over her after all. He forgave her the lapse, and he silently asked God to forgive her as well.

Of course, anytime they could, the men put their heads together and compared their claims in Natchez. Mr. Hanover had put his name to just over four hundred acres to the south of the village, quite near, they soon discovered, to Josiah's claim. Once they realized they would be neighbors, many of their differences melted away, and Josiah found that even Hanover's boys were less obnoxious than they seemed at the onset of the voyage.

Robert Hanover and his wife, Tess, had more schooling than either Josiah or Abigail, and both could read and understand Dr. Franklin's pieces in the *Pennsylvania Gazette*, something Josiah had difficulty with no matter how he concentrated. When Robert Hanover spoke of the Territory, therefore, Josiah listened closely.

"It's really part of West Florida," Hanover told him one night as they sat out under the vast sweep of stars. " 'British West Florida,' the mapmakers call it; did you know that?"

Josiah shook his head. "Tell me what else you know." He felt humbled before the man sometimes, a feeling he normally disliked. But he admired him greatly, and so he put his pride aside.

Hanover pulled out a paper from his coat pocket. It was well creased in accustomed folds. "I've read this to Tess so many times," he confided, "it's a wonder I've not worn away the print. This is from the report made by Thomas Hutchins, a geographer who came through eight years ago. 'The soil at this place,' he says, 'is superior to any on the borders of the river Mississippi.' "

"That's promising," Josiah said eagerly.

" 'It will produce crops of Indian corn, rice, hemp, flax, indigo, cotton, pot-herbs, and pasturage,' " Hanover went on importantly. "He also tells about the climate—do you want to hear that, too?"

"Of course!"

Hanover smiled. " 'A healthful place which is elevated, open, airy, and the situation of the country renders it less liable to fevers and agues.' " He looked up at Josiah. "Makes it sound a regular Eden."

"Could I show that to Abigail?" Josiah asked. " 'Twould make her feel better, I expect."

Hanover handed it over with an air of indulgence. "You know, we're lucky men, Josiah. Sooner than we think, there'll be no more land in Natchez for the latecomers. Together, we have near a thousand acres! Imagine what a man could do with such a fortune!"

"Praise God," murmured Josiah.

"Indeed," replied Hanover crisply. "Of course, it's still technically British land, but I expect once the Patriots have run the English off our shores, we'll have no trouble with them on the Mississippi. I have several of the Indian mounds on my claim; do you as well?"

"Yes, three of them that I've found so far," Josiah said. "What do you suppose they were for?"

Hanover lowered his voice. "Sacrifices, they say. Human sacrifices." He cleared his throat and raised the volume again. "But the savages have been wiped out now, and we should have no more trouble from them. Thirty years or more, I understand. Some of my land is their old pasturage—"

"Mine, too," Josiah said. "You can see where they planted their corn rows."

"I mean to sell off part of the parcel soon's I find a buyer with ready cash. These days you can get richer speculating on land than plowing it."

Josiah knew that many men took up a large claim simply

to sell it off to latecomers, but he could not work his mind around to the thought of letting go of the land before he scarcely had his hands on it. ''You going to get your slaves in New Orleans or wait until we get upriver?'' he asked Hanover.

''Neither,'' Hanover said, ''and I'd advise you to take my example, Fleming. I'm buying mine direct from the West Indies and having them shipped upriver. The ones in New Orleans are ruined by the French, I hear, and the ones in Natchez are too dear. I'm going to the source. They'll be fresh, cheap, and they won't have learned any bad habits.''

Josiah said, ''That sounds like the smart thing to do.''

''It is!'' Hanover said jubilantly. ''Lets us two throw in together, we'll be neighbors eventually after all, and I'll show you what I know about how to get rich.''

''And what will I show you?'' Josiah asked.

''Whatever you can,'' Hanover assured him. ''Whatever you've got at all, Fleming, bring it to the partnership. I vow you'll not regret it, for we shall share whatever Natchez has to throw at two newcomers. It'll take a lot of Territory to best the two of us.''

Josiah put out his hand. ''Neighbors, then,'' he said. ''And may God bless us both.''

''Amen!'' Robert Hanover said triumphantly.

That night, Josiah waited until the children were well asleep and then knelt at Abigail's side, whispering to her so that the Hanovers could not hear his words. ''Abby, I talked with Bob at length this evening about our properties, and he has proposed an arrangement where we work the land together as partners. He may well sell off some of his parcel— well, for that matter, we may do the same, if we decide later. Anyway, he thinks we should—''

''Partners with Robert Hanover?'' she looked at him, surprised. ''I thought you scarcely admired the man.''

''That's not true,'' he admonished her. ''I do indeed respect and admire him; I simply found him overbearing at times. I still do. But the fact remains, we shall be neighbors in the wilderness, and we may well need his help. He will need ours, and all of us will need the Lord's.''

"Neighbors we will be, indeed, but partners? That's quite another dealing altogether.''

Josiah shrugged. "It matters not what we call it. We'll need to depend on each other, and I find Robert Hanover to be a man of no small ability—''

"How do you know?'' she asked quietly. "You scarcely know the man.''

"I've been in close quarters with him now for several months. I know him better than a dozen acquaintances in Stonington.'' He peered at Abigail with some impatience. "What is it, Abby?''

She frowned, silent for a moment. "I do not trust him, Josiah,'' she said softly. "I think he is—he is a man who cares more for appearances than truth.''

Josiah thought before he spoke. "Do you say he's a liar?''

She shook her head. "I say he does not love the truth. Not as you do. Not as he should.''

Josiah sighed and took her hand in his. "Few of us are perfect, Abby. I expect we shall find many in the Territory who do not think as we do. Who don't act as we see fit. But we will have to work together and—''

"Do what you think best then,'' she said rather shortly. "Why do you bother to ask me at all?''

"I ask you because you are my wife,'' he said patiently. "But I cannot always follow your commands.''

"I hardly *command* you, Josiah—''

"Yes, you do, Abby. You do, indeed.'' He looked over to where the children slept on, undisturbed. "But let's not speak of this now. Perhaps as you grow to know Robert Hanover better, you may be well pleased with his character. If not, we can deal with that in Natchez. Surely, I'll do nothing if you are not content.'' He squeezed her hand briefly and rose, climbing into his upper berth.

"Josiah,'' she murmured up to him, "you are a good husband.''

He dropped his hand down to her so that she might hold it as she slid into sleep.

As they neared the Gulf, the *Providence* hit a space of mild seas and stagnant winds, and they found themselves becalmed for almost three weeks. For day after day, they sat roasting in the open sun, with not enough breeze to move the ship more than a half mile in the water. Men stripped nearly naked to keep themselves from fainting in the heat, and even the women took off whatever layers they felt modesty could omit, mostly staying below out of the sun.

But the compartments were no less fetid and smothering, and soon they would be driven updecks again, hoping for the slightest breeze and a space of shade. Captain rationed water and set up a small sail to catch whatever dew might fall in the dawn. Josiah led prayers on the aft deck morning and evening for deliverance, but God seemed to be busy elsewhere, for still the ship was stuck fast.

At first, the children found the motionless ship a new delight, for they could climb about her now with less danger of falling, and the seamen paid them no mind at all. But after several days of no motion and constant sun, they lay in the scant shade and panted like weary hounds, moving little.

Josiah leaned over the side of the ship, watching the sealife abound. He envied the flying fish, who carried their own sails and needed no wind to flash through the air or water, the dolphins who could leap as high as the prow of the *Providence*, dancing and splashing in the water as though in delight and play, and even the whales who glided by the ship, winking huge eyes in curiosity, as if they wondered what these humans wanted with this particular piece of the sea.

They waited and waited, drifting aimlessly. When they were down to a scant three more days of water, they caught a small breeze and managed to sail out of the calm, into rolling ocean once more.

Four days from New Orleans, Abigail gave birth to a son.

She labored for eight grueling hours, calling out for her mother, her sister, for death even in her pain and fear. Finally, the child was born. The sailors named the boy "Atlantic."

Thrust early into life, Atlantic was a mewling, fragile boy with no hair and the thin, wizened face of a little old man. But Abigail suckled him with she-bear determination, and when she was not feeding him, she was crooning to him quietly, urging him to live. He must have taken in her words with her mother's milk, for Atlantic seemed to grow before Josiah's eyes, rounding out within a few days, turning wide, wise eyes onto him whenever he moved into the infant's gaze, and taking the rolling ship with aplomb, as if it were his natural cradle.

"Our family is finished," Abigail announced to Josiah the night after Atlantic's birth.

Though he knew what that meant, knew that for the next decade or more their embraces would have to be cautious and infrequent, Josiah readily agreed. Four children were more than he'd expected, as much as a man had a right to expect surely, and all that Abigail could safely deliver.

"I am content," he told his wife. And he believed that he meant it.

The pod of dolphins had followed the ship for more than twenty leagues, leaping clear of the vessel and riding the bow waves for the sheer pleasure of the mutual movement. They numbered six: a mated pair, two older sisters, and two yearlings who had not yet struck out on their own.

They were saddleback dolphins, named for their distinct side markings, an hourglass pattern of yellow-tan on their sleek black bodies. The male was nearly ten years old, more than eight feet long, and still a robust breeder, though he now took longer to nuzzle his mate into readiness than he might have three seasons before.

The female was his third mate, a smaller, brown-black an-

imal with a tipped dorsal fin, who had the habit of calling
constantly as she rode the waves. He was so used to her
noise, he scarcely listened for her call anymore. She produced lovely calves, and more often two than one, but she
sometimes left off nursing them before they were fully
ready, and the calves' resulting barks, groans, and chirps of
pleading added to the chaos of the pod.

Nonetheless, she was a sleek swimmer, a vigorous hunter,
and she rarely turned him away from breeding. He found her
more appealing than her sisters, and so he stayed with the
pod, never straying away as he might have with a less exciting female.

Delpha, for that was his name, was now cruising the water
directly to the port side of the *Providence,* making an occasional jubilant leap, enjoying the music of the ship. His sonar
was so keen that he could hear the smallest scrape from the
inside of the hull, and he knew man was onboard, in fact reveled in that knowledge. Like many of his kind, Delpha was
drawn to these white-faced mammals, and he swam with the
boats trying to catch glimpses of the people aboard, pleased
when he caught their attention.

Now his mate, Stena, moved closer to him in the water.
Delpha could sense her mood, could almost see into her
inner spaces with his sonar, and tell if she was ready for
breeding, was hungry, was lonely for his touch. He grazed
alongside her, brushing her with affection, never diminish-
ing his speed. From behind them both came a burst of clicks
and squeals from the yearlings who traveled side by side.

They had spotted a school of smelts, and they veered off
from the ship's wake to investigate. Within seconds, the two
sisters joined them, and the four burst through the school
joyously, gorging themselves on the tiny silvery smelts, and
leaping high out of the water to excite the fish into jumping.

Stena wheeled in the water and turned to join her sisters,
and Delpha knew she was hungry, for her call changed to
one of excitement as she heard the smelts. Suddenly, however, her call changed again to the sharp rise-and-fall cry

which was the desperate summons for aid, and he turned abruptly to hear for himself what was wrong.

A marauding shark had torn into the school of smelts, a large black-tip who cut through the water like a serrated knife, jaw agape and body twisting in a rising frenzy. The yearlings instantly scattered, and the two sisters added their voices to Stena's cry for help.

Delpha felt a cold anger come to him, and he sped to his mate, who was no more than a body's length from the shark now, playing the avoidance game which was necessary with an enemy of this size. Like most dolphins, Stena could choose whether to run or to fight a shark, if not caught unawares and attacked without warning. But when calves were near and feeding was good, it was the dolphin's way to hesitate and decide whether to flee or fight.

Stena had clearly decided to attack, but she could not bring herself to make the first blow. Delpha wheeled between her body and the shark's, flapped his powerful tail for leverage, and rammed the shark in the side with all his strength, clicking furiously as he did so to warn the two sisters back.

The black-tip crumpled under the blow, recovered, and then turned with open jaw to punish the dolphin for his bravado. The shark's white eye rolled back in his head, the unmistakable sign that he intended to fight savagely, and Delpha rolled away from his bite, squealing in anger and fear. He circled the shark swiftly, coming at him again this time from the other side, and rammed him with all of his power once more, bruising his nose badly this time with the blow.

The yearlings meanwhile had circled back to see the battle, and Stena clicked to them anxiously to keep away, the whole while calling to her sisters for help.

The shark twisted once more under Delpha's punch and this time turned quickly enough to catch Delpha's side and rake his lower body with a jagged tooth. Bleeding now, Delpha turned to face his enemy once more. As he took a huge healing breath, Stena attacked from the opposite side, ramming the shark with all her strength, squealing in rage as she did so. Her two sisters rushed in, encircled the shark and barely avoided his snaps and twists and angry writhings. Biting at his flanks and tail, they nearly dragged him away from Stena, but she came at him once more from a distance, ramming him this time so hard that she shoved him two body lengths in the water.

The shark flashed his tail, whipped up the surface water, rose nearly out of the sea, and rushed away from the smelts. Delpha could tell by his lowered head that he would not return to the attack.

He hurried to Stena's side, moving alongside her and nuzzling her belly anxiously. She half rolled on her back, accepting his caresses, and then thrust her snout toward his. He could hear the spaces within her nose and mouth, could "see" that they were injured and sore, and he clicked to her gently, comforting her for her injury. The yearlings swarmed them now, curious and anxious to see the blood in the water, needing to reassure themselves that their mother was without serious injury.

Delpha knew that his own injuries were slight and would heal quickly, and the feelings of anger were slipping away, the distraction of rage that made him feel as uncomfortable and bruised as his nose was now. He circled his mate and yearlings, and when the two sisters approached, he enlarged his circle to enfold them as well. When he had pulled the pod back together and he sensed that they had told each other the story enough times to heal the fear, he gently prodded them to keep moving again, following the wake of the ship.

As he leaped high into the air, he could see that the vessel still sailed on, oblivious to the battle which had just been won beneath its hull, still rolled across the great sea with a power and majesty which drew him despite himself.

The dolphins hurried to catch the men in their boat, leaping high out of the air once and again to catch sight of them on the decks if they could.

* * *

The *Providence* sailed up the Mississippi, reaching the
port of New Orleans in the second week of September, just
ahead of the storm season. A full month behind schedule,
she carried far fewer trade goods than Captain had hoped for
and a new passenger besides.

New Orleans looked low and hazy in the late summer
heat, her buildings squatter, less lovely than the more gracious Charleston. The river levee allowed them to ride as
high as the houses, and it seemed they could look down into
the courtyards rather than up. The maze of crowded streets
leading down to the docks were busy with people, and the
brightly colored houses seemed to call out "foreign," even
though they were still in America.

"It's the French and Spanish influence," Josiah explained to Abigail. "They like exotic colors on their
homes."

She sniffed suspiciously.

Many of the houses were built of brick from the ground up
to the first floor, and the second floor was wrapped round
with galleries to catch the breeze.

Anxious to disembark, the passengers crowded the deck
of the *Providence* like refugees from another country, their
bags and children clustered around them. The customs officials who boarded spoke French to them first and then, only
reluctantly, heavily accented English. Josiah stood alongside
Robert Hanover, for they had already decided that they
would find conveyance upriver for their two families together. To his surprise, Mr. Henderson asked if he could
throw in with them as well. " 'Twill be easier to get a larger
boat than a smaller one," he argued, "and three purses to
pay will be better than two. We might not share the same
politics, but we will be neighbors, nonetheless. What do you
say?"

Josiah agreed readily. He glanced at Robert. "Only if you

keep your opinions on the war to yourself,'' Hanover finally said firmly. ''Agreed?''

Mr. Henderson bowed formally. ''You have my word on it.''

The three families disembarked, with hearty handshakes from the captain and best wishes from the crew. Abigail carried little Atlantic on her arm and her valise in the other hand. Ruth struggled with a bag too big for her, and Lamon and Jane each carried what they could. Josiah dropped a coin in a black boy's cap at the dock and got the rest of their trunks dragged to a waiting buggy. They were headed for a small inn on the dockside of New Orleans, where they would make arrangements for their passage upriver.

As they rode through the streets, Abigail murmured in surprise, ''I've not seen a single woman without paint in this town! Is that the way of the French then?''

Josiah shrugged. ''I suppose. But you'll see no wigs and paint in Natchez, I can assure you.''

''Praise God,'' she replied. ''Ruth, please sit up straight. It is not seemly to turn your entire body around to stare.''

''But Mother,'' she said, ''did you see that lady's beautiful dress? All lace with ribbons down the front to her toes!''

''Rather impractical, I would say,'' Abigail commented, ''with the mud in these streets. Wear it an hour and spend three hours brushing it clean—''

''Papa, what is that on the roofs of the houses?'' asked Lamon.

''New Orleans mud, they call it.'' Josiah smiled. ''They crush up the oysters from the river and mix it with clay and tar. They say it never leaks.''

''They should use it on their streets,'' Abigail offered.

Unlike the straight avenues of Eastern cities, the streets of *La Nouvelle Orleans* were narrow and twisting, following the curves of the river. Open gutters were clogged with offal, sewage, stagnant rainwater, and the dung of too many horses. The stench rose in the heat and hung like a fog about their noses.

A black man walked by dressed in a fine yellow waist-coat, followed by a servant who carried his valise. "Freedmen of color," Josiah said quietly. "There are many in the Territory, and some of them keep their own slaves."

"And this is allowed?" Abigail asked.

"There is little that is not," Josiah said in a low tone. "But we will be here only long enough to get what we need and head upriver."

"That's a blessing, then."

They came to the inn which was to shelter them, their buggy stopping just ahead of those buggies carrying the Hendersons and the Hanovers. The three families quickly found their apartments, settled their belongings, and the men left once more to arrange passage. By nightfall, they had hired a boat large enough for all three families and a small crew of four men to take them upriver. By the end of the second day, they had purchased what provisions they felt they could not find in Natchez, and by the morning of the third day, they were once more down at the river, loading up their boat for departure.

"I shall not miss New Orleans," Abigail said firmly. "The French can keep it, so far as I'm concerned."

Ruth gazed at the more than two dozen tall masted ships which lay at anchor nearby, each of them going to some exotic port or another, their flags fluttering in the river wind. Men stood in bunches all about them, haggling over goods, and other stevedores hoisted bales, loaded barges, and simply lay in the sun on the coiled ropes. Piles of crops lay on the docks: figs, watermelons, pecans, pumpkins, and other strange fruits and vegetables she had never seen before. "It is very beautiful," she murmured.

"I like the gingercake," Lamon declared. The only time Abigail had released the children from the inn was for a single visit to the public market, where they saw the street sellers offering oranges, bananas, sherbets, oysters, and gingercake for sale. Lamon had gorged himself on this New

Orleans specialty, and Abigail feared she would never hear the end of his desire.

Josiah, Robert, and Phillip Henderson were directing the loading of their families' goods. When Robert went to reprimand his sons and keep them off the crew, Phillip asked, "Did you notice how little we hear of the war in this town?" with a cautious glance at Hanover. "You'd never know a rebellion was happening in the colonies at all if you only had ears in New Orleans."

Josiah nodded. "They speak of only the Indians here, as if the rest of America scarcely existed."

"Did you hear of the recent troubles with the Chickasaw to the north?" Henderson murmured. "I did not mention it to Margaret, of course; she's got enough on her these days."

"Is she still feeling ill?" Josiah asked. Margaret Henderson had come down with a slight fever that morning, and she was listless and subdued even now.

Henderson put on an optimistic air. "You needn't worry about my Meg," he said jovially. "She's a strong woman. She'll not hold up the works. I heard the savages attacked a village north of Natchez—"

"I heard it was more than a hundred miles to the north," Josiah said firmly. "Let's not speak of it now. By the time we get there, it will undoubtedly be all over, if it ever gets to Natchez at all. The Indians are scattered and without arms these days; I doubt they can make much trouble."

Henderson considered that a moment. Finally he said, "You're right, of course. You, there!" he turned, calling to one of the hands. "Tie that trunk more securely, if you please!"

Finally, they were ready to leave the dock, and each man led his family aboard the large raft. There were seating areas enough for six, covered areas for sleeping, and small space in the middle of the raft encircled by the lashed trunks and hogsheads of provisions. The four hired crewmen, two white men and two black men, seemed to know the river and the raft well enough. They pushed off from the dock when all

the families were safely seated, one man at the tiller, three
more poling, and Josiah, Robert and his sons, and Phillip
Henderson poling as well, four on each side of the raft, as
they pulled away from New Orleans. Carefully, they maneuvered around the anchored ships, sometimes rowing, sometimes poling, sometimes leaping onshore and towing the raft
through the shallows.

Once they were out on the Mississippi, they made better
time, and the boatmen began to sing a riversong. Ruth complained of the sun and took shelter under the canvas sleeping
area with Margaret Henderson. The rest of the passengers
settled down as best they could to the last segment of their
long journey to Natchez.

The first night on the river was difficult, for every noise
from the banks caused the women and children to startle and
ask what beast made the sound and whether or not it was
likely to try to get to them on the raft. None of them was
anxious to set foot on the shore, even to do their necessaries
in the brush. Josiah would have thought that Abigail would
be eager to explore solid land after so many months at sea,
but she wanted only to sit silently under the canvas shelter
with Atlantic in her lap. During the night, Margaret Henderson grew worse, her fever rose alarmingly, and the women
took turns nursing her and laving her brow with river water.

Sometime in the night Abigail noticed that Ruth, too, was
weaker than she had been the day before. Jane alerted her
first by complaining that Ruth would not wake up nor speak,
no matter how she prodded her. When Abigail handed Atlantic to Jane and went to see how Ruth was, she came back
to Josiah with a grim mouth and anger in her eyes.

"She has the same fever Mrs. Henderson has," she said
shortly. "I might have known this would happen."

"How bad is she?" Josiah asked, alarmed. He had been
instructing Lamon on the way to properly coil the anchor
line, and he rose instantly to go to his eldest daughter.

"There's not room under that shelter for another body,"
Abigail said, waving him away. "She's hot as a brick and

nearly out of her head, is how she is. Mrs. Henderson has used up almost all the quinine. When do we reach the next town?''

Josiah hesitated.

''There *is* another town, is there not, between here and Natchez?''

''Not really,'' Josiah said honestly. ''Fort Adams is upriver, and we may well find all we need there, but there's no town—anyway, not a place which you would call a town—not until we reach Natchez.''

''And even Natchez is hardly a town, is that right?'' Abigail demanded. She was growing angrier with each word; Josiah could see it.

He nodded. ''But we'll get whatever we need for her, Abby. Please do not despair. God is with us—''

She snatched Atlantic from Jane's arms and came close enough to speak so that no one could hear her but him. ''Do not say that again to me, Josiah. Not until my children are safe and we are once more under a decent roof. If God is with us, He is playing a mighty cruel joke on us, indeed.''

Josiah bowed his head, unable to think of anything else to say. He knew from experience that if Abigail felt her children threatened, she lost all reason, and she would not be fair in her casting of blame. Once Ruth was well again, she would be easier to persuade, but not now. While he stood watching, she went once more to Ruth's side, pulling Jane and Lamon after her. Like a brooding hen, she gathered her chicks under her wings and turned her back to him as though he were a marauding hawk rather than her favored rooster.

He went to the edge of the raft and sat, melancholy and empty. Always, it had been thus. Abigail was a wonderful wife so long as all was right in their world. But when a crisis struck, she was filled with fear which translated to anger. He could not count on her to maintain her spirit before disaster. He wondered how she would fare in such a wilderness as Natchez. He could tell, by her words, that she was expecting more of a settlement than Natchez might be. He only could pray that in the nearly nine months of his absence, the village had grown closer to being something she could abide.

Robert Hanover came and sat beside him, lighting his pipe and gazing out over the river toward the western bank. "Your daughter is worse?" he murmured.

Josiah nodded, suddenly unable to speak.

"Wives don't take such things well," he said gently.

"Mine does not, that's certain."

Robert waited a long moment, and Josiah was thankful for the quiet. The river seemed to him such a deep, wide comfort after the constant motion and turbulence of the sea. The smells of dank, wet vegetation, mud, and unseen water creatures were primordial and basic, warm and soothing after the bracing, salt briskness of the Atlantic. Somehow, he felt safer here, for he felt that the river welcomed them in a way the ocean did not.

"Mrs. Henderson may well not last out the night," Hanover said then, almost as an aside. "She's near out of her head now, and her lungs sound full of fluid."

Josiah gazed at him. "Do you know anything to do for her?"

Robert shook his head. "She was likely too frail for this trip. Henderson should never have brought her."

"Perhaps I could be blamed for the same thoughtlessness," Josiah murmured. "Ah, God, I simply could not spend another year on that barren ground."

Robert awkwardly patted him on the shoulder, gruffly as a man will do when he seeks to comfort and does not know how to do it. "None of us could," he said. "But God listens to you, Fleming. I doubt He'll turn from you now." He rose and left Josiah alone, facing the river.

Josiah looked up at the moon, almost full now and hovering over the water like a benediction. If Ruth were not ill, if Abigail were not estranged, he would feel as if it were a beacon, a sign from all the angels that he had taken the right path, that his destiny was secure. But with a sick child, everything else was ashes in his mouth. Ruth was his favorite, truth be told. She had most of his heart the first time he held her; the other two had only the pieces left after she had her fill. He prayed often that no one would ever know how much more he loved her than any other living thing—only Abby probably knew the truth.

He bowed his head and prayed silently for long moments, beseeching God to save her. The fevers on this river could be mortal, he knew, and swift as the reaper's scythe. Grown men with vital, healthy constitutions were sometimes felled in as little as a night. But Ruth had youth on her side. That, and an indomitable spirit which was larger than her father's and mother's put together.

He rose abruptly and went to where his daughter lay. No matter how it might anger Abigail, he would see her. Perhaps if he only held her, it would help them both make it through the long midnight hours.

When he knelt over Ruth, ignoring Abigail's frown and hush of silence, she opened her eyes and turned her head toward him. "Papa," she whispered. Her lips were dry and caked with spittle. He was shocked at how wan and fragile she looked, how much of her was already taken since only that morning.

"Ruth, you must not give in to this," he said to her firmly. "Pray to God to be with you and He will take away the fever."

"I am," she said weakly. "The angels speak to me, Papa."

Abigail took in her breath in a gasp of alarm, but Josiah ignored the implication. "That's good, Ruth," he said, taking her hand. "You are a good, strong girl, and I love you. Do you know that I love you?"

She smiled faintly, her eyes closing again.

"Pray for strength, Ruth," he said again, leaning down and kissing her cheek. "Natchez is waiting for you."

"Natchez," she whispered, slipping away again.

Josiah put an arm around his wife and another one around his two children. Lamon and Jane instantly nestled to him as though for comfort. "Tomorrow, we will all be rested and we'll be strong again," he said with more confidence than he felt. "The river is very beautiful from here on up, and we're almost there."

"How much farther, Papa?" asked Jane wearily.

"See the moon?" Josiah pointed outside the canvas as the two children craned their necks to see where he pointed. "When the moon is thin again, we'll be in Natchez. We'll be home on our own land."

Abigail's body finally yielded to the pressure of his arm, and she leaned against him. Together, they slept thus, waiting for the dawn.

For two days, they struggled upriver to Baton Rouge, the small village which the Acadian people were settling about a hundred miles north of New Orleans. The currents were swift in this part of the river, and it made more turns and twists than an angry serpent. The men worked hard to make sometimes less than twenty miles in twelve hours. By the time they reached the little village, Margaret Henderson was dead.

She had slipped away the night before they reached Baton Rouge, with little to mark her going save the sudden sightlessness of her eyes. Abigail was tending her in that hour, the time before dawn which seems to claim so many fragile spirits, and she instinctively turned to Ruth and put her hand on her brow, praying that her own daughter had not followed the woman's example. But Ruth seemed cooler, her face less twisted with pain.

At the touch of her mother's hand, she awoke and smiled slightly. "Ruth?" whispered Abigail, "how do you feel?"

"Better, I think," she murmured weakly. "Is there any water?"

Abigail reached quickly for the pewter jug and poured off the top so that the river mud at the bottom would stay undisturbed. She held her daughter's head so that she might drink. "I think you're cooler," she whispered. "Perhaps the fever has lessened."

"It feels so," Ruth said after she'd taken several large swallows. "How is Mrs. Henderson?"

How like Ruth to ask, Abigail noted. "I'm afraid she's no better," she said carefully to her daughter. "But you are, that's certain. You're younger and stronger—"

Ruth focused then on her mother's face. "She's dead?" she asked faintly, sensing the truth.

Abigail dropped her head and nodded. "I did not want to frighten you. I think she passed a quarter-hour ago."

Ruth turned her head to gaze at the other bulk of comforter and rumpled clothing in the corner of the shelter. "I think I felt her go," she murmured. "I thought I heard her voice calling, so clearly. Just a few minutes before you woke me."

Abigail looked carefully at Ruth's face and took her hand. Even though she seemed better, there was a chance she could slip from them as well. "Perhaps it was only the cry of a river bird," she said softly. "The creatures are so many and so loud on this river . . ."

Ruth squeezed her hand. "Don't be afraid, Mama. I'm going to live."

Abigail's eyes filled with sudden tears of relief. Her daughter had always been older than her years, and she was never more grateful for that quality than now. She sighed deeply and arranged the comforter at her daughter's throat, simply to have something to do to keep her eyes from watering. "I should go and tell Mr. Henderson that she's gone," she murmured.

"Do you think we will ever get to Natchez?" Ruth whispered, almost as though she were afraid to speak her doubts aloud. She seemed loath to let her mother go.

"Of course we will," Abigail said quickly. "Your father is not a man to let his dreams die that easily."

Ruth was quiet for a moment. "I don't believe it's going to be so beautiful after all," she said then, reluctantly. "How can it be that much more beautiful than what we've already seen?"

Abigail frowned slightly. "It will be beautiful because it will be ours." She patted Ruth's hand. "You'll learn soon enough to see things through some man's eyes, child. You might as well begin that practice now. Your father says it is worth it, and so it will be." She smiled down at her. "Now let me go and break the news to that poor man. We should be in Baton Rouge by midday. Perhaps we'll be able to rest there a bit and get a decent bed and a cup of coffee. If I have to drink this river water the rest of my life, I'd like it mixed with something better than mud."

Ruth smiled at her mother's effort at wit. She knew then she would live after all. She closed her eyes to gather her strength for the coming hours.

When they reached Baton Rouge, they found a preacher to say a service over Margaret Henderson, and she was put to rest in the burial ground to the west of the village. It was surprisingly full, considering the settlement had fewer than fifty souls living there. All of the families and the hired men attended, but Ruth was unable to leave her bed at the small inn they found to shelter them down by the Baton Rouge landing. Soon after the burial, Jane joined her there, complaining of a sick headache.

When Abigail went to her, she was alarmed to feel how hot her skin was to the touch. "Ah my Lord," she moaned to herself, not wanting Jane to hear, "she's taken ill as well!"

She went to Josiah as soon as she had made her two daughters comfortable. "Jane has the fever," she said to him wearily, once she got him alone. Mr. Henderson had gone into the village to see to his affairs, and the Hanovers were in their rooms. She began to weep with fear. "She's so small, she hasn't the strength that Ruth has!"

"Dear God," he groaned, holding her to him. "What shall we do?"

His indecision suddenly enraged her, and she pushed him away, turning on him in a fury. "What shall we do? Why ask me this now, Josiah? You made the decision to bring us here, to uproot the children and wrench me away from my family, and now one is barely holding on to life and the other—my Jane!—may well be taken away from us by the next morning! And now you ask me what we should do! What we should have done is never to have left Stonington!''

''There was nothing for us in Stonington,'' he said wearily. ''You know that, Abby, as well as I—''

''There was nothing for *you* in Stonington, Josiah, but the rest of us were doing well enough, thank you! At least we could raise our children without these plagues and fevers taking them. I can deal with measles and the flux and the other diseases flesh is heir to in my own country, but these fevers come in the night and take away the soul and I can do nothing to stop them! There's not even a doctor who can help . . .'' She stopped and sobbed once, a harsh and unforgiving sound in the little, dim room. ''Nothing but pitiful burial grounds with sad little markers and not enough room for another body.''

He embraced her again firmly, ignoring her efforts to push him off. ''Abigail! Abigail, you must not lose hope! Ruth is recovering, and Jane may well not be taken with the same fever, or not nearly so bad, you can't know that yet. Where is your faith? Pray to God for comfort, Abby, and He will answer your prayers.''

She sobbed now, openly. ''He has answered little enough of those lately. I prayed we would not come to this wilderness, and we are here. I prayed we would be in Natchez before the birth of our child, and he is here and we are still weeks from our own land. And every day I pray for my children, yet two of them are in peril!''

Josiah held her tightly, letting her weep on his chest until she was almost under control once more. He gently bent her to the floor, his arm still around her, and helped her to put her hands together in supplication. He led her then into prayer, repeating the words, ''Help us, Oh Lord,'' over and over again, together with the Lord's Prayer, until she was calm. Then he helped her to rise.

Her eyes were clear once more, and her face was stoic.

She took his hand off her wrist. "If Jane dies," she said calmly, "the children and I will be on the next boat back to Stonington." And she walked quickly from the room.

Mr. Henderson made the painful decision to stay in Baton Rouge. He asked Hanover to sell his land for him at the best price he could get and send him the proceeds. "I'll remain here with my wife until then," he said forlornly. "And after that, I don't know. Maybe go to New Orleans. Maybe back East. I have no more heart for Natchez."

Josiah would remember the next forty-eight hours for the rest of his life, and there were moments within them when he wanted that life to cease forever. Jane's fever rose at an alarming rate once they were on the river again, and someplace north of Baton Rouge, before they reached Fort Adams, Atlantic took sick as well. Tess Hanover, who had been able to spell Abigail and nurse Atlantic when Jane could not be left alone, also felt ill. It was a terrifying spate of hours when the men and boys had to keep poling, keep moving the raft northward, making what progress they could, and the women fought for life in the cramped, damp, haphazard shelter that the small pieces of canvas provided, moving the sick ones from shade to sun as they could, sieving water through their skirts to get out the mud, and laving fevered flesh over and over with filthy cloths.

By nightfall on the second day from Baton Rouge, Jane was no longer conscious, Atlantic was very hot to the touch, and Tess Hanover was every bit as sick as Ruth had been before her. Ruth and Abigail showed Lamon how to care for his little brother, for Jane and Tess seemed to need more expert care. At dawn, Lamon brought the baby to his mother, his face woeful and frightened.

"Mama," he whispered to her as she lay exhausted next to Ruth on an open planking. "Mama . . ." He touched her lightly on the cheek, and she woke with a start.

"Does the baby need milk?" she asked, taking Atlantic in

her arms. He had refused her breast most of the day, sucking instead on a cool, wet cloth.

Lamon did not answer but only watched his baby brother with wide eyes.

Abigail wearily opened her bodice and turned the baby to face her, and then she saw that the infant was unmoving and cool to the touch. His fever was gone. She laid him down on her lap and gazed at him, then lifted him again and held his chest to her ear, feeling with her hand for any sign of breath from his tiny, open mouth. Atlantic was dead.

"The baby won't breathe," Lamon said softly, sorrowfully. "I tried to make him, but he won't do it."

Ruth stirred at Lamon's voice, waking and rising up on one elbow. She stared at her mother in confusion and then at the baby in her lap. Her eyes widened in horror. "Is the baby dead?" she whispered.

Abigail said nothing. She lowered Atlantic again to her lap and laid her hand on his head as if to shield him from the darkness. "He's not breathing, Lamon," she said gently, "because he has decided to go to heaven."

Ruth stifled a sharp sob, and Abigail reached out with one hand and touched her shoulder, hushing her gently. She could not face Josiah now.

"The baby went to heaven?" Lamon asked in bewilderment. "All by himself?" He seemed amazed that a tiny boy could make such a decision.

"Yes. But God will shelter him, and when you go to heaven, you will see him then. We'll all be together again."

Lamon looked at Ruth as if for assurance that this must be so. Ruth nodded to him confidently, through her tears. He bent and looked carefully at his baby brother and then sat down next to his mother. "Will I be going to heaven soon?"

She shook her head. Somewhere, she was surprised at the stillness in her heart, the feeling of great, cold calm. "Not for a long, long time," she said.

His face screwed up then and he fought back tears. "But

what if I get sick and die, Mama? Like Ruth and Janey and 'lantic!''

"Ruth did not die, and Janey hasn't died; Atlantic was just too little. You're a big, strong boy, and you're not sick at all, are you?" She felt his head. "Do you feel sick, Lamon?"

He shook his head and nestled closer to her.

"Then don't worry. I won't let anything happen to you. You're my only boy left." She hugged him tightly and then turned to pick up the baby. Ruth moved closer to her on her other side. Dawn would be soon enough to tell his father. For the few brief hours of darkness left, she wanted her remaining children to herself. She held the three and sat watching the river move past the anchored raft, and she did not think of God once.

After a while, Lamon dozed off on her shoulder, and Ruth saw that he was asleep. "Mama?" she murmured.

"Yes?"

"Why did Papa have to bring us so far from home?"

What was left of Abigail's heart broke then at the deep sadness and despair in her eldest daughter's voice. She sighed and thought what she might say. She did not want Ruth to share her bitterness. "Papa did what he thought was best for us all," she whispered. "Try to get some rest, Ruth. Tomorrow will be hard enough."

"But how could it be best?" she asked desperately, ignoring her mother's suggestion. "How could it be best for Janey? How could it be best for Atlantic? It isn't best for anyone but Papa!" She began to weep again in sorrow and frustration.

"We cannot know that yet," Abigail said gently. "Try to have faith in God and in your papa."

"God did not bring us to this awful place," Ruth whimpered. "Papa did."

Abigail could say nothing more. Her own throat hurt so badly, her heart ached so intensely that she could scarcely keep from throwing herself into the dark water and letting out her final breath in resignation. She could only hold her daughter close and croon to her, hoping the dawn would bring them some solace.

The next morning, Tess Hanover was dead also. Jane was still alive, but she showed no response to any stimulus. Weeping, Robert Hanover and his sons poled and prodded the raft now in a desperate pitch of sorrow and anger, shouting at the men to get them upriver faster, as if he were somehow leaving death behind.

But they were not. Within sight of Fort Adams, Jane also breathed her last. That afternoon, they buried little Atlantic, Tess Hanover, and Jane Fleming, six years old, in the common ground outside the fort.

Josiah wept so hard at the gravesites that he thought his heart would burst in his chest. He felt a physical pain in his body like a deep, killing wound that would never heal. Abby leaned against him, weeping quietly, half in shock. Ruth stood to his left, her face pale and trembling, still hardly able to stand for long periods of time. Lamon and the Hanover boys were white and starkly grim, suddenly older by a decade, it seemed. No longer the boys they had been in New Orleans.

His family was decimated, Josiah knew, and would never be the same, no, no matter how much healing time passed, no matter how many more babies might come to replace those gone. They would never be whole again.

And still, they were at least a hundred miles away from Natchez. How much more torment could the river deal them?

Abby did not speak again of leaving, though Josiah had no confidence that she might not once she reached Natchez and a larger populace. She talked to him only when she had to now, and with monosyllables which spoke volumes of her pain and her loss of faith. He knew she blamed him for everything—Atlantic's birth, Atlantic's death, Ruth's sickness, Janey's death, Lamon's wizened, old-man face, her own pain and misery—every bit of it was on his shoulders and would be until the day they laid him to rest alongside his children.

In his own mind he felt guilt, but he also felt a secret sense of betrayal, that Abby so firmly resisted his dreams. Had always done so, it seemed to him now, since the very first time the midwife put a baby in her arms. Until Ruth's birth, he had come first in her heart. After Ruth, and with each succeeding child, she had retreated farther and farther from him, becoming less and less vital to her like a receding star from the sun.

Sometimes it seemed to him that she was the queen bee, the core of the family, and he was no more than another worker bee to serve their needs. But then his sorrow and guilt overwhelmed him again, and he lost any resentment. He felt only the deepest sense of loss he hoped he would ever have to endure.

Robert Hanover moved through the next day in silent shock, and Josiah expected he would come to him, as Henderson had, and say that he could not go on. But instead, he announced that he would go to Natchez and make his fortune, as Tess would have wanted him to.

"And find another wife, no doubt," Abigail sniffed when Josiah told her. "And her scarcely cold."

"He could more easily find a wife farther south, say in New Orleans, than he will in Natchez," Josiah reproved her mildly. "He loved her, and he will mourn her loss all of his days. But he has his sons to think of, his dream is still alive, and that's why he's going to Natchez."

"Dreams." She repeated the word with such scorn and despair that Josiah feared to say another. He retreated then to go and comfort Lamon and Ruth, who sat together at the side of the raft, silent and bewildered. There was nothing else he could do for his wife.

It was harder to leave the dusty, ugly settlement of Fort Adams than it had been to say goodbye to Stonington. There were living souls in Stonington but none so dear as those dead ones in the earth next to the Mississippi. Both Josiah and Abigail could not, in fact, make a final sort of farewell to the place, and told Lamon and Ruth that they would come back and get both their children once they were settled in Natchez. The details of that retrieval, mercifully, the two siblings did not ask, and so they once more set out for the northern bends and turns of the great river.

The Mississippi was banked by swamps for the first twenty miles or so upriver from Fort Adams. Heavy, primeval trees laden with moss grew right to the edge of the river, and the land on either side looked scarcely firm enough to hold them upright. The hired men were loath to step off the raft in these wet places, for they feared all manner of snakes and sucking sands. And so the progress seemed slow, endless, and heartbreakingly arduous. The mosquitoes tortured them from late afternoon until past midnight, and they could hear the noises of the wild beasts closer now than they had before.

Often, the poles did not reach bottom, or if they did, the mud was too soft to gain purchase. And so the men had to do what they called ''cordelling,'' which seemed to Josiah the most killing job he had ever witnessed. There was simply no other way to get upriver.

Almost every bend in the Mississippi had a reverse current or eddy. These upriver currents were usually close to the riverbank and were used to full advantage when they could. But how to get around the next point and into the next eddy was the real problem.

This is where the cordelle came into play. The men would put a line ashore and pull the boat as far as they could possibly drag it, each one watching carefully where he put his feet, and also peering overhead for any low-hanging serpents. They then tied the toe line to a large tree ahead of the boat, and the man who remained on the boat would set his rudder against the current. This caused the raft to move forward to abreast of the point where the line was tied. Then the men onshore would tug and pull into the next eddy, and the process was repeated over and over, through the struggling hours.

The rudder man had, of course, the choicest position, and occasionally fights would break out among the hired men as to who might have been due a turn at the rudder next. Often, Robert or Josiah had to give up their turn so as to placate the men and keep them working, for money alone was insufficient motivation when the task was so grimly difficult.

Only once did two of the men erupt in a fight so fierce that Josiah was unable to stop it. As best he could tell, it centered around a young woman named Ella back in Baton Rouge as well as the coveted rudder, and before he could quell the argument, each of them had drawn knives and lunged at each other. One man, an Irish stevedore, slashed at the Creole sailor from New Orleans, and drew first blood across the man's cheekbone. In a flash, the Creole stabbed him in the neck, and he fell bleeding to the muddy bank.

Lamon screamed, for he had seen the fight begin, and as Abigail hurried him back into the shelter, Robert and Josiah and the others disarmed the Creole and turned their attention to the Irishman.

He was bleeding heavily, cursing his opponent in a tongue that was half Gaelic, half rude English, and with a final blaspheme on his lips, he died. Josiah said a prayer over the man, and they buried the Irishman in the Mississippi mud.

Robert pulled him away to say, "We'll need another hand. And as much as I'd like to run the Creole off or shackle him for the authorities, we dare not, lest we be unable to get two more to replace him. He's a strong mule, and with Danny gone, I doubt he'll fire up again."

Josiah gazed calmly at Robert, unable to believe that he was in this position. He would have to keep the man on, expose his family to a murderer, else take the chance they might never reach Natchez at all. But Robert was right. There was little choice.

"Where can we get more hands?" he asked.

"The Homochittos are upriver, not ten miles. We'll hire

two more men at their village, and likely be better for it. The Indians know this river like no one else.''

Josiah shook his head. Murderers and savages, and his were the only two females left onboard. "Would you suggest such a thing if your Tess were still alive?'' he murmured, half-knowing the answer already.

"I'd have no choice,'' Robert said firmly. "And neither do you, I regret to say. My boys are already doing the work of grown men, so unless you wish to put your wife and son to work on the rudder, there's nothing else for it.''

Josiah shook his head. "Let's just get there,'' he said wearily. "Surely nothing else can plague us between here and Natchez now.''

The small flying squirrel sat on the thin edge of the limb, as far away from his nest hole as he dared to go when his mate was off foraging. Very soon, it would be dusk, and he sensed the shadows lengthening more quickly now with every passing moment. Within the nest he could hear the squeaks and murmurings of his offspring, a litter of four naked, blind pups born just five nights before. Like him, they grew more active as the night approached.

He was Volan, the only flying squirrel species in the lower Mississippi, a smallish gray-brown creature with snow-white underbelly, a flattened gray-brown tail, and a loose fold of skin between his front and hind legs. His eyes were unusually large and black, even for a squirrel, and with them he watched the ground carefully.

The nest was one he had returned to year after year, mating and then persuading his mate of that season to build in this old woodpecker hole in the beech tree, high above the riverbank. Volan knew, from past seasons, that the great water often rose high and spread over the forest and the swamplands, flooding nests which were made too low and carelessly in smaller trees.

This beech was his, and he had claimed it again and again from younger males. Just as he had claimed his mates.

Volan scratched his hindquarters rapidly, snatched the flea off his back claws, and shifted his position nervously. His mate had been gone most of the afternoon. He was hungry himself, but he dared not leave the pups without guard. Small as he was, he was a fierce fighter when something of his was threatened, be it his pups, his nest, or his mate.

This litter was born of the first mating, another thing Volan had learned to do every breeding season. Let the younger males squabble over mates too long and end up with only the late summer breeding to make their nests and have their pups. Volan always chose the first breeding, even if he could not have his first choice of mates.

Normally, Volan slept most of the daylight hours away, for like the rest of his kind, he was nocturnal. But with the pups growing so quickly and his mate needing to forage well to fuel her milk supply, the hours of rest were fewer. And no squirrel could afford to sleep away the most dangerous hours, those just before dusk.

A bluejay landed on the branch several feet above Volan's head and cawed raucously at him, warning as always of danger. The jay's calls were so frequent as to be almost meaningless, and Volan only chittered at him in annoyance and then turned his back to the noise.

Far below in the brush, a female raccoon waddled slowly toward the river. No doubt she had a nest hidden nearby as well. Volan watched her carefully, for raccoons occasionally dared to attack nests, particularly in hard storm seasons. But this one showed no interest either in him or his tree.

The wind was low on the river this evening, a fine summer night in the making, Volan saw. Surely his mate would return soon, and he could hunt the summer crickets he savored. More carnivorous than most of his squirrel cousins, Volan ate whatever insects he could catch, and even an occasional minnow from the river shallows. He also feasted on all the acorns, nuts, seeds, and berries which the other

ground creatures sought, and he did his best to keep his fat
layers high at all times of the year, not only in the season of
the falling leaf. In that way, he sensed he was stronger, more
ready for danger.

A small scratching at the base of the beech caught his attention instantly. Expecting to see his mate returning, Volan
bent far down and focused on the source of the noise beneath
him. To his instant alarm, he saw a large black snake nosing
about the base of the beech.

Volan froze, holding his breath in terror. This was the
thing he feared most, of course, as did all of his kind. Neither
owl nor hawk nor fox took as many pups in one season as the
snake, and many grown squirrels as well, if they were not
very strong and very smart. The jay darted by overhead
screeching, "Viper! Viper! Viper!," a warning too late and
of no help whatsoever.

Now as Volan watched, the black snake shoved its large
nose into the grasses and small brush at the roots of the tree,
and then stared up the long trunk appraisingly, its black
tongue flickering in and out. Volan knew so long as he did
not move, the snake could not see him, but his scent and the
scent of his mate were on the tree. The snake knew they were
there.

Volan knew that if his mate returned now, the snake
would likely catch her, for she would be almost helpless on
the ground. Yet if she did return, she could perhaps help him
fend off the serpent, leading it away from the pups. He could
do nothing but stay perfectly still and wait to see what the
snake would do.

The black snake seemed to find a place on the beech trunk
which most especially intrigued it, and it raised itself high
off the ground and edged several feet up the rough bark.
Volan still stayed perfectly still. He knew that the snake
could not hear the noise of the pups; he wondered if it could
sense the vibrations they made within the tree.

The black snake began to climb the beech, and Volan
could see now that it was out of the brush that it was nearly

half the height of the tree. Noiselessly, Volan scampered to the branch just above the one he had just occupied, and he froze once more, unsure what his next action should be. If he'd been without mate and pups, he would have long since flown from the tree. If his mate sat within the nest, he might have had the courage to confront the snake, the two of them together. But alone, he was not certain what he could do.

Meanwhile, the snake inched cautiously up the tree, never hurrying, never veering from its course, its long tongue flickering in and out constantly, telling it the route the squirrels had taken most recently. At the base of the tree, Volan heard an angry chittering, an alarm call of frantic desperation, and he looked to see that his mate had returned.

She was a smallish gray, and this was only her second breeding season. Fertile with ample milk, he expected she would make a good mate for several seasons, should he be able to keep her. And should she be able to survive.

The snake had now reached a branch less than three feet from the opening to the nest. As if they sensed danger, the pups were strangely quiet. Volan's mate had scurried up the tree and stopped on a branch away from the snake, screeching angrily at it and stomping with her forepaws. But she dared come no closer.

Volan made the decision in an instant, leaping from his upper branch onto the snake below him, reaching behind the snake's head and biting with all his strength. The snake tightened its grip on the branch and reared back its head, snapping Volan like a spring and knocking him against the beech. Volan let go, reeling in shock, barely grabbed a claw hold on the branch, and scuttled to safety. The snake then went swiftly into the nest and devoured all of the pups as easily, as quickly, as if it were drinking cool water from the river shallows.

Volan watched in silent horror. His mate was silent as well. Finally, with never another glance at them, the black snake slid down the beech tree, a noticeable bulge in its belly, and back into the brush, heading toward the river.

Volan's mate moved quickly up the tree and into the nest, chittering frantically for her pups. She then erupted from the nest and attacked Volan desperately, chasing him round and round the beech, up and down the great trunk, in a frenzied spiral of frustration and confusion, nipping at his tail and making squealing noises like an angry pig. He had never been chased so hard, even by a rival male, and he felt fear of his mate for the first time in his life.

Finally she stopped, panting heavily. She went back to the nest and went in again to search for the litter, ignoring him now. He listened outside the hole, panting himself and wary of her next move. But she was silent. Indeed, they were all gone.

She did not come back out of the nest, and finally Volan followed her into the hole, his nostrils and whiskers quivering violently with the overwhelming odor of viper. His mate cast a baleful eye on him, screeched fiercely, and bit him soundly on the shoulder, close to his left ear. He did not return her ferocity nor did he run, but only lay down beside her, panting slightly.

Although he was very hungry, Volan did not leave her side through the night. Several times, she rose and hunted frantically again for the pups in every niche of the hole, as though she had forgotten their fate all over again. Finally, as dawn came to the woods, she subsided and seemed calmer once more. The scent of the snake was diminished enough so that the nest no longer seemed fouled.

Volan's mate was curled beside him. He nosed her, gently at first and then with more determination. She woke and he urged her outside the hole. Bewildered, she followed him to the end of the branch, and he cast himself into the air, the great skin fold between his legs stretching out like bat's wings, his tail flat in the air ruddering his direction. She followed his jump, and they landed gracefully on the ground, a good distance from the beech. Once landed, he mounted her vigorously, wasting little time with preamble.

Several moons later, as the geese were beginning to fly,

Volan's mate littered four more squirrel pups, but this time she would not be persuaded to nest in the old woodpecker hole.

At long last, they made Natchez, arriving at dusk on a cool day in late October. Nearly two months later than they'd planned, two children fewer than they'd planned, but at least they were alive, Josiah told himself. And he praised God aloud as they finally stepped ashore.

The little village sat on a bluff high above the river, two settlements, actually: Natchez-Over-the-Hill and Natchez-Under-the-Hill. The upper village was one street of small houses, none of them substantial by Stonington standards, but all of them relatively tidy and well appointed. The lower village was a hodgepodge of dockside inns, two taverns, and shanties which housed the business establishments of Natchez, both of good and ill character.

Back from the river sat Fort Panure, once Fort Rosalie, renamed when the British took over the Natchez Territory. The sturdy stockade walls seemed the most comforting sight Josiah had seen in six months, British or not.

Robert Hanover took his boys to one of the inns near the docks; Josiah ushered his family to a boardinghouse on the upper bluff, for he felt sure that Abigail did not wish to see water nor boats for several days.

In fact, the very words "boardinghouse" and "inn" implied more than Natchez could offer in truth. The inn was nothing more than a poor hut open to one side where the horses were stabled. If Robert asked politely, he and the boys might be served a mess of mush and milk or some fried bacon. Their beds were simple straw pallets on the ground. The boardinghouse offered cots, and perhaps a piece of fresh meat or fish, but was little more luxurious than the inn. At least it was a good distance from the docks.

After settling his family in one small room, Josiah and

Robert set off immediately to check on their claims at the land registry office at Fort Panure.

Abigail's last words to him rang in his ears as he walked the single street of the village. "Natchez has far to go before I'd call it a town," she had said. Now that he saw it through her eyes for the first time, he had to admit that she was right. When he'd seen Natchez nearly a year before, it had seemed a bustling, growing settlement, full of strong men with adventure in their hearts. The shining hope of free land had flashed in his eyes and blinded him.

He had not thought of such things as Abigail would, such as how they might find and acquaint themselves with decent, educated folk, how Lamon was going to get his schooling, how they might furnish their house once they built it, and how Ruth might find a suitable husband in the Natchez wilderness. She had not yet asked him those questions, but he knew she would soon enough.

"Do you plan to marry again?" he suddenly asked Robert. He knew it was a baldly put question, but he guessed the man would answer.

Robert Hanover looked at him askance as they entered the stockade walls of the fort. "Surely," he said with brisk confidence. "If I have to, I'll import a wife from New York or Long Island. But I doubt I'll have to go to such expense. No doubt there're wives a-plenty in New Orleans. My boys will need a woman in the house, and so will I."

He said it so matter-of-factly, he might well have been discussing the purchase of a new carriage.

"Why do you ask such a thing, brother Josiah?" Hanover grinned at him. The man was taller, a fact which always made Josiah feel younger, less acquainted with life's wiles somehow. "Are ye thinking to shed your own?"

Josiah was instantly and deeply offended for Abigail, but he could not stop a rueful smile. "She's a good woman," he replied. "Change is harder for them than for us, I think. She'll grieve our lost children for the rest of her life. She was happy in Stonington. But this . . ." He gestured around the fort to the straggling Indians leaning lazily in the sun, the black slaves hoeing the dusty corn rows, the soldiers in motley uniform, the settlers in ragtag clothes, and the rivermen in skins and filthy trousers. "This is hardly paradise, to her eyes."

"Well, ye shouldn't have promised her such," Hanover said cheerfully. "Tess knew we were headed for a grand adventure in the wilderness, and she didn't expect a fine feather bed every night."

"I imagine she didn't expect the fever, either," Josiah snapped, rankled. "If you'd lost one or both of your boys, I misdoubt you'd be so full of high spirits." In that moment, he pictured Jane with her lively curls, and he felt despair flood over him. "Abigail will likely never be the same."

"She's still a healthy woman," Robert said. "You can have more children, if you've a mind."

Josiah shook his head, too dispirited to argue. Robert Hanover was a good man, he knew, but he was not speaking with his normal sensitivities. No doubt he, too, was still in shock over his loss. Perhaps he was even afraid.

They reached the claims office and introduced themselves to the clerk. After some checking of his books, the man said to Josiah, "I'm sorry, Mr. Fleming. Your claim was forfeit due to nonsettlement. Only last month, in fact. Mr. Hanover's is still valid, but yours has been reregistered in the name of"—he turned some more pages in his ledger—"a Mr. Whitehall, as of September fifteenth, I'm afraid. He is the new claimsholder of record, sir." The clerk was a young man, and he struggled hard to keep his voice and face in tones and planes of authority. And yet Josiah could see that he feared a confrontation.

"My claim is lost?" he asked, bewildered.

The clerk dropped his eyes. "I'm afraid, sir, that the law is quite clear. If you do not settle your claim within a year of record, it is forfeit. Mr. Hanover recorded his claim a month after yours, and so his is still intact. But yours is reclaimed, sir. I'm sorry."

"The whole parcel? All five hundred acres?"

"The claim is kept intact, sir."

"And there is no appeal?"

"Not once the new claimsholder has paid the registration fee, sir. Now if *he* does not settle the land within the year, you may file a new claim yourself, but until September fifteenth of the next year, he is the rightful owner."

Robert Hanover put his hand on Josiah's shoulder to steady him. "Do you know if the new owner has broken ground yet?"

The clerk shrugged, clearly eager to move the two men out of his office as soon as he could. "I have no information on that, sir. Perhaps you could inquire at the livery, if the man has bought a team for plowing."

"Well, do you know if there's another parcel within close proximity to Mr. Fleming's original claim which might be available for claim by him now?" Robert would not give up so easily.

The clerk opened a large mapbook and scanned it quickly. "There are several large parcels still open, but I can't say how they might compare to the other claim. You are welcome to go and ascertain that for yourself, of course."

"What about Phillip Henderson's claim?" Robert asked quickly. "He's not coming to Natchez after all; we left him in Baton Rouge."

"Well, of course, we should have to have him come and relinquish his claim in person, sir. You understand that we cannot take your word upon it alone."

"When is his time up?"

The clerk consulted his journal. "December second."

"More than two months," Josiah murmured.

"Thank you," Hanover said, taking Josiah's arm. "We'll be back. If you have any other message, you can leave word at the White Apple Inn."

Josiah could scarcely move, could not think at all. He had come all this way, had sacrificed the lives of two of his children and the health of the others, his wife's goodwill, perhaps the future of his family—for nothing. He was without land. And so, therefore, he was without promise of any kind. He could not imagine how he could possibly tell this to Abigail. He would rather throw himself off the bluffs of Natchez and break his head on the rocks below. He felt the pressure of Robert's hand on his arm as though from a very great distance, and he mechanically moved his body in the direction the man was leading him, out of the claims office and out of the fort.

"Don't despair," Hanover was saying to him. "Likely we can find another parcel; maybe one you'll find just as promising. Or if not, perhaps the man will want to sell off part of his—you don't need five hundred acres after all, man! We'll go there immediately and speak with him, and if he's not in a mind to sell, we'll mark off a new claim for you. In the next year, he may well change his mind, and then you could make him an offer off your first crop, or maybe Henderson's land will do."

The words meant nothing to Josiah; he could scarcely make sense of them. All he could hear over and over in his head was the sentence, "Your claim is forfeit, sir." It sounded like judge and jury all together.

Dazedly, he looked around Natchez as they walked back to the White Apple Inn. He could not decipher this news somehow in his mind. An underlying panic kept rising up in his heart: How could he ever tell this to Abigail? What words would soften this dreadful news? How could he possibly keep her by his side in Natchez?

And then he realized that he might have to go back to Stonington after all. If he had no land, there was nothing to keep him here. Nothing to persuade Abigail to stay. An image came to his mind then: the thought of arriving back in Stonington harbor, facing his father-in-law a failure, with no land, having sold what he had there, and telling them that he had lost two of his grandchildren in the bargain.

That was impossible, he knew. He shook his head unconsciously. There was no way in God's world he could go back to Stonington now. Even if Abigail took the children and left, he would not go back. He could not. He would truly rather be dead. And so he must convince her to stay. Must get new land, somehow. Must show her that he could care for his family, no matter what.

"I don't think we should waste any time," Robert was saying firmly. "We must get upriver to our claims."

"I have no claim," Josiah said hollowly.

"Yes, but you shall." Robert waved that away impatiently. He was not a man to dance with despair for long. "We must get upriver as fast as we can and find this Whitehall and make him an offer. Or find you new land." He turned Josiah to face him. "We're partners, still, Fleming, and don't forget that. We'll weather this as we've made it through all else. Don't you dare give out on me!"

Josiah gave the man a wan smile. "Since we're partners, then, would you care to share in the explanation to my wife?"

Robert chuckled ruefully and slapped him on the back, propelling him several feet in the direction of the inn. "I'd rather swim all the way to New Orleans. I'll go tend to the boys and see to our provisions. We'll need to hire a new man to get us the last way upriver."

"Go and get the axes sharpened and the handle replaced on that one of mine," Josiah said, still feeling disoriented. "We'll need to knock together a shelter the first hour we get off the raft."

Robert strode off in the direction of his own inn, and Josiah admired once more the determined set of the man's shoulders. Squaring his own, he turned and walked quickly to the boardinghouse where he had left his family, while he still could borrow some of Hanover's courage.

The next morning, they left Natchez with one new hire and what provisions they had been able to muster together in short order. Josiah took his position at the pole, keeping his back to Abigail. She sat huddled on the little raft under the canvas shelter, holding to Ruth and Lamon as though they were the only lifelines to solid ground.

The scene the night before had been every bit as terrible as he had feared. He knew there was no way to tell Abigail such a thing gently, so he simply told her the facts as quickly as he could, rushing on to what the solutions might be, what hope they might still have, almost in the same breath. Thank God, Ruth and Lamon had not been witness to their mother's words.

"My father was right," she said to him scathingly. "You're not just a dreamer, Josiah. You are a damned fool!"

Shocked, not only by her blasphemy but also the hatred in her eyes, Josiah had been unable to summon any defense. Some part of his mind registered a stifled retort, that it was not his fault that the British had waylaid them off Long Island. It wasn't his fault that they'd been becalmed. It wasn't his fault that she had delivered Atlantic early, leaving him weak and vulnerable to the fever, Lord God, it wasn't his fault that Janey had died! But he could say none of it.

And when she saw that he would not stop her, the rage and pain of the last three months poured from her mouth like rancid ale, stinging him and watering his eyes with shame and lost illusions. Never would he be able to forget her words. He doubted she would ever forget them, either. He knew in his soul that their marriage was likely never going to heal, not only from the losses they had endured, but from the way she had taken those losses.

He begged her not to tell the children yet, not until he had a chance to see some of the vacant claims, but she would not reply.

There was nothing for it but to go on. He did his best to follow Hanover's lead, putting his shoulder into the pole, choosing to battle the river rather than his sorrow, and he did his best to ignore the baleful eyes which burned into his back. Someday, perhaps, Abigail would be herself once more. Until then, he had no choice but to care for her and his children as best he could.

White Apple Village lay less than a day's travel upriver from Natchez, if conditions were favorable. If the river was tempestuous, as it seemed to be this month of October, it might take them two days or more. But the new man was strong and able, and Hanover poled and pulled like a starving man in sight of a banquet. Josiah envied him so much he almost hated him, but he fought down that bitterness and thanked God in his heart that he had such a friend, for indeed, he would be far worse off without him.

After a full day of poling, they turned the raft into Saint Catherine's Creek, the last ten-mile stretch before they would reach the southern boundary of Hanover's claim. It was a rougher water than the Mississippi, but the men's spirits were high, knowing they had come so far and were almost within reach of their destination. Lamon left his mother's side to come and help pole, ignoring her strident call for him to come back to her.

"Your mother wants you with her," Josiah said to his son as he took up a pole and leaned into it, looking alarmingly like a young man.

"I know," he said calmly, "but she can wait a bit. We're almost there now."

Josiah was struck by a wave of love and respect so strong for his son that his eyes filled. He turned away and put his shoulder to the pole with new vigor, all of his weariness wiped away.

They had been on the Saint Catherine for an hour or more when they reached a place on the river where two whirlpools fought for control of the currents. All the men stepped off the raft now to pull it upriver by the towropes. The current was strong, and Hanover shouted instructions to the men, trying to keep the raft from turning into the whirlpools. Both Robert's boys jumped off to help turn the raft, and Lamon started to follow them, but Abigail called to him to stay, and he sat back down again, close to his sister.

The raft twisted against the towropes and snagged on a partially submerged willow tree. Debris from the strong current had lodged against the tree—broken branches, leaves, and smaller trees afloat from the upper river. There, the whirlpool was deepest. The raft wedged tight against the willow, despite the tugging of the men and Robert's shouts of directions, and as Josiah watched in horror, the raft began to sink. Josiah quickly tied his towrope to a tree and ran to the bank, calling to Hanover to come and help him, but Robert was busy trying to get the men to pull harder in a different direction. Josiah began to crawl out onto the willow from where it was still rooted in the muddy bank. And then, in that instant of terror, his weight snapped the willow loose from its own roots, the raft broke free, and capsized into the water. Josiah grabbed the branch above him and dangled with his feet in the current, shouting for Hanover to help. Abigail screamed once and reached for Ruth, but the two women were rolled into the rushing water, their skirts over their heads, their hair tangled and loose in the moving debris. Lamon was thrown over a boulder. Josiah saw his son snatch for the rock in desperation as the current pulled him under it, and then he could not see him again. He watched in frozen, screaming horror as his wife, his daughter, and his son, along with all their worldly goods, their provisions, and the raft, sank from sight under the rushing waters. He let go of the branch and fell into the water, not knowing what else he might do to save them, but the shock of the cold water snapped him to the harsh realization that he, too, might well perish in that moment. He could not swim; neither could his children. Abigail could not have kept afloat even if she had the skills, for she had donned all her skirts to keep them dry.

Josiah grabbed at a low-hanging branch as the men raced alongside the river now, shouting to one another and trying to help those who were fighting the current. He could not see any of his children or his wife, and he finally managed to struggle ashore. As he came to the muddy bank, one of the men ran to help him and he shouted, "Leave me! Find my children!'' but even as he hollered the words, he knew their impotence. He had felt the current almost take him; he had little hope they could survive these strong waters.

He could hear, fainter and fainter, the calls of the men one to another, as they struggled to get down the shore of the river, moving aside heavy brush and climbing from rock to tree, trying to keep from falling in and still trying to see behind every boulder or submerged tree which might hide a child or a woman. He lay exhausted on the muddy bank, his face on his arms. He could not weep. He felt numb and cold into the very depths of his soul. Over and over he prayed, ''Lord God, save my family,'' like a machine which knew only one rhythm and could not turn itself off.

It seemed to him then that a long while had passed, perhaps he even fell into a state of unconsciousness, for when Robert Hanover knelt beside him, it was as though an entire day had gone by. Robert helped him sit up, his face sorrowful and dark. Behind him, Josiah could see his two boys waiting, their faces also full of fear and confusion. ''We couldn't find them,'' Robert said starkly. ''What do you want to do?''

Josiah leaned against the mud bank, trying to clear his head. The last time he saw Abigail, she was fighting to keep her head above the water, crying out in fear, her hands grasping at air. He closed his eyes, willing that scene away. ''Keep looking,'' he said hoarsely. ''Recover whatever you can.''

''My God, I can hardly believe this!'' Robert cursed. ''We cannot be five miles from my claim.''

Dazed, Josiah began to walk upriver.

''Where are you going?'' Robert called to him.

''I'm going to see my land,'' Josiah said. ''Find my wife and children. Find their bodies, if you can.'' And he walked off, not looking back. He could not watch Robert Hanover with his sons. Not now. He did not have the strength for that.

* * *

Josiah wandered upstream, moving away from the water, following the contours of the earth in whatever direction they seemed to take him. He was blind to what he passed, deaf to whatever birdsong and insect buzz surrounded him, plodding on and forcing his feet to move despite his aching desire simply to lay himself down and die. The faces of his loved ones swam before his eyes: Abigail, young and shy with light brown tendrils peeking out from her bonnet, gazing up at him with trust and love; Abigail huge with child, cooking something over the black oven, looking over her shoulder to laugh at some nonsense of his; Abigail lifting up her mare's hoof and digging out a rock, her hands steady and determined. Abigail. His wife and helpmeet. The mother of his children.

Ruth, his first child, the closest to his heart. Her first baby smile, toothless and wide, her eyes crinkled and shining. Ruth toddling along beside him to the barn, carefully carrying a pail of chicken feed, her little feet bare and brown. Ruth lacing up her boots, a young woman now, helping Jane to lace up her own brogans patiently. Ruth. Prettier than her mother, stronger than her brother, probably the best of the lot. She survived the fever only to drown less than five miles from their new home, a home she trusted her father to take her to safely.

And little Jane. Perky and saucy, full of questions, bright as a new day and the child who would likely have been their greatest comfort in their old age. Jane would have been with them the longest, for Ruth would have her own home soon. Her own husband. Jane was most like her mother in temperament; most like her father in gesture and movement. Jane never even got to see Natchez at all. And her body might be the only one which rested in a place he could find, after all.

And Lamon, his only son. All his plans and hopes had been, truly, for Lamon. Ruth would marry and leave them, eventually Jane would find her own husband as well, but Lamon, he had hoped, would stay on the land, would work it as his own, would be with them and bring grandchildren to them, would make all the hardship and sacrifice ultimately worthwhile. Lamon. The child he was often harder on, asked more of, was less tender with—his son. Gone just as surely as his wife and his two daughters.

All of them gone, in a breath, a heartbeat, so quickly that he could not comprehend their going even as he saw the scene over and over in his heart and mind's eye. They were there, and then they were not. At least with Jane, there was time to see her going, time to understand the finality of her death. But with Abigail, Ruth, and Lamon, it was as if they had been plucked from the earth by the hand of God Himself, and he could not even find their last footsteps.

As Josiah walked, he began to speak aloud to God. At first, it was only a prayer, something almost intelligible, asking for help and strength. "Please God, help me now. Be with me now," he kept murmuring over and over. But gradually, his prayer became a litany of questions. And finally, a rising tide of rage.

He had rarely been angry with God before, surely never with the vehemence he felt now, and part of him was appalled and bewildered at the emotional pain such anger brought him. A piece of his mind stood back and watched as he brought God to task, and he wondered if it was his soul who watched, realizing that he might well be damning himself to eternal separation from all he had once loved.

He raged aloud as he strode the land, "God, how can You have allowed such a thing to befall us? Abigail was a good and righteous woman; Ruth and Lamon were mere children, as innocent as the day they first drew breath. And I have been steadfast in my faith through trial which might have turned another man's heart to stone! But You turned from me when I needed You most, God, I cannot forgive You! I will not accept this with a simple 'Thy will be done.' God! My Lord God, why did You allow this to happen!"

Raging thus, Josiah crossed the land and did not see where he came from or where he was going. Again and again, he called out to his God, blind in his pain and near-fainting with heartbreak. He screeched aloud, he shouted to the sky with raised fists, and he finally fell into exhausted whimpers of bewilderment and aching loneliness. He threw himself down beneath a tree, opening his arms to the sky and willing himself as dead as his wife, as silent and cold as his children. He did not wish to see another hour of daylight or breathe another chest full of sunlit air. In that way, he fell asleep finally, too weary to take another step or speak another word.

Sometime hours later, Josiah awoke in a state of such numb exhaustion that he could scarcely move. For a brief moment, he thought—hoped—that he had only had a terrible dream. And then he awoke enough to realize that it was not a dream at all. His family had perished. He was outstretched under a tree. A stark chill had come into the air with the departure of the sun, and he was cold to the bone. The moon was thin, just as he had predicted it would be to Lamon and Ruth when they finally got to the end of their journey. He closed his eyes again, softly weeping with despair. He had no one. He had no land. He was as meaningless to the world about him as if he had never been born, never taken a step or uttered a word. Once again, he wished for death, but he knew that God would not grant his wish any more than He had listened to his prayers. He felt like a fool for addressing this vast nothing which paid him no heed. God was as dead to him now as his children.

Josiah closed his arms about his body to conserve his heat and closed his heart as surely. Never again would he speak the name of God, not in his own mind and not aloud. There was no room for God in the wilderness; God did not dwell here. Josiah now doubted if He dwelled anywhere at all. Let those in the safe, warm comforts of Eastern cities natter about God and His dictums, he vowed; I will speak His name no more.

He closed his eyes again and let the cold take him. There was a very good chance he would be dead by dawn. He wished for nothing else.

* * *

A voice awoke Josiah many hours later, and when he struggled to open his eyes, a man's face blotted out the faint dawn light. Someone was kneeling over him, speaking to him now. Someone was attempting to lift him from the ground, move him from his imagined coffin of despair. He feebly fought to lay back down again, mutely cursing once more the wilderness and any man who was a piece of it, but the man was too strong for him. He was lifted, half-dragged against his will away from his frozen place on the ground, and he fainted again from the pain of moving his body against his will.

Josiah awoke once more, this time on a rough pallet against a log wall. He took some time and let his eyes adjust to the dim lamplight, moving slowly over the roof above him, the wall to one side, the expanse of wall a distance from him, the crude chair and table with no one there. He was in a cabin, he guessed. Where, he did not know; whose, he did not care. He was alive, that much he could feel. He was alive, and Abigail was not. The children were not. He rolled on his side with a groan of despair and closed his eyes again.

By the morning of the second day, he was reluctantly forced to admit that at least one part of his body refused to die. His stomach was aching for food, and his mouth yearned for water. He felt a hundred years old, and at once as stupidly naive as an infant. He had believed. He believed no longer. Not in love, nor in faith, nor in God. But most fiercely, not in himself.

Because, as he told himself as starkly as he could, over and over again until he could no longer comprehend the words as English: he had killed his own family. Not by design, but by carelessness, by selfishness, but his own sheer stubborn will, he had killed them, one by one.

He rose on one elbow and looked about the cabin. A man sat in the far corner, dozing in a chair. He looked to be about Josiah's age, though his beard hid much of his face. A reddish beard with no gray, a strong set of shoulders. Likely the shoulders which hefted me here, Josiah thought. "Mister," he called out softly, testing his voice. When he heard it, he scarcely knew it as his own. "Hey, mister," he tried again, louder now.

The man stirred. "Ah, you're awake at last," he said, straightening and stretching. "You must be hungry."

"Dry," Josiah said, croaking on the word like a dessicated frog.

The man rose and brought a jug of cool water, helping Josiah to drink. Josiah gulped it, gagged, and almost brought it back up again. To take it in was to take in life, and he was not at all sure he wanted to do so.

"Go on," the man said softly. "You've been out for two days. God knows how long you were walking. Drink more."

God knows, Josiah rolled his mind over the words. God knows nothing, stranger, I am witness to that much at least. But he concentrated on the water. And then on the soft bread the man brought on a wooden trencher, the smell and feel of it in his mouth as sensual as his first touch of Abigail's breast. But with it, the sadness welled in him so strong that he began to weep once more.

The stranger said, "I know your story, Fleming. Your friend, Hanover, will likely come to see you soon. He's been here twice a day since I found you. He told me of your loss. You have every cause to weep."

"Did he find them?" Josiah forced himself to ask.

"He found them and buried them," the man answered. "When you're strong enough, I'll take you to them."

Josiah forced himself to rise, leaning against the wall to quell his dizziness. "Take me to them now."

The man took his arm and led him out the door, still clutching the bread in his other hand.

The doe walked carefully into the clearing, twitching her ears back and forth for the slightest disturbance, her nose high and tasting the breeze. She was a white-tailed deer with a red-brown coat, white eye ring, and a brown tail edged with white. Like many of her kind, she had a dark stripe down the center of her tail, and she used this stripe to signal her intentions as it contrasted with the white of her tail when she jumped or ran.

Coue was a three-year-old doe in her second season of breeding. Last spring, she had had her first fawn, a small spotted creature now gone from her side. She did not know where. This season, she would likely have twins, for that was the way of her kind near the Great River, where there was plenty of good grass and ripe fruit in the summer.

Coue felt the urgings in her blood now as the leaves began to change colors and fall to the ground. Soon, she would be ready to mate. She stood quietly in the clearing, listening intently. There was sign of buck all around her, obvious to any deer which might come this way. Polished scars marked the near trees, where a buck had lowered his head and rubbed his antlers against the bark. One such mark, she noticed, was larger than her front hoof, the sign of a very large buck. Or a very old one.

Coue snorted through her nose and stamped her front hoof. The sign of the buck made her nervous. She lowered her head to graze and twitched her tail again but could not enjoy the drying grasses. It was almost dark, usually her most favored time of the day. But now she ripped alternately at the foliage and then raised her head, listening again. The grasses did not satisfy her.

A crashing from the nearby brush made her freeze. Normally, she would have bolted for cover, flashing her white tail in alarm. But now she stood her ground, for she knew a buck watched her. Silence from the brush. The smell of him came to her now, a strong odor of rut, and she lowered her head again, pretending to browse.

He came into the clearing, a large tan male, likely the one who had made the deep antler scars on the beeches. He stared at her boldly. She did not return his gaze. He strode

closer, shivering his shoulders and pulling his lips back from
his teeth to smell her scent on the air. She ignored him, turning her flank away, still mouthing the stiff grasses. A jay
called raucously from a pine tree nearby, but neither of them
started, neither deer even seemed to note his call. It was a
diverting, dangerous dance they had started, and little would
now distract them from each other.

The buck circled the doe cautiously, still sniffing the air,
jerking his shoulders and stamping at her insistently. She
stopped and raised her head, gazing calmly at him. She was
not, after all, a first-season mate. She knew what she wanted,
and she was ready. He moved closer now and nosed her
flank, and she stood still, not shifting away.

Another noise from the brush now, and she raised her
head. It was likely the only sound which might have distracted her, the noise of another buck nearby. The buck at
her side squealed angrily like a large pig and stamped his
front hooves, snorting and tossing his head. From the brush,
another buck emerged and stared boldly at the buck nearest
her. He snorted a reply, stamped his hooves, and moved
closer.

Coue appraised this newcomer. He was not so large as the
first buck, but he was younger. His coat held the scars of
several fights he had already sustained with other bucks. His
antlers were not so wide, but he showed no fear. The new
buck came toward them, moving to her side with bold confidence.

With that, the first buck squealed again and tossed his antlers at the intruder, the younger buck turned, and the two of
them squared off, almost pushing Coue aside in their eagerness to vie for her. She moved to the side of the open glade,
watching them impassively. It was not the first time bucks
had battled for her thus, and she really did not care which
one bested the other.

The two bucks pushed and shoved one another with their
antlers, their haunches, their necks and shoulders, sometimes coming together with a loud scraping sound, some-

times with a clash of horn which shivered through the forest. They panted and snorted, pawed and drooled in their frenzy, forgetting both the doe and their surroundings. In an instant when they separated to rush together again, a musket shot rang out, a puff of smoke from the nearby brush, and the older buck stopped short in his forward momentum. Coue bolted for cover in panic, away from the fearsome gunfire, the younger buck followed her, and the old buck stood, trembling and facing his ultimate enemy, bleeding from the neck. Coue stopped when she was in deep brush and looked back.

The old buck had crumpled to his knees now, his neck twisted at an odd angle. A man came toward him from the edge of the meadow, already pulling out his knife. She cowered and fled noiselessly into the deeper shelter of the thicket, trembling herself now with fear and excitement.

Later, the young buck found her again, mounted her, and quelled her fear. She thought no more of the old buck, and of course, she never saw him again.

Two years passed before Josiah was able to wake in the morning without the leaden feeling of despair so heavy that he could barely bring himself to rise. Two years before he no longer visited the graves of his children and wife daily. Two years before he could hear the name of God spoken in his presence and not have to fight back a sneer or a contemptuous rebuke.

But the healing was not complete, he knew as much. Every time he saw a child—a boy, a girl, of any age, it did not matter—he felt such pain and loss that he could not bring himself to speak. His envy of those who still had their children around them made him silent and cold with those he might have drawn to him for comfort.

Indeed, there were others in the settlement who had lost children, to accidents, to the harshness of the journey, to the fever. But he could take no solace among them. If they had a child left alive or a wife with potential for more children, he reckoned them fortunate, no matter their loss. No one, he felt, had lost more than he had, and so no one, he knew, could offer a word of understanding.

Thus, except for Robert Hanover and his sons, Josiah was all but alone for two years. He rarely ventured into the little settlement of Natchez; he never set foot inside the chapel or another man's home. Indeed, it was so many months before he could no longer hear Abigail's moan of rebuke echoing softly in his head that he almost had forgotten how to converse normally without her background chorus.

Josiah and Robert worked Robert's claim together for the first year, and Josiah asked nothing but his share of the crop and a place to refuge among those who asked no questions. After the first year, he was able to make his own claim, land which abutted Hanover's on one side. It was a smaller parcel than his first claim, only three hundred acres, but it fronted Saint Catherine's Creek and was mostly level. Josiah found it easy to ignore the rushing water and see it only as a resource for his stock. He never went there for pleasure.

So he built himself a tidy little cabin with the help of Hanover and his sons, and he moved into it one day in the late fall, almost two years after the death of his family. He left it only to retrieve Jane and Atlantic from their graves in Baton Rouge, a grisly and grim sojourn he hoped he would soon forget. He brought them back and buried them on his land and waited for the despair to overwhelm him again, now that he was alone without the tumult and distraction of Hanover and his boys. But he found to his surprise that some part of his heart was cold and dead. It felt little pain. It asked for no comfort. Indeed, Josiah wondered if a part of him had actually died with his family, so bereft from his heart did he feel.

But he turned his mule into the field and readied the earth for a late crop of peas and winter cabbage, making his body go through the motions, assuming it would need to be fed through the next few seasons at least.

Robert Hanover came to see him often, though Josiah could not honestly say why. There were days he had barely a word to say to another living person, and then Hanover had to make all of the words himself. He never seemed to have any problem doing so. Other days, Josiah was almost glad to see him, just to see another human face and hear another voice besides his own and the mule's.

"You ought to get a dog," Robert said once when he came with a bushel of potatoes to share. "A man should not be completely alone, even in the wilderness." He said it in a mocking tone because, as far as Robert was concerned, Natchez was more paradise than wilderness. But behind the wry humor was genuine concern. Josiah could see that plainly.

"Just one more thing to take care of," Josiah said. "One more mouth to feed."

"One more thing to run off, you mean," Robert said. "It'd do you good to have to care for something again, man."

Josiah waved his arm expansively. "I got three hundred acres to care for. That looks to me to be a full-time endeavor for most any man." It was the most he'd spoken aloud all week, and the effort exhausted him. He thought to lead the conversation away from himself. "Have you found yourself a likely candidate yet?" Robert Hanover had been looking for a new wife since they first put the roof on his cabin. So far, none he had seen suited him well enough to settle on one.

Robert grinned. "As a matter of fact, I have. The prettiest little bird on the river, to my mind. She arrived just a few weeks ago with her family—I've already met her father, a good man, if a little rustic. Goodwin is the name, Sarah is hers, Pennsylvania German stock, solid Methodist, though he's no Bible-thumper, they've taken a claim to the north, two hundred acres of good bottom land. Too close to the river, I told him, but there's little enough choice these days." Robert lowered his voice. "She's got hair the color of ripe wheat, I swear, and just as ripe herself. I mean to have her by spring, if she's willing."

Josiah thought on this news for a moment. These days, he did nothing in a hurry. "How old is she?"

Robert laughed, shaking his head. "Who knows? Who cares? She's old enough, to my mind, and to her father's, too. When there's so few mares to choose from, a man'll ride whatever can walk. He's got one other he'd marry off quick enough to a good husband, the elder sister. She's a widow, plump as a pouter pigeon. You interested? I know the two of them would rather be neighbors, given the chance."

Josiah shook his head gently.

"Well, that's an improvement, at any rate. Six months ago, you'd have thrown me off your porch for even suggesting such a thing. So now we've progressed to a shake of the head. Before long, we might get to a shake of the hand. And from there, you're as good as promised."

Josiah smiled ruefully in spite of himself. Hanover's humor was infectious when it wasn't annoying. "It'll be a cold day in hell," he said mildly.

Robert chuckled amiably. "Well, there's some who say this place bears a marked resemblance to that region, and it gets colder here than I'd have bet, so anything's possible."

"When's the wedding?"

"Ha! I haven't even asked her yet!"

"But you will," Josiah said calmly. "And she'll likely say yes."

"Then I'll post the banns fast, before she can change her mind. There's not enough women in the settlement now, and there are more sojourners coming in every day, most of them bachelors or widowers. A man's got to think of the future."

Josiah said nothing.

"A man's got to think of the future," Robert repeated more gently, "and let go of the past." He put out a large hand on Josiah's shoulder and shook it with rough affection. As he descended the porch and mounted his horse, he shouted back up to Josiah, "I want a wedding gift, old man!"

"What's that?"

"I want to see you dance with the bride's big sister!"

Josiah watched him ride off, wondering how it was that Bob Hanover managed to carry the vitality of a man twice his size, how he kept his spirits up no matter his losses. He had no wife, he had no real faith in God, yet he rode his mount with the straight spine of a young man, kicked him with relish, and laughed as the dust roiled by. If I were a bitter man, Josiah thought, I would be envious of my friend. Indeed, I could not stomach him in my life at all.

Josiah reflected on the mysteries of it all for a long while that afternoon. Robert Hanover would likely marry the woman, he was that determined. He might even have more children; young as she was, it was likely. His land would be rich, his wife fruitful, his sons strong and devoted, and his life full and content. All without a single prayer of thanksgiving to God or a genuflection to His power. Meanwhile, Josiah sat on his sagging porch all alone, pondering his fate at the hands of a God who did not heed his prayers, even when they had been constant and heartfelt.

The sparrow fell, Josiah concluded, without a thought, without even a glance from God. And so did man.

He turned his gaze outward now and saw that the mule was idle, the fields still needed work, the roof on the little cabin needed mending in one corner. He stood up and strode with determination to the mule. If Robert Hanover could remodel his life, so could he.

The wedding took place at the Hanover cabin less than a month from Robert's decision to woo. Josiah arrived at the celebration carrying a small jug of homemade brandy from the apple trees on his property. He set the gift on a table covered with pies, cakes, and sweetbreads, and headed for the knot of people behind the house. A fiddler was tuning up on the stoop, and Robert had a short woman tucked under his arm, the two of them smiling and speaking to their guests. Robert was well dressed as always, immaculate small-clothes, cutaway coat, a volume of ruffles, and carefully tied peruke.

Josiah recognized most all but the bride's people, but he hung back for a moment, suddenly uncomfortable. The woman at the bride's elbow, plump and elder by several years, was obviously the widowed sister.

Robert looked up then and hailed him over. "Come and meet my wife!" he called, signaling the fiddler.

"Have you already said the vows?" Josiah asked, bewildered. He had assumed that he would be witnessing the ceremony itself

"Oh, I decided not to wait. We were married by the preacher yesterday when he came upriver to baptize the Bowen baby, so there's nothing left to do but cut the cake and dance the wedding dance!"

The fiddler broke into a tune then, a slight and merry melody which brought smiles to the faces all round. Robert introduced Josiah to his bride, Sarah Goodwin, her sister, Jane, the elder Goodwins, and a small raft of neighbors whom he already knew. Josiah shook hands dutifully with all but the bride. For her, he bent and boldly kissed her cheek, murmuring, "Robert Hanover is my best friend. I am very happy for his good fortune."

She smiled and lowered her eyes. "Thank 'ee, Master Fleming. He has spoken of you so often." She turned to her sister. "Jane, we should be certain Master Fleming has his fill of your good apple cake."

"Don't forget your wedding gift!" Hanover laughed, bowing to his bride and turning her toward the fiddler. "Let's not waste the music!"

Quickly, the dirt yard was filled with moving couples. Hanover's two sons grabbed up some neighbors' girls, older couples jogged about awkwardly but happily, and even old Mr. Goodwin took his wife by the arm and moved her in a sober turn or two. Their departure left Josiah standing alongside Jane Goodwin Hoffman with the nearest nondancing couple more than ten yards away.

He cleared his throat and bowed to her shortly. "Do you care to dance, mistress?"

She returned his bow and took his arm.

The fiddler was warming to his task now, and the music jittered to a faster pace. The couples kept up, most of them twirling about the circle, barely avoiding collisions. Mistress Feeney and Mistress Powers danced together, rather than be left at the sidelines. One old man jogged happily by himself in the center of the yard, urging the fiddler on. Hanover and his bride looked as if they had danced together before, her bright hair glowing on his dark jacket shoulder.

"You come from Pennsylvania, then?" Josiah asked his partner politely.

"Seems a lifetime ago," she said softly.

He looked down into her face and saw there a sadness which he knew showed in his own. At that, his heart softened toward her, and he no longer felt burdened by the weight of her in his arms. "How did you lose your husband?" he asked, knowing that such a question was unheard of after such a brief acquaintance. But something in her eyes said that he could ask.

"Mr. Hoffman got the fever, just south of Memphis," she said. "It took him in two days. My son, too. A week later."

He was struck to silence. He had not known that she had lost her child as well. Then she was as he, bereft of mate and family all at once. It was clear she had no other child. She had no one save her sister and her parents. More than he had, of course, but little enough.

"How old was your son?" he asked quietly, feeling suddenly that the happy music of the fiddler had dropped far away from them, receding like the cries of a bird on the wing.

"James was six."

He gazed down at her again in surprise. "The same age as my Jane."

She squeezed his shoulder firmly. "I know. Sarah told me

of your great loss, Mr. Fleming. I understand more than most here what it has cost you.''

To his alarm, his eyes watered suddenly. He slowed his steps, his hand still on her waist. ''It cost me my heart.''

She nodded solemnly.

He gazed away, attempting to gain control. ''Quite possibly my soul, as well.''

She dropped her eyes to give him a chance to recover. Josiah noticed vaguely that the dancers had quit and moved to the table of pies and cakes. Hanover glanced his way curiously; Sarah looked once and then away. There seemed to be a conspiracy of agreement to leave the two of them alone.

Her voice was low and soft. ''When I lost my husband, my heart was broken. When I lost my son so soon after, I turned away from God and vowed I would never praise His name again. But now I understand that God did not take my son, the fever did.''

''Neither did God save him,'' Josiah said.

She looked up at him, a faint smile at the corners of her mouth. ''You are not afraid of God. That's good. It was not God's job to save my son. Perhaps my son and God had an agreement that I knew nothing of. Perhaps my son's life was fated to end as it did, or it was merely a trick of fate. But I know now that God's love is with me, whether I can bring myself to love Him or not. And I do not need to understand more than that to live my life in His grace.''

Josiah dropped his head and let his eyes water freely, the first tears he had allowed himself in so many months of arid, cold silence. ''I have missed that grace so much,'' he murmured. ''Almost as much as I have missed my children.''

She took his hand and held it in both of hers. ''You have not lost your soul, Mr. Fleming. It shines from your eyes.'' She smiled and tugged gently at his hand. ''Come. Let's have some of my apple cake. It's the best in the whole district, if I do say so myself.''

Josiah allowed himself to be led to the table, scarcely shamefaced at what must show in his face. To his relief, most were too busy enjoying the company and the good food to pay him much mind. The bride was seated before her groom, and he was telling stories to entertain her and their guests, of the Indians who used to live on his land. He had several humorous theories about the uses of the mounds which still stood on many of their claims, and Josiah heard the laughter of the party as he moved slightly away, still being led by the hand.

She stopped at the long table before a cake which looked ravaged. ''You can see it's good, the locusts have been at it well enough. But there's enough here for two good pieces,'' and she cut a large slice for Josiah, holding it out in her hand. He took it from her gratefully. It gave him something to do with his hands and his attention. She picked up a smaller piece for herself and ate from it slowly.

''You know,'' she said thoughtfully, ''I have a theory about death and loss. Do you wish to hear it?''

Actually, he did not, for he feared he might weep again. But he silently nodded for he wondered how this woman could speak of her loss so calmly. Perhaps he could take some of that calm for himself.

''There are big losses and little losses all of our lives,'' she said gently. ''No one escapes them. The little losses get inside our minds and hearts and are in and out again rather easily, I think. We make no changes in our minds and hearts to accommodate them, because we don't have to. But the big losses. They are very different, indeed. They move inside our minds and hearts and stay there quite a while. They force us to make a space for them, to accommodate and learn and make peace with their presence for the rest of our lives. And in that sense, they change us forever. But we can decide how those changes will be. We can choose our own lessons.'' She stopped and took another bite of apple cake, chewing in a measured fashion.

There was little which would be rushed about this woman, Josiah could see.

''The worst thing about a great loss,'' she continued, ''is

feeling that it is out of our control. That something was taken from us which we deemed absolutely necessary to our survival, all without our permission. When Mr. Hoffman was taken, I felt that way.''

"No," he said then. "That is not the worst thing."

She looked up at him and cocked her head, waiting for his answer.

"The worst thing is the knowledge that you somehow caused the death."

"That is not knowledge," she said firmly. "That's a belief. You *believe* you caused it, but in fact, it's likely you did not. And you can shed that belief as you have shed others in your life."

"How?" he asked bleakly.

"By supplanting it with another. By believing that things happen sometimes for no reason. Or there is a reason, but you cannot know it. And by believing that God loves you, no matter how the world at large may not." She finished her cake and wiped her hands on a small handkerchief. "You cannot control the events of life, Mr. Fleming, that much is certain. But you can control what they do to your mind and your heart. My theory is that the largest despairs give us the chance to learn the largest lessons. To grow very quickly to a state of grace and understanding."

"And what lesson did you learn, then, from the deaths of your husband and your son?" He deliberately did not mince his words, for her composure almost angered him.

She took a deep breath. "I learned that I do not need to know what will happen next. That I can go on with my life, even love my life, with my heart and mind rearranged around these losses. I can choose to love again and believe again, if it pleases me to do so."

"And what if it does not please me to do so?" he asked, rather sourly, setting down the remains of the apple cake.

"Then of course, you will not," she said placidly. "And your lesson will be one of stubborn loneliness and guilt all the rest of your days." She smiled to take the sting from her words. "Do you honestly think that is what God would wish for you, Mr. Fleming?"

"I scarcely know what I think, much less what God may think," he said. "But I thank you for your kind words, Mrs. Hoffman. And now, if you will permit me, I will take my leave of the bride and groom and hie me home."

She bowed her head respectfully, her face still placid. "Go with God," she murmured.

He glanced back at her but did not make a retort.

After he had said his goodbyes and mounted his horse, her words came back to him again during the journey back to his own cabin.

Whatever else the widow Hoffman might be, she was not a simple woman. And her words would not simply go away.

Hanover had been married nearly a season before Josiah finally visited once more, invited so many times to dinner that he was embarrassed to decline one more time. He dressed himself in his only good coat, the same he had worn to their wedding dance. He had not had it on, of course, since then, and as he pulled it from his closet, he smelled Jane's scent on his right shoulder.

He arrived late, and dinner was already on the table. With a boisterous welcome, Hanover shoved aside some plates and bowls to make room, his two boys amiably moving aside their long legs to allow him to sit by his friend. Sarah immediately popped up to attend to something on the stove, blushing and nodding to him a welcome.

Josiah looked around the cabin with amazement. He would not have believed that one woman could make that much of a difference in so short a time. Where once the floors were rude clay, they now were swept and sanded properly, with fresh rushes for warmth and softness. The table had a heavy cover on it, so none of the stained timbers showed, and the smoking tallow candles had been replaced by bright Betty lamps which gave the whole room a warm, welcoming glow. By the fire, kindling was stacked neatly, pots were filled with simmering substances, and the mantel was empty of Hanover's collection of dried squirrel tails and pipes. A single Indian basket of dried flowers gave added color to the hearth.

Even the pots which hung on curved hooks by the oven were scoured and shining.

Hanover's boys looked clean and well fed, and Robert himself was florid-faced and jovial, smug as a country squire. He beckoned to Sarah, pulling her forward and hugging her round the hips. "Bid a proper good evening to my wife, Fleming. You'll fall to your knees in gratitude when you taste her roasted capon." Josiah smiled and bent to kiss her cheek. He felt like an imposter, at once too old and mean-spirited to be with such a happy company. But he took the noggin of warm ale that Sarah offered with thanks, and he watched her carefully as she brought trencher after trencher of food to the wide table.

She was younger than her sister, less plump, more vivacious. Like a robin to a wren, he thought. But then, he realized, she'd likely never suffered much loss in her life, so of course her smile could afford to be ready, her laugh a lilt of unthinking joy. He wondered what Sarah and Robert would find to talk about, once they tired of their bed. With a hard pang, he thought of Abby, then. No matter what, they had never suffered for want of things to say to one another. He wondered if he would miss her for the rest of his days. Even just the touch of her bare feet against his under the coverlet at night was a comfort. Likely he would never take such comfort again.

"Have you heard the news?" Robert was asking, reaching for the bowl of snap beans.

"I've not been away from my fields for a fortnight," Josiah said patiently to Hanover. The man was in and out of Natchez as often as Josiah was in and out of his barn, it seemed, and every new political twist and turn of the war for independence enthralled him. Josiah had long ago discouraged him from riding over with every bit of rebel gossip up from New Orleans or down from Memphis—

"We're going to revolt against the Spanish and take back Natchez for America." He leaned forward eagerly, with a mouthful of fowl in his jaws. "Less than a week, I wager. More than a hundred of us are in agreement. Galvez is going to meet his nemesis at Pensacola, and we have news that there's a British warship off the coast at Biloxi with orders to retake the river."

Josiah gaped at him. "You are surely not going to join this mad scheme?"

He nodded fiercely, including both his sons with his look. "We shall take arms to restore liberty to this region, and stand together. We cannot live under Spanish rule—have you forgotten the Inquisition, Josiah? No decent Protestant will be safe once they secure their position. We're better off striking while Galvez is busy at Pensacola. We'll hold the fort for the King or deliver it to the Americans, whichever finally wins this war. But we won't be governed by His Catholic Majesty!"

Sarah quietly brought her own plate to the table now and sat across from her husband. Her face showed no fear of his words. Josiah felt he had mistakenly opened the door to a foreign country and wandered in among crazed strangers.

"But you've just been married," he said lamely, realizing as he said it that it mattered not a whit to anyone here.

"All the more reason to take up arms and defend what is mine," Hanover said, gesturing now with a half-full noggin of ale. "Shall I see my wife insulted by Spanish louts and cutthroats? Shall I see my lands taken from my sons and given to some Catholic latecomer with the ear of the Spanish King? I'd rather join the ranks of Colonel Hutchins and his men and fight the Spanish now, while they're still weak."

Josiah bowed his head and took another bite of the roasted fowl on his plate. It was excellent, basted with cream and some sort of herb, likely rosemary, he guessed. His mind was wandering wildly, he knew, but he could not seem to put two cohesive thoughts together in a row.

It was only the year before, in 1779, that Governor Galvez had marched upriver from New Orleans, determined to enlarge Spain's claim to the territory while the English and Americans were busy worrying each other's boundaries. Spain controlled Louisiana, but the British had managed to retain a hold on much of the lower Mississippi territory. Spain saw that Britain might well lose her war with the American colonies, especially once France declared her sympathies with the revolutionaries. Spain declared war on Britain and sent Galvez to seize the British forts along the river. Yellow fever had just swept through once more and left the settlers weakened. Galvez had quickly seized Baton Rouge and Natchez with his force of regulars, militia, and armed slaves and Indians, then turned south to Pensacola. They had taken Fort Panure with scarcely a ripple, and Josiah could see no way his life had altered because the flag flying over the fort was a different one. The land still needed plowing, the crops still needed harvest, and the price for indigo was still holding stable, if he could only wrest it from the caterpillars.

Now, some of the planters at Natchez were determined to capture the fort back again—why he could not imagine or care. And his dearest friend, the man who had likely saved his life and certainly his fortunes whatever they might be, was now going to join the retired officers and Loyalists who infested the district—Colonel Anthony Hutchins, Captains Blomart and Lyman, Christian Bingaman and Jacob Winfree and the rest of those restless old soldiers—in a military coup against the Spanish garrison at Fort Panure. It was impossible to take another bite, now that the totality of the plan and its potential for disaster was clear to him. He set down his fork and leaned back from his plate.

"Sarah," he said politely, "have you no persuasion that can stop our Robert from this mad effort?" He ignored Hanover's sudden dark glower.

To Josiah's surprise, she smiled gently at him. "I am proud of my husband," she said softly. "Likely the Spanish will be defeated at Pensacola, and they will surrender easily to Colonel Hutchins and our men with scarcely a fight."

Josiah scoffed openly, snorting into his noggin now. He did not care if Sarah thought him rude; he thought her silly enough in her blind faith. "I have never yet seen the Spanish do anything without a fight, and I cannot imagine why Robert should expose himself to such danger needlessly. We have been under Spanish governance now for a year, have we not? Have any of us been visited by instruments of Catholic torture? Have our lands been confiscated, our crops taken, or our souls been overmuch threatened by the papists among us?" He was angry now, and his words came more freely. He took a final bite, reluctant to give up the trencher before it was emptied, and pushed it away with what he hoped would be taken as a gesture of disgust.

"Sometimes when men go mad, it is the duty of their women to stop them with gentle reason. What does it matter who governs the fort, so long as we are left to govern our lands and our fate as we see fit? The only Spanish we ever see are in the fort; every settler is either American or British, depending on their sentiments, no matter what flag flies over the stockade walls. Let it be the Spanish, the English, or the Natchez, for all I care. Sooner or later, the Americans will take all of this territory for their own; why not wait and let them fight the Spanish for you?"

"That is like you, Josiah," Robert said, his frown now gone. To him, it was a sparring of wits, like any other. "You have retired from the battleground of life and are content to let others do your fighting for you. Your living for you, too, it seems. But some of us are not ready for the mustard plasters and the walking canes just yet, and we cannot abide a Spanish flag flying over our territory."

Josiah leaned back and gazed at his old friend. A sadness came over him then and blew away his anger like a cool breeze over an open flame. "You will arouse a sleeping lion," he said to Robert, "and the open-handed rule we have seen from the Spanish will tighten like a fist. Even those of us who are willing to live harmoniously with them will be punished for your rebellion. If you win, you gain only time and your pride. If you lose, you will likely lose your life, your lands, and your neighbors will be punished with reprisal, whether they supported your attempt or not." He sighed and made as if to stand. "I thought you had more sense."

"And I thought you had more courage," Hanover replied swiftly.

"And I thought we invited a friend to share a meal," Sarah said calmly. "Now sit, Josiah, and take up your knife again. There's yet pie to be passed." She rose and went to the stove, her straight back clearly brooking no disagreement.

Josiah was surprised. She had showed little spine until that moment. He wondered suddenly what she would look like with a nine-month belly. No doubt Hanover would have good fortune on that score as well. He sighed and settled back, unwilling to fight anymore. Robert would do what he would do, and no amount of words from him or anyone else would sway him. Probably Sarah had learned as much already.

"Calm your fears, old man," Hanover said amiably. "We'll rout the Spanish out of Natchez fast as you can say 'Bob's your uncle,' and Galvez will have his hands too full further south to turn his army north again. This land was meant to be American soil. It's bad enough to let the British traipse it temporarily, but to defile it with Spanish papists is unendurable."

"It's amazing what men can and cannot endure," Josiah said calmly. "Well, you've made up your mind, and I'll say no more on it. But if they ask me, I'll swear myself neutral."

"They won't give you that choice." One of Robert's sons spoke up for the first time, his young man's voice sounding far too passionate in the tiny cabin. "You must swear allegiance to the King of Spain or see your lands taken for his pleasure.''

"Then I'll swear allegiance to His Majesty with a smile and two fingers crossed behind me," Josiah replied. "Soon enough, they'll be gone, and someone else will ask for the same vow. I'll give it again just as easily to the next in line.''

Hanover's two sons looked horrified, but Robert only grinned. "Don't let him rile you, boys. He's a man of honor, and he'll do what's right when tested.''

"If these pies go untested, I'll forswear myself," Sarah pretended to pout prettily. "Now not another word about fighting and flags, or I'll leave you all to scour the pots by yourselves. Josiah, perhaps you might favor us with your opinion on the digging on the savages' mounds that Colonel Hutchins is having done on his claim. I understand they have found relics and piles of old bones, though no one can say how old they are. Why do you think the Indians piled up all that dirt?''

Most in the territory knew that Colonel Hutchins and several of the older settlement families had begun to explore the interior of the mounds on their properties. Some felt to disturb the ancient sites of the Natchez was unChristian; others saw no need to leave such mounds intact within their property lines. Sarah led them on a lively discussion of what the mounds might have been for and whether or not they should be left in peace, the pies were consumed with the proper praise, and all talk of war was silenced.

As he rode home deep in thought, Josiah remembered the way Sarah looked at Robert when she expressed an opinion. It was as though she asked permission with her eyes. Abby never did that, not even when they were first married. Somehow, he had always loved her more for that willingness to say her mind without asking his leave.

He wondered if Hanover were not more of a fool than he had ever guessed. He seemed so eager to follow others, so willing to take a young woman to wife who offered little other than that she was there and ready to wed. Oh, she was

pert enough and easy to look upon, but she had little substance to her. She would never survive the hard times, not in
flesh or in spirit. A man needed a woman to stand beside
him, not behind him—

He stopped himself abruptly from that line of thought. He
had lost his wife, his family, and his faith, Josiah reminded
himself. He would not lose his friend as well. He resolved to
think no more on Hanover's choices, for good or ill. He
would not be his brother's keeper.

Two weeks later, a buggy pulled up outside Josiah's porch
right about noon, the first buggy he had seen in more than
two years. Sarah held the reins for a prancing roan, and
alongside her sat Jane. They halloed brightly and were getting down from the buggy seat before he could scarcely recover enough to lend them his hands.

"We had to come and show you!" Sarah chirped at him.
"Robert had it built special, and the wheels were brought up
all the way from New Orleans! Isn't it cunning?" She patted
the horse happily. "Though where we'll find to drive it, I
certainly don't know. Mr. Fleming, you recall my sister,
Jane?"

"Of course," Josiah said, remembering his manners with
a bow. "Whatever are you two doing out here today?"

"You must excuse Sarah," Jane said confidentially to
him. "She could not rest until she had shown off her new
conveyance to anyone who might be within a ten-mile
stretch. I've brought you a pie as apology for our intrusion,
however, and we won't stay but a minute." She had him on
his own front porch before he scarcely knew her arm was
through his. "So this is the Fleming plantation," she said
approvingly. "Robert says you have made great progress in
a short while." She unlinked her arm from his, proferred the
bundled pie, and stood with her hands on her hips, surveying
his claim as though she considered its purchase.

Josiah was instantly rankled, both by her demeanor and

also by Sarah's constant background chorus. Even the buggy somehow annoyed him. But he brought the two women inside and poured cool cider, offering to cut the pie as they watched.

"Oh no," Jane said quickly, "that's for you, Josiah. Keep it for yourself later. Neither of us needs more indulgences of that nature," and she rolled her eyes in mock reprimand at her own wide waist.

"I have heard you have wonderful luck with your late cabbages," Sarah chimed in then. "Mine are riddled with worms. May I step outside and see for myself?"

It was a transparent diversion, but Josiah bowed and let her step out on the porch again, directing her behind the cabin to the kitchen rows. He was, of course, then left alone with Jane, exactly as Sarah had intended. He gestured to one of the willow chairs and took the other. He put his feet up brazenly on the porch rail and waited.

Jane sighed with contentment and began to rock. She said nothing at all.

He waited, slightly confused, thinking at any moment she would begin to speak. But still, she did not. Sarah seemed to have fallen off the earth altogether, and the silence of the place settled over them like a fine dust. She did not hum, she did not prattle, she scarcely even made a noise with the rocking. Jane was waiting him out.

Once he realized that, he relaxed completely. He need do nothing, he saw then, nothing at all, and he could wait the woman out until the cabin fell down over their heads, all in contented silence. The long moments stretched by, broken only by distant bird song and the buzz of the autumn insects foraging the bright air. "Your parents are well?" he asked then, willing to speak now that he knew he was not obliged.

She nodded, smiling at him. Still she said not a word.

He smiled to himself. She was a crafty cat, this one. He knew what she wanted, and by God, he would not give it up until he was ready—no, *unless* he was ready, willing, and able! "You must miss your sister, now that she's under Hanover's roof."

"Umm," she nodded. "Some. But she's happy."

He realized with a dawning respect that she could not be made to speak any more than he could. Indeed, it was just possible that she had no more need for idle chatter than he did. He waited a good long while in silence, willing her to speak. She did not. That blasted Sarah must have walked the entire three hundred acres by now and investigated every living thing upon it.

He sighed mightily. She did not glance at him. He shifted his weight slightly so that he faced her more openly, and she did not shift her gaze away from the open fields. Her face was open, calm, and at peace. She seemed almost not to know he was on the porch at all, much less care. With some small agitation, he said, "Hanover tells me that Colonel Hutchins plans a rebellion—"

"Please don't feel you must entertain me with conversation," she interrupted him gently. "I know what Mr. Hanover plans, and I do not agree with his ideas. But more important, I am perfectly content simply to sit here and enjoy the fine day." She turned back again to the sight of his empty fields and seemed to sink even deeper into the rocker.

Josiah leaned back and closed his eyes. An easiness came over him, a sense of rightness that he could not really comprehend, but he did not question. It was nice to have her here, actually. So long as she asked nothing of him, so long as she did not take away from the air with her voice, she was a comforting presence on his porch. His thoughts whirled away to the past, and as always, pictures of Abby, of Ruth, of Jane and Lamon came up for him then—and he realized once again that a woman sat upon his chair with the same name as his youngest daughter. Amazing that he had thought of that twist of fate so rarely. One Jane was so very different from the other. And yet, there was one thing they had in common—a determined cheerfulness which was at once a provocation and a source of joy.

If one would let the joy come into his heart, that is.

Steps now up the back of the porch, and Sarah bustled upon them, all energy and light radiance. The mood changed immediately. Josiah sat up, unwilling to be thought dozing with Jane beside him.

"What in the world?" Sarah chuckled. "The two of you ran out of things to say already?"

Jane smiled quietly at her sister. "Not at all. But it wasn't necessary to say them all in one afternoon."

"Well, of course not," Sarah bubbled. "I guess you two know best what you want, goodness knows. Josiah, your kitchen rows are neat as any housewife's; you put mine to shame. I guess worms are just too embarrassed to attack your cabbages—it would be almost a sacrilege to bring disorder to such a garden!"

Jane rose and took her sister's hand. "We'll be going now," she said gently. "Let's leave Mr. Fleming to his work. We've taken enough of his time, I'm sure."

Josiah rose from his chair, somehow understanding that he need make no false protest to Jane and therefore not to Sarah, either. He bowed politely to them both, thanked Jane for the pie, and helped them into their buggy. Sarah waved effusively, still trying to extract a promise from him of a return visit even as the horse was pulling away. Jane waved once, warmly, and then settled herself to face the front, her back straight and balanced against the movement of the buggy up the rutted road.

It was tempting to go back to the rocker and take the rest of the afternoon trying to recapture the peace he had felt moments before Sarah came back among them. But he knew that such contentment was a rare blessing, something which could not be pursued. He went to his chores with a renewed energy and a sense of having rested profoundly.

That night, Josiah sat before his fire thinking over the events of the day. It was clear enough what was coming toward him, as though he were back on the raft and he could see the current bringing debris and flotsam in a steady, oncoming rush. It was intended that he marry the widow Jane. Hanover wanted it, Sarah yearned for it, no doubt the parents wished it, and quite likely, Jane desired the union as well.

But what did *he* want in all that? Marriage itself did not appeal to him; that much was certain. He felt no need to have a woman about the place again, did not miss the comforts provided by a wife, and had no intention of being a father again. Down that road lay too much pain. The world was too dangerous a place to invest one's heart in something which could perish so easily.

On the other hand, it was not unpleasant to have Jane on his porch. Quite possibly, something in nature, something in the human heart, could not abide a man alone. Could not tolerate a woman alone, either. Something in the scheme of things moved them together. He did not believe that something to be God, not anymore. But he had to admit that the rhythms of life all around him seemed to argue for folks to go through life two by two.

Perhaps he did miss the comfort after all. The last two years had felt so empty, so desolate, that almost anything would be an improvement over that feeling of loss and despair. He was tired of envying other people's happiness. Josiah leaned over and tapped his pipe against the rocker, spilling the tobacco ash onto the porch. Would Jane be the kind of woman who would clean it up without a fuss, or fuss all the while she swept, or not sweep at all? It was impossible to say. He was canny enough to realize that however she might be now, marriage could change her. And yet, she had been married before. That much was in her favor. Unlike most men, he did not wish to have an untried woman. Virgins did not appeal to him, nor did the youth and gaiety of such a thing as Sarah.

No, there was something about the widow Jane which drew him. No small part of it, he guessed, was that they shared the same sort of sorrow. There were few enough women in the settlement and none of them had caught his eye. He wondered if his eye could ever be "caught" again in that fashion. He did not believe in love anymore, not really. Not any more than he believed in God.

But the realization made him feel empty and sad again. Was he destined to live the rest of his life alone, tending his cabbage rows and his acres like a miserly old rustic? If he wanted a wife—which he really did not—Jane would be the best of the bunch. She would likely not expect too much, and she was capable of leaving a man to his own thoughts.

So the question was: Would she be worth taking the risk?

He thought it over well into the night. He realized that he did not love her; likely he would never love again. But he felt warm affection for her when he thought of her, and likely if she annoyed him, he could take his leave and she'd survive. She was not a woman to perish if a man did not carry her through life.

As he fell asleep, he told himself that he could do a lot worse than ask the widow to take him on. He put the question to the universe at large: If it's a good idea to marry the woman, make it happen easily, he said, almost aloud. It was not a prayer, exactly, but it was the closest thing to a prayer that Josiah had expressed in more than two years. If it's meant to be, I'll know it. It will happen with little effort on my part. If it's not meant to be, it will not. And with that last thought as comfort, he slept easily through the night.

The next morning, without wasting another moment, he went to see the widow Jane. It occurred to him as he rode that he was nearly thirty-five years old and likely half his life was gone. It was time to begin the second part of this journey through the world, wherever it might take him. It made him feel solidly rooted to know that this woman would travel it alongside him. And he had no doubt that she would. He supposed he had but to ask her.

Four hours later, he traveled the same route home again, a betrothed man. As he had expected, she said yes to him easily, with little of the relief or excitement he might have anticipated or desired. Even in her acceptance, she was sensible. She told him, too, that her sister Sarah was expecting a child in the spring. He could see that being a part of a family was as important to Jane as being a wife.

All the way home as his little mare traveled the rutted path, he thought of how he wanted his life to be in this second half. He knew instinctively that if he did not plan it, it would take him unawares and where he might not wish to go. Somehow the planning of it made him feel it was already arranged to his liking.

As the shadows lengthened, he passed by one of the larger mounds on his property. There were four mounds on his claim, scattered over the roads like signposts. No doubt the Indians used them as waystations in their travels, perhaps places of worship or refuge. He dismounted for a time and sat beneath a tree, letting the mare rest and graze. A hundred feet away, the mound rose up before him, nearly half as many feet high in the air.

So many hands it must have taken, he thought, to bury the dead, to give the priests something to lord over the peasants. Probably a generation of workers had worn themselves out carrying the buckets and baskets of earth. No doubt they had the women do the major part of the labor. Most uncivilized tribes did so, he knew. While the men occupied themselves with gods and war.

The mound was surprisingly naked of most grass and brush. One would think, Josiah reasoned, that the seeds would grow easily in the soft earth. Perhaps it was true what the superstitious said about the mounds, that nothing would grow there since the Indians had been driven from the land. Or perhaps the natives did something to the earth to keep it barren and smooth. It was an impressive sight to gaze upon; that much was certain.

If he closed his eyes, Josiah could well imagine the scenes which took place there. Every settler knew the stories of the ritual sacrifices, the stranglings of hundreds of people upon the death of one of their Sun Kings, women and children in-

cluded. What ghastly tragedies have taken place in the name
of God, he thought. The name of the god did not matter,
truly. If the faith was strong enough, people would do anything in appeasement.

Someday, he thought, it would be satisfying to discover
what was at the core of one of these mounds. They were,
after all, his property now. Perhaps within lay buried some
ancient Spanish shield or sword. Perhaps even gold or silver.

But for now, he would leave them be. Let the others pil-
lage the places of the poor savages. Surely he had enough to
think on and plenty to do simply to keep himself in corn and
cotton.

The mare turned willingly toward the stable, sensing that
she was more than half the way home. It suddenly occurred
to Josiah that he would likely need to buy another horse,
since Jane would need a mount as well. That was an expense
he had not figured on, and he frowned as he rode. There
would be other expenses to taking a wife, none of which he
had tallied up in his mind before he had asked her to wed.

Well, it was a closed bargain now, regardless. But he
would not buy a buggy, he told himself. Not by a long sight.
The widow Jane could ride a decent horse or walk, just as he
did. He would not woo her. He would not be a fool like Robert Hanover over a woman. He had wooed once in his life,
his Abby. He would not do it again.

A month later, they were married in a simple, short ceremony on Hanover's porch. It seemed less of a trial to the few
guests to have them come a lesser distance, and Josiah's
house was another few miles farther from the village.

No fiddle this time, fewer cakes and pies, and only a handful of guests arrived to wish them well. Josiah wondered if
Jane would feel cheated, but she seemed content enough
simply to stand by his side and repeat her vows to the
preacher. Sarah beamed at them both as if she had invented
them, and Robert pumped his hand in congratulations so vig-

orously that Josiah felt he might well go into his wedding
night with only one competent wrist.

Hanover had loaned them the buggy for this first night's
conveyance, the better to get Jane's small trunks to his
house. They arrived at dusk, and he helped her down from
the buggy feeling suddenly quite ill at ease. He wished they
could simply sit on the porch as they had that once, rocking
in silence. Now that he thought on it, that was really all he
wanted her to do.

But Jane bustled about putting her things in place with a
minimum of fuss and remarks and then asked him if he was
hungry. When he said no, she repaired at once to her rocker
to watch the sun go down. He hurried to join her, as though it
were now a ritual as vital as any other consummation of the
marriage.

Long into the darkness, they sat in communal silence.
Once he asked her if he could get her a lap robe, but she only
smiled and shook her head. He only had to ask her one question before he understood that she preferred not to speak.
Like a benediction, the silence settled over them.

After the insects had died down and the birds had stopped
calling, she finally rose and stretched. "I'll ready myself for
bed now, Josiah," she said softly.

He nodded. He knew that he should give her ample time,
and certainly he was in no great hurry himself to join her.
Curious, he thought, that he felt no lust for this woman,
though it had been many years since he had been close to
female flesh. It was as if that part of him had gone as silent as
his heart. But he also felt no fear. He sensed that whatever
happened would be acceptable to Jane. He would not need to
physically bind them if he did not wish to, nor would she
reprimand him if he did not.

At last he rose and followed her. The bed sat on one side
of the room, there being no separate apartment for sleeping
in the little cabin. This was the practice in all of the cabins he
had seen in the settlement, and he no longer thought it
strange. But what was strange was to see Jane sitting up in

the bed, waiting for him, her white lace sleepbonnet in place, her white nightgown buttoned up under her plump chin.

He retired behind the screen, undressed quickly, and climbed in beside her in his drawers, blowing out the candle. The darkness was as deep as the silence. He lay down carefully, unsure whether he should reach for her or not. Thank God she was not a virgin, he breathed with relief. He could not have taken any more anxiety. At least she knew the ways of a man. Or he could hope as much. He listened for her breath to see if he could get a clue as to her expectations. It was steady and even. He rolled to face her.

She also rolled to face him, gracefully, with little movement of the bed. He would not have thought a woman of her size could move so well. She whispered, "It is so quiet out here."

"Yes," he breathed.

"More than at father's. Here, even the insects seem stilled."

"The owl in the live oak out back will start up soon enough," he whispered. "Just to warn you."

She smiled. He could see just enough to make out the contours of her face. "I've heard owls often enough," she replied.

Silence again. Finally he moved his hand slowly to her hip, resting it gently on the curve where it met her waist. "Jane," he began softly, "it's been a lifetime since I've—"

"Please don't fret," she said gently, putting a finger on his lips. "We have all the time in the world."

How did she know what he intended to say? he wondered. What if he was about to say that it had been so long since he'd been with a woman, and he could scarcely wait to enjoy her? Or that he was terrified to try? Could have been either extreme. Sometime soon, he would have to train her not to jump to those conclusions so fast. The truth was that he was nervous about approaching her. But the fact that she seemed to understand that did not make him feel more powerful or in control of their circumstances.

To cover his anxiety, he moved his hand up the curve of her body and touched her breast softly, through the light cotton of her nightdress. Now her breathing changed, and a charge of expectancy thrilled through him, instantly arousing him to desire. He began to caress her, thankful that he, too, was not inexperienced with a woman. Suddenly it seemed like an eternity since he had been held or had held another. His hands trembled slightly, and he hoped that she would not feel the tremor.

She leaned forward and kissed him softly, with a lingering gentleness which instantly hardened him and made him almost wince with the painfulness of his longing. Caught off-guard by his own body's need, he returned her kiss, again almost ashamed at the trembling in his lips, his fingers. Then he felt her own lips tremble as well, and he felt a stronger surge of power and confidence. He moved his hand from her breast to her face and stroked it, pulling her closer, kissing her more deeply. Tasting the dark, murky heat of her mouth, kissing her nose, her cheeks, her eyes, forcing himself to move more slowly than he wished, remembering her words that they had all the time in the world.

She reached down with one hand and grazed his chest with her fingertips, running her nails down slowly over his ribcage, his belly, and resting low on his groin. Her mouth under his opened and softened, and he heard a low murmur of pleasure come from deep in her throat. He was flooded with gratitude to her, to fate, that he had somehow found a woman with a capacity for passion, and he felt his body begin to move of its own accord.

He found to his delight that the years fell away, the past receded, and loving her was at once as new as the spring flowers and as familiar as the heat of the sun. As they joined together for the first time, a brief stab of longing for Abby came into his heart, but he shoved it aside ruthlessly. Abby was gone. The present, the future was moving under him willingly right now.

* * *

The seasons moved more quickly now for Josiah. Once Jane came to live with him, the regular movements of her about the cabin created a rhythm which hastened and ordered the days, made the weeks spin by as though they marched to her cheerful tune, and brought spring round again as regularly as wash days. There was nothing she could not do well enough, and much she could do better than most, he came to realize. She needed little from him but affection. So long as he gave her a solid hug at breakfast and held her through the night, no blighted crop or dried cow or dust-marred linen dimmed her contentment.

Once, after a year of marriage, he had tested her—feeling particularly bold that day with male pride—by deliberately withholding her morning hug and keeping slightly away from her in the bed that night. Slightly prickled that she said and showed nothing in the way of disappointment, he did it again a second night. And then again. After five mornings with no embrace, she burned the bacon, dropped the frying pan full of hot grease across the floor, and dissolved into hearty sobs, the first he had seen her display in their entire marriage.

He never teased or tested her that way again. It would have been like withholding the evening's ration of corn from a hardworking mule.

The second year of their marriage, she joyously presented him with a son, after an effortless pregnancy and an easy birth. He had seen mares labor more at foaling than Jane did at delivery. But he did not miss the shining triumph in her eyes as she handed him Josiah Lamon Fleming, a plumped and lusty infant with a preternaturally early smile. This one was to make up for what they had both lost, even as they both knew that was impossible. It was Jane's way of victory over death, of holding up a banner for life even in the midst of tragedy. He had never loved her more than at that moment.

Two years more, and she gave him a daughter. He searched the smooth, peachy baby's face for signs of Ruth, for any semblance to Jane. There was not a smidgen of similarity. They named her Anne Elizabeth. This baby would not be bound to the past, would suffer no responsibility to make up to anyone for anything. And so he was content to let the memories recede still further. He rarely thought of Abigail at all anymore, and when he realized that, he would be scorched by guilt and pull away from Jane for a time. But she never allowed his distance for long. Soon she would be cajoling him with a clever story about something Josie had said or done or plying him with apple cake or coffee with extra cream or Anne in his arms. And then the guilt would recede with the memory.

In time, the war with the Spanish also was only a memory. They ruled the settlement with a light hand on the reins, most agreed, and the only reason they knew they were under Spanish government at all was the flag flying over the fort. The attempted coup had been briefly successful, but when the rebels discovered that the Spanish had won in Pensacola instead of suffering the expected defeat, and further that troops were massing offshore to support Governor Galvez in his holdings in the territory, they retreated in panic. Some of the best men in the settlement and their wives and families fled across the river to escape what they were sure would be Spanish reprisals. Most were never heard from again.

Despite his bluster, Robert had not, after all, joined the actual battle but had contented himself with reviling the Spanish from the safety of his own home. All of them were grateful that he'd been spared.

Loyalists flooded the Natchez region, but when the war with Britain ended and the settlement was officially American, few let the change make any dramatic inroads into their day-to-day lives.

The crops continued to need attention, settlers still crowded into the region searching for good land, and more and more planters switched to cotton. The indigo worm savaged the blue-stalked fields which had been the staple for Natchez planters for a decade or more. After the third failure in as many years, few attempted anything but cotton.

And cotton served them well. The short staple would not answer in markets outside the Territory, but the good long staple fetched near eighteen pence at McGillivray & Strothers, the buyers in Natchez, and a good hand could pick near eighty pounds a day. Josiah found it unnecessary to buy much of anything that came from the ships in Biloxi, New Orleans, or Mobile. They grew two crops of corn a year, ample vegetables, the forests provided enough game, and the corn and apple whiskey the settlers made was a fine substitute for wine. After five years of decent crops, even with some failures, Josiah had prospered enough to purchase four slaves from the market in Baton Rouge.

He paid nearly five hundred for a prime fellow known in the Territory and four hundred for a woman to help Jane in the house. That and two other field hands gave him a crew, and they lived in small log shanties he built to the rear of the stable. The woman was married to one of the hands, else he might not have taken her, even though every planter knew that women made better pickers than the men. Jane had protested she needed no help, indeed did not wish to have a black servant about her kitchen, but he could not leave the woman behind, the man begged him so to take her.

"She work good for you, mas'sah," the man pleaded with downcast eyes. "She strong as any man, an' she cook better den mos'."

Now he was a slaveholder. He knew the God of his father, his own God for most of his life, did not smile on such decisions, but he had not spoken to his God for so long, he pushed that concern away. He told himself that slaves in the Territory were treated better than most, surely better than in Georgia or Alabama. They got winter and summer clothing, a heavy blanket, hats and shoes, plenty of pork and beef rations, and a pig pen and poultry yard they could keep themselves. They did no night work, their quarters were comfortable, and they got all the wood they needed for fuel.

It's a principle of expediency, Josiah told himself. They can't be just turned out like hogs or cows to forage, they need taking care of, and we need them to bring in the cotton. A fair trade, to his mind. He was at peace. Or at any rate, he had as much contentment as he expected to have at nearly forty. He did not look for joy anymore, though it came to him on occasion. He wished only to avoid further pain.

The only place he could perceive it might come was from his children. These two were somehow even more precious to him than the four he had lost, and yet he could never allow those feelings to swell in his breast too high, could never let them bloom as strongly as they might, for fear they would overwhelm him. That he would be lost in that love again.

He was good to them and loving, of course, but he kept them, most particularly his daughter, Anne Elizabeth, a heart's length away. She was a beautiful girl, with a nimbus of light, frothy hair about her blue china eyes, a fairness of skin which appeared ill-suited to any wilderness life, and a small, delicate structure which seemed almost birdlike in its grace and vulnerability. But she was not fragile. She learned early on to assess which lap in the house was most open to her, which arms most eager to take her in, and it was to her mother she went.

Sometimes Josiah caught her watching him in the firelight, her pale blue eyes open, frank, and assessing. There was nothing childlike in her gaze. And so because he believed she might see into his soul, he kept it from her. He could not afford to invest love there and lose it. She was too light and fey, he believed, to escape harm. And he would die if she did. And so he did not let her close enough to hurt him.

Little Josie, on the other hand, was a rough-and-tumble boy with little of Anne's softness or beauty. Even as a young child, he was vigorous in his exploration of the cabin and reluctant to be restrained by his mother's arms. Never one to lie about and simply gurgle at his own toes and fingers, Josie learned by the age of three months to pull himself up and out of his cradle, rocking himself to the floor with a resounding thud.

That was just the preamble. By five months, he could scoot across the floor on his belly, reaching crablike for everything from sharp firetongs to hot embers. He drove his mother to distraction and it was finally Josie who made Jane's acceptance of the new black servant inevitable. She simply needed one more pair of hands and another set of eyes, not for the house or for Anne, a full two years younger and far more docile, but for Josie. Else the boy might kill himself before his fifth birthday.

Josiah got used to seeing the young boy toddle along after Nelly, a tall black woman, silent and watchful as a guard dog. In time, Anne toddled along behind the two of them, often taking Nelly's hand when Josie would not. The threesome ranged over the fields and the bracketing woods, sometimes down to the creek, often into the stables to see the new calf or to feed the chickens. Jane preferred the house to herself anyway, she said, and she was grateful to have some moments without having to have a hand on Josie, lest he break something or himself.

One night when Anne was just four, she came to her father's knee and stood there, watching him light his pipe. She leaned against his leg, and he waited to see what she would say. Clearly she had chosen her time, for Jane was putting Josie into his bath, and the house was relatively quiet.

"Papa," she said clearly in her high, soft voice, "is Nelly a slave?"

He looked down at her. "Of course she is. So are Moses and Joe and Red. What else did you think she was?"

She lowered her eyes. "I thought maybe she came to stay with us to help Mama."

"Well, she did."

"But she has to?"

He hesitated for a moment. "I suppose she does. If your mama doesn't wish her to, she'll do something else. But she belongs here, and she works for us, just like the men do."

Anne thought that over quietly. Her face showed a distinct concern.

"Is something troubling you, child?" Josiah asked.

"Mama says that God watches us," Anne said slowly. "And that God loves each of us the same. Nelly says that God loves her, too."

Josiah's mouth turned down. His own conscience was not completely quiet on the subject, and he had hoped to avoid a conversation about the morality of slaveholding until the children were much older. That Anne should question such at her young age was amazing to him. And alarming. "And so you wonder what God thinks of Nelly being your papa's slave?" he asked, eager to get it over.

Anne shook her head firmly. "No sir," she said clearly, with no trace of confusion in her tone.

"What, then?"

"Does God love her as much as He loves me?" she asked her father without shame. "Because I don't think He does."

He watched his daughter carefully, not at all sure he liked what he saw in her small face. There was this assessing quality, this need to weigh portions of things—whether it was a piece of cake or God's love—and see if she had been equitably treated. Where had that come from? "You don't think God loves Nelly as much as He loves you?"

"No sir," she maintained stoutly. She thought for a moment, and then she smiled, a lovely, soft smile which lightened her face and his heart all at once. "But I don't think we should tell Nelly, do you, Papa?"

"No," he said, confused and bewildered by the control she seemed to have over herself and the conversation. "No, I suppose not. It would hurt her."

"Yes," Anne said serenely. "Night, Papa." She patted his knee fondly and skipped away to see what her mother was doing with her brother.

Josiah leaned back and breathed out a sigh he had not realized he was holding. This one would bear watching, he told himself. If he could stand it.

* * *

A young family of foxes lived quite close to one of the smaller mounds on the Fleming land, in a den cut back from the streambank. They were red fox, the small doglike rusty fox of the southern region. The male, Vulpes, had a long bushy red tail with a white tip, and he was as vigorous and healthy as a four-year-old dog fox should be. The female, Vixen, smaller and darker in color was a cross phase fox, reddish-brown with a dark cross across her shoulders. They both shared the snowy-white underparts, chin, and throat of their species.

They had found each other six months before when the ice was forming on the little stream. It was not Vixen's first breeding season, and she knew that sometimes the largest fox was not necessarily the most promising mate. But Vulpes followed her incessantly for two days, keeping all other males well away from her tracks. When she finally allowed him to mount her, she was satisfied that she had made the right choice for this season's litter.

Vixen had dug the den with her mate's help, and in it she whelped eight kits in early April. It was an old badger hole on a slight rise with a view of all approaches and two escape holes in the upper rise of earth. She lay out on the lip of the den now, watching her kits gambol in the sun. All around her were cache mounds where game was stored and scraps of bones and feathers littered the ground.

Vulpes was an excellent hunter.

The kits were two months old, and she no longer had to predigest their food and regurgitate it back to them. For a week Vulpes had been bringing them small mice and other rodents to kill, but Vixen usually had to do it for them. Two kits in particular were poor pouncers, and she wondered if they would survive separation from her, which would be coming in only two more passes of the moon. She watched them play impassively, the smaller females still not as strong as the males, but more eager to learn. Her male kits liked to loll in the sun. But they were healthy, well marked, and without birth injuries of any kind. She was quite content.

She could not know that her kind were relative newcomers to the Mississippi River region. Like the men who lived too close to her, her ancestors had come from far across the ocean, a water she would never see. Imported by men who wished to chase the red fox in the hunt, generations of her species had swiftly colonized all of the territory down to Florida, from their early releases in New York, New Jersey, Maryland, Delaware, and Virginia. And so Vixen and her kits were no more a natural part of the land where they lived than the men who hunted them.

But she adjusted far faster, expanded into new territory far more quickly than man ever could.

Now Vixen watched her kits with mild attention, for the sun was warm and few enemies prowled at this time of the day. Dozing, she kept her eyes open as much as she could, and her ears twitched attentively to the squeals and happy growls of her litter at play.

There were no changes in the air, no new sounds to disturb her, but something made her suddenly open her eyes on the very brink of dozing. Simultaneously, her fur rose on the back of her neck and shoulders, and a ripple of fear stroked her back like a breeze. She sat up and stared down the mound toward the stream. She could see nothing to alarm her. The kits still played, tumbling over and over each other and yipping in the tall grass. She turned and looked toward a copse of thick brush to the other side of the den.

And there it was. Not the slightest movement betrayed it, and no scent came to her, but Vixen's keen eyes saw the slow deadly gleam of the lynx's eyes as it stared unblinkingly at the kits, crouched in the tall brush, not three leaps away.

Vixen's lips pulled back from her teeth in a rictus of stark fear and rage. She rose and barked once, sharply, and the kits swirled in a moment of confusion, racing toward the den as she had trained them to do without hesitation. Without warning, the lynx leaped up the packed dirt toward her, snarling now and lunging with one claw outspread toward the fleeing kits. Vixen snapped viciously at the lynx's face, yelped in anguish at the answering swipe of claw, and turned to bolt down the hole after her kits as fast as she could move. Another claw swiped at her flanks as she shoved herself within the dirt, and she cried out in pain, for the claws had shredded fur and skin down to deeper muscle, despite her speed.

Inside, the kits tumbled over her, whimpering in fear and confusion, nipping at her jaws. She whined and snarled at them for silence, crushing them beneath her against the back of the den, attempting to squeeze them into the earth as deeply as she could. Outside, she heard a barking, snarling attack, and she knew that Vulpes had returned from the hunt.

Vixen pushed the kits behind her, snarled once again at them for silence, and moved as close to the outside of the hole as she dared. She knew the lynx could dig them out but was unlikely to do so while being harassed by her mate.

But harassment was likely all he could do, for the lynx could kill him easily enough with the right swipe of the claw or a well-placed bite, for it was twice the size of Vulpes and stronger too. She steeled herself for what would surely be a fight to the death, for if the lynx killed her mate and turned on her, she would defend the kits with her life.

She heard the battle before she could see it plainly, and her fur rose again in terror, an involuntary snarl coming from low in her belly. Vulpes was not simply trying to annoy the cat, was not satisfied with attempting to divert it, he was fighting the lynx as he might another fox, snarling and biting with a fury at anything he could reach. She knew then that her mate would be killed, and a sharp pang of loss coursed through her as if she herself had been savagely bitten. But she did not hesitate. She backed down the narrow opening of the den to where it widened slightly. Here, she had given birth. Here, she had slept with and suckled her kits to their present health and an age where they would soon be able to survive without her. But if she did not move fast and without fear, they would not survive the night.

She gave a low chortle in her throat, commanding them to follow in instant obedience. Her tone warned them that no play or hesitation would be tolerated. She crawled on her belly up the sloping end of the den toward another exit, one she had carefully dug and then concealed which opened onto a hidden part of the stream bank, under a large willow root. It was very tight about her shoulders, but she pushed herself through the dirt and the darkness, sensing that her kits were right behind her.

The hole had slightly caved in upon itself, but she was able to wriggle and bite at the earth sufficiently to excavate her shoulders and then her whole body, cautiously emerging into the light and looking about for the enemy. She could hear nothing from the entrance to her den, not a hundred feet away, and she knew that her mate must be dead. Perhaps the lynx was injured; perhaps it was digging even now where it had last seen her disappear. But very quickly, it might well bound up the bank to investigate the possibility that she had done exactly what she had done. She herded the kits out quickly into the brush and pushed them into a shallow depression in the streambank, tumbling them onto each other with a rough urgency. They knew to be still, and not a single kit whimpered despite her hard nudges and nips. Once she had them in place, she hurriedly dragged several fallen branches over them, pulling and digging at clumps of brush until she had them partially hidden. She then whirled away silently, freezing them to silence with her parting growl.

She crept to the top of the bank and looked down to where she had lain in the sun only an hour before. The lynx was gone. Her mate lay on his side, his legs crumpled and drawn close to his belly in a posture of pain. She sniffed the air, grimacing in fear, for she was certain the big cat must still be about. Perhaps even now he was stalking her. But finally, she could not wait another moment. She crawled on her belly down to where her mate lay, whimpering softly in terror and confusion.

She stopped again, feet from him, sniffing the air for signs of life and danger. She could smell blood everywhere, could see it on the ground and on her mate's fur. But she could not see the lynx, nor could she catch his scent. Finally, still whimpering with fear, she crawled to her mate's belly and smelled him cautiously. His belly rose and fell in shallow breaths. He was still alive. She crawled closer and began to nose his belly, his mouth and nose, whimpering loudly now, trying to rouse him as she once roused her pups from their birth slumber. She licked him where the blood was flowing, and pulled gently at first one paw and then another. He opened his eyes and shivered violently. When he saw it was her, he struggled to rise. She barked at him and whirled away.

She uncovered her kits and led them quickly back down to the den, taking them inside the front entrance again and commanding them to stay still, deep in the birthplace. They whimpered when they hurried past the still form of Vulpes, but they did not disobey her or hesitate. Then she emerged from the den again and began to lick and prod him once more.

In two hours, she had him on his feet, and he staggered weakly down to the stream to drink. He was badly injured, but he would live.

Two months later, the kits grew old enough to leave the den and find separate territories, some as far as one hundred and fifty miles distant. Breaking all patterns and customs of her kind, Vixen stayed the winter with Vulpes and mated with him a second season. She knew she would not find a better mate for her pups no matter how far she ranged.

It was a fine spring day in 1791, and Josiah and the hands had finally finished putting in the cotton for the season. The warming weather was irresistible, a promise of a fine year and an excellent crop. When Jane suggested they take a walk after the midday meal, perhaps even make an adventure of it, he found himself agreeably nodding his head. Josie and Anne capered in delight, immediately rounding up every conceivable treasure or tool they felt essential for an outing to the Indian mound a half-mile from the cabin.

At seven, Anne was already more elegant and finely boned than either her mother or father before her. In fact, as Josiah watched his daughter order her world and her brother about as though she, not he, were the oldest, he marveled that such a child could have come from their union. She was long in the bone with an almost imperious small face, long neck, and perfectly molded head. Her hair was a gilt airy frame around sharp blue eyes which looked far older than her years.

He could remember, even now, that her early cries were somehow different from her brother's. Josie had been a sturdy pup, sleeping and nursing with ease, gurgling happily at his toes and fingers and any face which loomed over his cradle. Though he was foolhardy, he required nothing but a guarding eye and a firm hand. Anne, on the other hand, demanded—nay, commanded—much more than that from the first breath of her life. Her cries were strong and indignant, piercing and constant, and the cabin was suddenly much too small for them all with the simple addition of her tiny body.

Josiah had asked Jane, was something wrong with the child that she cried so much? He could not remember any of his babies insisting on so much attention, seemingly so . . . *angry* . . . at the world.

"She's a strong girl," Jane said mildly, as undisturbed by his anxiety as she was by Anne's tumult. "She simply is unwilling to be left unattended, I think."

Josiah was annoyed at that. The child would be spoiled by the time she was weaned, doubtless, and if she or her mother thought that life would provide such constant attention, they would both need to be taught otherwise and in a hurry. And he resolved to ignore the infant's wails. But Anne would have none of it. And one night, when she had screamed for more than two hours, when he had forbidden Jane to go to her as usual in an attempt to teach the child that her very survival did not depend on an instant set of arms to hold her and tend to her every need, he finally gave up and himself lifted her to their bed to be rocked into instant silence. Once she had what she wanted, she fell blissfully asleep. It seemed to him that night, as she chortled and gurgled in quick contentment, that there was a note of triumph in her voice which made him recoil.

But he told himself that an infant of that age could not possibly be so canny. She simply needed more than most. He sighed. Surely she would grow out of it soon. Once she could understand speech and make her needs known, she would grow to understand the ways of the world and the needs of others.

Josiah had to admit ruefully, as he watched his small lovely daughter race ahead of her brother up the trail to the mound, that she had grown to understand the ways of the world quite well, at least as they worked in the Fleming cabin: she said what she wanted and she got it. Simple as that. And not because she was the weakest, but because she was the strongest and was somehow able to convince those around her that what she wanted was due her. More a distinct and completed small person than a child, she had a perfection about her that drew the eye and made her somehow splendid in her despotism.

Josie, however, was as sweet and easy a child as his sister was beautiful. From a rambunctious toddler, he had become a boy who made few demands on his world. Two years older, he seemed now to be younger than Anne, and Josiah guessed he would always be under her direction rather than the other way around. That troubled him, for a son must learn strength, no matter what else he brings to the arena, Josiah knew. A woman could afford softness, but not a manchild. He did not run ahead with Anne's purpose, but ran up, explored a bit, picked up this or that, and then ran back to show it to Josiah or his mother with pleasure and generosity. Always, he was aware of where the other members of the family were on the trail, whereas Anne simply ran on ahead, confident that the others would follow.

Josiah worried more for Josie than for Anne, because he knew that his gentle abstract nature would likely be torn rather than tempered by life. Only last month, he had discovered Josie hiding in a small space under the cabin, between the porch and the house itself. It was so tiny a space that he would not have thought his son would have fit in it, much less sought it out. But when he called Josie, he could see that the boy had been found out in his secret spot. He had sought out a cage where he could watch the world in peace and safety.

Anne said, when she heard her father asking Josie why he would sit in such a spot for hours on end, "He likes to pretend he doesn't belong to us. That he's just a visitor," she said blandly. "He watches us all the time."

Josiah had frowned and let it go. Later when he questioned Jane about it, she only shrugged and brushed off his concern. "Every child has secrets," she said. "It's likely a healthy thing, all told. I remember doing something like that when I was a girl, it was an old pickle barrel in the basement—"

"But you were a girl," Josiah said, still not persuaded. "Boys don't generally seek out such hiding places from the world."

Jane smiled. "Well, this one does. Don't fret so, Josiah. He need not be just like you to do well in this world."

And so Josiah had let it be.

Now they approached the mound, Anne already having run nearly halfway to the top. She stood up and crowed at them, her hands on her little hips like Colossus straddling the world. Josie helped his mother spread out the blanket and open the basket, and they soon were stuffing themselves with Jane's good cold chicken and cakes, buttermilk and early wild strawberries. Josie began to dig industriously in the dirt at the edge of the mound, proclaiming his intention to dig to the middle of the thing and discover its secrets.

Anne, on the other hand, relished the view from the top nearly forty feet above them, over and over and at the top of her voice.

Josiah lay down with his head in Jane's lap, and felt himself almost ready to doze in the soft sunlight. Jane was playing idly with his hair, and her touch was soothing. "Josiah," she murmured, "you know the cabin is really getting rather cramped as the children get older."

"Mmm." He felt so indolent and heavy, he wondered if he really had to ever leave this spot.

"It would be wonderful to have more space. More privacy. Soon, the children will need to sleep in separate rooms, and I'm thinking perhaps if the next crop is good, we could put on an addition to the back, perhaps a sleeping area and a space for sitting in the evening."

Josiah let his thoughts wander. Usually when settlers wanted to enlarge, they built a second cabin next to the first one with a piazza connecting them and a long porch. They called it "two pens and a passage." But somehow, that seemed not enough. A big house, perhaps.

He opened his eyes. The idea of it appealed to him, actually, once he got past his surprise. The land seemed to call out for more than they had planted on it somehow. It need not be grand, but he was, after all, no longer a bachelor. Even if he could not quite get used to the idea, he was a husband again and a father. Jane would love something better, though she would never complain. Anne might. And though the indigo crops had failed, the cotton was doing well. Very well, indeed. "I agree," he said mildly.

"You do?" she asked happily.

He nodded, noting with satisfaction the pleasure in her voice. "In fact, perhaps we should consider building a new house altogether. Something large enough to keep us comfortable until the children are grown and gone."

"Oh, Josiah!" she gasped. "That would be wonderful!"

"Nothing too grand," he said quickly, "but something more than a cabin." He did not want to duplicate Robert's error; that much was certain. Hanover had begun to build when Sarah had her first child and went on to add to the house with each succeeding birth. Now that their children had grown to a tribe of five, the house was huge, sprawling, without plan or grace. Josiah knew that "Hanover's Folly," as it was jocularly referred to in Natchez, would ever be the source for mocking amusement, no matter how it might end. Such was not what he envisioned for his own family. "Something in keeping with the climate and the land," he said thoughtfully. "Not like they build in the East."

Josie's sweet voice piped up, with an unusual note of troubled concern. "Will the new house be very far from the old one, Papa?"

Josiah glanced over to his son. He had not even been aware Josie was listening. "Probably not. Why?"

Josie hesitated. Anne came careening down the mound to investigate, announcing importantly, "He wants to make sure he can still get to his secret place anytime he wants."

Josie looked up at his sister, and Josiah saw the look of gratitude in his face, the soft biddable love which washed over him for the girl, and his heart hurt for his son. The world was going to torture him with its casual cruelties, its losses, its careless indifference to him, if he did not do something to steel his spine somehow. His voice was sharper than he intended. "Likely, we'll tear it down. Or turn it to slave quarters. You're too old for a hideyhole anyway, son, and if you've got time to waste dreaming under a porch, I can put you to better use with me out in the fields."

"Yessir," Josie said sadly.

Jane glanced at Josiah with quick dismay but she said nothing. Anne's eyes flashed with swift anger at her father, and she turned away, picked up a rock, and threw it with all her strength to the top of the mound. "Come on, Josie, help me dig a tunnel. Those old Indian bones are probably right near the top.'' The boy scuttled after his little sister, and Josiah sat up abruptly from Jane's lap.

"You're making a lapdog of him. He's got to get harder, or the world will eat him up."

She looked away and said nothing.

Somehow her silence angered him more than anything. "And Anne is turning into a little harridan. She needs taking down a peg or two, to my mind."

"Well, then, I'm sure you'll do so," Jane said coolly. She rose and dusted off her skirts. "I am of the mind that they will get all they need of hardship once they leave us; they needn't practice for it in the bosom of their family."

He began to pack up the basket, not meeting her eyes. "He's got to be raised as though he were not a substitute for the one you lost, Jane. You'll do him no good at all keeping him a baby with your coddling."

She turned on him with the first real edge of anger he had heard in her voice for a good while. "It's good we're building a new house, Josiah. It will give you something constructive to do besides tell me how to improve the children." She walked away around the perimeter of the mound, suddenly showing vast interest in the slope, the incidental diggings, the very dirt itself. He walked the other way, in no mood to be near her. As he rounded the circle, he came within view of his two children high above him, and Josie called to him and waved happily, clearly all hurt now quite forgotten. Josiah waved back, shading his eyes from the sun. From the bottom looking up, both of them appeared to be two perfect sun-children, wreathed in fire about their brows. He dropped his head in the glare, his eyes watering fiercely. Would he ever, ever be able to forget the pain and simply live his life? he wondered desolately. Perhaps the Bible was wrong all along. Perhaps one did not need to die to experience hell. Maybe each heart carried around its own perdition, a yawning pit of despair always available to cast itself into, whenever the sins grew too great for the mind to forgive.

He pushed the thoughts and the pain away, picked up a

digging stick, and began to worry the edge of the mound. The house should be large, he decided then. Large enough for them to live in it without rubbing shoulders.

Josiah bought one more slave that spring, a carpenter who had some experience in building, and he loaned out his best field hand to a neighbor in exchange for a month's work from a slave who knew the making of brick from the red Natchez earth. By the end of summer, the new house was almost complete.

And though Josiah had cautioned Jane that it would not be too grand, in the rising of it, that caution somehow went the way of the spring flowers. In fact, the house seemed to grow in the night of its own volition, like the cotton stalks themselves. White and tall, with angular lines and branches of rooms added on as afterthought, the Big House, as they had come to call it, became exactly that.

The Natchez earth provided the bricks, the yellow poplar and live oaks lent their strength to the walls themselves, and it seemed as though the land grew the place from invisible roots set deep and heretofore unknown in the soil of Fleming's claim. He had set the house on a small rise above the fields, well away from their first cabin and within sight of the Saint Catherine. Now that he no longer avoided the river, it seemed to him that the house should somehow be as high above it as possible, as though it watchdogged the water and the land.

Starting as one story, the Big House soon became two, and the simple porch turned into a wide veranda which embraced the house on three sides, opening the bottom floor to the breezes and the open air. Columns became necessary to support the wide, flat roof, and windows began to march around the front and sides as though they were sentinel eyes and glass was as easy to procure as the red clay.

Jane took as much pleasure in the growing of the house as she had when the children bloomed in her belly. She applauded the drawings, crowed over every progression, and wanted to talk of nearly nothing else but the Big House and its rise. Josiah wondered sometimes if the folks in Natchez were beginning to mock him as they had Hanover, but as the wagons and buggies ventured out from neighboring claims to discover what he was doing, his pride of the place grew apace with its walls.

Robert and Sarah took as much interest in its building as if it were part of their family, and it was now nothing unusual to see their own five children capering about the grounds, running in and out of the construction with Josie and Anne.

It was finally complete enough to occupy in the first hot weeks of September. The furnishings had been arriving for a month, stored in the barn, the old cabin, wherever they could find space away from the sun and the dust. Josiah knew he would need to make a splendid cotton crop, not just this year but for the next three, to pay for the bed, the tables, the chairs, the carpets that Jane had brought up from New Orleans, but somehow he did not care. For the first time in many years, he found that he did not expect calamity.

That alone, he realized, made the Big House a blessing. He told Jane they needn't fill it with furnishings all in the first year and she agreed, but somehow the piles and stores of commodities and necessaries kept growing. He remembered Hanover's rueful laugh, that a house was worse than a woman for keeping a man to the plow, and he knew it was true. It was now a living thing which must be fed, and he guessed he would work hard the rest of his life to be worthy of the Big House, even as it belonged to him.

They moved in and expanded to fill the floors, incredibly—he would not have believed they could use so much space. But when the night came that the two children slept in their new rooms, the two servants in their adjoining cubbyholes, Robert and Sarah in another room, their children filling two more, and Josiah and Jane bedded down in the largest room to the front of the upper story, he felt an expansion in his chest of fulsome pride and power that buoyed him so he could barely close his eyes. The Big House had risen under his hands, and he had made a thing on the land which would outlast him and, likely, his children. For a moment, he knew how the men who had built the mounds must have felt: they had somehow recorded their lives in a tangible way, piling up their dirt, their rocks, their trees, the land itself as evidence they had walked it. Had owned it. Surely, he thought as he drifted into contented sleep, nothing could ever dislodge them again.

The Big House stood now in a field of white, cotton on all sides as if it rose from a large down coverlet which turned alternately green, white, or red with the seasons of the crop. In a month, the chickens had decided to live around the porch rather than under the porch of the old cabin, and birds were nesting in the upper eaves. Josiah was surprised to see how quickly it felt like home, and he thought he might never tire of looking out the upstairs window and seeing the men work his fields out into the distance.

In the second season they lived there, a final caterpillar attack laid low the remainder of the indigo fields, and Josiah turned resolutely to cotton for every last acre of his claim. "For good or ill," he told Jane then, "we're sticking to cotton and nothing else. This land was made for it, I believe."

So far, his decision had been profitable, for cotton prices kept going up every harvest, and with no war between nations to bottle up the shipping lanes, markets were open worldwide to whatever they could get downriver to sell. New Orleans was afloat in a sea of cotton, they said, and all of it going for good money. Josiah and Robert joined with several neighbors and hired a crew to take their bales downriver. The same crew was hired by New Orleans merchants to bring imported goods up to Baton Rouge and Natchez for eager buyers, and both sides were amazed at their profits.

Natchez was growing swiftly now, from a wilderness settlement to a prosperous town. It was the frontier, "the

West,'' the jumping-off place where everything seemed possible. The immigrants who flooded into the territory came to better their fortunes, with the conviction that the United States had a just claim to the country and would soon assert it. Josiah heard fewer Loyalists holding forth at the livery, the butchery, or the general store about the virtues of British rule. Most of the newcomers had lately left Pennsylvania, Virginia, or the Carolinas, where some of them had taken up arms for the colonies. They brought with them more culture, enterprise, and wealth than the earlier settlers, and the successive Spanish commandants at Fort Panure were mostly gentlemen, fond of etiquette and pomp, and Catholic, of course, but they made no attempt to proscribe the Protestants who owned the land.

Josiah heard the tales of the religious frenzies taking place in Massachusetts and elsewhere, where men were forced into taking oaths of faith, convents were burned, and ministers silenced. Religion in the East seemed to be so much more severe, it seemed to him, and fanatics had bled beliefs into politics and politics into the pulpit.

But in Natchez, their community of Protestants prospered under the Catholic dynasty, with no persecution or civil disturbance. Even the gambling dens and brothels at the bottom of Natchez, along the docks and twisted streets where the thieves and sailors drank and caroused, had been cleaned up and sorted out into minor vice and diversions.

There were still lands to be claimed with little expense. A man could arrive on a Sunday and be landed by the end of the week, simply by finding an unoccupied parcel, presenting a request for order of survey, and paying a small fee for issuing the grant. He then went to Alexander Moore or Peter Walker, plantation owners who usually lent monies to the newcomers for their first crop, and signed into indebtedness, promising to pay annually one-third of his debt out of first crop until the debt was paid and he could fund himself. He then went to the John Shields store in Natchez to discover that current prices delivered to the dock for shipping to New

Orleans were: cotton, $4 per hundred weight in the seed, or
$25 clean; pork was $5 per hundred weight, beef was $4,
corn was four reals per bushel. Good land would yield about
fifteen hundred to two thousand pounds per acre of black
seed cotton, the seed procured from Georgia or Jamaica.
Based on prices and his land, he'd make the decision what to
plant or what brood stock to buy, and he was on his way.

Natchez was now formally divided into two distinct
towns. Natchez-Under-the-Hill was where the flatboats and
keelmen docked, with hardware and feed stores, blacksmiths
and buggy shops, taverns and poor inns. Most of the buildings were set on pilings to protect them from the river's ris-
ings, and they were shuttered even in the daytime, giving the
streets a squalid, furtive aspect. Natchez-Over-the-Hill was
lined with wide streets, bigger houses, and orderly gardens.
Here sat the court house, the churches, and the finer resi-
dences, overlooking the Mississippi below. Silver Street, the
steep incline from the water up the bluff, joined the two
towns to one, and it always teemed with folks these days,
buggies, wagons, and horses and mules. It was dusty and
bustling and noisy, the nearer it got to the docks.

Natchez was only a tiny island in the wilderness, however, and the fields and swamps and forests surrounded it
closely like an embrace. Every time Josiah made the trip by
wagon into town, he still hurried to finish his business so
that he could be back to the Big House by dark.

One evening as he traveled the rutted pathway, near to one
of the smaller mounds on his property, he heard a strange cry
in the forest. He pulled the mule to a stop and sat forward on
the wagon, listening. Something about the cry made him
edgy, and he listened to the silence for a long moment before
clicking the reins against the mule's neck and bidding him
on.

Again he heard the cry, and the mule snorted nervously in
reply. This time, Josiah did not stop. The mule had picked up
the pace perceptibly, and he steered him well clear of the
overhanging pines. The silence of the forest around them

seemed immense, larger than the river, the sky, the world. The shadows were long and the night would be on them soon, but Josiah felt sure he would be pulling into his own stable by the time it was good and dark. If nothing stopped him.

He drove the wagon along, watching from side to side until finally he felt the edginess diminish, and he began to relax. Whatever had made that cry must have been traveling away from him, he thought, and he began to imagine the warmth and company waiting for him at home. As he rounded a bend in the road, the mule stopped suddenly and snorted loudly, erupting into a short squall of a bray. Josiah looked up to see a cougar lying in the middle of the pathway, staring at the approaching mule and wagon with defiant calm.

Josiah yanked the reins and reached for his musket under the seat. It was a large lion, golden in the dusky light, and it did not turn away at his approach. Neither did it flinch at the sight of the musket. Josiah spoke softly to the mule, who quivered and snorted but held his ground. His large ears cocked to the lion, who began a singsong whine-snarl low in his throat. To Josiah, the song was clear enough. The cougar wanted his mule. At the very least.

As he primed and cocked his musket, he puzzled on it. There surely must be ample game for the lion, and stock at neighboring plantations abounded. Why would he take the trouble to approach a harnessed mule—surely not the most passive of prey—with a man on the seat above him?

Now the lion rose languidly, his switching tail the only indication that he was excited. He walked closer to the mule, his shoulders rising and falling in that characteristic frontal shrug which expresses power and supreme control in a cat, and just as Josiah was ready to raise the musket to his shoulder and take aim, the cat veered off into the forest, melting away in seconds to invisibility.

The mule, meanwhile, brayed angrily and shivered all over as if he had waged the battle complete in his mind. Josiah waited a moment, then set aside the musket and took up the reins once more. They walked on. He realized that he had never been that close to a cougar before, and he wondered what it could mean.

Finally, he had to confess himself content with the small explanation he could devise: the cougar simply wanted him to know that he was there. That it was his forest, his trail, his piece of the world as much as it was any man's. He knew just how close to come and just how long to stay, and the contempt in his eyes had been easy enough to read.

For a good while after that incident, Josiah did not feel himself so safe and civilized after all. Natchez seemed, after that evening, just a little farther off and the forest seemed ever so much closer, especially in his dreams.

The seasons passed in the Big House, and the Fleming claim turned in time into a plantation. Josiah bought more land and imported more slaves as he put more of his acres to cotton, for the crop required many hands to bring it to harvest. Each pair of hands cut into his profits, of course, but only in the short term. Within two years, most able slaves paid for themselves, and often they bred more workers in the process. The old cabin had been turned over to them, more quarters added, and the families lived there now, raising their own vegetables and chickens in the same rows that Jane had used when they first wed.

There was a certain rightness to it which pleased Josiah when he walked over his land and saw that most all of it was put to good use.

Josie and Anne were growing well and thriving, so far as he could see. Anne was becoming lovelier with each passing year, and Josie was growing taller, though he still had a softness to him which bothered Josiah when he stopped to think on it. But the plantation required so much of him, he thought about the children less and less. Jane taught them their letters and numbers and everything else she thought they needed, and when he discovered that his son or daughter could actually read one of the few books in the house, he was as surprised as if Jane had just announced the mule could cipher. None of his other children had had such skills. But then life was changing all around him.

One day Anne came to him with a sober face and stood around at his desk until he finally looked up from his journal with curiosity. "What is it, child?" he asked.

She looked down at her clasped hands. Such hesitation was unusual in Anne. At ten, she had generally the upper hand in the children's wing, over her servant, Dory, and over her brother. "Papa, do you believe in God?"

He raised his brows in what he hoped was a good indication of mild disapproval. It was not good for a child to ask her elders such questions, surely—

"Because Dory said you don't. And when I asked Mama, she said to ask you."

He thought for a moment. That Jane had referred the question to him was almost more interesting than that it had come from Anne in the first place. "I see," he said carefully. "And what are you doing talking of such with a slave, Anne? I shall have to speak to Dory about expressing her opinions on my beliefs or lack of them."

He had rather hoped that this alone might quell Anne, for she was fond of Dory and had often taken her side when Jane found fault with her service. But Anne's face did not betray any anxiety. She stayed right to the point. "Well, do you, Papa? Mama believes in God, and Dory believes in God, and most everybody else seems to, looks to me. Do you?"

"No," he said shortly. "But that is my business alone, Anne, and I'll thank you not to discuss my beliefs with outsiders."

Now Anne raised her brows in an eerie facsimile of his own expression. "Is Dory an outsider?"

"She is a servant, and as such she has no business giving her opinions about God or much else of importance."

"What about Mama?"

He frowned. "What do you mean?"

"Well, does she have business giving her opinions about God?"

"Of course, if she wishes to," he said, trying to soften his voice. He was aware that he was perturbed with her questions, but he was not quite sure why. He decided to forgive whatever trespass he imagined. "Your mother is a wise and wonderful woman, Anne. You would do well to be like her in all ways."

"But she believes in God," Anne said with small determination. "And you don't, Papa. So I won't either."

"Why not?" he asked, bewildered.

"Because if you believe in God, you have to be good all the time." She smiled a charming smile, one which he saw would be a deadly weapon in her feminine arsenal when she was just a bit older. "I don't know if I'd like that."

Despite his annoyance, he found himself smiling back at her. "Lots of people who believe in God aren't good and plenty who don't believe are good enough. When you're older, you might feel differently about all this."

"Did you used to feel differently?" she asked blandly. She was watching him carefully, though she appeared to pose the question without real concern for the answer.

He looked at her deeply for the first time in what had been, he knew now, too long. Anne was small and beautiful, grave and possessed of a powerful adult dignity. She was brighter than her brother, possibly more intelligent than her mother. Perhaps she would, one day, be smarter than he was as well, Josiah thought. They would have her only a little time, that much was clear. The world would beckon, and Anne would answer and be gone.

There was an odd radiance which wrapped around Anne, which gleamed from her hair and her eyes and her very skin, which seemed warm and cool all at the same time. She had a way of keeping a distance between herself and those closest to her. Her light was at once a magnet and a cloak behind which she stood, inviolate and separate at the core. With a small shock, Josiah realized that he truly did not know his own daughter very well. Did any man? he wondered.

He reached out impulsively and drew Anne to him, enveloping her in a warm hug. The words they had exchanged troubled him, but he did not want her to see that. "God and you will have your own truce," he murmured into her hair. "When you get older, you'll see. We'll talk again another time about this, if you wish."

"No, Papa," she said clearly. "That's all right. We don't have to." She returned his hug and then disentangled herself, skipping out of the room lightly and unconcerned.

That night, Josiah sat down on the bed while Jane was getting ready for sleep, watching her comb out her long, dark hair. It was the hair of a much younger woman, really, with little gray, thick and heavy as a mare's tail. Her body had thickened, of course, but it still had vitality which drew him. He contemplated her movements as she drew on her cotton gown and smoothed some sort of emollient over her arms.

She caught his gaze in the glass and smiled. "After all these years, it's still good to feel your eyes on me." She turned coyly, lifting her hair off her neck and shoulders. It was a move Abigail would never have made in a thousand years, even when she was young and winsome. He grimaced slightly, pushing the thought away.

She saw his look and turned to him, her brow creasing with concern. "What is it?"

He took her onto his lap to reassure her. "Nothing important, really," he said. "I had a conversation with Anne today which was a little—peculiar."

"About?"

He hesitated, wondering if he really wanted to wade into these waters. He smiled painfully. "About God, actually. And my lack of belief therein. I gathered she'd been talking with Dory. She said you also told her that her father did not subscribe to the—to the consensus of the majority." He knew his tone was wry, but he did not care to alter it.

She peered at him closely. "And that troubled you?"

He shrugged. "I suppose not. Certainly Anne didn't seem the least bit fazed by it. In fact, as I recall, she said she thought she might throw in with my side of the question."

Jane rose and looked down at him with sadness. "That would be a very great tragedy for her," she said gently.

"Why?"

"Well, has such a decision made you happy?"

He sighed and looked down at the wood plank floors, the expensive carpet brought up from New Orleans which softened and warmed the room. There was much here to content him, much that was certain. "I have made myself happy," he said. "God had nothing to do with that. He did not help me, and He did not hinder me, I suppose. In that, I can call myself happy."

She laughed softly, and he looked up with surprise. "Are you so very sure, my husband? Do you really suppose that you have done all of this"—her waving hand took in the house, the room, and by implication herself and their family—"by yourself?"

"Of course not," he said quickly. "You have partnered me from the beginning—"

"Do you not see the hand of God in the faces of your children? In the beauty and richness of your land? In your own health and prosperity?" Her laugh was gone now, and she looked at him as from a great distance. Sadly, as though she were leaving on a vessel where he did not wish to go.

He gazed down again at his lap. Finally he said, "I have to confess there are times I wished with all my heart that I could believe again, Jane." He looked up at her earnestly. "With every bit of my heart. But I cannot. I've tried, and I simply cannot accept the idea of a loving God in my life anymore."

"Why not?" She put her hand on his shoulder. " 'Tis an easy thing, really. Most come to it quite naturally. It seems a man must make a very great effort *not* to believe."

"I cannot forgive," he said, his throat going rough at the

edges. "I cannot forget, and I cannot forgive. I wish by all heaven that I could."

"You cannot forget your first family," she said evenly. "That I understand. I sometimes think of mine, of course, and I always will. But what is it you cannot forgive?"

"That God did not save them!" he cried out suddenly, a wrenching, hurtful sob of anger and desolation. "I had been faithful to Him all of my life! You could ask any man who knew me, I was one of His servants. Goodness? I worked hard at goodness. And what did it matter? My family drowned as surely as if I'd been a drunken, faithless heretic. God did not keep His part of the bargain!"

"He did not save your children—"

"Or my wife." He said it to hurt her.

"He did not save your children or your wife," she continued calmly, "and so you cannot forgive Him. You cannot forgive God."

"That is correct," he said, rather coldly. "And you needn't speak of this more to Anne; she'll have to come to her own decisions in her own time. Whatever they are, they will be what is best for her. I shall not try to sway her, but neither should you—"

"It seems to me," Jane said smoothly, ignoring this last, "that it is yourself you cannot forgive. Which is ironic, Josiah. Because God forgave you in the instant of your lapse."

He gaped up at her. "Are you saying that their death was my fault?" He could not believe she would say it. He knew he would die if he heard the words from her mouth.

"Do you think it was God's fault?" she asked.

"How can you not blame God for the death of your son?" he stood up, raging. "How can you simply accept the loss of your husband and your son with no sense of vengeance? No anger! An innocent boy, taken in the bloom of youth—what kind of God would arrange such a death?"

"He did not, of course; the disease took my son. Do you think it was God's fault that your family was taken?" She did not waver from her question or her gaze.

"Yes," he finally whispered. "I must believe so. Otherwise, it must be mine."

"It was your fault," she said gently. "Your fault, Josiah, that they came upriver. Your fault that they were on the raft, in the water, that they fell into the water, your fault for you married Abigail and created them in the first place, you made them and you unmade them. Just as it was my fault that my husband died and my son died—and their fault, too. And no one's fault at all. We are all at fault, every one of us, and every one of us innocent as newborn babes. God does not take us up or smite us down, He does not arrange our deaths or our lives. He simply loves us. And we must do nothing else but love Him in return."

He took her hand and gripped it firmly as it lay on his shoulder. He knew Jane meant to comfort him, at bottom. She meant to shock him, possibly jar him into painful recognition, but she meant finally to heal, if she could.

She was a good woman, and likely worth two of him in any God's eye who might be watching.

"I cannot," he said sadly. "I understand what you are trying to do, and I am grateful, I suppose, for your efforts. But I cannot, Jane. I will not let such a God into my heart again. I will not believe."

"I'm sorry for you," she said. "It must be terrible to have so little love in your life."

"I feel I have enough," he said, rather stiffly.

She shook her head. "You will never forgive yourself, my Josiah, until you forgive God. And you will never truly know love until you forgive yourself." She embraced him.

He drew her back into his lap again, for whatever else, her touch was a comfort.

"Would you wish such on your child?" she whispered into his neck. "Anne is going to need to believe in love with all her heart, I think. More than Josie."

He sat and thought on this. She was likely right. Josie would believe in love all of his life and never question it, and so it would come to him easily. The love of his fellow man, of a woman and family, and the love of God. But Anne would have a hard time believing in anything, most of all in love. And so she would need all she could find. He did not know how he knew this of her, but he knew it nonetheless.

"Well, I can't lie to her and tell her I believe if I don't," he said.

"No," his wife said, "but neither need you speak of it with her. Do you speak of everything in your heart? Simply tell her it is a matter for each individual soul, and that you are still deciding for yourself. Can you say that much with honesty?"

He stroked her hair, suddenly so grateful for the weight of her in his lap. "I can say that much."

She laughed ruefully. "And of course, it may not matter a whit what *either* of us says to Anne, she is already so certain of her own mind. Was your Ruth anything like her?"

"I don't know that anyone is anything like her. She is a—unique child. Hardly a child at all, in fact. I get the feeling that she just skipped that stage somehow and went on to become an adult. Possibly out of boredom. I sometimes wonder if it isn't she who should be groomed to care for these lands and this house when we're gone, rather than Josie."

She shook her head. "Some man will care for her. Josie will need to learn to care for himself and likely a family, besides. I've never had a daughter before; you have. Did you see none of this in your youngest or your eldest?"

He shook her head. "Anne is her own woman. Already, she is her own, complete and entire. My Ruth was nothing like her."

"I suppose you're right in that few are," Jane said soberly. "And it will likely take all our wit and courage to mold her into a seemly woman."

"But we shall have God's help in that?" he asked wryly.

She smiled lovingly. "We shall, indeed."

* * *

The next time Josiah took the entire day on horseback to oversee the plantation, he insisted that Josie be mounted on his pony and ride alongside him. Josie did not balk, but neither did he greet the proposal with happy enthusiasm. He mounted his fat dappled gray, however, and reined him in behind his father's horse silently, sitting up straight as if to be ready for whatever might be coming.

Josiah had taken Josie along before, of course, but never for the whole day and always sitting behind him. Those times were more obviously for amusement. Today was different. Today would be the beginning of Josie's education as a man.

The day was bright and hot already by eight as they set out across the fields. Jane waved them farewell from the front porch as though they were setting off for an expedition into the wilderness. Cook packed a meal of cold bread, cheese, and apples, and Josie had it tied importantly to his saddle. As they were mounting at the stable, Anne came racing round the corner, her hair flying back behind her like a flag. "I want to go too, Papa!" she shouted urgently.

He leaned down and gave her a quick hug. "Today is Josie's time, Anne. You can go another time."

She looked at him, horrified. "But I can learn, too! I can ride!"

It was true that she rode her small white pony every bit as well, with as much control and courage, as Josie did his gray. But that, of course, was not the point. "Not today, Anne. You can go another time."

"There never is another time," she said glowering. "Josie gets to see how to boss the slaves and make the cotton grow, and I get to see how Dory washes the linens and how cook makes the pies. It isn't fair!"

Josiah laughed kindly, ruffling her hair. "You speak to your mama about it, Anne. I'm sure she can find other things for you to do today, without following along after Josie." And he mounted, doing his best to ignore Anne's fierce frown.

Josie smiled down at his sister with affection. "It's going to be so hot today, Annie, you're lucky you get to stay in the shade."

"Oh, Josie, you're such a fool," Anne said desolately. She turned and stalked out of the stables, her shoulders stiff with rejection.

Josiah sighed and turned his horse toward the Big House. They walked by in a line, and Jane happily waved and called out encouragement, but Anne was nowhere to be seen. Likely she would spend a good hour hiding herself in some secret place, rehearsing the small revenge she might take. His heart hurt for her, but he knew that she must be made to understand her responsibility as a woman. It was not too early to begin her training. Her will must be bent—not broken but definitely inclined—to her proper place or she would be discontent and unhappy all of her days.

"Josie," he said firmly, "keep up close to me today. I don't want to have to shout at you."

"Yes, Papa," the boy said quietly, and he kicked his fat pony to make him go up.

They walked the horses out on the edge of the first field, a vast expanse of acres of cotton, tall and green and healthy in the sun. In the distance, they could see the gang of hands working, their hoes rising and falling like dark sticks against the white sky. It was weeding time in the fields, a necessary round of hoeing and grubbing out suckers so that the crop would be strong. Hard, hot work which the slaves must be kept to with sharp words and sometimes threats of punishment, for the bending and pulling and hoeing broke even the strongest man's back by the end of the long day.

The gang boss looked up as Josiah rode up and dismounted. Josie glanced at his father and dismounted as well, taking hold of his father's reins and holding his own. "How are they working today, Samuel?" he asked. The same question he asked each morning.

"Passable, Mister Fleming," the man answered, as usual.

"One man out sick, another feeling poorly, but we'll get this lot done by noon, I 'spect."

"Which man's complaining?" Josiah asked, letting Josie hear the sternness in his tone.

"Dan, come up!" the overseer called out sharply to the row of men. Six of them kept working, their heads down, their backs moving rhythmically in the sun. A seventh man looked up, dropped his hoe, and strode reluctantly toward the horses.

With the man before him, Josiah looked him up and down, an obvious frown on his face. "What's your complaint, man?" he asked. He saw that Josie was watching the slave carefully, his eyes shifting often to his father's face.

The man said nothing, only gazed at his bare feet.

"Tell Mister Fleming what's troublin' you, man," the overseer said.

"My leg," the man said quietly.

"What's wrong with your leg?" Josiah asked impatiently.

"It ache me bad."

Josiah knew this slave well. Dan was a decent worker, likely getting too old for hoeing. He couldn't say how old the man was, but he looked to be in his midforties. Slaves often looked younger than they were, though, and he could be older yet. His back was still good, and his arms were strong, but his legs gave out early on long, hot afternoons of hoeing and bending. He turned to Josie. "What should we do with Dan today, son?" He asked the question soberly, as though he expected to follow the boy's advice.

Dan cut his eyes quick to the boy and then dropped his head again.

"I don't know, Papa," Josie said miserably.

"Well, you must decide," Josiah said firmly. "This man belongs to you, same's your pony. Or will the day I'm gone. It's not too soon to figure out how he should be best used. He says his leg aches him. What do you want to do with him?"

"Let him sit down and rest?" the boy asked, looking up at

his father. His voice was very small in the vast fields, and the morning seemed suddenly heavy and still.

"And when the rest of the crew complains their legs ache or their backs ache or the sun is in their eyes, will you let them sit down and rest, too?"

Josie dropped his eyes now, matching the demeanor of the slave. "No, Papa," he said.

"Perhaps it would be better to think of something else that Dan could do today which would not make him use his legs quite so much. And then tomorrow, when his leg no longer aches, he can rejoin the hands. What do you think?"

"I think that's a good plan," Josie said quietly.

"Put this man to the stable today," Josiah said to the gang boss, "and let Red put him to work. Tomorrow, we'll see how that leg holds up with a hoe."

"Yessir," the overseer said. "You heard the master, boy—go pick up your hoe."

The slave glanced once at Josie, but not at all at Josiah. He went back to pick up his hoe, and the overseer said, "Want me to move them to the next field when we've finished here?"

"I want both finished by sundown," Josiah answered, taking his reins from Josie and mounting. The boy moved quickly to get astride his pony, not looking toward the field hands. They rode off to the edge of the field again, and Josiah said, "That was good, son. You see the proper way to handle the hands. You can't just let them sit down, or they'll all be sitting down. In fact, I'll be letting Red know he's to work Dan well today, or all of them'll get the notion they can take their ease in the stables anytime the hoe gets too heavy. You need to take care of them, as you would the stock, the fields, and everything else that belongs to you. And you also want to remember that they can only be pushed so hard, then you'll get nothing good out of them at all." He laughed mirthlessly. "You heard your Uncle Robert say that his slaves own him, not the other way around. Sometimes I think he's right."

"Yes, Papa," Josie said.

They rode their horses to the rear of the farthest field, the one which they'd only just recently seeded to cotton, Josiah pointing out things which he thought Josie should notice and remember. "You remember we had indigo here two years ago," he said, "until the worms took it all. And just as well, I think, because the soil was going dry with that crop. Cotton's better all round. Someday, you'll need to rotate this field to another seed crop, perhaps beans or corn, to let the soil rest. But for another few years, cotton will do well here."

Josie looked up at him from the rows of plants high on either side of his pony. "Where will you be, Papa?"

He grinned. "Oh I'll be here, I imagine. But I might not be willing to work so hard as I do now. You'll have to take up the harness then, boy, and make this land your own."

"Yes, Papa," he said.

"Pull up here, and I'll show you something," Josiah said, dismounting. He took the pony's reins and led Josie to a place in the field where the cotton plants were taller and wider than in some other rows. Josie got down and stood beside him.

"See how much stronger the cotton is here than over there?" Josiah asked. "What do you think is the reason?"

Josie looked carefully at the plants and the soil, doing his best to please. Finally he said, "I don't know, Papa."

"Well, it might be they get more water—do you think that's it? Or maybe more sun?" He opened his arms expansively. "Do you think it's just luck?"

Josie looked again, just as carefully, but he could see no obvious difference. He tried manfully, however. "Not just luck," he said.

Josiah patted his shoulder with some impatience. "Of course not, son. Look closer. These rows are different because they're a different plant altogether. See the leaves? Fatter and wider and more of them. Different kinds of cotton! I'm trying an experiment with a different seed I got

from the West Indies this year, Petit Gulf, and I think I'll
switch the whole field to this next season. No difference in
water, none in sun, and certainly it's not luck . . ." His
laughter had a bit of mockery to its edges. "It's a new cotton
altogether. We'll take near one hundred and fifty pounds a
day per hand. It's a long fine staple, free of rot, with stronger
stalks and larger bols. Now do you see?"

Josie nodded soberly. "Yes, Papa. It's a better seed."

"Exactly!"

They mounted again, and as Josiah led his son over the
fields, back and forth, he talked of the cotton, of prices, of
the market conditions, and of the way a man could get
cheated at the merchant's scales. Once he looked back at
Josie and thought the boy looked a little dizzy in the sun.
"Are you listening to all this, son?"

"Yes, Papa," Josie said quickly. "I'm listening."

"Good!" Josiah called heartily and turned his horse back
toward the Big House. They stopped as they passed one of
the smaller Indian mounds at the edge of the largest cotton
field. "You might wonder why I don't take this down," Josiah said, pointing to the hill of dirt. "Some men would, I
imagine. Perfectly good ground, a waste of acres to leave it
standing."

Josie smiled up at him innocently. "Because the Indians
built it?"

Josiah shook his head with some disappointment. "Why
would that matter? Beavers likely dammed the river, too,
time and again before we came to this land. That doesn't
mean I'd leave their piles of sticks and logs in place, does it?
No, not if it suited me to have the water flow. Think again,
boy."

Josie dutifully frowned and pondered, but he finally had
to shrug his shoulders. "Tell me, Papa," he sighed.

"Because it's a legacy for you, son."

Josie goggled up at him, surprised.

"The longer they sit, the more valuable they are—or
rather whatever's inside them. Might be nothing more than

bones, or maybe Spanish treasure or Indian silver. But the older the relics, the more folks pay for them. So I'm leaving them for you to oversee. Those mounds, these fields, and that house''—he gestured widely to the Big House in the distance—''will be all yours one day. Your responsibility, to guard for you and your sister, maybe for your mother, too, when I'm gone. Do you think you can do that?''

Josie seemed stunned, like a rabbit caught in the glare of a hunter's torch. He finally nodded feebly.

''Good,'' Josiah said briskly. ''Now let's go to the stables and see if that Dan's loafing in the shade.''

Josie thought in that moment that he hoped for nothing more fervently than that Dan was hard at work at something, anything, so that his father would not have to take him to task again. And after that, he hoped for this day soon to be over.

At the edge of the newest cotton field, a young squirrel had made her nest in a small hill of dirt, its entrance partially hidden under an outcropping of rock. Had she been more seasoned in breeding, she would have known to put her nest high, but there were few trees on that acre, most having been taken down by the men in the fields for the white-blooming plants. She dug the nest well, however, and allowed ample room in the birthing chamber for movement, two exits well away from each other, and several storage chambers for roots, nuts, and seeds. There, she gave birth to six naked, blind babies in the latter weeks of the month of May.

Indeed, had she been an older, wiser mother, she would not have even chosen this vicinity to nest, much less that elevation. For within her acre also dwelled one of the larger and most formidable foes in any kingdom, a five-foot eastern diamondback rattlesnake.

The snake made his home in a similar outcropping of rock, several hundred feet farther from the trespasses of man. In the winter season, he had denned with more of his kind farther from the great river, but as the weather warmed, he moved to the fields to be nearer the rodents, birds, and other prey which took up the seed the men put down and waited for whatever insects they might unearth.

The snake left his den at dusk, moving cautiously over his territory in full hunting alert. It had been a week since he had taken food, not an unusual spate of time. When he hunted, he fed himself to satiety and then let his body rest completely before gorging again. He had recently shed his skin, something he did now only two times a year. When he was young, he had shed twice that often, and so was twice as ready to strike when that state came on him, leaving him anxious, irritable, and nearly blind with the unwanted scales about his eyes.

Twice in his youth, he had been badly injured by striking at prey more out of annoyance than hunger. Bitten once by a squirrel, scratched savagely by a rabbit, he had learned to use his venom judiciously. Bite once, well, and then move away and wait for the toxin to do its work. Be patient. Take the prey only when it is subdued, his experience had taught him.

Now he was a more careful hunter. As he moved over the ground in a fluid, liquid searching, he never dropped his guard. He might be the largest predator in his territory, but he was hardly invulnerable—he had learned that lesson painfully. He rounded a small hill of dirt and stone and stopped in his quest abruptly. The smell of squirrel was strong on his tongue, and he immediately began to turn his head from side to side, pinpointing exactly its source. The tracks were in front of him and to one side, heading uphill. He stopped and waited, coiling slightly.

Under his belly, he could sense the ground was soft and newly disturbed. Easy to dig. He moved slowly up the hill now, keeping his head low and his tail quiet. So slowly did he move that a man watching might wonder if the snake was making much headway at all. But within moments, he was another twenty feet closer to the rise of the hill and the out-cropping of rocks.

Now he could feel the vibration under the earth of activity, and he knew what he had only suspected before. A squirrel had nested nearby in the soil, unusual enough in this territory. But more intriguing still, she had birthed a litter of pups somewhere close beneath him. This he could not know for certain, but every instinct told him it was so. He moved closer to the rocks, searching for the opening to the den.

As he was within a dozen feet of the entrance, the squirrel popped her head outside her hole, saw him, and froze in terror. The snake froze as well. As he was considering his options, however, they quickly narrowed, for the female squirrel chittered angrily at him, stamped her feet in defiance, and rushed not away from him but two feet closer.

The rattler instantly coiled in a partial-defense posture, ready to strike and kill. Now there was no question that she had a litter, and likely her first, for few seasoned mothers would stand and fight, he knew. He did not deign to rattle.

The squirrel chattered again, coming another foot closer, and threw loose dirt at his head with her front paws, trying to drive him off. The rattler rose on his last coil, darted away from the shower of dust and soil, and lowered his head again in anger. His tongue flicked in and out, and he sensed that the sun would soon be too hot for him to be so exposed. He lengthened his neck and moved closer to the squirrel, staring her down.

She whirled and retreated back into her den, chittering in fear, and he followed her slowly, relentlessly. The snake had half his body within the hole when he stopped and tried to feel the slightest vibrations around him. The earth was warm, dark, and comforting. Somewhere ahead of him was the litter. This time of year he expected that they would be blind, naked, and completely helpless. He would not need to expend the slightest effort or venom, and the meal would last him for several days at least.

The tunnel narrowed, turned, and suddenly opened

slightly as if the squirrel had considered a storage area and then reconsidered. The rattler paused and listened. He could hear her now, pattering quickly to and fro. She was moving her babies. He moved ahead faster, turned another corner, and she met him squarely, face to face, her eyes huge with fright and anger. Her head filled the narrow tunnel, her eyes black and bottomless with determination. She chittered at him again and pushed sand violently toward his eyes, kicking with her front paws frantically. He reared back with what room he could find and struck at her, embedding his fangs in her cheek. It was only a partial blow, but he knew he had injected enough toxin for her size. He pulled back as best he could and watched her.

The squirrel squealed in pain and backed frantically away from him, her face already swelling swiftly, her eyes nearly shut with the agonizing burning of the venom. He followed, came to another chamber, and stopped. She was struggling to pick up the last two remaining kits, tiny, pink things no larger than medium-sized caterpillars, one in her paws, another in her swollen jaw, and limped with them blindly up the escape tunnel toward the light. Clearly, she had taken the rest of her litter to freedom.

He moved forward cautiously, and she kicked savagely at him, striking him about the head, scratching him down his neck, and simultaneously staggering upward, her eyes almost closed now from the swelling.

The rattler stopped and waited. The scratches burned, and his eyes were flecked with debris and dust. She might not die. Some squirrels did not, he had learned, for somehow they had developed the capacity to live through his toxin in ways which larger, stronger animals did not. So many generations had been bitten, they simply had to reach a higher tolerance and so they did. Nonetheless, the poison was extremely painful and often made them very ill and helpless. There was still hope.

The squirrel had disappeared now with the last of her litter, leaving the snake alone in the darkness. She would

surely not go far, he knew. And so he waited. He had learned
to wait very well.

Finally, as the daylight was completely gone, he came out
of the exit of the squirrel den and onto open ground, coiling
and listening. He could not sense her near. He flicked his
tongue over the ground, questing to and fro. There was a
scurry of tracks and scent, but he could not be sure which
way she had finally chosen. As if she had run to and from,
back and forth a dozen times, the trail was confused and broken. He coiled and waited. Perhaps she would be back. Or
perhaps another prey would happen by.

He waited for several hours into the night and finally slid
back down the hill in quest of easier prey. Wherever she had
escaped with her litter, he did not care to follow.

It had been cool that night when Josiah and Jane went to
bed, and so when he awakened much later in the darkness,
the sense of heat within the house seemed strangely disturbing. He opened his eyes, unsure what exactly had caused him
to come to consciousness. The room was dark, familiar and
comforting in its vague outlines. There, his shirt lay over a
chair. There, in the corner, Jane's dressing robe hung by the
large glass. All as usual. And yet something was out of place
elsewhere in the house. He could feel it clearly. He lay quietly and listened. A hissing sound from a distance. And then,
as he wakened completely, he was sure of it: the smell of
faint smoke.

He rose instantly and went to the door, opening it quietly.
The hissing sound was louder now and the smell of smoke
unmistakable. He went to the hall and peered down into the
darkness. The view from the landing was of a portion of the
stairwell and, a floor below, the hallway into the dining
room. A glow came from the rear of the house, a dancing
warm lightness which could only mean one thing. A fire in
the kitchen.

He went back into the room and tugged his dressing robe

off the hook, glancing at Jane. She was still deeply asleep. No sense to wake her unless it was a real danger—

He hurried down the stairs quietly, thinking perhaps that cook had come in and started the fire for some reason, though he could not imagine why she would need to start so early, and as he passed down the first floor hall, the smell of smoke was so strong that his alarm rose with every step. When he stepped into the dining room, he saw instantly that the wall which separated the dining room from the kitchen was burning.

The kitchen was likely completely ablaze. He turned and ran for the stairs to wake his family, and behind him, in that instant, the wall into the dining room suddenly collapsed upon itself. What had been a quiet fire was now a fiery sheet of crackling timber and roiling smoke. He shouted now as he ran to the upstairs, and Jane met him at the landing, her eyes wide, her hair askew. "There's a fire in the kitchen!" he called to her. "It must have been burning for hours; it's in the walls to the dining room!"

"Oh no!" she screamed, a shocking sound in the stillness.

"Get dressed at once," he said, trying to keep his voice calm. "I'll get the children."

"Josie!" she wailed. "Anne!" And she tried to lunge past him.

"Go on, Jane!" he shouted to her, yanking on his coat and trousers and pulling her back into the room. "I'll get them ready; you get dressed, and take only what you absolutely have to save!"

As he hurried down the long hallway to the children's rooms, the smoke was now thicker on the second level, rolling in soft, evil-smelling clouds below his knees and higher. He could feel the heat rising from the first floor, running up the walls as though it were the scout party for the flames to follow. He sensed that the fire was worse than it appeared from the outside, likely racing within the thick walls and only bursting out of confinement when it ran out of ready timber. He cursed himself for not having kept the kitchen separate from the rest of the house, as so many planters did.

Opening the door to Josie's room, he shouted to his son to awaken. The room was so dark he could scarcely see his son's bed, but he heard him murmur and shift in his sleep. The room was already smokey and an acrid smell came from the rugs as though they were being heated from underneath. He roughly shook Josie awake and was bundling him into his clothing when he heard a scream from Anne's room farther down the hall. And then he remembered that Anne's room was almost directly over the kitchen.

He left Josie, shouting, "Get down the hall to your mother, son! Get out of the house!" and raced to Anne's room in the eery, glowing darkness. Now the smoke was much thicker, and he could hear Jane and Josie calling to each other, crying in fear. He burst into Anne's room and saw that half of the floorboards were smoldering from underneath. Anne had evidently just awakened, and she met him at the door, pulling her riding cape over her shoulders. "Papa, my room is burning!" she cried out, pushing past him in a frenzy of terror, coughing and wiping her eyes.

"The kitchen is afire!" he shouted, picking her up in his arms and rushing back down the hallway again to where he had last seen Josie. Her cape flapped around his waist and legs as he hurried, and he felt the fear in Anne's arms as she gripped his neck hard. Now the hallway was dim with smoke, and he coughed violently, his eyes tearing. "Jane!" he shouted, reaching the bedroom, thinking perhaps she had already taken Josie down the stairs as she should have. The low growl and crack of the flames was louder—even in the front of the house they could hear the fire moving swiftly through the downstairs. *Where was Jane?* "Josie!" he shouted, barely able to call out past his coughs. Anne was crying and coughing in his arms, and he was suddenly exhausted with the weight of her but he did not dare put her down.

He couldn't see Jane and Josie in the bedroom, so he

turned and went for the stairs. By now he could barely see the floor for the smoke, and he felt as though his lungs were on fire along with the rest of the house. He pulled Anne's head under his coat, and started down the stairwell. The banister was hot under his hand. He stopped and stared. How had it spread so quickly? The fire had reached the bottom of the stairs; he would have to move very fast and sure as a goat to save them both. As he started down, he heard Anne whimpering to herself, and he was flooded with sorrow—the Big House and all in it would be lost, he was certain. Nothing could save their belongings; they would have to start all over, maybe go back to living in the slave quarters until they could rebuild. He almost swayed to his knees with the feeling of waste and loss and agonized frustration. It seemed to him that all of his life had built up to this one moment, and none of it had returned to him what he had invested.

He was on the stairs now, holding Anne with one trembling arm—she was suddenly so heavy!—and trying to balance himself with the other on a banister which seemed ready to give way beneath him at any moment. He had to move quickly, for the flames were already encroaching onto the stairs, eating rapidly where his feet must trod.

Anne had stopped whimpering now, and he sensed by her weight that she had fainted, possibly from the smoke, which burned his lungs and made him dizzy and sick even to make the smallest exertion. He wanted suddenly to lie down on the stairs and stop moving, but he knew that it would be sure death for them both. He gathered his strength and began the descent, one step at a time, feeling with his feet as best he could before putting his weight on any one smoldering place. The heat was now killing, and his face felt swollen and hot to the touch. Halfway down he knew he could not last another five minutes, so he hurried, crashing down the stairs without regard to which ones might hold him, burst through the flames at the bottom and, yanking Anne's cape off her body as it caught fire, struggled to make it for the door.

Twenty yards from the door, which was open to the night, he could hear the cries of the slaves outside as they rushed to and fro, attempting to help stop the flames. He cursed himself for not training them for exactly this circumstance, cursed himself for not keeping the cook fires well away from the house, and then when he finally stumbled out on the porch and away from the house, cursed himself once more for not moving faster with Anne.

She was unconscious; he could see that the instant he laid her on the ground. Her face was flushed and swollen from the heat, but her body felt clammy and cool. Her breathing was shallow and barely perceptible. He shouted for help, and two of the house slaves came running. Dory came up then and kneeled beside Anne, weeping over her still figure.

Josiah was chaffing Anne's hands and calling to her, laving her face with the water one of the slaves brought. He shouted for Jane, and Dory said, "Oh Mister, Missus not wid you? Ah, Josie! Josie!" she began to cry, throwing her hands over her face.

"Missus and Josie came out long before me," he said to her. "You, boy, get buckets on that porch!" The slaves were bringing what water they could, but with no one to tell them what to do, their efforts were disorganized and largely futile. Josiah gazed up at the Big House in despair and wonder. The entire upper floor was burning now, flames licking out of the windows into the night like malevolent flags. Smoke curled high into the night sky, and somewhere inside the bowels of the house, he heard a timber creak and fall with a hissing crash.

Anne stirred under his hands and opened her eyes. "Thank God," he cried, and pulled her to his chest. "Anne, you're safe now," he soothed her as she began to cry weakly, still coughing and gagging. "Dory, get her warm and away from the house. Don't let her out of your sight." He stood up and began to run around the house, shouting for Jane and Josie. The slaves looked at him as though he were mad. Finally, with growing fear, he stopped one of the hands and asked him if the Missus and the boy were in the quarters. The man rolled his eyes wide and white, obviously terrified to tell him no. "I ain't seen 'em, Massa," he said. "We all think dey wid you."

Josiah stopped, frozen in fear. He gazed up at the burning house. If they were still inside, they were lost. But he had seen Jane with Josie! Told her to get out! She surely went down the stairs to safety well before he carried Anne out!

Josiah ran to the front of the porch again, where the flames had not yet ravaged the windows and door. He screamed Jane's name, Josie's name, again and again, beginning to weep with frustration and fear. He called for the slaves to bring buckets, and when they did, he threw them into the inferno frantically, dousing himself and trying to work his way back inside what used to be the grand entryway of the Big House. But the flames were high and fearsome, the smoke overwhelming, and the heat from the interior of the house hit his skin like a baked brick. He could not force himself forward, and even as he tried, the slaves clamored and cried and clutched at him, trying to keep him back from the fire.

He sank to his knees finally, weeping and cursing the house, God, and his life which had brought him to this point in time. If he went into the building to try to save his wife and son, no guarantee they were even still alive, he could well lose his own life and leave Anne an orphan. Or he could keep his life and lose everything except his daughter. Everything but Anne and the land.

He covered his face with his hands, feeling the blisters rising already on his skin from the heat. The land had led him here, finally, his lust for it, his need to have it for his own. Ah my God! he cried to the skies, have I killed my second family now? All the despair and guilt and agonizing sense of having failed in his duty as a husband and father, all the feelings which had crippled him for months after the death of Abigail, of Lamon, of Jane, of Ruth, all of them came washing over him again as if they were newly minted in his wretched heart. If it had not been for Anne, he would have thrown himself into the flames, fought his way to sure death, and died there with Jane and Josie, willingly, eagerly, just to have the pain in his mind and heart cease forever.

Anne. She was all he had left of value. Except for the land. Now, he cursed the land and all it had seduced him to do. Anne. He stumbled to his feet, weeping so hard that he could barely see. He staggered toward the quarters, calling out his daughter's name. The slaves still worked to try to put the fire out, watching him go by as though he were a moving specter. Afraid of such grief and helpless rage in a white man, they cowered and cringed away from him, many of them weeping openly in confusion and frightened sorrow.

Josiah reached the slaves' quarters and opened Dory's door, wanting only to hold his own flesh and bone close to him for whatever comfort that might provide. Anne lay on a rough pallet in the rear of the little cabin, pale now and somehow smaller than her years. "Did you find Mother and Josie?" she asked him weakly.

At the look on his face, she began to weep, covering her face with her arms. "Oh, Papa! God hates you after all!"

Her words shocked Josiah to the strongest sense of protective duty he had ever felt. "No, Anne," he said quickly, "don't say that. Don't ever think that. God has not taken your mother and brother. God did not start the fire, and God did not let them die in it." He sat on the side of her pallet and embraced her. Dory bowed her head and left them alone. He knew that Anne's words would be passed quickly from slave to slave before dawn.

He rocked her as he had not since she was a very small child, soothing her until she stopped sobbing. "We may never know why this happened," he said to her finally, when he thought she could hear him and remember. "But we don't have to have someone or something to blame to be able to accept it. Perhaps I was to blame . . ."

"No, Papa," she groaned.

"Or perhaps cook was to blame for leaving the fire too

high, or the man who built the fireplace and the flue, or the man who made the staircase too light, or your mother for not following my directions, or Josie for not waking and dressing fast enough, or the wind for blowing the flames too high. Do you see what I mean?'' His heart was breaking, but he tried to keep his voice level and strong. She needed that from him now.

"Mama," she cried brokenly. "Mama and Josie are gone."

He knew she needed to say it to begin to believe it, but her words cut him as keenly as if they were blades. "But we are alive," he said. "You and me, Anne. And we don't know why that is so any more than we know anything else."

"Mama!" she sobbed, shaking in his arms.

He held her very tightly, weeping over her head, rocking them both into the dawn. Finally, she fell asleep, exhausted, in his arms, and he held her, his eyes closed against the coming day and the pain he knew would follow like a lifelong disease.

The dawn came late that morning, as though the sun, too, were reluctant to see what havoc had occurred in the night. When Josiah and Anne stood before the smoking wreckage that had been their home, their lives, they clasped hands tightly. Neither of them could say a word. Behind them in a silent circle, the slaves stood and watched.

Josiah gazed at the fallen black timbers, tossed every which way like a child's jackstraws. Here and there, a standing piece of the house revealed, like a ghostly sentinel, what had been before. The upstairs had fallen in on itself, of course, and the downstairs was no longer recognizable as separate rooms. The two chimneys still stood, black and smoking. He could see pieces and particles of things which had not burned completely, but most everything was gone or ruined beyond use.

Anne's grip on his hand was tight, as though he were the

only anchor which held her to the ground. He kneeled beside her and put one arm around her shoulders. They were so small and thin, his heart ached for those slim bones which now would have to carry so much more than they should have for her age. "Perhaps you should go back to the quarters with Dory," he said softly. "We'll be sleeping there for a good while, until we can start a new house. You don't need to stand and look at this, Anne."

She shook her head so violently that she shook off his hand as well. "I want to find Mama," she said.

"No, Anne," he said firmly. "Neither of us needs to see that. I'll have the men clear away the debris and prepare caskets for your mother and your brother. But you should go on now with Dory." He turned and signaled to the woman to come and take his daughter away.

Anne shrieked, a high, wild keening more animal than human, her eyes wide and unseeing as she fought off Dory's hands. "Mama!" she wailed. "Maa-maa!" Her call was so piercing, so loud and painful to hear, that many of the hands behind her burst into fresh tears, wailing with her.

Josiah simply stood with his head bowed, fighting back his own despair. He knew that he must be strong now, for her, for all of them, and he wondered where he could ever find the courage to face the rest of his life. To help Anne survive. Ah my God, he began to pray fervently, his eyes closed, be with me now. Help me, God, for I cannot face this pain alone. It had been years since he had prayed, but it was all he knew to do in his agony. He did not question why. From somewhere in his memory, the words of a favorite hymn came to him, and he began to sing, very softly, "Nearer my God to Thee." Through Anne's high shrieks, he still kept singing, slightly louder now, not touching her, waiting for her to calm. From behind him, he could hear a few of the servants taking up the song, until finally all of them were singing the hymn, or trying to. Anne's sobs and wails began to subside. Finally, with one shuddering sob, she fell silent once more.

He finished the hymn and put his hands together in prayer. Aloud, Josiah said, "Oh God, be with us now in our hour of need, for we cannot face our sadness without Your love in our hearts."

A few straggling black voices echoed, "Amen."

And then from somewhere in the wreckage, Josiah heard a faint wailing call, a murmured and nearly indistinct cry. It sounded like his name. He lifted his head and stared at the house in wonder. He glanced at Anne. She was standing, staring wide-eyed and open-mouthed at the smoking debris of the house. She had heard it, too.

Josiah took her hand and walked a few paces closer, knowing that he was risking not only their hearts but perhaps even their sanity. Then he heard the cry again, this time more distinct. A second, high voice joined the first voice. "Papa!" he heard, he was almost sure of it.

Anne tugged at his hand. "Papa, it's Josie!" she screamed, running now to the nearest pile of timber.

Josiah followed her in a terror of dread, hope, and rising confusion, calling, "Anne! Anne, don't go in there!" But she was already climbing over the charred remains, calling out, "Mama! Josie! Mama!" He heard, to his amazement, answering calls, and he shouted for some hands to follow him. Back to the rear of the house, they struggled with the timbers, pushing debris aside, and finally came to the place in the floor where the cellar stairs once stood. Under a pile of scorched and fallen wood, bricks, and ruins, they could hear two voices calling for help.

"Sweet Jesus," Josiah breathed. "They're in the cellar!"

"Mama! Josie!" Anne screamed. "Papa, they're alive!"

The slaves had been hanging back, their eyes wide and fearful, but once they heard the voices themselves, they broke into a buzz of excitement, and every hand bent to pick up timber and bricks, to move aside the debris, and to uncover the door to the cellar. As they worked, they could hear Jane and Josie within, calling to them, and every cry made them work all the faster. Josiah finally pried off a final huge black log off the floor, wrenched open the door, and pulled Jane and Josie up to the morning light. He held his wife and son in his arms, weeping; Anne threw herself around her mother's legs, grabbed at Josie desperately, and the four of them rocked and swayed, crying and laughing all at once.

"Thank God, thank God," Josiah said over and over, kissing Jane on her hair, her cheeks, her brow, lifting Josie into his arms, Anne into his arms, somehow able to hold them all as with the strength of ten men.

"I couldn't get out the front door," Jane was saying weakly. "We tried to get out the back, but the flames were too high, so I thought the cellar might be safe, with the earth all around, but then we were trapped, and I thought we would perish!"

Josie cried, "We called and called, but no one could hear us!"

"We thought you were dead!" Anne cried to him. "In Mama's bedroom, we thought you burned all up!"

He laughed then, a boy's chuckle of delight, "Shoot, we were downstairs before *you* were, Annie. You never saw Mama run so fast in your life!"

Josiah felt a blanket draped over his shoulders. Dory had come from behind with a covering for her missus, and he wrapped Jane in it, realizing all at once that her dressing gown was burned half off her body. Fortunately, she had only small burns on her legs. Josie had nary a burn on him, Jane had held him so firmly. Anne was untouched; he had only a few minor burns. His family was unscathed. He could not let go of them.

As they walked back to the quarters, still holding on to each other, the servants trailing behind, Josiah said, "I thought I had lost you. Lost everything, except Anne. I thought it was happening all over again," he murmured to Jane. Anne and Josie were skipping ahead gaily, already full of themselves for having weathered their great adventure. The loss of the Big House and everything in it had scarcely touched them yet.

"But you told me to get out; did you think I had not?" Jane asked him. "It never occurred to me that you might think we'd not escaped. I figured you were looking for us in the swamp or the forest, half-worried to death; thank God you dug that cellar so wide and deep—"

"I thought you were burned to death, both of you," he said, his voice graveling with emotion. "And I prayed to God to give me the strength to bear it."

She squeezed his waist with her arm. "So then, something fine and beautiful came out of such a night." She smiled up at him, and he thought in that moment, he had never seen a lovelier woman. What a miracle she was, he realized. What miracles she had given him in their two children. If a man had such miracles in his life, could he be anything but thankful to God for his good fortune? No matter that he would have to rebuild, he had done so before. When his family was lost, he rebuilt. Now his house was lost, and he would rebuild again. God had been behind the rebuilding, not behind the loss. And he did not need to know what would happen next to know he would survive it and even find happiness again somehow.

A year later, Josiah stood and gazed out over his fields, past the high, flourishing cotton, to the edge of the trees where the tall chapel stood gleaming and white in the sun. It was a simple, gracious building, tall and narrow with a single rose window at the top through which the light burned in the morning and evening with a fiery glow. He sat there often, at the end of the day, musing over his life and murmuring to God. Under the rose window, it seemed to Josiah that prayers most likely went higher and faster to whatever listened.

He had no doubt, these days, that someone or something did. Even if it was only the same great and timeless forces that moved the winds and made the water course down its banks. It was a vast mystery to him, as were so many things in his life these days. And that was how it should be. For without mystery, there was no wonder in life.

The land, for example. He did not understand it much more now than he had twenty years before. Yet it produced and thrived—or did not—without his judgment or permission. He never felt closer to his land than when he sat in the chapel. He supposed the Indians had felt the same way about their mounds. Men needed a place to go to talk to the universe and its gods.

He turned as he heard Anne come from the back of the quarters, the next earliest riser after himself. Jane and Josie would sleep half the morning away, if allowed. But Anne was always up early, afraid something might happen which she would have missed.

She came up behind him and took his hand. "You going to town today, Papa?" she asked, yawning and smoothing her hair down with her other hand. She as luminous and lovely, as always.

"You want to come with me?" He had rarely taken her before, but it was time for Anne to understand more about the buying and selling which kept the plantation running smoothly. Josie did not seem to care much about it, and since the fire, Josiah had come to see his daughter in a different light. She was always going to be the stronger one, no matter her sex. And that was all right, after all. Neither of them needed his judgment to flourish. Only his love.

She grinned up at him happily. "Without Mama and Josie?"

He nodded. "We won't be back until dark; are you sure you want to be gone that long?"

"We have a lot to do," she said importantly. "I'll have to get ready." And she ran off to her small sleeping space.

Josiah gazed around the room. The same small quarters which had first housed them when they wed, the same quarters where the children were born. They would likely be here now for a year or two, for he had used his capital to build the chapel first.

Someday, he knew the Big House would rise again, but for now, the old slave quarters and the chapel would do. There was even a certain rightness to it.

Jane came out of their sleeping room, pulling her robe about her and lifting her face up to him to be kissed. "She's so excited," she murmured, nestling under his arm. "You'd think you offered to sail her all the way to New Orleans. She's gathering enough belongings together in her sack to keep her a fortnight."

"What can we bring you?"

She laughed softly. "You mean besides my mile-long list? Nothing. But yourselves, back safe and sound."

In the rear of the little cabin, they could hear Anne giving Josie clear and querulous direction about getting up and getting ready for his day, the first duty of which would be to say goodbye to her as she drove off in the buggy to Natchez. Her voice rose and fell melodiously and seemed as much a part of the morning as birdsong and sunlight.

Josiah turned once more to the window, Jane at his side. "I can remember saying once a long time ago that sometimes a dream comes true just because a man refuses to give up." He smiled down at her. "Or something like that. But actually, there's another way to look at it."

She looked up curiously. "Which is . . . ."

"That sometimes, just by the giving up, the letting go, the dream comes true all by itself."

"Yes," she murmured.

"With a little luck," he added. And then, as though in an afterthought. "And with the grace of God."

She chuckled low in her throat, squeezing his waist, and raised herself high on her toes to gently kiss his cheek.

In 1794, Eli Whitney obtained a patent for his cotton gin, the machine which was to convert much of the South forevermore, and for good or ill, to the blessings and curses of King Cotton. But two years later, in 1796, one David Greenleaf,

an ingenious slave who worked as a mechanic on a plantation outside of Natchez, perfected the first toll gin for his
master, making him a rich man and the Natchez region independent of Whitney's invention. In fact, many felt that the
slave's gin outperformed Whitney's both in speed and quality, and within three years, every Natchez planter of consequence built his own.

Natchez was soon awash in black-seed or Creole cotton, a
perennial which produced more than two thousand pounds
to the acre, so much that the early roller gins could not keep
pace. Cotton invigorated the Natchez planters and also
strengthened its handmaiden—slavery. In 1784, there were
fewer than five hundred slaves in the Natchez District. By
1798, that number had swollen to twenty-five hundred, more
than half of the white population. Fat, wide land lay ready
for the taking, it seemed to every newcomer. The fields whit-
ened with the soft, lightly packed bols until Natchez was the
capital of a cotton empire, the El Dorado of the age.

In early spring of 1798, under the terms of the Treaty of
San Lorenzo, Spain left Natchez forever to the United States,
and President John Adams and Congress renamed it the
Mississippi Territory. But naming it was not enough; taming
it was becoming essential. The great Indian nations of the
Chickasaws, the Choctaws, and the Creeks still occupied the
vast heartland that separated the Mississippi from the older
eastern settlements. Spain still held the land to the west of
the great river and New Orleans to the south. And the settlers themselves seemed prone to what the new governor,
Winthrop Sargent, called, "unrestrained democracy." He
wrote in his journal, "From the best intelligence I have been
able to procure, there prevails here a refractory and turbulent spirit, with parties headed by men of perverseness and
cunning. They have run wild in the recess of Government."

PART TWO
1830–1865

People live in cotton houses and ride cotton carriages.
They buy cotton, sell cotton, talk cotton, think cotton,
eat cotton, drink cotton, and dream cotton. They
marry cotton wives and unto them are born cotton
children

—EMORY M. THOMAS,
The Confederacy as a Revolutionary Experience

In the first year of the nineteenth century, the Chickasaw Na-
tion was persuaded, by threats and largely empty promises,
to give up some of their lands to the United States and the
new President, Thomas Jefferson. In 1805, they signed away
more, after General Andrew Jackson told them they must.
The Creeks rose in a fury to stop settlement on their lands,
but they lost their war and retired, a conquered nation. By
1820, the Choctaws were forced to follow their example, and
by 1830, all of the tribes within the newly surveyed Missis-
sippi Territory had ceded the remainder of their lands and
agreed to migrate to new lands in the Indian Territory.

Jackson promised them thirteen million acres in Arkansas
and Oklahoma for their five million acres in central and
western Mississippi. He contracted to provide food, furnish-
ings, guns, and ammunition to those who moved west. When
they proved reluctant, Jackson told them they would be
slaughtered or forcibly removed. The chiefs, still objecting,
signed the treaty, giving up all of west-central Mississippi to
the white settlers, who were already crowding them out. The
exodus of the Indians was completed when Jackson assumed
the Presidency, and the Indian cessions tripled the acreage
available to land speculators and settlers almost overnight.

So began the process which would transform Mississippi
from a growing Southern territory to a state famous for its
stubborn and unique isolation. As America moved toward

industrialization, Mississippi became more determinedly agrarian. As towns and villages grew and prospered elsewhere, few thrived in Mississippi, for settlers flocked to the new open lands instead. As the nation became critical of slavery, Mississippi became more dependent on it to survive, and as schools blossomed in established counties, education remained dormant in the Territory. Towns like Natchez, Vicksburg, and Jackson stayed small, dominated by cotton barons and tribal politics, a pattern that for more than a century would keep Mississippi one of the most rural and backward states in the nation.

Mississippi was becoming peculiar. And isolated in its peculiarity.

In 1815, the first steamboat reached Natchez from St. Louis, ushering in a new age of travel, but it did not change Natchez so much as Natchez changed the newcomers. The men and women who came up and downriver on the steamboats were looking for excitement, and Natchez obliged. Natchez-Under-the-Hill had a countrywide fame for vice of all kinds, and the magnificent estates of Natchez-Over-the-Hill were the most opulent and hospitable of the era. The city seemed, in short, to offer something for everyone. Natchez was beginning to have a reputation for being given to extremes.

In 1817, the Territory achieved statehood, but it was almost twenty years later before the first planter's bank was established. Mississippi rolled in cotton profits, wallowing in what old-timers would call its "flush times." Prices rose like smoke, doctors and lawyers needed no training or license to hang out a shingle, and duels to the death were common on public streets.

If you had come to Natchez in spring, say in the early years of the nineteenth century, the smell of wisteria, the buzz of katydids in the trees, the dark wetness of the shadows would have been most seductive. Black faces were everywhere, and their music and laughter wafted up from the fields and out from the quarters. White folks were well

*dressed, well fed, and well satisfied with themselves, presid-
ing over cotton palaces second to none in the nation. You
would have been charmed by a vast flat countryside which
drowsed in the heat with an air of being, already, faintly
overripe, almost ruined. And completely self-contained.*

*Behind Natchez, indeed, all around it, was the world of
the piney-woods whites, the squatters, the people back along
the bayous, and the folks on their way west. But they did not
matter much to Natchez. All that mattered was the land and
the richness to be taken from it. An ethos, a special sort of
Southern religion, had taken root in this region, a feeling
that nothing would ever change, that nothing could ever topple or diminish such a kingdom rooted in such a land.*

*Meanwhile, the Mississippi's yellow-brown current, vast
and slow as it curved against the land with a timeless air of
volume and omnipotence, took its own way to the Gulf.*

Arden sat sewing in the sun-washed room as the sheer
linen curtains undulated in the light spring breeze. The high-
ceilinged bedroom to the rear of her grandfather's house was
her favorite, and she had made it her own with her trousseau
strewn about like so many frothy waves lapping a sand
beach. Only three more nights, and she would likely never
sleep in her grandmother's rice bed again. She would leave
Graced Ground, her family's plantation, forever. And even
though she had never lived there, she already felt its loss.

She glanced up from her stitches to rest her eyes, as the
nuns had taught her to do over long years of training. Across
the fields of cotton, to one side of the simple white chapel
that her grandfather had built, the graves of her grandmother
and grandfather rested under a copse of live oaks. They
would have been happy to see her today, sewing such perfect
linen for Martin's pleasure. They would have been happy
with Martin himself, she knew. Just as happy as her Uncle
Josie was with her decision. Far happier than her own
mother was; that much was certain.

When she had been very young, the saga of her mother's love for her father had been one of the more romantic tales of her imagination, something she warmed herself with while within the cold walls of the cloister. She had heard it often enough, from Portia, from Uncle Josie, from Anne, herself. Josiah and Jane Fleming, her grandparents, had built Graced Ground on the ashes of their first Big House, with the profits of a cotton empire which seemed to spring up from the fields almost overnight. In less than ten years, they were wealthy—and then they were gone—buried next to the graves of Josiah's first family, leaving Uncle Josie, their son, at the reins of an ample fortune.

Meanwhile, their only daughter, Anne, had fulfilled her mother's fears. She met, loved, and married a gambler bound for New Orleans, a man with little to recommend him, Uncle Josie said, but a handsome face and a reputation for spectacular poker luck. Josie said it had nearly killed his father. When Arden was six, she was sent to the Catholic Sisters to be a pious, modest, and obedient child. Everything her mother was not, Portia said.

Arden learned to love the nuns, even to love the dusty cool shadows of the cloister and the endless quiet of the long hallways and the gardens. Her mother saw her often, but a riverboat was no place for a child, she said, and her place was with her husband. Arden knew the truth of that, even at six.

Six years later when Portia was given to her, she had someone of her own then, and she came back to the house in New Orleans to live. But her father did not share the house with them for long. When she was thirteen, he was killed in a duel.

Arden's grief was nothing next to her mother's despair. She honestly thought, for a few months at least, that Anne Lawrence would lose her mind. When her mother finally surfaced from her most intensive mourning, she was somehow softer at the edges than before, as if she no longer had anything worth keeping for herself. And Arden was left with the firm conviction that she never wanted to love a man quite so much as that, for when they went away—and they too often did—they took too much with them.

Martin was a good man, she told herself again as she had a hundred times since she had accepted his proposal. He might not be dashing; he might not look, as her Uncle Josie said once of her father, like "he was going to the devil at a hard gallop," but he was a fine man. He offered a secure life, a safe love, and he deserved the very best she could give him. As the master of River Reach, he was likely used to the best, after all. She remembered something that her mother had told her after her father's death. "You can't have a better investment than a plantation," Anne Lawrence said. "Houses burn down, stocks fall and fly to the winds, and men lose their money or leave or die. But a plantation is a solid thing. It's always there."

Arden bent her head again to her task. The final set of damask sheets to do, and then she was finished at last. Six night dresses, four petticoats, a dozen light chemises, two morning coats, four sets of fine lace undergarments, and four sets of sheets . . . any girl in the state would be proud to be married with such a trousseau. Martin would be pleased, she hoped.

Portia made her small scratch at the door, a familiar sound which somehow was more intimate than a knock. Without pausing, she entered and began to pick up the sheets tangled at Arden's feet. "Dat wind bring up de river dust sure, Miz Arden," the slave said, the gentle rebuke her usual tone.

Arden scarcely heard the scold in the slave's voice anymore, so used to Portia's manner was she now. Portia had been hers for five years, since she was twelve and put into long skirts. The tall, silent West Indian slave had been a gift from her mother, and the woman would always think of her as a little girl who needed guidance. Arden took no offense. In fact, she knew for Portia, a mild reprimand was a declaration of love.

Portia gathered up the sheets, folding them carefully and

clucking audibly over imagined creases and dust in their laced edges. ''I 'spec Mas' Martin see to it his sheets don' touch de floor,'' Portia sighed with mock sadness, as though Arden was heading for certain disaster if she allowed such a calamity to occur again.

''I expect you're right,'' Arden said mildly, ignoring Portia's invitation to a verbal scuffle. The slave needed to exercise her will like a horse needed to exercise his legs, but Arden was not ready to have her mood of tranquillity broken. ''Come and tell me if this ivory trim is right, Portia,'' she said placatively. ''In this light, it looks almost yellow.''

Portia took her time folding the sheets and only when she had arranged them on the cupboard to her satisfaction did she come and inspect Arden's work. Of course, it was perfect. Arden had not spent so many years in the hands of the nuns to turn out linens with mismatched lace. But Portia examined it critically, taking it from Arden's hands and holding it up to the light. ''It look right to me,'' she said. ''Could be jus' de light make it yellow.''

''Good,'' Arden said happily. ''Then that's the last of it. Martin Howard will have the best sets of sheets in the state.''

Portia scoffed lovingly, handing the lacework back into Arden's hands with more gentleness than when she had taken it away. ''Mas' Martin gettin' more den de best sheet,'' she said, again with a mock scold. ''He gettin' de best gal, too.''

Arden smiled in reply, and Portia took it as a signal of agreement. She sat down beside Arden as easily as though she had a right to the chair. Arden wondered how Portia would fit in at Martin's plantation, River Reach. His manservant, Joseph, ran his household like an army troop, for Martin took little interest or notice of the small details of his estate. Portia would likely begin skirmishes with Joseph the day of the wedding which would escalate to battle campaigns before the wedding guests returned home. Joseph was a tall, ebony stalk of a man, with a face grim as any African warrior, ageless and proud. He brooked no trespass

from the rest of Martin's people, and only slightly more
from Martin himself. He and Portia would be worthy adversaries.

Arden sighed and closed her eyes, leaning back into the
sunlight. It was so pleasant, after the chill of February, to
feel the growing heat of March. She had no doubt Portia
would be the victor, so might as well let the wars begin.

Portia took her sigh for weariness and patted her hand
with fond affection. "My baby be all worn out 'fore de weddin' even get here. When your mama due to 'rrive?"

"She should have been here a week ago," Arden said,
still not opening her eyes. "But you know Mama. She'll
come when she's good and ready and not a moment before."

Portia frowned. She made no secret of the fact that she did
not approve of Anne Lawrence, Arden's mother. In fact, it
was likely that very disapproval which persuaded Anne to
give her to Arden, finally. Anne could not abide a slave in
her presence who did not show the proper awe for her beauty
and charm. Portia was too valuable to be sold but also too
opinionated to survive in Anne's presence for long.

"She be late for her own wake," Portia muttered.

"There's really nothing for her to do anyway," Arden
said mildly.

"Nothin' 'cept be a mama to her only baby," Portia
grumbled. "Ain' got much time left to do dat, an' she miss
what chance she got."

"Nothing new in that," Arden said. "Now, tell me what
you know about the doings over at River Reach."

Portia opened her eyes wide. "What make you think I
know de goin's on an' weddin' fuss over to Mas' Martin?"

Arden grinned and patted the black hand, almost as familiar to her as her own. "Stop stalling, Portia. I know you
know most everything of interest that happens in any house
for ten miles, because if the slaves talk about it, you know it,
and there's not much they won't talk about. Were they able
to get the magnolias I wanted for the banister?"

Portia nodded importantly, all pretense of ignorance

dropped in the instant. "An' de cook make dos lil' lemon cakes you so set on, more'n a hundred of them—"

"A hundred won't be near enough!" Arden sat up with alarm. "I told her two hundred, and even that might be a squeeze, if Martin's people come from Vicksburg, and you know they will, even if they act like they might not 'til the last minute. Tell her I said two hundred, Portia, and tell her quick!"

"I tol' her," Portia said calmly, "don' you worry a thing 'bout it, Miz' Arden. She say, ol' Joseph say Mas' Martin say her make a hundred orange an' a hundred lemon. So dat what she do."

"Well," Arden said, scarcely mollified. "If that's what Martin wants, I suppose it will be all right. So long as we have two hundred at least, all told. But she's going to have to learn to mind me, Portia, and so's Joseph. And now's not too soon to start."

"Don' you worry," Portia soothed her mistress. "She learn dat de day we unpack de trunks, I see to it. An' so dat Joseph, too."

Arden stood up and went to the window, peering now down the road to the river. The Saint Catherine glistened in the near distance, visible from the upstairs windows. She had heard the stories of her grandfather's lost first family often enough, knew where the gravestones leaned, farther down the hill then he and Grandmother were buried. But the tragedy never seemed much of a tragedy, at least not when her mother told the stories. As if it had all happened a hundred years before to people she shared no kinship with at all. A fine barouche was coming up fast up the road. "Mother's here, at least," she said, feeling the first weariness of the morning settle on her now.

Portia turned and gazed out the window, assessing for herself. "Good she could spare de time," she muttered dryly.

"Now, enough of that," Arden replied, letting a little sharpness show in her tone. "She's here, that's all that matters. I'll not have you spoil things by fussing with Mama and going about with your lower lip pushed out like Uncle's mule—''

"I don' say a word," Portia hushed her. "I don' spoil your weddin' day for nothin', Miz Arden, don' you worry 'bout me." She hurried to the door to call to the upstairs gal that the buggy was arriving, adding over her shoulder, "Your mama think I struck dumb, I be so still, you see—''

"I doubt that," Arden said, half to herself in the empty room. She watched as the buggy pulled up the wide, circled drive and stopped before the high-pillared porch of Graced Ground. She heard her Uncle Josie's voice call out a welcome, and she watched, not moving, as her mother stepped down from the buggy into his portly embrace. Were any two siblings ever less alike? she wondered, not for the first time in her life.

Uncle Josie was plump as a country squire, with a florid face and wild, thin hair which never seemed to take to a brush or a smoothing hand. His clothes were the finest available, yet on him they always looked rumpled and strained at every buttonhole. He was nearly at the half century mark, yet he still had the eyes of a boy: kind, merry, almost shy, and his mouth had ever a hopeful smile, as if he hoped he'd please you but didn't quite expect to without an effort—but he was ready to make that effort.

Anne Lawrence, his younger sister, seemed older in all ways save those of the flesh. She looked taller, though she was not. She seemed wiser, and she likely was. She was beautiful, slightly haughty in demeanor, striking in her poise, and luminous in her ability to attract and keep attention. Blond and slender, she had no fragility of the spirit which showed in her face, as Josie had. She looked as though she had always had the very best in life and expected nothing less.

Arden was taken with her each time she saw her, especially from a distance. She enjoyed watching her, pretending that she was not her mother and wondering what lovely woman that was—and suddenly saying to herself, "That is the woman who bore me,'' and then falling in love with her all over again. When she could no longer see her mother, she turned and hurried down the stairs, holding her skirts as the nuns had taught her, moving as gracefully as she could. As her mother preferred.

"Arden!" Anne cried in pleasure when she saw her descend, moving out of her brother's embracing arm. "Can you ever forgive me? Why, I meant to be here a fortnight ago, but the journey was so dreadful—well, I knew it would be, and so I simply put it off as long as I could and could not bring myself to begin it!"

"Mama!" Arden cried, holding her tightly. At seventeen, Arden was exactly her mother's height, though Anne had more strength to her spine and steel to her shoulders.

Anne pulled back and looked into her daughter's face. She beamed up at Josie. "Isn't she lovely?" she exclaimed. "Won't every man in the state be absolutely stricken to see her wed?"

"Yes, indeed," Josie said happily. "Martin Howard's a lucky man!"

Anne made a mock scowl, pulling off the tight kid gloves she wore in all weather. "Too damned lucky if you ask me—"

"Mama!" Arden's eyes widened in alarm. "Please don't let's start—"

"Oh, stop fussing, chick," Anne said, patting Arden's cheek and wisking her toward the stairs as if she still owned them, "I won't say a word against your precious beau, since I can't talk you out of the man. I guess it's too late now, anyway, I understand half the county is descending upon us in a matter of days."

"Hours," Josie said, almost a little hesitantly. "In fact, I wasn't sure if that was your buggy or the Hanovers. They're due to come in anytime, and the Chadwicks and the Kingsmiths right after."

Anne grinned. "A full house—my favorite hand." She languidly mounted the stairs toward the room she assumed to be her own, pulling Arden after her. "Josie, you let us two set and chat a bit and then we'll be down for supper directly. I'll be needing a tumble of your good Madeira, some ice, and a spate of quiet, and I'll be new-made by the time the sun goes down."

Josie almost bowed to his sister, as always simply buoyed along by her wake. "I'll send it right up, Anne. So good to have you here!"

The door shut on his words, and Anne threw herself back on the bed, laughing low in her throat. "That sweet silly man hasn't changed a whit," she said, shaking her head.

Arden smiled, a little stiffly, and sat down in a chair a ways from the four-poster. "You seem well rested, given your long trip."

Anne waved her hand lightly. "Oh, I stopped for two nights in Natchez. I wanted to see how the old town has changed. Some ancient friends I haven't seen in a lifetime— so I'm fine. Are you all ready for the big day?"

The question took Arden back a little. Almost her mother might have been asking if she were ready for a special outing, or maybe a ball—not the most monumental moment of her entire life. "I guess I am," she said slowly. "Anyway, I think most of the arrangements are almost completed."

"No second thoughts?" Anne smiled teasingly at her.

"No," Arden said firmly. "Mama, I know you don't like Martin—"

"It's not that I don't like him," Anne said quickly, "I just wonder what you're going to find to talk about once the dew's off the cotton, child. The man is dreadfully boring, to my taste, but that's not the point. I wonder if he's got enough—enough *life* in him, Arden, that's all."

"He's a wonderful man, and I'm marrying him in two days," Arden said quietly. "I wish you'd not say anything more about him, Mother."

Anne gazed at her daughter with a bemused expression. Finally, she sighed and sat up, plumping the pillows about her. "You're right, chick. I won't say another word." She cast about for a change of subject and brightened. "It sounds as though half the state's coming, at any rate. Is your Uncle Josie quite crazed with it all?"

"Completely." Arden smiled. "I believe he's lost ten pounds in the last week, fretting."

"From where?" Anne laughed, rolling her eyes. "The man gets bigger each time I see him. Soon, none of his blooded hunters will carry him, and he'll have to ride around on one of his prize mules. If he doesn't keel over with apoplexy first."

"He's such a dear," Arden said, shaking her head at her mother's scandalous words.

"He is that," Anne agreed, subsiding.

A knock at the door and Portia bustled in, carrying a tray with a bottle of Madeira, ice, and two glasses. She bowed stiffly to Anne, who watched her with ill-concealed amusement. "Miz Lawrence," she murmured. "You have a pleasant journey?"

"Not that you give a damn." Anne grinned. "Arden, you still keep this lazy uppity nigger under your wing? Why, I'd have thought you'd have sold her south by now, sure. Martin surely won't put up with her sass for long."

"Mother . . ." Arden groaned.

"Did you tell her to get along with me?" Anne asked her, ignoring Portia completely, who had puffed and ruffled herself to half again her size, like an insulted black bantam hen.

"Yes, and I'd appreciate your doing the same," Arden sighed.

"I don't guess I'll need to worry, since she's bound to do the gettin' along," Anne replied, reaching for a glass and the wine. "You can go now, gal."

The slave turned on her heel and stalked out.

Anne chuckled and poured an inch of wine in the other glass and offered it to Arden. "That nigger is spoiled to death."

"You gave her to me!"

"And I should have known better. She thought too much

of herself when *I* had her, now she thinks she *owns* you, child. You'll have to hobble that black nag and get her in the traces before Martin Howard does it for you."

"He'll do no such thing," Arden said mildly. "He knows that Portia's my say-so."

Anne laughed. "If you say so, chick. Now," she said, taking another long swallow of the Madeira, "what can I do to make you happy, my dear?"

Arden smiled. "I think we're almost ready. Portia tells me that it's been a whirlwind at Martin's, and the chapel is all cleaned and ready. They'll fill it with flowers in the morning—"

"I'm still wondering why you'd want to wed in that old chapel," Anne said. "It'll hardly fit all your guests, and it was never intended for a grand *fête*, just private prayers."

"I think it'll be beautiful," Arden said. "And the plans are all made. So really, there's not a thing you need do except be here with me."

"What about your gown?"

Arden hesitated. "I decided against wearing yours, Mama. I hope you won't mind much. It fit me, but it just didn't—"

"Fit you," Anne ended her sentence. "That's fine, child, whatever makes you happy. When I got married, styles were more glamorous, and I was on my way to New Orleans. Women wear such frumpy dresses these days!" At Arden's frown, she continued, "Not that your gown will be frumpy, dear, but I liked the older styles better, I guess." She grinned. "A woman with a nice bosom wasn't afraid to show a bit of it, and a man appreciated what he saw."

"Well, if I wore that gown in the chapel," Arden said, "half the county would be appreciating me before Martin did." And then she blushed at her mother's laugh. "Anyway, I'll show you my gown after supper. Uncle sent away for it all the way to Boston, and it's absolutely beautiful."

"Then there's not a thing I can do," Anne said, rather satisfied. "I knew you'd take care of everything, Arden; you always were such a grown-up girl."

Arden set down her glass and stood up. "I expect you'll want to rest a bit before supper?"

Anne stood and embraced her daughter, pulling her close and quiet. "You've grown to be such a fine woman," she murmured. "When did that happen?"

"I don't know," Arden said quietly. She pulled back and looked at her mother. Even in the strong sun coming now into the room, the setting sun which turned the room to a warm glow, even now Anne looked like Arden's older sister rather than her mother. At forty-six, her mouth was unlined, her brow wide and pale and without a single furrow. Arden laughed then lightly, a younger, less robust version of Anne's own laugh. "Likely when you and Papa were out dancing somewhere."

"No doubt." Anne smiled. "You tell Josie I'll be down directly, and then I'll whip him at poker."

Arden went out the door quietly, closing it behind her, and Anne went to the chair by the window. She opened the window wide and the smell of the roses, gardenias, and cinnamon pinks came up from the garden below. She gazed out over the vast fields of cotton which radiated out from the house like the spokes of a wheel. Beyond, she could just make out in the hazy dusky shadows the white chapel. And behind the chapel, she knew lay the bodies of her mother and father. They would be so proud of Arden now. Her eyes watered, and she did not bother to wipe away her tears. They felt soothing, cleansing, cooling. She took a final long drink of her Madeira and leaned back, listening to the sounds of the Big House settling down for the evening.

Arden's wedding day dawned clear and warm, and for a moment, as she appraised the sun from her upstairs window, she regretted the high collar and long satin sleeves of the ivory gown from Boston. But then she reminded herself of how fine she would look in the dress, how pleased Martin would be, and how faultless his relations would find her, no matter what they might think of her mother's past. It was worth a little discomfort to feel so certain of approval.

Portia bustled in, already bristling with indignation, and it scarcely eight o'clock. Over her arm, she carried Arden's clean linen, especially prepared and scented for her wedding day. "Dat mama o' yours goin' to shock de whole county 'fore she through," Portia grumbled. "Black! An' all her bare arms an' her whole bosom showin' for de worl' to see! Mas' Martin's folks goin' see dat woman an' wonder what der boy marryin' into, no matter how good his bride be lookin'. De apple never fall too far from de tree, dey goin' to say, Miss Arden, an' your mama one scand'lous-lookin' set o' branches do she wear dat gown!"

Arden looked up from her toilette and replied, "Good morning to you, too, Portia. Have the Hanovers come down to breakfast yet?"

"Yes'm, an' de Kingsmiths an' de Ebbits, an' your uncle say de churchman comin' soon, but you better go an' tell your mama to wear her nightshirt 'fore she wear dat ol' black gown—"

"It's not black," Arden said mildly. "It's deep purple watered silk. Really rather beautiful in the light. And I know it's a little *décolleté*, but Mama is from New Orleans, and that's the style there. I'm sure it will look lovely on her—"

"You already seen it, den?" Portia asked, shocked.

"Of course. I asked her to show me what she was wearing the night she arrived. I suppose it would be nicer if she wore something a bit more—a bit more conservative, but she wants to wear it, it's all she brought, and I'm not going to make a fuss over it now."

"Well, I 'spect Martin's folks will!" Portia sputtered.

"Then they'll have to do so," Arden said, leaning forward and dusting her cheeks with powder. "I prefer to pick my battles with Mother, and this isn't one of them. I'm getting married in two hours, Portia, do you think I can have a

little peace?'' She began to brush out her long dark hair.
Arden's hair was like her father's, thick and wavy and deep
sable brown. Before she pinned it up, it came halfway down
her back. Normally, she wore it quite simply, in a roll atop
her head with small fringed bangs to soften her brows.
Today, she had decided to let one of Martin's upstairs maids
dress it, for the woman was said to be a genius with hair.
There was a knock at the door. ''That'll be Jessie,'' she said
to Portia. ''Let her in and then go be sure my gown's
steamed and ready.''

Martin's maid, Jessie, stepped shyly into the bridal bedroom, ducking her shoulders under Portia's baleful gaze.
''You look mighty young,'' she said to the little slave. ''You
sure you know how to dress Miz Arden's hair proper?''

''Yes'm,'' she piped up, brandishing her basket of tongs,
brushes, pins, and pomades. ''She be beau'ful when I done
wid her.''

''She beau'ful now,'' Portia scowled, and she shut the
door firmly behind her.

An hour later, Arden was dressed, her hair piled on her
head in a cascade of artful curls, powdered and perfumed
and garlanded with small white roses at her waist. She stood
at the long cheval glass, the one Uncle had brought back
from London, her mother gazing at her with approval. ''You
look . . .'' Anne hesitated, searching for the right words.
''You look like a perfect bride,'' she finally said, smiling
softly at her daughter.

''But do I look . . . beautiful?'' Arden asked wistfully. She
knew she would never be as striking as her mother, that men
would never find her as powerfully appealing. Her mother
often told her she was fine, she was good, she was graceful—but she could not remember her mother ever saying she
was beautiful. Just once, she yearned to hear that. From
Anne's own lips.

Her mother said quickly, ''Of course you are, chick.
Every bride is beautiful, don't you know that?''

"She more beau'ful den most," Portia grumbled from behind them.

"That's for certain!" applauded Uncle Josie from behind her. "Arden, your groom waits downstairs, and the preacher says the front rows are getting fidgety!"

The moment was lost then, and Arden turned quickly, embraced her mother, kissed Portia's cheek, and took her uncle's arm with the poise and surety of a woman who knows exactly where she is headed and why. Before she left the room, however, she took the large corsage of white camellias from Portia's hands and turned to pin it in the middle of the bodice of Anne's low-cut gown. Anne looked bewildered, trying to catch a glimpse of herself in the mirror before they left. "Shouldn't this be at my waist, child? It feels like the prow of a ship out in front of me."

"It's gorgeous, Mother," Arden said firmly. "Please wear it for me; it will make me very happy."

"Oh," Anne said, for indeed the flowers did artfully conceal much of her cleavage. "Well, if you're sure—"

"She sure," Portia said loudly, leading up the rear. "An' if we don' get to dat chapel, de folks goin' to melt down to puddles an' pour out de door!"

Martin waited at the foot of the long, curving staircase, his hand outstretched to take Arden from her uncle. He was dressed in a light gray coat, a tall hat, and fawn trousers. A tall man with slight shoulders, he looked for all the world to Arden in that moment like a graceful heron, all gray and white and angled patience. "My dear," he murmured to her as he tucked her under his arm, "you are beautiful."

She beamed up at him, saw only him in that moment, and they stepped out onto the gallery of Graced Ground, walked down the long rows of slaves bowing on either side of them, to the chapel, filled with friends and families from three counties.

* * *

Later, Arden would confess to her mother that she could recall scarcely a moment of the actual wedding ceremony. "Most brides don't," Anne teased her. "They're in a fog, some of them most of a year! Anyway, until they find out they're pregnant."

"Mama," Arden had scolded her, "you talk like a girl gives away her mind the day she gives away her hand."

"I couldn't have said it better myself," Anne retorted. "Well, if it's any consolation to you, the ceremony was perfect. Short and sweet and completely refined, just the way you wanted it."

"Yes." Arden smiled, reaching for a memory or two. "It was, wasn't it?"

She had stepped down the aisle of the chapel on Martin's arm, rather than on Uncle Josie's, for that was how she had wanted it to be. If her father had been alive, of course, he would have been the most natural choice. But even if he had been, she might still have preferred Martin. For Martin, after all, would be her supporting arm for the rest of her life— what better way to symbolize that promise than to have him take her into the chapel, down the aisle between the rows of upturned faces, all smiling at her eagerly, to where the preacher stood waiting, to have him help her arrange her train and settle her flowers in one hand, and then stand, ready and vulnerable with an open heart to God, for Him to make them one? Who better than Martin?

In a blur, she recalled the preacher's words, Martin's answers, her own small replies, soft and scarcely more audible than the cooing of the doves in the chapel rafters. And then they were down the aisle again, surrounded by well-wishers and outstretched arms, turned cheeks to kiss, helping hands into a buggy, and the quick ride to River Reach.

One memory which stood out above all others was the first view of the large, white house which would be her home forever now, as the wedding carriage came up the wide circling drive. She had not seen the house in more than a month, and somehow it looked larger, cleaner, and more impressive than it had before.

River Reach was the only house in Natchez that had a wide veranda all way around the foundation. Two stories of white, fluted pillars supported the two wings of the house, six of them on each side. Green shutters banked the many windows, and the roof gleamed in red slate. On the top of the house, a large cupola perched, ringed by a white widow's walk. Black fretwork from New Orleans trailed about the upstairs gallery, and a long row of live oaks led to the circular drive. Wisteria climbed up one side of the house and chinaberry trees flanked the rear. Beyond the house and to the rear, the quarters made two rows of tidy cabins. Two smokehouses, a dairy, a gin, the laundry hut, the tool shed, two poultry houses, a blacksmith foundry, a large stable, and a graveyard made up the rest of River Reach, one of the most gracious estates in the district.

And now she was its mistress.

As at Graced Ground, the slaves formed two long rows to bow the couple home—but the lines were longer, their numbers almost twice as many. That pleased her, too. As she descended the carriage on Martin's arm, her train gathered over her wrist, the slaves shouted, "Welcome home, missus! Good luck, mas'sa!" loudly, happily, as though they were truly pleased for them both. She smiled, waving to them, and only stopped when she caught the gaze of Joseph, Martin's man, standing at the top of the steps to whisk them inside. Joseph frowned and shook his head slightly at Arden, and Arden instantly dropped her hand.

Joseph was right. It was important to get off on the right foot, and she must have their respect. But she had no more time to think about it, for the carriages began arriving then, circling the drive and disgorging the more than two hundred guests and family who had come from miles to celebrate their wedding week.

Now Arden stood in what was her new bedroom at River Reach, the room she would share with Martin that very night. Anne was helping her remove her veil and her train, for now that the wedding feast was over, it was time for the dancing. "We should go down the stairs together," Anne said eagerly, "arm in arm like two sisters. You with your dark hair and light dress and me in my light hair and dark dress, what a picture we'll make!"

Before Arden could answer, a soft knock at the door announced her new husband. "Martin's here," she murmured to her mother. "Perhaps I should go down on his arm instead."

Anne pulled away slightly, her face crestfallen. "Well, of course. I suppose you should." She laughed ruefully. "But you'll have the rest of your life to descend together, just one last chance to greet your guests with your mama on your arm. Come in, Master Howard!" she called out gaily. "Come in and claim your bride!"

Martin came into the room, his eyes seeking out Arden immediately. His smile was soft and full of love, and Arden instantly felt her body sway toward him like a flower to the sun. "Mama wants us to go down together just once," she said, taking Martin's arm and squeezing it in entreaty. "Would you mind awfully? It would make such a pretty picture, the two of us, with my dark hair and white dress and her light hair and dark dress, don't you think? Just this once?"

Martin smiled and bowed his compliance at Arden's mother. "Of course, Madam Lawrence. I'll come along behind."

"Oh, that's splendid!" Anne said, clapping her hands together with girlish enthusiasm. "You're a sweet soul, Martin, I knew it from the first. Now, Arden, let's go greet our guests!" And Anne led them both from the room, linking her arm through Arden's as they reached the top of the stairs. Below them, down the wide, winding staircase to the bottom foyer, what seemed like a sea of faces looked up, waiting and smiling, some of them already clapping in appreciation of the arrival of the bride, which signaled the beginning of the dancing.

Anne laughed and waved at the people, Arden waved and smiled, and the two of them descended in step, Martin trailing behind. As they came to the bottom step, he took Arden's other hand and swirled her away into the crowd of well-wishers. "Unless you want to dance with your mama, too," he chuckled lightly, "I believe this one's mine, Mistress Howard."

She raised her eyebrows in surprise at his wit and laughed aloud. Martin was many wonderful things, but clever? She'd not suspected—but she had no time to think, for he turned her into the crowded ballroom, the people fell away to make room for their first waltz, the orchestra sprang into a sprightly air, and he whirled her about the floor. Martin was not an accomplished dancer, but he could make sufficient progress around the floor to acquit himself, and Arden had already learned, in the two times they had danced before, that if she exaggerated her dips and bends, they looked graceful enough. Three turns around, and other couples hurried to join them, so it no longer mattered, and she was so happy to be in his arms she cared not a whit what picture they made.

Once, as they whirled past, she saw her mother standing next to a handsome older gentleman, gazing up at him and smiling winsomely, both of them holding punch glasses, which she had no doubt her mother had not fetched herself. All in the space of a half of a waltz, Anne had found herself a companion! Arden smiled at her mother as she danced by, and her heart was light and full of joy.

The dancing and festivities lasted well into the evening, when finally couples began to drift toward their carriages. Many were staying at neighboring plantations, crowded into any spare room which could hold them. Every room at River Reach was full, as was every available bed at Graced Ground. Some few had already started back to Natchez, but many would stay well into the week, enjoying the wedding frivolity as long as they could make it last.

Arden wanted to end her evening before she was too tired

to appreciate her wedding night, so she said goodbye to her mother while others were still dancing the last few waltzes. "I'm going up now, Mama," she said to her quietly when she could get her alone. "Portia will tend to me, and I'll see you in the afternoon over at Uncle's tea." Josie was having a light dinner for them on the gallery of Graced Ground, a gathering which would likely extend once more into the evening hours.

"So soon?" her mother asked gaily, embracing her and kissing her cheek. "So eager to start married life?" She laughed low in her throat. "That bed will wait, chick, the dancing won't."

Arden smiled and glanced over her mother's shoulder, looking for Martin. He saw her and came to her through the crowd, stopping to shake one more hand and accept yet another kiss on his cheek from a tiptoeing lady.

"I think I should stay here tonight," Anne said impulsively. "Someone else can take my bed at Josie's and I'll stay right here with you and Martin. That way, we can breakfast together, and take the buggy over to Uncle's later on."

Arden pursed her lips slightly. "Well, Mama," she began hesitantly, "I don't think that will work. Everything is planned, you see, and all the beds here are full up—but we'll be over to Uncle's in the afternoon, and I'll see you then—"

"Oh, mercy, there's surely room for one little ol' mama in this big house! Martin, tell your bride you can surely find space for her mama. Just a little pallet will do, I don't need much. Tell her you're not about to send me out in the night air all the way to Graced Ground!" She was smiling and laughing, pulling Martin to her as though he were her next dance partner, and Martin looked at Arden quizzically for his cue.

"Mama," Arden began softly, trying to mollify her mother once more, "there really isn't room, quite honestly—and Uncle Josie will be so disappointed if you don't go home."

That was all Martin needed to hear. "Madam Lawrence,"

he said smoothly, with more authority than she could recall hearing in his voice ever before, "we should love to have you stay with us any other time, but Arden's right. The plans are all made, folks have already unpacked their bags and settled into their rooms, and I'm afraid you'll have to wait until tomorrow to see your daughter once more."

Anne narrowed her eyes at Martin, though she kept her smile intact. "Are you telling me there's not a teeny ol' broom closet left for your bride's mama, not in this whole big house?"

He smiled graciously at her. "It's hard to believe, I know, but it's God's own truth. We're full up, with no room at the inn. But I'll tell you what," he continued as he moved her toward the door and the waiting carriage. "We'll make a special point to come over to Graced Ground a little bit early, so you and Arden can have a private chat before the folks set down once more. That'll be better anyway — she'll be rested, and so will you, and you can have her all to yourself for a bit, would that please you?"

Anne put on a mock scowl "Well, if I can't have my way, I guess I'll take yours with as good grace as I can muster." She smiled brilliantly up at him. "But don't think I won't remember this, Master Howard! You surely have bested me this night, but there'll be others!" She laughed gaily, climbed inside, and waved to both of them as the carriage pulled away with her safely tucked within.

"Neatly done," Arden murmured to him as they went back inside.

"Oh, I'm certain I'll pay for it many times over," Martin said mildly, "but for now at least, we've got a bit of privacy."

Arden laughed up at him as they passed through the phalanx of more than a dozen couples still left in the house, went up the stairs where folks were milling about and readying themselves for their own beds, calling back and forth to them and each other. "Is that what this is? Well, I'm certainly glad Mama's not here to intrude!"

Martin stopped, one arm around her, and gazed down into her face. "Did you want her to stay?" he asked swiftly, looking stricken. "I thought you wanted—"

"No, no," she reassured him, pulling him to the top landing and toward their room, "this is exactly what I wanted."

He laughed then and made as if to chase her within. "All right then, bride, no more complaints!"

With the wedding over, Arden was anxious to settle into her new home and begin her life as a married woman. She had one prickled moment with her mother, when Anne suggested that it might be a wonderful idea for her to live on at River Reach for a time, perhaps sending for her things in New Orleans and closing up her house there for "oh, at least a season or two. You know," her mother said happily, "it's been so long since I've been close to my brother and my only baby girl, it would be wonderful to get to know them both all over again."

Arden had such a division in her heart at her mother's request that she lay awake next to Martin for several nights, pondering what to do. It was not an unreasonable suggestion; many widows moved in with their children for their entire lives, especially once the grandchildren began to come. To have an extra pair of loving hands to help raise them seemed only sensible. It gave the old folks someplace to be needed and safe shelter, it gave the young a sense of the continuity of life, and it gave the daughters some breathing space.

But would her mother's presence at River Reach accomplish those things, in fact? Anne was not old; she had her own life and friends, she needed no help from Arden with her support, and there were no children for her to help raise. And as for her daughter's breathing space . . . well, Arden had some qualms about how much of that space Anne might devour.

And then there was Martin. She gazed over at him in the

darkness, his shadowed form rising and falling gently with his breathing. She loved him so much. He was gentle and knowing and intelligent. His thin arms felt strong around her, refuged her and encircled her, made her feel safe and cherished in a way she had never felt before.

She wanted him to be happy. Wanted them to be happy together. What might happen to that happiness with Anne there every day, every hour, to oversee it?

She replayed a favorite memory in her mind, a time she had come upon him in his study, and he had kissed her fervently, backing her onto his wide desk and caressing her with abandon. She had laughed and blushed and pulled away, surprised that he was careless of who might come upon them.

"I am master of this house," he mock-blustered at her, "and if I wish to take my woman on the floor itself, then I shall do so, by God!"

"Not this one, you won't," she teased him, gathering her skirts as though to run.

But he caught her and pulled her to him fast. "You only run so I'll want you more," he murmured. "You're a teasing wench, aren't you, and you know exactly what you're doing . . ."

Arden knew with the instinct of an older, more experienced woman that Martin was, in the secret places of his heart, a basically shy man who was less a rake than even . . . Josie. But she also sensed that Martin's desire would be piqued by such play, if she could only bring herself to forget her own shyness in his embrace. "I do," she murmured to him with a low, vibrant promise in her voice. "And I might even be able to teach *you* a thing or two, Master Howard."

"Oh?" There was a sudden mix of apprehension and eagerness in his face.

"Yes." She laughed, whirling away from him. "And the first thing is the gavotte, sir. Rumor has it that you cannot dance a step, and it's the latest thing in three counties!" She took his hands and moved them into position at her waist.

He groaned theatrically, but he kept his hands where she had placed them. ''Who would start such a vicious rumor?'' he asked plaintively. ''Why, I can gavotte with the best . . .''

''Let's see it, then!'' she challenged him, and she turned into a sprightly step, pulling him to follow. Of course, he stumbled and shambled, for he did not know the gavotte from the mazurka, but he put up a game front for a moment before he pulled her to him once more.

''Enough,'' he murmured, kissing her. ''What else can you teach me, mistress?''

''What else would you wish to learn?'' she whispered, so close to him that his breath was moving in and out of her mouth along with her own.

''How to keep those eyes dancing exactly as they are to-night.''

''That, you already know, sir,'' she said. ''Better than any man alive.''

''Good,'' he had replied then he grinned and kissed her again. ''Then the gavotte be damned.''

Ever afterward, she was drawn to the study when Martin was there, hoping for the intimacy between them that the place seemed to encourage. He had allotted at least half the space in his study to his passion: the stars and the heavens. Martin was the only man she had ever known who was so interested in such other worldly things. He spent long hours many nights gazing at the skies and the stars with his telescope. It was a strange fascination, she had thought at first, and even when he persuaded her to put her eye to the glass and stare at the heavens, she could not quite understand his passion. But now even that interest seemed logical, given the depth of his soul.

He was so sweet, so strong when he loved her. His heart beat swiftly against hers, and she felt the wildness of his hunger rise, the only time he forgot to touch her with softness, and even still, she had never felt more complete. She could close her eyes and recall every nuance of his lovemaking. How he cupped his hands under her buttocks and lifted her against him, pushing her thighs open gently, still more open, how he shifted her to bring them both more pleasure, and made her body feel completely owned and mastered. "My love," he moaned urgently in her ear, and she whispered, "Say *Arden*," and he did, over and over like the wild cry of a swan. And then after, when they lay together talking quietly, his voice floating over her as gently as his touch, and his fingers would slide inside her sometimes, spreading the warm fluid, rubbing it into the flesh of her belly as they cooled. "My pink, pink lady," he'd say then, finding the perfect slow rhythm she had grown to love.

Being with Martin, naked in their bed together, felt like a sort of truth to her, a place of comfort and union she had never believed in, had not allowed herself to trust existed. She did not feel timid or small or afraid anymore. She felt alive with pride and joy.

And her mother in the house would alter those feelings; she knew it. Anne would take the pride, would somehow soak up the joy, for that was what she always did; that was her best talent. Arden could not bring herself to share this part of her life with her mother, no not even if the refusal made her angry.

In that moment, Arden made the decision to tell Anne she must go. She could stop at Uncle Josie's if she wished, she could see Arden often, several times a week, in fact, if that would make her happy. But she could not live at River Reach. Not now. Not yet.

Arden reached over and stroked Martin gently at the top of his head, where his thin brown hair felt silky as a child's. No reason to involve him in this decision or Anne's request. He would support Arden in whatever she wanted; she knew that much. But to refuse her mother would be too difficult for him. He would want to take that burden from her, but it wasn't one he should have to bear. She would tell her mother herself in the morning. Quickly, firmly, and with love. Her mother must understand—surely could understand, given her own passion and the decisions which came from those passions in the past. Her mother must have a life elsewhere, separate from Arden and her future with Martin.

Arden chose to speak with her mother the next afternoon, when the house was quiet and Martin was out in the fields with his new overseer. The gallery was warm and still, with only the smallest breeze coming in over the fields, and the scent of the magnolias was hypnotic. They had taken a light dinner, and Anne sat fanning herself quietly, gazing out over the cotton as though it were a vast sea and beyond lay another country, one she yearned to inhabit.

"Mother, I've thought long about what you said the other day," Arden began, "about wanting to stay here with Martin and me for a while, and I wonder if it's such a good idea."

Anne swung her gaze to her daughter and raised her brows in an appraising fashion. "Oh?" she murmured.

Arden smiled and cocked her head. "Mother, do you remember how it was when you and Father were first together?"

"Of course," Anne said impatiently, "I'm not so old that I'm losing my mind, chick."

Arden looked down in her lap, blushing at the memories she had of nights with Martin already, and so few of them had passed. So many more to savor.

"Master Howard pleases you, then, does he?" Anne chuckled wryly. "I'm happy for you, Arden. Many women do without such pleasure." She smoothed her skirts and put down her fan. "I never went without it when I had a say in the matter, but it's different now, with your father gone." She let the sadness creep into her voice. "Nothing's the same and never will be again."

Arden was instantly stricken with pity for her mother, but she also sensed that a game was being played out, and that she must win it. "Well, if you remember how it was with Father," she continued bravely, "then you'll understand when I say that I think it best you stay at Graced Ground rather than here with me, Mother. Martin and I, we need—

we need to begin our lives privately, without—company about us."

"I'm hardly company!" Anne said indignantly. "I'm your mother!"

"Yes, but to Martin—"

"Is this Martin's idea?" her mother snapped. "If so, I'll be happy to have a word with him, Arden, and you mustn't worry your head about it a minute more."

"No, Mother," Arden said firmly. "I've not spoken to him about this at all. This is my decision alone. I want to make a life here with Martin by ourselves, for the time being. I welcome your visits anytime, and I think it's grand if you wish to stay at Graced Ground forever, but I don't think it's a good idea for you to stay here at River Reach with us. Not right now. Perhaps when we have our first child—"

"Good Lord, Arden, you only just married the man! Surely you're not planning already—"

"I'm not expecting, no," Arden said patiently, "nor are we in any rush for such—such a circumstance. But I expect it will come soon enough."

"I expect you're right in that, at least," Anne said sourly. She sat for a long moment in silence. "Then I'm to pack my baggage and refugee over to Josie's, and send a note round with a nigger boy if I want to see my own daughter?"

Arden forced herself to laugh lightly, for she knew that she had won, but it gave her little pleasure. "Not at all, Mama. Uncle will be thrilled to have you, and we'll look forward to your visits several times a week, if you like, you needn't send notice. You'll probably have more fun at Uncle's anyway, he has guests round the clock, and any excuse will do for a *fête* or a supper. We'll likely have less to offer in the way of entertainment—"

"And retire by nine o'clock each night," Anne completed her sentence with a graveled innuendo in her voice. "Fine, then, I'll leave you to your connubial bliss, chick. Far be it from me to push myself where I'm not wanted."

"Ah, Mama," Arden sighed, "you'll always be wanted. Just give us a chance to get to know each other a little first."

Anne studied her daughter carefully for a long minute. "You know, Arden, you're older than you seem. Older than I was at your age by a long mile."

Arden smiled, a genuine one now. " 'Twas the nuns, Mama. If you had lived behind those high convent walls, you'd have been old at eighteen, too. But you didn't. And so, you're still young at forty-six."

Anne grinned. "Forty. And perhaps next year, forty again."

Arden felt her shoulders relax with relief. She had said it, her mother had relinquished the battle, and it wasn't as awful as she had feared. Perhaps she should continue their talk, since it was going so well. Perhaps she could find the courage to ask some questions she had always wanted to pose. "Mama," she started hesitantly, "what made you pick Father to marry?"

"You've asked me that before, Arden, don't you remember? Once every few years, you look in the mirror, try to see him in your face, and ask me that question again. I told you, I fell in love with your father the first time I saw him, and I never stopped loving him, not even when they buried him in the cold, hard ground."

Arden knew to ignore this last bid for pity. "But what made you fall in love with him?" she insisted. "What was so special about him?"

Anne sighed, leaned back in her chair, and picked up her fan again. "He wasn't ordinary, I guess. I could not abide the ordinary."

Arden thought about that for a moment. She knew, as well as she knew the lines of her own hand, that she would have an ordinary life. She relished that knowledge, actually, even as she knew that her mother despised it. They were very different in that. In many ways, truth be told.

Anne read her mind. "You are going to surrender to it," she said gently. "The ordinary. Aren't you, chick?"

"Yes, Mama," Arden smiled. "I believe that I will."

Anne closed her eyes and leaned back in her chair. "I know," she said resignedly. "I guess I've always known."

Arden had been married nearly a month before Portia and her nemesis, Joseph, finally wrangled themselves from open warfare down to a grudging truce. Martin's manservant was loath, of course, to give up territory to a newcomer, and Portia, naturally, was adamant about retaining her status as the one through whom all domestic orders must pass.

Martin was wise. The first order he gave Joseph the day after the wedding was that, henceforth, all household details were no longer his concern. "Miss Arden," he announced clearly and firmly to all of the house servants and the glowering Portia, "is your mistress now in all things. Whatever she says, however she wishes River Reach to be run, is how it shall be. Furthermore, I will not take it well if I must hear of petulance, laziness, or stubborn behavior. I expect all of you to work together like the family you are, and I will not be happy with disharmony." And with that, he had walked out of the dining room, pausing only to kiss Arden's cheek and squeeze her shoulder gently.

She was both grateful for his confidence and dismayed at his easy expectance that, therefore, because he said so, both adversaries would put up their swords. She could tell by Joseph's grim visage and Portia's victorious grin that nothing had really been solved. But Martin was a bit of a dreamer; she already knew that much. It was up to her to put his ideas of how a house should be run into practical realities of who should do what. And so she began.

The first week, she tried dividing the household duties into separate chores, putting Joseph in charge of some and Portia in charge of others. They instantly drew lines in the sand and commanded the servants into warring camps, until the wench who did the wash would not speak to the one who did the household ironing, and Ruth, who directed the four spinners which kept the plantation in cloth, refused to give any worsted or thread to Cassie, who did all the household sewing and mending.

Then Arden tried dividing the household in half, putting Joseph in command of the downstairs, Portia in charge of upstairs duties. That worked slightly better, though still the warring went on, mostly plaguing the poor housemaids who had continually to go from one general to the other, taking orders which usually conflicted. When both of them broke down in sobs, their aprons over their heads, wailing that they could not be in two places at once, could not please both Portia and Joseph and they'd fetch up sick if they had to go another day running their feet to the bone—finally, Arden called both combatants to her in the little office Martin had set up for her off their bedroom.

As they came in, sidling away from each other as though each held poisonous vipers in their pockets, she made them stand to each side of her large rosewood rolled desk. She kept her chin firmly set in anger, though one part of her wanted to laugh aloud at Portia's black glower, at Joseph's indignant glare.

"I've had about enough of both of you," she said sternly.

"Missus—" Joseph began.

"Miz Arden!" Portia sputtered.

"Silence," Arden said firmly. "Not a word from either of you. I'm disgusted with you both." Portia tried to catch her eye and keep it, but Arden refused to give quarter. "You've turned this household into a nursery of squalling, weeping babes in the space of a week with your jealousy and your petty complaints, one about the other, and I won't stand for it another minute." She glared at Portia. "Are you listening to me, Portia?"

"Yes'm," Portia grumbled.

"Do you understand what I'm saying to you, Joseph?"

"Yes'm," Joseph muttered, his eyes getting bigger and more angry. "I tell Mas' Martin dis won' work, but he—"

"You'll tell Master Martin absolutely nothing from this

day forward," she said smoothly. "I am your mistress now, as he told you clearly enough, and I will not have him bothered with such childish problems. And I *will* have this house run properly. Both of you look at me."

Both slaves looked up at her reluctantly.

"The very next time I hear any complaint, the next time Ruth or Cassie or Jessie or any of the others can't or won't do their work properly, both of you will spend the day under Moses' hand out in the fields. Do you want that?" She spoke softly, but there was no ignoring the steel in her voice.

Portia's eyes now matched Joseph's, wide and white as kitchen saucers. To work in the fields under Moses, the black crew boss, would be such a loss of face before the rest of the slaves that, likely, neither of them could ever hold their head up again. For a housenigger to be put in the fields was scandalous enough—but for a housemistress or manservant, who carried the master's keys and kept the master's personal linen, for such a slave to be forced into the field was tantamount to a public whipping. Worse. Any slave might be whipped, regardless of his or her station, if that slave disobeyed badly enough. A whipping would heal. But if Joseph or Portia had to take up a hoe and chop cotton, they might as well go move into the quarters, for the houseniggers would never take orders from them again.

Arden knew that well, but she did not let herself smile at Portia's stark look of fear, at Joseph's open mouth of shock.

"What if only one be bad," Portia started, "what if only one get de others riled?"

"Won't matter," Arden said stubbornly. "I will assume both of you are to blame, for it takes two to tangle, after all. If I see one more evidence of distress and chaos in this house, both of you spend the day with Moses, and the labor will do you both a world of good, I'd wager. Both of you are spoiled as week-old cream."

"Yes'm," Portia said quickly.

Joseph glanced at her in amazement. "Yes'm," he swiftly parroted.

"Now get out of here and work it out between yourselves what each will do and how it will get done. You've got one day to smooth over your differences. By tomorrow morning, I expect River Reach to run like clockwork."

The two slaves hurried out, already letting their shoulders brush in their exit, like two condemned prisoners in sympathetic despair. When they were out the door, Arden let her smile come up freely. What children they were, really. What dear, benighted, simple hearts they had. She had no doubt that they would now become comrades in as short a space of time as they had become enemies, and each would defend the other against all outsiders as eagerly as they had once denounced each other.

She rose and stretched languidly. Time to see what Martin was up to in his study. She went up the backstairs to the topmost part of the estate, to the large attic area which Martin had refurbished to be one of the two work areas he had in the house. Of course, his main office was downstairs, where he might receive his agent, the overseer, and any business callers. But in fact, he spent a large part of each day far away from those duties in what he liked to call his *sanctum sanctorum,* his pigeon coup, his pew. She knew she would find him there now.

Sure enough, she entered quietly to find him bending over his desk, poring over one of the largest of the huge volumes which were piled all about, notepapers here and there, and large rolled maps or scrolls leaning against each other in each corner. His precious telescope rested on a tripod, its lens facing out the single window toward the sky. Martin was actually out of place, and she smiled indulgently at him. He should have been an Oxford scholar or a scientist of some sort. He had no more business in a cotton field than Robert Fulton.

He turned and smiled at her, beckoning her forward eagerly. "Come and see this, sweet," he said. "You remember when I told you about the cyclone on the sun?"

She nodded enthusiastically.

"Well, this journal I've been reading says that these storms or cyclones are rather common, actually, and perhaps they might have some significance to farmers with crops—or not, they can't say for certain. But isn't that amazing? A maelstrom of fire on our sun, so many millions of miles away, and it might determine whether the corn crop fails or not in Mississippi." He shook his head in wonderment. "It's hard to fathom, isn't it?"

Arden recalled the few times she had looked into the shaded eyepiece of the telescope onto whirling masses of light and darkness, where no one had ever been or ever would be. He had shown her such secrets of the skies that few had seen: the Big and Little Dippers, Cassiopeia's Chair, the Seven Pleides, Orion's Belt, and the Milky Way. Spangles across the night darkness, they were alluring and lovely. Yet, she still could not really comprehend Martin's fascination. The stars were beautiful, but they had no sway in her world. She did not need to know their names nor study them to enjoy their brilliant distance. But she had concluded that he was somehow more to be admired because of his obsession. He must see and understand, somehow, more than she did.

"Ah, if only I had an equatorial," he murmured, his eyes still on his notes.

"What is that?" She went to him and put her hand on his shoulder.

"Something that holds the telescope in place, so that it keeps with the planets and the stars and the vision of them stays intact as they move."

"Well, why don't you get such a thing?"

He smiled up at her then. "Because it costs more than two good field hands, that's why. After the expense of the wedding and our guests . . ."

She dropped her hand unhappily. Because of her, he was unable to purchase what he seemed to want most.

He took her hand and squeezed it. "No, no, sweet, don't look bereft. I wouldn't trade you and our wedding for a dozen equatorials.'' He turned his gaze back to his notes. ''There's plenty of time for all that—see here, what I've been reading, it's really quite exciting.''

She sat down next to him and prepared to listen carefully. She had to give all of her attention to Martin's explanations, most times, to understand them even a little.

''Sir Isaac Newton, more than a hundred years ago, explained about the laws of gravity. You know all about that, of course,'' he began.

She smiled. ''Well, of course. The apple falls down to the ground, not up to the sky.''

''Yes, and planets are attracted to each other, directly proportional to their mass and inversely proportional to their distance from each other.''

''Yes,'' she said, growing a little bewildered. Arden had had what was considered the best education possible for a young girl in Louisiana with the nuns, yet when Martin began using words like ''inversely proportional,'' she grew a bit uneasy.

''But here's what's so exciting,'' Martin continued, moving his hands over a map of the solar system with the same reverence a woman might have used when touching an exquisite length of silk. ''The whole universe—down to the smallest creature on earth—is commanded by the same laws. The laws of attraction. Of fascination, if you will. Of allurements.''

''Allurements?'' This was beginning to sound more interesting.

''Yes!'' he said, grabbing both her hands in his excitement. ''Don't you see it, Arden? The same rules of physics which run the planets, the stars, the sun, the whole solar system, also run the universe. And those same rules run every living creature on earth, including man! That means that we are drawn to each other with a powerful force, the same sort of force that holds the stars in place round the sun, to merge or join or get closer somehow—our fascination with each other has the same basis as a fox to a vixen, a rooster to a hen, a stallion to a mare, a spider to his mate—that same energy pulses through each of us and makes us alluring to each other. It's a planetary explanation of love!''

She laughed delightedly at both his enthusiasm and his idea. "So the whole universe is powered by—love?'' She raised her brows. "What about God?''

"Well, of course, many believe that God is love and so that's not hard to accept. But think of it, Arden! The planets are drawn inexorably to each other, sometimes even to the destruction of their own individual orbits, their very existences as single stars! And the elements follow the same rules, each one trying to find and combine with some other element which it finds fascinating. Allurement! And every creature on earth follows the same laws . . .''

"But what about the laws of God?'' she wondered, still holding his hands and gazing into his eyes. Something in her thrilled to his words and sensed an essential truth there, but she also heard the words of the nuns drumming in her head, and often those words had little to do with love. Much less to do with allurement.

"The laws of God don't conflict with this, Arden,'' he said happily, as though the question alone hardly seemed worth the trouble. "It's the laws of man which don't seem to understand the essentials of the universe.''

"Martin, how in the world did you ever settle on such a course of study? I've never known another single soul who spent so much time thinking about the stars and the planets and—the whole universe before! Was it something your father taught you?''

He laughed. "Not hardly. My father was interested in land and money and my mother, in that order. Oh, he had his hands in politics, too, and I do think he enjoyed the judgeship he held for a time, but all in all, if it didn't grow in the ground or somehow get to his pocket, he couldn't be bothered. But I had a tutor when I was a boy who was a great reader. In fact, he'd rather have his nose in a book than give me my lessons any day of the week. And he got me reading

Emerson and some of the other Transcendentalists and . . .''

She dropped her eyes, not wanting to reveal her ignorance aloud, for she had never heard of these men or their ideas.

He caught her discomfort instantly. ''But that wasn't what you were asking me about, sweet. You were asking me about my singular passions, were you not?'' He smiled and touched her hand softly. ''I guess the best answer to that is that I am attracted to all things of beauty. Which is why I married you, of course.''

She hugged him spontaneously, suddenly not wanting to hear any more about the solar system or the laws of man, only wanting to hold him close to her.

''Ah, my dear one,'' he murmured, holding her and kissing her hair. ''What a treasure you are in my life.''

That was all she really wanted to hear, and she kissed his cheek and his nearest eye. ''Am I your allurement?'' she teased.

''One of the best,'' he said cheerfully, pulling away a little and spreading himself out again over his papers. ''Now did you want something, sweet?'' His brow was already furrowed over what he read.

''No, no,'' she said gently. ''I just wanted to see what you were up to. And now I know: explaining the universe.''

He laughed genially.

She went out and shut the door softly behind her. One of the best, he had said. Not the best. Not the only. One of the best. She sighed, not really with any sadness or disappointment, simply a recognition that men were truly different from women, no matter how much they might claim to love. For she would have had to confess, if pressed, that there was nothing more important, no ''allurement,'' as Martin put it, which drew her fascination from him. And yet for him, she was simply ''one of the best'' allurements in his life. Well, she thought, likely that's the way it's supposed to be, else they could not build their empires and run the world as they do. And that's why, she supposed, that women have children. They need to feel that they are, even if only for a few years, the sun in someone's heaven.

She stopped and gazed out over the fields of River Reach from the second-story window. In all directions, as far as she could see, the ground was green with abundant cotton crop. Prices were high and going higher, Martin said, and so they would likely be richer each year. Perhaps all of their lives. Rich enough that he might have an equatorial—or whatever else he might wish—whenever he wished it. Far in the distance, a crew of slaves worked the rows, their colorful headdresses moving up and down among the green. It was a verdant empire, stretching out over the land, settling something in her heart to a steady, contented beat. All was as it should be, she told herself. God had answered her prayers.

Portia came up quietly behind her. "Miz Arden," she murmured, "dat Joseph an' I work dis out, don' you fret."

"I'm not, Portia," she said calmly. "I know you will."

Portia hesitated. "You not 'rathful wid me?"

Arden turned and patted the woman's shoulder. "No, I'm not wrathful. I just want things to be nice here. For all of us."

Portia grinned with relief. "I wan' dat too, Miz' Arden." She frowned suddenly. "But dat Joseph, he don' wan'—"

"Portia . . ." Arden said, with a warning glower.

"Never you min'," Portia said quickly. "Der ain' no pro'lem wid dat Joseph. I see to it."

Arden waited. She knew there was more.

"Miz Arden," Portia said softly, "you didn't mean dat, did you? 'Bout sendin' me to dat Moses man?"

"No, Portia, I guess I didn't," Arden said gently. "Not unless you make me do it."

Portia smiled and touched Arden's arm as she passed. "I knew you didn't mean it, Miz Arden. I make sure dat Joseph mine his manners, don' you worry 'bout it no more."

* * *

There was a place on the Saint Catherine, right where it flowed into the Mississippi, where large boulders had built up the sides of the river to a height of several feet. And despite the erosion of the Mississippi, that height remained more or less constant, for with every rock the greater river managed to dislodge, the lesser deposited one anew.

A hundred and fifty years ago, there were species of fish in the Mississippi and its tributaries which have long since vanished. One of those species was a version of the Atlantic salmon, which tolerated higher temperatures than the northern variety and made its way up the Mississippi each year in the autumn to spawn in the rivers of its birth.

Each fall, the bears knew to gather at chosen places along the great river to catch the spawning salmon, for though they did not hibernate as long or as deeply as their northern cousins, the bears of the Mississippi region still gorged in anticipation for the coming colder months. One favored fishing place was the high rocked banks of the Saint Catherine as that river flowed into the Mississippi.

On this day in November 1835, a small black bear ambled from her den four miles upriver down to the place where the Saint Catherine emptied into the slower, deeper currents of the Mississippi. She was drawn by her instinctive knowledge that this was the time of the year when the salmon were spawning, but she could have fished the upper river without such a long walk.

However, it was only her second season, and she felt a need to be among her own kind. She was *Ursus americanus,* nearly black all over with a tan snout and small ears close to her head. She was small, only three feet at the shoulder and about two hundred and fifty pounds. The male she had mated with the previous May was almost half again as large as she was. Sometime this winter, she would give birth to cubs, likely two, and she would nurse them through the coldest months in her den, though she would eat little or nothing herself.

She needed to put on several inches of fat over her body to

accomplish this, and salmon were an excellent source of that final layer. She had already eaten all the berries, corn, grubs, bees, acorns, ants, and small rodents she wanted: salmon were now her obsession. When she had gorged on fish for a week or more, she would then stop eating entirely except for pine needles, twigs, and even bites of her own hair. This last roughage would pass through her digestive system and form an anal plug more than an inch long which would be voided only in the spring when she first emerged from her den. In this way, she would keep her den free of excrement for her three-month hibernation.

Ursus shuffled down the riverbank, snuffling the air for information about bears in the near vicinity. If you could have seen her tracks in the river mud, they would have looked as if they were made by a flat-footed, pigeon-toed man in moccasins, except that the large toe was outermost, the smallest toe innermost, and claw marks would be visible. Ursus stopped to smell very carefully at a bear tree, a live oak close to the water which had been scarred with tooth marks higher than she could stand, with its rough bark rubbed away in places where the passing bears had stopped to scratch their shoulders and leave their scent.

Many bears had passed this way, some of them quite recently. Most would be drawn to the salmon spawning, some few to the very place she was headed. She grew excited. She went on downriver, snuffling the air noisily and moaning occasionally to herself in anticipation of the good salmon she would soon eat. Ursus clambered over some smaller rocks, scratching her claws on the stones clumsily. She was not swift nor particularly agile, neither was she as strong as her bear cousins to the north. But she was clever and stubbornly persistent in her search for food, and so she was able to thrive, so long as she kept well out of the way of man.

Now she could smell the dank green smell which was the Mississippi, and she began to waddle a little faster. As she came within view of the place where the Saint Catherine and the larger river met, she heard a whiny singsong croon, the sound of another black bear close by. She shivered all over and slowed her pace, sniffing at the air carefully.

As she had expected, another female stood on the boulders fishing for the salmon. She could see her now, a larger, older bear, black as she was, taller at the shoulder and broader through the tail. Ursus groaned low in her throat, a call part-greeting, part-warning, for she could not anticipate her welcome.

The older bear turned, and Ursus could see her surprise. Evidently, the noise of the river had muffled her approach; the excitement of feeding had kept the larger bear too busy to be watchful. The boulders were littered with remnants of salmon, large tails and half-eaten heads. Ursus began to moan with hunger and appeasement, for she wanted to share the other female's fishing position.

There were plenty of places to fish, to be sure, but this one spot, tall and jutting over the Mississippi's deepest currents, was the best for a mile on this side of the great river. From here, Ursus knew, she could stand and swipe at the salmon easily, snagging them with her paws and lofting them onto the bank with little effort. She had come here for a single reason: to stand on the same set of boulders which was now occupied by another female black bear.

She came forward, muttering and groaning loudly, and the other bear turned to face her angrily. Ursus sat down on her haunches and wailed, much as a child might wail, hoping that the elder bear would allow her to come closer without incident.

But the other bear growled and coughed, warning her off. She turned again to the river balefully, as though Ursus was of no more consequence than the bothersome crows at her feet.

Ursus felt the frustration rise in her and she stood up, moving closer still. She wanted that fishing spot, and no other would do. No, now that she had come this far, she was stubbornly determined to take salmon here and no other place. She growled and opened her mouth wide in the char-

acteristic threat display of canine teeth which she knew
would invite attack.

The larger bear turned once more, growling louder, and
lunged at Ursus, her mouth opened as well. The two bears
came together, their jaws agape, and seemed almost to lock
mouths in a frantic, whining, jostling threat display which
was more attitude than injury. Both of them squalled in dismay and attempted to push the other back, but neither would
budge. Finally, the larger bear turned her back in frustration
and tried to fish once more, growling threats at her intruder
all the while.

But Ursus would not be ignored. Time and again, she
came on, sometimes whining like an annoying cub, sometimes nipping at the older bear and jostling her, often dis-
playing appeasement postures even as she kept trying to
engage the larger bear in small battle. Never aggressive
enough to injure, she nonetheless kept the older bear from
feeding, just as if she were a swarm of worrisome insects at
her shoulders, her head, and her flanks. Once, twice, several
times, the older bear would turn and try to slash Ursus with
her claws or her teeth, but Ursus stayed just out of reach, still
squalling and insisting that she must have that particular
boulder or die trying.

Finally, the older bear turned and clambered off the boulder in disgust, snarling and whining a loud complaint at the
unfairness of it all, and Ursus eagerly, happily climbed up on
the vacated rock, her head lowered and wagging in pleasure.
Neither bear had inflicted any real injury on the other save
stray tooth scratches and small bruises. Both had expressed
their desires forthrightly, but Ursus had been just a little
more stubborn, a little more annoying, than the older bear
and so had won her spot on the river.

Now she stood gazing into the water, seeing the salmon
throng the deep waters, relishing the thought of those which
would soon fill her belly. She paused to watch the older bear
amble off to another fishing site, a little saddened at the departing company. But she had her favored site, at any rate,

and that was why she had come. She moaned to herself with pleasure, swayed from side to side, and reached way down to the water to swipe at the largest salmon she could see.

Arden had been married seven years and given birth to two sons before she had to face the problem, once again, of where her mother might live. Uncle Josie, to the amazement of all who loved him, announced that he would wed the widow Hocker in the spring, adding her three children to his household and her five hundred acres of corn and cotton to his plantation.

"Can you imagine it?" Anne laughed when she told Arden the news. "Dear, red-faced Josie says he is in love at last!"

"Well, I wonder why it's taken him so long," Arden said, finally getting Owen's shoes buckled and setting him on the ground on his already moving feet. He was only two years old but could still run precariously after his older brother, Micah, shrieking all the while in mixed frustration and glee. Anne sat with her mother on the gallery, taking tea and cakes and watching as the boys ran in and out. As she had for seven years, through pregnancy and childbirth and illnesses and busy days, she set Thursday afternoons aside for Anne's visit, taking care that cook had the most delectable sweets ready for her mother's pleasure.

As usual, Anne gave the boys little attention save a hug for greeting and blown kisses at their ever-moving cheeks. She had been curious when Arden announced each pregnancy, seemed to lose interest as the months progressed with each one, and finally, when Arden gave birth, she was content to hold the babies briefly, dandle them on her knee and coo to them, and then give them back to the wetnurse and admire them from a small distance.

Actually, Arden could understand her mother's ambivalence. Micah had been a noisy, vigorous handful ever since birth, and Owen was turning out no different. Anne was not enthralled with the day-to-day mess and tedium of caring for small children, though she never failed to bring them pretty presents and sweets and greet them both with lavish affection. In fact, as Arden thought about it honestly, Anne was no different as a grandmother than she had been as a mother, and why should that be a surprise or a disappointment? Portia had several insulting comments to make about Anne's lack of womanly feelings, of course, but that was to be expected. The two of them had not, in seven years, taken to each other one whit more than they had from the beginning, though Arden had tried to get each to see the other's virtues. Now, she simply banned Portia from the gallery on Thursday afternoons, and her mother's visits were much more pleasant.

"Is she attractive?" Arden asked, turning to pour her mother another cup of tea.

"The widow? Lord, no," Anne scoffed, brushing aside Arden's offer of a third teacake. "But you know your Uncle Josie. He'd be struck dumb by a pretty woman, wouldn't know what to do with his feet, much less his hands."

"Mother!" Arden laughed, despite herself. "You are simply awful."

"Well, it's true and you know it. Your Uncle Josie is as stupid about women as he's smart about horseflesh, though why that should be, I can't begin to know. His father certainly wasn't that way, and I brought enough beaux around in his growing years so that at least he could get a hint at how things were supposed to work, but he was always messing about with his collections of this or that, and he never showed much of an interest in women at all." She lowered her voice in the loud whisper of a conspirator who cares not a fig if she's overheard in the next room. "I often wondered if he wasn't one of those—oh, you know, Arden, one of those men who prefer small boys or something."

"Mother!" This time, Arden did not laugh.

"But obviously, Josie's just a late bloomer," Anne chuckled, unperturbed. "Despite my joy at their pending union, however, this does rather unsettle my plans, you know. I don't relish the idea of sharing the house with the widow Hocker, for all her innumerable charms, much less her three wild Indians.'' She looked pointedly at Arden over her teacup.

Arden busied herself with the sugar and lemons for a moment, trying to catch her balance. She should have seen this coming. It was inconceivable that Anne would tolerate another mistress of Graced Ground, nor could she stomach three young children, not of her own blood.

"Arden, if you take another second to think this over, I'm going to be so insulted, I'll never set foot in this house again,'' her mother said lightly. "Surely you can't plead more time for passionate embraces with Master Howard—you're the mother of two already!''

Arden shook her head quickly. "No, Mother, of course not, and you are absolutely right, your place is here with us now. I was just thinking it through—how exactly it might be arranged best. You don't think Josie will be hurt?''

"I think Josie will be vastly relieved that he will not need to protect the widow from my sorry influences.''

"There *is* one more thing,'' Arden said slowly. "Though of course, it's not a problem, simply something to consider—''

"There's nothing to consider,'' Anne said sharply. "I'm too old to begin all over again in New Orleans. In that town, you're forgotten in six months, and I've been gone seven years. I scarcely think I need throw myself on the compassion of strangers—''

"I meant only,'' Arden went on with a small smile—it did so amuse her to get her mother riled sometimes—"that you'll scarcely be avoiding the hubbub of children at that house by moving to this one.'' She raised her head to let her mother see her smile, broader now and knowing.

Anne's eyes narrowed. "You don't mean to say that you're expecting again.''

Arden nodded happily. "In six months. And this time, I believe it will be a little girl."

"Oh for heaven's sake," Anne said with some annoyance. "Two children are already too many; do you need an entire litter?"

Arden opened her eyes wider in surprise and some confusion. She had assumed, of course, that her mother would be pleased. "But—well, most women I know have half a dozen or more. I scarcely think three is too many—"

Anne waved her hand as if shooing away a pesky fly. "Oh, do as you wish, you always have. I simply don't understand why you would wish to ruin your figure, your marriage, and possibly your life by saddling yourself with a dozen children—"

"Three is scarcely a dozen—"

"Once you go past two, you've changed the odds so much, you might as well have a pack of them. Now, it'll be three against two, and you'll never have a life until the last one is out of short pants. And Martin—"

"Martin is ecstatic about it," Arden said, rather shortly. "At any rate, it has no bearing on your welcome here at River Reach. Of course, we shall be happy to have you stay as long as you wish, and I think probably the large back bedroom will be best—it's the farthest from the nursery." She lowered her head so that her mother could not see her keen disappointment. "Perhaps when the baby comes, if it's a girl as I believe it will be, you'll be more—content with the idea."

Anne sighed deeply, looking away with some discomfort. "Oh, Arden, I'm sorry. It's not that I'm not happy for you, it's only that I wish you could have more out of life than a husband and three babies. There was a time, I remember, when I hoped you might make the Grand Tour of Europe, perhaps have a bit of adventure before you settled down to the role of wife and nursemaid. Remember how you used to love to dance?"

"I still do," Arden said softly.

"But do you get to do it often enough to remember that pleasure?" She smiled ruefully, more grimace than smile. "Does Master Howard enjoy the subtler refinements of such entertainments?"

"Occasionally."

"And do the two of you speak of the events of the day, or political changes, or anything else of interest beyond the children and the cotton crop?"

"Of course we do, Mama," Arden said stiffly.

"Oh really? What then do you think of President Jackson's latest disaster, chick?"

"What do you mean?"

Anne smiled grimly. "Only the worst calamity which could possibly befall this state, Arden. I mean his latest edict that the land offices will accept only hard money in payment for lands from now on—no more cotton specie, no more paper notes—I suspect Martin's aware of these small details, even if you're not. We're headed for a bust—everybody's talking about it in town—and you might as well be on the moon for as much as you know or care about it. And you can read and write better than most ladies in this county!"

"I'm sure Martin will discuss it with me soon, if it's so important."

"But why should you be waiting for the crumbs from that man's mouth to keep your brain working, Arden? I raised you to be more than some man's brood mare!"

"Mama," Arden replied levelly, "you scarcely raised me at all, if you want the truth."

"Well, I damn sure saw to it that you *were* raised, and I hate to see you sit here like a country mouse and grow dull as a stick just to keep Master Howard content. He's taking your best years, Arden!"

"Mama, why do you continue to make such remarks?" Arden said sadly. "Do you think I'll suddenly throw up my hands and wail, 'My God, Mama, you're right, I've made a terrible mistake, he's simply dreadful, and I must leave him right away?' What do you hope to accomplish by insulting

him to me? Except to make me not want you in our home?''
She sat back, suddenly exhausted, her hands over her belly
in the traditional protective gesture of a woman with child.
''I love him, Mother. And I love our life together. I'm sorry
if it's not the life you would have chosen for me or he's not
the man you'd have chosen''—she looked up meaning-
fully—''for yourself. But I'm happy. I wish you would be
happy for me.''

Anne put her hands up to her eyes and covered them,
erupting into soft sobs. Her action was so sudden that Arden
was as alarmed as she was surprised. ''Mama!'' she said,
going to her and embracing her, ''please don't take on so.
I'm sorry if I upset you—''

''No, no, 'tis I who am sorry,'' Anne said woefully.
''You're right, I've been simply terrible, and I beg your pardon. Please let me stay, and I promise I'll never make another remark about Martin or your life again.'' She looked
up at Arden through her tears, her face beautiful and sor-
rowed and full of remorse.

Arden felt such love and compassion for her in that moment, she would have done anything to keep her happy. ''I
doubt you could keep such a promise,'' she said, smiling at
her mother gently, ''and I'm not sure I'd want you to if you
could. I'll tell Uncle Josie you're moving in—''

''I already mentioned it to him,'' Anne sniffled.

''Good. Well, then, it's settled.''

Anne smiled up at her tremulously. ''Shall I go then and
pack my bags?''

''Absolutely.''

Anne rose and hugged her, bustled out the door, and she
was no sooner gone than Portia entered. Arden was leaning
against the porch, gazing out over the fields.

''Dis house ain' never goin' to be de same,'' Portia grumbled blackly. ''Ma'm goin' to turn it topsy on de first day she
come an' keep it dat way, sure.''

Portia never called Anne Lawrence anything but
''Ma'm,'' no matter how many times Arden had gently sug-

gested that "Mistress Lawrence" would be more appropriate. Anne did not deign to notice what Portia called her, what
any slave called her, unless she took it into her head to take
offense, and then nothing at all would please her. "No, she's
not, Portia, and you're not going to make it any worse by
looking for trouble, either," Arden said, not turning away
from the view. "Mother's getting too old to stay alone, and
now that Uncle's getting married, it's only right and fitting
that she come here to River Reach."

"So you decided, den?"

"Yes," Arden said firmly. "I am decided."

"An' Massa Martin say yes?"

Arden glanced at Portia suspiciously. "Master Martin
will do as I think best, I'm sure, Portia. She is my mother,
after all."

"I 'spec' dat's right," Portia said evenly. "Dat man do
set a store by you, I see dat much."

Arden could not suppress her smile. Somehow it pleased
her out of all proportion to hear Portia say such a thing.

"It will be good for the children," she said briskly. "And
Mother will bring a new spirit to this place, I have no
doubt." She smiled then, ruefully. "We'll all manage just
fine."

Portia appraised Arden carefully and, in the silence,
reached her own decision. "What I do to help, Miz Arden?"
she asked softly.

Arden turned then and smiled at her. "That's my good
and faithful Portia. You can keep the boys out from underfoot for the first few days, while Mama gets used to the
rhythms of the house. I'll give her Ruth for her own gal upstairs, and I'll tell Joseph to tell cook to make her what she
wants each morning for breakfast. Joseph will likely find her
charming enough, as he does most women with a handsome
figure."

"But what *I* do?" Portia asked, still determined to be of
some specific help.

"Never let her get you riled," Arden said smoothly.

"Dat goin' to be mighty hard."

She smiled ruefully. "If I can do it, you can do it," she said.

Just then, Micah and Owen raced up the stairs, slammed into the gallery, laughing and pushing each other into the walls and against the portieres, nearly entangling themselves and yanking them out of the rods, then slammed out again.

Portia hollered, "You young massas don' come in here now an' trouble your mama!" She halfheartedly grabbed at Owen as he whirled past, but Portia was not their nursemaid, and they knew it as well as she did. The boys minded their father and their mother, occasionally minded Joseph, who was in charge of their room and their meals and their clothes, but the rest of the slaves were just so much furniture to them as far as discipline was concerned.

Arden watched them career through the gallery with a fond resignation. Soon enough, they would need to be reined in, and the schoolmaster from Natchez would be coming out twice a week to see to their lessons. For now, they could run free.

"What your mamma say 'bout de new babe?"

Arden shrugged. "She is pleased, of course."

Portia laughed, a low, knowing chuckle. "She 'bout as happy as a treed coon 'bout dat, I wager."

"Why are you so ready to believe the worst about my mother? Once and for all, Portia, let's get this done with. She's coming here to live, she'll likely die here, and she will be grandmother to my children, maybe the only grandmother they'll have, since Martin's mother is too frail to make the trip from Vicksburg very often. Yet you will not believe a good word about her. Why is that? Say your piece and then I'll hear no more on the subject."

Portia narrowly scrutinized her mistress. There were limits to the freedom of her tongue, even alone with Arden. She did not know where the limits were, but she knew they loomed like a hidden animal trap under fallen leaves.

Arden gazed at Portia steadily, daring her to speak. She

knew that the one thing the slave could not do was hold her tongue.

"She not much mama, to my mind," Portia said reluctantly.

"Why do you say that?"

Portia sighed. "She a han'some woman, an' I 'spect de menfolk like her fine, but she put her onliest lil' gal away from her, an' let strangers do for her."

"So it's for my sake that you don't like her much?"

Portia nodded.

Of course there was nothing new in Portia's opinion, but now at least she had said it. "Can you, for my sake, forgive her?" Arden watched the slave steadily. She did not want to resort to threats with the woman, though she knew she had only to say the word and Martin would sell her and buy a replacement. Portia had been with her for too many years, had been too faithful and loyal to be treated like a slave. And yet, Arden had to remember that a slave was all she was. Moreover, Portia needed to remember that fact as well. "I would think," she said once more, "if I can love her, you can at least find a space in your heart to care for her for my sake."

Portia was silent. Uncharacteristically so.

"And for the sake of my daughter," Arden said softly. "For a daughter surely is what I will have next, and she will need a grandmother more than the two boys."

Portia nodded then. "I promise you once, Miz Arden, I never do nothin' to make you sad. On your weddin' day, I make dat promise."

Arden waited and watched. Clearly the slave was struggling with her own will.

"I make no trouble for M'am, Miz Arden. She your mama, no matter what." She frowned. "An' she dat babe's granmama, like you said."

"So you will welcome her and you will do as she says, just as if I gave you the order myself?"

"Yes'm," Portia said stoutly.

"Good," Arden said firmly. "Then let's start with deciding what you will call my mother when she comes to River Reach. Her name is Anne Lawrence. You may call her Madam Lawrence or you may call her Mistress Lawrence. Which do you choose?"

"Miz Lawrence," Portia muttered.

"That's settled then." Arden sighed deeply, leaning back in her chaise.

"Dat babe hurtin' you, Miz Arden?" Portia asked.

"And if she were, would you be angry with the poor thing and try to protect me against her?" Arden asked, her eyes closed.

Portia grinned as she went to her mistress and began to softly massage her shoulders. "Mos' likely. An' den you sell me South, sure."

"Most likely," Arden agreed.

That night, Martin and Arden made love with the practiced passion and the almost smug satisfaction of the long married. She found herself frantic for him at one point and pulled his face to hers, mouthing his jawline and his cheek. She bucked rhythmically under him, and she heard herself make senseless pleading noises, lifting herself against him and finally biting down on his shoulder and making him gasp. It was only afterward, when she felt their intimacy was once more secured and inviolate, that she told him that her mother was coming to River Reach to live.

Martin listened carefully, as he was wont to do, his hand resting on her head, his fingers buried in her thick, dark hair. She tried to see his face in the dim moonlight coming in over the four-poster, but he was in shadow. She finished with, "I know it'll be a problem at first, getting used to her being here all the time, but it's a big house, and we've got so much room. She'll be happier here than with Josie and his new family."

"Will you be happier, too?"

Arden turned to gaze at him then. "I don't need to be happier," she said with a smile. "I don't think I could be, anyway."

He smiled then, and she saw the glint of his white teeth in the darkness. "I mean, will you *stay* happy with Mama everpresent?"

"I think so," she said slowly. She lowered her voice as though others might hear. "I really don't feel I have much choice, Martin, so I might as well do it gracefully. I mean, she does have a point. We're not exactly newlyweds anymore, and now with another baby coming, it seems only natural that the children should have a grandparent close by. And where else is she to go?"

He laughed then, and she reached up swiftly to put her hand over his mouth. "Hush! What's so funny, Master Howard, I'd like to know."

"The whole world's her oyster, sweet, at least the part that's populated by men. She's got enough put by to do just fine, and any number of places would be more fun for her than River Reach. You make her sound like some poor bereft sparrow in widow's weeds, who needs a place to come out of the storm."

Arden smiled ruefully. "I know. Somehow she makes me feel that way about her, though I know she is perfectly capable of taking care of herself—"

"Or getting a man to do it for her," he added, grinning.

"But she is my mother, Martin," Arden said, trying to sound more severe. "There may be plenty of places she could go but where else really *should* she go?"

"No place else," he said easily. "I think she should come and welcome. I just want to be sure you're satisfied with the decision."

Arden sighed and rolled toward him. "And if I weren't, would you tell her she had to go back to New Orleans?"

He chuckled. "I like to think I'm a brave enough man, but I've no need to court death before my time. No, I would never tell her she couldn't stay at River Reach. I'd simply

build her a small house of her own on the grounds, so that
the two of you wouldn't have to sit across from each other at
the same table three times a day.''

"Ah God," Arden groaned, "that sounds so wonderful.
A perfect little miniature of the big house, that she could call
her own. But I dare not even suggest it. She'd be so insulted
and hurt, I'd never hear the end of it.''

"Well, let's see how she fares after a few months," Martin suggested. "When Owen and Micah finish with her, she
might be delighted to take a straw mattress in the quarters.''

Arden laughed happily and nestled closer to him, cleaving
her thigh against his, her leg thrown over his in a mingling of
warm skin and comforting weight. Very slowly, as though
his hand were featherweight and moved of its own accord,
his fingers began to trail upward on her spine, slowly,
slowly, up and down from her neck, tracing a soft pattern
down her bare skin to the very top of her buttocks. She shivered slightly, for his touch was like cool silk, and all her
nerves were instantly alive to him. She smiled quietly
against his neck. Even after all these years, she thought, after
all these times—

"I thought you might hurt me tonight." He pulled back
and grinned at her teasingly.

"I was desperate for you," she chuckled.

"So what was that calumny about us hardly being newlyweds?" Martin murmured as he pulled her to face him.

"Are you quite mad?" she whispered, as his hands
moved up her flanks softly.

"Quite likely," he said softly.

"You're asking for trouble," she groaned.

"Begging for it," he whispered.

"I am, sir, the mother of two, almost three. A respected
matron, wife to a man of dignity and standing in the community.'' Her voice was low and teasing and full of promise.

"Ah, yes," Martin said throatily, "but does the wretch
bring you pleasure, madam?"

There was no need for her to answer, for he was already

enveloping her again in his arms, moving his legs around her, and her moans, so sweet and deep, rising from someplace dark and private at the core of her belly, marked her delight, her joyful acceptance of his body over hers.

Martin was right. Anne was not in the house three months before she was fretful and waspish with the noise and the inevitable antics of two growing boys up and down the stairs, in and out of the doors, and constantly underfoot. Martin put four men to work on the building of what she was to call her "pigeon roost," and Anne was henceforth usually to be found out on-site, watching the house take shape and directing its erection as though she had built whole cathedrals on her own.

The higher her "roost" grew, the more her spirits matched it. When she was out near the construction, she was eager to have anyone, even Micah and Owen, join her in walking about, picking up this piece of wood or that brick, examining every nook and cranny of the work site. But once back inside the big house, she grew almost annoyed at its very walls, and she seemed to take pleasure in finding fault with small details of its construction.

"I suppose good clay was harder to come by when you were building River Reach," Anne said to Martin one night over dinner.

"No, not really," he said mildly. "The ground hasn't changed much in twenty years, so far as I can tell."

"Well, but I mean you probably couldn't find good artisans to make the brick back then." She smiled winningly. "It was likely enough just to get the walls raised and a crop in the field!"

He smiled. "I think you're right, Miss Anne. Your pigeon roost is going to be much more elegant than River Reach."

Anne laughed delightedly. "Well, now, I wasn't saying that exactly."

"No, no," Martin assured her with a wave of his hand. "I'm just pleased you're happy with it."

She clasped her hands together like a gleeful child. "I'm thrilled with it, Martin."

Arden could not help but laugh, her mother was so enchanting when she was like this, as much girl as woman, as beguiling as only a combination of the two could be.

"But Martin," Anne was going on, "do you think we might think about extending the balcony just the slightest bit? I mean, it will be lovely as it's planned, of course, and I'm sure I don't want to seem greedy, but I think it would be so much nicer if the balcony were wide enough to set a chaise out and take the air, don't you think? Maybe just a few more feet, and then I could have a double veranda!"

"It would be a nice place to have your evening Madeira," Arden said teasingly. Portia was coming through the dining room at that moment, having stepped back to speak to the cook, and she rolled her eyes at Arden, but she did not say a word.

Anne missed neither the tease nor Portia's response to it. "Hush your black mouth," she said archly to Portia's back. And then to Arden, she chuckled, "Absolutely right, chick, and my afternoon julep, too, if I've a mind to it. So what do you say, Martin, can you spare an old woman a few more feet of your good cypress wood?"

Martin thought for a moment, and Arden glanced at him, suddenly concerned. It did not seem like an unreasonable request, after all.

"I don't know if the bearing walls will take the extra weight," he murmured doubtfully. "On my original plans, I allowed only for a three-foot span—"

"Oh, I know you drew up the whole thing for me," Anne said graciously, "and Thomas Jefferson himself couldn't have done a better job of architecting, I'm sure, but I can't see how just a few more feet would hurt." She gazed at him steadily. "And it would make me so very happy!"

Owen had already been excused from the table, but Micah

was still helping himself to more ham. He glanced up at his grandmother curiously, an appraising frown on his brow, and Arden realized with a small start that her elder son had understood all which had passed—and was passing—between his father and Anne. He suddenly piped up, "Will it all fall down, Father?"

Martin looked up, amused at his son's perception. As Martin usually did, he took a moment before answering.

Anne filled the moment with a swift and teasing barrage. "Will it, Martin? Would it actually fall right to the ground if we went out a few teeny, tiny feet?"

"I don't think so," Martin said then, glancing at Arden with a silent plea. "But we'll have to heavy-up the pillars, of course, and perhaps add to the struts at the corners—"

"Excellent!" Anne said happily. "I do so appreciate it, Martin, and it will be lovely to sit out there in the evenings and watch the world go by my veranda." She winked at Micah. "If you're a very good boy, you can come and be my special beau, you handsome lad, and take a sip of my toddy when I'm not looking."

"Mother . . ." Arden said warningly.

Micah grinned and ducked his head, snatched a final piece of ham, and bolted from the table.

"Miss Anne," Martin said gently, "I can't help but wonder what you must have been like when you were a—a *very* young woman."

She rolled her eyes. "I'd have eaten you alive, Master Howard."

"I am sure," he said smoothly. "I feel right well nibbled, as it is."

Arden laughed then and broke the tension. She stood up and reached for the port decanter. "You two need a drink, I believe," she said lightly, "and this baby needs a little something to settle her down as well, if I'm going to get a wink of sleep tonight." She poured them each a small glass of the ruby port and took a sip of her own gratefully.

"She kicking good?" Anne asked solicitously, eyeing her daughter over the rim of her glass.

Arden nodded ruefully.

"Good," Anne said with small relish. "We need another fighter in this family."

Martin groaned, downed his drink, and covered his eyes dramatically, while Anne giggled and patted his free hand in mock consolation.

Arden's third child was due in the autumn, just as the final touches were being added to her mother's cottage out back. In addition to the wider porch, Anne had cajoled Martin into adding extra windows, a small music room for the piano she wanted to order up from New Orleans, and two-room slave quarters at the rear. When Arden had protested that they surely needed no more space for slaves, and certainly not separate quarters at that, her mother insisted, even offering to pay for the extra expenses involved herself.

Anne was planning, she said, to invest her monies in two good breeder slaves, women who would be mated to strong field hands or perhaps skilled laborers, and then give birth to more slaves which would be sold for high profits in the New Orleans, Natchez, or Baton Rouge markets. These breeder slaves would have to be kept away from the rest of Martin's slaves, lest they breed indiscriminately with inferior stock.

When Arden expressed her dismay at such a plan, her mother only scoffed at her. After all, she pointed out, there were excellent gains to be made from slaves these days, and just because she had no land didn't mean she needed to miss out on that investment opportunity. "They'll be well treated, and their offspring will bring good cash money," Anne assured her. "And anyway, what's the difference? Your niggers have their little broom-jump weddings, and then six months later, the wenches are heavy with child. Martin gets new help, and he doesn't waste time wringing his hands over it, I assure you."

"But we don't sell our people off this land. And certainly not their children," Arden said.

"Not so far you haven't, but if they keep breeding like they do, Martin may well see the wisdom of that policy soon enough. It's a waste of money to feed more than you can work, and I'm told that well-bred hands of good stock can fetch up to eight hundred dollars in Natchez."

"For young children?" Arden asked, shocked. She had never heard of such prices before. Clearly, President Jackson's new hard-money policy was having a stark effect on the slave market as well. No wonder Martin had not purchased any new hands lately—she must remember to ask him about this.

"Soon as they're good and weaned and can be trained," Anne was saying. "And my agent says the price will go even higher by winter. You mark my words, the time'll come when I make more from my two breeders than Martin makes from fifty acres of good cotton, and a lot less trouble in the making of it."

Arden shook her head slowly. She could not argue with the economics of it, but the idea of two mothers on her land knowing that their children would be taken from them was too distressing to consider at length. She put her arms around her huge belly in a protective circle. "Mother, don't let's talk about this anymore right now."

"Are you all right, chick?" Anne asked gently, putting her arm around her shoulders.

Arden hugged her, as much as her stomach would allow. "I'll be better when I'm lightened of this girl-child."

Anne cocked her head. "You still so certain that's what it is?"

"As certain as I am that Micah and Owen are not."

Two nights later, Arden's prediction proved true. She was delivered of a strong, healthy baby girl, light of hair like her grandmother, fine of features like her father and her mother.

"We'll call her Felicity," Arden said wearily as she held the infant in her arms after six hours of strong labor. "Because she will bring us so much joy." Martin smiled down at her and kissed her brow.

Portia took the child from Arden's arms to wrap it in the warm cloth she had readied.

Anne asked, "Why not just call her Joy, then? It's less of a mouthful."

"I think it's a fine name," Martin said. "Owen, Micah, and Felicity. A beautiful name for a beautiful girl."

"I'll call her Lacey, for short," her grandmother said, stroking her soft hair and gazing at her. "Lacey Howard. Sounds like a woman I would like to know."

"Mama," Arden said, "would you settle her in the nursery now? I need to rest."

"And moon together over your third little triumph," Anne added. "By all means. Miss Lacey and I know when we're not wanted anymore." But she smiled and crooned to the child as she went out the door.

"You make such beautiful babies," Martin said as he stroked her face softly. "I knew you would, the first time I met you."

"Oh, you great liar," she teased him wearily. "You only wanted my body for reasons of lust. You never gave a thought to the children that would come of it."

He chuckled ruefully. "You're right, of course." His fingers went down to her breast and cupped it very gently. "I'm glad to have my own sweetheart back again." He stopped when she winced slightly. "I'm sorry, is that too much?"

"Just for now. I'm so very swollen."

"Was it worse this time?"

She smiled tiredly. "Not as bad as Micah. He was the worst of all three. That boy didn't want to come out for anything."

"Are you very sore?"

She watched him under lowered lashes. "You don't fool me a whit, Master Howard. You just want to know when I might be able to muss your sheets once more."

He smiled. "It does seem like it's been a year."

"Well," she murmured, "perhaps you might hold me now, if you're very, very careful."

He put his arms around her and put his cheek to hers, murmuring to her softly. She lay back and let him stroke her, more and more intimately, sighing as he bent to very gently take her breast in his mouth, tonguing her softly, his warm breath moving over her nipple and then lower to her belly. She fell asleep like that, with the sound of his voice humming gently in her ear and the feel of his arms around her tightly.

Aquila, the golden eagle, plummeted earthward in a vertical dive, crying "Kee-kee-kee!," his high-pitched scream which sounded more like anger than courtship. He dropped as a missile, wings closed, homing in on the great brown female that spiraled upward from the cliffs of the Natchez below him.

On a collision course with the ground, the plunging eagle suddenly spread his wings, pulled out of his dive, and shot upward past his soaring mate. He brushed her wing tip, side-slipped into another dive, and broke off into a spectacular series of rolls and loops, his golden hackles catching the sun.

Now the female nosed over into a sequence of dives, rushing so close to the male that he could hear the whine of the wind through her feathers.

Aquila circled her tightly, calling once more and dipping his wings in homage to her power. It was a nuptial flight by a bird who had captured man's imagination for centuries. Shakespeare called him a "feather'd king," and his image led Roman legions and Persian armies into battle. Indians and Scots Highland chiefs wore his flight feathers as symbols of courage and rank. When falconry was the most popular sport, the privilege of training and flying the golden eagle was reserved only for emperors and kings.

But Aquila was unaware of his species' renown. A large male of seven seasons, he was all dark with a pale golden nape. His bill was smaller and darker than that of a bald eagle, but he was a better raptor because of his flying skills. There were few of his kind left along the Great River where it made its southern flow, but Aquila had managed to find and entice a female to these Natchez cliffs, and he did not intend to lose her now. Truly, he feared no adversary save man.

The Great River provided him with fish, and the nearby fields, spreading farther and farther out from the water each year, provided him with other prey: newborn lambs, chickens, and rabbits which were lured by the man's corn. Aquila could eat a pound of flesh a day and more, when he could get it. To stave against failure in the hunt, he cached food high in the treetop sometimes, saving excess for the following meal.

In other times his kind, *Aquila chrysaetos,* had flourished. Far before his memory, brown eagles had nested in large numbers in the Mississippi River region. But no more. Man no longer left them to hunt unmolested as they once did on these lands. Too often, Aquila came upon broken bodies of other eagles, shot at, wounded and left to starve, and those nests built in too-accessible cliffs were sometimes pillaged and destroyed.

There was a time, well before his memory, when man had lived in peace with the raptors, capturing them only occasionally for the theft of a few feathers. A favored trick of the Natchez Indians was to pinion the wings of a falcon so it could fly only a few hundred yards. They tied a ball of feathers to its talons together with many hair nooses. When an eagle, soaring several thousand feet above, spotted the falcon carrying what appeared to be food, it hurtled down to steal a meal. The falcon rolled over and threw its feet up to protect itself, and the nooses caught the eagle's talons. Then the two birds fluttered to the ground, where the hunters easily captured the eagle, plucked out two of its most coveted feathers, and released it to fly again.

Aquila had no experience with such captures, but somewhere in his genetic memory, he had the knowledge that men were capable of much trickery.

But he was determined that this season's aerie would be undisturbed, despite the growing numbers of men in the cluster of houses beyond these cliffs. He had hunted these lands for three seasons, and he felt a fierce territoriality for this place on the river, these fields, and these rocks which would shelter his young. His homeland stretched nearly a hundred square miles. If he could persuade his mate to nest here, he would be content.

Aquila had had a mate the previous season, but she was killed. He did not know how she died; he only knew that something had damaged her spine and wing so badly that she could not fly. He suspected man had attacked her. He mourned her through the cold months, for his kind stayed together for nesting season after season, adding to their aeries and brooding the young as partners. But then he had rare fortune. He found another female to court. He had fiercely defended his territory against other raptors and lesser birds; now the homeland would be held, his line would continue unbroken. If he lived, he would stay on these cliffs for thirty years or more and raise his eaglets with the same mate throughout those seasons.

Now he spiraled upward as swiftly as he could fly, higher and higher until he felt the air thinning beneath his wings. He looked down at the earth below. His eyes were telescopic, microscopic, monocular, and binocular, and about eight times finer than man's. He could spot a rabbit at half a mile up, and his circling mate who was riding the air currents was easily visible as a dark spot against the lighter water. At thirteen pounds, she was heavy and larger than he was, a healthy female in the prime of her breeding life.

Their courtship ritual was soon over, and Aquila covered her quickly while both of them were perched on a jutting rock over the site of his aerie. That she allowed this site for their consummation reassured him. In time, over successive nestings, the aerie would be added to and improved with layers of sticks, and might weigh as much as a ton before one of them finally died. He was filled with protective pride for his new mate, and he guarded her carefully that night, sleeping only fitfully as she rested.

A month later, she carefully laid two eggs in the aerie, which she had reconstructed to her own taste. A careful housekeeper, she had lined it round with pine boughs to keep the nest tidy. Likely, she would not allow uneaten prey to pile up and putrefy. She brooded the three-inch-long mottled eggs for thirty-five days, and Aquila took his turn incubating the clutch, hunting for her while she sat them and then taking food from her in his turn.

Finally, two hatchlings emerged from their eggs, a male and a female eaglet. Covered with white down, their huge gray eyes and gray beaks pointed up to Aquila each time he came to the nest. They would not begin to have feathers for about six weeks, and in that time, they were most vulnerable to accident, enemies, or starvation. If either parent became unable to hunt, they would die.

Aquila took his guard position on the rock above the aerie and watched as his mate dropped a dead rabbit into the nest. The female eaglet was always the first to claim the food. She fought her brother off, grabbed the rabbit, and covered it with her wings, snapping and screeching at him.

The male fledgling squawked at the edge of the nest but did not attempt to recover the prey. After a few moments, Aquila's mate landed on the nest and appraised her two eaglets. She knocked over the young female with one stroke of her wing, tore up the rabbit, and divided it equally between both siblings. Ignoring the protests of her daughter, she then flew off once again to find more food.

The eaglets grew quickly, fed well and often by two hunting parents. When it was time for them to fly at thirteen weeks, the female no longer dropped the food in the nest but circled the nest on the wing, holding the prey so that the eaglets could clearly see the lure. The female eaglet was the first to attempt her wings. She screeched loudly in her frustration and fear, but she flung herself from the edge of the aerie, flapped clumsily, and managed to stay aloft, finally landing awkwardly on the outstretched limb of a live oak upriver. Aquila's mate instantly flew down to her and offered her the largest portion of the rabbit she held in her talons. She took wing again, circling the nest and tempting the male eaglet to fly. He would not.

Aquila watched for days as his mate tried to get the smaller male to fly. She would fly upwind to within a few yards of the next, then roll over on her side, exposing her prey. The hungry young female, who by now was more able with her wings, watched her intently. As her mother circled, she flew from the nest, maneuvered alongside her, and tried to snatch the food. Aquila's mate made a strong downward stroke of her wing that sent the young eagle head over tail and forced her to land on the slope below.

The male eaglet then let out a frightened cry and lunged over the edge of the nest, flapping wildly, trying to reach his mother and the food. He could not, but he managed to keep himself aloft well enough to land not far from his sister. When he did, his mother landed beside him and gave him the largest portion of the bloodied young fox she carried. He screamed his triumph, covered the prey with his wings, and watched his sister with a fierce eye.

Unconcerned, the female eaglet tore at her portion of the fox, protecting it from him and also from her mother as she ate.

The flush times of Natchez ended dramatically in the late 1830s, but it was to be years before those who lived through them recognized the end for what it was. In the summer of 1839, a yellow fever epidemic swept through the town, likely coming from one of the steamboats, percolating into a deadly simmer in the shanties and brothels of Natchez-Under-the-Hill, and finally erupting overnight in the big houses on the shaded streets of the city. For two weeks, the stench of burning tar filled the town, as the mayor ordered smoke pots burned on every corner to rid the air of the unhealthful "miasmas" which were thought to have caused the contagion. The three physicians in Natchez labored day and night, going from house to house, offering what small comfort they could, but little could be done against the raging chills and fevers, the acute nausea, the brutal vomiting, and the final exhaustion which claimed the unfortunate victims of the disease.

The weary doctors could soon tell, simply by the smell and taste of the patient's vomitus—whether brown or black, merely rank or putrid—whether or not he or she could be expected to survive. And many did not. The graveyards of the city and the nearest plantations, both public and private, were quickly filled in that late August, as more than two hundred people succumbed.

Arden kept close to the house and the quarters that summer, watching for the first signs of the epidemic, but to her vast relief, River Reach was not struck by the disease. She suspected one reason might have been that Martin had drained, filled, and planted so much of the land around the house that the unhealthy miasmas which came from wet earth simply were fewer on the plantation. Martin kept out of Natchez that season, sending his driver in for him, and even when supplies grew low and Arden yearned to see friends in the city, she stayed home and contented herself with her children and the company of those few who ventured out the dozen miles to see her.

It seemed to her then that the most important thing she could do for her family was keep them healthy. And that extended to her slaves as well, a part of the larger family which kept the machine of River Reach running for the good of them all. She went through the days in a fever, reading all she could find in her herbals, roaming the fields and the woods for roots and flowers to make her medicinals, thinking that if she could only prepare a large enough pharmacy, they need never fear disease as so many did in town. She had

two of the hands build her a drying shed out to the rear of the
quarters where she hung bunches of yaupon, horsetail, flat-
root, and sweet gum bark to dry and strengthen the good
juices so that she might prepare them for oils and tisanes.
She found rattlesnake plant and prickly ash and slippery elm
and a host of other shrubs and leaves, each one noted in her
herbals as having some specific power over an ailment, and
she hoarded them as one might hoard gold against misfortune.

Finally, after a month of prayer and caution, the disease
seemed to move south, leaving weakened victims and
mourning families in its wake. It was not the first yellow
fever epidemic to hit the town, nor would it be the last. But
this particular contagion seemed to usher in a series of
calamities the likes of which Natchez had not had to endure
before.

Two months later, as the contagion was dying away, a fire
spread from the shanties below the bluff to the city proper,
and more than forty buildings were either destroyed or extensively damaged. Then cotton prices fell hard, and many
planters faced ruin. Martin saw drastically lower profits that
season, but he had enough in savings to wait out the poor
cycle and hope for a better year to come. A month later, the
Mississippi Railroad, after completing twenty-eight miles of
track, abruptly decided to end all further construction in Natchez, thus isolating the region from the trade of north central
Mississippi.

And then on May 7, 1840, while half the town was still
reeling from financial shock and personal loss, Natchez was
struck by a tornado. Shortly after one o'clock in the afternoon, when most of the city was just sitting down to dinner,
the sky suddenly grew dark as night, and the winds which
had been blowing rose to a gale force. A distant roar moved
closer from the south, and within five minutes, Natchez was
in ruins. The tornado crossed the Red River some forty miles
out of Alexandria, Louisiana, swept across Natchez Island,
and hit just south of the Natchez bluffs. The winds left a

swath two miles wide, leveling Bellevue, the Briars, and many other palatial estates.

The tornado sank the ferries, sixty flatboats, and six steamboats; made the river rise by eight feet in less than five minutes; and drowned more than three hundred people. On land, the winds toppled the Steamboat Hotel, Brown's sawmill, the Mississippi Hotel, the railroad depot, the City Theater, the Presbyterian, Methodist, and Episcopalian churches, Magnolia Vale, the Planters Hotel, and some of the finer homes which graced the bluffs.

The winds were high at River Reach, four trees toppled, and part of the roof needed repair. At Graced Ground, the chapel where Arden was married suffered damage to its steeple and glass windows. But they were fortunate. They did not realize how fortunate until they drove into Natchez the following week, and then Martin and Arden were shocked at the extent of damage.

Almost a thousand people lost their lives, and many more lost their homes and their businesses. New Orleans, Baton Rouge, and Vicksburg sent help and volunteers, but many people felt Natchez was doomed to slide into oblivion. She had simply suffered too many blows in too short a time.

But finally, with a stubborn nobility which would serve them well in the years to come, the citizens decided once more to rebuild, and the 1840s ushered in a new era of prosperity, dimming the memories of disaster with each new, prosperous cotton crop.

Felicity grew into a lovely child, much like her grandmother before her, with a light nimbus of frothy golden hair around cool, blue eyes and a porcelain face of delicate features. Only her mouth was her father's, narrow-lipped and usually smiling. From her mother, Felicity acquired a hundred gestures, a turn of her head, the movement of her hands, and a low, soft voice. She was, in sum, a delight to all three adults who lived in her house and who loved her to distraction.

By the time she was five, she was already completely in charge of both her servants and usually at least one of her brothers. She was imperious with women, wheedling with Joseph and her father, and blithely adept at getting her way. Martin rode her round the plantation on his white mare, holding her safely before him and letting her touch the crop to the horse's neck. She learned early the proper tone to use with the field hands and the overseer, one of firm and dignified expectation that they would do exactly as she wished when she wished it.

Arden had to take her aside at times and reprimand her, in fact, for such a tone, when it was directed at her brothers, her father, or at her Uncle Josie.

And when Felicity was reprimanded, she had several strategies. First, she would swiftly, indignantly, turn her head away, as if to block out the distasteful view of a scolding face. Then, if the indignity continued, she would put her hands to her ears. If Arden took her hands down and insisted that she heed the correction, Felicity instantly burst into tears. Only upon mollification would she then promise to try to do better. Arden realized early that to chastise the child was to invite a larger storm than her offense often warranted, and she learned to pick and choose her battles with Felicity for the sake of household harmony.

Martin was little help when it came to disciplining his daughter. Where he had no difficulty scolding the boys or curbing their excesses with punishment if need be, when it came to Felicity, he seemed to turn deaf, dumb, and blind. Once when she had gone into his astronomy study without permission, a place which was off-limits to the children without supervision, and while there, had turned his telescope away from the window so that she might look down the shaft more easily, Arden was horrified at her trespass. She knew well enough that it would take Martin several hours of concentration to put the instrument back where he had it and find his exact line of sight once more into the heavens.

But Martin barely scolded the girl. "Next time," he said mildly, "you must ask Father before you touch anything in his special room. Will you promise to do that, Filly?" He had adopted that pet name for her when she was old enough to be delighted by it, and he used it now as a form of verbal caress.

"I promise, Father," she said solemnly.

Later when Arden asked him why he had not punished her for breaking his rules, he said only, "She's a bright child, sweet, and I hate to curb that curiosity. At least she has a thirst for knowledge."

Arden suspected that her daughter had more a thirst for going through doors which she knew she should leave closed, but she let the matter drop. Still, it troubled her that Felicity was growing up with so little reins on her desires. And her grandmother was no help at all.

From Felicity's birth, Anne Lawrence had taken the child to her heart as she had neither of the two boys before her. As though she had been somehow a product of her own body, her own soul, she laid claim to Lacey, as she called her, with every opportunity. If Arden wished her to dress practically, so that she might be outdoors, romping with her brothers, Anne moaned that the child looked so winsome in lace and crinolines that it seemed a shame to dress her in anything else. For a time, Felicity was so struck by the sense of her grandmama's opinion that she refused to wear her little cotton shifts and demanded that she be dressed for a ball each and every morning. Arden finally fought her to the ground on that one, but for every time she managed a victory, her mother seemed to win a greater war.

Once she had come upon Felicity holed up in Anne's room when she had looked for her for a while, wondering where the child had got to, and found her before her mother's long, gilded cheval mirror. Anne beamed behind her on the bed. Filly was dressed in one of her mother's long

ballgowns, with it pinned up so that she might walk without
tripping. Pinned, too, in the back, it hung on her small shoulders with a deep plunge down to midchest. Filly preened and
strutted before the mirror, fluffing her hair with a saucy
smile, practicing her flirtations.

"What in the world?" Arden had asked as she stepped
into the room. "Filly, I've been looking all over for you."

"I'm at a grand *fête,* Mama," Felicity answered gaily. "I
am the prettiest lady in the room, and all the handsome gentlemen want to dance best with me."

"Well, I'm not surprised," Arden said mildly, "for you
are very pretty, indeed. But I wonder if you should be showing so much of your pretty shoulders, child. You might make
all the fine gentlemen think you're not as sweet as you are
pretty."

"Nonsense," Anne said tartly. "Gentlemen like pretty
shoulders more than they like sweet, Lacey, and don't you
forget it."

Fortunately, Filly was scarcely listening, so entranced
was she with her own reflection. Also, she missed the glare
Arden shot her mother over her head. "Mama, I need a red
dress!" her daughter said suddenly, racing to her and clasping her knees in heartfelt supplication. "Granmama says
every young lady should have a red dress!"

"Maybe in New Orleans," Arden said, laughing ruefully,
"but I think there are likely a whole passel of young ladies
in this county without one. When you're older, child—"

"No!" Filly shouted, stamping her small foot. "I want a
red dress now!"

Arden stopped and frowned at her daughter solemnly.
"Filly, you know I don't like that tone. Perhaps you're too
young to wear any dresses at all still, for only spoiled children speak like that to their elders. If you are, indeed, a
young lady, I expect you to act like one."

Anne laughed merrily and went to Felicity, unpinning the
back of the hem so that it suddenly fell down to the carpet.
"Come on, chick, your mama doesn't like to play make-

believe. We'll do this another time, when we're all in a better mood. Run along now and see what she needs doing—''

"No, Granmama, I want to play here with you!"

"Run along now," Anne said gently, "and then you can come back another day." She ushered Arden and Filly out the door and silently closed it behind them.

"Oh Mother, you ruined it," Filly said angrily. "I never looked so pretty, Granmama said."

"Well, your grandmother is wrong," Arden said firmly. "You look far prettier in your own sweet dresses, of which you have more than any three girls in Natchez. Now don't you dare fuss, miss," she said warningly as she saw Filly begin to work herself up into a hissy.

"All right, I won't," her daughter said suddenly, turning off her tears as instantly as she seemed to turn them on. "I'm going to see Papa."

Arden had sighed as Filly hurried before her, up the stairs to invade Martin's study. No doubt the subject of the red dress would be brought up again with deft maneuvers, and she could only pray that he would stand fast against such nonsense. Sometimes she wished she could spank Anne Lawrence instead of Felicity.

And yet she was loath to dampen her mother's love for her daughter, believing that both of them would be happier for that affection, as passionate as it sometimes threatened to become. She honestly felt no jealousy—no, even when she plumbed her soul in the depths of the night, she could not admit to that. She was not jealous, truly. She knew that her daughter was hers forever, and she did not begrudge her grandmama's piece of her heart. But sometimes, she wished for a stronger ally against all three of them—Felicity, Grandmama, and Father—than simple, obdurate Portia.

Portia loved Felicity well enough, but she refused to be taken in by the child's whims and wiles. "Dat gal goin' to be spoil rotten," she said time and time again, pushing out her lower lip in disapproval and annoyance.

"I know it," Arden sighed. "I do my best, but between

her father and her grandmother, she can always find someone to take her side.''

"You got to put your foot down hard," Portia warned,
"an' put it down right on dat chile's neck. Else she be worthless when she grow up, an' bossy to boot. She order ol' Cassie round like she a mule wid a saddle, an' I hear her tell
Owen dat her mama love her best an' her father love her
best, an' nobody love Owen best at all.''

"What did Owen say?" Arden asked worriedly.

"He tell her dat if she get any meaner, he goin' to tie up
every baby doll she got an' hang dem from de peach tree, an'
ain' nobody love her no mo' if she don' stop bein' such a
dog in de manger, an' besides his daddy love him best.''

Arden laughed. "Good for him.''

"He be right, too, leastwhys 'bout de part dat nobody love
her if she don' stop bein' so wicked," Portia said solemnly.
"Ain' nobody goin' to marry wif her if she don' get more
sweetness." She glowered. "An' I misbelieve her gran'-
mama be de one to teach her dat.''

"Portia . . ." Arden said warningly.

"Well, I cain' hep it, Miz Arden," the slave said suddenly. "Dat woman can raise de blisters wid her tongue!''

"What's she said to you?" Arden asked. "No lies, now,
because I'll know if you're lying, and I'll whip you, I swear
it.''

Portia sighed hugely. "Ain' no use in me tellin' you, Miz
Arden, she your mama, an' you bound to love her, no matter
what. But I tell you dis, she ain' goin' do dat lil' gal no good,
an' Cassie an' Lucy an' Jessie, dey say de same thing.''

"Oh, Portia, they'll say whatever you say, and I don't
care a whit anyhow. Filly's a smart girl, and her grandmother loves her, and I don't want to hear another word.''

"Well, den, I don' say another word," Portia said stubbornly, her chin jutted out like a plow.

"Good." Arden nodded in agreement then, but she was to
remember Portia's warning years later when Felicity was ten
and no more manageable than she'd been at five.

Felicity had been in the habit of taking afternoon tea with her grandmother on Anne's veranda for many months, and as much as Arden worried what her daughter might be learning there, she did not have the heart to curtail the visits. Each afternoon, Felicity put on a clean frock, usually one which her grandmother had had made for her especially in Natchez by her own favorite dressmaker. After brushing out her hair and putting on a fresh ribbon, she traipsed over to her grandmother's and there the two of them sat into the afternoon, sipping tea and chatting.

At first, Arden could not see how her mother kept Felicity entertained each afternoon for sometimes two hours or more, but little by little, Felicity herself began to explain the attraction. "Grandmama says I look best in pale colors," Felicity told her mother gravely. "I think that red dress is likely too small for me anyway, so we should give it to some other little girl." And then later, "Grandmama says I'm too old to wear my hair down with no styling or curls. She says I should be in long skirts with my hair up by the end of this season." And then again, "Do you like my voice, Mama? Grandmama says I have a pretty voice and I should read aloud for an hour every day to practice, just like a bird practices its song."

In short, her grandmother was spending the time with Felicity talking chiefly about the girl and how attractive she was and would be. What child would not be entertained, at least temporarily, with such a topic? But as the months went on, Arden began to be somewhat resentful about the time Felicity spent on her grandmother's porch. When she asked her daughter, she said only, "Oh, Grandmama's teaching me stuff, Mama. About being a woman." She said that last with such a touching tone of importance, as though her grandmother were imparting to her a priceless and rare gift of self, that Arden could not bring herself to laugh.

However, on one afternoon a week later, she made it a point to come up from the quarters in such a way so that she approached Anne's house from the rear, and came onto the veranda below them quietly without calling out, realizing as she did so that anyone who looked could see that she was eavesdropping on her own mother and daughter. But she did not care. She wanted to hear this for herself.

Anne was in the middle of a long anecdote about the dancing master who had taught her the most essential social graces when she was perhaps only a few years older than Felicity. "He was so suave and handsome," she was saying confidentially to her granddaughter as she slowly brushed and arranged her hair, "that I nearly swooned each time he touched me. Which he had to do, of course, to teach me the proper deportment. My shoulder, my waist, my hand . . ." She laughed lightly. "I can still feel it even after all these years, Lacey. Can you imagine?"

Felicity answered her grandmother's laugh with one of her own, shockingly similar in tone and quality. It did not sound like Filly's laugh at all. "But did he ever—did he ever touch you anyplace he shouldn't?" the girl asked finally.

Arden winced and frowned.

"No, but I finally learned that it was great fun to let him think that he might," Anne said teasingly. "After I grew bored with the lessons, I was still vastly amused by the man's fumblings around me. This man who was so charming and suave, was after all, just a man like all of them, I figured out. And when I gazed up at him through my lashes and smiled a certain way at him, he tumbled over his feet and his own tongue, gawky as any schoolboy."

Arden sighed sadly. This was not what she wanted Felicity to hear. It might well be Anne Lawrence's reality, but she did not wish it for her daughter. Was there no middleground between the nuns and her mother? She was ready to stand up and announce her presence when Felicity's voice stopped her.

"Grandmama, are you truly going to sell Hanna's little boy-baby?" Hanna was one of Anne's breeders, a slave who had produced four children in eight years, all of them sold at auction in Natchez when they came of age to be weaned.

Lately, Felicity had been down to the quarters with Arden to learn the doctoring of the slaves and their husbandry. In fact, Arden had her supervise the spring cleaning of the quarters this year, and watch while the women worked. All the little cabins were emptied out and the contents sunned, the walls and the floors scrubbed, the mattresses emptied and stuffed with fresh hay, the yards swept, the ground under the cabins sprinkled with lime, and the walls whitewashed inside and out.

The cleaning happened twice a year, in the spring and the fall, and it was high time, Arden told Martin, that Filly learned that one of her responsibilities would be, one day, to see to it that her people lived in a healthy manner. "In the long run," she'd told him, "she'll need to learn less about doctoring if she learns more about keeping them clean."

And so, Filly had more occasion, these days, to see that Hanna's little boy, a little black nubbin they called Cake, was nearly grown enough now to be taken from his mother as all the rest had been before him.

Arden held her breath, waiting for Anne's answer. Filly was old enough now to feel compassion for Hanna's pain and her boy's coming despair. This was surely one area of opinion where her daughter would break openly with her grandmother.

"Of course," Anne said smoothly. "Why wouldn't I?"

"Well, Cake's so little," Felicity began, "and Hanna's still grieving for the last one gone . . ."

"How do you know such a thing?" her grandmother asked sharply. "Have you been down to Hanna's quarters? I told you not to go there, didn't I?"

"Mama took me with her to doctor Hanna last time, when she had that boil come up, and she—"

"Why in the world would she do that?" Anne demanded.

"Well, she says it's important," Filly said with some confusion. "She says my first duty to learn is to tend to the sick among our people. She says they must be strictly and regularly tended to, three times a day if they're poorly, and to watch over the changes 'til they get better.''

Anne laughed then, mockingly. "Oh for heaven's sakes, Lacey, I never heard anything so ridiculous in all my born days. Do you think Caroline Hampton's mama does such a thing? Or Mrs. Kaye or Rebecca Nevins, or any of your other neighbors? Is your mama trying to put the poor doctor out of business? You have to go, I suppose, if she makes you, but as for messing about in the quarters, why, I can't imagine such a thing! You're apt to catch the headlice or something worse—imagine that, in your beautiful hair!"

Filly was silent for a moment while Arden listened, her anger rising in her slowly like heat up an iron spike. When her daughter finally spoke, Arden could hear the bewilderment in her voice, and her heart turned in her chest. "But Grandmama, Hanna was weeping so hard. The whole time she suckled that boy. Crying like her heart was going to break in half."

"They all weep and whine like that, Lacey," her grandmother said shortly. "Some more'n others, and Hanna's a weak-spined sort of woman with no more sense than a goose."

"Well, she's all but made herself sick over it, Mama said. Nothing else wrong with her except plain grieving. If you was to keep just one of her children for her, maybe put him to work round the place where she could see him, she'd be well quick enough." Felicity took a deep breath, but she said no more.

Arden was pleased at the girl's gumption. She smiled quietly to herself. How would Anne get out of this one?

"It'll be years before that boy's old enough to earn his keep," Anne said smoothly, "and I can sell him right now for good cash money."

"Why would anybody buy him, anyway? What can a little boy like that do?"

"Why, he can tote water, he can tend sheep, he can gather up firewood, help out with the tenders, sweep the yard, run

up to the big house with eggs, pick worms off the tobacco—
any number of things, I imagine. Leastwhys, the folks who
will buy him will know right well enough what to put him
to.'' Her voice turned sweet and tender. ''Now Lacey, you
needn't fret over ol' Hanna and her nigger-boy. He'll have a
good home with folks who'll take good care of him, better
than she could, that's for certain. He'll grow up to be a fine
man, and his mama can be proud of that. You can't be worrying yourself over things like this, Lacey, you listen to me
good now. When your father sells off his colts in the spring,
do the mares carry on and pitch a fit? When your mama
takes the eggs from under the hens, are we all supposed to
stand about and wring our hands and fret over their
squawks? Not by a good sight. Hanna will forget that boy
just like the mares forget their colts by next season and the
hens forget their eggs. Soon as she gets another baby in her
arms, she'll be fine. And she can't do that 'til she weans this
one, so the sooner we get him weaned and gone, the happier
she'll be.''

''Yes'm,'' Felicity said glumly.

''Do you see what I'm saying to you, child?'' her grandmother asked her kindly.

''I see,'' Felicity said. But her voice betrayed her confusion.

Arden could think of no finer time to interrupt, so she
called out, ''Hey, you two, can a mama come up and set a
spell or is that veranda only big enough for two?''

''Come on up!'' Anne caroled out gaily.

Arden noted that Felicity did not echo her grandmother's
call. When she climbed up the outer stairs to the upstairs
porch, she saw that her daughter was fighting hard to keep
back tears. Anne was either blissfully unaware or was studying to seem so.

Arden put a light hand on Felicity's shoulder. ''I hate to
interrupt this lovely tea party,'' she said playfully, ''but Cassie says if you don't come and stand still for that dress you
want her to finish, she won't get it done in time for you to

wear it to Caroline's *fête*." Felicity's best friend, Caroline Hampton at the next plantation over, was having a birthday party in two days, and Felicity had her heart set on an organdy dress with billowing ruffles and matching pantelets.

"Oh, that Cassie's so slow, I swear Josie could have had that dress sewn up by now. You're not firm enough with them, Arden," her mother said petulantly. "You let them run that house and everybody in it."

To Arden's surprise, Felicity added, "Yes, Mama. After all, who is she to tell me what to do, she's just a nigger slave."

"Filly, we don't use that word in this house, I've told you that before. It's ill-bred and ignorant." Arden frowned at Anne, daring her to contradict. Her mother sipped her drink and said nothing.

"Well, I'll come, but only because if I don't, Cassie'll pitch such a fit, she'll never finish the dress at all. Grandmama's right, Mother, you spoil her to death." And Felicity got up, flounced off her chaise and down the steps and out across the yard to the big house.

When she was out of earshot, Arden said, "Mother, I don't appreciate you filling her head with your views on how to properly manage the hands. She's upset about Hanna and the sale of her children—"

"I've explained that to her well enough," Anne said evenly. "She doesn't look the least upset to me."

"Well, I *want* her to be upset by such a thing," Arden said firmly, "and a little less upset about whether or not her dress will be finished on time!" She turned from the banister where she had been standing, watching Felicity walk across the wide expanse of verdant lawn. She took a deep breath, trying to keep her temper in check. It did no good to get in a shouting match with her mother; she knew that well enough. She could never win such a battle, for she was never willing to take it as far or as furious as Anne Lawrence was prepared to go. Usually, she would begin to weep, mostly in anger, well before they got the argument escalated to where Anne was satisfied. "Mother, I know you love her, and I am grateful that you spend such lovely time with her. Really, I am. But you must be careful what you teach Felicity. She will need to live in a world far different from yours."

"Well, of course I know that, Arden. After all I'm not a fool," her mother said, yawning widely and covering her yawn with a graceful, well-manicured hand. "But I daresay some things will never change, and the niggers are one of them, and pretty dresses are another, and the ways of a man with a maid are likely a third. These are the things we speak of, mostly, and so I don't think you need worry about Lacey. She's a smart gal, much smarter than I was at her age, and she'll make out just fine." Her mother laughed lightly. "She knows I'm just an old woman who loves her and loves to prattle on in the lazy afternoons about the old days."

"Everything you say to her," Arden said stiffly, "she takes as gospel. As though it came from God on high."

"And so it does." Anne yawned again. "I'm just as much His instrument as you are." She rose, groaning slightly and standing upright with a bit of difficulty and ceremony. "And now, if you'll excuse me, it's time for my nap. All this talking just wears me out."

She descended the stairs lightly and with no trace of hesitation. She is ageless, Arden thought weakly. Daunting, ageless, and totally without a sense of guilt. She sat down in the chaise her mother had just vacated with a sense of deep fatigue. What a nice way that must be to live one's life, she thought then. Had it not been for the nuns, perhaps I might have the same resources.

A movement in the side corner of her vision caught her attention then, and Arden turned to see Hanna coming up toward her mother's cottage, carrying her mother's clean linen in her arms. Behind her toddled her boy, Cake. He was a fat and thriving child, black as an anvil and full of himself. He stopped often behind Hanna, picking up stones and small twigs, throwing them clumsily at imagined adversaries and shouting out for his mama to watch him. Hanna looked older

than her years, almost gray at the temples, though she could
not be yet thirty. Four times, she had borne children and
three times seen them sold from River Reach before they
were five years old.

Cake was past four, to the best of Arden's memory, and
likely he was the next to go. Everything in Hanna's step and
the bend of her back said that she knew that as well as anyone on the plantation. Arden could not imagine what that
must feel like—to give birth to a child, to nurse it and tend it
and love it, only to know that, all too soon, it would be gone
from you. Likely, Hanna would never see her other children
again. Never even know if they were alive or dead, unless
she simply happened to get word by the grapevine, extensive
and all-reaching, which the slaves had among themselves.

Would you try not to love the child at all? Would you be
able to live each day, knowing how temporary the child was
in your life? But on the other hand, Arden realized—an argument her mother might well make if she thought of it—
aren't all children essentially the same way? They are, each
of them, only in our lives temporarily and can be taken at
any time by a power out of our control.

Arden watched Hanna as she came closer, her slow, lazy
tread as aimless and careless as though she barely cared if
she got there at all. She was heavy with another pregnancy,
and her breasts hung on her chest like two emptied feed
sacks. Arden wondered how much of a slave's tired demeanor was despair and how much was inherent laziness, as
their detractors claimed. There was nothing slow and lazy
about Cake; that much was certain. What sort of man would
he make in a dozen years?

As the two of them neared the house, Hanna did a curious
thing. She silently pointed at the copse of azaleas which
clustered close to Anne Lawrence's cottage. Without a word
or a hesitation, Cake disappeared into the bushes like a rabbit. Only when he was completely hidden and invisible did
Hanna then knock on the door. Anne's servant answered,
Hanna greeted her and handed her the linens, they ex-

changed small pleasantries, and then the door closed again. Cake did not reappear at his mother's side until she was once more well away from Anne Lawrence's door, out of sight of most of her windows. And then, Cake burst from the azaleas as though from a chicken coop, hopping and crowing with the excitement of hiding. He bent again to pick up another stick, threw it high in the air, and followed along behind his mother back to the quarters.

Christmas season came to River Reach that year with a special fervor, for it was to be the last when both boys would be at home. In January, they were to be sent to West Point on the Hudson, where they would be graduated, Martin hoped, with earnest goals and a fine, classical education.

"I know it is largely a military academy," he told Arden privately, "and I don't want them to be soldiers, by any means. But it's superb for teaching them to lead, it's attracting some of the best minds in the country, and they will meet many young men there who will be their peers in later life. Some of the finest sons of the best families will be their classmates, and it is no small honor to get an appointment to the academy."

"I know," she said. "Were it not for your father's stint in the legislature so many years ago, they would not have been accepted. Certainly *my* family's name alone would not have been sufficient."

"Well, they'll learn a good deal about managing men there," Martin added, "and the education they'll receive will be first-rate, I hope. Actually," he confided, "they won't need much of their lessons to run River Reach, but the discipline will do them no harm, they'll get comfortable with the idea of command and order, and what ideas they'll experience! That alone is worth their departure, I should think. They've outgrown Master Frieberg . . ."

"So has Filly," she said quickly. Master Frieberg was the tutor at River Reach, hired to give all three children their lessons since they were quite young. A middle-aged teacher from Boston, Master Frieberg traveled to five plantations in the county and came to River Reach once each week. He had managed to teach the children the rudiments of reading, numbers, and a little history, but his visit was hardly the highpoint of their week, and Arden often suspected that the hours she spent with them over their books were far more productive than the lessons he was able to devise.

"Well, and Filly shall have something better when it's her turn," Martin said. "But for now, I think the boys must be seen to, sweet, for they're growing fast and will have the responsibility for everything." He beamed at her proudly. "They'll leave here boys and come home to us young men."

"Yes," she said faintly, trying to match his happiness. To see her two boys gone from her seemed unusually hard to bear this winter, for Filly was growing away from her as well. She sometimes felt she had only dreamed her children, rather than borne them. And Martin had changed over the years also. They still loved each other, it wasn't that, she told herself often. But the people they had become over the long seasons of life no longer seemed to satisfy their deepest dreams. Martin was always so busy now, either in the fields, at his desk, or up at his study poring over his charts and maps of the universe. They had lost that enchanted realm they once inhabited, Arden thought wistfully, where they were everything to each other. And in exchange, they had a family and an empire. "Do you have plans for Filly as well?" she asked.

"Well, not just yet, of course," he said with a smile. "She'll need to stay under her mama's wing a mite more, I'd say. But in time, she could go to Columbus Institute for young ladies, and that's fairly close to us, or even up north, if you think she'd do better. A girl these days needs even more education than a boy, for the boys will only run the land, but a girl must run a husband."

She could not help but smile then, despite her sense of emptiness. A few nights later, Martin sat them all down and told Owen and Micah that he had arranged their appointments to West Point. After telling them of the fine futures which might be theirs, he added, "And I hope that you both will resolve that you will faithfully and tirelessly labor to see what you can accomplish there. After all, it's not every young man who gets the opportunity—"

"We will, Father," Owen said eagerly. "Won't we, Micah! West Point!" He was always the more enthusiastic of the two.

Micah nodded thoughtfully. "I expect we'll be rubbing elbows with a lot of sons of politicians, Father?"

"And planters and generals and important businessmen from all over the country. I want you to be educated away from the South, Micah. And you, too, Owen. The world is changing, and I should think you would want to be part of that change. So improve your minds and rein in your tempers"—with that, he looked pointedly at Owen—"and refine your manners."

Felicity giggled at that, and Arden shot her a reproving glance. She rolled her eyes at her mother, but she kept still.

"I truly believe, boys—and this is for you, too, Filly—" Martin went on, "that it is the cultivation of the mind and the controlling of the temper which elevates men a portion above the vulgar herd. It matters less how much land they have than how much grace and elegance they bring to their bearing." He surveyed his children one by one, his expression solemn. "Do you understand me, all of you?"

"Yes, Father," they all said obediently.

"Excellent, then," he smiled. "Mother, do you wish to add anything to my remarks?"

Arden tried to match his dignified bearing. She stood and faced all three of her babies, so suddenly grown and so irretrievably gone from her in many small and intimate ways. "Just that it's well to avoid low company, my sons. Try to associate only with refined individuals, for your manners soon tell what company you keep. Recollect, dear boys—especially you, Owen—that you have a name to preserve."

With that, Felicity laughed again, infectiously and merrily, tossing a pillow at Owen in delight. "Yes, *Odin*. Don't forget you have a name to preserve!"

At that, Martin and Arden could not help but join in the laughter, for it was true that Owen had been nicknamed "Odin" by his sister when she had first learned about the Norse myths from Master Frieberg. "Odin" because he was the God of Thunder, for Owen was given to unrestrained and unseemly flatulence anytime he got overly excited—which for Owen, seemed to happen regularly as the clock struck the hour.

Owen leaped on her for revenge, of course, which was exactly what she had planned. As Micah joined in and all three children and all available pillows swiftly ended up on the oriental rug, Arden laughed and shook her head, glancing at Martin first to be sure that he shared the humor.

Martin had sunk down in his chair, his eyes wistfully following their antics, his mouth softly smiling in an almost painful joy. And in that moment, she knew that he loved them as she did; that he would miss them even as much in his own way. She went to his side and caressed his brow softly. "We've been blessed," she said softly.

"Always," he answered her.

Finally, finally, Christmas came round, and the cotton was laid by, and the year drew to its natural end. Arden had been very busy, for it seemed half the people in the quarters were down with some sickness or another. "You coddle them," Anne told her shortly. "One gets sick and the other sees that it's a good bargain, and before long, every boy's down with some imagined fever or another, all so they don't need to work a lick. Put a few of them out in the fields, fever or no, and you'll get them back into shape soon enough."

"Or get them into their graves," Arden said shortly to her. "I expect I can tell, Mama, who's playing possum and who's sick as a hound."

Arden had been in charge of the health of Martin's people since she came to River Reach, learning a little more each season about how to keep the hands well and content. She held little truck with the leeches, lancets, and blistering that kept most of the physicians in the county in practice. Instead, she used poultices of linseed oil, herbs, onions, potatoes, and various roots which she collected in the woods behind the plantation. She used the inside bark of the willow tree for pain, the magnolia kernel against fevers, sassafras for tonic, and the wax myrtle for dysentery. She was proud of the fact that at most times of the year, less than ten percent of her people were out of the fields for sickness of any sort.

She told Filly again and again, "You must consider their health your most important job. You need to *feel* that it is above all your other duties and bear in mind that they must be attended to like children, but most especially when they are ill. Remember, three times a day—"

"Yes, Mother," Filly said dutifully as she joined Arden in her rounds.

But Arden knew that for every admonition she offered Filly, her grandmama offered another much different opinion.

Particularly in the winter season, the sickness always increased. And this year was unusually damp and cold, and the hands, especially the old uncles and aunties, complained of aches and pains with more regularity. Even Martin groaned as he left the bed these days, saying that his knees ached like those of an old plow horse.

The earth was frozen fast and early, hard enough to strike a match on it. The skies were unyielding, iron-gray and scudded with clouds day after day with no rain. The fields were griddled with ice in the rows, and the leafless trees stood stark about the house as though this were New England, not Natchez. "De cold come on too fast," Portia said glumly. "Seems like, even de sun be out o' time dis year."

Arden asked Martin privately, "Dear, do you fear next year's crop, if this cold keeps up into spring?"

"My sweet, I'm a farmer," Martin said ruefully.
"There's nothing I don't fear. But I did take the precaution
this harvest of directing my factor to send our money overseas to Liverpool. No sense keeping it in Northern banks another year, with the way things are going. So don't you fret.
We'll have enough to eat, I wager, even if the Mississippi
freezes over."

And so cold or not, aches and pains or not, Christmas
came at last, and Arden assembled the boys and Felicity on
the front veranda, and Martin called Joseph to bring out the
house servants and the special morning punch. Felicity was
dressed in one of her best day gowns, her hair done in long
curls down her back, her green velvet gloves and green morocco slippers a perfect touch for the season. Anne had taken
much pains and pleasure in dressing her for the occasion,
and this outfit was commonplace next to what she would
wear for the various Christmas *fêtes* she would attend over
the week.

Owen and Micah looked like slenderer versions of their
father, with brocade vests and long jackets, their stylish
stove-top hats making them seem even taller than they were.
Anne wore her finest long cloak, made of beaver skins and
otter tails, as regal as any foreign queen. Portia lined up the
servants, each one in her widest skirt and whitest apron.
Portia's head kerchief was pinned with scarlet flowers. At
Martin's signal, Joseph rang the big iron bell which was only
used for emergencies or this special morning.

And there they all came, up the hill from the quarters.
Aunt 'Becca led the tenders, those children of a young age,
up to the big house for their parade. She had her head kerchief tied to high points, and she strutted proud and slow as
an old, fat goose. Behind her, two by two, the little negroes
danced in their new trousers and shirts, giggling and shush-
ing each other, crowing aloud when they saw the veranda of
the big house lined with the white folk and the house people,
all come to see them parade. Aunt 'Becca brought the little
ones round, herded them into proper order, and said, "Min'

you' manners, now!'' and they quieted down, their eyes
white and gleaming, their faces wreathed in huge grins.
Then all at once, they shouted, ''Cris'mas gif! Cris'mas
gif!,'' their hands waving in the air.

At that, Felicity and Arden stepped forward with baskets
of oranges, whistles, little cakes, apples, and hard candies.
The children came up one by one to get their treats, making
their bob-down bows and curtsies and murmuring, ''Thank-
ee, ma'm,'' then bouncing away, shouting and capering
under Joseph's inspection and Aunt 'Becca's repeated orders to ''Be good, now! You there, Jack, you min' yo' manners, boy!'' until Joseph waved her away. Then, completely
out of order now and all parade form forgotten, the children
ran away back to the quarters, shouting with delight at their
new treasures.

And then came the older hands, pressing forward almost
shyly, many of them silent but grinning their delight at the
master and his ladies on the veranda of the big white house.
Joseph came forward with bundles, handing out each
gravely, with Martin taking the time to say a word to each
slave and patting the backs of a few special workers. Each
man was given a new pair of trousers, a new pair of shoes, a
wool blanket, and a shiny dollar gold coin. They all took off
their hats to Felicity and Arden, gazing respectfully at the
houseservants, who smiled regally at them from their preferred position of the upper reaches of the veranda. The women
came forward then, to receive from Joseph a new skirt, a
new pair of shoes, a length of calico cloth, and—to Arden's
great pleasure—their own shiny dollar gold coin.

''They should get one, too,'' Arden had told Martin the
first year she'd been at River Reach. ''No woman should
have to beg her man for something for herself or her children.''

He had agreed, and forever after, the women had taken
their own coins from Martin's hand, bowing and murmuring
their thanks shyly, slipping away, clutching the coins and
biting them furtively as they'd seen the men do. Then the

whole passel of them broke out in cheers and laughter and dancing, as they trooped back to the quarters.

Later in the day, Arden filled three large tables with food, pulled up chairs, and invited the grown hands to feast together. She read to them from the Bible then, as she did every year, and led them in the singing of "O Come All Ye Faithful" and the Lord's Prayer. The tables groaned with pork and eggs, fried chicken and ham, puddings and cakes, and fresh oranges and apples. A large cauldron simmered with boiled molasses, and Moses took it off the fire, laid it out in slabs on the grass, and when it cooled, they pulled it into candy. Uncle Dan tuned up his fiddle and they danced to "Possum up the Stump" and "Arkansas Traveler," jigging and clapping and celebrating until dusk. Felicity danced too, with her brothers and her father, and Arden took a turn or two with Martin. Even Anne, putting aside her cloak, took Micah by the arm and showed him how to waltz, calling out to Uncle Dan to slow the music down to her taste.

Once night came, then the family moved inside to have Christmas dinner and gifts among themselves, and the joyous noise from the quarters continued until midnight.

As the evening ended, Arden went to Owen's room and then Micah's room in turn, telling each boy that she loved him, that she knew he would do well at West Point, and that they would be missed by everyone at River Reach while they were at school. As Martin passed her in the hall, on his way to say his own private farewells to his sons, he saw her cheeks wet in the lamplight. He embraced her silently, holding her and stroking her hair. Then he released her, and she went to their bedroom to let go of the last of her grief.

Cake was sent away soon after, despite Hanna's attempts to keep him out of sight from her mistress. He was loaded onto the buggy which went into Natchez each week, along with the extra eggs, the corn, and three dressed shoats for trading. From there, he would go to the block, where male slaves of any age fetched a pretty price. Arden was coming back from the quarters that morning where an outbreak of croup had laid low two of her hands, and she saw Hanna bring Cake to the wagon and stand quietly while he was set in the back by the bushels of corn. Dick, the driver, was teasing him loudly, trying to make him laugh, but Cake kept his eyes pinned solid to his mother, who stood alongside the wagon silently.

She had dressed him in the best cloth she could find, a faded red coat she must have made for him from dress scraps and a pair of long trousers, likely the first he'd ever worn. He was barefoot, but he looked older than his age under his broad felt hat.

Cake stood it well until Dick called out "Get up" to the mule and the wagon lurched forward. Then he wailed aloud once, a piercing call which shivered Arden's heart. At that, Hanna began to sob, running alongside the moving wagon and reaching up to her boy, trying to touch his trouser leg in a last farewell. Dick's mouth turned down in a silent grimace, and he hurried the mule to a trot, but Hanna was young and strong, despite her belly, and she was able to keep up, nearly to the drive. Then, as the wagon pulled away from her and Cake's wails grew fainter, she stumbled and fell into the dust, weeping and pulling at her skirts as if to pull every vestige of civility off her body, hitting at her belly as though to erase the child within.

Arden stood silently, tears gathering in her eyes. She was not able to look away, as much as she wished to, was not able to stop the wagon, even though she felt she should. She glanced back at Anne's porch, but her mother was nowhere apparent. With a heavy sigh, she walked out to where Hanna still lay in the dust. She touched the slave on the shoulder and spoke to her softly. Hanna shivered away from her hand as though it were poison to her skin. Arden could see she was trying to stifle her sobs against her arm, trying to grieve more quietly, but the wracking pain made her sound like a howling cat, less human than animal. Arden bent then and pulled her upright, holding her by the shoulder. ''Come now, Hanna, let's get you out of the sun,'' she said wearily. ''There's no use for this, you know. You'll only break your heart.''

Hanna was incoherent, her face old and wrinkled well past her years. Arden was momentarily shocked at the change in the woman. It seemed to her that only a few years before, Hanna had been one of the healthiest, most vigorous young slaves on the plantation. She took her firmly by the hand and led her back to her quarters, leaving her on her bed to finish her grieving alone.

As Arden walked once more past her mother's house, Anne called to her from the porch. ''I should have sent him away a bit sooner,'' she said sadly, ''I blame myself. I let Hanna keep him too long. She got too attached to that one. Poor nigger.''

''Don't call her that,'' Arden said, low and weary.

''What should I call her, then?'' Anne's brows went up in slight indignation.

''We call them servants or people or hands or negroes, Mother, you know that. I've said it a hundred times.''

''That lil' ol' gal? She's not a servant, that's for sure,'' Anne said lightly.

Arden said nothing more to her mother. There was nothing she could say, really. Nothing that her mother would understand. She went up the steps to the big house, and there at the window, Felicity stood, still gazing outside. Likely, she had seen everything.

Arden went to her daughter and put her hand on her shoulder, turning her gently around. Felicity's face was wet with tears, but her mouth was firm. ''I don't see why they can't be taken off after dark,'' she said fretfully. ''After Hanna's asleep, so the whole house doesn't have to hear her carrying on like that.'' She wiped at her eyes with a hand small and delicate as a peony blossom. ''She rolled in the dirt just like a dog,'' she murmured, almost angrily. ''Father shouldn't allow such a thing.''

"Perhaps he shouldn't," Arden said, keeping her temper in check. "Perhaps he shouldn't allow it at all. But so long as your grandmother insists on keeping her people like so many brood mares, Hanna and Carrie are going to be weeping every few years, when one of their babies is sent away."

"Carrie doesn't carry on like that," Felicity said, angry now at her mother since there was no place else to direct her despair.

"Carrie did, when Jim was taken off, but you just didn't see it. She'll weep all over again when Rose is sold, so if you don't want to get yourself upset, best keep away from the windows on that day." She knew her tongue was sharper than she intended, but her daughter was frightening her in some fundamental way she could not define.

"I guess I'll do just that," Felicity said defiantly, stalking away.

Arden leaned against the window sadly and watched her lovely daughter mount the stairs. Her body was lithe and strong, tender and soft all at once. And so, of course, was her heart. Arden wondered if the same could be said of her soul.

She loved her so much! And yet her daughter gave her more pain than both boys together. Filly was her mirror and she was Filly's as well. When she looked into Filly's face, she saw her own grown young again—and also her mother's. She had sprung from her womb like a slippery fish and had been swimming away ever since. How to hold her! How to let her go?

Arden turned and looked out over the fields, wishing in that moment that Martin would come riding up on his horse, strong and straight in his saddle, carrying his whip with that off hand air of command he had always, unconsciously and effortlessly making her feel rooted to the ground again and safe. Filly was whirling away from them in a way the boys never had, maybe never would. And only she could see it; only she would suffer the loss. She knew it as surely as she knew that the fields would always be there and the rains would come once more.

*   *   *

In 1850, the first full-blown secession crisis hit Congress,
when California was admitted as a free state and Utah and
New Mexico were being organized with no mention that
slavery would be allowed within those regions. The Southern states had staunchly supported the Mexican War in the
hopes that slave territory would be expanded. Now they understood finally that their "peculiar institution" would
likely be banned from the lands they had helped win, and
they were affronted. John Quitman, Natchez planter and
Mississippi Governor, became an outspoken partisan for
Southern expansion. Jeff Davis, United States Senator for
Mississippi, had fought in the Mexican War as commander
of the famed Mississippi Rifles. He joined Quitman in demanding that slavery be allowed in the new territories.

Other men, some said cooler heads, were more inclined to
accept the compromise of 1850. Many planters knew they
had the most to lose from war, and they had few illusions
that the South could win. Some had traveled in the North; all
did business there, and they had an economic stake in its rail-
roads and banks. Martin was not the only planter who expressed private concerns about the coming confrontation. At
supper, when guests were present, he sometimes said mildly,
"I don't know why we can't stay in the Union and keep our
slaves as well. It seems to me that we need some constitu-
tional guarantees to protect us, and the North needs our cotton at prices only slave labor can produce."

"Sometimes I wish to God we'd never had slaves at all,"
Arden said quietly.

"So do I," Martin agreed. "But we've got them now and
we can't do without them. I figured it out the other day. One
acre of cotton has seventy rows, each one more than two
hundred feet across. That's nearly fifteen thousand lineal
feet to the acre. Say a man had fifteen acres . . ."

"He'd starve," scoffed Anne. "Leastwhys, in Natchez.

Why, I don't know a man who's got less than five hundred—"

"Just for the sake of argument," Martin said patiently. "Just to make his crop, a man's got to pass over his ground twenty-two times a season, plowing and planting and hoeing and weeding and cutting and clumping and what all—so he'd travel more than nine hundred miles on that fifteen acres. Nine hundred miles!"

"And we've got more than eight hundred acres," Arden said, amazed.

"Exactly. And we've not got as much as some. So you see why I say, we can't do it without the colored. We'd *all* starve, like as not." Martin shook his head. "Yet I wish it weren't so. And I hope the North will let us work out something which will let both sides keep their honor."

Sometimes he met with agreement, but sometimes, even at his own table, he was all but shouted down by neighbors and friends who called his compromising attitude near treason to the Southern cause.

In his own house, Anne Lawrence was often the first to call his thinking muddle-headed, the loudest voice of resentment against any Yankee interference in States' Rights. "Why, when we joined this Union," she said indignantly at the table, "it was supposed to be a government with the consent of the governed. Any schoolboy knows that! Well, we no longer consent, that's plain enough. And so they've got to let us go, I say, and if they try to stop us, they'll have such a fight on their hands—"

"Mother," Arden said calmly, "I insist that we not make our dining table another Waterloo. Surely, there is room for different opinions without such fiery rhetoric. When Martin expresses his hope that we can avoid war, he's saying no more than a dozen other good men in high places are saying—"

"And a good lot of them fools and cowards," Anne cut her off short. "Not you, Martin, of course," she added solemnly to Martin, "but we have our share of both in Congress and our own Mississippi legislature."

"Why, Grandmama," Felicity said earnestly, "you sound like you *want* a war to happen. Wouldn't that be a terrible thing for everybody?"

A long silence lay about the table then, and Martin smiled at his daughter fondly. "You are absolutely correct, Filly," he said softly. "It would be terrible, indeed. And I'm sure your grandmother does not wish such a calamity on us. Perhaps we can hope our fools and cowards slow us down just enough to think before we exchange bullets . . . or insults, overmuch."

"I'd rather see a war than have us bow to dictators," Anne said defiantly. "We have a duty to the constitution to defend it—"

"You know, it astounds me," Martin countered mildly, "how logic changes over the years. How is it that we Southerners have come to equate bondage for our slaves with freedom for ourselves and rebellion against the nation with loyalty to the constitution? It really does baffle me."

Arden smiled.

Anne did not. "If we have to have a war to get things right again, then I say, let's get on with it."

"Another paradox. You seem to be saying that only by waging war can you achieve peace."

"Oh, you are such an infuriating man!" Anne finally sputtered, standing and throwing down her napkin on her plate. "You've completely ruined my appetite!" And she stalked out of the room.

Felicity said quietly, "Father, I wonder if it's such a good idea to rile her so."

"I suppose you're right," Martin said wearily. "But she's so wrong-headed these days . . . along with half the county, it seems." He sighed. "But I will try to remember myself hereafter, Filly. No sense in any of us going without our supper, after all."

Felicity smiled at him then and held her tongue. Arden

wondered what an effort that must have been for her, and she doubted that the effort would last for long.

Meanwhile, Natchez was spreading and thriving, and cotton profits were sailing sky-high once more. A good thing, Portia said often, that the Master was rich, the way Felicity was growing. "Needs a new dress 'mos every week, an' ain' happy wid home-grown lace, no m'am! Miss Filly say dat de French got a way wid fabric dat is nigh unmistakable!" Arden sighed and ordered up another gown, for Portia was right. Filly was growing fast.

And so was Natchez. Some wag named the town "the Versailles of the South," and her citizens did their best to live up to that fame. At Pharsalia Race Track, the finest blooded horses in the state, like Hardheart, Pelham, Lexington, and Le Comte, raced in two- and four-mile heats. Fortunes were won and lost in the space of moments, but it was said—with much pride—that no man won or lost more graciously than a Natchez planter.

Steamboat races were frequent and the excitement they produced frenzied enough so that outlying folks traveled to the river to be part of the spectacle. All talk of crops or politics stopped for that race, while men and their ladies placed wagers, planned outings, and argued with their neighbors over which ship would best the other. The captains of the two steamboats visited the finest houses, drank imported wines, flattered the women, and generally attempted to best the other in boasts and wit. They stripped the racing vessels of every encumbrance, threw off the spars, tossed over the deck chairs and the sideskiffs, and even sanded the gilding off the rails, took off their kid gloves, and shaved their mustaches—all to lighten the ships for speed.

One season, Anne insisted that the whole family had to go and see what all the fuss was about, just once, if they expected to count themselves as loyal Mississippeans. So Martin dressed up the buggy, Arden and Felicity fussed over their finest gowns, and the entire entourage rode into Natchez to stay at the best hotel and watch the steamboats come in.

It seemed to Arden that most of the countryside was abandoned for the streets of the city that evening, most particularly the bluffs and the houses overlooking the river. The rival boats had started upriver at Vicksburg, and they were due to round the bank at Natchez about dusk.

They walked down toward Natchez-Under-the-Hill, again at Anne's insistence. As they descended Silver Street, the throngs around them thickened. The narrow alleys and steep backways of the little town, more a village really, nestled under the city of Natchez like a bedraggled chick under a hen's wing.

Down to Water Street they walked, and here the buggies were so crowded that they could scarcely pass. The low, broken, half-sunken sidewalks were jammed with those walking. Fashionably dressed young men smoked and lounged, highly rouged females beckoned to sailors, Kentucky boatmen, negroes and negresses, mulattoes, pigs, dogs, and dirty children moved through the finer-dressed crowd hurrying to the docks.

As they came to the bottom of the street, Arden knew for certain that bringing Felicity had been a mistake. In fact, it was highly likely that no woman in Martin's household should have been there. If one listened and looked—which Arden tried not to do and tried, also, to divert Felicity from doing—one could see and hear profanity and revels, barrooms and brothels, the clink of silver at a dozen roulette and faro tables, in short the whole underside of life not allowed within the parlors of Natchez, proper.

"I do wonder," Martin said with some discomfort, "if we might have watched the races from the bluffs just as well." He had Felicity by one arm and Arden by the other, Portia crowding Felicity so close and glaring so fiercely that no one dared approach her save her family. "Whoever said Natchez had feet of clay told no lie."

"Nonsense," Anne said airily. "This is the stuff of life, Martin! We're as safe as in the finest parlor in Natchez."

Suddenly a dockhand shouted out, "Steamboat a-comin!" and the crowd surged forward with shouts of glee. Martin hurried Arden, Anne, and Felicity to a high point on the bluff, away from the throngs, and there in the distance, they saw a moving light. First one, and then the other appeared, two specks like two stars, off in the immensity of the black river and the velvet-dark sky, slowly getting bigger and bigger, sliding closer. Torches were lit all up and down the street, bells rang out, and the steamboats came on, faster now, bigger, finally so close that, in their lights, the onlookers could see their long white lines, the gingerbread trim of their turrets, their towering smokestacks, the roustabouts shouting on the decks. Horns blew, cannons boomed, men shouted, "Steamboat comin'! Steamboat comin'!"

"I do hope the *Defiance* is as fast as they say," Anne said happily. "I placed a healthy wager on her."

"You placed a bet on the boats, Mama?" Arden asked, amazed.

"Of course I did," Anne replied with a chuckle. "Why should the menfolk have all the fun?"

"I took the *Liberty*," Martin said.

"Of course you did," Anne purred at him.

But as the two boats pulled closer, Martin began to grin just like a boy, for the crowds were shouting, "*Liberty! Liberty!*" and it was clear that Martin had won.

"Ain' nothing like it!" a man crowed at them as he went past. "Nothin' on land nor water!"

One steamboat pulled in, rammed the dock, and then the other, right behind it, like two huge white cows jostling for space at a single trough. The throngs set up a cheer, the bands played, and as they walked back up the hill, Arden saw ladies gasping and fanning themselves from sheer excitement.

Martin said, "I wonder if there's anyplace else where fortunes can be won or lost so quick as Natchez."

"Wasn't it brilliant!" Anne laughed, clapping him on the shoulder.

"Mama, I do believe you had more fun than the roust-abouts," Arden murmured.

"I believe I did!" Anne crowed. "I don't even mind losing. The spectacle was worth it!"

"And Mama, do you know what I heard at the hotel?" Felicity asked, all aglow with the giddy thrill of being in such a place at such an hour. "Miss Jenny Lind is coming to Natchez to sing! At the Methodist Church! The Swedish Nightingale, they call her; Papa, do you think we could get tickets?"

"Well, Filly, I don't know," Martin hesitated as he steered their little troop back up onto safer streets and toward the hotel. "How much will the tickets be?"

"Fifty dollars," Anne said staunchly. "And I'll buy them for you, Lacey, if your father won't. Why, it isn't every day that a young lady gets to see such a thing."

"That won't be necessary," Martin said smoothly, taking Arden's arm in one hand and Felicity's in the other. "I'm sure we can afford such a luxury once in a while." He smiled at his daughter. "The Swedish Nightingale, eh? Who will come to Natchez next?"

"Owen and Micah, I hope, and on a slower, safer vessel," Arden said shortly. "That will be the only thing which might bring me to these streets again anytime soon."

Anne laughed at her daughter, patting her on the shoulder as she might have comforted an aging aunt, and gaily pushed ahead through the crowds toward the music which flowed out of the open doors of their hotel.

It was in 1855, while Owen and Micah were home for the holidays, that Anne decided it was time to send away Hanna's fifth child, a four-year-old girl named Pansy. This time, at Arden's suggestion, the child was to be collected early in the morning, before dawn. Hanna had been told she must say her farewell inside her own cabin, and so though Arden lay awake next to Martin that morning with a heavy heart, she was relieved she would not have that scene burned onto her memory once more.

To her surprise, a soft knock came at the door. Portia's whispered "Miz Arden?" galvanized Arden immediately, and she moved from the bed, already grabbing for her wrapper, her mind filled with foreboding. She slipped her feet into her shoes, opened the door, and stepped outside onto the shadowed landing.

Portia had the lamp in her hand and Arden's cape and physic bag. "Dick say come quick, Miz Arden, dere's trouble wid Hanna."

"What sort of trouble?" she asked as she descended the stairs quickly, taking the bag from Portia with one hand and buttoning up her cape.

"Don' know, ma'm. He say de lil' gal is sick."

Arden groaned aloud. She stepped out, leaving Portia to close the door behind her. Surely Hanna did not think she'd stop fate with such an excuse; better to get it over and done now, rather than put it off 'til it's only harder—

She walked quickly across the wet grass, noticing the single lamp which always burned in her mother's room, no matter the hour or the season. It was impossible to tell whether Anne slept well or not, for the light or its lack was no clue. She reached Hanna's door and pulled it open, her hand instantly going to her mouth in horror when she saw Pansy on Hanna's bed.

The little girl was naked and whimpering in pain. Her legs were both bent at awkward angles, her kneecaps jutting away from her thighs as though disconnected and floating free. Hanna sat, white-faced and silent, gazing at the floor. Dick hovered against the wall, his hat in his hand, his eyes wide and frightened.

"You can go now, Dick," Arden said quietly. "We'll not take Pansy this trip."

"Yes'm," he said, relieved, going out the door.

Arden went to the child and tried to touch her leg, but Pansy shrieked in fear and pain at the slightest movement. "Both these legs are broken," Arden said calmly to Hanna. "And badly."

"Yes'm," Hanna said, her voice small and sleepy, as though she were a small child just awakened.

"Did you do this?" she asked.

Hanna looked at her daughter as if seeing her for the first time. "No'm," she murmured. "She fall 'gainst de bed."

Arden gazed down at the suffering child. Strong desperate hands had twisted those limbs. "Look at me, Hanna. She didn't fall. She was deliberately maimed."

Hanna lifted her head, and she gave Arden a brief, burning glance of hatred and shame and pleading, all at once. "No'm," she repeated then, her voice dull. "She fall."

"Child, did your mother do this to you?" Arden turned to the little girl.

Pansy closed her eyes in pain and shock. She only whimpered, trembling and clasping her hands tightly together in the bed linens. Arden opened her bag quickly and pulled out her bottle of laudanum and a spoon. She dosed the child heavily, watching as she greedily took down the liquid as though it were salvation. "This will make you sleep and take away some of your pain," she said wearily. "Tomorrow, the doctor will come and set your legs, child." She turned to Hanna. "With luck, she may walk again. She's young enough to heal."

"Yes'm," Hanna replied, no emotion at all in her voice.

"Cover her up," Arden said shortly, "lest she catch her death on top of everything else."

She took up her bag and left the fetid, shadowed cabin, walking swiftly back to the big house. Her heart was squeezed tightly with pain like a mouth which had tasted straight vinegar. As she passed the tall oak, when no one could see her, she stopped and vomited once in the dirt, gasping and coughing as though to rid herself of a powerful toxin. She leaned against the tree until she could walk again without weaving. Then, she went back upstairs to lie down beside Martin until dawn.

When morning came, of course, there was a flurry of chaos, all of which had to be reordered with a minimum of noise and acknowledgment, lest the other slaves and the children be upset more than was necessary. When Anne heard what had happened, she went white with shock and then pink at all the edges of her face and mouth. Rigid with anger and disgust, she marched to the breeding cabin, where she stayed just long enough to see for herself how ugly the scene was within. The doctor came and set Pansy's legs. Her high shrill shrieks of pain were awful to hear, and Anne demanded that Hanna sit and witness every one.

The doctor reported that it was highly unlikely that Pansy could ever walk normally again, for even though she was young and healthy, the bones had been broken in several directions and their healing would be painful, slow, and possibly inadequate. "When the victim is as young as this," he said, "the mending often halts the natural growth or anyway slows it. She may well have both legs crippled or at least unnaturally short for her torso, if she walks at all." He looked away over the fields when he told Arden and Anne this news, as though the hazy sunshine might somehow soften what he had only just witnessed. His mouth was set and hard with distaste.

After the doctor left, Arden went upstairs to see Felicity. The boys had taken an early breakfast, quiet and subdued by what they knew was happening in the quarters. They'd quickly saddled their mounts and gone out to hunt pigeons on the Trace, and for that she was grateful. By the time they returned at dusk, the worst would be over.

But Filly was still in bed. Now that she was nearing sixteen, she had begun to sleep later and later each morning, putting off her lessons until late in the afternoon. This was rather a trial for Arden, who was by nature and discipline an early riser. But this morning, she was glad for Filly's ability to sleep through most turmoil.

Felicity was sitting upright in her bed when her mother knocked and entered, and her face told Arden immediately that she already knew at least part of the circumstances of the day. She sat with her back to the window, which was in itself an unusual place to find her. When she saw Arden, she asked quickly, "Has the doctor gone yet?"

"Yes, he has," Arden said softly. "Did Nell tell you what happened?" Nell was Filly's personal maidservant and had been since she put on long skirts. Nell also was a woman prone to hyperbole and dire predictions, and Arden would have preferred the news to have come to her daughter from almost any other quarter.

"She told me Pansy fell and broke her legs." Felicity studied her mother pensively. "But I don't believe her."

"Nor do I," Arden said, "but that's Hanna's story."

"Hanna's a fool and a liar," Felicity said with small venom, "and she should be whipped for doing such a wicked thing! Poor Pansy!"

"Poor Pansy, indeed," Arden agreed smoothly. She sat down on Felicity's white wide bed and fingered the soft coverlet carefully. "What about poor Hanna?"

"Hanna is only being selfish," Felicity said swiftly. "She wants Pansy to stay with her, and she's only thinking of herself. Grandmama says that Pansy will have a much better life away from here, that she'll likely serve some fine mistress in Baton Rouge and live in a nice house—"

"And what does that mean to a four-year-old child?" Arden asked softly. "All Pansy knows is that she's leaving her mother. And all Hanna knows is that she's losing her child." She reached out and touched Felicity on her hand. "If I had to face such a prospect, that someone was going to take you away from me when you were too little even to understand, much less take care of yourself, I think I'd . . ." She stopped, and her voice thickened. "I don't know what I'd do, but I know I couldn't stand it."

Felicity was silent, her head bowed.

"What your grandmama is doing is wrong," she said qui-

etly. "You must know that, child. It might be right according to the law, but it's wrong according to God."

"Grandmama says that it's in the Bible."

"What is?"

"That nig—that they're supposed to be slaves, and they
have to mind us."

Arden remembered then the passage that Anne had quoted
once or twice smugly, from the New Testament. It was from
Ephesians, and it went something like, slaves be obedient to
those who are your earthly masters, with fear and trembling.
It was an argument she had heard from others as well, lately,
when talk of the Compromise rose at supper tables. The jus-
tification by the very Word of God. "Just because the Bible
says they are to be slaves doesn't mean we should sell away
their children from them, Filly. We have a responsibility to
care for them with kindness. You must feel that someplace
in your heart, don't you?"

Felicity nodded slowly. "But what Hanna did was wrong,
too," she murmured.

"Yes, you're right," Arden said, standing now and caressing Felicity's head. "And I imagine your grandmother
will see to it that she is punished for it, well enough."

Felicity turned her gaze upward, studying her mother.
"You don't like Grandmama much do you, Mama." It was
not a question.

Arden's face fell. She did not want her daughter to wonder about such a thing, not ever. "That's not so, Filly. I love
her very much. She's my mother, after all. But I don't always . . ." She struggled to find the right words.

"You don't always like her much," Filly finished for her.

"Oh heaven's, Filly, she's my mother. Of course I love
her with all my heart, sometimes even when I don't wish
to." Arden sighed. "I don't always like what she does. Let's
leave it at that."

"Nor do I," Felicity said in a still-smaller voice. "But I
don't always like what you do either."

"You don't?"

Felicity shook her head. "But I love you anyway. Like you love Grandmama, I guess. It's like I have no choice, somehow. Even if I want to be different from you, I can't seem to." She smiled ruefully. "But I'm not going to stop trying."

Arden smiled and hugged her. "You are my heart, dear girl. And that remark heralds your becoming a young woman," she added lightly. "I would scarcely expect anything else. Now dress and come down for breakfast, Filly. I doubt anything else horrible will occur betwixt now and supper, at any rate."

But Arden was wrong. Before the day was through, Hanna had been sent on the wagon instead of Pansy. Sent to be sold at auction, sent away from her daughter forever, never to return to the only home she had known. Sent, despite her screams and wails of grief. Away, down the road, tied into the wagon so that she might not throw herself under the wheels in her despair.

"If you let one slave get away with that sort of mischief," Anne said to her daughter staunchly, "the rest will be looking to try the same. Pansy will be ready to breed in a few years . . ."

"She's only four years old!"

"They come to season faster than we do. And I can get a new wench easier than I can ever trust Hanna again. If she doesn't know how to act, let her go work in someone's cotton rows. That'll bring her up short quick enough."

"So it did her no good at all," Arden murmured sadly.

"None whatsoever," Anne said firmly. "And it's good that the rest of them know that as well."

Arden thought for a long moment. "Mother, I want you to consider what this—business of yours—is doing to the rest of us. It's not good for the children to see it, and it's painful for me and for Martin. I don't want to force you to stop, but I wish you would consider what the effects of this sort of— brutality—might have on the rest of the household."

"Brutality!" Anne frowned. "For heaven's sakes, Arden,

what in the world are you prattling about? Is it brutal when
you take the eggs from under your setting hens? When you
kill a shoat before its mama's very eyes? When you take
away the yearling colt and pen it away from the mare while
she cries for it and runs a furrow in the next corral? It's life,
Arden, and if that's brutal, then I guess the children will just
have to learn to live with it. You worry too much about
them, child. Lacey is a lovely girl and much smarter than
you give her credit for, if you ask me. She knows the facts of
life, and she understands the difference between a slave and
a white man, same as she knows the difference between her
mama and her daddy.''

Arden put her hand on her mother's shoulder. ''That's a
wonderful speech, Mama, but it doesn't make me feel any
better. Hanna's no setting hen, she's a human being. She's
got a mother's heart, same as you and I do.''

Anne scoffed, brushing away Arden's words with an easy
shrug. ''Next, you'll be saying she's got a soul. I guess you
think all your preaching's taking root.''

Arden had started preaching to the servants at least once a
month, letting them gather under the chinaberry trees on
Sunday afternoons. She knew well enough that the penalty
for any slave caught reading or writing was five hundred
lashes and the loss of a thumb; the penalty for a master who
allowed such a trespass was five hundred dollars. But she
reasoned that reading to them from the Bible was not akin to
teaching them the words themselves, and she felt it her duty
to teach them of God. ''I think it makes them better people,
whatever else they may be,'' she said.

''Well, they're slaves. Hanna's a slave, Arden, and nothing you do will change that a whit. A mother's heart!'' She
laughed angrily. ''She's nothing but a black wench I bred to
Simon, because he's got a strong back and he gives little
trouble. Her get will bring a good price, and if Pansy breeds
true, her grandbabies will fetch close to nine hundred dollars
on the block, maybe more if the Yankees get more riled than

they already are. That's all I need to know about Hanna's mother's heart.''

Something snapped in Arden's head then, a single strand of love, a simple fiber which had kept her loyal to her mother no matter how she trespassed what Arden called morality. And she felt suddenly light and free.

"If you insist on continuing to breed and sell slaves like they were common stock, you'll have to do it someplace else besides River Reach.'' She felt her mouth turn rigid at the corners and her heart harden. Now she had said it, and as she heard the words, she only regretted she had not said them sooner.

"What are you saying, child?'' Anne's brow was thunderous with contained anger. "That you'll send away your own mother rather than send off a few lazy black wenches . . .''

"I'm saying I'll no longer tolerate slave breeding at River Reach. Not if you insist on sending off the babies from their mothers. If you want to breed them, fine, but the offspring will stay here on this plantation.''

"That's fine with me, if Martin will meet my price,'' Anne snapped.

"Martin won't buy a single one of them.''

"You're mighty quick to speak for him.''

"That's right, I am,'' Arden replied. "You can stay, Mother, but your slaves must go. I'm not going to watch poor Pansy grow up, crippled and miserable, only to see her put to the same despair her mother faced year after year.''

"And why should I wish to stay?'' Anne said coolly. "When you've already accused me of brutality? Why should any mother want to inflict such agony on her only daughter? Indeed, if I am such a burden to you, child, I can be gone by the morrow. Me and my poor, benighted wenches will just hightail it back to New Orleans, where folks know the difference between a nigger and a mother well enough!''

Arden took a deep breath and said the words she never

thought she could bring herself to utter. "Perhaps," she murmured, "that would be best, then."

Anne glared at her for a long moment. "I see. And I suppose your ridiculous husband has pushed you to this moment of triumph?"

Arden felt another secret fiber snap. She wondered idly how many more were in her heart and head, tying her to this person who even now seemed almost a stranger before her. "No, Mother," she managed to say, holding her voice steady, "I've not discussed this with Martin. But of course, the decision is mine to make. And I have made it."

"That I am to be driven off like a plague of locust?"

"No, that you are to stop breeding your slaves like so many milk cows."

"If I do, I'll have no cash money of my own and will have to ask you and Martin for pin money when I want to go to town and buy a new frock. You'd likely enjoy that. Thank you very much, but no, sister child, I will not accept your *generous* offer," she said formally, pulling herself to her full height and dignity. "Tell Dick to have the wagon ready tomorrow morning. I'll be leaving with the first light. I'll stay in Natchez until I can get a boat south to New Orleans, and I'll not trouble you further with my bestial manners. And," she added with no small malice, "I'll be inviting Lacey to join me. I suspect that New Orleans will be a heady lure for a young girl of sixteen. She'll learn more in one month in the Quarter than she'll learn on this cotton farm in the next five years."

"You may not take her," Arden said quickly, her throat thickening with alarm. "She's too young to go so far."

"Well, I'll ask her, nonetheless," Anne said smoothly. "And you can be the one to tell her that she must stay here in this backwater, just so you can have her company." She smiled a lovely and gracious smile. "I think you'll have a bigger fight on your hands then you had with me, child. I don't envy you one whit." She turned and went into her house and shut the door firmly. Then she opened it again.

"Please tell Lacey I'll wait on her for tea, as always, Arden.
I know she'll not disappoint her grandmama." She went
back inside, leaving Arden alone on the narrow veranda,
standing in the dappled sunlight.

It seemed to her in that moment that her whole life with
her mother had been building to this one conversation. This
single confrontation between them had been coming for
years. Decades. Perhaps since she herself had been a small
child. She glanced up at the big house. Filly was no doubt
still upstairs, likely readying herself for her afternoon visit
with Grandmama, one of the highpoints of her day. She
looked out to the fields. Martin was out there someplace
with the overseer. He would not return until supper.

Martin, she cried silently, I need you now. I have always
needed you more than you needed me and never so much as
when I'm losing something else which I love, namely our
daughter. Why was it that, so often, her husband was just out
of reach when her heart ached most for him? Sometimes she
felt that, even as he lay next to her at night. Just out of
reach—just beyond the touch of her voice, her heart, her
fear. It was enough that she had had to birth her children
alone; did she also have to bear the pain of raising them
alone as well? Did other women feel so lonely for a partner
to bear the burden as they saw their children spinning away
from them like stars into a dark and unknown orbit?

But Martin is not here, and I must act now, without him. I
have two choices, she realized then quickly. I can tell Felicity of her grandmother's intended offer and tell her also that
she may not go, thereby ensuring that she will insist on
going—or I can let her grandmother tell her and hope that
she will not accept. There is always time to tell her no when
she has heard the offer and accepted.

Arden went up the walk then, resolutely, past the cook in
the kitchen and up the stairs to her own bedroom, where she
intended to wait out the siege. Anne would do what she
threatened to do, and she would make her offer as seductive
as possible. Filly would bear the whole burden of acceptance

or denial. And there was nothing she could do but wait. She took up her embroidery hoop, settled herself by the window where she could not see her mother's house, and began to take fine, even stitches, smoothing out her mind even as she smoothed the linen under her hands.

An hour went by. Two. The day pulled away from the earth slowly, like a great ship moving away from land to the sea. She heard the clatter of her sons returning to the house, their calls to one another, the noise of their descent upon the kitchen, but she did not go down to them. The shadows grew denser, longer, and then came the knock at the door. Arden knew instantly that it was Filly. She called out softly, "Come in," and she turned so that she could see her daughter's face. She felt sure that the moment she saw her, she would know what had transpired in her heart.

Felicity came into the room hesitantly, and Arden's hands froze. The girl's face was full of fear and defiance, all at once. She was ready to say no to someone, that much was certain, and she was scared of her own decision. "Mama, Grandmama is leaving," she said abruptly. "She said you told her to go."

"That's not so," Arden said gently. "You know better, I think."

"What did you tell her, then?"

"I told her that she was hurting too many people by selling off those babies. That I couldn't abide it anymore, and I don't want my children abiding it, either. I gave her a choice of staying with us and giving up her slaves, or going elsewhere. She chose to go elsewhere." She shook her head. "You know your grandmother, child. She will not be told what to do. But I love her, and I'm sorry that she's going."

Felicity came in and sat down on the bed, staring at the wooden planked floor and the cloth rug as though she were only seeing them for the first time. She traced a delicate pattern with her white slipper.

"Do you believe me?" Arden asked quietly.

"Yes, I guess so," she said finally. "Anyway, Grandmama's leaving, that's the end of it. And she wants me to go with her.''

"I know," Arden said. "She told me that she would invite you, despite what I said."

"You told her not to ask me?" Felicity asked sharply.

"I asked her not to, because I felt you were too young to be faced with such a choice. But of course, your grandmother will do as she wishes. Always has."

"I'm not as young as all that. Plenty of girls my age are made wives already—"

"And plenty are made sorry at that, too. Your father and I had hoped you would want to have a fine education and meet new and interesting people before you decide to marry."

Felicity thought on that for an instant. "She asked me to come with her and to live with her in a big house in the French Quarter. She said I could have two servants of my own and a dressmaker and a carriage to take me out on visits."

"And whom would you visit?"

Felicity hesitated. "New friends, I suppose. Grandmama knows everyone, she says."

"She certainly used to," Arden said calmly. "But that was a long time ago."

"Well, anyway," Felicity said with sudden impatience, "I told her no."

"You did?"

Felicity nodded. "She fussed a bit and wheedled, but I don't really want to go. If she tries to talk you into it, Mama, stand firm. I think I'd rather go to Columbus, like we planned." She rose and smoothed her frock. "Maybe I'll visit her next season, if she wants me to, but I don't think I'll go right now."

"I'm glad," Arden managed to say carefully.

"Papa wouldn't like it," Felicity added.

"That's true."

She rose and went to the door, pausing just as she was going out. "You know, I remember we used to be so close,

Grandmama and me. I loved her so much, and she loved me so much, there were times I used to pretend I was her little girl instead of yours.'' She said it easily, with some small wonder. "But it's all different now. I know she loves me, but I don't know if she really . . ." She hesitated, searching for the word. "I don't know if she really knows much what love is, after all. Sometimes, it's as though she would rather be stirring things up than doing what might be best for everyone.'' She smiled slightly. "It's probably better she goes to New Orleans for a while, Mama,'' she said solemnly. "You two were simply not getting along.''

Arden smiled in relief. "I'm afraid you're right, dear.''

And her wise and lovely daughter went out the door.

A few months later, Arden and Martin drove Felicity into Natchez to put her on the train for Columbus. Up until the last, Arden had planned to go along, for although Felicity was being met by Martin's second cousin, Milly, a lady of middle years with two daughters already safely ensconced in the Columbus Institute, and although she would be well chaperoned while in her home and then taken to the institute to board there, it still seemed like a mighty long journey for her to take alone.

But Filly had wheedled and begged and finally firmly declared that she simply *would* go alone, despite her mother's expectations. "Mama,'' she said with her jaw frighteningly reminiscent of her father's, "I'll feel like a fool if you persist in tagging along. Aunt Milly will think I'm a child, and she'll treat me like one the whole time I'm under her roof, if she sees you and Father won't even let me out of your sight for a single day's travel to Columbus!''

"But Filly, it simply isn't done. A young woman traveling alone for eight hours! Without proper chaperone . . .''

"Mama, it's closer to seven hours, and it's done all the time! Six of my friends went off to school this year alone, and I doubt a single mama traveled with them.''

"Well, I know, but of course, most of them took their mammies along, but with all the talk of war, your father is reluctant to let any of our people stray too far from home. They could fall into some abolitionist's clutches and run off so fast—did you hear that Doctor Linus's boy, Sam, ran off just the other day? Took a mule and lit out for Memphis, they say."

"Mama, I don't want Nell to come with me and I don't want you to come with me and I don't care a sour fig for Doctor Linus's Sam. I want to go alone, and I simply won't hear of anything else. If you insist on coming, I'll stay home, I swear it." Felicity spoke those sentences with a brilliant smile on her face and a wheedling tone, but Arden had no doubt she meant every word.

That night, she told Martin that she really didn't think it necessary to accompany Felicity to Columbus. "After all," she said, "Cousin Milly will be there to pick her up at the station, and it's less than eight hours on the train."

Martin looked up from his book in surprise. He'd been buried in one of what she called his star books all evening, and she saw the familiar glaze of bewilderment on his brow as she called him back to the reality at hand. To come all the way back from the outer galaxy to his horsehair chaise must be a bit of a shock, she smiled to herself.

"Besides, Filly swears she'll die of humiliation if I force myself on her, and she won't go at all." She let her smile show now. "You know how she gets. She looks more and more like you, dear, every day."

"What do you mean?"

"I mean, she's got a mind of her own, of course, nothing we haven't known for seventeen years. But sometimes she can jut out that delicate jaw of hers in such a way as to make one think she could carve meat with it if she had to."

"And *I* do that?" he asked, amazed and not a little affronted.

She nodded calmly, her head bent over her stitching. She was glad it gave her the chance to hide her grin. "Just as often as you think you can get away with it. Filly's just like you, my love.''

"Well, then she shouldn't get away with it!" Martin replied. ''I don't know that a strong will's such a good thing in a young woman, after all. Should we encourage her stubbornness by giving in to it?''

With that, Arden could no longer hide her amusement. ''No, I suppose not,'' she chuckled, ''but I guess it's a little late to start raising her different now. We should have done something about that chin when it was smaller, but we didn't. Oh, I tried many a time, but between her grandmother and you, my dear, I fought a losing battle often enough.''

"Me!"

"Yes, Martin, you. 'Twasn't I who let her knock the telescope out of whack and didn't even bar her from the room, and 'twasn't I who let her have her own pony and her own servants and her own dressmaker by the age of eight.''

He thought for a moment, half put off by her words and half amused. "Well, I scarcely think I need take the blame for my daughter's disposition all by myself, but I guess that's not the point at hand. If she won't have you with her, then I suppose I should accompany her.''

Arden laughed aloud. "You do that, my love. You tell your Filly that her papa won't trust her for eight hours on a train, to be delivered up to her matron aunt. You may well find yourself traveling all alone, but by all means, you tell her. Match her chin for chin.''

Martin thought again. Finally, he sighed. "You think she'd be that upset?''

Arden shrugged. ''Perhaps she'd allow you when she won't allow me, who knows?''

He was silent for a moment and then he shook his head. ''No. She's right. If that's what she wants, that's what we should do. If she's old enough to leave us and go to academy, she's old enough to take the train there unescorted.''

Now it was Arden's turn to be amazed. ''Really? You will truly let her go alone?''

Martin grinned. "Of course. If our Filly wants to run without a saddle for once, I'll let her. You know, the best mares need the biggest pasture. If you put them in a small field, they'll just jump the fence. But if the field is big enough, they take no notice of their confinement and remain content within it. Filly needs a bigger field than most, that's all. And besides," he added with a twinkle, "the fence will still be there; she just won't see it."

"What do you mean?"

"Jack Nevins is going to Columbus on that same train on business; he happened to mention it the other day at the bank. I'll drop him a note and ask him to keep an eye on Filly. He can sit right behind her, if need be, and she won't even know he's there."

Arden smiled and shook her head. "I should have known."

"So you tell our strong-willed daughter that her mother and father will give sway to her wishes. She may go on her journey unescorted."

Arden chuckled again. "Oh, you are simply dreadful. A master strategist and cunning adversary."

"No," he said, sliding back into his book. "Just the father of a beautiful daughter."

It was early summer, and as usual, the great river was in flood. Each rain pushed it beyond its banks until it seeped, then ran with muddy currents over the rocks, the levee, and wide into the fields, turning melting farms into mud and stinking up the Natchez region with decayed vegetation, drowned creatures, nightcrawlers, and the silt of a thousand miles.

Floods were a fact of life on the river. Usually coming in the spring, when rain and snowmelt filled the streams and rivers that drained the upper Mississippi, they generally did not bother those farms more than five miles from the river-banks. But this year, something unusual was happening many miles to the north. It rained enough to saturate the earth and then, instead of stopping in the beginning of the summer heat, the jet stream swung south, and cool, dry air from Canada dropped down and collided with warm, moist air pumping up from the Gulf. Thunderstorms raged over the Great Plains and could not escape to the east because of a high pressure area stalled over the whole Atlantic Coast. The storms stayed where they were born, and the rains kept coming and coming.

In Iowa, on the upper branch of the Iowa River where it junctured with the Mississippi, the farms there saw more than three feet of rain, a year's worth in four months. In Kansas, the Missouri, north of its joining with the Mississippi, had more than twice its normal rainfall that spring, and the early summer was the wettest on record for Minnesota, Illinois, Iowa, and the Dakotas.

By late June, the river at Natchez was over its western banks by more than a foot, and it was even worse farther south where levees were the only things standing between the planters and disasters.

Natchez, on its high bluffs, was protected well enough, but Natchez-Under-the-Hill was being eaten away every day. Graced Ground and River Reach were both far enough away from the Mississippi that the flood waters did not reach them, though the waters of the Saint Catherine were high, brown with mud, and over its banks by half a foot. The lowlands began to be marshes, and even the higher fields were gradually inundated with several inches of mud and water. Farmers closer to Natchez and south of the bluffs worried that cotton might be lost, and Martin wondered aloud what they might do for their neighbors. "It's not impossible that someday the river could come for us as well," he said quietly to Arden. "It never has, but that doesn't mean it couldn't."

"What would we do?" she asked.

"Run to the top of the mounds, I guess, and wait it out," he said thoughtfully. "They're the highest ground for

miles.'' But when he saw the look on her face, he stopped
and hugged her warmly. "But don't worry, sweet, that's not
likely. We'll send some sugar and flour and bacon over to
the church, and they can give it out to those who need it
most.''

She had let him comfort her, but then she stood and
watched the Saint Catherine from her upper window. She
could just see it in the distance, winding, shining in the sun.
Much farther from the house than at Grace Ground. She
wondered what the river was doing in New Orleans. Surely
they would have heard, if there was trouble so far south. She
went to the chiffarobe in the corner of the room and pulled
out two extra sets of blankets to add to Dick's wagonload for
the less fortunate farmers closer to the river.

That night, they had a heavy drenching of rain, the third in
as many evenings. The next morning, the lowlands surrounding River Reach looked like a marsh. Cattle stood low-
ing in a sheet of water and mud, and the cotton looked as if it
grew from a shallow lake in some of the lowest fields. For
almost a week, the water stood like that, dropping slowly to
less than an inch over the soil but never actually drying out.

The slaves could not work the fields, and the stock could
barely move. Mud covered everyone from morning to night,
and tempers were short, waiting for the sun to finally take
away the wet. But what they did not know was that something else waited as well.

In the layering of water, millions of mosquito eggs which
had been attached to the grasses, dormant and invisible,
were incubating in the sun and the water. The larvae were
eating rapidly for several days, then turning into pupas. Two
days more, and adult mosquitos were pulling themselves out
of their pupal shells and drying their wings in preparation for
flight. From the windows of the big house, no one could see
the natural chain of events happening in the low fields surrounding River Reach, nor would there have been a thing to
do about it had they known.

Arden was in the quarters near dusk, tending a slave's

ringwormed scalp, when she felt the stinging on her arms and neck. She slapped at her neck absently, then waved her hand back and forth across her face to ward off a half-dozen singing mosquitoes. "They're going to be bad tonight," she murmured to the slave, rising now to go.

"Always is, wid de water up," he murmured, slapping at his own arms.

She stepped outside and glanced west toward the setting sun. There was a humming sound coming from the marsh, louder than she had recalled it on usual summer nights. She began to hurry toward the house. Then she saw it: a solid black cloud extending from the ground up to about thirty feet in the air, moving toward her from the river. She picked up her pace and began to run. Other clouds were forming in the distance and not so far away. As she raced past the quarters, she could hear the slaves shouting to one another and cursing the stinging insects, and she saw Martin galloping toward the house on his white horse, his hat pulled low over his eyes and his neckerchief up over his mouth.

Arden ran up the back stoop, shouted to Joseph to shut the windows, and raced past the gawking servants toward the upstairs, hollering directions as she ran. Already, the insects were inside the house, and she went from window to window, slamming them, sometimes straining to pull long-opened windows shut which had swollen from the damp and the heat tight within their frames. All the while, she could feel the stinging on her face, her arms, even, she imagined, under her skirts on her legs, and she thanked God swiftly that the boys were so far north, that Felicity was in Columbus, too far from the river to be plagued.

Martin came up to the second floor then and helped her slam down the windows on the south side of the house. "Is it locusts coming?" she panted. "The skeeters are so bad tonight, I can scarcely see straight. What are those dark clouds forming?"

"More mosquitoes," he said grimly. "I've seen the like only once before."

"Well," she said lamely, "at least they won't eat the crops."

"We might lose worse than the cotton, if we're unlucky," he said, and he turned to hurry down the stairs again. She followed him at a run, ignoring the wails of the servants and their worried, plucking hands, as they tried to keep the mosquitoes off their skin. He was pulling on his heavy oil coat, despite the muggy heat of the coming night, and wrapping his face in his kerchief again. Then she heard the screams of his horse tethered outside, and she ran to the window to watch. The dark clouds of mosquitoes were still coming across the sky, and some of them were already upon them. Martin's prize white stallion was covered solidly with mosquitoes. He bolted straight upward, snapped his halter, and crashed down on his side, struggling and kicking. Martin got to him and yanked him up, helping him regain his footing. Martin hurried him away, the horse still whinnying and bucking, and Arden heard then frantic bellowing coming from the stables, as the cows were attacked by the swarms, and loud screams came from the quarters.

The view from the windows was obscured now by the swarms of insistent mosquitoes, and Arden could not see how Martin was managing to make his way to the stables. The stinging along her arms and neck was nigh unbearable, for even with the windows closed, so many insects had already come in that she would be welted and scratching for days. But the poor slaves in the quarters! Not even a thin glass between them and the swarms!

Martin came rushing back inside the back door again, wiping and slapping at his legs and face. His eyes were almost swollen shut above the protective kerchief, and he was gagging and coughing, yanking off his clothing. "The damn skeeters get in your nose and mouth," he gasped as she and Portia ran to help him. "We'll likely lose some cows, they're running blind and falling down, and when they do, the bugs clog their nose and mouth so bad, they can't breathe. The horses are going crazy, bucking and screaming, they'll kick out their stalls before this is through, the bugs swarm on their eyes . . ." He coughed again and gagged up phlegm. "I'm sorry, I feel like I've eaten about a million of the damn things."

"What about the crew?" Arden asked worriedly. She knew the field hands could not possibly have made it to shelter before the mosquitoes struck.

"That could be our biggest problem," he said. "The poor devils likely were covered before they knew what was coming."

"Oh Martin!" she cried. "What about the women in the quarters? And the children?" She ran to the window and looked out. "Look, they're leaving!" she shouted. Martin hurried to her side. The clouds of stinging insects were moving across the land now, toward the river to the west. She and Martin grabbed hats and coats and went out the door again, rushing toward the quarters.

They lost two children that swarming, both of them infants left unguarded when the mosquitoes struck in force. Three head of cattle, a horse which had to be destroyed with a broken leg, and about a dozen chickens. All of Martin's prize doves were dead, smothered under the weight of a million insects which had clogged their eyes and beaks so badly, they could not breathe. But the mosquitoes then fell to their usual tolerable level, and life looked as if it might go on.

Early the next morning, as they finally got to bed, Arden said, "You were very brave last night. I was terrified, but you stayed calm. I haven't seen you like that too many times in our lives." She reached up and stroked his shoulder as he lay next to her. "You were wonderful."

He took her hand and silently kissed her palm. "Should I arrange crises more often so you can admire me with regularity?"

"Heavens no." She thought for an instant. "Should I admire you with more regularity, crisis or not?"

He smiled in the dim light, and she heard it in his voice.
"Of course."

She hugged him hard. "You are my hero."

"Good," he murmured, holding her as they fell asleep.

It was a Sunday, and Filly was home for a few days' holiday from Columbus Institute, having passed her history
exams with honors. She had specially requested a picnic,
and so Arden woke early and padded downstairs before
Portia could bring her coffee. She took a cup from cook and
went out on the veranda to watch the sun rise over the land.

Of course, the hands were already in the fields, for their
day started with the bell at four in the morning. The cotton
was high now; its red and white flowers, so like hollyhocks
in form, made the fields appear pink from a distance. She
closed her eyes, relishing the coolness which came from the
earth, left over from the night.

The fields had regulated her life for so many years, she
could visualize them in all seasons, even with her eyes
closed. Midwinter, when the cotton stalks were burned and
the crop laid off; then mid-March when the women were
sent to the fields to scatter the seed. Then they were sent out
again, with the boys this time, to cut back the growing plants
to a stand, so that only three sprouting plants would survive
in each clump. Then out and out again, to hoe and weed and
chop. As the long rows began to form, the blossoms came
on, creamy white, red, sometimes pink as the evening
cooled, but lasting only a day or so and then gone for another
year. After the blossoms came the form, the queer square in
the center of which appeared the fruit, the cotton bol. Those
green hard balls were the center of the universe then, as they
grew and grew all summer through the baking heat.

Then early in the fall, they dried, popped open, and the
long white staple showed with the black seeds. Once more,
the crew went through the rows, this time with large cane
and willow baskets, picking and plucking, one row at a time.

Then to the gin, then packed, and the bales bound in cotton sacking for the steamboat to New Orleans.

They'd work until eleven o'clock, again by the bell and the call of the overseer. As the heat of the day came on hard, they'd stop for dinner: a little pork, some cornbread, cabbage, maybe some mustard or turnip greens, a swipe of molasses, then they'd sleep until three when the bell called them again. From three o'clock until sundown, they'd labor the rows, and the hum of their singing drifting to the house would gently waken all the family inside from their afternoon naps.

Filly, like the boys, was gone from this world now, perhaps never to return in the same way. Already, after only a single term at college, she was less interested in her studies than her father liked, more interested in the young men who vied for her attention than he knew. In some ways, Arden reflected, she was more like her grandmother than her mother. And yet, at seventeen, it was time—

It suddenly struck Arden that she did not know her own daughter's mind or heart nearly so well as she once did. She was grown now—when had that happened?—and she was very likely being courted by some young man who would wish her to wed. She had promised to finish two years at Columbus at least, promised her father that, no matter what, she would have that much education. But Arden well remembered the heady lure of love. Could Felicity withstand it and keep her promise?

The boys were out of school now and off on their trip abroad—a trip their father had insisted upon before they settled into the management of River Reach. "It will round them out," he had said to Arden, "make them gentlemen, rather than just scholars. And I suspect, make them appreciate their native land, the more they gallivant about a foreign one." And so her Micah and Owen were in the company of one Master Crutchfield, a man fluent in French and manners continental, for six months across the wide, wide ocean, acquainting themselves with what Paris and London and Munich had to offer.

She sighed deeply, savoring the smell of the good, dark coffee. She was almost finished with the job of raising her children, of starting them off properly in their lives. Almost, too, was Martin finished with the task of running River Reach. Soon, Felicity would be wed; the boys would come home and take over the plantation, and maybe then—who knows?—she smiled at the thought. Perhaps she and Martin might see a thing or two themselves before their eyes hazed with age forever.

She stretched and stood now, hearing Portia's quick scuffle behind her.

"You cain' sleep, Miz Arden?" She came round and peered into her mistress's face with concern.

Arden squeezed Portia's shoulder with affection. "Too excited, I 'spose. With Filly home, seems like there's too much to do to sleep away the day."

Portia grinned. "She look good, don' you think? She done growed nigh three inches, looks like. No wonder dos boys buzz round her like she made a' molasses."

Arden glanced quickly up at her. "She say anything about that to you, Portia?"

" 'Bout what?" Her face took on an air of innocence.

"Which men, in particular, she has allowed to pay court to her?" As Portia bridled, clearly pleased at being the owner of possibly valuable information, Arden kept her face bland. The slave was nearing fifty, old enough to know better, and yet she still took inordinate pleasure in having a secret which someone else might yearn to know.

Portia rolled her eyes and put her hands on her hips, looking for all the world in that instant like a black version of Anne Lawrence herself. "I 'spect she got too many to winnow down jes' yet, Miz' Arden, but she say dat Daniels boy got de inside track in de race."

"James Daniels? Judge Daniels' boy?" Arden smiled slowly. "Well. I must say, that's a nice piece of news so early this morning." The Daniels plantation, Rosewood, was more than two thousand acres of cotton, corn, and excellent horseflesh. Judge Daniels' pacers were making a name for themselves as far afield as Mobile and Memphis, and James Daniels, his younger boy, was surely due to take some small part of that world with him when he wed. "Did she say if he has made his attentions to her seriously?"

Portia crossed her arms now obdurately. "Now, Miz Arden, you best ask Miz Filly dat, 'cause if she want her mama to know, I 'spect she say so. Young miss got to have an ol' ear to talk to what ain' her mama, now, don' she? Ain' you had some ol' ear like dat yourself when you was growin'?"

"Yes." Arden laughed lightly. "The nuns. They had a passel of ears, all right."

Portia grinned again. "Well, Miz Filly ain' got no need o' nuns. Like as not, she got no need o' nothin' but what she got, an' dat be de truth."

Arden looked up then as Felicity came down the stairs, saw them in the morning light, and came to them with two quick hugs. "Mama, it looks like a glorious day for a picnic, doesn't it? Portia, did you tell Mama all my secrets?" Her smile was warm, but Arden saw that her gaze was direct.

"No, ma'm!" Portia huffed, indignant.

"Secrets, Filly, tell me, tell me." Arden smiled, enveloping her lovely daughter in a hug. The girl smelled of warm sleep and fresh hair and unsullied promise, smooth and pungent as new milk. She pulled back and looked into Filly's face. Her smile changed to one of teasing mystery, and in that instant, Arden knew that she was grown. Somehow, in that year, she had moved away from her childhood and from her mother's controlling protection. She was a woman now.

"Well, if you really must know, Mama, there's a certain young man who has been paying me quite a bit of attention," she said archly. And then her voice changed to the giggle of a young girl again. "Mama, he's so wonderful!"

Arden felt a surge of love for her and an equal surge of

anxiety. Her heart was so untouched. So precious and perfect, like a just-opened blossom. She drew her daughter down to the chaise and waved Portia away. "Tell me," she said, holding Filly's hands and watching her eyes.

"Papa will be furious!" Filly moaned.

"Why should he be furious?" Arden asked instantly. "Filly, have you been foolish . . ."

"No, no," she said impatiently, "but I know that James should have asked permission to call first, and his father and my father should have met, and his mother should have written to you, but Mother, it all happened so quickly, and with the war coming and all—"

"Filly, what war? What are you talking about?" Arden jounced her daughter's hands with some exasperation. "Tell me right this minute, what have you done?"

"Well, nothing, Mama," Filly said indignantly, "but war is surely coming. James says so and so does everyone else. We can't allow the Yankees to tell us how to run our business, after all! And with all this coming on so fast, it scarcely seems to matter much if all the niceties are preserved, before a girl accepts a young man's proposal of marriage."

"Felicity!" Arden gasped. "What have you done!"

Her daughter straightened abruptly and took away her hands. "James Daniels has asked me to consider his proposal, Mother, and I have told him I shall. That's all. He hopes to be allowed to call on Father next week—surely you know his father, Mama, there can't be any question of the man's family—"

"Filly, you've never even *met* his family!"

"No, but I know about them, of course—everyone does. Judge Daniels may well have more questions about our family than we do about him."

"I doubt that," Arden said a little stiffly. "River Reach may not be as large as Rosewood, but your father is not likely to give away his only daughter so lightly, just because a man raises fast horses and more cotton." She stood and paced to the window, gazing out over the fields. "James

Daniels,'' she said softly. "How did this happen so quickly, Filly?"

"I met him at Letty Carter's birthday *fête*, Mama—you remember I wrote you about it? Since then, he has written me, oh, scores of letters, and been to see me twice—"

Arden turned around quickly.

At her mother's look, Felicity hastened to add, "Oh Mother, it was all perfectly respectable; we've scarcely been alone for two seconds since we've met. But James says he knew the moment he saw me that we were destined to be together."

Arden's thoughts were whirling, and one in particular struck her as strangely ironic. Martin's theory of allurements and the look on Filly's face when she said James Daniels' name: they were all of the same cloth. "James Daniels," she repeated. "Are you in love with him?"

"Oh Mother," she murmured, closing her eyes. "I don't think I can live without him."

To Arden's own surprise, laughter bubbled out of her then at the rapt look on her daughter's face. "Oh Filly, you dear, lovely child . . ."

"Why are you laughing at me?" Felicity asked, bewildered. "Didn't you ever feel that way about Father?"

Arden nodded, unable to speak for her laughter. "Of course, of course I did. Still do, I suppose, but I guess I just never thought that you would feel that way, or at least not yet!" She sat down beside her daughter and hugged her firmly. "But I'm so very glad, my dear. And if you love him that much, then whatever comes of that must only be to the good."

"Oh thank you, Mother!" Felicity exclaimed, bursting into happy tears. "Then you'll help me tell Father about him?"

"I will, child, on the condition that you'll remember your promise to your father about finishing two years. And I only hope that Master Daniels knows what a rare treasure you'll be giving him."

A few hours later, Dick brought the carriage round, and Arden and Felicity took their places on the velvet seat, shaded under the canopy. Cook's basket, plumped with ham and chicken, peaches and pickles, cakes and sweetened tea, rested between them, and Martin rode *en cheval* beside them, his long riding whip held at attention like a banner into battle. They drove down the road, cut toward the Trace, and followed the river along that well-worn path north until they reached the largest mound in the county.

Emerald Mound was partly on Martin's property, partly on acres belonging to Graced Ground, and it was their favorite spot to picnic. When the boys were young, they clamored to climb the Indian site on any outing, as did most boys from surrounding plantations, and so it was not unusual to arrive for a picnic and find evidence that other families had been there recently.

But today, to Arden's relief, they had the spot to themselves. Emerald Mound was a huge hillock in the middle of a cleared field, an ancient mountain covered with short green grass and little else. It was always a puzzlement to Arden that the mound had not been taken over by brush or trees— almost as though something in nature wanted it left as the savages had intended. On either end of the mound, two raised platforms of grassy earth rose even higher than the height of the mound itself, likely places where they enacted their superstitious rites, custom said. They climbed the mound up more than forty feet and spread their quilt and basket out in the shadow of one of the higher hillocks.

Arden could see that Felicity had taken special care with her toilet today, and she wore a soft flowered bonnet with pale peach ribbons which her father had given her last birthday. She smiled to herself. Filly was no fool when it came to men, that much was certain. In that, she was more like her grandmother every day.

It was a beautiful day, one in which every bird making its home on or near the Trace was singing in joy at its simple existence. Warblers and bobolinks, jays and sparrows, mockingbirds and thrushes made a cheerful noise at all corners of the surrounding woods. The tulip trees were lush with blooms and the honeysuckle sweetened the air. The heat rose from the earth with a soft, enveloping odor of green, and it seemed that cold, like death, could never come again.

Martin was asking Felicity about her classmates, her lessons, and her impressions of her teachers, as always well entertained by her tales, his attention completely on her every gesture and turn of phrase. Arden felt very grateful, in that moment, to have a husband who loved her daughter so completely. Likely, his love was the best insurance she could have that she would choose a mate wisely. And then she heard Felicity say, "Father, I think you'd like him, actually. He's a fine person. And Letty's mother speaks very highly of him . . ."

Arden sat a little straighter, set down her chicken leg, and prepared to arbitrate on her daughter's behalf.

"You've made no promises, is that correct?" Martin asked. Quite calmly, Arden thought. Many fathers would have been infuriated that their daughters even entertained a man's hopes without their consent.

Felicity hesitated. Finally she said, "Not exactly. But he knows how I feel."

"And how *do* you feel?" Martin asked gently.

"I want to marry him, Father," she said firmly.

"That's what you want," he said patiently, "but that's not how you feel. How do you feel about the man, Filly?"

She dropped her eyes shyly. "I love him."

Martin turned away, and Arden could see the mixture of gladness and sadness in the lines of his mouth. "Well, then," he said after a long moment. "I suppose I must meet this young man as soon as he decides to favor us with a call." His voice was light, teasing, as though he were discussing Felicity's newest frock rather than a potential mate for life.

"Oh, he wanted to come sooner, but I said I had to speak

with you first, Father! I begged him to wait until you were ready to receive him . . ."

"I don't know that I'll ever be ready to give away my daughter," Martin said wryly, "but I'm ready to receive the man, at any rate. But what about your education, Filly?"

"Oh, I intend to finish my two years, Father, just as I promised. And perhaps I may even do a bit more, we'll see. I'm doing well, you know, and that was even with the attentions of Master Daniels to divert me."

It was true. Filly had made excellent marks in her classes, and her instructors seemed pleased with her progress. "I will have your word on that, Felicity," Martin said solemnly. "You know how strongly I feel about the value of education, even for a young woman."

"Yes, Father," she said winsomely. "I promise."

"Very well," he said, rising and extending a hand to Felicity. "Then let's take a walk, and you can tell me exactly why you believe you love him." He was smiling down at her, and she rose into his arms with the same ecstatic fervor that Arden had seen on the faces of nuns when they embraced the statue of Christ in the chapel.

Arden wanted to weep with love and relief. Instead, she simply sat and watched them walk off together, arm in arm, her daughter's long skirts trailing softly in the grasses, her husband's hat inclined down so that he might hear the girl's words more clearly. She picked up her chicken leg again and began to eat with the first real appetite she had felt all day. He better be good to her, she thought then, this James Daniels. Because she knows what a man's love feels like well enough. She will surely never settle for less.

Along the Natchez Trace, an ancient wilderness trail which was now widened and deepened by the frequent passage of man, the soil was soft and dark and silted, unlike the rich loam of the cotton fields of River Reach and Graced Ground. The soil of the Trace was largely loess, deep deposits of windblown top soil formed during the Ice Age when glaciers covered the northern half of the American continent. At this time, nearly continuous dust storms swept in from the western plains and covered the region of the Trace with windblown dust to a depth of as much as ninety feet.

The loess rested on the sands and clays of an ancient sea. It originally covered a vast region but had gradually eroded away, to be replaced by the rich top soil which supported the cotton and corn of Martin Howard and other planters. Eventually confined to a strip east of the Mississippi River from three to thirty miles wide, from Baton Rouge south into Tennessee, the loess supported a vast array of native plants, delicate wildflowers, and the animals which depended upon them to survive.

Where the Natchez Trace passed over the loess, it formed sunken roads, some as deep as twenty feet, with the exposed roots of oak and sassafras and myrtle twisted and gnarled into the passageway like so many claws trying to take back the forest for its original inhabitants.

One of the original inhabitants of the Trace was also one of its oldest, *Dasypus novemcinctus*, a small creature which the Spanish conquistadores first saw when they followed the game down the Trace. They named the creature "the little man in armor." It was the nine-banded armadillo, America's only mammal shielded with heavy, bony plates which covered its head, body, and tail. Between its front and back plates, a midsection of nine narrow, jointed armored bands permitted it to curl up tightly and protect its soft underparts and upright ears. Its little body was sparsely haired with brownish fur, but it usually appeared to be stained darker, for it burrowed in the soft loess of the Trace and assumed its color.

One of these creatures, named Daspy, lived in a burrow along Saint Catherine's Creek where the water was slow, cool, and deep, and she ate the many insects she found in the soft dirt there and along the edges of the water. This young female of three seasons was about two feet long and ten inches high.

Daspy was an excellent digger, as were all her kind, and her burrow extended deep into the riverbank. If you had come along the entrance, a hole about eight inches across, you would have seen her tracks scattered about, four toes in front, five toes in the rear, frequently obliterated by the drag marks of her long, scaled tail. If you had examined her scat, you would think that Daspy ate only the moist clay of the river, for it was like clay marbles. In fact, Daspy ate a good bit of earth while she consumed her insects, for she usually had to dig to find each meal.

While Daspy dug for her insects, an activity she had to do most of the day to nourish herself, she grunted like a small pig. The almost-constant noise she made while she ate, burrowed, or tracked from place to place along the river made her easy to find, and so a vulnerable target for predators. But Daspy could run surprisingly fast, burrow with amazing speed, and when threatened, roll herself into a tight ball for defense. In this way, she was able to survive the bears, cougars, bobcats, wolves, and foxes which might enjoy her mild, porklike flesh.

Daspy had given birth the previous spring to her first litter of piglets. A male armadillo had found her in the autumn season, when the leaves of the sassafras trees had carpeted the Trace. After mating, she drove the male away and began to build a nest of leaves in her burrow. Fourteen weeks after breeding, the single fertilized egg in her uterus implanted and divided into quadruplets. Her four identical piglets were born in the early spring.

Her children were well formed, with open eyes, and could walk within an hour of their birth. Their skin was soft, however, and they could not defend themselves against enemies, and so Daspy kept them very close to the burrow as the spring warmed the earth around the Trace. When they could root about for ants and worms, when they could find crayfish and small minnows on their own, she taught them to swim the shallows of the Saint Catherine.

She stood on the riverbank and gulped air to inflate her belly so that she would float, jumped into the deeper water, and grunted for her piglets to follow. One by one, without hesitation, they imitated her, gulping air, squealing with fear and anticipation, and leaping into the water. She then showed them how to walk underwater on the stream bed where the current was slow and the water was shallow. Only after they could do all these things did she drive them away to hunt for themselves. And then she waited for another mate to come and find her.

There was a time, before Daspy's memory, when her kind was more plentiful along the Trace. But then man came, following the game and the buffalo from the north. The first men caught many armadillos, for they ate of the mild meat and used the shells to make bowls, utensils, and ornaments. Men who came later trapped her ancestors and shot them for food. As the men passed on, however, her kind grew in numbers. Now, Daspy found that more than one male pursued her each autumn. Indeed, she was often mated by two or three. It did not matter. She drove them all away once her urging was passed. She never knew who fathered her piglets, nor did she care.

Now, on an autumn day when the wind was still warm from the great river, Daspy was digging intently downstream from her burrow after a crayfish which was attempting to evade her by burrowing under a large rock. The crayfish was the largest one Daspy had seen in three days, and she was determined to remove it from its refuge. She grunted in eagerness as she dug, turning on her side to insert her long, clawed front toes in after the hiding creature.

With incredible speed, she snatched the crayfish as he scuttled up out of the rock, ignored his pincers, and cracked his carapace right through the middle of his jointed body. While he still wriggled and fought to escape, she held down his tail with one toe and chewed off his head, grunting more loudly now with enjoyment.

Suddenly, Daspy became aware of a noise behind her, and she turned quickly, already arching her back to coil up for trouble. It was another male coming upstream, grunting a greeting to her. She half snarled, half grunted a warning, swallowing the rest of the crayfish before he could demand a share. Then she turned to face the oncoming male, her tail stiff and angry with resentment.

Daspy was not yet in season, and any intruder, male or female, into what she considered her territory, was likely to receive a sharp warning and a fight, if necessary. But the male was eager to woo and he came on, ignoring her grunt of rebuke.

She ran toward him, squealing angrily, and as she came closer, he froze, his head high, his tail stiff behind him. She was fearless, stamping her front feet and chomping her jaws as though she intended to eat him ears first. He hesitated a moment and then turned tail to run, but she was not satisfied. As she chased him, he was grunting in dismay, but she was grunting even louder. They came closer to the Trace, the flattened, deepened trail which defined the traffic for the animals, man, and the cattle and sheep which man sometimes drove to and from the great river.

The male armadillo plunged down into the Trace, glancing back over his shoulder at Daspy as though he did not believe she would follow. But follow she did, right into the Trace and halfway across. As he ascended the other side, she stopped. From a near distance, she could hear a coming thunder. A rumble which got swiftly louder and louder, and she turned to confront yet another intruder.

In that instant, a carriage pulled by two fast horses rounded the corner of the Trace and was on her. She rolled immediately into a tight ball, her head tucked in, her stomach protected, her front forepaws clutching her chest in terror. One of the horses gave her a glancing blow as it passed, and she spun like a coconut back to her side of the Trace and out of danger. The carriage was far past her and out of sight, out of sound, before she cautiously unrolled herself and looked around.

The male intruder was gone. The thundering terror was gone as well. She sniffed the air. The smell of the water behind her drove all memory of danger from her small mind, and she remembered the crayfish she had eaten some moments before. She turned and waddled back up the embankment and toward the river once more. Daspy's territory was safe, her burrow secure. She thought of nothing now but her demanding stomach.

Every Sunday, Arden took her Bible in hand and walked to the rear of her mother's house to meet with the servants under the spreading magnolia tree there. Near half of them came, some Sundays as many as forty folk from the quarters, to sit on the grass at her feet and listen to her read. Martin teased her, called her his "preacher lady," but she knew he was pleased that his people heard the word of God. Many Sundays, the mothers brought their children, plunked them down firmly with whispered admonitions to be still, and she would glance up from her reading to see their eyes agog, their mouths open in wonder.

For many of the slaves, those who did not often need her healing, it was the only time she saw them up close all week.

Arden had never forgotten her mother's admonition about the penalties for slaves if they were caught reading or writing. Though she had known of those punishments vaguely, her mother's words had made them somehow more stark and ominous. To sit reading to her people and picture Moses, who leaned against the magnolia there before her, his great hands cupping his knees, to picture those hands minus a thumb, was disturbing. To picture little Patsy, the ten-year-old gal who brought water to the crew in the fields, enduring five hundred lashes—which would likely kill her—made her eyes swim and her hands tremble as she held the Bible before them. To be sure that neither she nor they were ever accused falsely, she took care that they never saw a clear glimpse of the printed page.

Besides the Bible, Arden used the time with the slaves to make small announcements about who was ill or who was healed, which little cabin might be expecting a child, or what the weather forecast was for the next week. Each cabin had its own small garden behind it from which the slaves took their collards and their turnips and their sweet potatoes, and they watched the skies as anxiously as Martin did when a storm was due.

If she had any other news which might concern them, she took pleasure in passing that along as well. She knew, of course, that they often knew the news before she spoke it, thanks to the amazing telegraph system of the slaves, but she preferred they hear any details from her own lips rather than from the gossip chain.

And so this Sunday, she was pleased to tell them that Miss Felicity had accepted the proposal of Master James Daniels, son of Judge Daniels, owner of Rosewood plantation. Her people broke out in excited grins and laughter, and a smattering of applause circled the little group, so pleased were they at the news.

"Dat Rosewood bigger den River Reach, ain' it, ma'm?" asked one of the hands.

"Yes, it is," Arden said. "And so our Miss Felicity best keep her wits about her, to mistress such a place!" She laughed lightly. "She may not be so fortunate in her people as I have been."

They squirmed in delight at her praise, beaming and pushing at each other.

"De weddin' gonna be here or Natchez?" Letty asked from the back. Letty was the seamstress, and she had the rare fortune of being taken with the family when they moved back and forth between River Reach and the new house Martin had just finished in Natchez on Commerce Street. He had said, a year ago, that he wanted a place for Felicity to entertain her friends and for them to entertain as well, a place away from the fevers and moist heat of the summer months, a respite from the dawn-to-dusk work the plantation demanded. And so they had bought a grand home on Commerce, a two-story Queen Anne with a gabled porch and six bedrooms. As lovely as it was, Martin had ordered many changes and additions to the house, and so it was only recently that they had moved in their furnishings. Already, Arden loved it almost as much as River Reach. And those servants who had been to see it liked to pass themselves off with grand airs as somehow more important to the Master and Mistress than those who had to stay behind.

"The wedding will be in Natchez," she said reluctantly to Letty, seeing the downcast faces which followed those words. "It's so much easier for guests to attend, and since Master Daniels is a member of the Episcopalian faith, he'll want to have the service in his own church, I believe." She brightened her tone to include them each particularly. "But the wedding party will come out to River Reach to bring you each some wedding cake and punch, and I do believe the bride will have a special gift for each of you to remember the occasion!"

The faces turned bright again then, and the buzz of excited speculation rose round the circle at her feet.

"And another piece of lovely news," Arden went on. "Mistress Lawrence, my dear mother, has decided to come again to live with us." She lowered her voice in a confidential tone which she knew riveted their attention. "You know, she's getting on now, past seventy though she scarcely looks it, of course, but Master Martin and I feel it best she be close to us in her remaining years, and she has agreed, to our great relief."

The servants did not take that piece of news with near the joy with which they greeted Felicity's upcoming nuptials, but most of them tried to smile politely with pretended contentment and interest. Dick, the driver, asked, "She be stayin' here or in Natchez, ma'm?"

They all listened closely for her answer.

"Likely she'll spend more time in Natchez," Arden said smoothly, "for she does enjoy her little card parties and folks coming and going about her. But of course, when we come to River Reach, she'll come along some of the times. I know you'll be pleased to see her again, all of you, and make her welcome." She gave the group a meaningful glance, and not a pair of eyes slid away.

"Yes'm," Dick answered solemnly for all of them.

"And perhaps the best news of all," Arden went on, "Master Owen and Master Micah will be returning soon, and they'll be coming to River Reach to take over much of the management from their father." She smiled on them happily. "I know many of you remember the boys from when they were in short pants, and isn't it grand to think that they will be the masters of such a fine plantation as this?" She made a gesture to encompass the big house behind her, the vast fields, and all of them as well. "Master Martin says he'd like to spend a little less time in the saddle and a little more time with the grandchildren he hopes to have soon. Master Owen and Master Micah learned much at the academy and their traveling, and I know they will be equal to the task. I'm sure you'll be pleased to see them again and work for them as well and as loyally as you have for Master Martin and myself."

Once again, the faces were beaming, and Bill, the drover who handled half of the cotton crew in the field, spoke up. "Dat Massa Micah, he a bri' penny, dat one. An' Massa Owen, he no fool. We bes' be on good 'havior now!" The slaves laughed genially. It was as though they were somehow consulted in the decision, included in the transfer of power, and they felt the pride of the trust Arden placed in them as she shared her personal news.

"Massa Martin don' wan' to run de place no more?" a man asked curiously. In his voice was the bewilderment of a servant who could not understand that anyone might conceivably tire of mastering others.

"Not so much as he has," Arden said. "But don't worry your head, John. He'll keep his hand in for a good while yet. We won't let those boys run amok." Once more her people laughed along with her good-naturedly, although she had no doubt that a few of them did not understand her words or her jest.

She picked up the Bible again and opened to Ecclesiastes, one of their favorite parts. As usual they began to hum and sway with her voice, hypnotized by the very rhythms of the words. She read on into the afternoon, as the sun grew lower and the shadows lengthened. Her favorite part of the week was Sunday, submerged in the word of God with her people all about her.

Later, as dusk was coming to the fields, she was out on the veranda having her iced lemonade, when Moses, the old driver, went on past on his crotchety mule. He was one of the few servants allowed his own animal, since he'd been with Martin forever and was getting too lame to get about very well or very far. She laughed to herself quietly when she heard him say to his mule as he kicked him in a futile effort to make him hurry, "You needn't think 'cause I got religion, I cain' cuss you! I done made a 'ception in your case!"

Owen and Micah now occupied their old bedrooms at River Reach, but Arden knew that their time in the big house was limited. Already, they were talking about moving into Anne's house or perhaps building new places of their own in separate corners of the vast acreage which made up the plantation. Neither of them really wanted to live in their grandmother's old home; both of them were courting young ladies in Natchez and could see ahead to a time when they would need more room for their own lives. And that was how it should be, Arden said to Martin contentedly in their bed in private. Thank God they had the land and the resources to offer both of their sons a fine beginning.

Over supper one evening, they sat long over their port and

cook's excellent cherry trifle discussing the boys' plans for
River Reach. Like most young men, they had large dreams.

"I think the war is coming faster than a bullet," Owen
said, struggling to keep a grin from his mouth. He knew his
father hated the idea of a battle between the states and was
an ardent Union supporter. But he had been filled with the
war fever at West Point, and there was much talk of war
overseas. He was half afraid he might miss it. "The North
won't let us leave in peace, and they won't let us manage our
own affairs as we see fit. It's no different than when we re-
belled against England, and waiting for them to strike the
first blow is not in keeping with the spirit of our revolutionary fathers!"

Martin looked up from his plate with dismay. His younger
son tended to be more volatile than his elder, but he had
hoped that both would hate the thought of war as he did.
"You sound like the fire-eaters at the *Free Trader,*" he said.

The Natchez *Free Trader* and the Natchez *Courier,* the
two newspapers in town, were equally adamant about the
rights of the South, but the *Free Trader* was by far the more
violent proponent of a revolutionary approach to those
rights. "War will lay waste to this country and make a hell
of our lives," Martin added. "Thousands will be killed, millions of dollars wasted, and for what? So that young men can
feel like heroes. I, for one, hope we're not too hasty to act.
The issue is too serious for heroics. Let's leave the decision
to Lincoln—"

"Lincoln!" Micah exclaimed. "If you leave it to that
devil, we'll all be hoeing our own corn or starving by winter.
If he gets elected, Father, this country will explode!"

Arden could feel the anger rise in Martin and feel, also,
his effort to control it. She reached over and laid a hand on
his.

"I think Congress learned a thing or two from the John
Brown tragedy," Martin said, keeping his voice level.
"Men paid too much attention to a fanatic, gave him far too

much public voice, and turned him into a martyr. Perhaps if we had just ignored the fool—''

"Ignored him!" Owen sputtered, "Father, John Brown was telling the slaves to rise up and cut our throats!"

Martin shook his head. "Well, he's dead now and so are others who died in vain. And Harper's Ferry is not Mississippi and one man does not make a cause. Lincoln is a wise man, I'm sure, and he loved the Union. If he loves the Union, surely he will not strike the death blow—''

"And death blow it will be, too!" Owen crowed. "We'll whip the Yankees back so far north they'll freeze to their saddles!"

Martin went on patiently, "At any rate, I would hope that we would not be the first to strike it."

Micah said solemnly, "It's different for you, Father. You're nearing the time when these issues will hardly concern you. And you didn't go away from here once in your whole life. You don't know what it's like to go someplace and have everyone look down on you because you're from Mississippi, to have them ask you how many times a day you beat your slaves, to try to explain that slavery might be wrong but just setting them free is an even greater wrong. Those who don't live here can't possibly understand how our lives are and how to change them—or even if change is necessary. And I'm damned if I'll listen to someone a thousand miles away tell me how to run River Reach!"

Owen drank down his port in a swift swallow and banged the glass on the table. "Hear, hear!"

"So you both believe we should secede from the Union?" Martin asked, his voice hollow with disappointment.

"Yes!" Owen said.

"I think," Micah added soberly, "that we might be allowed to leave without bloodshed. And I would pray for that choice, Father. But if we are not allowed to exercise our free will, then we will have no choice but to fight for our freedom. Just like our forefathers did against a tyrannical government."

Martin sighed and put his hand over Arden's, glancing at her with sadness. "Then we are doomed. Because if young men like yourselves, who have been educated and offered the best futures, still desire war, then war will surely come. And we shall surely lose. Come, my dear," he said to her gently, pulling her up from her chair and her unfinished port. "Let us retire and leave the field to these firebrands." He softened his words with a smile. "I'm sure they won't go to killing Yankees before breakfast, at least. In the meantime, perhaps we can get our rest."

Arden touched her sons on the shoulders as she followed behind their father. "Be sure to put out the fire and don't leave your hounds in the kitchen, boys. Cook has such a hissy when she must trip over them in the morning."

As she ascended the stairs behind Martin, she murmured, "Do you really believe war will come, then?"

"Now I do," he said glumly.

"Then I want to move to Natchez," she said firmly. "If war is coming, I want to be close to neighbors. Mother would rather live on Commerce Street anyway. Give the boys a free hand for a season, Martin, and let them prove themselves. Or if you won't, then resign yourself to sleeping alone at least part of the week. Because I don't want to be here when war comes." She took a deep breath. It was the strongest statement of feeling she had ever made to Martin, and now that she had spoken, she was almost afraid of his response.

He turned and stared down at her on the shadowed stairs. "I see now where the boys get their thirst for rebellion, dear wife. A fire-eater in my own bed!"

Dismayed, she reached up and took his hand. "No, Martin, I didn't mean to sound such a harridan, but if you honestly believe war is coming—"

"I do," he said calmly. "And we'll move into Natchez within the month." He put his arm round her shoulder then and led her into the bedroom, closing the door behind him with an air of closing out the rest of the world altogether.

"Now come to bed, sweet. I feel older than my years tonight."

She embraced him warmly, holding him close and murmuring to him of her love.

Felicity's wedding was the largest, most opulent that Natchez had seen in a decade. Judge Daniels was determined that his son's nuptials reflect his own rising position in the state legislature, and Felicity caught the fever early on in the plans. Rapidly the *fête* grew and grew like wild mushrooms after a rain.

With every addition, every new guest, every increased extravagance, Martin grew more and more disturbed. "It isn't the money," he explained to Arden and finally to Felicity as well, "it's a matter of simple good taste, it seems to me. To flaunt our good fortune might invite just its opposite."

"Oh, Papa, that's so superstitious!" Felicity laughed. "I don't think God has given us such happiness just to hide it under a bushel. And for heaven's sake, do you think Judge Daniels has such concerns?"

"Obviously not," Martin said dryly. "But I wonder what the rest of the county must think of us, putting on such airs."

"The rest of the county would be stricken with disappointment if we didn't," Felicity said. "Folks need something right now to cheer them up, with all the danger of war and all. It may well be the last gracious wedding this county sees for a while, if Lincoln gets his way."

Martin subsided then, especially when Arden added, "A girl only does this once, dear. I have never regretted all the expense and trouble of our own wedding, I know that much."

And when Owen and Micah announced that they had proposed to their two sweethearts and would be declaring their engagements on the occasion of Felicity's wedding *fête*, Martin gave in completely.

When all was said and done, more than five hundred people came from all over the county, some from as far away as Vicksburg and Memphis. The Episcopal Church was filled to overflowing, the wedding guests ate more in three hours than Martin normally spent for the entire working accounts of River Reach in one month, and the dancing and festivities went on for five full days. Felicity's gown, sent up from New Orleans by her grandmother, was a wonder of lace, seed pearls, and tiny diamonds sewn all round the bodice and hem. Arden suspected that it had come from France and been reworked by her mother's personal dressmaker. "Likely," she whispered to Portia, "the bodice alone cost a thousand dollars or more."

Portia had rolled her eyes in mock terror. "Leastwise, it *got* de bodice in it, anyhow. 'Cause Filly goin' wear it, no matter what."

James Daniels was a fine young man, both Arden and Martin agreed, and if they had to give away their daughter, they had the consolation of feeling comfortable with her choice. Owen was marrying Miss Hanna Collins within the week and Micah was betrothed to Miss Mary Hamilton, due to wed a month later. Both young women seemed lovely, devoted, and of good family.

Arden did her best not to picture what the house on Commerce Street would be like with her children gone and her mother back again in permanent residence. It had been more than five years since Anne had left River Reach in anger. More than a year passed before her letters warmed, more than two before she visited once more. And now, finally, all past injuries seemed to have been forgotten. That was one thing fortunate about Anne, Arden thought—she had a quick fuse but a short memory. Arden almost looked forward to her presence once more.

"It will be good," she told herself relentlessly, "to have Mother near now that the children are out on their own." What she did not say to herself, not even in the privacy of her own heart, was that she also hoped, once Felicity, Owen, and Micah were started on their lives, that she and Martin could resume theirs again on a renewed and intimate level.

Martin was so preoccupied with the coming war these days that he scarcely thought of anything else. Even River Reach got less attention than was needed, until the overseer complained that he needed another driver if Martin did not intend to be at the plantation more than a day a week. Martin hired him another driver and cut his trips to River Reach even more.

He spent long hours poring over papers and proposals from the legislature, discussing some of them with Micah and Owen, hoping always that wiser heads would prevail and war would be averted. He told his sons, "If war does come, promise me you won't rush off with some fools just because a soldier's beating a drum. That's not our style. If you feel you must go, then I expect you to go as officers and gentlemen in a regiment chosen for its excellence."

"Yes, Father," Micah answered for them both. "Do you think, then, that war is certainly coming?"

Martin shrugged sadly. "Last year, I would have said no to such a question. Today, I cannot say. I do know that intelligent, reasonable men don't seem to be able to do what this country has always done best and what democracy demands: compromise. You know, we have over a thousand people at Graced Ground and River Reach, maybe more, and I don't believe in slavery. One of the first things I'd do if I could was get rid of them. But I don't see any other way out, not as things are now. Why, down in Louisiana, the colored outnumber us six to one. Six to one! And it's not much different here. Who would take care of them? What would they do if they didn't work the fields? And who would work the fields if they didn't?" He shook his head. "It's a sorry state, son. I don't believe in slavery nor in secession, but I can't think of any alternatives. So when you ask me, will we have war, I have to wonder who is going to come up with the compromise that will keep us from it."

And the more Martin read and thought, the more he pulled

away from what was happening right under his nose. Arden was at first bewildered by his detachment from her but she tried to tell herself that it was only temporary. Surely other thoughtful men in Natchez had the same worries, and likely their wives suffered from the same neglect.

Felicity's wedding pulled Martin up and out of his depression for a brief spell, but then he plunged back in again once all three of them were out of the house. Anne announced she was sailing back to New Orleans, "just to tidy up some business affairs, but I'll be back again before the holiday season gets under way, so don't rent out my bed!"

Martin and Arden were thus alone together, aside from a dozen personal servants, for the first time in twenty-five years. After a month of that condition, Arden was forced to recall some words her mother had told her once. "Love is attention, Arden," Anne had said to her when teased about the rapt solicitations of an elderly beau. *"Attention.* Never forget that. If you want to know what a man loves, look to see where he spends his time."

As she reflected on those words of her mother, one of the rare occasions Anne had offered advice about men and little enough at that, she had to admit to herself that perhaps Martin had changed more than she'd realized. For attention, these days, was certainly something she could not get from him easily.

Anne Lawrence arrived back in Natchez in the midst of a time when the town was in a state of uproar, like most of the South. It was November 1860, and the heat of the summer seemed only just past. But the coming winter promised to be one of more heat than any summer could provide: the dreaded Lincoln had just won the nomination. Mississippi Democrats had walked out of the nominating convention, South Carolina had already organized a secession proclamation, and the only question seemed to be whether Mississippi should secede immediately or wait for some other state to go first.

Felicity and James came into town from Rosewood to visit and to welcome Anne back to Natchez. The short business trip Anne had planned had stretched on through that holiday season and then into the following year, and despite Arden's letters entreating her mother's return, Anne had always "just a little more to tend to, dear, and then I'll take the next boat directly, I promise."

But she was here, at last. Never one to miss a chance at irony, Anne Lawrence had booked passage on the *Liberty,* the very boat Martin had bet on for the one race they'd witnessed together. "She did that on purpose," Martin had said wryly when he heard her choice.

Natchez-Under-the-Hill was not quite as nasty these days, but it was every bit as teeming. More so, with the news so urgent each day from the North. Arden held her skirts as high as she dared as they walked to the dock, and even with Martin and James flanking them, she was nervous for her own safety and Filly's even more, especially in her present condition . . .

"Do you feel well enough?" Arden murmured softly to her daughter, taking her gloved hand in her own. "Your grandmother would surely understand if you waited for her back at the house."

"No, she wouldn't," Filly said good-naturedly. "And I'm fine, really, Mother." She put her handkerchief to her nose for the lavender scent she had there. "So long as I can keep the stink out of my mouth, I can make it."

James bent down to hear her words more carefully. She reassured him in the same way, taking his arm and patting his hand.

Arden smiled at him. He was so gentle and solicitous of her, she only prayed he would continue such care as their marriage weathered the years. So many men began in love and ended in apathy—or worse. She smiled up at Martin.

She hoped fervently that Felicity would have the same good fortune.

The *Liberty* was pulling into view now downriver, rounding the bend and giving three mighty blasts on her horns. Shouts of "Steamboat a'coming!" rose up around them, and the busy pace of the sidewalks quickened even more. Natchez-Under-the-Hill was thronged with strangers. The news from Washington seemed to charge the people with the need to do something, anything, and men flocked to the docks to meet passengers, hoping to get fresh information and perhaps stir themselves up to greater heights.

The *Liberty* sidled and bowed up to the docks at last, her whistles blasting and her smokestacks steaming. Up on the topmost turret, Arden could see the small figure of her mother waving her handkerchief. Somehow she stood out, even with taller shoulders crowding around her.

"There's Grandmama!" Felicity cried with delight, her voice suddenly that of a young girl again. She giggled happily and squeezed James's arm, almost jumping up and down.

They waited impatiently while the roustabouts threw the ropes and lowered the gangplanks, cleared the decks for the passengers to exit, and the captain stepped to the dock to doff his hat and bow his passengers ashore. There was a thick flurry of traffic, and Arden stretched herself as tall as she might to see her mother, and then Martin spied her coming up the dock, a negro porter on each side, her wide-brimmed flowered hat bobbing and bouncing as she gave each of them orders with every step. She swept her full and lustrous skirts aside, closed her parasol with a snap, and then she was among them.

"Arden!" she cried. "Lacey, my darling child!" she embraced them both together and then each of them in turn. "My heavens, you're absolutely stunning!" she said to Felicity, "and Arden, my love, you look well fed and prosperous as a country squire's wife!" Once she stepped out of the women's embrace, she turned to Martin and said, "And

here's the country squire himself!'' patting the round of his
stomach under his buttoned vest. "I see the threat of war
hasn't thrown you off your feed, Master Howard. And this
can't possibly be your young husband, Lacey? Why, he
looks twice as handsome as he did in his wedding coat!''
Anne Lawrence turned all her glowing attention on James
Daniels.

To Arden's surprise, James colored like a schoolboy and
doffed his hat awkwardly. "It's my great pleasure to see you
again, Madam Lawrence,'' he said hesitantly. His words
seemed almost rehearsed, and Arden realized with a start
that Felicity must have somehow spoken enough about her
grandmother's pending arrival to make the man nervous as a
cat.

"Mother, do you know Justice Daniels' horses swept the
quarters this last season, and James has plans for making
Rosewood one of the finest breeding stables in the South?''

"Well, that's just fine, just fine!'' Anne said amiably. "If
that evil Lincoln lets us keep a single piece of horseflesh for
ourselves, I'm sure we'll all thank you for it, sir!'' She
turned then and monitored her baggage, and the men put the
women in the carriage. Arden quickly studied her mother
once they were out of the sun. She looked older, admittedly,
but not old. She was still beautiful at nearly seventy-five, her
eyes still had a remnant of the snap and bristle of youth, and
her hands were hardly lined at all with fewer spots than
Arden's own. "Mother,'' Arden said without thought, "how
in the world do you keep your hands so perfect?''

"I never do a lick of work,'' Anne said laughing wryly.
"And I sleep with them in buttermilk and lemon juice every
chance I get.''

"I suppose I'll need to follow your example,'' Felicity
said. And then she added shyly, "The doctor says that it's
not at all unusual for a woman's skin to get speckled as a
guinea hen when she's expecting.''

"I've heard that,'' Anne said blithely, turning to look out
at the throngs moving up Silver Street. Then Felicity's

words caught her attention. "Expecting!" She turned with eyes huge and mouth open in aghast surprise. "Lacey, don't tell me! Are you pregnant already?"

Felicity blushed beautifully. "We've been married more than a year, Grandmama."

"Well, for heaven's sakes, I suppose you're going to follow your mother's example and have one after another, every other year, like a damned darky!"

"Mother, that's uncalled for," Arden began severely, but she needn't have worried. Felicity was more than able to state her own indignation.

"James and I love each other," her daughter said stiffly. "Just because you didn't want children doesn't mean I shouldn't. In fact, I should think you'd be proud to be a great-grandmother and still look no older than my mother."

"But I had hoped for so much more for you, Lacey! The Grand Tour of Europe, the chance to meet fascinating people! It's hard enough to do all that when you're a wife, but once you're a mother, you might as well start sewing your shroud, because you'll be dead to that world and anything else exciting."

"That's what you said to me, as I recall," Arden said softly. "So many years ago when Felicity was still just a whisper in my soul."

"You did?" Felicity asked her grandmother. "You made Mother feel small and stupid for wanting me?"

"I did no such thing," Anne retorted angrily. "I merely pointed out to her that she had enormous potential . . ."

"Which I wanted to spend on my family," Arden finished quietly.

Felicity was silent for a moment, gazing at Anne with new and appraising eyes. "You once loved me very much, Grandmama," she finally said calmly. "I would hope that you didn't love me simply because you thought I'd do and be all you once wanted for yourself. So that you could take secondhand joy from my life for your own. You didn't, did you?"

"Of course not," Anne said. "I loved you for yourself, Lacey, and I still do."

"Good," Felicity said. "Then you'll still love me even if I have a pack of babies round my feet, right?"

Anne took her granddaughter's hands and squeezed them to her cheeks. "Oh, Lacey, I am happy for you, of course, but I just don't want to see you suffer! Women have such trials with their children, from the bearing of them to the burying of them! You're just a child yourself, my dear, and to think of you in pain and torment! Well, I just can't stand it . . ." And she leaned back on the velvet-tufted carriage seat, fanning herself in despair, her eyes closed grimly.

"Suffering is part of life," Felicity said serenely. "We can't run from it lest we run from joy as well. And how would we know we were happy if we hadn't known unhappiness at one time or another? It's all part of it. Part of the bargain God strikes with each of us."

"Well for heaven's sakes, Felicity," Arden murmured softly. She was, in that instant, slightly in awe of this beautiful young woman beside her. Where had she learned to speak with such assurance about things past her years? "You surprise me, child."

"She surprises me not a whit," Anne said with a twinge of sour weariness. "Marriage does that to you, makes you old and wise too fast. You were smarter, Arden. You stayed within the safety of the bosom of the nuns long enough to enjoy your girlhood, at least. Lacey will be a mother before she's even old enough to be a wife, to my mind."

Again to Arden's surprise, her daughter laughed lightly. "Ah, Grandmama, you haven't changed a bit; you still don't give ground even when you're outnumbered. But you're right, I'm no longer a girl. And I doubt the nuns would want me now." She laid her hand on her stomach protectively. She giggled then, a girlish trill which was infectious. "But James does."

"I see he does," Anne said with a wry grimace. "Oh well, I'm delighted for you both, of course, and I'll be the

doting *great*-grandmama—dear God, I can scarcely believe
it!'' She groaned theatrically. ''Promise you'll tell anyone
who asks that I was wed at twelve and had your mother at
thirteen.''

Arden laughed then, too, and glanced out the carriage.
They were coming down Commerce Street now, James and
Martin both riding their mounts alongside. They made a
handsome pair, and she was proud to have her mother see the
new house, resplendent with its new portico and other additions, white and shining and bedecked in the last of the autumn flowers. Martin knocked with his whip on the carriage
door and called out, ''We're home, ladies!'' She could hear
the pride in his voice.

The carriage stopped, and they alighted. Anne grasped her
hands together at her breast and laughed delightedly. ''Why,
Master Howard, it's simply grand!'' She had not seen it with
the new additions.

Martin beamed and bowed her up the long steps. ''Well,
we certainly hope you'll be very happy here with us, Anne.''

Arden cast him a quick glance. To the best of her knowledge, she could not recall him ever addressing her mother by
her given name. She looked to see if Anne Lawrence bridled
at the familiarity, but to her relief, Anne seemed not to have
noticed. She was too busy exclaiming over the added or-
namentation on the veranda railing and the clever Victorian
trim at the windows. Felicity sidled up alongside her mother
and murmured softly, ''Well, it looks as if we have her back
for good, Mother. Are we glad?''

''Yes, we are,'' Arden said firmly, pulling her family into
her house at her side.

Portia met them at the door, bowing Anne Lawrence
within with a ''Welcome back, Miz' Law'ence. Was de trip
tol'able?''

'' 'Bout as tol'able as I expected,'' Anne said archly,
looking about the room as though it might not pass inspection. ''I see nothing's much changed on the inside, anyway.''

"Portia, tell cook to have Mistress Lawrence's julep ready directly and a plate of her good lemon bars sent up to Mother's room right quick," Arden said smoothly, taking Anne's arm and gliding her away.

A halloo from behind them made them all turn in surprise. James's older brother, Leonard, was rushing up the path to the house, waving his hand in excitement. "Have you heard the news?" he called as he came. "It just came over the wire!"

James and Martin turned as one to greet him, Anne coming forward with an air of expectant pleasure like a receiving madam, but when she heard his next words, she froze with horror, her hand to her mouth.

"Lincoln's been elected! The scalawag got nary a single Southern electoral vote and a minority of the popular vote, but he's willy-nilly the new President of these United States!"

"Not this one!" Anne said hotly.

"That means war, for certain," James replied.

"Oh no!" Arden cried. She put her arm around Felicity, who had instinctively reached for her mother's hand.

"You're sure the voting is completed?" Martin asked. "He's been declared by Congress?"

Leonard nodded. "And will be sworn in before we can do a thing about it. That black Republican will be our President, unless we do what we've promised to do and secede, taking the whole Cotton Belt with us!"

"Let's all go inside, at least," Martin began. "We needn't stand out on the veranda."

"I'm going to tell Father," Leonard said to James. "And I'm going to enlist in the morning. Will you come with me?"

Felicity gasped and took her husband's arm, but he paid no heed. "Of course," James said calmly. "We'll sign on together."

"Surely there's no need to hasten this tragedy," Martin

said, his brows knotted in despair. "Lincoln has said he does not want war."

"South Carolina will secede inside a week, mark my words," Leonard said.

"And the rest of the South will follow!" Anne added. "Of course you must go, it's your duty!"

Felicity began to weep softly, one hand on her husband's arm, the other in her mother's.

"Please take the ladies inside," Martin said to Arden swiftly. "James, I know you're anxious to go with your brother, but I beg you to consider your family . . ."

As Arden ushered her weeping daughter and indignant mother into the house, she heard Martin add, "Surely you can delay your decision for a time; we may well get news in the next few days which will make war unnecessary . . ."

And then she closed the door on the men and took both women by the shoulders, moving them upstairs out of the eyes and ears of the entire household. "Don't think about this now, Filly. You'll just make yourself sick, and maybe all for nothing . . ."

"Well, she said she wanted to know all about life, suffering and all," Anne said. "Now I guess we all will, whether we want to or not, thanks to those devil Yankees." She went resolutely into the room prepared for her and, without even a backward glance of comfort for either of them, closed the door.

Leonard was right, of course. South Carolina seceded from the Union within weeks of Lincoln's election after deliberating less than twenty-two minutes in special convention. Cannons roared in the Carolina Citadel, bells chimed in the church steeples, and crowds cheered in approval as they marched through the city.

The text of the secession proclamation was wired quick as sound to Natchez:

We, the people of South Carolina, in convention assembled, do declare and ordain that the union now subsisting between South Carolina and other states under the name of the United States of America is hereby dissolved.

When the news reached the streets of Natchez, the town exploded in a frenzy of celebration and sword brandishing the likes of which Arden hoped never to see again. Men drilled in small, colorful troops in the open streets, regiments were formed right and left, and not a single supper hour passed without talk of politics, war, and the rascal abolitionists. Martin was so disgusted with South Carolina and her "hotheads," as he called them, that he decreed he would never eat another bite of rice, her chief export product, nor would he allow a grain in the house. When Anne rebuked him for disloyalty to the Confederate cause, he replied that "the whole state was one vast insane asylum," and he hoped the insanity was not catching.

But his hopes were soon dashed. In January 1861, Mississippi followed South Carolina's example and seceded from the Union of the United States. The Natchez *Free Trader* was jubilant. "Bring out the cannon and let it roar its loud, reverberating approbation!" it exulted.

Martin immediately banned the paper from his house.

James and his brother, Leonard, joined the Adams Troop, named for their county. Worse still, Micah and Owen signed on as officers with the Adams Light Guard, leaving the overseer and his two hired drivers in charge of River Reach and departing for Memphis the day after James's departure.

Felicity was brave and without tears as she bade her husband goodbye on the Natchez docks. With her head high, she sent him off in a new uniform she had had made hastily, a new pair of boots, a beautiful wool coat, and a promise to write every day faithfully, no matter what might come between them. "God will take care of you, my husband," she said cheerfully, "and He will watch over me as well until you can come home to us." Arden was amazed at both her faith and her courage, and she wondered where this new Felicity had been hiding all these years. In fact, when Owen and Micah left a week later, she was ashamed to say she could not meet her daughter's good example and wept uncontrollably as her two boys rode down the street toward the docks and their waiting ship.

Martin attempted to console Felicity, but she rebuffed him gently. "I am happy to see my husband and my brothers do their duty," she said calmly. "I'm sorry you can't be proud of them as well."

"It's not a matter of pride," Martin tried to tell her, "it's a matter of waste! War is always unnecessary and always a terrible waste."

Felicity went back to Rosewood to be surrounded by James's sister and mother, where Arden could only assume they consoled each other mightily with thoughts of glory in battle and the righteous cause their men had gone off to serve. She had never felt so lonely for her daughter in her life.

Martin plunged into a state of depression which made him unable to speak. He sat in his study, surrounded by his beloved astronomy instruments, and Arden could not get him to come out for more than a week. Finally, in despair, she sent a note round to Felicity asking her to speak to him. Martin and his daughter stayed behind closed doors talking for most of a day, and only Joseph, Martin's ancient retainer, was allowed to shamble in and out delivering interminable pitchers of fresh mint tea. In the evening, Felicity descended the staircase on her father's arm, quiet and pale but calm. Martin took supper with them that night and, from then on, seemed to accept with resignation the end of his nation as he had known it.

When Arden questioned her daughter later, Felicity said only, "Father hates war. But he hates chaos even more. He says he will work and pray that the dissension will be short, the Union soon repaired, and my baby will grow up under one flag and one government."

Arden thought that hardly sounded like Martin, in truth. "Did he say he was afraid?"

"No. And I told him that we need him more than ever now, with James gone and the boys, too. He's the only male who can take care of us." She took a deep breath. "He may be the first to see this baby born, before his own father."

"Don't think of that now," Arden said quickly. "You'll only get yourself upset. Did he . . ." Arden hesitated. She felt embarrassed before Felicity. "Did he mention the boys? Did he ask for me at all?"

"He asked for nobody, Mother," she said soothingly. "He didn't ask for me, either, really, but he didn't want to break my heart so he let me in." She patted Arden's arm. "He's getting older, you know. Men get sometimes—a little odd when they get to a certain age. They seem to lose their capacity for hope, some of them." She assumed an almost maternal air. "We mustn't let that happen to Father."

"Isn't it odd," Arden mused, "that women don't seem to have that happen to them so often? Your grandmother, for example . . ."

Felicity laughed. "Grandmama hasn't lost her capacity for *anything*, least of all hope. So long as there's a new frock to be considered, a new man to meet, or some trouble to stir up, she's ever hopeful!"

Arden shook her head. "She is hard-pressed to contain her glee over the coming battle, as though she scarcely realizes that Owen and Micah and James might be in it."

"She's a child, for all of her years," Felicity said quietly. "I love her, but these days I've come to know her for what she is—a lovely, naughty child."

Arden gazed at her daughter. "Marriage has changed you mightily," she said finally. "Are you happy, then, with your choice?"

Felicity said, "Yes," quite quickly, Arden noted. "I guess I see life for what it is these days. More than I did before James." She held her stomach lightly. "And of course, the baby changes everything, too. People who used to be so important to me . . .'' She hesitated, then thought better of what she had intended to say. She smiled brightly. ''You and Father will always be important to me, of course, and the rest of my family.''

''But you have a new family now,'' Arden said softly.

''Yes,'' Felicity said. ''And my husband's ideas now must be the ones I embrace. I hope Father can understand that in time.''

That night, Arden lay alongside Martin quietly, wanting to turn to him and speak of her concern. But he was still, his back to her, stolid and impenetrable. She felt so lonely for him, yet she knew she must respect his sorrow. Indeed, if she allowed herself to think of it, she could scarcely lift her own head out of her own sadness. Both boys gone, mounted on their best light-footed mares, each with a new suit of clothes, a servant, and their mother's kiss—none of which would stop a Yankee bullet.

She pushed the thought of their peril from her head. Likely, the war would be brief; they might not even see battle at all. Most in town said that once more states followed Mississippi's example, the Union would dissolve and Lincoln would have to declare defeat. She unconsciously put her hand on Martin's hip, stroking him without thinking of it, as one might pat a big, much-loved hound for comfort.

He turned to her then. She could tell by his eyes that he had not closed them once that night.

''I should never have sent them to West Point,'' he said earnestly. ''All that military bravado and the glory of distant battlefields.'' His eyes flashed in the darkness. ''Just so much bullshit,'' he said, his voice low with scorn.

Arden was mildly shocked. Martin rarely used profanity or low language of any kind.

''They got a good education,'' she murmured. ''Latin and Greek and the mathematics, remember?'' She stroked him comfortingly. ''History and philosophy and surveying and oratory . . .''

''And what good did it do?'' Martin asked her. ''Now

they think that war is glorious, that being a soldier means linking arms and clinking tankards—do you remember that song they used to sing?"

She grimaced wryly. She had finally forbade the verses in the house.

" 'To our comrades who have fallen, one cup before we go,' " Martin mocked quietly, " 'they poured their lifeblood freely out *pro bono publico*, no marble points the stranger to where they rest below . . .' "

" 'They lie neglected,' " Arden finished, her voice low with sadness, " 'far away from Benny Haven's, O!' " Benny Haven's was the tavern where West Pointers gathered to drink and dream of military honor.

"And that's what will happen to them now, I fear," he finished. Gloom furrowed his brow and curved his mouth down.

"Ah God!" she cried out, stricken then by the picture he had made in her mind's eye. "My boys!"

He pulled her to him quickly. "Don't let me take your hope, Arden. I'm a fool, a selfish fool. I let my own fear for them infect my good sense. Odds are good that Lincoln will make whatever concessions are necessary to keep us from war. And if we do go to war, it's likely to be over quickly— the boys will hardly even get their saddles busted in before they'll be home again. Please don't let my cynicism infect *your* heart, dear one, or we truly will be lost." He kissed her softly. "You're my mainstay. You know that."

"I do," she said, covering her fear with a tender embrace. "And you're right, of course. Likely, the boys will be home again before the roses bloom."

She stroked Martin into sleep, holding him until she felt his breath deepen and his body relax. Gently, she pulled herself away from him then and to her side of the bed, where she lay half the night trying to drive her fears away. Over and over, the refrain from the military air drifted through her thoughts: "they poured their lifeblood freely out . . ."

Sometime before dawn, she soundly, silently cursed Lin-

coln, Mississippi, abolitionists, and all men with the worst
blasphemies she could muster and only then did she finally,
finally fall asleep.

In March, however, the boys were not home yet. That
same month, Lincoln took office, and Natchez ran all flags at
half-mast, as though someone in high office had died. In
April, when the trees were all in bloom and the azaleas a riot
of color, Natchez held a collective breath, waiting to hear the
worst from Washington.

Letters from Micah and Owen were rife with humor and
wry accounts of their sojourns in Tennessee. They could find
little to praise about military life, but they adjudged their
own troops head and shoulders above those Yankee troops
they'd seen.

"The typical Yankee foot soldier," Owen wrote,
"doesn't know his left foot from his right, nor his backside
from his front. He takes cold easily, fills the barracks and
tents with the racking uproar of his coughs, is short-winded
and queasy in the belly as a nervous filly, and what's best of
all, for us at least, shows a surprising bewilderment when it
comes to his rifle. Micah says these Northern boys are all
pasty-faced mechanics and apt to run at the first sight of battle. I, for one, pray he is correct in his assessments."

Arden read and reread the letters, writing back almost
daily, sending along blankets, better shoes, a new set of
buckles which Micah specifically requested, and tobacco
when she could get it. She told herself that usually officers
were kept to the rear, for they were too vital to risk.

In April, the cruelest month of all to get such news, the
wires were ablaze with the firing of Southern gunboats on
Fort Sumter, South Carolina. For a week, the papers in Natchez spoke of little else, and almost overnight, the town was
emptied of young men, all bound for glory on distant battlefields.

Martin began to collect vital statistics which he held to

him like naked swords: The North had twenty million people, the South only nine million. The North had more than a hundred thousand manufacturing plants; the South less than twenty thousand. Massachusetts alone produced over sixty percent more goods than all of the Southern states combined, Martin said woefully. The North had more than twenty thousand rail lines; the South less than ten thousand.

Arden's head whirled with the numbers and she finally pleaded with him to leave her ignorant of any more such facts. Martin apologized, but within a few days, he was back again at the table with little else to discuss. It was as though he could not help himself.

"The people of this state—this whole damned country—don't know what they're getting into," Martin told her. "This land will be drenched in blood, and God only knows how it will end. It is all folly, madness, a crime against civilization. They speak so lightly of war!" and here, he slapped the Natchez *Courier* on the breakfast table. "They don't know what they're talking about. War is a terrible thing."

Arden listened silently, her heart filled with anguish. Martin kept forgetting that, with each word, her mind twisted desperately to Owen and Micah and James and a hundred other young men she knew well. Their poor mothers! At least they did not have to hear their husbands predict ignominious defeat and a bloodbath, of that much she felt sure.

"We are bound to fail," Martin went on, as though he spoke to himself. "Only in our spirit and determination are we ready for war. In all else, we are woefully outmatched, with a bad cause to start with . . ."

At those words, Anne came into the dining room, her head high and her nostrils flaring as though for battle. Clearly, she had heard enough to ignite her. "Martin, I sincerely hope you don't share your fears with anyone outside these walls, or you're apt to be hung for treason in the marketsquare!"

"No," he said tiredly, "I know better than to try to reason with a frenzied mob . . ."

"It seems to me," Anne said, taking her seat and unflapping her napkin like a banner, "that the Yankees are the mob, Martin. We want nothing more than to be left alone to go our own way and mind our own business, but *they* started it."

"I cannot deny that they occupied Fort Sumter," Martin said. "But only after the Confederate Congress declared war on them. Still, I cannot understand why Lincoln would take such a step."

"Because he's a ruthless dictator!" Anne replied, pouring her coffee with a shaking hand. "He wants our unconditional surrender, and he'll settle for nothing less! But he forgets some small details, Martin, as you have evidently done. We Southerners are used to command; we have to be to keep our niggers in line. Our men know how to ride and shoot, and one of them is worth ten Yankee factory workers who never picked up a rifle in their worthless lives." She smiled ruthlessly. "And I'm sure, since you know so all-fired much about war, Martin, that you must realize the great disadvantage any invader must face: our men will be fighting on their own soil, for the lives of their women and children. I think the Yankees will find them fierce as a nest of hornets bothered in their own tree!"

"I had not forgotten that advantage," Martin said, "but I don't think it sufficient to win this war."

"Now, Mother," Arden said, "I wish you wouldn't get yourself all upset first thing. No matter what either of you say, the tide will go as God will have it."

"Oh, Arden, don't be such a ninny! God hasn't a thing to do with it, 'tis a bunch of fool men with their blood up, bound and determined to have their way as usual, and the Devil take the hindmost." She turned back to Martin with a dismissive gesture to her daughter. "And as for your amazing remark that we're going to battle for a bad cause, I'd like to know, Martin Howard, what you think a good one would be. You might as well tell the Yankees they can come down here and take our houses and our horses and our land, as let them take the niggers out from under us—or worse yet, set them free to wander and rob at will!''

''They'll do just that, I fear,'' Martin said, rising and bowing politely to Anne and Arden. He dropped his napkin on the table as though it suddenly disgusted him.

''What?'' Anne asked.

''Take our houses, our horses, and our land,'' he replied calmly. ''And then we can sit under the chinaberry trees and mourn the days gone by. We'll all starve together.''

''Bah,'' Anne said to his back as he left the room. ''Arden, I hope you warn your husband not to speak of such when he's out and about; I swear, folks will not forgive such naysaying, not when war is on us. Seven states have seceded; they can't all be wrong. We must stick together now against the common enemy.''

Arden said quietly, ''I'm not quite sure who that is anymore, Mother.''

Anne leaned toward her daughter, her face narrowed with anger and her eyes flashing. ''Well, let me tell you, daughter, your two boys and your new grandbaby's daddy are sure enough, and when the bullets are flying, you better pray to God that they don't forget it!''

Arden rose to follow Martin. ''Whatever else, Mother, never mistake my silence for agreement. He is my husband, and I will believe what he believes, forsake what he forsakes, and take joy in what makes him jubilant.''

''You make pretty speeches just like Felicity! And what comfort do they bring her? How did I ever raise such a goose for a daughter and a slave for a granddaughter! Both of you think your men walk on water.''

''This is a big house, Mother,'' Arden said calmly, ''and I daresay there's room enough in it for opposing views.''

''I'm sure that's what Jefferson Davis hoped before he was forced out of Congress, chick!''

Arden held up one hand for silence. ''Let's agree to disagree, Mother. I'll ask Martin to air his views to me alone. I'll thank you to keep yours outside this house.''

"I don't know what we'll find to talk about over supper, then," Anne grumped, reaching for her second waffle. "I might as well go back to New Orleans. The man has no common sense and—"

"Enough, Mother," Arden said stiffly.

Anne looked up and assessed her daughter carefully. "I hope," she said softly, "for your sake, that all who are near and dear to you return unscathed from peril, my dear. For if they do not, you'll have small comfort from Martin's philosophies."

"I'll take my comfort where I always have," Arden said firmly. "From my husband's arms."

Anne gave her daughter a mock salute. But its effect was diluted by the fact that Arden was already out the door and gone.

Felicity received a letter from James at least once a week; Arden from Owen and Micah almost as often. All three men claimed to be writing more often, but the letters were usually late, sometimes waylaid, or simply never delivered at all. Nonetheless, the women watched and waited for them eagerly.

Owen's letters were full of humorous anecdotes; Micah's dry and newsworthy, spare in detail. "My men have no objections to privileges of rank," Owen wrote, "accustomed as they are to the same sort of hierarchy in civilian life. But let a shopkeeper or a merchant be promoted above a planter! Then you'll hear the planter shout, 'God damn you, I own niggers up country!,' and all hell breaks loose until I promise him special privileges and ingratiate myself to him as best I can. I hope you'll excuse my language, Mother, but I fear I can hardly express myself these days without profanity. It is all such a complex charade, this army, considering all of us are sleeping on the same ground and marching through the same dust. But at least I have learned all the words to 'Lorena,' 'Aura Lea,' and 'Home, Sweet Home.' Some of them are Yankee songs, to be sure, but my men are democratic in their choices. They ask only that a song makes them laugh or weep.''

Owen said that his men showed a penchant for gambling on anything and, lacking cards or dice, they'd bet on races between lice. "Everpresent in camp and on our persons," he reported, "the louse is much respected in my regiment in trials of speed. The men stage races with their favorites on any flat object, but one of my soldiers boasted a champion speedster which could not be beaten. After several trials wherein the competitors were each placed on their owner's plate to see which would vacate it first, it was found that the famed speed of this man's louse was due to his heating the plate before each contest. The following day, the losers were avenged, however. They staged a louse fight and the former speedster was soundly licked by his combatants. If I could get my men to fight Yankees as eagerly as they lose money on their lice, we'd win this war in a fortnight.''

Micah informed them that many of the men were woefully unprepared for battle, despite mind-numbing drills and long hours in the sun at target practice. "My Kaintucks prefer bowie knives to rifles and think a Bible will stop any bullet," he wrote. "Sometimes I recall that I joined the army to fight Yankees, not make men walk pickets and miss their sleep. Yet if I do not, discipline will falter. As it is, there is altogether too much breaking ranks for berry picking along the roadside," he added.

James's letters, at least those parts Felicity shared, spoke much of honor and duty. "What is life without honor?" she read to them, her eyes bright with proud tears. "Degradation is worse than death. We must think of the living and of those who are to come after us, and see that by God's blessing we transmit to them the freedom we have ourselves inherited.''

To Arden's great relief, Anne managed to hold her tongue at such recitations, murmuring only, "The boy has his father's gift for oratory, does he not?" Privately, Arden hoped that James's letters were, in other passages, tender and more ardent than those Felicity read aloud.

She remembered so clearly the look on Felicity's face when James left months ago. Standing at the Natchez docks, he had embraced his father, kissed his mother tenderly, and then turned to Felicity. They exchanged a long look. Clearly they had already said their goodbyes. Felicity held out her hands and he took them in his. "God keep you," were her last words.

"And you," he replied.

And then he was gone, as they all were, the handsome young men on their shining horses, and all that was left of James were Felicity's bulging skirts which barely hid his expected child.

To her dismay, Arden realized that she missed her boys more than she missed her only daughter. They were in peril, and not more than an hour passed that she did not yearn to see their perfect young faces. Felicity's absence was somehow more bearable. The truth is, Arden thought sadly, that it's not the sins of the fathers that are visited on the third generation but the sorrows of the mothers. One girl, unmothered, makes another so. For all my love of her, I cannot seem to be her proper mother. She recalled her own mother's plain words. Anne had said once, when Arden asked if she ever thought of remarriage, "I know all about love, and I don't want it. I gave it up. It hurts too much." Was Arden teaching the same lesson to her own daughter? Or did life simply and relentlessly teach that lesson to women more than it did to men? She did not know the answers. She could only resolve to do her best to bear up under her despair and worry and try to keep Martin and Felicity from seeing her pain.

Meanwhile, the letters kept coming. Micah said that diarrhea was now as feared and hated as any band of Yankees. The boys got it from eating green corn and unripe fruit as they marched through the land, and the sufferers, trotting white-faced to catch up with the column, could only wince and joke about it, though it was scarcely funny when it was your own bowels so tortured, Micah reported. Owen said his prowess since the disease was excellent; he could hit a dime at seven yards. Micah said his men had sore feet. Many had been without shoes for a week on Virginia's rocky roads.

Four more states seceded, Tennessee being the last. The Confederacy was now complete; Jefferson Davis was President, Alexander Stephens of Georgia was Vice President, and the capital of the Southern Cause was proclaimed to be Richmond, Virginia.

Lincoln called for 175,000 troops to quell the "insurrection," refusing still to call it war. Confederate leaders had no such qualms, named it revolution, and Southern men and boys flocked to enlist in a hundred local troops, guards, regiments, brigades, and cavalries named for their towns, their counties, their states, even for their homesteads.

The virgin battle of the war which blooded Mississippi was the first battle of Bull Run, and the Natchez papers were full of eyewitness accounts. Anne crowed over that first overwhelming victory and read aloud at the breakfast table when Martin was not there. These days, he took little breakfast, just coffee and fruit, and then up once more to his study to mull over his papers in gloomy silence.

"The Mississippi Regiment was there in full glory!" Anne read gleefully to Arden. "Union troops of thirty-four thousand strong led by Brigadier General McDowell ran in retreat, together with sightseers and Congressmen who came out from Washington to witness the expected Union victory. All of them fled in panic before Confederate troops led by General Beauregard and Thomas Jackson's brigade of Virginians. It was a rout!"

"Do they mention casualties?" Arden asked.

"Not in this article. That'll come later, I suppose. But they say that General Bernard saw the Virginians standing fast and said, 'Look, there is Jackson standing like a stone wall.' Like a stone wall! Isn't that magnificent? The Yankees will think twice before trying something like that again!"

"Well, those may. But unfortunately, there are a lot more of them where those came from," Arden said.

"Don't you dare be pessimistic this morning, chick," Anne said happily. "This news is simply too wonderful not to cheer. Remember Micah's last letter? Where he said that according to the Northern papers there were only two political parties now, the Patriots and the Traitors? He said he wanted to be ranked with the latter, and so should we all."

"Yes, and I remember Owen's last letter," Arden said. "When he mentioned that the new march in his regiment went something like, 'Saw my leg off, saw my leg off, saw my leg off short!'—I doubt they made that up for the sheer humor of it."

"Oh, you are hopeless," Anne scoffed. "You and Martin are getting to be like peas and carrots; I can't tell one from the other these days. You both go around with the same long faces and the same glum predictions . . ."

"Well, speaking of glum predictions," Arden said, hoping to change the subject, "do you know what a bolt of buckram costs this week, and that's if you can get it? Forty dollars cash! In my whole life, I never thought I'd see such piracy in broad daylight. Two years ago, you might give five dollars, and that's if you wanted it at all. And the same with flour and butter and molasses and turpentine—and don't even talk about sugar. Not for love nor money. Mary Springer told me yesterday that she gave ten dollars for a pack of needles. And was grateful to get them for that! I don't know what we'll do when the war actually gets started."

"It has gotten started and likely ended there too," Anne said firmly. "We've seen the worst of it. Mary Springer is a fool and so are you if you spend your husband's money on needles now. Wait six months, and we'll be back to having anything we want."

"I hope you're right, Mother," Arden said softly. "If you are, you'll be able to lord it over everyone else in town, for most folks are saying this will be longer than we thought."

"It won't be the first time most folks were wrong," Anne said shortly. "Nor the last."

In August, Lincoln announced a new income tax for all citizens of the United States. All adults making more than eight hundred dollars a year had to pay three percent of their income to the federal government.

"Got out just in time," Anne chuckled as she read the papers. Despite Martin's edict against the *Free Trader*, Anne smuggled it in under her bodice so boldly that everyone in the household knew of her defiance. Martin chose to ignore the trespass.

He said, "We may well laugh now, but how shall we amuse ourselves if we lose this war and the tax collector comes to reap our fair share of the war bill, Madam Lawrence?" He had retrenched to his old formality with Arden's mother since their battles began.

"First of all, we shall win this war," Anne said genially. "And likely, before we do, someone will take it into his head—a Northerner, probably—to rid the land of this Lincoln creature, once and for all. Attack a man's purse and even the most ardent Unionist will pull out his pistol." She grinned. "Mark my words, Martin Howard. That lanky monkey will not serve out his term."

In August, the Union Navy seized Forts Clark and Hatteras on the Carolina coast. Natchez was outraged. In October, Confederates chased a whole pack of Federals down Ball's Bluff on the Potomac at the Virginia-Maryland line, and the Mississippi Regiment was there to help. Natchez was jubilant. As the list of more than a thousand Union casualties was printed, and among them such prominents as the grandson of Paul Revere, the son of Oliver Wendell Holmes, a nephew of James Russell Lowell, and the Senator from Oregon, Ned Baker, fire eaters in the town began to predict that Washington would be put to the Confederate torch before the year was out.

In November, Federals retaliated and took Port Royal, South Carolina, bottling up the state and her nine billion dollars' worth of cotton as tight as a lyncher's noose. The winter dragged on, with a bleak Christmas in store. Only Owen's letters raised Arden's spirits: his last told of a massive campaign in which his regiment was supremely victorious. "The whole brigade formed with courage, and you never saw such a snowball fight in your life. Not a Captain or Colonel kept his hat, not a General was uncovered with white. We charged them and took two dozen prisoners, I'm happy to say." She read and reread that passage, for the pleasure of the rare smile it brought her.

With so many men gone and few allowed furlough, Natchez anticipated little holiday gaiety and no festive spirit. Sugar was harder to get, rum was too dear for all but the most frantic occasions, and it had already become a question of honor for the matrons and misses of the town to wear last year's Christmas gowns, rather than buy Northern goods.

"Every bolt of silk and lace is bought with Confederate blood," Anne said staunchly. "I will receive no woman with that stain on her bodice." Fortunately, most of the women in Natchez felt the same way, and so Arden's parlor was spared the turmoil of Anne Lawrence ordering out a traitorous female acquaintance. Even Felicity, mild Felicity who was huge with child now and barely able to get about at all, was determined to attend a few select Christmas gatherings, if only to show that she wore her homespun cotton and wool with pride.

And then it got worse. The Union Navy bottled up the Pamlico and took Ship Island, the last defense of New Orleans. Now Wilmington, Charleston, Savannah, and New Orleans were imperiled, and Federal gunboats were moving up the rivers and inlets and occupying the towns of Beaufort and Port Royal, taking with them some of the finest old plantations of the South. Right behind them came the abolitionist missionaries, spreading freedom fever.

"You must forbid your niggers to leave River Reach,"

Anne told Arden when she heard the latest news. "Once they find out about the war, they'll run wild and kill us all in our sleep."

"Nonsense," Arden said staunchly. "Our people have been treated fairly, and they are members of this family. Besides, they know about the war, and I can't stop up their ears, Mother. Portia and Cassie and Lucy come in and out of town most often as we do, and they'll tell the others whatever they know."

"You and Martin have spoiled those darkies for years," Anne said tartly, "and I told you as much the day I first came to River Reach. Now I guess you'll see that I was right all along when they up and leave you at the first sign of a Yankee uniform."

That night, Arden did something she had avoided for many months. She turned to Martin in the night and sobbed, letting him see her fear and frustration. He said nothing, only held her very tightly for a long while and let her weep out her despair wordlessly until she had only dry hitching breaths left to expel.

"This is very hard, isn't it," he murmured.

She moaned against him. "I get so tired sometimes," she said. "So weary with not knowing. With waiting and waiting for some word."

He patted her softly, aimlessly. It seemed that he did not know what else to do. "Do you think we should leave here?"

She shook her head. "We can't. I can't leave Felicity. I can't leave my mother."

He was silent for a long while. "We could take them with us."

She knew what an effort that cost him, to offer to take Anne Lawrence anywhere at all. "No," she whispered. "Felicity can't travel and Mother won't."

"Then we must stick it out." He sighed deeply. "But it's very hard."

She realized that he had repeated himself, something he

rarely did. She pulled back and gazed at him in some confusion. Something was missing. Somehow, he was not as much comfort as she had hoped. "Yes," she said finally, with a sense of disappointment.

"I knew it would be," he murmured. And then he released her gently, easing himself back down on the bed. "Try to rest, Arden. Try not to worry."

"Yes," she repeated. There was nothing else to say.

In the last week of December, Felicity's little girl was born, a healthy, red-faced child she named LeeAnn, after her grandmother and Robert E. Lee. Anne was, of course, puffed with pride and victory. Arden was simply relieved to see her daughter safely delivered. With so many men called to action, Natchez had now only one physician available, and as it was a point of honor to do without a new gown, so it was also a point of honor to do without a doctor for something so simple as birthing a child.

Arden held the tiny, perfect infant in her arms and gazed into her face, seeing Felicity again as she had been so young. She felt a fierce protective love surge through her, leaving her wet-eyed and cleansed of the sorrow and fear of the last year.

This was her first grandchild. The first real promise that life would continue, no matter how many crazed men attempted to bring it to a bloody halt. She had not thought it possible to love a baby any more than she had loved her own children, and yet if asked, she would have had to admit that yes, she somehow loved LeeAnn more. The space in her heart for a child was larger now, with Martin so far out of it, with her own three grown and gone. The need to touch that perfect skin, to gaze into the soft blue eyes, to fondle the silken hair, was more powerful than the need to breathe, Arden realized. The wonder of this new life was somehow much more of a miracle with death now much closer at hand.

She watched her own mother with LeeAnn, remembering

that when Felicity had been born, it had been the only time Anne Lawrence showed a spark of maternal love for any of her children. Perhaps she had felt a bit of what Arden felt now: the perfection of loving a child who was her own yet not her own, her blood but not her charge.

Felicity was going to be an excellent mother, that much was evident from the start. As competent as though she had birthed a dozen, she swaddled LeeAnn, put her to suck, bathed her and dressed her as smoothly as she seemed to do most else in her life. Ignoring her grandmother's rebuke that "only darkies suckle their own children," she proudly nursed LeeAnn for the first few weeks of her life, giving her to the wetnurse only reluctantly, as though she understood that in gaining her freedom, she was also losing a large place in the infant's soul.

But there was no time for any of them to dote upon the new baby or spend languid hours in the rapt contemplation of her future. Bad news came into Natchez so fast and regularly that they could scarcely recover from one event before the next one was upon them. It was the second year of the war, 1862, and it already seemed that it had been going on for a lifetime.

Owen and Micah were now with General Robert E. Lee on the Atlantic Coast, together with hundreds of South Carolina volunteers. Lee had ordered his soldiers to dig in for the impending Union attack, and Owen reported the storm of protest which followed. "Those at work with the shovels are complaining vigorously. Digging isn't fit work for a white man, they say, and a brave man wouldn't hide behind earthworks in the first place. They're calling Lee the King of Spades, Father, and I know you'd be amused at that and plain amazed at what the Tennessee boys call him behind his back—'Granny Lee.'"

Micah reported that General Butler was doing the same fortifications on the Virginian peninsula, taking slaves to do the work. "The servants say, 'I's contraband,' and cross what the Yankees call the freedom line to work for the Federals. Wish they'd do the same for us.'' He added laconically, "The mud here is apparently bottomless. Guns and wagons bog past the axles and then sit there, stuck until the millenium, I suppose. I saw a mule go almost completely out of sight in one of the chunk holes, all but the tips of its ears. Of course, it was a smallish mule.''

Arden noted that it had taken more than a month for their letters to reach Natchez, and she wondered how any nation could survive with such a slow post. And for that matter, without buttons, needles, corsets, simple medicinals, and pots and pans. With railroad lines threatened and ports blocked, the list of things she could not buy grew longer and longer every week, no matter how many Confederate dollars she sent with Portia to the Mercantile Store. The bottom had gone out of the slave market, and gold was selling at a premium of fifty percent, but still Natchez tried to keep doing business as usual.

It was becoming increasingly clear that this "rebellion" as Martin called it, this "revolution" as Anne declared it, would not be the ninety-day affair predicted when it began. General Grant and his Federals took Fort Donelson on the Cumberland River in Kentucky and Fort Henry on the Tennessee. Much of Johnston's army had been lost, and suddenly Nashville—oh, Nashville!—was lost to the enemy.

All at once, the war was very close, indeed. The year before, it had seemed a far-off thing, and aside from letters and fear and the deaths of other boys and the deprivation of material goods, Arden had felt mostly safe from its ravages. Now war was closer, and she felt a queer numb panic and frozen fear settle over her so deeply that it seemed she would never truly be safe again. Folks were evacuating from Nashville and pouring into Memphis—Memphis! Just up the Trace and within a few days' ride!

Folks said Memphis was nothing but a huge hospital, with hotels and houses and even stables and churches jammed with the wounded. Eight out of ten amputees died, the papers reported, victims of erysipelas, tetanus, and shock, but many more were sick with dysentery, measles, and typhoid fever.

Now Arden knew that Micah and Owen were imperiled not only by Yankee bullets but by disease as well. She began to collect parcels of herbs, medicinals, and powders to send to them, in a frantic haste to ward off what she imagined to be a horde of pestilence which followed every regiment like Death himself.

A reporter sent his impressions to the *Courier,* which printed the following: ''Nashville is now deserted, all of the stores and the most of the better homes are closed; the State House is abandoned, the legislators and Governor have fled. This journalist repaired to a hotel, found it closed and bolted, but kept on ringing, determined to get a bed for the night. Finally a colored man swung the door ajar and stood there grinning broadly. 'Massa done gone souf,' he said.''

Owen and Micah had seen their first battle, their most recent letters said, but not at the front. They were at Roanoke Island when General Wise surrendered to General Burnside, turning over two and a half thousand troops as prisoners and thirty-two cannon. Norfolk was likely next, and maybe Richmond shortly after. They were not taken as prisoners because their own brigade was too far to the rear. Also, the Yankees simply could not handle any more than they already had. ''But they could have had us, Mother,'' Owen said. ''We were lucky.''

''The problem,'' Micah's letter added calmly, ''is that Wise and his regiments ran out of powder for their cannon. We hear there is none to send. If that be the truth, we're not far from coming home, likely in defeat, but coming home nonetheless.''

Arden began to pray secretly that he was right.

Martin said, upon reading their letters, that war would be coming to Mississippi next, likely to Corinth on the border of the Tennessee. ''It will come faster to us than to other states,'' he predicted, ''for two inescapable reasons. First, we're located in the heart of the South, and we've got the

Mississippi River along our western flank. If the Yankees take the river, they've got the hammer to break the back of the Confederacy. And second, we're the most hotheaded of the secessionist states, and they hate us."

"More than South Carolina?" Arden asked, surprised.

"I am shamed to admit it, but yes," Martin said glumly. "And of course, we have the great good fortune to claim your mother's personal saint, Jefferson Davis, as a native son. You watch. Grant will see that we get it fast and hard. Our best hope is that it will be over soon."

Word came from James that he was at Corinth now with Generals Johnston and Beauregard. His regiment's task was to keep the Memphis and Charleston Railroad from the Yankees, and "keep it, I mean to," his letter to Felicity claimed, "or fall on my own sword in shame." To Arden's alarm, Felicity read that passage aloud, beaming at her mother with pride. "Isn't he a wonderful man?" she said softly, her eyes shining. "I know that with James between us and the Yankees, we'll be as safe as we can be in these terrible times."

"Yes," Arden could only murmur. She scarcely recognized her daughter anymore. James must tend to his own fate, Arden decided then. Live or die in glory, whatever God decreed. It was all she could do to keep Felicity, Anne, Martin, and LeeAnn in some semblance of health and good humor. She put thoughts of her own boys away from her. They were not in the fighting now, thank God, and the more trenches they dug, the better she slept at night. All eyes turned north now, for Grant and his troops were less than twenty miles from the Mississippi border. Sooner or later, he would strike hard, for the railroad was almost as important, Martin said, as the river itself. The Memphis and Charleston ran east-west across northeast Mississippi from Corinth to Iuka and then followed the south bank of the Tennessee across Alabama to Chattanooga. There, the railroad branched and one fork went south to Atlanta and on to Charleston and Savannah. Another fork went up to Richmond. "It's the artery of the Confederate body," Martin said. "And Grant will do his level best to cut it and bleed it dry."

For three days, Natchez held its breath, waiting to hear when the battle had begun. The wires hummed on April 7 that the guns could be as far south as Vicksburg. Estimates were that Beauregard attacked first, leading his forty thousand men against Grant's seventy thousand, and that the Mississippi Sixth led the charge.

The breath of the town went out then, not with relief but with a groan as though it had been punched hard in the vitals. Too many Natchez men, good ones, young ones, were in the Mississippi Sixth, and what could Beauregard be thinking of, with those odds, if they were true?

Now Felicity called with her carriage for Arden each day to accompany her to the offices of the *Courier*. Though her father would not allow the paper in the house, the list of dead and wounded came through their wire and was posted outside the door after supper. Felicity said she could not bear making the trip with James's mother and sisters, for they could not remain calm, no matter if his name appeared or not.

And so Arden went with her, the two of them hidden under their widest hats and veils, for it was simply too painful to see the carriages roll up, filled with wives, mothers, sisters, some of them weeping already with fear. Arden had thought of asking Martin to go for Felicity, but she knew that her daughter would not hear of it. She was determined. That chin was out, even under the veil; the back was straight even as her hands shook in her gloves. Felicity asked her driver to stop at the office, and she descended with grave dignity, doing her best to ignore the weeping women on all sides. A father, a husband, a son, a brother—Arden did not know who was lost until Felicity came back to the carriage, and she would not allow her mother to take her arm and walk her there. Arden sometimes still did not know who was lost and who was not until she read it in the paper the next day, for Felicity read no farther than the D's—if James Daniels and

Leonard Daniels were not on it, she turned resolutely back to
the carriage and had her driver wheel for home.

"How do you stand it?" Arden asked her quietly. "I
don't know that I could do this more than once."

"Yes, you would," Felicity said tightly. "You would if
your own husband were out there. It's the least I can do."
And then her breath caught in a stifled sob. "Somehow I
feel, so long as I come and look, his name will not be there.
But the first time I miss, that's when he'll fall!" She
clutched her mother's gloved hand. "Thank you, Mother.
No one else would understand."

On the second day of fighting, details began to come
along with the news of the fallen soldiers. Johnston had tried
to catch Grant's men by surprise but had moved too slowly.
They were waiting for him. Also, too many Confederates
stopped at the mess sites and rummaged in the Yankee tents
for food and other treasures, one journalist reported, so that
their comrades to the front missed their support sorely. Men
who read the reports swore loudly; their women wept with
shame and frustration.

The second day of fighting, once more James Daniel was
not listed, nor was his brother, Leonard. Felicity closed her
eyes in prayer as she sat alongside her mother, this time letting her driver take the carriage at a slower pace back home.

The worst news of all came in shortly after: General Johnston himself was killed and the Yankees were still standing
fast. Beauregard alone was unable either to destroy or to
move Grant's troops. After the loss of more than ten thousand men, the Confederates withdrew, leaving the field open
for the Federals to move deeper into Mississippi at last.

The mood in Natchez went from fearful hope to ominous
panic. The Yankees were now close, too close to be ignored.
And there was real doubt they could be stopped. Shiloh, a
little log church whose name meant "the place of peace,"
brought none of that to Mississippi.

Ten days after the battle, a letter arrived from James's
commanding officer with his regrets. James Daniels had

fallen, alongside his brother, Leonard, on the second day at Shiloh. He was cut down by enemy fire, the commander wrote, while trying to rally his men. "We lost more than a thousand men in one hour in that skirmish," he added, "and we might have lost more had it not been for Daniels and his brother. They will be sorely missed from our regiment, from our hearts, and from the glorious cause for which they died. My sincere regrets, Madam."

Felicity received the news, drove her own carriage directly to her mother's door, went in, and handed her mother the letter. Arden had only to look at the flourishing black border, the heavy penstrokes, and Felicity's pale, set face to know what it said. "Oh no, Filly!" she screamed.

Felicity turned to face her father, who had just come into the room, smiled wanly, and fainted dead away into his arms.

The summer dragged on, long months of blistering heat, damp air, and a suffocating fear. Shortly after Shiloh, the Union Navy took New Orleans, capturing the largest seaport in the South. The Crescent City, larger in population than any four Southern cities combined, had also been the center for important blockade activity. Here, the sleek, low, ghostly runners made their escapes and their elusions, usually by the dark of the moon, running with smokeless coal, telescopic funnels, and feathered paddles to keep them invisible to the Yankee gunboats. With names such as *Let Her Be*, the *Fox*, the *Leopard*, and *Banshee*, they slid in and out of New Orleans under high risk, bringing as many as ten thousand Enfield rifles, a million cartridges, two million percussion caps, four hundred barrels of powder, and a large quantity of cutlasses and revolvers. The South could not survive without them.

New Orleans erupted in rage and frenzied frustration when the news came that the city was taken. For days, crowds milled in the street, brandishing knives and pistols and howling for resistance to the end, burning bales of cotton and crates of rice, screaming, "The damned Yankees shall not have it!"

But have it, they finally did.

When the Federals took New Orleans, they hit a killing blow at the South's war supplies and also, for Natchez and the rest of Mississippi, blocked the last escape route on the great river. Now Natchez was trapped between Federals above her to the north and below her to the south.

When Anne heard the news that her beloved New Orleans was at last in enemy hands, she took to her bed in despair. Arden was alarmed, and she called for the doctor to come for her mother, despite the fact that he was too busy already with more pressing wounds and diseases. He came, he spent an hour alone with Anne in her room, and he pronounced her sound enough, except for a racing pulse and a strained heart. "Keep all further war news from her," he said gravely. "She's too old for any more shocks."

The next morning, Arden went to her mother's bed to find her passed into death. She was lying on her back in her best lace sleeping gown, her hands at her breast, her face calm, her eyes closed as in sleep. She was cold and still, but lovely. Remote. Her few wrinkles were relaxed, her skin as perfect as ever.

Arden sat down carefully next to her mother and took one of her hands. She waited for the grief to pour over her like a tide. But it did not. She could feel only small sorrow, some sense of regret, and an infinite relief, both for her husband, her daughter, and yes, for herself. Anne Lawrence was gone, and with her, a different era. A different sort of womanhood. Certainly, a different sort of mother.

Arden smoothed her mother's hair with her pearl-handled brush and then rang for Portia. Portia would know what should be done. She was suddenly too weary to do another thing more.

Portia came into the room warily, saw Arden sitting there,

and then gazed in surprise at Anne Lawrence's composed face. "She pass?" Portia whispered.

Arden nodded. "Sometime in the night, I suppose. Doctor said she couldn't take any more shocks. Perhaps it was her heart."

Portia moved closer. "She don' look like she suffer none."

Arden smiled sadly. "She never did."

Portia put her hand on Arden's shoulder and peered into her face. "You goin' to bear up, Miz Arden?"

"Yes," she said quietly. "I'm going to bear up fine. But you must do this for me, Portia. I can't seem to make myself." She looked up at the slave with fond affection. "Will you take care of Mother for me?"

Portia nodded resolutely. "I do ev'r'thin', Miz Arden, don' you worry none. You go to your room now," she added, pulling Arden up gently by the arm. "I see to Miz Lawrence jes' fine. I make her right afore God an' nobody see her 'til she ready."

"She'd like that," Arden murmured tiredly. "You call me when everything's set." And she went out to her room and closed the door, trusting that somehow, between Portia and Joseph and the rest, her mother would be readied for death at least as well as she was cared for in life.

She sat down on her chair and picked up her needlework, turning so that the light from the morning fell on her hands. Outside, the streets of Natchez were coming to life as they did every morning, with or without war, with or without Anne Lawrence.

I am no longer a daughter, Arden told herself. Never, for the rest of my life, will I fill that role. Never will I be responsible to a parent, need to please or gain approval from one, be embarrassed by a mother, disappointed by a father, never again will I be taken care of in that way or loved because I am part of someone else's flesh—I am no longer a daughter. I no longer have a mother.

And in that moment, Arden felt the deep ache of grief, the

yearning and hot anguish that she had felt when she was only six, and the nuns behind their cold walls and gray veils kept her from her mother's arms. Or at least she had thought that to be true. She had cried so hard then, "Mother! Mother! I want my Mother!" But no mother came to her. She sometimes felt that she would cry the very heart out of her body, would weep her eyes out of her head. But still no mother came.

And when she did, at last, come to see her, Anne Lawrence was loving and gay and so very beautiful, kissing her cheeks over and over and petting her hands, but never really looking at her, staying such a short while, telling her over and over how much she loved her and missed her, but when Arden begged to be taken home, "Oh, darling, you know how happy that would make me! But it's simply not a good idea for you to come home now. Your father is so very busy, and we'll be leaving soon for Memphis, you remember I told you that I'll bring you something pretty and special from Memphis? And when we come back, I'll come straight away to see you, I promise . . ." and then she would be gone once more.

One day, Arden found a small gold button out in the garden right after her mother departed, and she knew it was from the jacket her mother had worn. She immediately hid it away in her pocket, holding it and fondling it over and over, for it seemed to her to hold all the love, all the soft words and tender touches, that her mother might have given her if she could. She knew it was a sin to keep such things from the nuns, knew, too, that it was wrong to covet material objects and make from them something to love as she should have loved God. But for many years that button kept her warm at night in a way nothing else did, until she finally put it away with her other scant treasures and never looked at it again.

Arden had missed her mother every hour of every day for so many years that finally, she had no choice but to stop. She must stop wanting what she could not have or die of the wanting. And so she put away her dreams of being with her mother and did her best to be such a good, sweet, mannerly child, so bright and charming, that her mother would want to visit more often, stay longer each time, and perhaps some-day take her home again. She prayed to the Virgin Mother for strength and love, as the nuns taught her to do, and in time, she did not expect her mother to be who she was not.

But now her mother was gone once more, and this time forever. She would never again embrace her with that spe-cial warmth, never again scold her or tease her or laugh at her misgivings, never again be that beautiful beacon she longed for—longed, sometimes, to be. Her mother was gone.

Arden put one hand to her eyes and wept harder than she had in months, sobbing as she had when she was six. Not for the mother who was gone, but for the mother she had waited for all of her life who now would never come at all.

Anne Lawrence was buried at Graced Ground next to her mother and father. Josie wept hard at the gravesite, an old man now, palsied with gout and trembling legs which seemed far too small for his body. He was even more sor-rowed than Arden. More distraught, too, than Felicity, who stood stolid and numb with LeeAnn in her arms. Somehow, in the chaos and everyday deaths of war all round them, the simple passing of an old woman, no matter how lovely, seemed not of much import in the grand scheme of things. Few mourners made the trip out from Natchez, and only the slaves made the funeral seem well attended.

Owen's wife, Hanna, sang for them all "The Bonnie Blue Flag":

We are a band of brothers and native to the soil,
Fighting for the property we gained by honest toil,
And when our rights were threatened, the cry rose
    near and far,
Hurrah for the Bonnie Blue Flag that bears a Single Star.

Hurrah! Hurrah! For Southern Rights Hurrah!
Hurrah! For the Bonnie Blue Flag that
    bears a Single Star!

It was fitting, Arden thought. More fitting than any hymn. Martin stood by, his hand at her back for support. "It's well," he said to her as they left the burial ground, "that she went before the South does. She couldn't have borne the despair of that."

Arden glanced at him then, quickly affronted by his words. They seemed to imply relief at her mother's passing, and she could not abide anyone echoing a sentiment she fought down so hard in her own heart. But she repressed a retort, telling herself that he meant no insult. He had simply grown a bit clumsy at comfort these days.

"Now we're in mourning on all sides," he said to her that night in bed. "Like most of the families we know. Has Felicity allowed visitors yet?"

Felicity had not allowed a single caller since James's death except for a single visit to his mother and sisters and two visits from her mother, and even those visits had been strained and awkward. She had shut herself up in their town house with LeeAnn and the few servants she had left and made no response to those who might extend their condolences. So many families were stricken now that the usual mourning rituals were impossible. "No," Arden said sadly, "but I doubt anyone has noticed much. They've all got their own losses to deal with."

"And more to come, I fear," he murmured.

"Oh God, Martin, don't let's talk of death anymore. I'm sick to the heart with it." She moaned this last, turning her head away from him as though he carried a contagion.

"I'm sorry," he said softly. And he turned to the other side of the bed.

* * *

Soon, there was little time to mourn, even if Arden had been so disposed. Owen's latest letter said that they had seen hard battle and won it. "I want to get the whole regiment drunk at my expense!" he exulted. "I want to shout the rebel yell from a rooftop, I want to fight a small man and lick him!"

Micah's letter said, "The problem of deserters is one of discipline, of course, and I strive always to keep my men in tight order. I find that punishment is the only way to keep some of them in line. Last time I rounded up three men in continuing retreat, I shouted at them, 'Stop, men! Don't you love your country?' and one of them hollered back, 'Yes, by God! And I'm trying to get back to it just as fast as I can!' I could not, in my heart, condemn his sentiments."

Meanwhile, the Mayor of Natchez got news that Admiral Farragut's Union gunboats were coming to the city to demand surrender. Without hesitation, he wired to the Federals his immediate compliance. Natchez was now in Union hands, though those hands were still far downriver.

When the news rocked the city, Martin invited one of his friends, a city councilman, to come to supper, hoping for a fuller explanation. He politely questioned the man about what seemed to be a rather precipitous action, and the councilman answered as wearily as though he had had to answer that same question a hundred times before. "We had no choice, sir. We have no forces, no fortifications, absolutely no means to defend ourselves at all."

"We have bluffs as high as Vicksburg," Martin said.

"Yes, and no cannon for fifty miles to put on them," he replied. "Governor Pettus seems to think Vicksburg a better place to take a stand, and Jefferson Davis doesn't seem to care about either city." He waved away Martin's further questions as one would a pesky fly. "It doesn't matter, sir, not a whit. Whether we surrender or not, the town is theirs. By surrendering, we need not worry about being shelled at least. And they didn't get any of our cotton, we saw to that."

Arden said mildly, "Yes, that was a dreadful sight. The whole riverfront ablaze . . ."

"The only currency this county has, going up in smoke," Martin added grimly. "Now if we had to buy cannon, we couldn't. I had no bales standing ready to ship, but if I had, I wonder how I would have made myself light that match."

"At the point of a gun, you would have, sir," the councilman said impatiently. "And that's what it took for a few. But it's done now, and if you please, I'd like not to speak of it again while I have my plate before me." He took another bite of chicken, one of the few left, Arden supposed, in the city. "I've been given the appelation of this fine bird all too often these days, and I frankly wish to hear it no more."

And so the town of Natchez was formally under Union rule, though not a soldier was in sight. As went Natchez, so went the rest of the river. Except for the four miles of water under the Vicksburg bluffs held staunchly by confederate cannon, the whole of the Mississippi was now open to Union gunboats. Everyone knew that Vicksburg would be Grant's next target, but the papers said that the city could not be attacked from the rear because of the Yazoo bluffs, or from the north because of the flooded delta country, and only a fool would face the open cannons on the river itself. "Vicksburg is impregnable!" claimed the *Courier,* but many wondered privately if the Union General knew the meaning of the word.

Martin Howard's was not the only house in Natchez where there had been dissension about the war, Arden discovered as she went from home to home to pay her respects and condolences to those friends who had lost someone in battle. Many of Martin's friends were beginning to see that they had more to lose by continuing to fight than by surrender. And though they were despised by both sides, there were enough Confederate deserters hiding out along the Trace to add a growing voice to those who wanted the war stopped at any cost.

Plantations on the outskirts were being looted and barns

were mysteriously being torched, some said by the Yankees, some said by malcontent Confederates. River Reach had been fortunate to escape damage or loss; Graced Ground was likely kept safe by the presence of Josie and his wife, but many others were not so lucky.

The last letter Arden received from Micah had pleaded for cooking vessels of any kind she might be able to find. "My men have not a single vessel to cook one morsel of bread," he wrote. "For God and the country's sake, if my fair-promising but never-complying quartermaster does not send me some skillets or ovens or pots or anything that will bake bread or fry meat, my men will rise up and leave me on the field. Mother, send what you can . . ."

But she could find nothing to send and no way to send it, to her intense frustration and despair.

And Owen's last letter seemed to come from another time and place altogether. "When we open our eyes in the morning, we find the canvas roofs and walls of our tents black with flies. It needs no morning reveille to rouse the soldier from his slumbers. The tickling sensations about the ears, eyes, mouth, and nose caused by the microscopic feet and inquisitive suckers of an army numerous as the Yanks themselves will awaken my regiment from innocent sleep to wide-awake profanity more promptly than the near beat of the alarming drum."

"This last letter seems to have been written in the hot months. Do you think the boys are no longer together?" she asked Martin.

"No, I think they are still together," he reassured her. "But there's no guarantee they put paper to pen simultaneously."

She tried to comfort herself with that, for there was no other explanation she could endure.

Refugees began to stream from Natchez to points of safety, out west, farther south, wherever they thought the Yankees might not invade. Even more refugees poured back into the city, however, from the outlying plantations and

farms. No one wanted to be on isolated ground when the
Bluecoats came like a deadly tide. Folks began to fear their
own slaves, for talk of "freedom comin'!" was rampant
among them, and no one forgot John Brown's warning that
"the crimes of this guilty land will never be purged away but
with blood."

River Reach was still producing some cotton, of course,
for Joseph and Dick and Samuel kept just enough slaves
working. Many had run off, but Martin spent more and more
time on horseback among them, telling them that even if the
Yankees won, they would still have a home on the place.
More of them feared being turned out than feared being
bound, it seemed, at least on Martin Howard's land. But
there was no ready market for the cotton and no way to get it
out of port safely. Fortunately, Martin had sent much of his
money overseas to Paris and Liverpool, but the cotton was
not so easy to liquidate. He could do nothing but store it in
large bales, hoping against rot or an errant torch, until somehow, Natchez and the river were open once more.

In July, after seven days of hard fighting, General George
McClellan's army had to retreat from its lines around a be-
sieged Richmond to the muddy waters of Harrison's Landing, where the Union troops were finally transported away.
This was a small victory, but the news was not enough to
make the South jubilant, for the death letters were coming
hard and fast. Thousands and thousands of young men had
been killed at places like Gaines Mill, Trent Farm, Savage
Station, and the bloody slopes of Malvern Hill where General Stonewall Jackson prayed in his tent while thousands of
Confederates died trying to take an impossible defensive position.

After several weeks of hard mourning, during which time
she scarcely ate or spoke, Felicity roused herself to care for
LeeAnn and to pull her life back together. When Arden went
to her daughter's home again, she saw that all of the mirrors
were turned to the walls, the curtains drawn, and the large oil
painting of James in his uniform with drawn sword was

draped in black. The stench of the dye pots out back, where the servants stirred all of Felicity's clothes into black mourning, filled the steaming air both outside and inside the large house.

Arden found Felicity upstairs in LeeAnn's nursery. She was rocking the baby silently, her eyes fixed on the window which faced the slowly winding river. When Arden came in the room, Felicity said softly, "I'll never remarry, Mother. And so I hope Owen and Micah live through this carnage, for LeeAnn will need an uncle or two to make up for her father's loss." She looked down at the sleeping baby and kissed her gently. "He never even got to see his child."

Arden's heart ached at her daughter's words. They sounded so final, so hopeless. "You're a young woman yet," she said. "It's too soon to speak of such, naturally, but I'm sure you'll want to marry again one day. James would have wanted you to."

"No, he would not," she said firmly. "You can't know that, of course, but he would have wanted no such thing. We spoke of it before he left. He was a man of great honor, and he believed that marriage was eternal, regardless of the life or death of either spouse. If I had died giving birth to LeeAnn, he never would have married again—he told me so. Like an old swan, he said," and she gazed out to the river again. "An old swan who never takes another mate if the first one is shot by a hunter. He just lives alone and leads the flock and rides the winds."

"Oh Filly . . ." Arden tried to speak.

"No, Mother, just listen." Felicity took a paper from her bodice. It was well worn and creased, obviously read and reread a thousand times. "We hurled rocks when ammunition ran low. I look on the body of a man now as I once looked on the carcass of a horse or a hog, I have seen so many dead. My shoes are gone, my clothes are gone, I'm weary, I'm sick, and I'm hungry. My comrades have all been killed or scattered to the winds, my brother's dead, and my family's land is likely gone, perhaps my family as well. I've suffered all this for my country. I love my country, dear Felicity, but if this war is ever over, I'll be damned if I ever love another country again. But I have no lack of confidence in our cause, nor does my courage lack nor falter. I am willing to lay down all my joys in this life to gain freedom for my child. Dear Felicity, my love for you is deathless. My memories of you, however brief, sweep over me like a strong wind and bear me home to you in my mind, and I am deeply grateful to God that I have known your love. If I do not return, never forget how much I loved you, nor that with my last breath, as it escapes me on the battlefield, I will whisper your name. Forgive my faults and the pains I have caused you, and how thoughtless I have been, but oh Felicity, if the dead can come back to earth and live among those they love, I shall always be with you and our child. In the brightest day and the darkest night, always, always. And when the soft breeze fans your cheek, it shall be my breath passing. Do not mourn me dead, Felicity, for I am only waiting for you. Please wait for me until we shall meet again. Your loving husband, James.''

Arden wept quietly as Felicity finished the letter and folded it carefully back into her bodice. She turned away and wiped her eyes.

After a long moment, Felicity said, ''You can understand then, Mother. I will wait for him.''

A tired anger rose in Arden then, at that dear foolish man—a boy, really—who had said such passionate, thoughtless things to her daughter and so wed her to him, even in death. And at her daughter for holding on to such eloquent, beautiful nonsense. But she knew better than to speak to Filly of that now, for her daughter would never hear the words.

There must be thousands of mothers trying to comfort thousands of daughters now, she suddenly realized, all over the South. Many of them, widows themselves. She touched her daughter on the shoulder. All that mattered now was Felicity and LeeAnn. "Whatever you wish, Filly," she said simply.

In the forests surrounding Natchez, most particularly in those along the Trace where the creeks were quick and the trees were denser, the Red-bellied woodpecker, *Centurus carolinus*, sent his loud, oft-repeated *churrr* into the bright, hot air. Robin-sized, he was about ten inches of determined bird energy, with barred black and white back and pale buff belly. Like the other males of his species, he had a bright red crown and nape and a smaller red patch on his lower abdomen which attracted females from all quarters.

Zebraback, as he was called, was much loved by the farmers in his region, and that was well, for his kind was numerous. He ate vast numbers of wood-boring beetles, grasshoppers, ants, and cotton worms. His loud chuck-chuck-chuck call and knocking drill could be heard more than a quarter-mile from his nest.

Nesting season was over now for Zebraback, his mate long since flown, their four white eggs brooded in his tree cavity now only a few remnants of old shell. Chicks gone, mate gone, he was busy storing food for the winter, usually acorns, beechnuts, and wild fruits—those he might snatch from the greedy, swift hands of squirrels and raccoons.

Zebraback was hunting for the perfect hollow tree, an occupation which particularly obsessed him during courting season but which was always on his mind no matter the time of the year. The hollower the tree, the farther his rapid-fire drill would resonate through the forest, and the more females could hear him. In his prime, he had attracted no fewer than four females at a time, and he had flushed and preened himself, the red feathers on his head standing up and out like flame.

He was an older bird now, his drill less powerful, but he still attracted fine mates. Now, he was merely hunting for food, a no less compelling activity than mating, to be sure, particularly at his age. He picked a fine oak tree, hollowed in many places, and began to drill vigorously.

Zebraback could hit his sharp bill on the treebark eighteen times a second, more than ten thousand blows per day. Because he had no cavity between his brain and his skull, his brain was not bounced about by his drilling, he felt no pressure or pain, and the pad of cartilage between his beak and his skull as well as the muscles there supported the brain without damage, no matter how hard the tree or how frequent his drilling.

In fact, if farmers had known more about Zebraback, he might not have been so well tolerated. For the bird was so powerful, so tenacious in his quest for a mate and for food—and also so plentiful—that he and his kind could actually kill whole stands of trees by drilling through to heartwood.

But here along the Trace, Zebraback killed few trees, for the insects were so plentiful he did not need to drill very deep. Now, he drilled with all his might, searching for bark beetles, one of his favorite meals.

The din he made halfway up the tree was so loud that he could not hear what approached below. A feral cat prowled the bottom of his oak tree, black and white striped, just as he was on his back. The cat was gaunt with hunger, and his eyes glowed wild with fear. Long fed by his humans, he had been abandoned for several weeks when they left their small farm near the Trace to refugee to Natchez. Alone and left to fend for himself, he had had some small luck with mice in the fields, but now it was growing late in the year, and he sensed that when cold weather came, he would die if he did not learn to hunt more effectively.

He had come to the bottom of Zebraback's tree, following the noise of the drilling. Twice before, he had hunted the strange, knocking birds, but never caught one. He intended to succeed at this hunt today.

He watched the drilling bird for long moments, hiding behind the tree and growling low in his throat, unable to keep still. He glanced about nervously. At any moment, he might

be attacked himself, by a raccoon, a fox, one of the many
dogs which prowled these forests, wild as himself and huge,
or a snake or—

The drilling stopped, and the cat shrank against the tree,
still as the air itself. The bird cocked its head, peered intently
into the hole it was digging, and then began to drill again.
The cat knew it must act quickly. It sprang silently as far up
the tree as he could, on the opposite side of the tree from the
bird, held on with his claws, and leaped up twice more until
he was on a branch just above the bird's head. Panting, he
clung to the branch, trying to melt himself into its thickness.
He watched and flattened his ears, unable to see the bird directly. The din from the drilling was deafening at this close
range, but his empty stomach pressed him forward.

The drilling stopped abruptly, and the cat inched around
the branch where he could see the bird. The bird spied the cat
in the same instant, and he squawked in alarm. In that moment, the cat sprang, grabbed the woodpecker, lost his footing, and fell down, down to the brush below, the bird in his
jaws.

The fall nearly knocked the cat senseless. He had fallen on
his side, and he had no wind, could scarcely open his eyes.
He felt the bird struggle feebly, however, and he gripped his
jaws closed as tightly as he could.

Zebraback twisted in the cat's teeth, trying to peck the animal squarely in the eyes. He managed to peck once, twice
even, but the cat only growled and gripped him more tightly.
He could feel his wing was broken, and the pain in his back
was a slow, growing terror. Zebraback called out, strongly
once, crying out his pain and fear, then more softly, as his
eyes glazed over, and he knew only black silence and the
cessation of all pain.

The cat lay still, trying to recover his breath and his
strength. He felt numb along his back leg, and his back was
already sore and tight. He knew he would likely not hunt
again for a good while, perhaps not even be able to walk
away with this prey. He waited a longer while, still holding

the dead bird in his jaws. Finally, slowly, he rose and tested his limbs. One was broken, he knew that by the sharp pain. Dully, he dragged the bedraggled, limp bird to the shelter of a bush and began to try to eat.

He knew, with the instinct of a wild creature, though he had not been one for long, that this would likely be his last meal. He determined to eat what he could, to live as long as possible. Already, a fire was in his limb, and his head felt light from the pain. But he ripped open the bird with as much strength as he could muster to feel the warm blood on his muzzle one last time. Growling again, he yanked at the woodpecker's small body, warning all who might be within hearing that this was his kill.

Natchez was gloomy, expecting the worst, with danger looming in all directions. Mail was erratic and slow, roustabouts no longer swarmed on the docks for there were no cargoes to unload, the wharves lay idle, and warehouses formerly bulging with cotton and sugar and grain yawned hollow. Money was so scarce that a grim joke was the present currency: that an olive oil label would pass for cash because it was greasy, smelled bad, and bore an autograph.

Prices were exorbitant, and many items were simply not to be had for love nor money. Meat was fifty cents a pound and often not fit to eat, butter seventy-five cents, coffee just shy of two dollars, if you could get it—in contrast to cotton, which had fallen to five cents a pound. Salt was scarce and sugar such a luxury that it was saved by would-be brides for months for a simple wedding cake.

Arden quietly began to take in needlework and sewing to earn extra money for the household. There were still women in town who could not sew for themselves, and with so many of the slaves gone, there were too few hands who were skilled. She was careful not to let Martin see her work, however, for she knew he would be pained by her efforts. Word of mouth was enough; she had as much as she could do, and so long as she would accept payment in Confederate dollars, she had ample customers. But she never referred to them as customers, even in her own mind. They were simply friends who needed some help, she told herself. And if Martin asked, she would tell him the same.

As she went out to collect or deliver her work, she saw signs of change all around her. Natchez always seemed to inspire high-running sentiments, usually in contradictory directions, it seemed to her. She often saw treasonable slogans chalked on fences: "Union men to the rescue!" "Now is the time to rally round the Old Flag!" "God bless the Stars and Stripes!" There were whispers of secret Union meetings and talk that if the Yankees did show their faces in town, a few certain merchants and planters might well be there to welcome them properly.

Occasionally, a frustrated mob would bloom abruptly, out of some saloon likely, and up and down the streets they would march, men half-drunk with rage and whatever else they had to drink, brandishing knives and pistols and howling for resistance to the end, hoping to stumble on a pack of Yankees to tear to pieces.

But most often, Natchez stayed behind locked doors and shuttered windows, enduring the heat, the sorrow, and the fear in isolation.

Arden visited Felicity almost every other day. Her granddaughter was blooming into a beautiful healthy child, as though no war raged round her, as though she had not been born into sorrow. Felicity gave her every bit of love she could muster; Arden could see that much. But there were times, and it showed, that her daughter had little to give. Arden wondered if this would be another daughter raised with a question in her heart where love should have lived, but there was nothing she could do but try to keep both of them afloat in a sea of troubles.

When she could, she also made frequent visits to the new wives of Owen and Micah, though both young women had retreated to the bosom of their families as though they had never been wed at all. Each visit was as much torment as consolation, for they had no more recent word from the boys than Arden had and could do little to fortify each other with courage and hope they scarcely felt.

On September 2, the Union gunboat, *U.S. Essex* sailed into Natchez waters and docked. When the townspeople saw a genuine Yankee gunboat settled at port, a fine frenzy settled over them like the summer dust, and the Silver Grays quickly rushed from house to house, assembling their weapons and themselves in a controlled panic.

The Silver Grays were a company of those males left in the town after fourteen companies of gray-clad soldiers had marched down the hill to the boats when the war began. Men too old or too young for war had banded together to form the only defense Natchez had. Now, at last, they were to see battle, after futile months of patrolling the river for exactly this terrifying spectacle: Yankees on Natchez soil.

Before the Grays could assemble properly, word came from Natchez-Under-the Hill that the Yankee sailors had plundered a dockside warehouse, taking hay, rice, and some hogs. One hapless negro roustabout was forced aboard the gunboat, together with a supply of coal.

But the Yankees were back aboard their ship by the time the Silver Grays reached the plateau. They drilled back and forth a while, letting the sailors see their weapons, and then they went to their homes for supper.

Martin was sitting at the head of the table, reading a month-old copy of *The New York Times* which he had been fortunate enough to borrow, when a boy rushed into the dining room, gasping in horror. "Colonel! Colonel Martin, sir! The Yankees are coming up the hill again, and we don't know what to do! Should we fire on them?"

"My Lord!" Arden moaned, turning to stare at the white-faced lad. It was Clara Mill's son, Douglas, the only Mill boy still home from the war. A beardless youth no more than thirteen, he wore the gray uniform well, but the musket on his shoulder looked obscenely out of place. Oh, why had

Martin ever accepted the position of Colonel of the company!

Martin moved quickly for his coat, grabbing his own musket as he followed Douglas out the door. She heard him say, "Run ahead, boy, and tell them to hold their fire until I get there," Douglas took off like a rabbit, and she hurried to her husband and grabbed at his coattail.

"Martin, let them take whatever they want, don't fight with them!"

He unloosed her fingers gently. "I suspect they'll do so without my permission, my dear," he said, patting her. "Don't fret, I feel no need to be a hero today."

Martin's horse was already brought round, and he mounted and rode quickly toward the docks, his bayonet clanking against his bootheel.

"I cannot stand it," Arden said softly to herself, sinking into the chaise on the veranda. She let her thoughts whirl away from herself for a few moments, trying to recall the feel of Owen's hand in hers when he was quite small and they would go to pick berries. He liked to hold the middle fingers of her hand, like a cow's udders, and pull at them rhythmically as they walked along. His small voice rose and fell alongside her, like a bird chirping as it hopped, telling her of this or that which he deemed vastly important. And now, he was somewhere out there in the country, possibly wounded, certainly ill-clothed and badly fed, if not worse. And Micah. Her solemn, owl-eyed Micah . . .

So ironic! Her mother had accused her of surrendering to the ordinary, as she recalled, as though that were something to be devoutly dreaded. How she ached for the ordinary now! How gratefully she would embrace it, if she could only have the tedious details of the everyday returned to her in all their banal and beautiful moments.

She pulled her thoughts sharply back to this moment. She remembered something Martin had told her long ago: that the Indian name *Natchez,* given by other Indians to the earliest inhabitants of this region, meant "men who run to war."

The irony of the name was certainly not lost on her now.
Portia silently came out onto the veranda with her shawl,
placed it round her shoulders, and took a seat next to her.
She did not speak, only shared the vigil.

Suddenly, shots rang out from the direction of the docks,
and Arden froze, her hand in the air as though reaching for
someone unseen. "Oh God, Portia!" she cried. "They've
started the war!"

"No'm," she said, "they jes' scarin' dem off, meybe."

The shots continued for a few moments, sporadic and
seemingly without pattern or control. Long moments of silence followed. Arden and Portia did not speak, wondering
what might come next. Finally Arden said, "Let's go inside.
It won't do for us to be outdoors, no matter what's coming."
She wondered briefly, frantically, if the baby and Felicity
were able to hear the shots, told herself that all would be well
soon, that Martin surely was not in any real peril, but her
heart was in her throat, and her pulse raced as though she had
climbed two flights of steps in double-time.

They were no sooner indoors than the bombardment
began. Shells screamed over the city, explosions followed
rapidly, some of them far, some altogether too near, and the
servants shouted and hollered in fear as Arden herded them
down in the cellar, grabbing for lamps and hushing them as
best she could, clutching her Bible to her as though it were a
life raft in a stormy sea.

Through the next three hours, shells exploded, they could
hear racing buggies and screeching horses, and the smell of
smoke and powder was acrid, even in the cellar. She led her
people in prayers, reading to them as calmly as she could,
letting them raise their voices in song as loud as she could
stand to drown out the noise of war from without.

Every time her thoughts turned to Martin, she resolutely
turned them to the situation at hand. It was her duty to care
for those who depended on her right here and now: if God
was indeed as good as she believed, He would care for Mar-

tin, for Felicity and LeeAnn, for everyone else she could not touch or see while she did this duty as best she could.

Finally, after another long hour of silence, she led the servants back upstairs again, set them to their tasks with a firm hand, and waited. Martin came home quickly, his mouth grim, and his eyes filled with sadness. "Stanton Hall was struck, so were Magnolia and a few others," he said quickly to her first inquiries.

"My Lord, it sounded as though half the town was destroyed," she said, weeping softly on his shoulder.

"No, actually, we were quite fortunate. Damage is neglible." He turned away then, wiping his eyes. "We are such fools," he murmured. "I knew that even when I gave the order to fire on the ship. What could we hope to do against them?"

"But you couldn't just let them loot the town!"

"Why not?" he asked. "Why not let them take whatever they want without a fight? They're going to take it, regardless."

Later in the evening, they heard that two had died in the Yankee attack. One was an elderly man, felled by an apparent heart attack; the other a ten-year-old girl from an exploding shell. Martin wept then, the first tears she had seen him shed since South Carolina seceded. And no matter what she said to him, he would not be consoled. The next day, he turned in his uniform and his bayonet and resigned as Colonel of the Silver Grays.

Finally, finally, letters trickled in again from Owen and Micah, and Arden felt she could breathe a little easier as she went through her days. To her enormous relief, the letters arrived dated in October, after the terrible news of Antietam in Sharpsburg, Maryland, the worst battle in the war so far, where more than twenty-five thousand had died. Right along with her relief came guilt, for she knew too well how many doors were wreathed in black mourning crepe in Natchez, for the husbands and brothers and sons and fathers lost. She grieved for all of them; so did Martin. But at least their two boys had been spared.

And yet, Arden wondered if the letters were getting through in the order they were written, for Owen's last letter spoke of snow once more. "The weather is as cold as the world's charity," he wrote. "I counted out on inspection yesterday, thirty-one men in my troop who did not have a sign of a shoe on their feet, yet I must compel them to perform as much duty as those who are well-shod. Our brigade is being cut up soon, some to go here, some to go there, into other brigades as needed. The men don't like it much, and more run off when put to strange officers. It's like they've lost their family a second time, and then they lose their nerve."

Lincoln issued the Emancipation Proclamation, and slaves all over the state began to rush northward as though they themselves had been personally notified by the Savior that salvation lay north of Richmond. Though it would not take effect until the first of the year, its impact was swift and brutal. River Reach and Graced Ground now had too few hands to make a crop, even diminished ones. Martin rode out to Graced Ground to see Josie and his wife and then over to River Reach, where he told his slaves they were officially free. He came back into Natchez with Joseph riding next to him on the buggy seat. Of more than two hundred people, he now had only five left. Josie, he said, had only three, and they were talking openly about leaving, to the indignation of his wife.

They heard that great camps were being set up in Tennessee, northern Mississippi, Missouri, and Arkansas to accommodate the refugee slaves. Some were such bad places, the slaves whispered among themselves, that a man might beg to go back to his master rather than die there, half-starved and sleeping in the mud with no blanket.

In October, Corinth, Mississippi, fell to the Yankees and in December, Fredericksburg, Virginia, fell to Lee. That winter, Josie died, and Arden wept as hard as if she'd lost a brother. It seemed to her that her family was as diminished and torn as the leaves of the trees, ripped by winds they could not stand against and swirled to the ground alone.

Josie's wife said she was convinced he had died of sorrow. "He never was the same when those boys walked off the land," she said bitterly. "He fed those men and clothed them, and they never took a harsh word from him, and they up and left him same as he'd whipped them every day of their life! Now I wish he had," she added. "They broke his heart, those niggers, some of them born on his land and raised alongside him, like kin. The day the last bunch ran off, he just took to his bed and never wanted to get up out of it again."

Josie was buried in the chapel cemetery, next to Anne and his mother and father. He was an old, old man, Arden tried to tell herself, and he had lived a good, full life. With so many young men falling, it scarcely seemed fitting to weep for a man near eighty who had come to his death without shame or violence. But weep she did, and she knew that her tears were as much for what else seemed to be passing with Josie: a time of grace and elegance and gaiety, a place of beauty and order and peace. It was all gone now. Even the land was changed; even the air which lay above the land felt sere and desolate, as though the magnolia would never bloom again, the cotton would never flower.

Felicity stood alongside Martin and Arden with LeeAnn in her arms, of course, but she did not sing at Josie's gravesite. Arden realized with a pang that she had not heard her daughter sing since James had died. Was it possible that she would never sing again? No, she pushed that thought from her mind as soon as it entered. Spring would come again; she simply had to believe that or go mad. Spring would come, the war would end, and someday, things would be right once more. Never, ever the same, but somehow right again.

Josie's wife, twice widowed now, booked passage to New Orleans, there to take a ship to London. She said she would not come back to that benighted land, no, not if the war ended tomorrow. "You watch," she said. "Even if the Yankees win, the niggers will be slaves again in a hundred years. And then some fools will try to get them free again, and on and on it'll go. But I'll not stay here to see this house surrounded by Yankees. Nigger Yankees at that." And she packed her trunks and left before the soil on Josie's grave was even dry.

Graced Ground was left to wither like untended corn. As much as it grieved Arden to lock it up, board up the chapel windows, and leave the gravesite abandoned, she had no choice. She could not stay, and there was no one to take on the responsibility.

As Martin turned the carriage back to Natchez, she wondered that she could bear up under her sorrow. If someone had told her, years before, that she would lose her loved ones in this way, that she would see Graced Ground abandoned, her people all gone, her daughter and husband in despair which ground their spirits down so low, if anyone had warned her, she would have flung aside their warnings and declared them mere doomsayers. Nothing could be that bad, she would have said, and if it were, I could not stand it. But it was, and she could. Somehow, with so many losses, so many people gone, it was hard to care much about the land and the house, as important as it all once seemed, where once, the loss of Graced Ground alone might have bent her to the ground.

Now all that mattered were those close at hand and the food one might eat at the next meal.

In January of the new year, 1863, the Confederates lost at Murfreesboro, Tennessee, and in May, they won at Chancellorsville. But the cost of the victory was terrible: General Stonewall Jackson was wounded by his own men accidentally and died four days later. The South was plunged into mourning, a state of gloom which only deepened as the months of this third year of the war went on.

In July, details of the terrible fighting at Gettysburg, three days of the bloodiest fighting of the war, came over the wires at Natchez, and Arden began once more to wait anxiously for letters from her sons. It had been several weeks with no word, weeks which alternately raced by and dragged with brutal slowness, and there were times when she could scarcely believe she had ever had another life, ever had other concerns beside providing the barest provisions for her household and keeping her family's spirits up, her own sanity intact.

And then the worst blow, Vicksburg fell to the Yankees: an unconditional surrender by General Pemberton, Mississippi's best hope, to General Grant, her worst fear. For weeks, Grant had laid siege to the city, forcing the troops and the citizens of Vicksburg into caves dug into the bluffs. It was whispered that folks were eating dogs and horses, rats and other vermin before Pemberton finally declared defeat. It was said aloud that next the Yankees were coming south, right through Natchez.

It was bad enough in January when the slaves threw down their hoes and walked to town, pilfering, swarming, bewildered and scared. Now, the Yankees were coming. Women who had only sneered at straggling slaves now barricaded their doors and windows with heavy furniture, armed themselves with butcher knives, and buried their jewels and silver. Next time Martin drove out to River Reach and Graced Ground, Arden sent her silver and what jewels she had left from her mother with him, wrapped in a soft cloth. It was risky to send them, but riskier to keep them in Natchez now. "Bury it all out at the mound," she told him, "and don't even mark where you put it. We'll find it well enough, when we can, but I won't lose my mother's gold and diamonds to them, not if I can help it. Oh God, Martin, the Yankees! Here, in Natchez!"

On July 13, Arden was just finishing up with cook after dinner when the clamor from the street brought her to the front door. "The Yankees are here! The Yankees are here!" folks were shouting, running to their homes and hurrying their horses off the road. From a distance, Arden could hear the sound of whooping and screaming, as if a pack of wild Indians were coming up the hill from the docks. She raced quickly up the stairs, calling for Portia to lock the doors and windows, and found Martin leaning out the upstairs windows watching a regiment march up Commerce Street. ''My God, they're here at last,'' he said.

Within a half hour, pickets were stationed at every house on the street, the yards were filled with soldiers, and a Yankee officer rapped hard at the front door. Arden and Martin met him together. To Arden's shock, she saw that some of his men were negroes, in uniforms, with bayonets on their shoulders. Just like the widow had warned. Thank God my mother isn't alive to see this, she told herself quickly. She'd have swooned away or shot someone, that was certain.

''Sir,'' the officer announced with no bow or preamble, ''we have occupied this city, and we shall be headquartering at Rosalie.''

Arden gasped. Rosalie was the grandest mansion on the river in Natchez, perhaps one of the loveliest estates in the South. But more than that, it housed their friends, the Wilsons, had seen the pomp and ceremony of huge weddings and *fêtes*—it was the finest Natchez had to offer. Rosalie! Gone for Yankee headquarters!

The officer spied Portia hovering just behind Arden's shoulder and he saluted her as though Arden were invisible. ''Step forward, please, ma'm,'' the officer said to Portia.

She stiffened, her eyes big as plates, but she obeyed him.

''Is this your master?'' he asked her curtly.

''Yessuh,'' she said.

''Is he a good, kind master?''

''Yessuh. Marse Martin a good man,'' she replied, her voice quavering. She never once looked at either Arden or Martin.

''Give me an example, if you can.''

Portia thought for a moment. ''Marse Martin never

whupped us, suh. An' he always call de men by der given name. He say it disrespect to call dem anythin' else.''

"Has he ever mistreated you?"

"No, suh."

"And your mistress? She ever whip you?"

"No, suh!" she said, a little more indignant. "My marster an' missus treats us good."

"Shall we let this man go, then?"

Arden gasped again. "What do you mean, sir?" She felt Martin tense beside her with anger, doing his best not to speak.

"I mean that we are arresting all Confederate officers, ma'm," he said, "and your husband was an officer with the defending troops of this city—"

"He is an officer no longer!" Arden said desperately. "The troops you speak of surrendered, sir! Surely no arrest is necessary—"

"I am aware of that, ma'm, and we are making exceptions if the negroes vouch for these men." He bowed curtly. "I'm afraid the pleas of other Confederates, wives or otherwise, will not stave off arrest and punishment." He turned back to Portia. "Shall we let him go, then?" he asked again, rendering Arden once more invisible.

Portia looked then at Arden and Martin and back again to the officer with genuine fear. "Yes, suh! Please let Marse Martin go, suh! He a God-servin' man, a peace-lovin' man! An' ef'n there was more like his kind, they wouldn't be so many of your kind comin' down here an' killin' folks!"

A small burst of rueful laughter came then from the troops at attention behind the officer.

"That'll be enough, Portia," Martin said then quietly. "Thank you for speaking on my behalf."

"You welcome, suh," she said, matching his dignity.

"You know you're free now, do you not?" asked the officer.

"I know dat, suh," Portia said. "I choose to stay on wid my fambly."

The officer shook his head slightly. "Well, be that as it may, this house is under confinement, and we will picket here until we have further orders. You may come and go as you please, sir," he said reluctantly to Martin, "so long as you do not interfere with my troops."

Martin bowed to him curtly, silently. He then slowly closed the door. "Ulysses S. Grant will sleep in Bob Wilson's bed tonight," he said wonderingly.

"And where will Jane Wilson sleep?" Arden asked anxiously.

"Wherever she may," he said with a great weariness. "*How*ever she may. Like the rest of us."

So Natchez was occupied. Mail was intercepted now, and Arden had no hope that any of the letters she had watched for so long would get to her until after the Yankees left once more. And who could say when that might be?

General Grant was at Rosalie, and in Clifton, another mansion on the river, troops were quartered in every room in the house. Armed soldiers walked the streets with easy affrontery, and black men strolled and loitered, speaking to any woman they encountered, black or white. Tabby, Jack, Rose, and Dora had long since left for the North. Only Portia, cook, Joseph, Cassie, and Lucy were left in Arden's care. She sometimes wondered what she would do with them now. So many mouths to feed, and not enough work to keep their hands busy.

She often dreamed of white bread and white cake, tea with real sugar, and coffee with good cream. When she awoke, she was hungry, sad, and angry all at once.

Felicity brought LeeAnn over to visit now daily, as though she dared the Yankees to try to keep her at home. She walked the streets with her mammy behind her carrying her baby, under her ruffled parasol as though nothing had changed in her world at all. Usually she arrived livid with indignation at the glances and remarks of the men she passed.

But one afternoon, she came to the house with one of the

few genuine grins Arden had seen on her mouth in months. "Whatever has happened?" Arden asked her.

Felicity took LeeAnn on her lap and bounced her happily, then set her toddling off to find a flower just off the veranda. She laughed ruefully. "I shall surely go to Hell, Mother, but I don't care."

"Filly, what have you done?"

"You know that pomegranate bush in the front yard? Well, that Yankee who's torn up my flower beds and put his horses in my garden came and asked me this morning if it was good to eat. I told him, yessir. Why, just help yourself. He asked me how do you eat them, can you imagine?"

"I guess they don't have pomegranates up North?"

"Not where this fool's been, at any rate. So I told him, just bite it. Like an apple."

"Oh, Filly!"

"He did, Mother! You should have seen his face! That ol' pomegranate was hard and green as a lime and bitter as gall." She laughed happily, wiping her eyes finally and shaking her head. "He gave me such a tongue-lashing . . ."

"You're lucky he didn't have you arrested."

"The day a Yankee arrests a woman in this town will be the day that God deserts them once and for all. The impudent scoundrels have no more manners than monkeys!" Felicity said, her mouth turned down in a sneer.

That sneer, and too many like it, was soon enough the cause of even more discomfort for the women of Natchez. Union officers quickly grew exasperated with the way the ladies drew aside their skirts on the streets as they passed, raised their parasols, and ignored their bows and doffed caps. Southern men might be cowed but Southern women gave few signs of fear and fewer still of reverence. The Yankees were galled.

Then four ladies left the Episcopal Church rather than join in prayers for the protection and health of President Lincoln, and all four were swiftly slapped with Special Order No. 49 from Brigadier General T. E. Ransom, Commanding Officer of the Union Headquarters at Rosalie. The orders were posted to their front doors, to wit:

"Mrs. ———, whose public conduct was insulting to the Flag of the United States and the officers and soldiers of this command, is denied the protection of that Flag and is hereby notified to leave this city and our lines within twenty-four hours, with her family. She will be allowed sufficient transportation for a reasonable amount of baggage and household goods. The Provost Marshal will be charged with the execution of this order and will take inventory of the effects of Mrs. ———, occupying her premises for the use of the Government of the United States. The property retained by the Provost Marshal will be confiscated for the benefit of the Government."

Mrs. Wilbourn, one of the banished ladies of Natchez, left behind, Arden heard, sixteen rooms of mahogany and rosewood furniture, four silver services, and china in the amount of three dozen each of plates, cups, serving platters, and saucers. Not to mention the house and all her goods within.

Arden and Filly, along with most of the other women of the city, had to watch in quiet horror as Yankee officers paraded through their homes and played their pianos for the benefit of negro soldiers who were invited to take seats on the sofas. At Filly's house, the soldiers stripped all but her bedroom of linens, mattresses, and pillows. From Arden, they confiscated all of her medicines such as quinine, paregoric, peppermint, calomel, or camphor, most of her foodstuffs, and whatever soap, perfumes, and hairbrushes they could carry off. And there was not a thing to be done about it.

Martin could only stand by, helpless, while they pillaged his house, his study, his papers, his beloved books and astronomy maps. When he objected, asking them with dignity to leave him his papers at least, they laughed and took them away. "Paper's at a premium, sir," they said with mock civility. "Too many men are suffering from the diarrhea—that rich Southern food, you know, sir—to leave it behind."

Several homes were taken over for the use of the negro soldiers, one for a dormitory, another for a hospital, still another for an encampment for the white officers who led them. Negro regiments drilled daily up and down the public streets, and whenever a citizen was to be arrested, the white officers seemed to take special care to see that a squad of negroes was sent to take the offender away.

Vast numbers of the slaves on the outlying plantations now flocked to Natchez, sleeping in the gardens and lolling on the streets in a bewildered and disorganized fashion. Many of the men were put into the regiments for training, but the women and children and old men were put in a confined camp Under-the-Hill, where the soldiers told them they could not leave without a special order from Congress. There, they began to die at the rate of twenty or more a day, for lack of water and food and proper shelter.

Meanwhile, the Confederates won an expensive victory at Chickamauga, Georgia, and the Yankees drove off the Rebels at Chattanooga, Tennessee.

And then the winds began to shift in Natchez. After several months of occupation, many of the most ardent secessionists in the city were becoming Union supporters, however grudgingly. Union officers were increasingly entertained in some of the finest homes, in the hopes those homes would be left standing. Young ladies who might have wept as the handsome men went off to fight for the Cause now found it acceptable—even pleasant—to go out riding with Yankee officers and welcome their suits.

By Christmas, Arden was almost as depressed as Martin. Felicity barely left her home anymore, for the Yankees on the street. What mail came through was so censored that they could hardly tell the date or the disposition of the troops which Owen and Micah led, and those letters so infrequent they scarcely took any comfort from them at all.

Savage fighting went on, the reports said, at Wilderness,

Virginia, and Spotsylvania that May, and both sides claimed victory now, despite huge numbers of casualties, both Union and Confederate. They heard that Lincoln had called up half a million more men, and Jefferson Davis began drafting men between the ages of seventeen and fifty.

"Thank God you're too old," Arden said to Martin without regard to how it might sound to him. "I couldn't stand it."

Martin said nothing, only looked out at the bluecoats loitering in his yard and picketed before his door with distant eyes. "Perhaps it will all be over soon," he murmured.

"Let us pray that it is," she said wearily. These days, neither of them spoke their fears aloud. There was no need to, for they were the fears of every parent in the South with a son in battle. The Cause was no longer their chief concern; they wished only to see their boys back home safe once more.

Grant tried to take Richmond at Cold Harbor, but Lee held him off. It was said that the frontal attack by Grant, a desperate move, was more suicide than war. Thousands of Federal soldiers were killed in a matter of minutes, thousands more were killed at Petersburg a few weeks later, and thousands more killed or wounded at Marietta when General Joseph E. Johnston stopped Sherman's "march to the sea" less than a week after that. And still, the Yanks kept coming.

One night, Portia came to the veranda where Arden was sitting, trying to rally her spirits sufficiently to go to visit a sick friend a few blocks away. Martin had taken Joseph and gone to River Reach, "simply to see if it's still standing," he had said.

To Arden's surprise, behind Portia stood the rest of the negroes, Cassie, Lucy, and cook. "We is goin' to de Yankees," Portia said abruptly. She raised her hands and closed her eyes as though God Himself had inspired her. "Yessum, we is goin' tonight!"

"Why, Portia!" Arden gasped. "Whatever do you mean?"

"We's gwine to Freedom!" Cassie shouted. "Das what she mean, missus! Freedom, Lord!"

Cook cried out, "Gonna get dat mule an' forty acres!"

"Gwine to de Yankees!" Lucy began to shout and cry, but Portia hushed them all. "We is goin', Miz Arden. Don' you try to stop us. We is goin' tonight!"

Arden began to tremble. "But Portia, you've been like my own family!"

"Come on, brethren!" Portia turned to call to the others, ignoring Arden. "Git yer freedom! No more work! Plenty o' vittles! Come on to de Yankees wid me!"

Cassie and Lucy and cook, all of them together with one voice and shuffling feet, hurried past Arden then, off the veranda and out into the darkened street, led by Portia at the front of their little troop, shouting at them to keep up and get to Freedom.

Arden stood in amazement and horror, watching as they all hurried off, struck to the soul that her last view of Portia was her back, and she never once turned again to wave farewell. She sank slowly down again into her chaise on the porch and sobbed.

When she finally dragged herself up to bed, it was to sleep alone in a house for the first time in her entire life. She fell into exhausted slumber with Martin's pistol clutched firmly in her hand.

Sometime in the night, she heard a noise and abruptly awakened. She sat up, still holding the pistol. A sound of movement downstairs . . . stealthy, soft movement as though the feet knew what they wanted and where to find it. She stayed still and silent, willing the intruder away. Whatever you want, just take it and leave me alone, she prayed. Then came a small tap at the door. Her throat was thick with fear, so throttled that she could not speak.

"Miz Arden?" came a cautious voice. Portia.

Arden leaped from the bed, pistol in hand, and yanked open the door, ready to shoot to the death Portia and her small band of betraying thieves—

"Miz Arden, don' shoot me!" Portia cried in terror, her hands to her eyes.

"What do you want?" Arden said coldly.

Portia took her hands from her eyes and said, "I took dem sorry niggers to de Yankees, Miz Arden. Dey is lazy an' triflin', jes' eatin' up all de vittles an' we is better off widout dem. I led dem to de Yankees. Let *dem* feed dem!"

Arden sat down slowly on the bed, Martin's pistol now beside her on the coverlet. "You didn't mean it, then?"

" 'Bout leavin'?" Portia asked, round-eyed. " 'Course not, Miz Arden! I never leave my chile, but you got lil' enuff dese days to share, an' I kin do what needs doin' round here, an' Cassie an' Lucy, dey ain't fit to work no more, an' cook, she fixin' to run off anyhow, so I jes' figure, round dem all up an' take dem off 'afore Marse Martin come back an'—"

"But Portia, you know you are free, don't you? You are free to come and go now as you wish. The Yankees told you the truth."

"I know dat," Portia scoffed, "but what I need wid freedom? I gots fambly, an' if you got somebody to do for, you ain' free, no matter how many Yankees say so. No, Miz Arden, I won' run off, I don' need dat kind o' freedom, nohow."

"Oh, Portia!" Arden cried, falling into her ample black arms and weeping again in relief.

"No need for dat, Miz Arden," the old black woman said softly. "I ain' goin' nowheres, don' you worry none."

Some of the worst news of the year came in the early winter. Sherman had taken and burned Atlanta. That lovely, gracious Southern capital lay in smoldering ruins after the inferno which was General William Techumseh Sherman was passed. The Natchez *Courier* reported that he was insane. Few doubted the paper's charge.

It had been five months without a letter from Owen or Micah, and Arden was unable to hide her anxiety from Martin. She had tried, through most of the chaos and fear, to keep as cheerful a countenance, as hopeful a spirit as she could. It was hard enough to do so with the deprivations they endured, the death of James, Felicity's sorrow, Martin's own skepticism and despair—but she could continue so long as she knew her boys were safe. No news was hardly good news these days, however—of that she was certain.

The Confederates had tried to take Natchez back twice, once in a brief skirmish outside of town and again that month, when almost four thousand men under General Adams attempted to take the garrison from the Yankees. Both attempts failed, but in the interim, the Confederates did what they could to damage whatever the Federals might deem valuable, burning buildings and cotton, stealing stock, and clapping negros into irons whenever they found them away from the city, running loose.

Between the two armies, Natchez had little left to save.

Martin spent more and more time out at River Reach now, for he had been able to hire a few freedmen to help him, and he was trying to bring in a small cotton crop and the corn. Besides, he said, the streets of Natchez were so galling to him, with the Yankees loitering and glaring on every corner, he could hardly bring himself to ride from Commerce to Market.

"You know," he said, "time was that I loaned money to anybody who needed it, mostly. Neighbors and friends, they knew to come to me, and I usually said yes. But now I'm in debt. Got enough cotton to sink a steamboat, but not enough cash to buy our supper for a week. Oh, not so bad as some, because I put some overseas, but I can't get it now, to save my life. So I owe men. For the first time in my life, I can't pay my debts."

"Nobody can," Arden said softly. "You remember what you told me about Robert Spellman?"

He nodded. "Yes. A man of substance. A man with five hundred acres on the taxrolls. And he had to sell it off and build himself a log cabin to keep off the rain. And when his wife died, he had to sell his three sheep just to pay for her coffin." He shook his head. "Well, I'm a trifle better off, but not much. And I'd rather have a man shoot at me than ask me for money that I owe him and can't pay him. I hate to even go on the streets anymore, for I feel like dodging men lest they dun me. If I live a thousand years, I don't think I will ever get over this feeling."

Sometimes she wanted to shout at him when he talked like that, to shout and scream, "It's only pride, Martin! What does it matter! Swallow your pride and do what must be done! Like *I* do." Didn't he wonder why so many linens and frocks and baby clothes were floating through the house these days? Was he blinded as well as bent by this war?

Pride. Male pride. It was what got them where they were in the first place, she told herself with quiet anger. But she never shouted at him. She only put on her shawl and set out alone, on foot, to do what must be done in town and bring back what she could find for them.

Arden was tempted to go with him to River Reach, but there were so many stragglers, deserters, and negroes wandering the Trace and the surrounding countryside, he told her she was safer in town. Sometimes she wondered.

For the first time in her marriage, they slept now many nights apart. Martin's absence only fueled her despair, and she rarely slept a single night through these days without being awakened by her fears for Owen, for Micah, for Martin, for LeeAnn and Felicity. Her family seemed to be dissolving around her, despite her efforts to hold them safely in her hands.

"The boys should have come home," Arden fretted to Martin when she felt he could hear it. "They've done their duty. They only signed on for a year, and that was three years ago."

"They could have left the army legally more than eighteen months ago," he said, "but you know they can't do that. They won't desert their men. Not after West Point."

"Oh God, it's not fair that they should still be fighting when so many are not," she moaned.

Martin shrugged. "War isn't fair, dear. We knew that at the outset."

Portia was Arden's only solace these days. She was much older now, and she moved slowly on her spindly legs. She and Joseph had forged a truce between them long before, and now they were actually affectionate with one another. She could not manage the work of the house alone, of course, but she did what she could, Arden did the same, and the rest slipped by. Somehow, it all seemed much less important than it used to, before the war.

"Before the war," they said to one another over and over, "remember when cook used to make those delicate cream pastries, before the war? How we took our picnics out to the river, before the war? The horse races, the grand *fêtes,* the price of cotton!" All of it was before the war. No one said, "after the war," for it was difficult to believe, after so long, that it would ever be over at all.

It was in December when Martin went out to River Reach to see to the cotton. The harvest was over, so small a crop she wondered if the effort had been worth it, and now it was time to lay the fields by. Each time he returned, it seemed he had bad news these days. The corn was dry, the horse was stolen, someone had ripped up part of the barn for firewood—each trip meant a new loss to be tallied.

This time she could tell by his face as he came into the sitting room that the news was worse than she'd expected. "Well, is the house *all* gone, then?" she asked with some small exasperation. These days Martin's face alone could sometimes prick her annoyance, with his woeful sad eyes and heavy mouth ready always to utter the most doeful predictions.

He sat down quietly, his hands together, and his head bowed. A sudden chill ran up Arden's spine, and she touched his shoulder. "Tell me quick," she murmured. "It'll be easier that way."

"Owen's home," he said softly. "He left his command two months ago and made his way down the Trace." He looked up at her then. "And oh my dear, our Micah's gone."

She clenched her fists together so hard that the pain kept her upright. "How?" she managed to ask.

"He died at Petersburg. Owen was with him when he died." He shook his head. "Owen was wounded, too." At her gasp, Martin added quickly, "But he's healed. That's what took him so long to come home. He had to travel slow and by night."

She felt that hands were gripping her throat, hard cold hands with no life and less compassion. "Why didn't he write?"

"He said he couldn't put it in words." Martin bowed his head again and wept softly. "Ah, Arden, our boy. Our first boy is gone."

"I must go to Owen," Arden said, standing abruptly, her hand still on Martin's shoulder. "Take me to him now."

He did not resist her, though he had only just returned from the plantation and must surely be weary to the heart, she knew. She took a quick hour to pack what she might need and get Portia in the carriage, and they drove out of the city as though hunted by the forces of good. "My boy left his command," she told herself a few times, just to test the idea in her mind. At first, she felt keen shame at his act, picturing what her friends would say, what Felicity might think, what those who knew them well would whisper—

And then she resolved to think on it no more. Micah was dead; Owen was alive. For now, that was enough to think on for any mother. At any cost, he was alive. And must be kept from the Yankees.

She was horrified at the changes she saw in the countryside as they rode on, the empty fields, the houses in ill repair, the stables yawning and empty of both stock and conveyances—but most of all the idle negroes, packs of them it seemed to her, loitering on fences, leaning against shady trees, sitting on rickety porches as though they had not a thing to do all the livelong day, their women among them with their bright kerchiefs on their heads, their children running loose, half-naked in the winter sun.

She was more appalled at her first sight of River Reach in a good while, for her housewife's eyes saw immediately that the veranda sagged, covered with vines, that the windows were broken and filthy, and the steps were covered with brush and debris. The house looked like an abandoned woman, ill-used and unkempt. But none of that mattered, she told herself as she stepped over the threshold. Only Owen mattered now.

He met her in the foyer and swept her into his arms, suddenly half again as broad through the shoulders and taller than she remembered. "Mama," he said softly, and she could feel the tears behind his voice.

"My son," she said, her own tears rolling from her eyes without her volition. "Thank God you're safe."

His face crumpled like a boy's, though he strove manfully for composure. "Micah's gone," he choked out.

"Yes, I know," she murmured. "It must have been terrible for you. But you're safe, and you're home now. Try not to think about it until you're rested."

"No, Mother," he said, his voice growing rough again with thick emotion, "I have to think about it, and think about it fast. I'm a deserter. They shoot deserters, when they catch them."

Arden turned to Martin with dismay, still holding on to Owen. "But he's an officer! And he's served more than three years!" she cried out, as though he could somehow equalize the unfairness. "Let someone else stand up before those cannons!"

Martin said, "That's not the point now, Arden. It's the Yankees. He's an officer, and he deserted. If he's taken prisoner by either side, he may hang. He will surely be sent to one of their prison camps, if he isn't shot, and frankly, he'd be better off before a firing squad. We can hide him, I suppose. Or he can go west and disappear. But it will be hard to keep him hidden. Someone's bound to see him, even if it's only Portia and Joseph. They scarcely miss a thing that goes on . . .''

"We won't talk about this now," Arden said firmly. "He's only just got here. Owen, you must come and tell us what you can about Micah, son, while the details are still fresh in your mind."

He laughed harshly. "As though I'll ever forget them." He let himself be led into the sitting room and there, until the shadows grew dark and deep, until they had to light a candle to see each other's faces, he spoke of where he had been and what he had seen.

Owen and Micah had been, with thousands of other young men, under General Stonewall Jackson at battle after battle, and they had come to know the man who led them fairly well. "He rode this close-coupled, thick-necked, ox-eyed creature, taken from the Yankees on the field. Little Sorrel, he called it, but we called it Fancy," Owen said. "They made a strange pair, the undersized animal and ol' Jackson, tall as he was. He wasn't exactly close with the men, you understand, though we respected him. He seemed to commune with his own spirit, a sort of one-idea man. Two things he believed in absolutely, the bayonet and the blessings of the Lord. I remember once, we lost a courier, killed while delivering a message in the thick of fire. Boy was only fourteen. 'Very commendable,' Jackson only said and went back to the matter at hand."

"What did Micah think of him?" his father asked softly.

"Micah thought the man spent too much time talking to Providence and not enough time talking to the men," Owen said sadly. "But we followed him bravely enough." He had been recollecting for a good while now, and Arden could see the weariness on him like a gray cloak about his shoulders.

"There were so many battles," Owen said quietly. "The things I've seen, no man should have to see and keep living. The sights and the smells . . . corpses swollen to twice their size, the odors so foul that we all sickened and fell to the ground, vomiting profusely. For the rest of my life, I'll remember that smell." He paused, looked at his father, and continued. "I remember once, after a hard battle into the night, the rain came before daylight and fog filled this valley where we'd been fighting the Yankees for—oh, I guess twelve hours or more. Down in the valley in the fog, you could hear the boys, even if you couldn't see them, this babble of cries and wails and groans from the wounded who had lived through the night somehow. The cries for water!" He paused again as though for strength. "And then the sun came out and burned the fog off, and you could see, down there on the slope, the bodies of five thousand of us, like a carpet of cold or suffering flesh."

"Five thousand!" Arden gasped.

"Just in one battle," Owen nodded. "About half of them dead or dying, the rest of them alive and moving and trying to get help." His smile was ghastly. "Gave the field a singular crawling effect that I'll not soon forget."

He looked at his mother's horrified face and added, "But there were other times. Times I'll also remember. Last Fourth of July, we were on picket duty to observe the enemy, a small regiment of Bluecoats overlooking an open field. Someone figured out that the field was full of ripe blackberries, so our boys and the Yanks made a bargain that for one day at least, they'd hold their fire, and they went out together, like girls on a picnic, leaving one man on each post with the arms. For hours, they gathered berries together and talked over the fight and traded tobacco and coffee and newspapers as peacefully as if they hadn't been engaged in the last seven days in butchering one another."

"Was Micah there?" Arden found the strength to ask.

"Oh yes." Owen smiled, a genuine one this time. "Micah told his men they better eat all they picked or he'd put them on drill for slacking. He didn't have to tell them that, of course, we got so little to eat toward the end, most anything was welcome."

Arden touched his arm. "You do look dreadful thin, son."

He shrugged. "We all do. The Yanks have got the uniforms, the powder, every luxury in camp. My men had no transportation save their feet, and most had no shoes at all. Our food was as indifferent as our beds. But we fought! Lord, how we fought."

"How were you wounded?" Arden asked.

"It was before . . . before Micah." He paused for strength and then went on, speaking as though he told the tale to strangers. "The first ball that struck me was so close that the musket's breath was hot on my face, and I fell forward across my gun, my left arm useless falling under me. I didn't feel pain right then, only numbness everywhere. I felt as if I had taken an awful blow, but I couldn't tell where I was hit. Then I was struck again . . ."

Arden cried out aloud.

Owen shook his head. "This time in the thigh, by a ball that fair lifted me off the ground. I bled a lot, but I didn't lose consciousness. For some hours, I lay there, and then my men carried me back to the rear to the surgeons. During those hours, I thought of more things than I have in my whole lifetime." He paused, and his voice lowered. "I had a horror of dying alone, you see, and I couldn't find any of Micah's regiment around me, much less Micah himself. The more blood I lost, the colder I got, and I shook so hard I thought I would shake to pieces. I was cold as ice and still I wanted water. Finally, the surgeon got to me, but he had no chloroform. I watched him while he laid open my flesh, and I marveled that it looked so like cutting fat pork, so smooth and pink. It hurt more than the bullet, but by then, Micah was with me. He stayed with me throughout the operation." He stopped and collected himself. "And I recovered. As you can see."

"Can you tell us about Micah now, son?" Martin asked softly.

Owen nodded slowly. "It was at Petersburg. After Jackson died, we were sent to support General Beauregard out of

Richmond. Grant invaded us, and we had to keep him from the capital. Ol' U. S. Grant. The Yanks told us that stood for 'Unconditional Surrender.' Well, we fought for two days, stern and relentless as ever, I suppose. Supplies were low, and victuals were down to cornmeal and rank bacon, little enough of that. The stock were so hungry they were chewing away the wagon beds, the bridle reins, the halters. One mule even ate my horse's tail. We were pinned down in ditches, and the shells came screeching through the air almost constantly. We were low on water, and what we had stank so badly we had to hold our nose to drink it. But the men kept up their spirits as best they could. Anyway, we kept up the shelling, but so did they. Micah was two men away from me, in the brush, and we were fixing to move our men forward, when I heard him cry out. A bullet caught him in the neck. I got to him quick, but he knew he was dying. He couldn't speak, but I saw it in his eyes.'' He looked away from both of them. ''I don't think he knew much pain, at any rate.'' He paused, in thought. ''I spent the whole night talking to him, but of course, he was already gone. I buried him the next morning, and my leg pained me as much as when I was shot. But there was no time to rest, I was back in command of what few men I had left, and we fell under murderous fire. I tried to rally the men, mine and Micah's also, I rode up and down commanding them, entreating them to rally, beseeching them by all they held sacred and dear, to stop and fight, but without success. We'd had scarcely any food for thirty-six hours, we'd been under fire so long with no respite, and our casualties were so high, our wounded so many, that we had nothing left. Not just my brigade, but all of them. They had just had enough. We had to fall back. I gave the order to retreat and . . . I kept on going.''

Arden was weeping quietly. She did not know when she had started and now she wondered when she would stop. If she would ever stop. Owen was alive. Alive but his heart would never be the same. Perhaps his soul, as well. And Micah was gone forever. She put that away to think on more when she could endure it. For now, she had two children left, both of them bereft. She gathered her strength and dried her eyes, reaching for her husband's hand. His eyes, too, were wet.

"When this is over," she said firmly, "we'll go and get Micah and bring him home. Will you be able to find him again, son?"

"Yes," Owen sighed. "I still see the place in my dreams often enough. He'll be where I left him. I marked it well."

"What made you . . ." His father hesitated. "What made you quit, son?"

"The horror of it, of course," Arden said quickly, angered that Martin would need to ask.

"Tens of thousands of young men are living through that horror still," Martin said evenly. "I just need to understand it, my dear. I'd like to hear him tell me, if he can."

Owen was silent, looking down at his hands. By now, the shadows were long in the room, the corners dim and distant as another country. "You know, at West Point, we were pretty well indoctrinated with the idea that a good officer looks after his men. My men were green as grass when I got them, and they were veterans when I left them, but I couldn't take care of them—not even feed them properly. Half of my men who died did so not from bullets but from sickness." He looked up pleadingly. "How long can men march on cornmeal and hog fat? How many times can a man weather pneumonia and flux and fevers and chills and still keep on pickets in the rain with no shoes and no coat and no blanket to cover him when he does go off-duty?" He dropped his head again. "But so long as Micah was with me, I could stand it," he said quietly. "First our negroes left us—"

"They ran off?" Martin asked sharply.

Owen nodded. "Near the end of the first year. Woke up one morning and they were skedaddled. Took my purse and Micah's bowie knife with them. Then we got our horses shot from under us, and there weren't more to be had. We were officers with no mounts." He shook his head. "A sorry thing to see. But we finally got some sorry nags from some farmer's plow, and our men still followed us bravely, so that was all right, I guess. But once Micah was gone, I just . . ." He stopped, bewildered. "I just didn't have the stomach for it anymore." He paused. "I don't know how to explain this, Father, but it wasn't that I was afraid. Truly, it wasn't that. It was that it wasn't fair. The men were good men, but I couldn't ask them to keep fighting without shoes and food. I couldn't take care of my men! And I couldn't make myself do it another day."

Arden listened closely, taking her son's hand in hers.

"But I know now what I'm going to do," he said, his voice more firm. "I'm going to go back to Richmond. I have to. My men are mostly all gone, but they'll give me another command. I'll just tell them I was wounded and forgot myself for a spell. They'll take me back." He laughed mirthlessly. "Hell, they might give me a medal, if I survive. I guess I just needed to come and see you, to tell you about Micah. But I'm strong now. It's almost over, I think, and I want to see it through. I'm going back."

Martin said nothing.

Arden pulled at Owen's hand in alarm. "You don't need to decide right now, son."

"Yes, Mother," he said quietly. "Yes, I do. The Yankees will take me, sure, if I stay. I'm better off at the front." He smiled. "It won't be much longer now. We're losing this war fast."

"Is that true, son?" Martin asked intently. "We suspected it, of course, but the papers here—"

"We've already lost it, so far as I can see," Owen said. "But I've stayed with it this far, and I want to see it through to the end." He thought for a moment. "You know, I did every day and without a second thought what at another time would have been the event of a year. Perhaps of a lifetime. Things I would have gladly gone a lifetime without ever having to do at all. And I hated every minute of it. Yet, I know I must go back."

A long silence hung over the room. "You know that we lost James," Arden said finally.

Owen nodded. "Felicity wrote us. I'm so sorry. Is she well?"

"Well and the mother of your niece, LeeAnn," Arden said. "Will you see her before you leave again?"

He shook his head. "The longer I stay, the more likely they'll capture me. I dare not come into town, and if she comes out here . . ." He shook his head. "Just kiss her for me and tell her I'll see her soon. The sooner I'm gone, the better for all of you. They don't need much excuse to arrest the whole lot of you, if they want to." He looked up at Martin. "I'll leave with first light, Father. With your permission."

Martin shook his head. "I cannot agree, in all conscience, Owen. What of your wife? What of Micah's wife?"

Owen grimaced sadly. "Micah's wife wrote him a year ago, telling him that she could no longer endure their separation. Madam Mary Hamilton Howard told him that she had come to believe that the Federals were right—"

Arden gasped. "She didn't!"

Owen nodded. "He had no plans to return to her. From what he heard, she was out riding with Yankee officers, dancing with them . . . he couldn't take it."

Martin closed his eyes in pain. "This war has ruined everything. What of your wife, Owen? Does she know of your wound? Of Micah's death?"

"I stopped writing to her after Micah died, just as I stopped writing to you."

"We thought the letters weren't getting through!" Arden said.

"Well, that may be true. But I also stopped writing. I simply couldn't put the news to paper. Anyway, I want to see her, but I can't expose you and her both."

"We can get you into town safely for a short while," Martin said firmly. "You must see your wife. You must see your sister and your niece. And then if you wish, I will take

you myself to Jackson. I believe from there, you can get a
train heading north.''

Owen bowed his head silently. Finally, he raised his eyes
to his father. ''Yessir. Perhaps you're right. If I can get this
far without being caught, maybe I can get in and out of Natchez for a night without them catching on. What about the
negroes?''

''They're all gone,'' Arden said. ''Everyone but Portia
and Joseph.''

''Not a single hand left?'' he asked, appalled.

Martin put his hand on Owen's arm. ''That's the least of
our troubles now, son. Let's see to some supper for you now
and a good night's rest. And then in the morning, we'll figure out what's best to do.''

Owen picked up a knapsack at his feet. ''Mother, I have
Micah's—a few of his things.'' His eyes welled up again.
''Not much, I'm afraid. We didn't have much to show there,
at the end. But I figured they better be in your hands, not his
wife's.'' He hesitated. ''His widow's.'' He looked up,
watching her face. ''Do you want them now?''

She nodded, mute with sorrow.

Into her hands, Owen carefully placed Micah's Bible, the
small leather housewife she had given him, his penknife, his
pipe, and his captain's bars. She held them reverently for
long moments, feeling her firstborn's spirit still hovering
around them, through her, with all of them as vividly as
though he were only in the next room. And then she saw a
small leather pouch—two of them, in fact, nearly identical.
''What is that?'' she murmured.

Owen smiled grimly. ''Just a piece of home. We each carried it, full of dirt from the mound. Sort of like good-luck
charms, I guess. Micah said that it was the place where warriors had walked, and we were warriors, so it was fitting.''
His smile faded. ''Not much luck came from them, though,''
he added, his voice faltering. ''Not for us, and not for those
we swore to serve.''

"You keep those," Martin said then. "Maybe that's what brought you home safe to us."

Arden embraced him then and watched as his father walked Owen upstairs to his room. She sat and held Micah's pipe in her hand, marveling at the worn bowl, the smooth stem, the warmth of the thing, as though it had only just left his palm.

Portia came into the room, and Arden could see she had been weeping. Of course the old slave knew all, without being told. "Don' let him go back der," Portia pleaded quietly. "Dey kill him, too, Miz Arden."

"I can't keep him here, if he's sworn to go," Arden said, a calm descending on her now. "Damned few asked their mothers when they left the first time, and they're hardly going to ask us now. They'll do what they're going to do because they're men, and they think they have no choice."

Portia never even blinked at her blasphemy. "God keep him, den," she said in despair.

"Yes," Arden said quietly. "God keep them all."

The next morning, they rode back into Natchez, with Owen between them, hidden as much as possible in his father's old oilcoat and heavy hat. Once inside the house on Commerce Street, they sent word to Owen's wife and Felicity to come that night to an early holiday supper. "We won't take no," Arden said on the notes she sent round to both of them. "And Felicity, I want to see that granddaughter of mine, most especially."

At the appointed time of seven, both ladies' carriages came up the circled drive, and they hurried up the steps of the house, Hanna exclaiming over how much LeeAnn had grown since she had seen her last. Both of them rushed in the door, simultaneously discarding their wraps and calling for Arden and Martin. Arden met them, kissed their cheeks, hugged LeeAnn and bustled her out of her mother's arms deftly, then turned to lead them into the parlor, where she had the doors closed and the curtains drawn.

Martin and Owen rose from the sofas to meet them, and both women stopped in their tracks with small cries of alarm and wonder. Hanna was first in Owen's arms, and Felicity sagged down on the sofa slowly, staring at the two in silent embrace as though she could not believe her eyes. "Is the war over?" she murmured at last.

Owen put Hanna gently aside and went to his sister. He extended his hand and pulled her gently into his arms. "No, Filly, not yet. But I think it will be, soon. I am so sorry for your loss. James was a good man."

"Yes," she said faintly. "Where is Micah?"

Owen glanced at Arden and then said gently, "He's gone, Filly. I came home to tell you because I couldn't put it in a letter. He died at Petersburg."

Felicity burst into tears. "Dear, good Micah! I guessed as much as soon as I saw you. You wouldn't be here without him, I know, if you had a choice."

Hanna was weeping then, as was Arden, and Martin and Owen embraced them in turn, doing their best to add what comfort they could to what the women provided for each other. LeeAnn watched, owl-eyed and solemn, from Portia's arms at the door.

When they were calmer, Felicity went and brought LeeAnn in and sat her down on the sofa. "This is your Uncle Owen," she said. "He knew your daddy, and he is a hero, too, just like your daddy was."

LeeAnn appraised Owen carefully. "Are you a soldier?" she asked finally.

"Yes, dear," Owen said, smiling down at her.

"Where is your gun, then?" she asked bluntly.

LeeAnn already had the probing directness which her mother had at that age, Arden noted. "He has a gun, LeeAnn," she said smoothly. "And a uniform, too. He's a very good soldier."

"Well, then," she asked, "why isn't he fighting?"

"I'm going back to do exactly that," Owen said to LeeAnn and the room at large all at once. He turned and embraced his wife. "I'm sorry, Hanna, I have to go back. I can't stay in Natchez, and I can't leave my men, what's left of them. I think it will be over soon, but I have to stick it out to the end."

"Oh God, Owen," she wept, sinking back on the sofa. "Must I say goodbye to you all over again?"

"But not for long this time," he said. "We shall all be home soon."

"Not all of us," Felicity murmured. And with her words, they were all struck to silence.

"Arden," Martin said then solemnly, "I must tell you now that I am going with him."

Arden was struck to stark silence, her eyes frozen on him in shock. "No," she whispered.

"I must. Truly." He met her gaze steadfastedly.

She began to weep then, slumping alongside Felicity and Hanna. LeeAnn took one look at her grandmother weeping and began to wail now for the first time, for though she had often seen her mother weep, her grandmother's tears were entirely strange and new. Portia swept in, gathered up the child, and coaxed and coddled her out of the room.

Martin knelt at Arden's knee. "My dear, I know this must seem foolhardy to you, but I have made up my mind. I am going with Owen back to Richmond. The war may well be over by the time we get there—"

"Or you may be captured and hung before you get across state lines!" she cried out, clutching at him.

"Perhaps, but I doubt that," he said. "But I can no longer stay here in Natchez, enduring the Yankees and their insults, nor can I let my only son go back to the front alone."

"But Father, you're all we have!" Felicity cried. "You're too old for war!"

"If I'm not too old to protect my family, then I'm not too old to protect my country," he said simply. "You have each other; you will be safe now with the Yankees in control."

He turned to Hanna. "Will you stay here with my wife and daughter? I ask it for both Owen and myself."

She nodded. "Yes, Father. I'll stay here with them."

And then he turned to Felicity. "Filly, will you bring LeeAnn and keep your mother company here until we return? We will travel lighter and keep our spirits higher, knowing that all of you are under one roof and keeping each other safe."

Felicity stared at her father, amazed. "You are really going, then?"

"I must," he said simply. "Will you come?"

"Yes," she answered softly.

"But Martin!" Arden cried, "what can you be thinking of? It's hundreds of miles to Richmond, and the Yankees are everywhere!"

"I believe we have a better chance of slipping by them with two of us," Martin said. "I have some contacts which may help us, if we need them, and I think Owen will be less conspicuous with an old man along."

"Father, don't do this for me," Owen said.

"I don't," Martin replied. "I do it for myself."

After another hour of talk, Felicity took LeeAnn up to bed, Hanna and Owen retired, and Martin and Arden followed them up the stairs. Once behind their door, Martin turned and took her in his arms. "My love, I hope you can understand that I have to do this."

"All I understand is that you're leaving me," Arden moaned. "You're leaving me alone with the Yankees all about us and nothing but women to tend to."

"You're safer here in Natchez with the Yankees firmly entrenched than you'd be anyplace else," he said. "And you need souls to tend to, whether you know it or not." He smiled at her. "Be they women or children or orphaned chicks. I'll be back in no time, Arden—"

"You can't know that! You may never come back at all!"

He held her tightly, and she could feel the urgency in his embrace. "Yes, I will, my dear. But I must go. I must find

Micah and bring him home. I must do what I can to help
Owen. And most of all, I must get something back that I lost
somewhere, a few years back.''

She pulled back and looked into his face with bewilderment.

''When they started this war, I railed against it because I
didn't believe in war as a solution, but also because I didn't
have much faith in what they were fighting for. Those men
who went to battle had a certainty that I lacked. Whatever
else I may have said of them—what fools they were, what
hotheads—they had an assurance that they stood for something. That when they picked up a sword, they did it for a
reason.''

''They did it to protect their slaves,'' she said bitterly.
''And what good did it do?''

''No,'' he said, shaking his head, ''that wasn't why Micah
and Owen fought, dear, and it wasn't why most of them did.
Most of those men never even owned a slave in their lives.
They did it because they thought that such things as bravery
and patriotism and freedom mattered, and they were willing
to stand up for those things with their lives.'' He kissed her
softly. ''I, unfortunately, was not. But now I think it's a good
thing for men to have such a faith, though I still think war is
a terrible waste of lives. Not having those beliefs is an even
more terrible waste, I've come to see. Perhaps I was just a
little too wise for my own good. Just a little too glib on the
subject. And I think I've lost something I need very much to
find once more. A faith in something. And the courage to
back that faith with action. Micah did it. Owen is doing it.
And I want to be part of that before it's over.''

''You said war was the worst evil in the world!''

''So I did. And I said those who wanted to join the fight
were young fools. But those young men *believed*—as I don't
seem to anymore—and their faith made them innocent. Not
fools at all, but innocents. They spent their shining youth
like bright coins, and I stayed home, frugal and pennywise,
yet I feel empty and wasted now and they, forevermore, will

be able to say they took their place in history. That what they did mattered.''

''But Martin,'' she said desperately, hating herself for having to say the words, ''you're twice the age of most of the men who'll be fighting with you.''

He smiled grimly. ''That's so, my dear. And they might turn me away with laughter when I show up on the field. But at least I'll show up.'' He thought for an instant. ''I hope you can understand this, Arden. I feel like I've learned something I never knew before. I used to think that the luckiest men were those who had some sort of passion about something, you know, as I did with my stars and my maps and all. But now I know that life is passion *and* action, and if a man doesn't have both, he's only half a man. I think now that it is required of a man that he share the events of his time, at peril of being judged not to have lived at all.'' He patted her gently. ''I can't watch life through a telescope at a distance forever, Arden.''

She began to weep again, softly, into his shirtfront. ''I can't stand it,'' she murmured. ''First Micah and now you.''

He held her tightly, kissing her cheeks tenderly, her brow, her eyelids. ''I promise you, Arden, I'll be back. And I'll bring both of our boys with me.''

She looked up at him then and saw in his eyes the flicker of the young man he was once, the man she had loved so deeply for so many years. He was alive now, where he had not been for the past long months. She thought about what he had told her so long ago, about allurements. How the pieces of life are drawn to each other, the smallest particles of things, just like hearts, like souls, like flesh.

Martin had it only half-right, she realized. He thought, like most men, that life happened in the big events, in the wars, the births, the deaths, the taking and leaving of office, the buying and selling—but that was only what showed on the surface. In truth, life happened even more in the spaces between those events. Life was the pauses. The intervals. Just as love happened in the spaces between two people as they were drawn together, irresistibly as two stars or planets, heedless of the consequences when they merge.

"Tell me that you can stand it, Arden," he said softly. "I cannot leave you unless you let me, for by my very soul, I love you more than my own pride."

She knew then something which she guessed her mother did not ever learn, and she learned it, she realized with wonder, from Martin. And it was simply this: that love had unequaled power because love was the power that unified the whole world and everything in it. The nuns said that God ruled the world. But it was not God, it was love, the ultimate gift God had given the world. Martin said that the law of gravity was love in action. But it was more than that, really. Love was the equalizing, harmonizing, balancing force that was constantly at work throughout the universe. Love could cost a lot, sometimes more than she could pay, but not loving always cost more, in the long run. And those who feared to love with their whole hearts, like Anne and perhaps now, Felicity, too, often found that lack of love was an emptiness that robbed the joy right out of life.

She could feel, in that moment, the pain of her mother, the pain of her grandmother, too, within her own body. She took her time in answering him.

"I can stand it," she said finally, after a long pause. "I understand why you must go."

As he kissed her then, she felt his own tears mingle with her own, and she knew that even if he perished, he at least was completely hers once more, now that he was also his own.

Before first light, while the streets were still asleep, Martin Howard and his son, Owen, left the house on Commerce Street with Hanna's small carriage and an extra mount, carrying only what goods they could hide under the seats and within the floor compartment.

Arden, Felicity, and Hanna stood at the window, waving them goodbye, without even the comfort of a light to keep them in view. As the carriage rounded the drive and disappeared into the night, Joseph said to Arden, from where he stood with Portia behind her, "They be all right, Miz Arden, you see. De Yankees ain' been borned yet what kin outsmart Marse Martin."

"They don't have to outsmart him," Arden said. "They only have to outshoot him."

"Not another word, Mother," Felicity said then firmly. "We will see them both back to us by springtime. As God is my Savior, I know it. Now pray with me, both of you."

"You're right, Felicity. As always," Arden said. And obediently, gratefully, she tucked her hand in Hanna's arm, pulled her gently beside her to their knees, and followed Felicity in silent prayer.

In April, the victorious Union Army, with bands loudly playing "The Girl I Left Behind Me" and "Dixie," marched into the capital of the Confederacy, having made of Richmond a smoldering ruin. Regiments of negro soldiers entered the city, and crowds of former slaves came out to greet them, cheering wildly. The next morning, President Lincoln came to what was left of the city, accompanied by his son, Tad, who clutched his hand as they walked through the rubbled streets. Lincoln walked to the Confederate White House, where General Weitzel, in charge of the triumphant Union troops, had his headquarters after Jefferson Davis had abandoned it. When negroes on the streets saw Lincoln, they wept and cheered, shouting "Glory! Glory! Glory!"

At the Southern White House, Lincoln, who looked pale and exhausted, sat down in Jefferson Davis's chair, and the Union troops broke into a loud hurrah. He would not live another year.

Three months later, Martin Howard rode back into Natchez with Owen, bearing the body of his elder son, Micah. They had never even reached Richmond before the battle was over, yet both men looked far older than when they'd left. But then, so did Arden, Felicity, Hanna, and LeeAnn. Martin told Arden, ''I feel that I have lived more in the last few months than I did in the last thirty years.''

They drove out through the countryside to River Reach, and to their amazement, only the double chimney was left standing, charred and dark and ghostly. The big house was burned to the ground, along with every bale of cotton. Two outbuildings leaned precariously, the barn was also torched, but the little house which Martin had built for Anne Lawrence stood untouched. It appeared to have been housing a band of deserters for weeks.

''It looks like it happened at least a year ago,'' Owen said wonderingly. ''I can scarcely believe it.''

''Thank God we took most everything of value when we left,'' Felicity said dully. ''It's all gone now. All of it.''

''Well, not all of it,'' Arden said. They were walking about the house, kicking at lumps of charred wood and turning over strange compositions of burned materials they could not identify as ever having been their own. ''Mama's old house is still there.''

Martin shook his head. ''Wouldn't you know it?''

''And the land. The land is still here,'' she said, turning and spreading out her hand. The others turned to follow her gesture. It was July, and the fields were dotted everywhere with straggling cotton plants, come up from roots, from dropped seeds, all by themselves with no cultivation at all, as if they were determined to flower and bear fruit, with or without the help of man.

''And we're still here,'' she said finally, softly, turning to look at her family, one by one. Her eyes settled on LeeAnn. ''We've lost one and gained one.''

''Lost two,'' Felicity said faintly.

''And gained two,'' Owen said, his arm around Hanna. ''Are we going to rebuild?'' he asked his father.

Martin shook his head. ''Taxes are already too high. Now that the war's over, they'll eat us up. Better to sell the land now, when folks still want it.''

"Sell River Reach!" Felicity gasped. "I can't believe you would!"

"Why not?" her father asked her gently. "It's time to think about the future, not the past. We've got Graced Ground, that's enough for any family, I should think. With no slaves, what do we need all this land for anyway? With the money we'll get for this land, we can buy more cheap land to add to Graced Ground if we want to, or we can simply feel safe again, for the first time in a good while. Frankly," he said with a half-smile, "I think that'd be a nice change."

"But your father built this place," Arden said. "And his father before him brought the land together."

"Yes, and they each took what they wanted from it and so have I. It's time to let it go, I think. Time to stop living for the past."

Arden realized in that instant that he was right. And once again, her mother had been both right and wrong. She had once told her that houses burn down and stocks rise and fall and men leave or die or stop loving, but plantations are always there—and so it was. But now the land was both burden and blessing. Martin was right. He was also far more courageous than she had known. If he could give it up, then so could she. "Good," she said then and met the surprised stares of both her children. "Your father is right. It's time to put it all behind us, and we can't take care of this place properly. Let it go to someone who wants it more than we do, and we'll make Graced Ground one of the finest plantations in Natchez once more."

"I never thought I'd see the day when you'd walk away from this place," Felicity said. "You always loved it so."

"I surely did, but it's time to love something else now." Arden looked at Owen and Hanna, their hands intertwined, obviously taking strength from one another. She looked at her daughter and saw that she, also, was gazing at her brother.

Filly set LeeAnn down to walk on her own two feet. "I

guess you're right,'' she said slowly. "If you all can stand it, so can I.''

Arden put her arm round Filly's waist as they walked back to the carriage. Behind them, LeeAnn toddled along, talking solemnly to herself about the summer sun and the white cabbage butterflies which flurried around her head.

"Doesn't it break your heart, Mama?" Felicity asked her.

Arden somehow found the strength to laugh lightly and squeeze her daughter gently. "My sweet, my heart's been broken a hundred times and by worse things than this. It just keeps healing up and ticking along, and I expect it always will.'' She glanced at Felicity closely. "How about yours?"

Filly leaned her head on her mother's shoulder in a way she had not in many years. "I guess it's still beating in here someplace, though I'd not bet my life on it.''

Arden smiled. "Yes, you would. You already have.''

"Mama,'' she murmured, "I just don't know what to do anymore." Her voice roughened. "I'm so lonely sometimes.''

"Of course you are, Filly," Arden said firmly. "Any woman would be, and you're too used to love to go without it the rest of your life.''

Felicity was silent for a moment. "You know, it's true. Papa was always so good to me, I guess I just got spoiled. And then James loved me so well . . .'' Her voice caught and skipped, ragged at the edges. "I still miss him so much!''

Arden squeezed her, still walking.

"I was so lucky," Felicity went on. "I felt so much love as a child.''

"You did?" Arden asked, surprised.

"Oh yes! You and Papa made my world so safe and happy. I thought it would go on forever. You were such a good mother to me.''

"I was?" Arden laughed aloud. "How lovely to hear you say so.''

"Truly, you were, Mother. And I never knew how hard it

was until LeeAnn. But now I know how much I was loved, and I miss it.''

Arden's heart swelled with love and pain and pride all at once, and she turned and stopped, embracing her daughter. ''You needn't miss it anymore, darling. Life's going to start up now anew, you'll see. And you should be a part of it.''

Felicity nodded slowly. ''You're right, Mama.'' She smiled tremulously. ''You generally are.''

''And as to LeeAnn, I think you are a wonderful mother,'' Arden said fervently. ''I'm very proud of you.''

''You are?'' Filly blushed.

''Completely.''

The two women walked on together then, arm in arm, their heads inclined toward each other, as LeeAnn skipped behind them, lisping a little song in an out-of-tune warble.

Later that afternoon, they buried Micah at Graced Ground, where he could sleep alongside his grandmother, his uncle, and his great-grandparents. To their relief, the house had suffered little damage. One side was scorched, as though a torch had been set to it and then smoldered out. The chapel had two broken windows and the door was off its hinges, but it was otherwise unharmed.

After the others had settled in for the evening, Martin and Arden walked over the land. Like the fields at River Reach, the vast acres round Graced Ground were dotted with a thousand errant, upstart cotton plants, each determined to live with no help at all. Even the corn rows held a few stragglers, and the garden patches back by the slave quarters were alive with twisting old vines, an occasional squash, and a few hidden melons, only visible with close inspection.

''We were lucky, really,'' Arden said to him as they walked. ''Many lost a lot more than we did.''

''We have always been lucky,'' he said.

She turned to look at him, her arms round his shoulders. She remembered how her mother said she feared that Martin would not have enough life in him to suit. How wrong she was. He had not only enough life to go on, but the substance and courage to start over. "You know, you do surprise me, Martin. Here, you've lost River Reach, or at least decided to let it go. And we've just buried our son. Yet somehow, you seem almost—content. Something you have not been in too many years."

He drew her closer and nestled her head on his shoulder. "I know," he murmured. "I scarcely understand it myself."

"Well, please try," she murmured. "For I need to learn it if I can."

He was silent for a long while. Finally, he said, "I guess I just came to see that it wasn't enough to be always looking for new vistas. I had to have new eyes." He turned her so that she was still in his arms but gazing out over the fields as he was. "You know, your grandfather was right when he picked this place. It *is*, truly, a graced ground."

After four bloody years and more than a half-million deaths, more than in all U.S. wars combined, the American Civil War was over. Americans would never again pick up swords and pistols to fight one another, for something had been settled once and for all time. The United States was a nation, and that nation stood for liberty for all men. They had defined ourselves as countrymen by denying that relationship and had finally come to a place where they could not imagine ever questioning that kinship again.

One-fourth of all the white males in the South were dead. More than ten billion dollars in property lay in waste. One half of all the livestock in the South was destroyed. It would take nearly a quarter of a century just to replace the horses. In Mississippi in 1866, one-fifth of the state's entire budget was spent on artificial limbs. Most every family was left with vivid memories of men who should have been alive—but were not. The survivors went home, but sometimes there was no home left and no family to greet them.

When the Emancipation Proclamation was law, freed slaves all over Mississippi threw down their hoes and walked to town. In Natchez, the Federals put the wandering, homeless negroes in a camp at Under-the-Hill. Called the Corral, hundreds were kept there under armed guard with no sanitation, no sewage, scant protection from the weather, and only those provisions which the town could spare. The ex-slaves, many of them women and children, drank from the river, fought off the sandflies and mosquitoes, and died at the rate of more than twenty a day. They were buried in pits, one on top of another, as they succumbed to scarlet fever, measles, bloody flux, and malnutrition. Once inside, they could not leave without a pass from Washington, D.C.

When the Federals withdrew and the survivors of the negro camp abandoned it, a wild peach orchard flourished on that site. It bloomed early and bore magnificent fruit, but the place was so feared by the freedmen that the fruit rotted on the ground, ungathered. Hades-Under-the-Hill, they called it, and for many slaves, it was their first taste of freedom.

PART THREE
1880–1885

I've known rivers:
I've known rivers ancient as the world and older than
  the flow of human blood in human veins.

My soul has grown deep like the rivers.

I bathed in the Euphrates when dawns were young.
I built my hut near the Congo and it lulled me to sleep.
I looked upon the Nile and raised the pyramids above
  it.
I heard the singing of the Mississippi when Abe
  Lincoln went down to New Orleans, and I've seen
  its muddy bosom turn all golden in the sunset.

I've known rivers:
Ancient, dusky rivers.

My soul has grown deep like the rivers.
                    —LANGSTON HUGHES,
                   "The Negro Speaks of Rivers"

The year 1880 in Mississippi was in many ways a remembrance of how the land had been before the terrible war years. Finally, finally, after fifteen years of peace, the healing was evident, even to eyes which still turned back with bitterness to the past.

The land scars of the battles were grown over now and less visible to the casual observer. The human scars were always harder to see and slower to heal. Widows had remarried or died, brothers had either reconciled their differences or resolved themselves to silence, and new families were born to take the place of those which had been ripped asunder. The military rule of reconstruction was over, and Mississippi was left to drone her way into the next century at peace. Every red-dirt farmer in the state was trying to put in a cotton crop, for prices were up to prewar levels, and even rocky, piney-woods farms seemed to glitter with potential.

The slaves were still as large a part of the Natchez landscape as ever. Now they were sharecroppers, as tied to the soil and their landlords as they had been once to their masters. At first, of course, they had had high hopes. Finely dressed carpetbaggers sold them bundles of nicely painted sticks to stake out their forty acres, and smiling politicians preached to them of the righteousness of their vote. But the nightriders and the Kluxers pounded the roads in their bedsheets with the cut-out eyeholes, and the hooves of their

*horses sounded like somebody beating a drum to war once
more. The nightriders burned crosses before shanties and
big houses alike, and the negroes saw soon enough that men
who'll burn what they pray to will burn anything.*

*And so they drifted back again to the land, knowing that it
would never be theirs after all, but it was all they knew to do.
The white landlords gave them little ramshackle cabins in
the middle of the cotton fields to rent, and they were then
beholden to those landlords for a furnish, a credit for food
for the babies and clothes for the wife, and hoes and plows
and seed. The landlord told them when to plant and what to
plant and when to hoe and pick, and he kept the books and
sold the cotton against which the furnish was charged . . .
and almost always, it seemed, they owed more at the end of
the harvest rather than less.*

*The Thirteenth Amendment was followed by the Four-
teenth and the Fifteenth, which promised full citizenship and
due process of law for all American men, white and black.
But those promises were soon drowned in the scramble for
what prosperity was left. Most negroes said they couldn't
tell much difference in this freedom over that ol' slavery, except that they didn't eat so good these days.*

Arden was sitting on the veranda of Graced Ground, her
fingers slowly adding yet another row of lace to the inner
lining of the bodice of LeeAnn's new frock. At seventeen,
her granddaughter had breasts that were still small and pert,
not at all like her mother, more like her grandmother, Arden
thought ruefully, and she liked to have rows of stiff lace
folded inside her bosom to add roundness where she thought
she needed more.

Arden sighed and put the lace down for a moment, resting
her eyes. She noticed that she could no longer sew for hours
on end without her eyes complaining, and if she pushed herself, she might get a crick in her neck worse than her arthri-
tis. But LeeAnn believed that nobody could sew like her

grandmama, and Arden would rather be blind than disappoint her. She gazed out over the fields to rest her eyes and let her stiffened fingers splay out and relax into the folds of her lap.

It was good to see the land green again, after so many fallow years. Good to see the folks working the fields, up and down the rows, the cotton wagons moving to and fro, the mules braying and groaning in the heat-shimmered air. It seemed to her that the war had been over only a few months, instead of fifteen years. But that was the way of it, when you got old. Time slowed and raced with little regard for your needs or feelings about it, one way or the other.

Portia shambled out and took her customary seat in the rocker beside her. "You need anythin', Miz Arden?" she asked, from long habit. Of course, she wouldn't fetch it, but she'd see to it that it was fetched. Portia was past seventy now and spry only in her heart and her mouth. But she still ruled Graced Ground and all which concerned her mistress as though she had the strength to take a slap at any servant who didn't step lively enough to suit her.

"Not a thing," Arden said contentedly. "Where is Master Martin?" These days, Martin seemed to spend almost as much time on the veranda as she did, gazing out over the fields with a pensive eye. Owen managed Graced Ground ably enough; Felicity ran the household with a firm hand, and with the aid of two agents and a score of croppers, there wasn't much left for either of them to do. Usually about this time, they set to arguing amiably about their past. The war was Martin's favorite topic, of course: why it happened, what it did, and why the South failed.

Arden preferred to discuss the children, their lives, and the years before the war. Or their travels. That was a favorite of hers on these somnolent afternoons. Right after the war, they had traveled to the continent, taken in the sights of Paris, London, and Bavaria. But for all Martin recalled, they might as well have read about those places in books. For Martin, the years that counted were the war years.

"He over to de barn. Wade Martin got hisself a new saddle, an' Marse Martin need to look it over." She grinned impishly. "Dat boy need to grow 'nother foot 'for he be able to set it proper."

"That boy needs to pay more mind to his books and less to saddles," Arden said sourly. "He's going to find himself out of his third school this year, if his father doesn't pull him up sharp."

Portia nodded. "Miz LeeAnn de smart one."

"Wade Martin's smart enough, he just doesn't apply himself," Arden said. "His father needs to make him take his studies more serious."

"You tell him so?"

"Course I did. But Owen's got a blind spot when it comes to Wade Martin, you know that. Ever since Hanna died, Owen can't seem to take a firm hand with the boy. And he needs it more now than ever." Hanna, Owen's wife and Wade Martin's mother, had died in the yellow fever epidemic of 1873, when her son was only seven. Since then, Felicity had done her best to mother Wade Martin and LeeAnn together, but the boy needed a father's discipline, something Owen was reluctant to give.

"Yessum," Portia said, nodding her agreement. "Since Miz Hanna pass, Marse' Owen don' seem to care 'bout so much no more."

"Well, that was seven years ago. Wade Martin's a young man now, nigh to fifteen. Time for Owen to make him measure up." Arden picked up her sewing once more and took a firm grip of her lace bobbin. "Shoot, Portia, you didn't take on so when you lost Joseph, and he's only been gone two years."

"Dat's so," Portia said, "but I be an old woman when he take me to wife. Owen still needs a woman, seem lak. I don' need no man." She smiled slyly. "Don' know I ever did." She frowned at Arden's chuckle. "But I slept true to dat man, whilst I had him."

Arden smiled. "I know that." Portia and Joseph had married soon after the war, to everyone's surprise and delight. In their sixties, they had gone to a preacher just like white folks, moved her worn carpetbag into his room, and except for the fact that they shared a bed, little else seemed to change between them. When Joseph died after a decade of marriage, he was buried at Graced Ground in the family plot behind the chapel. There, he slept with Micah, Josie, Anne, Hanna, and all those who had gone before. It was fitting, Arden thought. Probably even now, he was doing for them in death as he had done for them in life.

"You talk to Marse Owen," Portia said. "He listen to you better'n most. Tell him that Wade Martin goin' waste hisself on fast horses an' faster gals, if he ain' careful."

Arden sighed hugely. "Does it ever stop, Portia?"

"What?"

"Worrying over these children."

Portia chuckled wryly. "I 'spect not, Miz Arden. An' we ain' even took up Miz LeeAnn yet—"

Martin came on the porch then, and Portia rose, gave him her nod of welcome, and said, "I see to supper, Miz Arden." She knew to leave them alone in these golden hours of the afternoon.

"Well, the boy's determined to yank that gelding's mouth clean back to the river, if he has to," Martin said as he carefully lowered himself into his chaise.

Arden could tell by the way her husband moved that he had likely overdone this afternoon. He'd be asleep by nine o'clock. "I'd like to see him be a little less determined about his mount and a little more determined about his mathematics," Arden said. "Master Spring said if he failed one more examination, he'd be dismissed summarily." Master Spring was Wade Martin's tutor, the man hired to bring the boy to heel and keep him from being expelled from yet another school this year.

"And so will Master Spring," Martin said. "If he can't handle the boy, we'll find someone who can."

"His father should," Arden said firmly. "And I mean to speak to him about it."

Martin turned to his wife with a raised brow. "I swear, dearheart, don't you know you're supposed to get more feeble as the years pass? Instead, you get more hotheaded with each season. Just let Owen handle Wade Martin—"

"I will not," she said, snapping off a thread with her teeth. "We are a family, we live under the same roof, and I won't be still when I see my child *or* my grandchild going to ruin on a greased track. Why, if his mother were alive—"

"You'd have a passel less to do," Martin declared calmly.

"—she'd take him in hand quick enough," Arden continued as though Martin had not even spoken. "And in her stead, I mean to ask what Owen intends to do about his only son and the fact that the boy has been thrown out of two perfectly fine schools in less than six months."

Martin sighed hugely. Loudly. And rolled his eyes in the bargain. "And what will you do when Owen tells you to go chase yourself up that willow tree yonder, madam?"

She smiled winningly. "I'll tell him I'll move back to Natchez and leave him alone here with Felicity and LeeAnn. That always gets him."

"You *are* a hothead," Martin retorted. "You can't leave a family just because you don't see eye to eye. That's what your mama did, and you had a fit when she did it. That's what the South did, and that was our mistake. We should have seen that the family—the Union!—was more important than any one member in it."

"Well, if it was like a family," she replied quickly, "it was a ruinous one. The South was the wife with too many children to care for, and the North was the husband who wouldn't see to them properly. Why, we had no choice but to leave. Like any good wife, it was our duty to our children!"

And so, they were off and running once more, as they talked and retalked the war, their past, and their lives. What was most real to Martin, Arden knew, were his memories and opinions. And even those seemed to be more and more selective each year. She could remember, however, with great clarity and wonder, the young girl who sewed with the nuns, who worried over her wedding gown, who gave birth to two sons and a daughter. She could picture Micah as clearly as she could Owen, though he was fifteen years dead and his brother was just out to the stables.

But nothing was more real than Wade and LeeAnn, her two grandchildren, and for them, she did her best to remember it all.

Owen strode into the dining room, where Felicity was giving the daily instructions to the cook. He moved with his usual irrepressible energy and an air which defied the world to bring him anything but the best possible news. His sister glanced up and smiled at him, but continued her conversation. Once you started with cook and got her attention, Felicity had learned, it was well to keep to the end. The woman had cooked for them since Wade was born, but concentration was not the best of her attributes.

"And for my father's birthday *fête*," she finished up, "let's have your wonderful squab, Mary, shall we? He always loves that. Remember that will be a week from tomorrow, Sunday next."

The cook nodded and grinned at Owen. "I gots your fav'-rite on the stove, Marse Owen. Giblets an' gravy."

"Why, Mary, you spoil me absolutely!" Owen bantered with her as she expected. "You know I don't dare eat anybody else's giblets, they'd stick in my throat like a Yankee dollar. I'll be back directly, and I expect to see my plate piled so high I can't see over!"

She rolled her eyes and waved his jaunty bluster aside, shuffling off to her kitchen happy once more.

"Well, you're certainly in gay spirits today," Felicity said, reaching up to give her brother a kiss on the cheek. "Did Burnham meet our price?" She had sent Owen into

Natchez to meet with the cotton factor to see if their current crop could fetch a better price than last season's. "It seems to me that Graced Ground cotton should get better than market, unless he can come up with a good reason why not."

"So you said and so I told him," Owen said blithely, arranging his long legs on the dining chair, which immediately looked too small for his frame. "And he said he'd go as high as twenty, if that suits you."

Felicity thought for a moment. Twenty was just up from market, likely less than she'd have been able to get if she had gone herself. Still, it was more than they got last year. It would do. "Well," she said smiling hugely at Owen. "You did just fine, then. No wonder you're in such good spirits. I knew you'd bring Burnham around."

"So did I," Owen said, "but that's not why I'm glad. I'm bringing a young lady round to Pa's birthday supper next week, and—"

"You're doing what?" Felicity was in the process of leaving the room and she stopped, turned abruptly, and stood with her hands on her hips, staring at him.

"Now what do you look like that for?" Owen asked, instantly on the defensive. "I swear, Filly, when you stand like that you look more like an officer than I ever did."

"Which isn't saying much," Felicity said. "What are you talking about, Owen? This is a celebration for Father, it's for *family*. The man will be seventy-two years old—"

"You don't have to tell me my father's age," Owen said. "In fact, you don't have to tell me anything at all, Filly. This party isn't for you, after all, unless I've been sadly misinformed. And I'm certain Pa will be delighted to meet my lady friend—"

"Oh, of course he'll say so," Felicity interrupted, "just as he said so a half-dozen times in the last year. By all means, Owen, drag another 'lady friend' into our midst, and we'll all be polite and make her welcome, but just once, I wish you'd think of how it looks to the rest of us—"

"To you, you mean."

"No, actually, I had LeeAnn more in mind. And Wade Martin, as well, if you want to know the truth. What must they think when they see you bring round gal after gal, each one younger and more simpering than the one before."

"Bella didn't simper!"

"Bella was only two years older than my daughter!" Felicity saw the hurt in Owen's eyes, despite his denial, and she sat down suddenly, softening her voice. "Ah, my sweet brother," she said, "I know you're lonely. But you cry wolf so many times with these young things that when you finally bring around the one you want forever, we won't believe you."

"How do you know this one's not the one?" he asked. "I swear, Filly, you get older every year."

"That's what we're supposed to do. You're one of the few I know who manages to avoid it." She gazed at him a few, fond moments. "Well, then, tell me. What is her name?"

He grinned then and rolled his eyes in appreciation. "Shelly's her name, sis, and she's the best of the lot."

"And a lot you've had," she murmured wryly.

Owen pulled himself up to his full height, replete with dignity, wounded honor, and a scowl.

The solemnity of his face made her laugh despite her effort to remain serious. "Oh, Owen, you're such a scamp. Were you this bad before the war or was I just too young to notice?"

He thought about that for a moment. "I don't know. I think not. The war changed me, I'm sure. How could it help but?"

"Well, bring her then. I suppose another happy face to celebrate with Father will only be to the good."

"Actually, I was thinking of asking Robert as well. He and Tess haven't seen Pa and Mother for ages."

"Oh, Owen, I don't like that man," Felicity groaned. "He's a troublemaker. He can't talk on any subject but the negroes."

"You don't like too many of my friends these days," Owen said shortly. "I guess I'm old enough to choose for myself, however."

"It's true, I don't much like this current crop you're teaming with, that Robert Foote and James Bonny and Phillip Reston—they're all just nightriders, and they scare me to death."

"They're all gentlemen, Filly, and they belong to the same gentlemen's club that I do, that's all. And I'll thank you to say no more on the subject. About the time I start taking social advice from my little sister—a lady, I might add, who has scarcely been outside the bosom of her family for nearly twenty years—well, that'll be about the day I hang up my hat and turn up my toes forever."

"Fine, then," she said, "invite anyone you please, run with them too, but if you all get shot one night by a scared cropper, well, don't come crying to me."

Owen turned serious for a moment. "Just what do you know about the Knights, Filly? It's supposed to be a secret club, after all."

"You boys are such fools," Felicity said. "You think a few bedsheets keep your secrets? The negroes know who you are, and so does everyone else."

"Well, I've never ridden with them, and I don't know that I'd hold with such gossip anyway. The men I know are honorable, decent men, family men, most of them, and I know things like that happen in other counties, but not here in Natchez."

"Good," Felicity said. "Just so long as you don't ride with them."

He gazed at her a moment. "You know, you're sounding more and more like Mother every day."

"I know. And looking more like her, too."

Owen grinned, rising again and towering over her. "You need a man, Filly. Let me know when you want to let down the castle drawbridge and I'll introduce you to a few likely ones."

She waved him off. He kissed her lightly on the cheek and was gone. It was true, she thought then as he left, she did talk to him more like a mother than a sister. Well, someone had to, she told herself. He wasn't worth a lick around the place most of the time. He was dear, sweet Owen, and he would never have the spine he had before the war. And she supposed it was wrong to fault him. Something had happened to him then, had happened to a good many men in the South, and they were never going to have the faith they had before.

She stood and looked out over the fields from the vast bow window which faced the dining room. The croppers were spread out in the rows, much as they had been since she could remember. They looked no different from when they'd been slaves, really, except now they worked alongside their wives and children, and no foreman stood over them on a horse, carrying a whip.

It was a beautiful land, she told herself as she did almost daily. Worth everything they had to do to keep it intact.

A quick surge of rustle and noise behind her, and Felicity turned to see LeeAnn bounce into the room with little of the dignity one might have expected in a young lady of seventeen.

"Smoothly," Felicity said automatically to her daughter, an admonition she parceled out several times a day. "Move with grace, dear, as I've told you."

"Yes, Mama," LeeAnn said, scarcely pausing, "Is Uncle Owen back from Natchez?"

"Yes, he is, and I'm sorry to say that he was unable to obtain that watered silk you wanted. It's just too dear. I told you that before he left."

LeeAnn frowned ferociously, and Felicity almost laughed aloud at the effort such a grimace took from her daughter, whose normal countenance was one of joy.

"Mama! I told you that I *needed* that silk! Did you tell Uncle Owen not to get it for me?"

Felicity shook her head. "No, actually, I did not, and you can ask him yourself. I told you it was too dear and I told him as well. He decided to get it for you himself, regardless, but he couldn't find it, for love nor money.''

"Oh no!'' LeeAnn moaned. ''I'll just die if I don't find that silk. I need it for Jane's *fête* in one week!''

"What's wrong, for mercy sakes, with your lovely apple-green damask? It suits you beautifully, dear, and you've only worn it twice.'' Felicity touched her hand gently as she always did when she wanted to calm her daughter. It usually worked to pull her back to herself when she threatened to fly off into a hissy fit or worse.

LeeAnn sighed and slid down into the chair closest to the door. ''Well, I suppose it'll have to do, if Uncle Owen can't get the silk for me, he's such a dear to try . . .'' And then she sprang up again. ''I have to go see him and tell him at once not to give it another second's thought. He'll be devastated to disappoint me, I know, and he mustn't worry his head another minute.'' And she hurried out of the room.

"Smoothly!'' Felicity called after her.

LeeAnn turned and smiled at her mother, brilliantly, with the same vivacity Filly remembered in her grandmother. ''Thank you, Mama,'' she said. ''I'll try to remember.''

"And you might remember something else as well,'' Felicity said. ''Your uncle has a lot on his mind just now. Not the least of which is another young lady he's planning to bring to your grandfather's birthday celebration next week.''

"Oh no, not another one!'' LeeAnn shrieked with high glee. ''I can't wait to see Wade's face when I tell him.'' And she bustled away, her skirts swishing like a dozen mares' tails.

Martin's seventy-second birthday was celebrated on the following Sunday, out at everyone's favorite picnic spot, the largest mound on the property. Over the years, Arden had directed that trees be planted about the base, so that it was shaded on three sides. The fourth side was left open to the sun, as the original Indians had intended it, "for history's sake," she said.

Now a half-dozen buggies were parked in the shade, and the horses drowsed or nibbled the grass at the edges of the high hillock which dominated the landscape for miles. Owen had, indeed, brought his lady friend, one Shelly Ames, as well as several male acquaintances from Natchez and their ladies. Felicity drove over with Wade and LeeAnn, and Arden and Martin came in last, with cheerful bells ringing from the top of their carriage. Both cooks had tried to outshine the other, as usual, so there was enough fine and satisfying food to feed twice as many guests as attended.

LeeAnn and Wade took one collective look at Miss Ames, a bright and sprightly girl of no more than twenty, and promptly hovered about her, offering her first one delicacy and then another until she was quite dizzy.

"Do try these lemon cakes, dear Miss Ames," LeeAnn cooed to her. "They're simply luscious."

"No, you've got to leave room for another piece of cook's fried chicken," Wade insisted, pressing a large, greasy drumstick upon the woman. "And here, you won't want to miss my mama's sweet pickles. Well, she's dead now, of course, but we wouldn't dream of eating any other pickles than her own recipe. Here, have another bite . . ."

"Miss Ames, I do fear you've slighted my uncle's favorite!" LeeAnn said with near panic in her voice. "Why, he won't hear of a picnic without my grandmama's peach pie. Here, take this slice, it's small . . ."

They nearly had her on the run and slightly ill. As she escaped to Owen's side, they fawned over her and pestered her with first one request to race up the mound and then another to see who could find the prettiest wildflower, until the poor girl was faint with their attentions. And then, when they had completely outflanked her, they left her utterly and obviously alone.

"That's another one down," Wade said covertly to

LeeAnn as they ambled together away from the others, stopping every so often to inspect for perfect four-leaf clovers.

"And a gaggle more to go, no doubt," LeeAnn sighed. "Your pa has about as much sense as a gander when it comes to women. Why doesn't he ever pick on one his own size?"

"Likely, the older ones got too much sense to fool with him," Wade said shortly. "Hush now, here he comes."

Owen came up from the other side of the mound, dusting off his lawn trousers and pulling on his waistcoat as though he felt it suddenly too small. "Well, that was a fine little charade, you two," he said wearily. "What does that make? An even dozen you've managed to run off, all told?"

LeeAnn giggled, unable to keep up the pose of innocence. "Well, if you'd bring round a lady with a decent head on her shoulders, I guess we wouldn't try so hard to knock it off," she said.

"You're just like your mama," Owen sighed. "Nobody is good enough for me, and in the meantime, I'm supposed to grow moss like your granddaddy there, waiting for some woman who can put up with this family."

They stood and looked over to where Martin and Arden sat on chairs under the trees, flanked on all sides by family and neighbors and guests. It was a happy group, from a distance, and they could hear the rise and fall of varied voices, almost drowned out by the summer buzz of the cicadas in the trees.

"Where's your lady love?" Wade asked sourly.

"In the buggy," Owen replied. "She says she's got a sick headache and begs to be excused. I'm going to take her back to the house, but before I do, I thought you'd like to pay your respects and come back to join the party." He grinned wryly at them. "I doubt anyone will miss me much, but if your grandmama and grandpapa don't have their best grandchicks close by when I leave, the party will be over, so far as they're concerned."

"Oh, you don't have to go!" LeeAnn cried, genuinely regretful now. "Just because she's not well . . ."

"I'll just run her up and then come back for a spell," he said. "But you might keep that in mind, next time you decide your next campaign. When you chase off the guns, the soldiers generally go, too."

Wade grumbled, "Let her go, then, LeeAnn. No doubt you'll see her again at Jane's *fête*. She's no older than the rest of your friends."

Owen said sternly then, "When I need advice on women, son, I'll be asking a man who's had one or two before I come to you, is that understood?"

"Yessir," Wade said quietly. "Sorry, sir."

Owen clapped him gently on the back and steered them both toward the group under the trees. "Now, let me run this young lady to a quiet bed in a cool room, and I'll be back directly. Wade, go and sit next to your grandfather. The chances you'll have to take that seat are surely numbered."

The afternoon was a grand success after that, most everyone agreed then and later. Martin told tales of the old days with unusual wit and energy, keeping his audience leaning forward to hear him better, and even Arden joined in once or twice with remembrances which made them laugh or shake their heads at the poignancy of life. At one point, she said, almost casually, "I do wish we could remember where we buried the silver, however. That still troubles me after all these years."

"Mama, what are you talking about?" Felicity asked.

"Why, surely you remember? No, you were likely too hard in mourning still—well, your father came up here one night when the Yankees were coming and buried the good silver and some of Mama's best jewelry, like those emeralds my father gave her. And do you think he can remember where I put it?" She shook her head. "Someplace, right next to some Indian chief's treasure, I suppose, are a few trinkets of the Howard family, but I doubt we'll ever find them again."

"Mama, are you fooling or are you simply getting a little dizzy in the heat?" Felicity asked, amazed. "I've never heard such a tale!"

"It's the truth, sad to say," Martin chimed in. "I was in quite a hurry that night, and she wouldn't let me mark it for fear the Yankees would find it, and now I can't recall where it is. Oh, someplace in that far field," he said, gesturing, "but I couldn't pinpoint the spot if they held a gun to my head now. You young folks'll have to excavate it someday, if you've a mind. In the meantime, it's surely as safe there as in the Farmer's Bank of Natchez. Safer, if the Yankees ever decide to plague this county again."

"Oh, you surely don't believe they ever will again, sir!" one of Owen's Natchez acquaintances cried with what seemed to be genuine concern.

"I misdoubt that sincerely, sir, but you can never tell what a Yankee will do," Martin said. "I said it twenty years ago, and it's just as true today. I told them then, let me tell you young men what is coming. Your brothers, your friends, the husbands of your ladies, and the sons of your mothers will be herded at the point of bayonets to war, sir! I said as much even then, what, chick, twenty years or more ago?"

"At least," Arden said.

"I told them, you may, sir, after the sacrifice of countless millions of treasure and hundreds of thousands of lives, as a bare possibility, win Southern independence. But I doubt it, sir! I sincerely doubt it! You see, I told them, I know the North some little bit, did enough business there to know the Northerners, too. They live in a colder climate. They are not fiery and impulsive, sir, as our young men are wont to be. But when they begin to move, they move with the steady momentum and perseverance of a mighty avalanche. I said as much then, and it's just as true today, I believe."

The group nodded slowly with agreement.

"There's much talk about the Grand Lost Cause these days, but even then, I was one of many who questioned its righteousness. After all, the American people *as a whole*, not thirteen states, forged our great Union, and therefore, sir, they could alone have the power to dissolve it! That's a mighty strong argument, it seems to me, and I said it then, but few listened, leastwhys, not in this county.'' He chuckled grimly. ''Now, of course, plenty of them say they thought the same thing, But it makes perfect sense, sir! We could not allow the constituent parts of these United States to ignore laws enacted by Congress, any more than we could allow you, sir, to ignore those laws while your neighbors obeyed them. Those laws were supposed to represent *all* the people, and no democratic republic can survive if the minority flouts and defies and thwarts the majority! States rights be damned, sir! However, it was nothing more than anarchy then, and it still is today.''

''I have not heard the other side of the argument put so eloquently, sir,'' one of the Natchez guests said, ''even by Yankees themselves. I may not agree with your point of view, but I do see the reason behind your words.''

''Did I tell you about when they took over my carriage house?'' Martin continued. ''And nearly set it and the street afire?'' As he saw he had his listeners sure again, he started in, ''Well, it was after the siege of Natchez, when we tried to run them off and failed. The Yankees swarmed the streets like bluecoat rats that night . . .''

And so the sun went down slowly behind the mound to the west, and the sounds of the birds from the Trace began to dwindle before the birthday celebration finally began to wend its way back to the lights of Graced Ground, the Big House, and home.

It was Sunday, Felicity's favorite day of the week. As Arden had before her, Felicity took a certain pleasure in leading the black folks in prayer in the chapel at Graced Ground. Each week, the croppers assembled in the tall, light-filled church which her great-grandfather had built when the country was still a wilderness, the place where her people were laid to rest in the ground out back. Once they were all sitting in rows, she read to them of the word of the Lord.

On most Sundays, LeeAnn helped her with the readings and then led the families in song. LeeAnn had a singing voice like an angel, better even than Felicity's, and her voice was never better than when the whole chapel was filled with other voices following her lead. She was less patient with the scripture, and tended to fidget, but a single glance from her mother inevitably pulled her back to quiet decorum.

On many Sundays, Arden joined them, Portia slowly walking behind her, leaning on her cane. The colored croppers seemed to sense those Sundays when Miss Arden would attend, and their own attendance rose accordingly.

When Felicity looked up from a passage to see thirty or forty rapt faces shining up at her in the dancing motes of morning sun as it came through the rose windows of the chapel, she knew a sense of family and abiding peace which often escaped her during the rest of the week. At those times, she regretted she had not been married there. Perhaps if she had been, James would not have been killed, she told herself. Perhaps her long-dead ancestors would have watched over him a mite better . . . but then she put that thought right out of her mind. Sheer superstition. God took James when He meant to, and that was all she needed to remember.

On this particular Sunday, she had chosen as her reading the passage from the King James where Christ speaks of the two greatest commandments, that they should love their God with all their hearts and minds and souls and that they should love their neighbors as themselves. Mark 12, one of her favorites. She liked those images, when Jesus said that the poor widow who gave two mites to the treasury was closer to heaven, for she gave all that she had, above the rich men who gave far more out of their abundance.

There was something in those passages, she felt sure, which would move her folks to that high place they reached on many Sundays, when they bloomed into song before her like great shining blossoms of soul, and she could see and feel and hear the gratitude and love pour from their mouths. Their voices were like soaring birds then, particularly the young men and the young women, and that was her single greatest reward.

As she and LeeAnn walked from the Big House to the chapel, she smiled and said aloud, "Oh, I expect they'll be singing big this morning."

LeeAnn was doing her best to keep her skirts from the dust, as she planned to go with Owen into Natchez that afternoon to visit some friends. She plucked anxiously at her dress. "I should never have worn this frock this morning; I should have waited to change after service. But I don't know for sure when Owen's fixing to leave, and I don't want to hold him up."

"Well, the folks love to see you, however you dress, of course," Felicity said, "but I think they like it best when you put on a bit of a fuss for them. Makes them feel special, I suppose."

"Did you pick a long passage?" LeeAnn asked.

Felicity could feel the hopefulness there, though her daughter would never come right out and ask for brevity. To do so, she knew, would guarantee her mother taking her time with whatever she was planning, just to prove to her daughter that Sunday service was worth whatever else was kept waiting. But she smiled at her indulgently. "Not so very," she said. "The part where Jesus talks about the poor widow and the rich scribes and loving thy neighbor . . ."

"Oh good," LeeAnn said with relief. "They'll bowl you right through that one."

They got to the chapel and greeted some of the folks outside. As usual, the croppers had done their best to dress decently, but Felicity was struck by the difference from what she could remember of her own childhood.

In those days, the slaves had few garments, but they each had at least one "best set" for special occasions, sometimes no more than a simple red shirt for the men or a colorful cotton shift for the women, but something they kept extra nice.

Usually it was made from the cloth they got each Christmas
and saved all through the year.

But the croppers got no Christmas cloth and they had little
to spend on extras, so when Sunday came round, they did
what they could to pay their respects, but it was poor stuff,
generally. A man might have a clean shirt, a baby might
have something sewn special, but most of them simply put a
flower in a buttonhole and called it good. Bare feet, some of
them barely covered up, but at least they came. As usual, she
had to put those thoughts away, for she wasn't responsible
for their clothing anymore, no matter how much she felt she
still ought to be.

She bowed to those who waited for her outside, speaking
to each by name, and LeeAnn touched a few of the young
folks on the head, teasing some special ones and making
them laugh. Then inside the two women swept, their makeshift congregation at their heels.

Inside, the rest of the folks waited, turning to look at the
two women as though they were a bridal party. Felicity took
her place at the small altar, seeing with satisfaction that the
flowers were in place as she directed each Saturday. She
stood behind the pulpit and took up her Bible, smiling out
over the crowd. Quickly counting, she saw that they were at
thirty-eight. Not bad for a warm Sunday morning when
crops beckoned every hour of daylight. She held up her
hands as she'd seen the minister at the Episcopal Church do
in Natchez, gathering her folks to her with her welcome.
And they responded, as they always did, with a loud "Hal-
lejulah!"

She began reading, swaying slightly, unconsciously as the
words of the Bible made their magic in the warm, spring air.
The sense of life everlasting, of all things renewed and forever young, was as powerful as the words themselves, and
she felt herself growing quieter within her heart, still and effortlessly finding her way as a clear creek down a sloping
hill. Beside her, LeeAnn hummed, letting her voice rise and
fall at will with the words, and the folks swayed in time,

sometimes humming along. Sometimes a voice would warble higher than the rest as a bird will do when gathered at dusk, and the chapel was filled with a sense of community and contentment.

Then when the scripture was finished, LeeAnn began the singing proper, with her favorite hymn, "Praising My Savior," and the chapel rang then, their voices finally released, with the bass of the men and the high, soaring sopranos of the women, and as always, Felicity felt closer to James at that moment of the week than at any other.

The folks gathered outside the chapel after the singing, and she was satisfied to see that her words about neighborliness had made an impression. Croppers spoke to each other, some men shook hands who had not spoken before, their women standing aside shyly and nodding to each other, their children joining in a spontaneous eruption of running glee. Soon, they would likely be speaking more, and then perhaps sharing a supper or two. It was as it should be.

As Felicity and LeeAnn walked back to the big house, the girl said, "It's been a while since Grandmama came to chapel. They set such store by her and Portia, both. Especially since River Reach is gone to new folks, there's not too many of the old-timers left anymore."

"Don't let your grandmother hear you call her that!" Felicity laughed.

"Oh, she'd probably love it. Now Portia's another story. Oh!" she said suddenly, skipping as she remembered. "I forgot, I have to hurry! Uncle Owen's surely ready to leave now, I don't want to miss him."

"Child, he wouldn't leave without you."

"No, but he also will fuss so if I keep him waiting, it's almost not worth listening to him halfway to Natchez!" And LeeAnn rushed ahead to the house, waving back to her mother, who brought up the rear.

Felicity deliberately walked more slowly, watching her daughter as she hurried off. LeeAnn was young for her age in many ways, likely from being around Wade Martin as her only companion in her growing-up years. She'd had a decent education, she supposed, with Master Kimble, her tutor, but it was time she was with young ladies her own age more. Young gentlemen, too. She remembered that she was just about LeeAnn's age when she met James. But of course, those were the war years, and everything moved faster then. She frowned and rebuked herself softly. It was time to let her go. There was a whole world beyond Graced Ground, beyond Natchez even, and LeeAnn should have it all like an apron of ripe fruit for her own. She wasn't a child anymore.

As Felicity approached the house, she saw that Owen's carriage was waiting to gather LeeAnn up to go, and she came round front to wave them both goodbye. To her surprise, Owen was standing at the carriage speaking to LeeAnn, and his mouth was turned down in a disapproving frown.

"What is it?" she asked, coming upon them both.

LeeAnn's face was crestfallen, and she looked up beseechingly at her mother. "Uncle Owen says we shouldn't be reading to them from the Bible. The croppers. He says, it just ruins a good field hand."

Felicity's frown now matched her brother's. "What in the world are you talking about, Owen?"

"I'm talking about reality," he said, "and the facts of life as they are, not as you'd wish them to be, sister mine. You know the croppers need to keep their attention to the crops, or they'll starve. Pure and simple as that. And filling their heads full of wishes and high-toned words gives them too many other things to think about and fret over. Why, you might as well just take the food right off their tables, right out of their babies' mouths. Because they'll go hungry, sure enough, if they start mooning around after what they can't ever have."

"Salvation, you mean?" she said coolly. "Owen, I can't believe you're talking like this. Why, you must remember, Mama always read to the slaves, the same King James I read to them today."

"And Mama was famous in three counties for spoiling her niggers to death," Owen said. "Many folks, some of her neighbors even, didn't thank her none for it either."

"You sound like an ignorant piney-woods redneck farmer right now," Felicity said. "And I can't believe you mean what you say."

"Well, plenty of them do, that's for sure," Owen said. "Most of the folks I know—"

"Most of the *men,* you mean," Felicity said angrily.

"That's right, sister mine, most of the men. Because whether you like it or not, the men are still running things in this state and they're running things to suit the *white* men. Now if you don't like it, I guess you can march with the suffragettes in New York and take up with black folks and marry off your daughter to one, if that suits you. But on this land, I'd take it kindly if you'd stop agitating the croppers. I got to live in this county, too, and you don't make it any more comfortable for me, that's a fact."

"I don't make it comfortable for your mean-spirited ol' Kluxer friends, you mean," Felicity said, her eyes narrowing. She saw that LeeAnn had shrunk back into the carriage, but she wasn't missing a word. "Because this isn't you talking, Owen. It's that pack of nightriders you run with these days. I told you once before, they're too bent on mayhem to last for long. Do you think the Yankees won't come back? You think we can just keep on stomping the black folks down and not have them rise up and kill us in our sleep one night?"

He snorted derisively. "They tried it once or twice, as I recall. John Brown's body lies a-molderin' in his grave, sister, and so do a sight more who thought like he did."

"Well, that's not the point anyhow," LeeAnn suddenly added from the dim quiet of the carriage. "It's the word of God we're talking about here, not the vote."

"It's reading," Owen said, "and one thing leads to another."

"We're not teaching them to read," LeeAnn continued softly. "We're only teaching them to have faith."

Felicity started to speak and then thought better of it. LeeAnn was doing just fine.

"And I would think," LeeAnn said, her voice gentle and persuasive, "that even men who want to keep them in their place would see that faith is the one thing they can have of their own which will keep them happy where they are." She looked up at her uncle with trust and love. "Don't you want them to be happy at least?"

"Of course I do, sweet girl," Owen said gruffly. "I just don't want them to get big ideas and start a revolution. You know, there's some of that in the good book as well."

"I guess there is," LeeAnn said, "but we just tell them about trusting in the Lord and loving God with their whole hearts and souls, and that they will be rewarded in Heaven. Seems to me that's got to be a comfort for them, no matter how terrible their lives might be." She paused. "And you have to admit, Uncle Owen, their lives are pretty terrible."

Owen dropped his head silently. For a moment, no word was said at all.

Felicity said then, "What did you think when Mama read to the slaves, brother? Were you so all-fired against it then?"

He shook his head. "But they were slaves, then. They're free now. It's a whole different landscape."

"You mean, they're not your property anymore. But you still want to own their souls." Felicity deliberately did not look at Owen when she said that. She gazed instead out over the fields and spoke casually, as though she had only just thought of some incidental thing.

Owen fell silent again. He glanced up at LeeAnn, who smiled at him beautifully, winningly. He slowly smiled back. "Well, I suppose you're right, sister." He ran his hand through his hair as he often did when he was perplexed. "I guess I'm just a hotheaded fool."

"No, you're not," LeeAnn said loyally. "But Uncle, I do

worry sometimes about your—gentlemen's club. I know the croppers are scared to death of them, and I can't help think that they've got good reason. You . . . you wouldn't ever ride with them, would you?''

Owen shook his head. "No, LeeAnn, I wouldn't." He sighed hugely and slapped his riding gloves against his yellow fawn trousers. As always, they were immaculate and expertly tailored in the newest fashion. After a long moment he said, "I tell you what. I'll quit them." He grinned sideways suddenly at Felicity. "Hell, they're getting to be too rowdy, even for me."

"Oh, Uncle!" LeeAnn smiled, clapping her hands happily. "That's wonderful to hear. I've been so worried . . ."

"But if I hear of you two taking primers out to that chapel and teaching those croppers their letters, I'll burn the place down myself, you hear?"

"Yassuh," Felicity said with a broad imitation of a negro accent. "Yassuh, Mars' Owen!"

"Mars' Owen," he said, and laughed as he clicked to the horse and started off. "I like that, Felicity. Perhaps you can keep it in mind."

They trotted away, and Felicity could hear LeeAnn's giggle over the high-stepping hooves of the horse. There was happiness in that laughter, much relief, and sufficient love for them both.

Along the Natchez Trace, and up and down the fertile valleys of the Saint Catherine before the turn of the century, a small black animal lived and foraged who was scarcely seen by day—and would have been scrupulously avoided by the croppers whose cabins she waddled near at night.

Her name was Dorsa, and she was a long-quilled porcupine. Called *Erethizon dorsatum* in the north where she was more numerous, her kind was becoming quite scarce in the lower Mississippi region. But so were her enemies. As man moved over the fields and cleared the woods for his crops, the bobcats, foxes, wolves, fishers, and mountain lions who might have caught and killed her were moving out of the Trace and going north and west where man was not. Dorsa, too, would soon be gone and likely few of her kind would remain.

But now, on an evening in June, the scarcity of her numbers was not on her mind. Dorsa was pregnant with a single ovum she had been gestating since November of the previous year: seven months, a very long time for such a small mammal.

The male had found her in October, a large, black, chunky mate with a high-arching back, short legs, and poor eyesight like her own. His quills were quite full, indicating that he had not been molested or attacked recently, and she let him approach her without hissing a warning of defense. She had been in season for a week without a male approaching her, and she was ready for his courtship.

Dorsa had left her scat in the appropriate places, and she was slightly bewildered that it took him so long to find her. She was too young to have memories of generations before, when a female in season would have been badgered by so many males that she would have had to run from half of them and be mated by the other half. But so few of her kind remained in this region that now she was as eager as he was to mate.

A solitary creature like the rest of her kind, Dorsa approached the act of mating with gruff brevity and a maximum of caution. Her generic name meant "one who rises in anger," and she was completely capable of epitomizing her name. When the male began to follow her trail—patches of urine laid down which led to her den in a crevice shelter near the Saint Catherine bluffs and small piles of scat—she knew it at once. She saw his track about her territory twice before she actually saw him.

His trail was distinctive: toe in, almost like a badger but for two important elements. The pebbled knobs on the soles of his paws left a stippled track with long claw marks far ahead of the oval main prints, about three inches in length and six inches apart. A big male. His broom-tail swept out part of his track but there was sufficient remaining for him to judge his gait and his size before she ever saw him.

When he appeared one dusk, moaning softly outside the entrance to her cave, she went out at once and faced him. She was just awakening for her nightly hunt, and she was hungry and eager. She grunted in reply when she saw him, and she stepped forward, laying her quills back flat against her back in deference. Squeaking loudly, he approached her from the side, sniffing her from nose to tail.

She stood very still. She knew she must be sufficiently aroused to mate, or she would injure her mate as surely as she could any other predator. She waited for him to court her, letting her body relax.

He sniffed her round and round, grunting, groaning, and squeaking at her to arouse her. Finally approaching her gingerly, the male licked at her nose tentatively, pawed gently at her legs, and only when she had relaxed her quills and raised her tail over her back did he move behind her. As she presented herself, he carefully mounted her, mated, and then moved away from her once more.

Within a week of his departure, she sensed her impregnation. Always fond of salt, she now began to crave this substance even more as her embryo grew. Usually a strict vegetarian, Dorsa fed on leaves, twigs, and green plants like skunk cabbage, lupines, and clover. In the winter, she made do with the rough outer bark of pines, cedar, and hemlock. Actually, it was not the bark which she needed but the inner bark, or cambium, which sustained her. Now as spring came on again, she knew her single baby would be born when the wild roses were in bloom. And still, she was driven to find the extra salt her pregnancy demanded.

Dorsa feared little, for generations of defensive quills had made her kind almost careless when it came to danger. She waddled slowly, looking neither to the left nor the right, similar to the skunk who knew that he was not likely to be disturbed. The fisher was quite good at flipping the porcupine over to attack its wiry-haired but unquilled underbelly, as was the mountain lion. But since both of those predators were scarce, Dorsa and generations before her had become lax in their defense. She did not need to be clever; she had her quills.

When she struck an enemy—or even a perceived threat—her loosely rooted quills detached easily and were driven forcefully into her attacker. Once in flesh, the victim's body heat made the microscopic barblets on the end of the quill expand and become even more firmly embedded. The wounds usually festered, and the animal who had come after Dorsa usually found itself blinded, maimed, crippled, or unable to eat.

Dorsa had more than thirty thousand quills, each one a modified hair, solid at the tip and base, hollow down the shaft, and renewable quickly in case of loss. She felt herself, mostly, to be invulnerable, an unusual attitude for a wild creature.

Now she was on the hunt for salt. She knew there was little in the woods, for whatever salt was there was quickly licked off the stones or the plants by the deer and other animals which needed it as she did. But there was one place where she knew she could find what she wanted: the dens of man. She left the wooded cover of the Trace and waddled slowly to the open field. Up the rows she ambled slowly, her long tail dragging along behind her, her nose moving from left to right. Soon, she came to the little house in the middle of the field, a cabin where man lived.

It was night, and the calls of the frogs from the nearby irrigation ditch were loud and unceasing, a certain sign that no danger was present. Dorsa moved a little more quickly now, for even as protected as she was, she feared man. Up to the door of the cabin she waddled. She stopped, looked around, and listened carefully. Dorsa's eyes were weak, but her other senses were as finely tuned as they needed to be for this hunt. She soon smelled what she sought.

Against the cabin wall, next to the door, leaned several wooden-handled tools, long sticks which the men had handled again and again. The smell of the salt from their hands drove her forward. She knocked over a shovel to the ground, and it made a clatter, but she ignored the noise and began to gnaw on it fiercely, her eyes closed with pleasure. Suddenly, from within, she heard the stirring of the men. She arched her back, whisked her tail from side to side, and continued to chew.

A man opened the door and shouted something at her, and she dragged the shovel away from the door, still chewing as fast as she could. As he came to her, she faltered and dropped the wood, arched her back higher, and lifted her tail to strike.

The man stopped and shouted something, and Dorsa sensed that he was not going to touch her. Fortunately for her, the man did not know that a single blow to her nose with the very shovel she chewed would have killed her instantly. She bit through the shovel handle and carried it off as quickly as she could waddle, back down the row and through the field, back to the wooded protection of the Trace, dragging it to her creviced shelter.

Once within, she gnawed on the handle with care, sucking the salt from the wood fibers with deep satisfaction. When her offspring was born, she would lead it to the best salt source in her territory, showing it how to elude the men as she did. And their dogs. She would most especially show her offspring, and with some pleasure in the process, how to deal with the dogs of the men they might find on their lands.

The year LeeAnn turned nineteen, Felicity made a bold decision. She booked passage on the Greenville and New Orleans Packet Company aboard the new, luxurious steamboat *J. M. White* for the one-day journey up to Vicksburg. She reserved rooms for herself, LeeAnn, and for Arden, saving the news for a surprise for LeeAnn on her birthday morning.

"But Mother!" LeeAnn squealed in excitement. "How thrilling! How long do we get to stay in Vicksburg?"

"One week, at the Beauregard," Felicity said, amused and pleased at LeeAnn's pleasure. "Your grandmama thinks I have lost my mind, of course, but she wouldn't miss it for the world."

"Why does she think that?" LeeAnn asked, racing to her dressing room, where she began to pull frocks out onto the chaise, already planning her travel wardrobe. "I think it will be sublime!"

"Because she thinks New Orleans offers far more opportunities for a young lady to run amok than most, I suppose, and she says if we're going to go to all the trouble and expense, we might as well go there."

"How could she know such a thing? She was in a convent, wasn't she?"

"Yes, and too long ago to remember, I'm sure. But her own mother—your great-grandmother, child—was a great one for running amok, as I hear it, and New Orleans was her favorite place to do so. But we'll see how Vicksburg sets with us, and if we enjoy ourselves, perhaps we'll do New Orleans another time. I do believe it's time for you to see a little more of the world than Natchez Landing."

"The *J. M. White!* It's the biggest boat on the river, Mama!"

"Not quite, but almost," Felicity said. "I'm sure it will be more than enough excitement for a day and a night in each direction."

"Will Uncle Owen come along?"

"He must stay and attend to business," Felicity said, shaking her head. "And besides, he's been to Vicksburg a dozen times. No, sweet, this trip is for you."

LeeAnn ran and hugged her mother so hard that she almost lifted her off her feet, then ran back to her closet, pulling out enough gowns for a month in Paris.

A week later, Owen escorted LeeAnn, Felicity, Arden, and Portia down to Natchez-Under-the-Hill for their boarding onto the massive steamboat which idled, waiting at the docks.

Portia had a hard time maneuvering the stairway, but she managed, leaning heavily on her cane. Arden had insisted on bringing her along at the last minute. "I can't not take her," she told LeeAnn and Felicity quietly. "She's such a dear and been such a good and faithful servant all these years. I expect it'll be the last time she ever sees anything but Natchez, and she deserves it."

The *J. M. White* was one of the most impressive steamboats on the river. more than three hundred feet long and almost a hundred feet wide, it was ornate, monstrously commodious, and sumptuous in every detail. The women quickly stored their baggage in their rooms and then began to explore their ship, walking where they dared. Crowds of finely dressed passengers thronged the stairways and the wide promenades which wrapped the vessel, and since there were few ladies walking unescorted, Portia shambled close to them like a large, black watchdog, glaring at any young man who might gaze a moment too long at LeeAnn.

Felicity led them into the main cabin, and LeeAnn stopped, struck into silent wonder. "Why, it's grander than the grandest hotel," Arden murmured. When they looked up, the hand-carved moldings and gingerbread on the walls and ceilings were no less intricate than the stained-glass windows and skylights. Huge chandeliers with globes etched *JMW* hung overhead.

They peeped into the dining hall, which spread the full length of the ship, flanked on each end by a grand piano. More than a dozen chandeliers hung over the table, which seemed to stretch onto the other side of the river where Vidalia, Louisiana, slept, ignored by such magnificent craft. The chairs were intricately carved and upholstered in dark maroon leather, and the ceilings festooned with so much molding as to seem a giant, upside-down wedding cake.

They went by the gentlemen's salon and into the ladies' salon, which had wall-to-wall carpeting, smartly upholstered furnishings, and a huge mirror, astounding in the intricacy of its frame. On a small ledge to one side of the mirror stood a silver handbell to be rung for service. Outside the door, two boys in full dress waited with silver trays, to bring whatever the lady passengers might desire.

"Only one day and one night . . ." sighed LeeAnn.

"In both directions," Felicity reminded her.

"It take dat long jes' to make our way back to de cabin," Portia muttered.

That evening it was as though a whole new world opened to them, a world of glamour and easy, stylish living that had been going on, up and down the river, for years without their knowledge or participation. The women seemed more beautiful, the men more prosperous and elegant, than those they knew in Natchez. Even the river, which they rode like a huge magnificent white swan, seemed larger and more powerful than the water which edged the Natchez landing.

Always before, when LeeAnn was in Natchez with her uncle, she had enjoyed going to the bluffs to see what was being unloaded at the bottom of Silver Street. Perhaps this was the boat bringing the dozen new racehorses for Mister James Surget, or the mule trader would disembark with a hundred or more mules to sell, or maybe some new load of fancy carriages or the Phoenix Fire Company's new steam pumper had arrived. From the river came all things wonderful, and the steamboats ruled the river.

But now, to actually be aboard such a floating palace! That night, they dined on fine oysters and New Orleans shrimp, roasted capons, veal with dumplings and green peas, and mutton garnished with new potatoes. For dessert, there were pies and cakes, tarts, puddings, and sweet little confections such as candy kisses, cream figs, and lemon drops . . . and the music from the dance hall to the rear of the boat filled the night air with promise. LeeAnn begged her mother to be taken to the dance hall simply to see the people and watch them whirl and promenade.

"I am likely making a terrible mistake," Felicity said, glancing at her mother, "but I scarcely can see the point of bringing you on such a ship and then not letting you see all it has to offer. But you must promise me, we're only going to hear the music."

"Oh, Mama!" LeeAnn said gleefully.

"Things are certainly different than in my day . . ." Arden started to say.

"Oh Grandmama, you just set and rest yourself. We'll tell you all about it when we come back."

"Not on your life, miss," Arden said firmly.

Portia rolled her eyes and began to put her shawl about her shoulders.

"You needn't stir yourself," LeeAnn said solicitously to her. "We'll be back in a jiffy, I promise."

"I ain' fixin' to set here an' wonder while you traipse about," Portia grumbled.

"Oh, for heaven's sakes," LeeAnn said, now losing her patience. "Now, I have to drag the whole battalion along! You'd think I was still in short skirts! I'm nineteen—does anyone recall that fact at all? Mother, I'm going to the dance hall," she finished firmly with a toss of her head. "If you care to come along, be quick about it."

Felicity gasped, but Arden only chuckled wryly. "I can go just as fast as you can, pet, and Portia can stay here." She turned to the old, black woman. "Portia, you set here, and we'll be back soon."

"Don' rush on my account," Portia said defiantly. "I is comin', too." She glared at LeeAnn. "I jes' as free as you are, chile."

And so together, shoulder to shoulder like four horses in harness, the women made their way to the dance hall, which beckoned with gay music from the farthest corner of the *J. M. White*.

LeeAnn was dressed that evening in a lovely gown, which

dipped slightly at the neckline, one of her more daring choices. She bloomed like a glowing white rose at sunset as she stood at the edge of the ballroom, gazing at the dancers with a rapt expression. Portia had immediately taken a seat near the door, and she watched the proceedings balefully, as though she were affronted by every bar of music, every step of the waltz. Felicity stood close to LeeAnn, taking in the scene before her with a slight and wistful smile, as if she watched all the dancers from a very high place.

Arden was struck in the moment how very empty her daughter's life had been since James had died. More than twenty years of celibate solitude in a bed which surely must have seemed like a coffin more times than not, she thought. And yet she had rarely complained of loneliness, never once shown an interest in any of the young men Owen had brought round the place, a few of whom had certainly shown some interest in her when she was younger.

No, she gave every impression that LeeAnn was enough for her. LeeAnn and Graced Ground, that is, for the land had become more than a possession—it was almost a second child for Felicity now. Indeed, Arden thought as she watched LeeAnn being watched, Grace Ground might soon be Felicity's *only* child.

The stag line at the side of the ballroom had suddenly noticed LeeAnn, and an almost palpable ripple went up the scattering of young men, as though a silent bell had been rung somewhere right above their eyes. Many of them turned to her, a few murmuring something to their comrades. Within moments, one man, closest to the end of the room and bolder than his companions, approached Felicity where she stood close to LeeAnn, doffed his bowler hat, and bowed politely. "Madam, would you care to dance this waltz?"

Felicity was surprised, but she recovered her poise quickly enough. "Thank you, sir, but I do not dance." She smiled at him as she might have at Wade Martin.

He bowed once more, never ruffled, and asked, "May I

have, then, the pleasure of dancing with your lovely daughter?''

LeeAnn gasped and blushed, moving slightly away from her mother and toward Arden, as if for protection.

''You are very kind, sir,'' Felicity said, her smile slightly less warm now, ''but my daughter does not dance either. We merely stopped to listen to the music for a moment.'' She made as if to take LeeAnn by the hand. ''And we really should be going back to our cabin now.''

Portia rose as if by signal, bustled forward, and started to take her place on the other side of LeeAnn, puffing slightly like a tugboat with a special ship to escort.

Arden said lightly, ''Oh, I scarcely think one small waltz would hurt, Felicity.''

All three women turned to Arden in amazement, and the gentleman beamed, bowing now to the matriarch of the group. ''Thank you, madam. May I present myself? I am Edward Random, of New Orleans. I'm on my way to Vicksburg, where my family has several business concerns. I would be honored to be presented to your''—and here he hesitated slightly, unwilling to make a fatal error—''your niece. If I may presume upon your kindness.''

Arden smiled. ''My granddaughter, sir, and you do not presume at all.'' She turned briskly to LeeAnn, ignoring Felicity's look of shock, and said softly, ''LeeAnn, may I present Mr. Random, of New Orleans?''

Felicity found her voice suddenly. ''Mother, I really think we should be going back . . .''

''I hardly think a single waltz will topple the foundations of the world, Filly,'' Arden said mildly, ''and what will we do back in our cabins anyway? The music is delightful, I think, don't you, Mr. Random?'' She asked this last with an air so innocent that one would have to look closely to see the laughter in her eyes.

LeeAnn took her cue from her grandmother then and quickly reassessed the situation. She held out her hand to the gentleman and said, ''Sir, I am pleased to make your ac-

quaintance, but I'm afraid I must decline your invitation."
She blushed again, quite prettily. "I don't dance, you see."

The man did not hesitate. "Perhaps then you'd like to go a
little closer and see the pianist? I'm told that he is quite accomplished."

LeeAnn glanced at her mother for permission. Felicity
nodded slightly, still in amazement. All of them did their
best to ignore the hissing exhalation from Portia as LeeAnn
went off with Mister Random, her hand resting lightly on his
arm as though she had done such a thing a hundred times
before.

"Well, Mother, I can scarcely believe you did that," Felicity murmured when the two were out of hearing.

"Miz Arden, you gone clean out o' your mind at last!"
Portia breathed out with a huge sigh.

"Oh my Lord," Arden said impatiently, "you two act as
though she's made of spun sugar."

"Dat man gonna eat her up, too," Portia grumbled.

"Mother, we agreed we were only going to come to listen
to the music," Felicity said severely.

"And so we are. LeeAnn is just going to hear it a little
closer than we are, that's all. My goodness, the child is nineteen years old, Filly, and she doesn't even know how to
dance! That's disgraceful. She's not Wade Martin's age,
after all, even though he's her only companion. She's a
young woman, and you treat her like she's still a child."

"I think I can best be the judge of my daughter's social
needs, Mother. I'll thank you to respect my wishes on this
matter."

Arden reached out and held her daughter's hand gently.
"Of course, you are her mother, and I will respect your
wishes. But I think that perhaps, since you have not had love
in your life for so long, you might have forgotten how important it can be to a young woman like LeeAnn."

"Love!" Felicity snorted in disdain. "We're talking
about a simple waltz."

"And that's how it begins, often enough."

They turned and watched as LeeAnn walked through the crowd. Even some of the men who were dancing glanced at her as she passed. She was lovely. She almost shimmered with her joy at being who she was and where she was, in that exact moment.

"I'm surprised you've kept her as protected as you have for so long," Arden said to Felicity softly. "You've done a good job. But now it's time to let her go."

"But not to dat one." Portia frowned. "What kind o' name is 'Random'? Who his folks anyhow?"

Felicity said, "Hush, Portia. Mother's right. She should know how to waltz, at least."

Arden wrapped her arm round her daughter's waist. "And it wouldn't hurt you any to recall how to do it either, my dear."

"Don't go too far," Felicity replied shortly. "I'm not nineteen, and I don't miss dancing a whit."

"You're not in the grave either," Arden said smoothly. And when Felicity turned with a sharp retort, she said, "Oh, look!"

As they watched, the gentleman was introducing LeeAnn to the pianist. He stood from his piano, bowed low to her, and then reclaimed his seat, starting a sprightly air with a nod in her direction.

"I do believe she's made a conquest," Arden said happily.

"So now it starts," Felicity said, low and sober.

Arden turned to look at her. To her surprise, her daughter had bright tears in her eyes, as if she had just realized that if it were not this man, it would likely be another one. And sooner than she was ready to admit to that reality. Arden took her hand and squeezed it. "Don't let her see you cry, dear."

"She won't," Felicity said swiftly, wiping her eyes as LeeAnn came back to them, still on Mister Random's arm. "My sweet!" she called out gaily. "Did the pianist choose this song specially for you?"

"He should have," Arden said to LeeAnn clearly when she came up close enough to hear. "You were the most beautiful girl on the floor."

After the trip to Vicksburg, which each woman agreed was the highlight of the year, Felicity sat down with LeeAnn and helped her select a school to attend for the next two years. She, of course, had been tutored adequately as were most of the children of the more landed planters, but it was time for her to "sally forth," as Arden put it so cheerfully, to test herself against others her own age and the world at large. LeeAnn preferred to go to Atlanta, for many of her friends attended the academy there and had told amusing stories of their adventures, but Felicity was loath to let her go so far away.

"There are plenty of fine opportunities closer to home," she said to her daughter, "and I see no reason to add the trouble and expense of your traveling back and forth frequently from someplace so far away as Atlanta, when you can just as well get a good education right here in Mississippi."

"Where in Mississippi?" LeeAnn asked truculently. "Goodness knows, there's no decent academy in Natchez."

"Why do you say that?" Felicity asked in injured tones. "Miss Weymouth's school for young ladies is a fine old establishment, and I daresay any girl would be proud to be matriculated from there."

"Not a one that I know. Mother, I just don't see why I can't go to Atlanta with the rest of my friends."

"Not all of your friends are in Atlanta," Felicity said dryly. "In fact, a good many of them are no place at all except at home, likely where they should be."

"A dozen of them are married already."

"And is that what you want? To be saddled with a husband and a half-dozen babies already? For heaven's sakes, LeeAnn, show some good sense. You've got the rest of your life to be married, and a very few years to enjoy your freedom.''

''That's what I'm talking about, Mother!'' the girl moaned in a near-frenzy. ''My freedom!''

Owen sauntered into the room then, on his way out riding. He sprawled down on the chaise and mimicked LeeAnn's desperate expression. ''Lord, child, you sound like a raving abolitionist. Is Mama going to sell you South?''

''Just about,'' LeeAnn pouted. ''She wants me to go to some piddly ol' school in Natchez, when everyone I know is either already in Atlanta at Academy or on their way there. I'm already later than most to go off, and she still wants me to stay within hollering distance.'' She leaned forward with her hands clasped in her most dramatic manner. ''Tell her, Uncle Owen. Tell her I'll be shamed to death to stay here in Natchez, like a bitty baby who can't be trusted out of her sight. Why''—and here, the thought struck her all over again, rousing her indignation—''I don't even know how to dance!''

Owen laughed genially. ''I tried to teach you a few times, pet, but you were always too busy running off with Wade Martin, galloping after hoptoads or climbing up the scuppernog to lend an ear. Besides, if it's dancing you want, you needn't go all the way to Atlanta.''

''Oh! You're just as bad as she is!'' LeeAnn cried. ''You just want me to stay close enough to tease and torment, and I'll be an old maid for the rest of my natural days!''

''That's not true,'' Owen said mildly. ''I do think you should go to Atlanta. Or anyplace else your heart desires. You're nineteen years old, free, white, and pert as a songbird. If you want my vote—''

''I don't,'' Felicity said sourly.

''We do!'' LeeAnn protested.

''Then, I think you should go off and find out what your friends like so much about Atlanta.''

''Oh, thank you, Uncle Owen!'' LeeAnn clapped her hands and turned to her mother with raised hopes. ''Mama, you're the *only* one who thinks I ought to stay in Natchez. Grandmama and Uncle Owen *both* think—''

"When did you talk with your grandmother?" Felicity asked sharply.

LeeAnn saw instantly that she had made a strategic error. "Well, I didn't really *talk* with her about it, I only mentioned that we were thinking about Academy, and I said I wanted to go to Atlanta, and she didn't say she was against the idea . . .''

"Your grandmother felt I should stay in Mississippi, as I recall, when the subject came up of my schooling, so I scarcely think she'd approve of her only granddaughter going so far away.''

"Times are different now," Owen said gently. "When the subject came up of your schooling, we were heading for war, and besides, many women didn't go to school at all when you were a girl.''

LeeAnn decided to press the point. "At least you got to go to Columbus, Mother. Back then, that was almost as far away as Atlanta is today.''

"And she met your father there," Owen said. "A rather tempestuous courtship, as I recall.''

"That's it, then," LeeAnn said triumphantly. "You're afraid I'll run off with some rake or another—''

"LeeAnn!" Felicity warned.

"But Mother, I can find a rake just as easily here in Natchez as in Atlanta, if I've a persuasion in that direction, and you know it." She paused and watched her mother's face.

"LeeAnn, that's extremely unattractive," Felicity said as severely as she could manage. "You'll make me think you best stay home altogether and put the idea of academy right out of your foolish head." She frowned convincingly. "Rake, indeed!" But Felicity was beginning to sag in her conviction. Even Owen could see it.

"Mama," LeeAnn said gently, "do let me go. I'll make you proud of me, I promise. Atlanta is not so very far these days.''

Felicity sighed hugely. "I wish your father were alive today. It's not a matter of money, of course, it's a matter of—"

"Maternity," Owen completed for her. "A taxing burden, I hear, that many mothers are loath to put down, even when it's time to do so."

Felicity glared at him. "I thank you so much for your participation, dear brother. I don't recall inviting you to the discussion, but I scarcely think we could have managed without you."

Owen laughed amiably. "Oh, let her go, Filly. It'll be fun visiting her, lots more fun than dragging up to Vicksburg or Columbus. If she's going to go, let her really go."

LeeAnn kept still as a rabbit, knowing full well that a wrong word from her might well sway her mother away from where Owen was persuading her to go.

Felicity sighed hugely again. "Oh, all right," she said finally. "If you honestly feel that you simply can't abide the idea of Miss Weymouth's, then you may go to Atlanta to academy there. But you must promise me, LeeAnn, you'll concentrate on your studies, and you'll complete at least two years, no matter what."

"This sounds vaguely familiar," Owen grinned.

"Not another word out of you!" Felicity warned. "I'll have your promise, LeeAnn, or I'll change my mind in a blink."

"I promise!" LeeAnn cried, leaping into her mother's arms in gratitude. "Thank you, thank you, thank you!"

"Just don't make me regret my decision," Felicity said solemnly. "You're nineteen, but you're still very young in many ways. I expect you to use what good sense you have and to cultivate still more, do you understand?"

"Yes, Mama," LeeAnn said soberly. And then she turned to grin at her uncle. "Atlanta!"

* * *

Arden woke up one morning with a startled flinch at the bright sunshine coming into the bedroom window. Normally, Martin was up so early, waking her gently with his movements, that they were down to breakfast before the sun was so high. She raised herself on one elbow and gazed at him next to her, turned on his side, still quite deeply asleep.

She eased herself back down again. He deserved a little extra rest. Yesterday had been such a busy day, so much excitement, with LeeAnn leaving for Atlanta. Felicity had been in a tither for a week, getting them both ready for the journey, and not the least of her preparations was a long list for Owen of what he needed to do for Graced Ground in her absence. But finally, finally, they were loaded into the carriage for the drive into Natchez, finally put onto the train, and they all stood and waved farewell, blowing kisses and waving handkerchiefs until the train was out of sight.

"You'd think," Martin had said yesterday as LeeAnn and Felicity pulled out of sight, "that she was going to China. I wonder if any young woman has ever arrived at Academy with so many trunks."

"Oh, I doubt she'll set any records," Arden had said happily. "And didn't she look full of herself? It's way past time that she be on her own."

"Filly will likely weep halfway back to Natchez," Owen said.

"No doubt," Arden agreed. "But by the time she gets back to Graced Ground, she'll have her overseer's hat on again, you can be sure. And if there's something not to her liking, you'll hear about it quick enough."

"Tell me something I don't already know," Owen had said, laughing. "Pa, how did you raise such a headstrong daughter?"

Martin had replied with a droll smile, but the day had taken much out of him, Arden could see it at the time. On the way back, he had dozed almost the whole way, despite the bumpiness of the road. Let him sleep, she thought, lying back down and listening to the faint noise of the household below.

Portia was up as usual, she knew, already down in the kitchen, grumbling at cook and bossing the downstairs servants. She liked to think she was still in charge of the house, even if she spent most of the day rocking on the back porch in the shade. And cook would listen to her orders with scant courtesy, then heave a large sigh of relief when she exited the kitchen, promptly doing exactly as she pleased. Same with the upstairs maid, Sylvie, who had learned long ago that it was easier to pretend to mind Portia than to argue with her.

Outside, she could hear the croppers in the fields, the teams moving over the earth, the occasional snort or bray of a mule. And from somewhere out in the stable, she heard the rhythmic clang of the blacksmith, likely shoeing Martin's black gelding, who'd thrown a shoe the week before. The sounds of Graced Ground, as constant and reassuring as the wind moving through the oaks round the house.

As she did every morning, she wondered what was doing over at River Reach. Even though the house was gone, even though the new owners, a wealthy man and his wife from Virginia, had taken down her mother's house and sprawled a new big house over both the old foundations, the land was still there as she had known it for so many years. And the people were still on the land, some of them returned with their children. She never passed a day without thinking of the old place, the old times, the old folks.

After a good while, she eased herself out of bed, no longer able to waste away the morning. As she moved, Martin groaned lightly and opened his eyes.

"Good morning, darlin'," she said to him. "You're sleeping in like it's Sunday." She leaned down and kissed him lightly. "Did you weary yourself yesterday overmuch?"

"I guess," he said, his voice still weak with sleep. "I don't seem to feel like moving this morning."

"Well, that's fine, no need to," she said cheerfully. "I'll

just get up and tend to things, and you rassle those pillows a while longer.''

He said nothing, only closed his eyes again and rolled over away from the light.

She made her toilet quickly and quietly and let herself out of the room, noticing that he barely stirred the whole time. Once downstairs, she forgot for a while that he was still sleeping, as the usual bustle of Graced Ground swept her up in her normal routine. But after several hours when she still had not seen him downstairs, she went back up to see if perhaps he was ill.

She saw instantly that Martin was not himself. He had rolled onto his back, and his eyes were still closed, but his breathing did not sound like that good, deep resting breath of a man asleep. She moved quickly to his side and felt his cheek. Cool and clammy. There was an ashen color around his eyes which alarmed her. He still did not open his eyes or stir.

''Martin,'' she said softly. ''Are you going to sleep the day away?''

He did not answer. Neither did his eyes move.

She took up his hand and held it, shaking him slightly. ''Martin, are you ill?''

With a deep groan, he opened his eyes. She was alarmed to see how weary he looked. ''What time is it?'' he asked.

''Past eleven,'' she said calmly. ''Are you ready to get up yet?''

He thought for a moment, his eyes closed again. ''I think not,'' he said then, his voice low and weak. ''Arden, I . . .'' His voice faltered slightly. ''I believe I'll stay in bed the rest of the day.''

''Are you ill?'' She felt carefully for his pulse. It was thready and weak as his voice.

''I don't know,'' he said finally. ''Just let me sleep, sweet.''

She watched him for a moment longer, as he fell back into oblivion, his eyes closing again, his mouth dropping open

slightly. It seemed unseemly to sit and stare at him when all
he wanted was rest, so she went back out of the room again.
As she descended the stairs, she stopped Sylvie and said,
"Send John round to me on the veranda, I want him to drive
into town."

"Yes ma'am," the girl said, starting to hurry off.

"Wait, Sylvie," Arden said then, thinking better of it.
"Never mind. I think I'll wait a bit."

"Yes, ma'am," the girl answered again, glancing behind
her curiously at the mistress as she went back upstairs to her
duties.

No sense in sounding an alarm for no reason, Arden told
herself. It might be nothing; he's just overdone it again, as he
does sometimes. He's seventy-five, after all, and he's certainly allowed a low day now and again. If he's not up and
about by tomorrow morning, I'll send for the doctor then.

Martin slept that day away and halfway through the night.
Suddenly, about four o'clock in the morning, he woke and
called out for Arden quite clearly. She woke with a start,
reaching for the lamp. "What is it, dear?" she asked, leaning over him.

His eyes were open, but he did not appear to see her, much
less recognize her face. "Arden!" he called again.

"I'm here, Martin," she said more loudly.

He turned to her. It seemed to take him an enormous effort
to collect his thoughts and assemble his face. "Arden, I believe I'm dying," he said then, his voice stark in the silent
room.

She gasped and then frowned. "Why, Martin, whatever
are you talking about? Don't say such a thing, you're only
overtired. You'll be better by morning."

"No," he murmured, "I'll be gone by morning."

"Martin!" she cried then, genuinely alarmed, "why do
you say that?"

"Because I know it to be true," he replied weakly. "And
I have always told you the truth, my dear, even when I knew
it hurt you."

She thought for an instant. That statement was, of course, as true as all the others he had made to her in their life together.

"Where do you hurt?" she asked.

"Nowhere. And everywhere," he whispered. "I think I had some sort of a—perhaps an attack of some kind in the night. A collapse. I felt it when it happened, somewhere around my heart. Pain," he sighed and stopped. Too tired to go on. Finally, he whispered, "Now the pain is mostly gone. And so am I. I know it."

"I'll get the doctor immediately," she insisted.

He turned his head away and closed his eyes. "I beg you, Arden. Don't do it."

"Then what should I do?" she pleaded. Somehow she knew that Martin would have the answer, as he always did.

He did not open his eyes. "I would like you to leave me tonight," he said softly. "Please. Just go to another bed and leave me."

"But Martin! If you're ill . . ."

"I have always thought that a man should die alone," he said, his voice wavering and weak. "I understand that it pains you to hear it, but if you wish to make me more comfortable, leave me."

"Oh, Martin," she murmured, "I can't leave you. Especially if you think you're—you're dying!" She could barely bring herself to say the words. "Perhaps the doctor should be sent for, don't you think? If I roused John now, he could be in Natchez in no time."

"No, Arden," Martin said firmly. He opened his eyes. "You have always been an excellent wife. The best wife and mother in the county." He smiled faintly. "The best woman a man could hope to love in a dozen lifetimes. You have had the natural and rare gift of letting a man be a man. And I have loved you over all else . . ." He sighed and closed his eyes again. "You know that. So don't fail me now. I want to do this alone. No doctor. No friends, family, not even you to witness my . . . my journey. Please, Arden. Leave me."

She began to weep softly, plucking at Martin's pillowslip for lack of anything else to do with her hands. "Oh, Martin," she moaned softly.

"Please," he said again. And then nothing.

After a long while, she took herself up and out the door, edging out backward to see if he would change his mind and call to her to come back. But he did not. In fact, she could not even say if he knew she was gone.

She went into the room down the hallway, the room which had been Josie's before he wed the widow. There, she lay down on the wide tester bed where her uncle had slept alone, had made his plans for his life, had held the reins of Graced Ground for so many years in his plump, kind hands. Somehow, the bed comforted her. It still held the imprint of Josie's large body. She was reminded that life was going on, outside the walls of Graced Ground, outside the boundaries of Natchez, of Mississippi, even of the United States. So many people birthing and dying and making their way in their own time to where she and Martin were today.

Incredibly, she woke suddenly with a start to the realization that she had dozed. How could she have done such a thing? she asked herself with heady guilt. How could she have slept while Martin was perhaps dying in the next room! She rose in a flurry, pulled her wrapper about her, and hurried to their bedroom door. She paused and listened, almost feeling that she should knock. She heard nothing.

She hesitated. Martin had been so sure. So clear in what he wanted and what he believed he was experiencing—would it not be a betrayal of her love and respect for him to ignore his wishes and intrude? But could she actually leave him alone to die?

Or worse—could she leave him alone if he were *not* dying but only so ill that he believed himself to be dying? What if she could save him and did nothing? Surely some of her herbals might make him feel better—a tonic, perhaps, of fresh willow and that special sweet potato tea he liked when he felt bilious. With that thought, she gently opened the door, poised to withdraw again if he said a word, hoping almost that he would be asleep and he would never know she had trespassed his privacy.

Martin was not facing the door. He was facing the window, now faintly shadowed by the first vague light of dawn which made some shapes outside seem darker than others. She stopped, uncertain what to do next. But then, as he did not move, she stepped forward again and went to where she could see his face.

He was gone. She saw death as clearly in the lines of his jaw, on his skin, in the placid, white expanse of his large brow, as plainly as if he had been ripped asunder and all his vitals exposed. Martin was dead.

Arden sank back slowly into the chair by the bed and gazed at her husband. Even unto the end, he was right. Even about the time of his passing. And she had not even said goodbye! She had not told him she loved him, something she had rehearsed a hundred times in the last few years. She had pictured his deathbed so many times, what she would say, how they would embrace each other, even if he could not do so physically, how sure he would be, as he left her, that she would never leave him, not really.

And none of that had come to pass. She had said nothing. Had given him nothing in his going. He had done it in his own way, as he did everything else.

She could not weep. Not yet. Surely later, when his death became a fact for her, she would weep. She would have the rest of her life to weep. But now was the time to say all the things she had not said when she'd had the chance. She rose from her chair, slipped off her wrapper, and slid into bed next to her husband. From behind, she embraced him as she had a million times in their lives together, cleaving her body to his, her knees behind his kneecaps, her arm around his shoulder, her hand resting on his chest, her breasts against his backbone, her feet wrapped about his. He was warm and yielding to her touch, as firm and comforting as ever.

And there, holding him in the first light of dawn, she told

him over and over again how much she loved him, how much she needed him, and that she had believed herself to be the luckiest woman in the world for more years than she cared to count.

Martin's funeral had to have been one of the most well attended in the state, Arden thought. To her amazement, men and women came from all over, from as far north as Memphis, as far east as Birmingham, as far south as New Orleans, as far west as Natchitoches. Most everyone they knew in Natchez, at least fifty croppers and their families, freedmen she had not seen in two decades, and many men she did not know at all. She wondered how they had come so quickly; she marveled that they had heard of his death at all, yet nearly five hundred people witnessed Martin Howard being laid to rest alongside Micah, Anne Lawrence, Josie, Hanna, and all the other members of the family.

Arden stood with Owen and Felicity at her side, watching as the preacher said what he said, watched as the casket was lowered into the ground, watched, too, as the well-wishers came and took her hand, whispered their comforts, embraced her when they wished to do so. She watched herself from some high, safe place, up above the chapel walls, next to the spire. From there, she could see everything and feel nothing.

Not nothing, of course, but she could stand it, at least. She could stand it, so long as Felicity stood near, so long as Owen was next to her, so long as both of them could stand it. They had said their farewells and cried their tears in private. Martin would have wanted his family to comfort the other mourners and keep their own sadness to themselves, and this they did as well as they could. LeeAnn and Wade Martin wept, of course, and that was proper. They were still young. But Martin's sense of dignity and strength would have been satisfied, Arden thought that day, by the serenity on Felicity's face, by the firm purpose in the set of Owen's mouth, by her own gentle murmurings of welcome and thanks to those who had come so far to pay tribute to her husband.

Later, after many hours of doing what she knew she was supposed to do, Arden allowed herself to do what she had been wanting to do all along. She sat out on the back veranda, facing the river. Beside her was a strong julep and her two children. They all wept then, a little, in the dark shadows, sometimes laughing in between their tears as they remembered their father, her husband, and all the years which had passed.

"What will you do now, Mother?" Owen asked finally. "Will you want to stay here or move into town?"

She said, "I'm going to move into Natchez."

"Oh, Mother, you should stay at Graced Ground," Felicity protested.

Owen cleared his throat as though to speak, but Arden went on quickly before he could. "No, I've always loved that house on Commerce Street. Your father loved it, too. It suits me just fine."

"That's just as well," Owen said then, softly. "Because it's going to get a little more crowded at Graced Ground soon enough."

"Oh, Owen, don't start with that again," Felicity said shortly. "You've been threatening to marry one of your gals for a dozen years now, and I scarcely think tonight's the time to bring it up again, with Father only in his grave . . ."

"Actually," Owen said, "it's exactly the time to bring it up. It's exactly the time to make such a decision." He turned to Arden. "You know, Mother, it came to me today that I want what you and Father had. I want what you still have. I want someone to love and someone to love me, too. I want to have a partner in life, like you and Father had in each other. I scarcely had a chance with Hanna. It seemed we were together such a very short time. And since then, I've been sitting on the sidelines." He laughed ruefully. "I might be coming to the *fête* a little late, but at least I made it." He said this last pointedly to Felicity: "I am going to marry. And I will make a home at Graced Ground. It's way past time."

"Well, if it's a partner you want," Felicity said, "I hope you look for a woman more your age."

"I'm not looking at all anymore," Owen said. "I've already found her."

"Why, that's lovely," Arden said softly. "Who is she?"

"Miss Alva Blair," he replied firmly. "You don't know her, I don't think."

"And *you* haven't known her very long," Felicity said.

"Nope," Owen said blithely. "And that bothers me not a whit."

"Who are her people?" Arden asked.

"She's from Baltimore, Mama, and I doubt you've ever heard of them. They came down to Vicksburg after the war."

"Carpetbaggers?" Felicity asked, appalled. "Yankee carpetbaggers?"

"Yankees, yes, carpetbaggers, no. Her father is in trade in Vicksburg."

"What sort of trade?"

"Oh, what does it matter?" Arden asked Felicity impatiently. "Tell us about *her*, Owen. Where did you meet her?"

"At a friend's birthday gala in Vicksburg." He sighed and hesitated for a moment and then rushed right into it, as if determined to get it over with. "She's twenty-five, widowed, with a small son. She's pretty and smart, and although I've no doubt you'll find reason not to, Filly, she's likable enough. I see no reason to wait, actually. She has done me the honor of accepting my proposal, and I mean to marry her before she changes her mind." He looked pointedly at Felicity. "Likely, she'll be at Graced Ground by the end of the month."

"Well, for mercy's sakes," Felicity said in horror. "What's your hurry?"

He shrugged. "Why wait for happiness? Death can come at any time, to any of us. I'm tired of being alone."

"And have you told Wade Martin of this yet, son?" Arden asked.

"No, but I mean to in a few days. He'll be meeting her next week, when she comes to Natchez to visit her cousin."

"Who is her cousin?" Felicity asked.

"Oh, for God's sakes," Owen said impatiently, "you don't know her, I'm sure. She's not of your circle."

"But she will be soon enough," Felicity glared. "To bring a strange woman into our house—I don't even know her—and a little boy, to boot."

Arden said quietly, "It's Owen's house, too, Filly. You understood that from the start. If your brother wants to have a wife and a family, you can scarcely blame him."

Felicity fell silent.

After a long pause, Owen said, "Cheer up, sister mine, Alva's bright and full of energy. She can take some of this big ol' house off your shoulders."

"Mama, perhaps I should come into town with you?" Felicity asked in some confusion.

"And give up Graced Ground to a stranger?" Owen laughed. "Don't be foolish, girl, it's a big house, and there's plenty of room for all of us. Besides, nobody runs it like you do. Give Alva a chance. She's a sweet woman with plenty to recommend her, not the least of which is another son under the roof to help out."

"Of course, you can come to Commerce Street if you want to, Filly," her mother said. "But I should think Owen's right. You wouldn't be happy away from Graced Ground."

"No," Felicity said. "I guess I wouldn't." Her face suddenly crumpled with the first hard tears of the day. "Oh, I don't know what would make me happy anyway. Why does everything have to keep changing all the time? First Papa and now Owen . . ."

" 'Cause that's the way it works, little sister," Owen said

kindly. He stood up and went to her, embracing her. "And no one knows that better than Mama."

At his words, Felicity realized that Arden must be suffering a far greater confusion and grief than her own, and she turned to her mother, weeping anew. "Ah, Mother, I'm so sorry. Here we are talking about houses, when Papa is gone."

"That's all right," Arden soothed her. "Your papa loved to talk about all sorts of things, houses not the least of it."

"You seem so—calm about everything," Felicity said, gazing at her mother. "I imagine you've already done your weeping."

Arden looked at her strangely. "I imagine not. I expect I'll be doing some of that for the rest of my days." She turned and looked out the window over the fields. "For as long as they last, until I see him again. But I've done what I'm going to do for now." She turned back to her two children with an air of some briskness. "So. One more thing. I think I'll leave here for a while now and do some traveling on the continent. Perhaps up North, or wherever my fancy takes me. Likely, I'll leave within the month."

"By yourself?" Felicity gaped.

"By myself," Arden said firmly. "I know you'd offer to go along, Filly, but frankly, I'd rather be alone just now. For the first time in my life, I want to do it my own way."

"Well, I wonder if that's a good idea, Mama . . ." Owen began.

"I think it's a splendid idea," Arden said, "and I've been thinking about it for a while now. Even if your father had not passed, I might have done it, because I love to travel and he really didn't. But now, there's no reason to wait." She smiled at him sadly. "As you said yourself, son, death can come at any time, and I'm no more immune than the next old lady."

"Oh, Mother, you're scarcely an old lady," Felicity said.

"You're right. And I'll be just fine traveling alone. I'll stay in the nicest places, and I'll have a perfectly wonderful time. Now, I don't want a lot more conversation about this. I know what I want to do."

"Perhaps I could go with you," Owen said. "Or maybe LeeAnn."

"You need some coffee to clear your head," Felicity scoffed.

"What's wrong with my head?"

"Nothing, when it's not running over with foolishness," Felicity said dryly. "Mama just said she didn't want me to go; what makes you think she'd want you or LeeAnn? Besides, you're getting married, you said, and that'll keep you plenty busy." She turned to Arden. "You're right, Mama. You should do exactly as you please. You've earned the pleasure."

"So have you, chick." Arden smiled at her. "I keep waiting for you to take your own advice."

"Well, perhaps I shall," Felicity said. Suddenly her voice went graveled and throaty. "Now with Papa gone, and LeeAnn so far away. It just strikes one that it goes so quickly, doesn't it?"

Arden nodded. "More quickly every year."

Together, Arden sat with her two children watching as the sun lowered over the fields. Martin would have appreciated this, she thought to herself. It was just his sort of day.

LeeAnn had been in school two years, and Felicity could not believe the change in her daughter in that short time. She was no longer a girl; she was a woman, plain and clear. Her hair, once left to tangle in curls down her back, was now up in a sophisticated "cat and mouse" style of multiple rolls and fringed bangs. Her dress, always fanciful, was now less ruffled and more daring in cut and design.

But what struck Felicity most was LeeAnn's new poise and dignity. She no longer skipped; she glided. Felicity would no more have thought to warn her of her posture than she would have chided her own mother for unseemly table manners. Two short years at Atlanta Academy had accomplished more to make LeeAnn a lady than a dozen under her mother's watchful eye.

Felicity was both gladdened and chagrined to see that LeeAnn not only had made herself a life of her own—but had, in the process, become a woman of her own mind.

It was never more apparent then when she visited Natchez, which now seemed to her like a small town full of backwater country folk next to Atlanta's bustling sophistication. She gazed with wry amusement on the shops, the marketplace, the grand homes on Main Street, as though to say, "Well, this is fine and well for Natchez, of course, but in Atlanta . . ."

Felicity was visiting her mother in the house on Commerce Street when LeeAnn arrived by train from Atlanta. Arden was back from a long tour of London and Paris, settled in for a short two-month hiatus, and then she was planning to be off again. Felicity's visits to Natchez were becoming more frequent and extended, now that Owen, Alva, and little Will, her son, had moved into the rear upstairs wing at Graced Ground. Owen had gradually taken over more and more of the management and duties of the plantation—once more, to Felicity's mingled gladness and chagrin. In some place of her heart, she had hoped that always, she would have been able to roll her eyes at Owen's incompetence and heave a huge sigh as she shouldered what should have been his rightful responsibilities.

Now, he was taking those responsibilities on, and with more time to consider her choices, Felicity found herself often drawn to the lovely, serene house on Commerce Street.

Arden and Felicity met LeeAnn's train, as always, and as they drove her back to the house, she spoke of the new streetcars along Peachtree Street in Atlanta and the new Coca-Cola tonic being sold at Jacob's Pharmacy at the corner of Marietta and Peachtree Streets which, LeeAnn said, made her feel "absolutely divine!"

"What's in it?" Arden asked as the carriage came up to the house and the driver stopped.

"I don't know," LeeAnn said, "but it was invented by a Mr. Pemberton, and they say it cures nervous headaches and dyspepsia and mental depression—all I know is that if I'm weary or melancholy, it perks me right up. Oh, the house looks wonderful, Grandmama, you've planted new roses!"

As they got down from the carriage, Mrs. Whitaker was coming up the sidewalk, and she stopped to greet them with effusive kisses on LeeAnn's cheek. "My dear, Atlanta agrees with you. You look so very—intellectual! I suppose you've been mingling with the highbrows and the literary set, and you'll scarcely have the patience for poor ol' Natchez anymore."

"Not at all, Mrs. Whitaker," LeeAnn said smoothly. "It's always a pleasure to come home. And as for my new intellectualism, I daresay it's simply this new hat!"

Mrs. Whitaker was the new mistress of Lansdowne, a grand estate outside the city. She fancied herself an avid historian and Southerner, a stance which Arden had noted with some dismay was becoming almost a profession these days in some circles.

"And what is John up to these days?" Felicity asked, with an eye to the veranda. She longed for a cool drink and a shaded peace with her daughter. John was Mrs. Whitaker's youngest, closest in age to LeeAnn by a few years.

"Oh, he's most involved with the Knights, you know," Mrs. Whitaker said breathlessly. "In fact, I must tell you, Arden, there has been some rather spirited discussion, I gather, at their most recent meetings about croppers in the county learning to read! They're most agitated, I understand, and any planters who are helping them are going to hear from the Knights, to be sure! I do hope you're not still reading to them, Felicity. You know it's such a problem when they get foolish ideas into their black heads . . ."

"Well, I do read to them from the Bible," Felicity said, a little stiffly, "hardly what I'd call foolish ideas. And I scarcely think that can be anything but a goodness in their lives. But how did you know I did so, Mrs. Whitaker?''

"Oh, John told me, of course. You know, the Knights know most everything that goes on in this county, and when they feel some of the better families might need some help handling their people, why, they're very community-minded.''

"I don't think we'd need any help in that way," LeeAnn said then suddenly, and all three women turned to look at her in surprise. LeeAnn's face was pale, and her lips trembled in anger. Her eyes were bright with unshed tears, and she clasped her hands tightly as though to keep them from striking out. "To think that anyone would dare insinuate that my mother or my grandmother would do anything unseemly with the people on our land is quite insulting, it seems to me. My grandmother gave them the word of the Lord when they were slaves; my mother and I will continue to teach them what we can of their salvation now that they're free. If John and his pals have a complaint, I suggest they bring it up with my Uncle Owen. I shall certainly tell him of your concern, Mrs. Whitaker. And now if you'll excuse us, it's been quite a long trip, and I think I'd like to rest a spell.''

"Well, for heaven's sakes!" the old woman gaped and stuttered as LeeAnn took her grandmother's arm and led her up the steps to the house. She looked behind to make sure that Felicity was bringing up the rear.

As they drew out of earshot, Felicity said, "You do surprise me, child!"

"Not me," Arden said quietly. The amusement in her voice was evident.

Felicity glared at her mother. "I scarcely think it's necessary to start the war all over again right before our front gate the first day you come home. Perhaps you best take a bit less of Mr. Pemberton's nerve tonic, LeeAnn, and remember that compared to Atlanta, Natchez is a small town filled with small-town minds. They don't cotton much to outsiders, and you're beginning to sound like one!''

"Oh, Mother, how could you stand there and let that old cow say such things to your face! She all but called you out, or said that her precious John would tattle on you to all his crazy pals."

"Now, now," Arden soothed them both, "let's get ourselves something cool and light, and we'll all feel a lot better. Sam, take LeeAnn's bags up to her room; Betty, please bring us a tray and that pitcher of fresh lemonade out on the veranda. Filly, do calm down, you're pulling at your hat like you mean to pull down the temple and all the money-changers with it."

Felicity finally wrestled her large straw hat off her head and slapped it down onto a chaise. "Well, I can't believe it. She's home less than an hour, and already, I'll have to send around a note of apology."

"Don't you dare apologize for me," LeeAnn said to her mother, her voice low and scornful. "Not ever. I'm proud of our family."

"So am I," Felicity snapped, "but I feel sure there might have been a more diplomatic way to speak to Mrs. Whitaker, that's all. After all, I have to see the woman at every garden club meeting and her son is one of the more attractive men in Natchez."

"Not to me he's not," LeeAnn said, subsiding into the chaise, from which she plucked her mother's hat. "In fact, I hadn't thought of it, but now that she's called us out, I believe I'll make a special point to be in chapel next Sunday, and read to those colored croppers until my eyes ache."

"Oh Lord," Arden chuckled. "Welcome home, chick."

"Why do you find this so highly entertaining?" Felicity asked Arden peevishly. "You have to live in this town too, you know."

"So I do, and so I will, and I doubt Mrs. Whitaker will have much say about it one way or the other. And in the meanwhile, I'll be off gallivanting. Now, LeeAnn, tell us more about Atlanta and your new friends there and your studies. Your letters have been such fun! Owen vows he made the worst mistake of his life not going off to college and spending all those years at West Point instead.''

LeeAnn settled back and began to relax then, which was exactly what Arden had in mind. Felicity's mouth began to soften, and she took a final long drink of her lemonade, set it down with a small clang, and leaned back and closed her eyes.

The rest of the afternoon was serene and amiable, and when Owen arrived for dinner that night, LeeAnn was as charming and flirtatious with him as if he were her best beau.

Two days later, Felicity and LeeAnn were out visiting friends, and they stopped at Rosemary's Milliner's to see the new chapeaux styles. They had been having a running argument about whether or not Natchez was current with fashionable styles, and Felicity meant to show LeeAnn once and for all that it was just as possible to find the perfect hat in Natchez as it was in any shop in Atlanta.

As they emerged from the shop, Felicity triumphant and LeeAnn resplendent in her cunning new leghorn bonnet, a man greeted them on the boardwalk. Felicity knew he looked familiar, but she could not place him for the moment. He bowed and smiled, removing his hat and bending over LeeAnn's hand. He said to Felicity, ''I can't suppose you would remember me, madam, but I had the pleasure of your acquaintance and that of your lovely daughter on the *J. M. White* a few seasons past. Mr. Random, at your service.''

LeeAnn smiled winsomely at the gentleman and murmured, ''Why, Edward, how nice to see you again. Whatever are you doing here in little ol' Natchez?''

Felicity bridled at LeeAnn's tone, but she was diverted to more important matters instantly by the look in her daughter's eye. In that moment, she could have sworn that LeeAnn remembered this man far more clearly than she might have from a single meeting, more than two years before.

''Yes, I do remember you, Mr. Random,'' Felicity said, recovering herself quickly. ''You were so kind that night, to see that my daughter enjoyed the waltz music.''

"I would have enjoyed it even more had I been able to dance," LeeAnn blushed becomingly. "You might be happy to know that I can do so now, sir. One day, perhaps I'll show you."

Felicity goggled at her daughter in amazement. She wanted to ask, with some asperity, how it was that LeeAnn had learned to dance and, moreover, how she came to speak to a man with such poise and—by the way—hadn't she called him by his first name? But she bit back her questions. Obviously, she might learn more by her silence.

Mr. Random laughed warmly and bowed once more with grace. "I look forward to that immensely, Miss LeeAnn. I'm here on business, for about a fortnight, I should think. Perhaps I might call on you sometime soon while you're in Natchez?"

"I'm sure Mother and I would welcome your visit," LeeAnn said gracefully. "Shall we say this afternoon?"

"That would be delightful," he said.

"We're visiting with my grandmama."

"I remember the lady with pleasure," he said.

"The big white house on Commerce Street with the rose arbors in front."

"I know it well. Shall we say four o'clock?"

LeeAnn bowed gracefully, took her mother's arm, and glided them both away.

"Good heaven's, LeeAnn!" Felicity sputtered when they were well away. "What in the world are you thinking of?"

"Why, what do you mean?" her daughter asked calmly. "He's a perfectly respectable gentleman."

"I didn't say he wasn't, but then I could hardly say, since I scarcely know him. And neither, I trust, do you! And yet, you both act as though you are the best old friends from the country. Here's the carriage, let's go back now."

"I thought you wanted to call on Miss Sunett?"

"Well, I changed my mind."

They got into the carriage and Felicity held her tongue until they got back out again at their own front steps. She had a perfect horror these days of the servants hearing their private business, although when they were slaves, she would not have thought a thing about it. As they went into the house, she said, "And when did you learn to waltz, miss?"

"Oh, ages ago," LeeAnn said scornfully. "Owen taught me some, you know, and the rest of it I simply picked up, to the misfortune, I'm sure, of the gentlemen who were my partners." She glanced at Felicity with amusement. "Surely you didn't think I never went out to a single dance or ball or *fête* the whole two years, Mother?"

"Frankly, I didn't give it much thought. You certainly didn't dwell on it in your letters."

"I do believe I mentioned an occasional 'sally forth,' as Grandmama would say. Let's not make a mountain out of a molehill."

"How did he know you were visiting in Natchez?"

"I told him so, Mother. Don't you recall?"

"Did you?" Felicity thought for an instant. "And was I mistaken, or did you call him by his first name?"

"I did," LeeAnn said simply. "Once, I think."

"And you allowed him the same familiarity."

"Yes, I did, I believe."

"Well, I am surprised at you," Felicity said, almost relieved to have a concrete issue to rail against. "In my day, men and women were engaged before they shared such intimacies!"

"Really?" LeeAnn asked innocently. "That seems rather stuffy."

"Stuffy! I hardly think so. If you give out your first name to every casual Edward, Dick, and Harry that you meet one time on a passing steamboat, what will you save for your husband?"

"Well, I hope to save far more for him than my given name," LeeAnn murmured. "You must remember, Mama, times are different now. Women do a lot more things than they did back when you were my age. And besides, now that

I've called him by his first name once, I can scarcely go back to a stricter formality. *That* would be stuffy, indeed.''

Arden came into the parlor to greet them, all smiles and her arms full of fresh roses, cinnamon pinks, and gardenias. ''Look what a bounty the garden has given us this morning!'' she said gleefully. ''LeeAnn, I swear, the roses know you're home and are especially extravagant in your honor.'' And then she saw their faces. ''What's up, chicks? No decent hats in the entire city of Natchez?''

''LeeAnn's friend, Mister Edward Random, is coming to call at four o'clock,'' Felicity said morosely.

''And that doesn't please you?'' Arden asked with some bewilderment.

''No, not especially, although I'm sure it will please everybody *else* in the household,'' Felicity said shortly.

''Who is this gentleman?'' Arden asked LeeAnn.

''Oh, that man who took me up to the piano two years ago on the *J. M. White*,'' LeeAnn said with some impatience. ''Mother is determined to make a scandal out of this. The poor man simply stopped us on the street and said hello, and I invited him to call, and that's the end of it.''

''LeeAnn, do be a dear and go get me a vase for these,'' Arden said gently, ''my arms are near falling off. I can't imagine what I thought I'd do with all these once I got them into the parlor.''

LeeAnn went off and Arden turned to Felicity. ''What in the world is the matter with you, dear?''

''You mean, because I'm not anxious to have my only daughter take up with every strange man she meets on a steamboat?'' Felicity said sourly. ''Why, Mother, I can't imagine how I could be so small-minded.''

''Nor can I,'' Arden said pensively. ''She's not talking about eloping with the man, so far as I can see. She's only mentioned a simple visit under her grandmother's roof with her mother present.'' She lowered her voice and said even more softly. ''I fear you're making a fool of yourself, Filly, and turning LeeAnn into your adversary in the process.''

Felicity thought for a long moment, sinking down again into her chair as though she were suddenly very weary. "Ah, Mother, I know you're right," she said with an air of bewilderment. "But I can't seem to help myself."

"You might start by remembering how wonderful you felt when you first met James," Arden said. "I certainly do. You walked on air for months. I believe your exact words were 'I don't know if I can live without him.' "

"But I have," Felicity said sadly.

"But at least you had that grand feeling. So did I. Would you keep LeeAnn from having it, too?"

"No, not when she's old enough to know what it is and what it means."

"You mean like you did? You couldn't even be talked into keeping your promise of more school to your father, as I recall," Arden said with wry amusement. "Nothing would do but you have your James—"

"There was a war on, Mother!"

Arden sighed. "Oh, my sweet Filly, there *always* is, of one kind or another. LeeAnn's now older than you were when you met James and far older than I was when I married your father. Let her go."

"But she's not nearly—"

"Let her go," Arden repeated calmly. "Let her go or she'll run from you to any man who has the courage to steal her."

"Oh, God," Felicity moaned. "I wish her father were here."

"And I wish her grandfather were here. But in their stead, she's only got us. Let her go and have her life, Filly."

Felicity thought for a long moment. She pressed her hands to her eyes in silence. "You're right," she finally said. She stood up and wrapped her arms around her as though for support. "I'll greet this Mr. Random as though he's some long-lost cousin. I'll make him feel so welcome, he'll think she's not had a beau before in all her life. And then if she chooses him, it'll be for his own self, not to spite me."

"I always said you were wise for your years, child."

A few hours later, Mr. Edward Random was admitted to the light and airy parlor on Commerce Street, reintroduced to Arden, and set down on the best chaise in the room, flanked by LeeAnn and Felicity. The man endured the first few moments with poise and surety, and only when LeeAnn turned the whole of her attention and feminine charm on him did he begin to make the smallest of betrayals as to his nervous state.

"I was so pleased and surprised to see you again, Edward," LeeAnn said pointedly, with nary a glance at anyone but her caller. "Imagine right on the street as we were coming out of the milliner's! If we had been a moment later or earlier, we'd have missed you entirely."

"Yes, that's true," Felicity said amiably. "What sort of business do you pursue here in Natchez, sir?"

"I run a small import-export concern, madam," he replied, taking the glass of lemonade LeeAnn offered him in one hand and a plate of small teacakes in the other. "And I must confess to you a dark secret, LeeAnn—may I call you LeeAnn?"

"I think that would be fine," she said blithely, glancing at her grandmother but avoiding her mother's eyes.

"Well, my secret is this: I was visiting with the Hansens last evening, and Sara Hansen mentioned that you were coming home from Atlanta, and would likely be stopping with your grandmother for a spell. Quite frankly, I was on my way to leave my card in the hopes you might allow me to call on you when we ran into each other on the street. And Providence provided me with the perfect opportunity. So you see, I'm a very fortunate man, indeed!"

"You have the most interesting accent, Mr. Random," Arden said approvingly. "Have you traveled extensively?"

"Yes, where are your people from?" Felicity asked.

"I have traveled, and to a great many fascinating places," he said easily, "and one day, if it wouldn't be too tedious for you, I'd be pleased to show you some photographs I've taken of different spots I've been.''

"Oh, that would be wonderful!" LeeAnn said, laughing. "Mother, don't you think that would be interesting?"

"Yes, indeed," Felicity said smoothly. "What sort of places, Mister Random?"

"Oh, as far north as Vermont. As far south as Saint Augustine . . .''

"Florida?" asked Arden. "Now that's a place I've always been curious about. Do they have alligators in the streets, as they say?''

"Not in the streets, madam, but some folks do keep them penned out back like dogs for pets.''

"Oh my!" LeeAnn exclaimed, touching his arm for emphasis.

"And what other sort of places?" Felicity asked, a trifle shortly. Her daughter's gesture had not escaped her notice.

"Well, out west as far as the Alamo—and of course, London and Paris. I've been several times to the continent, on business usually, but it's always mixed with pleasure when you travel, don't you find that to be true, Miss LeeAnn?''

"I could hardly say," she said, suddenly shy. "I've scarcely been out of my own backyard.''

"Now that's not true, LeeAnn," Felicity said immediately. "Why, you've been to New Orleans and Atlanta—''

"And don't forget Vicksburg," he added.

"No," she murmured. "I won't forget Vicksburg.''

In that moment, it seemed clear to Felicity what she had suspected at the outset. Somehow, LeeAnn had seen this man before—again—and not only on the steamboat to Vicksburg. There seemed to be a current running between them, under the layers of air, unseen and barely palpable to others. And yet, how could that be? To suspect such a thing was to suspect her daughter of duplicity and, worse, a certain cunning in matters sexual which was more of an alarm than the man sitting next to her on the chaise.

Arden said, "Perhaps now that your education is complete, you might want to take a trip to the continent, sweet. Your grandfather and I never had so much fun as we did traveling all over the capitals of Europe, and I had a lovely time myself just this season.''

"Oh, where did you go?" Mr. Random asked eagerly.

Arden and the man were immediately engrossed in comparing anecdotes and memories of London and Paris, and LeeAnn glanced at her mother over the rim of her lemonade. Her gaze was cool and appraising.

Felicity knew then that her daughter had secrets, something she would not have admitted to herself before the arrival of this man into their parlor. The sure knowledge that somehow LeeAnn had not merely grown up but had grown past her made Felicity feel older than she had for decades. She had been so afraid of losing her daughter—and she had lost her nevertheless without ever even realizing she was gone. She felt in that instant like weeping, slapping the man, raging at her daughter, yanking her up by her graceful arm and out of the parlor, but of course, she did nothing. She said nothing. She merely felt the knowledge seep into her bones like cold water.

"And if you'd like, I'd very much enjoy taking you there myself this evening," Mr. Random was saying.

"I'd like that," LeeAnn said demurely. "Mama, have we plans for this evening which would prevent me?"

Felicity brought herself back to full attention. "I'm sorry, dear, where did you want to go?"

Arden said happily, "Oh, I think it sounds fascinating. They've had rave reviews all over the South, I hear."

And then Felicity guessed they were speaking of the Baptist Heavenly Choir, a group from Savannah which had been touring locally. LeeAnn had expressed no interest in hearing them before, but now she leaned forward and pressed her hands to her bodice as though such an experience would be like a visitation of angels. "No, no plans that I know of," Felicity said evenly. "I think it sounds like fun."

LeeAnn shot a sharp glance at her mother, and Felicity

was almost tempted to add, "In fact, I'd love to go along," but she refrained. "By all means," she said finally. "Sally forth and have a good time."

Eventually, Mr. Random took his leave with a promise to return for LeeAnn at seven o'clock that evening. As she waved him goodbye, LeeAnn turned to her mother and said, "I really don't know why you didn't ask him to supper, Mama. That was so embarrassing!"

Arden laughed lightly as she went up the stairs and called back to Felicity over her shoulder, "Yes, chick, I was simply mortified myself!"

"Oh, the both of you are impossible," Felicity said sourly, and she swept up the stairs, passing her mother like a galloping horse.

Over the next two weeks, LeeAnn and Edward Random were practically inseparable. Felicity was not surprised when her daughter came home one night and knocked on the bedroom door for a talk. But she was rather startled to see Arden behind her in the dim hallway.

"Do you feel like company?" Arden asked artlessly. "LeeAnn wanted to chat a spell, and she asked me to come along."

LeeAnn was flushed and bright-eyed from the night air, and she swept in, her gown all rustling and spangled. "Oh, Mama, the ball was *so* fine tonight! Edward is such a dear— and quite the best dancer on the floor, I swear." She prattled for a moment about who was there and what they wore, and Felicity watched Arden's face for a clue. Her mother didn't interrupt with questions as she usually did, but only watched LeeAnn fervently, her mouth soft with smiles.

Finally, LeeAnn settled down somewhat and said, "Mama, Edward wanted me to ask you something."

"And what might that be?" Felicity asked. She tried to keep her voice light, noncommittal.

"He'd like to call on you formally." She blushed and her

voice dropped. "To ask if we may announce our engagement."

There was a long silence in the room, and it was by that silence that Felicity knew that Arden had known what LeeAnn was going to say before she said it.

"Have you accepted him?" Felicity asked.

"No, but I want to," LeeAnn said quickly.

"You've known him only a few weeks."

"No, actually, I've known him a good deal longer. But there was simply a long interval in between," LeeAnn said carefully. "But that's not so important is it, Mother? Who he is matters much more than how long I've known him."

"That's true," Felicity said. "And who is he, exactly?"

LeeAnn sparked to anger at that one. "Why, you certainly know well enough, Mother. He's a businessman, a gentleman, a man who has traveled the world a good deal, he's a kind, good man, and . . ." And here, she hesitated, glancing at her grandmother for support. "And I love him." She bounced her chin slightly for emphasis.

"In only two weeks?" Felicity asked.

"How long did it take you to fall in love with James?" Arden asked, amused. "I know, with your father, I was in love the first time I saw him. The rest was just—arrangements, after the fact."

"I take it you're in favor of this match, then?" Felicity asked her mother.

"I wish the two of you would stop talking over my head like I'm not even in the room!" LeeAnn sputtered. "I'm a grown woman, and I tell you I've found the man I want to marry, and you two act as though I'm foolish as a twelve-year-old girl."

"When it comes to love," Arden said, "we can, each of us, be a twelve-year-old fast enough. But no, sweet, I'm not opposed to your engagement. In fact, I'm tickled pink." She gave her granddaughter a hug. "If you love Edward Random, that's good enough for me."

"Well, I guess that just goes to show how much easier it is

to be a grandmother than a mother. Because it's *not* good enough for me. I still don't have any idea who this man *is,* LeeAnn!''

"Well, ask him yourself," her daughter snapped. "He'll be here to speak with you formally tomorrow morning at ten o'clock, if you haven't other plans, and you can put him to the inquisition at that time."

Impulsively, Felicity reached out and hugged her daughter hard. She felt the girl stiffen and then, very gradually, relax. She took LeeAnn's face in her two hands and gazed into her eyes. "I just want you to be happy, LeeAnn. Don't you know that?"

LeeAnn looked down, disengaging herself from her mother's grip very carefully. "I do, Mother. But sometimes I think you only want me to be happy if you approve the way I get there."

Felicity looked up at her mother in dismay. Arden nodded to her gently.

"I think I'll toddle on off to bed," Arden said then with a huge yawn. "I don't think the two of you need me anymore, do you?"

"No, Mother, we'll see you in the morning."

"At the inquisition?" Arden grinned. "I'll bring the thumbscrews.''

As she closed the door, Felicity said, "Has your grandmother ever told you much about her own father?"

LeeAnn shook her head. "She didn't know him, did she?''

"Not much. He was shot in a duel in New Orleans when she was very young."

"Really! I never heard that before. Was he some sort of rake?"

"Some sort, I gather. He was a gambler on the riverboats, the way I heard it, and he came through Natchez, met and married your great-grandmother over the objections of her family, and she went off with him to New Orleans with never a fare-thee-well. When she had your grandmother, she put her with the nuns rather than be bothered with her, and when he died, she never married again.''

"So she really loved him," LeeAnn said thoughtfully.

Felicity shrugged. "You never knew her, of course, but she was a very beautiful woman. Very spoiled. I sometimes wondered if she knew what love was, after all. She was good to me but . . . she was always trying to get me to do something. Most often, there was a tug-of-war between my mother and my grandmother over who would rule the roost. And me. And my mother won, finally. But only because she had my father behind her. If she had been just herself against my grandmother—''

"As you are," LeeAnn finished gently.

"Yes. As I am. Well, the outcome could well have been quite different.''

"So you're afraid I'm taking after my great-grandmother and running off with a scalawag." LeeAnn made the statement calmly, as though it were an understood fact.

And when she did, Felicity saw in the moment that, of course, she was right. Without realizing it, she had been fearful of the past more than the future: that Anne Lawrence was coming to life again in her own daughter, complete with her patterns and fatal mistakes. "Oh, my darling girl," she murmured, "I suppose I'm afraid of exactly that.''

"But Mama," LeeAnn said, "how can you tell if a man's going to be a good man even if he seems so at the beginning? He might seem like the best of the lot and go bad after a few years, or he might seem a scoundrel and become the finest husband in the world for the right woman. It seems to me," she added, "that the whole thing is a wild card anyhow. Why not choose the one you love and hope for the best?''

Felicity could find nothing to argue with in LeeAnn's reasonable statement. In fact, as she thought on it for a moment, it was surprisingly wise for a young woman of her age and experience.

"You're right, honey," she said. "Of course, every mother's going to want her daughter to marry well—and that means a good man of substantial property and good family who has the respect of those who know him—but there's no guarantee those qualities alone will make him love her daughter. And if he doesn't love her, what good is all the rest?''

"Yes," LeeAnn said. "I know some friends who married what their mothers would have called 'well.' And they're not happy. Oh, they have everything their mothers wanted for them, all right, but their husbands don't cherish them.'' She took her mother's hand softly. "And Edward cherishes me, Mother. I know he does. And I believe he will forever.''

"Forever is such a long, long time," Felicity sighed. "Such an unknown, perilous eternity. There's just no banking on it. You know what Mark Twain said about marriage? He called it the supreme felicity and also the supreme tragedy. It can be both, you know, LeeAnn. And the deeper the love, the surer the tragedy and the more painful when it comes.''

"Oh, Mama, that doesn't have to be true!" LeeAnn said with the anguish of a new apostle.

"When you think of how easily we pick a man to spend our lives with, to spend our lives *on*," Felicity said, "it's a wonder any wives are happy at all.''

"Lots are," LeeAnn said staunchly. "Grandmama was, and you were, too.''

"Briefly."

"Well, that's a start. It's something to believe in.'' LeeAnn reached out and touched her hand. "Can't you believe in it for me?''

"LeeAnn, tell me the truth. Have you seen him other times? I mean, besides on the steamboat to Vicksburg and then in Natchez two weeks ago?''

Her daughter looked up, surprised. "No, Mother. He wrote to me when I was in Atlanta, quite regularly, and I answered him back, of course. But I never saw him. Not until that day outside the milliner's.''

"But you knew he was here.''

She smiled mischievously. "Yes. I knew he was going to be here, and I hoped we'd meet. There. Are you satisfied?"

Felicity smiled, despite the urge she had to weep. "No, of course I'm not satisfied. I don't know that I will ever be with the idea of my daughter going off with some man I barely know. But at least there's no chicanery going on, anymore anyway than always goes on between a man and a woman." She shook her head ruefully. "Give me a kiss, then, and go on to bed. I'll see Mr. Random in the morning, and we'll talk again after that."

"Thank you, Mother." LeeAnn got up to leave, and at the door, she turned and said, "I hope you find someone to love again someday, Mama. It's too wonderful to miss forever."

Mr. Edward Random came, he saw, and he was conquered. By noon, Felicity and Arden had persuaded him that though they were joyful at the pending engagement and though they scarcely could believe LeeAnn's good fortune at his proposal, it would be best, truly best for all concerned, if they would consent to a long engagement of, say, a year before they wed. Only in that way, Felicity and Arden together assured him, could they plan, organize, and bring to full bloom a wedding celebration that would be suitably grand, only in that time could they make the necessary arrangements, and only in all those months, a short enough time when they thought of it to send them once more into a flurry of anxiety, would they be able to settle all the tedious details and legal necessities of giving LeeAnn her rightful properties and inheritance.

Under the combined assault of Felicity and Arden together, Mr. Random was coddled and petted and flattered so adroitly that he scarcely realized he had been also controlled, delayed, and put off until he was back out to his horse. And by then, he was so exhausted and relieved that he scarcely cared, so long as the interview was over.

And so the engagement went on for a year, to LeeAnn's

occasional frustration. But each time she wondered aloud why it was necessary for a woman of nearly twenty-one to wait to wed, her mother assured her that she would not be sorry. By the end of the year, Felicity was finally reconciled to having Edward Random in her family.

He was not the man James had been, she knew, not the man her father had been, to be sure. Perhaps he was not even such a man as Owen had become. But he was LeeAnn's choice, that much was certain. Her love for him had done nothing but strengthen in the year of waiting, and so far as she could see, he loved her as much in return.

As the plans for their wedding began to solidify as surely as water turned to ice, as it began to look as if, in fact, her daughter would soon be gone from her, Felicity did not feel the terrible pang of loss she had feared and expected. It was time, she told herself so often that by now she believed it: time for LeeAnn and time for herself, as well.

Of course, LeeAnn wanted to be married in the chapel at Graced Ground, where her grandmother had been married before her. The old church had stood the years well, and except for some minor repair and propping up of a sagging stone foundation, the walls were still firm, the rose windows still gleaming in the light of the afternoon sun.

"It was a miracle, really, that the Yankees didn't burn it all down," Felicity was fond of saying to her friends when war reminiscences began. "They destroyed some of the big house, you know, just by quartering in it, and made a mess of the chapel. You remember, they burned River Reach to the ground, all except my grandmother's little cottage. But the chapel's still standing, and the big house, too, thank the Lord. Even Yankees won't burn down a place of worship, I suppose."

LeeAnn had refused to go back to Atlanta once she was engaged. "Mama," she said firmly, "I've had all the education I need or want. If Graced Ground is to belong to me and

Wade Martin one day, then I need to learn how to take care of it properly and run it like you did.''

"But LeeAnn, it will be years before you need to worry about that. Alva and Owen will live there for a good while, and you'll be the wife of a businessman, not a planter. And don't forget Alva's son, Will. He will inherit right along with you and Wade Martin. I think one more year at the academy would be good for you.''

But she continued to hold firm in her refusal until finally Felicity was weary of the subject. After all, she told herself, LeeAnn likely had all the education a woman in her time would need. She certainly was a wonderful and expressive reader: why, the croppers had come to prefer LeeAnn's reading of the Scriptures even more than Felicity's, judging by their attendance whenever she was back from Atlanta.

One night, Felicity and Owen were up late discussing crop prices and harvest schedules for the bottom two hundred acres when they heard the sound of hoofbeats coming hard down the road toward Graced Ground. Owen stood and went to the window. The rest of the house had been asleep for an hour or more, and the croppers never ventured out much at night. Visitors at this hour could hardly mean good news.

Felicity heard the sharp intake of Owen's breath as he looked out the window and she went instantly to his side. Five horsemen were coming fast up the road. They were carrying torches and, despite the hour, making no effort at silence. As they drew nearer, she saw that they wore white capes and white hoods.

"It's the Brethren," Owen said.

"What? The Knights!" Felicity gasped. "What are they doing here?" She turned on Owen angrily. "I thought you said you quit them!"

"I did! At least a year ago!"

As they watched in growing fear, the horses thundered round the back of the plantation house, the drum of their hooves sounding ominous and threatening in the dark silence of the night. The torches sped by like comets, and Felicity and Owen ran for the back door silently. Owen stopped at his office long enough to grab the rifle which lay above the mantel, and when Felicity saw him reach for the door with one hand on his weapon, she shrank back, appalled, suddenly understanding what this night might be about.

The riders had gone past the house and down the hill toward the chapel. They could hear in the distance the sounds of men dismounting and horses breathing hard, shuffling for position under the trees. The sudden crash of breaking glass made Felicity shriek in fear, an involuntary scream which she instantly regretted. Now the whole household would be up.

Owen was moving fast toward the men, and she heard him shout something in their direction. She turned to get the lamp, and Arden was already behind her. "Mother, go back to bed," she said sharply.

"Don't be ridiculous," Arden snapped. "Is it those damned night riders?"

Felicity was almost as surprised at her mother's quick assessment and language as she had been by the horses. "I think so," she said as she ran by. "Owen's already down there."

"Uncle Owen!" LeeAnn cried as she came into the kitchen. "They'll shoot him!"

"Go back to bed, LeeAnn!" Felicity hollered as she grabbed the lamp and ran out the door. "Mother, don't you dare let her come out here," she added as she slammed the door behind her and ran to catch up with Owen.

The horses were moving restlessly, and she could see dim shapes down by the chapel door. She heard Owen's voice rising in anger, and then a pistol shot rang out, and she screamed once more and ran toward the noise. The torches were moving wildly then, and she heard Owen's shout of warning. She suddenly realized that she was unarmed, defenseless, and if she were to be killed, her daughter would have no parent left at all in her life. She stopped and trembled, unsure what to do for an instant.

She could see that several of the torches—two, maybe three—had moved behind the chapel. She could no longer distinguish Owen from the other men. Now all of a sudden, the shapes were moving rapidly toward her again, some torches, then others joining them, and she picked up the lamp and ran back toward the safety of the house. As she reached the door, she saw over her shoulder that the men had mounted once more. The door burst open and Arden reached out and grabbed her shoulder, pulling her inside. "Where's Owen!" her mother asked frantically.

"I don't know!" Felicity gasped.

The horses were galloping away then, and all three women ran down toward the chapel. They found Owen on his back under the oak tree, a gunshot wound in his arm. "Oh my God!" LeeAnn cried, falling on her knees and weeping.

Arden said, "LeeAnn, go back in the house and get Portia up. Tell her to bring my bag."

Felicity said, "She can barely walk, much less run. LeeAnn, bring it yourself, and hurry!"

Owen opened his eyes and saw the women around him, and he struggled to raise himself up on his good arm. "Where are they?" he moaned. "Filly, get my gun!"

"They're gone," Arden said calmly. "Rest yourself, son. LeeAnn's bringing my bag, and we'll have you up in no time. You've got a wound here, but it's not a bad one." She had been probing his arm and pressing on the bleeding area. "The bullet grazed you, I think. It's not in there—"

"Owen, who are those men!" Felicity cried. "What did they want!"

"My former companions," Owen said angrily. "They figure now that LeeAnn's back, the Bible reading'll start up again."

"The Kluxers?" Felicity said. "Owen, I told you they'd be nothing but trouble!"

"Enough of that now," Arden said as LeeAnn came running up with the large black bag that had her medicinals.

"Let me bind this, Owen, and then we'll move you to the house." She began to work quickly, methodically, ripping his shirt off at the shoulder, pressing a cloth to the wound, and then wrapping it firmly with another strip of linen from her bag.

All of a sudden, Felicity cried out, "The chapel!"

They turned to look and saw that a strange glow was coming from the windows, from the rear of the building. The chapel was afire.

"Those bastards," Owen groaned, trying to raise himself.

"LeeAnn, run and ring the firebell," Arden said. "The croppers will come and help."

Felicity was already on her feet and running round to the rear of the building. They could hear her shouting and beating at the flames with her skirts. Portia hobbled up and said, "Lawd Gawd, Mas' Owen, dey shot you!" But he did not answer her. He pulled himself upright and, teetering once, regained his balance and ran for the stable. Arden heard then the clanging alarum of the firebell crashing through the night, and she ran after Felicity, calling behind to Portia for her to keep away from the building and go back to the house.

The next moments were a jumble of confusion, as Arden fought alongside Felicity to beat out the flames first with their skirts, then the shovels and blankets that Owen and the men hurried up with, then finally buckets of water brought by the frightened croppers. The garish light of the flames climbed higher, and the smoke billowed out of the chapel in high dark clouds up to the stars. The flames were almost under control, then escaped them, then were subdued once more, then raged up again. They fought back and forth with the fire, shouting directions to one another and sending back for more blankets, more water, and once Felicity saw LeeAnn race by with a shovel, her hair all undone down her back, her nightdress flapping about her ankles, her bare feet flashing in the firelight, and she called to her to stay back, but of course she never listened.

When it seemed that the fire at the rear of the chapel was

almost subdued, it spread anew to the middle of the building, and when Arden hurried around to where the people were working to put it out, she saw Portia beating with a blanket on flames which were higher than her knees. As she went to pull her away, the old slave's cotton skirt caught and flared up as fast as a frightened breath, and before Arden could reach her, Portia was afire. She grabbed the old woman and knocked her down, rolling her over and over, trying to smother the flames, all the while crying out for help. Two croppers ran to snatch them away, and they carried Portia outside the chapel and laid her on the wet grass in the dark. Arden stumbled after them and fell beside the old woman, who lay with her eyes closed and her face still, deaf to all the tumult around them.

Arden kneeled at Portia's side, scolding her loudly, and began to unbutton her basque and chafe her hands. As she pulled hard at her collar, a terrible pain roiled through Arden, a stabbing, searing agony which made her gasp and set back on her heels, reeling with the dizziness which followed. She slid down alongside Portia, holding her side, for it felt as though one of those nightriders had shot her, too.

The noise and chaos of the fire and the family and the croppers faded away from her as though she fell quickly down a long, dark well. She was vaguely aware of the wet grass beneath her light cotton nightdress, dimly able to move her feet somewhat, but she could not speak, could not get back up on her feet, no, not if the fire came to her very hands which lay clenched alongside her.

Arden thought for some crazy reason of the time when little Cake was sent off in the wagon to Natchez, and his mama fell in the dust, weeping and rending her clothes. She thought of the picnic she and Martin took on the mound the day he asked her to marry him. She remembered, so vividly that it drove the smell of smoke right out of her nostrils, the scent of Felicity's tiny fuzzy head the first time she held her, swaddled well by Portia's loving hands. She saw in her mind's eye the vast darkness of space and the spangle of stars and brighter planets through Martin's telescope that time he had told her about—what was it he had said?—she could not recall it all now, it was fading—something about love. About forces of gravity . . .

A voice from nearby, a darker face over her, blotting out the light of the stars. Portia called to her from very far away, "Miz Arden? Miz Arden, you fixin' to come along now?"

And then Arden thought nothing more at all.

The chapel was saved, enough so that when more than a thousand mourners came from four counties round Mississippi to pay their respects to Arden Lawrence Howard, the old edifice stood firm in the sunlight. The rose windows were patched with plain glass for the time being; the white-washed walls were scorched, but the roof was still sound and the walls were upright.

LeeAnn stood, whitefaced and silent alongside Edward Random, her hand twisted through his arm. The loss of her grandmother and Portia had hit her extremely hard, but she did not wish to weep anymore. Not before all of these people. Her mother was stoic and pale but silent. Her uncle wept openly without shame, his arm still wrapped from his wound.

Portia's simple pine coffin lay alongside Arden's own, the two of them looking quite small and stark. It was hard to believe two grown women lay inside and not two children. The minister spoke long over Arden, lauding her many contributions to the county, to Natchez, and to the lives of those for whom she was responsible. He mentioned Portia in passing as her good and faithful servant. He said, almost as an afterthought, that she had died the oldest colored woman in the county, according to those who knew her.

The croppers did not wait for LeeAnn to begin the hymns. They broke into song spontaneously the moment the preacher was finished. Arm in arm, they swayed and sang, until the music filled the chapel, overflowed out into the bright air, and hung on the wind like the scent of honey-suckle.

Arden was buried alongside Martin, and at her feet, Portia was laid down as well.

Over in the fields at the fringe of River Reach, land which no longer belonged to the Howards or the Randoms, the Saint Catherine made its way in a tortured curve to the Mississippi, dammed and diked and leveed by the Howard family for two generations, so that the rush of water could be controlled and used to the advantage of the land. There had been a time, before the first Revolutionary War, when the land had been planted to rice. Then the levee system was essential to the crop, and the Saint Catherine had been even more vexed as it twisted its way to join the great river.

Now the waters were mostly tamed, and the creatures who lived along the banks of the Saint Catherine were used to its spring surges, its summer diminishment, its occasional swelling with autumn rains. One animal in particular, the muskrat, knew the river as well as he knew the length of his own tail.

He was a large rodent, more than two feet in length not counting that tail, which stretched out another foot behind him, naked and flattened and tapered to a point. His name was *Ondatra zibethicus,* he carried a pelt of dense, glossy, dark brown fur, and at the mature age of five years, he weighed more than four pounds.

Zib made his home in a roomy lodge made of cattails, river grass, and other water plants, piled on a foundation of roots, mud, and small branches. Over the years he had built it stronger each nesting season, until it now towered over the river nearly five feet high.

A secondary platform was near to the house, his feeding station. It was there that he brought his meals, and it was usually littered with discarded grasses, cut vegetation, piles of freshwater clamshells, and crayfish tails. The feeding platform lay high and dry in the sun and was often messy, but the inside of Zib's lodge was immaculate. Like all his kind, he could not abide a filthy bed.

Zib was the best swimmer on the river, even better than the beaver who lived upstream. He spent most of his time in the water, propelled by his webbed hind feet and using his tail for a rudder. Unlike the beaver, he could swim backward as well as he could swim forward, and he could even chew underwater, for his mouth closed behind his protruding incisors—again unlike his ungainly beaver neighbor, who had to draw everything he ate to high ground or his dry lodge.

When he was younger, Zib had trained himself to stay underwater for as long as he could, and now, though he could not have told you the time, he could swim beneath the surface for almost twenty minutes at once. He was older now, and feats of strength and endurance no longer amused him as they once did. Now, he cared only for the new grasses in the springtime, the fresh crop of crayfish, and his mate of the current season.

Zib's lodge had three chambers, each one with a tunnel which led underwater. In the late winter, he lined one of the chambers with extra grass and left his markings, musky secretions from his perineal gland, on selected trees and stumps around his territory. He rarely had to wait long. The females were always in season, it seemed to him, and sometimes he had to drive away a mate so as to allow another, newer female to come into his lodge. The younger females would want to have a litter four or more times a year, sometimes even encouraging him to mate while they were still nursing. While he was never loath to mate, he sometimes yearned for the quiet of his lodge again, without the chaos and debris of mate and young ones in every nook and cranny.

Once, only once, he had made the mistake of taking two mates at a time. It was when he was young and eager, and it seemed that there would never be enough females in the world for his lodge. But in a single moon, the lodge was so crowded, the fights between the females so common, that he almost moved out and left them the lodge altogether. He waited another moon until the first litter was weaned, chased off one female, and soon thereafter, chased off the other as well. He had stayed celibate that time for several moons, before he was ready for the females and the trouble they brought once more.

Zib's only real enemies were the raccoon, the mink, and worst of all, man. The raccoon was a born bandit, and he was adept at peeling off the top of the lodge and eating the naked, blind babies within. The mink usually dug in from the bottom and was equally rapacious, capable of fierce fighting with the females over the fate of the young.

But man was the most dangerous of all. Zib could not know it but he carried on his back the reason for his peril. Muskrat fur was of vital importance to the fur trade in Mississippi and Louisiana, and even his flesh, called "marsh rabbit" by the small farmers, was considered a delicacy. The only reason Zib had not been taken in previous years was because the Howard family did not care to eat or trap him. He could not know that now, with the land all around him sold to strangers, he was once more in grave danger.

But this season, with the summer sun warm and the river calm, Zib had little reason for fear. He ate his fill, built his levees and dams and channels with industrious energy, and only occasionally foraged away from his river for the corn which was less than a half-mile from his lodge.

One day, as Zib woke from his long midday rest, he ventured out earlier than usual, when the sun was still strong but the shadows were growing longer. He had been too busy that morning to eat as he often did, and his belly woke him with a pleasant hunger. He dove through the underwater channel from his main burrow to surface in the deep, shadowed area of the river close to the bank. He saw instantly that the sedges were putting out new leaves since the last time he had fed there, and he eagerly swam over, pulled up large bunches with his teeth and paws, and swam back to his feeding platform to enjoy them.

With his mouth full of sedges, his vision was blocked somewhat, but he was so familiar with the edge of his platform that he did not hesitate, but clambered onto it, feeling with his frontpaws for a purchase. He pulled himself up, dropped the sedges, and turned to see a large cottonmouth coiled on the platform before him, sunning himself in black, malevolent silence. Zib squeaked in sharp terror and froze, but the snake was too fast for the muskrat to avoid his strike.

He felt the fangs sink deep into his flank, squirmed and twisted to escape, and then the burning venom pumped through his veins like fire. When the snake released him, he took one step toward the water and then his legs crumpled beneath him. Panting, he lay quiet now, trembling, as death overcame him, wiping out all pain, all effort, all memory.

"Mama, can't you make Alva make Willy keep his hands off the cake? It's going to be toppled over before I can cut it!" LeeAnn was struggling to get her veil off her head, as two gals with hot curling tongs and combs stood by. Her hair would have to be redone, of course, before the dancing began. "I saw him take a smidge off the corner, and I'd have cuffed him myself, but I didn't want to get frosting all over my gown."

"I'll ask her, I'll ask her, now don't get yourself all fretful, sweet, it was a beautiful wedding, and the reception will be even better," Felicity soothed her. "Lily, run go tell Miss Alva I said Willy is to have—"

"No, Mama, tell her yourself!" LeeAnn fussed. "I need Lily to help me with this mess." And she snatched the black maid by the hand which was not holding a hairbrush, and pulled her to the large cheval mirror, already giving her instructions how she wanted her hair fixed for dancing.

"All right, LeeAnn, I'll tell her right now," Felicity said, and she went out of the room, rolling her eyes silently. Lord protect me from brides, she told herself silently. LeeAnn had been in a state for a week before the wedding which only got more frantic as the ceremony approached. This morning, she had broken down weeping because the lace on her bodice would not stand up just so, and then she flew into a hissy when the orange blossoms for her bouquet would not drape over the little white roses at the right angle—all this worry and fuss just to marry Edward Random, Felicity sniffed a trifle sourly. As though the man might dare to say he was used to better.

She was reconciled to the match, of course, had to be now that it was done. But she would likely never come to love and respect him as a son, as she had dreamed she might when she pictured LeeAnn's future husband so many years ago. But no matter. So long as he kept LeeAnn happy and gave her healthy children, that was all that counted. The rest would come as it would. She stopped at the door to her sitting room and went out to the balcony, resting her hands on the railing and gazing at the scene below.

Way out to the road, the buggies were parked, and the grounds were swarming with friends and far-flung relations from three states. From the smokehouse came the smell of the cooking meats for the wedding banquet: hams and turkeys and chickens and lamb and pork ribs. The long tables under the trees were laid out with every sort of cold plate, salad, and pickled delicacy, as well as a variety of punches; children ran helter-skelter among the strolling couples, and from the downstairs ballroom, she could hear the strains of the orchestra tuning up. There, she could see Owen walking with Alva, meeting folks and shaking hands, accepting congratulations for his niece. Alva's light, graceful laugh wafted up to her ears, and she smiled. Owen was happier these days, and it was mostly due to that laugh and the love which came with it. Then she spied little Will, Alva's son, racing at the head of a pack of youngsters, bellowing like a banshee in glee, heading for the dining room double doors, and she pulled back from the porch rail and hurried downstairs. If that cake was their target, LeeAnn would skin them alive.

Felicity met Edward on the stairs coming up. He embraced her fondly. "Mother Daniels, it was a perfect wedding," he said to her gratefully. "I am so glad you made us wait so that it could be just right. I know LeeAnn and I will remember this day for the rest of our lives. I'm only sorry that her grandparents couldn't be here to see this day."

"Yes, so am I," Felicity said, and a small welling of sadness slipped over her heart. She had tried not to think of her mother today, but it was impossible. As they sat in the front row of the chapel, watching as LeeAnn came down the aisle on her uncle's arm, as she stood beside Edward Random with the soft rose light falling on her hair from the new windows, as she repeated her vows and tilted her chin to receive her new husband's kiss—with each moment, Felicity thought of her mother. Of her grandmother, too. At least half of her tears were for them. She was used to being without James at such moments, but to be without her mother as well seemed more loneliness than she could bear. She wanted to turn to someone and whisper, "She is so beautiful, isn't she? Ah, God, I pray she is happy!" but there was no one but Alva and Owen, the two of them sitting so close together she could not have stuck a playing card between their shoulders. And so, she kept her sadness and her joy to herself.

"I'm going to change," Edward was saying, "and then I'll be right down. Is LeeAnn almost ready?"

"Oh, heavens!" Felicity said. "The last thing I saw was an army of curling irons advancing on her hair, Edward. I have to go down now and keep Willy from the cake . . ." and she hurried past him, holding her skirts high on the curving stairs.

She rounded the corner of the dining room, delayed and impeded by at least twenty guests who wanted to embrace her and congratulate her and tell her how beautiful the wedding was, just in time to spy Willy about to snatch his second corner off LeeAnn's towering white wedding cake. "Don't you dare, William Henry Howard!'' she hissed, shutting the dining room doors behind her. ''LeeAnn will skin you alive!''

Willy flinched and stuck both hands behind him, immediately assuming the guilty air of a ten-year-old rascal caught out good and proper. ''I wasn't gonna, Granma,'' he said solemnly. ''I was only going to look at it.''

''Look at it, my great-uncle Josie's mule, young man, that other corner didn't just get up and flat walk out of here on its own steam.'' She was about to deliver a semiscorching lecture on the sanctity of good manners, weddings, and bridal cakes in that order, when Will took her gown in one hand and tiptoed to his full height, the better to whisper to her confidentially.

''I saw Wade Martin sneak a lick,'' he related behind one hand, ''and Papa did, too.''

''Why, that's the most dreadful fib I've heard all day,'' Felicity said, laughing and squeezing the boy's head in an armlock. ''You ought to be tied up with the horses, I swear.''

''I did, I did!'' Willy insisted, trying to escape her grip. '' 'Twas just after cook brought it out, an' nobody was around, an' they each took a big swipe at it!''

''Wasn't a big swipe,'' Owen chuckled as he walked into the dining room, Alva behind him. ''No more than a little chicken track, if you ask me.''

''Oh, you're both impossible,'' Alva said, then smiled at them lovingly. ''And William Henry, if I see you near this cake again before LeeAnn cuts it, I'll cut myself a peach switch and meet you at the shed, young man. Do you hear me?''

''Yessum,'' the boy said sadly. ''I'm sorry, Granma.''

Felicity grinned. ''Save your sorries, boy. If that's all the trouble you find to get into today, I'll be thanking Jesus on my knees tonight.''

Wade Martin stuck his head into the dining room then, his face a wreath of exasperation. ''Well, here you all are, I've been looking all over. LeeAnn says you better be at the bottom of the stairs in three minutes flat, or she's eloping the next time.''

"If there's a next time, *I'm* eloping. Or running away, I swear," Felicity moaned. "Come on, if she doesn't see our smiling faces, she's likely to turn right around and never come down at all.''

They hurried together to the bottom of the vast, curving stairs, the spinal column of Graced Ground, embracing guests and shaking hands and accepting fond wishes, making their way through the crush of shoulders as the orchestra struck up Mendelssohn's wedding march, just as LeeAnn had ordered. The crowd surged forward, and they made a half-moon at the stairs, gazing upward.

And down came LeeAnn on Edward's arm, a vision of white lace and flowing blond hair, her chin high, her eyes radiant. At the landing, she stopped and held open her arms as if to embrace the whole room. "Thank you all so much for coming," she said softly, her voice as beautiful and warm as her smile.

Wade Martin started the applause then, and a few of his friends shouted the requisite "Hurrahs!" as the couple embraced. Edward leaned forward and kissed LeeAnn's brow, his face betraying his love and pride. She took up his hand and returned the kiss on his palm.

"He's a good man," Owen murmured.

"I hope so," Felicity said softly.

"Don't worry," Alva added gently, "he loves her with all his heart.''

"He better bring more than his heart to it," Wade Martin said, "or she'll eat him alive. Our LeeAnn's no soft-shelled crab, is she, Granmama?''

Felicity laughed then, the worry of the morning suddenly vanished now that her family stood alongside her. "No, sir," she said. "She takes after her own grandmother that way. Edward best keep his wits about him!''

And then LeeAnn was among them, and the orchestra burst into the first waltz of the afternoon. Laughing happily, she kissed her mother, quickly embraced her uncle and aunt, patted Wade Martin on the cheek, and whirled away from them in a flurry of white and fragrant blossoms. Edward was close behind her in a state of addled joy, his eyes never leaving her, his hand gripping hers as though it were the only anchor in a turbulent sea.

"The man is oblivious," Wade Martin said mockingly as they flew by. "I give him short odds in this race. She'll beat him by a length, and he'll run round and round the track, grinning like a fool, with dust in his eyes."

"You should be such a fool," Felicity said lightly, tapping her nephew on the arm. "When are *you* going to bring a young lady home for us to make fun of, sweetheart?"

"When cows skate on moonbeams," he said, equally affably.

"Oh ho!" Owen laughed. "So sayeth the young Lochinvar. Your time will come, laddy, and sooner rather than later, I'd say." With his arm around Alva, he added, "And you better get going before all the best ones are taken."

"Oh, I don't know," Wade Martin said gallantly, with a short bow to both Felicity and Alva. "Looks to me like some of the best peaches stay the longest on the tree."

Felicity smiled and hugged him round the neck. "I swear, you get more like your grandfather every day. A regular Shakespeare."

"Or like his great-grandfather," Owen said, rolling his eyes. "Wasn't he the rake of New Orleans?"

"Only to hear Mother tell it," Felicity said. "I imagine he managed to keep Grandmama happy enough, long as he was upright."

"Upright," Wade Martin said, pretending to consider the problem solemnly. "That's the key, I do believe. Don't lie down, or they'll trample you to death."

From across the crowded room, a feminine voice called out then, "Oh, Wade Martin! I do declare, you mean old thing, you asked for the first waltz, and it's half-gone already!" Sally Huxley from BriarRose plantation was threading her way through the shoulders, smiling and bowing at friends and neighbors. When she reached Wade Martin's side, she plucked at his sleeve and giggled. "Come on, you rascal. I don't mean to miss another moment of it!" And she whisked him away.

"Oh Lord," Owen groaned. "Let it not be Miss Sally. She's got six sisters, and he'll not get an inch of land out of old man Huxley."

"Oh hush," Alva said, poking her husband. "A waltz scarcely means a wedding."

"Well, let's go spy them out," Owen said, pulling her toward the music. "If she bats her eyes at him any faster, she's apt to take off like a hummingbird around the room, and I'd like to see that."

Felicity watched them go, and as they moved away, the music seemed to get softer, the lights dimmer. The frivolity and excitement were receding away from her once more, she thought with a small prick of sadness. Just as always. A colored servant was coming through the crowd with a huge platter of champagne glasses, barely managing to balance her burden without tipping them all, for the hands which reached to lighten her tray. "Here, I'll take one of those," Felicity said. She took a glass, sipped it swiftly, and then looked about to set it down.

Immediately before her, a man was coming forward to make his introduction. She instinctively held on to her glass for something to help occupy her hands, smiled brilliantly at him, and made for the stairs.

"Don't run off, Mrs. Daniels," he said cordially. "I came all the way over here through the swarming hordes simply to thank you so much for inviting me to this splendid affair, and I doubt I have the strength to buck the current again." He bowed smoothly and doffed a fawn-colored hat of some softly mottled silk. It matched his coat and trousers impeccably. "John Duncan, madam, a grateful neighbor. Your brother was kind enough to allow me to share in your daughter's joy today, and I wanted to extend my thanks to you in person." He took her hand and kissed it lightly. "I've not been to a more gracious *fête* all year."

"Why, thank you, Mr. Duncan," Felicity said, coloring slightly. "I thought I knew most of Owen's friends and surely all of our neighbors. Have you only recently come to Natchez?"

"Yes, indeed," he said, slowly relinquishing her hand. "From Montgomery. I have bought the old Sanderson place, do you know it?"

"Whitewood? You bought Whitewood from Bobby Sanderson?" she gasped. "Why, I had wondered if it might be for sale to the right party, but I had no idea . . ." She stopped in some confusion. Whitewood was one of the finest plantations to the north of Natchez. Robert Sanderson had had more than six hundred acres of excellent cotton, fine stock, a perfectly charming house—and an invalid wife, a pallid homely daughter, and an old war injury which, it was said, plagued him from morning 'til night. No wonder the man wanted to sell out—but if she had known for sure it was on the market, she might have sent Owen over to see if it could be had at a bargain. And now some stranger from Alabama had whisked it away! "Well," she finally finished lamely. "I wish you the best with it, Mr. Duncan. Whitewood is one of the prettiest pieces of land in the county."

He laughed low in his throat, and she glanced up at him sharply. "Don't tell me you coveted it, too, Mrs. Daniels? Seems to me that every cotton farmer I meet lately had an eye on Whitewood, but nobody would put their money where their mouth was. Poor ol' Sanderson would have much preferred to sell it to a neighbor than some upstart from Alabama, but nobody would give him a tumble. So here I am, just another nasty newcomer with two feet planted firmly on old Natchez soil." He bowed once more. "Will you do me the honor of a waltz anyway, Mrs. Daniels? It might help the Old Guard to accept the stranger in the flock a little faster, if I am seen dancing with you at least."

"Of course," she said, rather shortly. The man was arrogant and just a little coarse for her taste, but to refuse him would be simply too rude, since he was Owen's guest and likely knew few folks in the crowd. She took his arm and let him lead her to the ballroom, her head high, her smile brilliant, and her step firm. One waltz, she told herself, and then I will foist him off on Owen.

Once on the floor, John Duncan took her expertly in his arms and began to move to the music, his body telling her instantly that he had waltzed his share of waltzes, foreigner or no. She found that she had to keep her wits about her to keep up, and she disliked him even more for making her feel awkward. A gentleman, her father always said, made a lady look good when he danced with her, however he had to do so. They whisked by LeeAnn and Edward, holding court at the sidelines, champagne glasses in hand. As she passed in a flurry, LeeAnn gaped at her in surprise, and Edward lifted his hand in a toast.

"A handsome couple," John Duncan said to her. He was barely breathing fast. "She is not quite so lovely as her mother, but she's still head and shoulders above every other young woman in the place."

"Thank you," Felicity said, concentrating on his movements. She could not think of a single other response. "I think they'll be happy enough."

John Duncan laughed. " 'Happy enough'! Oh, I do hope they can do better than that, Mrs. Daniels. All of us should."

"But few of us are able," she said stiffly, hoping the waltz would end soon.

"Then more of us need to set our sights a little higher," he said confidentially. "For indeed, we can be as happy as we decide to be, to my mind."

"Indeed," she said, glancing over his shoulder with what she hoped would be perceived as disinterested courtesy. "An interesting philosophy."

"I understand your father was quite the philosopher," he said then, bending her slightly over his arm. "I am so sorry that I never had the good fortune to meet him. I hear he was more entertaining than Voltaire and wiser than Jefferson." He added gently, "You must miss him very much."

She smiled reluctantly. "Yes, I do," she said. "And thank you for complimenting his memory."

The waltz ended then, and the couples stopped, the volume of conversation and laughter instantly much louder and insistent. "Oh, there's Owen!" she said, rushing off the dance floor. "I'm certain he'd love to see you, Mr. Duncan!"

"I'd rather have another waltz with you, Mrs. Daniels," he said, his tone suddenly gone wistful.

"Oh, I'm afraid I must see to my guests' refreshment," she bridled gaily, pulling her hand from his and moving away. "But do say hello to Owen, and thank you so much for the dance!" She turned away then and fled to the kitchen.

Much later, she spied Owen and Alva standing a bit apart, their heads together in private conversation. She came up and stood so close to Owen's back that she could rub her nose on his tweed shoulders. "Who in the world is that Duncan person you invited from Alabama?" she whispered.

Owen and Alva turned and pulled her into their circle. "He said he found *you* delightful enough, sister mine," Owen said. "You didn't like the chap?"

"Oh, he was all right, I suppose. A good dancer, for his age."

"For his age!" Owen laughed. "He's a year older than you, I believe, old woman, and spry enough for half of the widows in this county!"

"Fine," she sniffed. "Let him ask *them* to dance, then."

Alva put her arm round Felicity's shoulders. "He seems nice enough, for a newcomer. I suspect the man is rather lonely, alone over there at Whitewood. That's a huge house for a bachelor."

"He won't be a bachelor long," Felicity said, and rolled her eyes. "Not with that line and that hat."

"Well, it's just as well you weren't taken with him," Owen said, a little more soberly. "There is some scandal attached to Master John Duncan, though I'm not sure what exactly. But I have the suspicion it's more than just his divorce.''

''He is a divorced man?'' Felicity asked, appalled. To think that she danced with a man who had been divorced!

''Yes, that's the story I get. Some say he's more of a gambler than a businessman, but I wouldn't know about that. Anyway, I invited him because he's a new neighbor, and I wanted to make him feel welcome. But I don't know that we need go beyond that courtesy.''

''A divorced man,'' Felicity said wonderingly. ''Well, you may rest assured, dear, he's had his share of courtesy from me, at any rate. Let the rest of the widows take up the slack from here.'' And she saw that LeeAnn and Edward were momentarily free from the mob, so she hurried over to speak to them both while she could.

The newlyweds left shortly after for their wedding trip to Europe with plans to visit four capitals in four weeks. Wade Martin went back to the University of Virginia to finish his degree in law, and Felicity found, suddenly, that she had far too little to do and too few people to care for to be happy. She moved back to the house in Natchez, her mother's beloved Commerce Street home, and from those tall Victorian windows, she gazed out upon the streets of Natchez and wondered what she was going to do with her life now.

Somehow, it seemed to Felicity, that while she wasn't paying attention, she had grown far older than her years. She was only fifty, and she felt like seventy. She was weary of spending time with widows and charity work within a few months of moving back to Natchez, but she felt out of place at Graced Ground, now that Owen and Alva had the place running like clockwork. Always, she had despised elderly female relatives who hung around the younger folks, the spinsters who were pitiable in their uselessness and their

loneliness. And now, it seemed, she was to be included in
their numbers.

For the first few weeks, Felicity missed LeeAnn so terri-
bly that she thought she might never be happy again. Her
heart felt utterly empty, arid as a fallow field. She could not
recall feeling such despair, even when James had died. All
the sunshine was gone from the day, and the nights crawled
by like large crippled spiders, bleak and ugly. There was no
one she could confide in, no one to whom she might go for
sympathy, and she believed that somehow, to miss a daughter as much as one might miss a husband was almost unnatu-
ral. A freak of nature.

That's what I am, she told herself, an abberration. A
travesty of all natural order. She tried to tell herself to cheer
up, tried to scold herself into her usual energy, but she
scarcely seemed to recognize her own thought patterns. Always before, when she was sad or angry or fretful, she was
able to find some small lucid space in which to stand, a safe
spot from which she could take a larger look and reassure
herself that this, too, would pass. Now, she could no longer
find that part of her mind which calmed her anxiety. Her
thoughts went round and round like a squirrel on a wheel,
she was unable to sleep, unable to stop the spiral downward
into melancholy and brooding worry, and it seemed to her
that gradually and for the first time in her life, she actually
began to doubt her own good sense.

Felicity knew of many older women, whispered about by
their friends and family, who had such depression and went
slightly mad for a spell. They drank bourbon in the afternoon, they spent too much money on hats, they redecorated
their houses over and over obsessively, or they took to their
beds with laudanum. One widow, an elegant wealthy woman
from an old Natchez family, dyed her hair red, had a dozen
pairs of green morocco dancing slippers custom-made, and
took a steamboat to New Orleans on the arm of a fancy man.
Her family would likely never get over the shock.

There were at least two families in Natchez who kept

spinster aunts in small attic rooms. Tenderly cared for by faithful servants, they were not taken out on the public streets nor admitted to polite society. Like deranged pets, they were kept safe and fed, but they were not allowed their freedom lest they bring injury or shame to themselves or their relations.

Felicity was determined not to be numbered in their lot. And yet there were days . . . nights, when she almost wished for death, simply to end her aching sadness. She wished she had listened more closely when her mother was trying to teach her about her herbal cures, her tisanes, her root decoctions. Likely, Arden would have known either a curative or a swift dispatch into oblivion for her. But as it was, Felicity was too ashamed to speak of her mental state to a soul. And so, she suffered alone, each day determined to get past the supper hour; each night resolved to get past midnight one more time.

One day, she was walking back from the marketplace with as brisk a pace as she could manage when she saw a gentleman coming toward her who looked alarmingly familiar. Lately, Felicity had taken to walking all over town as much as she could, in the hopes that the movement of her body would help clear her head and lighten her heart. Coming toward her now, on a sidestreet shaded by a canopy of flowering mimosa, was John Duncan. Even without his fawn-colored hat, she would have known it was he.

For an instant, Felicity considered turning and going back so that she need not pass him, but she scolded herself angrily. Stop this, she told her mind, stop this at once. Simply nod courteously to the man, speak if he speaks, and then go on your way. Don't be a foolish old woman!

John Duncan saw her approaching and doffed his hat quickly, bowing to her with obvious pleasure. "Why, it's Mrs. Daniels," he said warmly. "What a surprise and delight to see you again."

"Thank you, sir," Felicity said cordially. "How have you been?"

"Excellent, excellent," the man said, "and have you now moved to your Commerce Street address?"

"Yes, I have," Felicity said. "How did you know we had a house in town?"

"Oh, I make it my business to be as knowledgeable as I can about the finest pieces of real estate in Natchez, and that lovely Victorian is one of the best, to my mind. Has your daughter come back from her wedding trip?"

"Not yet," Felicity said, a slight sadness in her voice.

"Ah. And you miss her mightily, I suppose."

Felicity found, to her surprise and alarm, that she could do nothing but nod. When she looked up at John Duncan, he was gazing at her with soft compassion. He put out his arm. "May I walk you home, Mrs. Daniels?"

"Yes," she said faintly, not knowing what else to do. Somehow the idea of his company was a strange comfort in that moment. As they walked, he talked on lightly, taking care to keep the conversation impersonal and entertaining. He told her of his trials with Whitewood in such a way that implied that he knew she, better than most women, would understand the victories and defeats of running a large plantation; he spoke of his family in Montgomery, his ailing mother, his sister, and she listened for mention of a wife, but he made none. He told her again how much he had appreciated the invitation to LeeAnn's wedding and the dance she bestowed on him, "for it was," he added, "my first real introduction to Natchez society, you know. I don't know how many years I might have knocked on that door without admission, if it had not been for your kindness." He carefully asked her little about herself, but he watched her with a rare attention which she found strangely appealing.

As they reached the front steps to her house, she turned to him abruptly and asked, "Would you care to come in for tea?" She had had absolutely no intention of making such an offer, and she had no idea why she said it, but she seemed unable to help herself.

He smiled eagerly. "Yes, I'd like that," he said. And they walked up the steps together.

The servants made a small flurry at his arrival, and Felicity was instantly chagrined. Quite obviously, their behavior said, a man had not visited this house in too long. He took an opposite chair from her in the parlor, and Felicity waited until he had been served before she took up her own cup and slice of Esme's good orange cake. Thank goodness it was a Wednesday, the day after baking day, else the man might have had nothing but biscuits to balance on his knee.

They spoke back and forth, of the wedding, crops, various mutual acquaintances, Wade Martin's progress at the University, the weather, and then finally, he set down his cup and saucer and leaned slightly forward toward her, his gaze suddenly more direct. "Mrs. Daniels," he said, "I don't suppose you know much about my past. Am I right?"

She hesitated. How did a lady respond to such a question? She guessed instantly that he was referring to his unfortunate marital history, something that should not be mentioned in polite society at all and certainly not to a casual acquaintance. She busied herself with her napkin. "I scarcely need to," she finally murmured.

"I see that you do know then," he sighed. "No doubt your brother warned you away from me. Many ladies in Natchez have been so warned, I warrant."

She glanced up at his change of tone. It was the same rather wistful tone she had heard once before from him as they danced, when he had wished for another waltz. It occurred to her with a blinding sense of amazement that the man was lonely. A man of some wealth, of good property, of a thousand business connections and family, a man, likely, with more responsibilities in a month than she might assume all year . . . and he was lonely. She felt a sudden kinship with him, and she let the stiffness of her shoulders relax, unbidden. "I don't know what other ladies may or may not know, Mr. Duncan," she said softly, "for I don't go out among them as I once did. I believe my brother did mention in pass-

ing that you had a wife at one time . . .'' She deliberately let
her voice fade to silence.

"I did," he said. "She left me for another man, I'm sorry
to say, and sued me for divorce. We are no longer man and
wife. I wish her well, of course, but I am quite relieved now
that we never had a child and were together for only a short
time. Five years, to be exact. And I've not seen her for a
decade. But yes, madam, I am a divorced man." He watched
her carefully. "I realize that makes me quite a liability, at
least socially."

She said nothing. She had never known a single person
who was divorced before. This was something which might
happen in New York, perhaps in Paris. But never in Mississippi.

"Frankly, Mrs. Daniels," he said with some hesitation.
"I would very much appreciate hearing your opinion on that
matter."

"Why?" She was genuinely surprised.

"May I speak bluntly?"

"I believe you already have," she murmured.

"I find you to be the most attractive, most intelligent, and
quite the most interesting woman I have met here in Natchez. I consider myself a most fortunate man to have made
your acquaintance, and I wonder if such a woman as yourself"—and here he faltered just a moment—"if a woman of
obvious taste and quality would ever overlook such a . . .
scandal in a man's past, enough to allow for friendship." He
let out a large sigh at the end of those words as though a
burden had been lifted from his chest.

Ah, she told herself with a small, internal smile. Mr. Duncan has found a woman he would like to woo and fears that
she won't let him past the front door. He hopes that I might
be able to gain him entrance in Natchez circles by letting the
world see that I, at least, find him acceptable. She felt pity
for the man. She knew what it was like to feel the outsider.
Indeed, she had felt that distance between herself and others
for what seemed her whole adult life. She said finally, "It is

not for me to judge another's decisions, Mr. Duncan.'' She looked up at him frankly. ''But if you are hoping that I might be able to help others understand your past, I'm very much afraid you'll be disappointed in me as a friend. For you see, I scarcely go out at all anymore myself. Perhaps you thought because of LeeAnn's wedding that I was some sort of''— and here she blushed awkwardly—''*grande dame* of Natchez. But that is not the case. Indeed, I've become more retiring than ever these days . . .''

''It's not the understanding of others I seek,'' he said quietly. ''It's yours, Mrs. Daniels.''

''Mine?''

''Yes. For I would like to call on you again. And again, if you'll allow me. And again after that.'' He smiled. ''That is, if you can overlook my shady past.''

She found herself smiling despite herself. It was hard not to, when he was obviously determined that she do so.

''What do you say?'' he asked.

She laughed aloud. ''Mr. Duncan, you're a rogue,'' she said, suddenly feeling more alive and powerful than she had in years. ''That's what I say. But a relatively charming one, I suppose. As to your past, we'll speak no more on it now.''

''And to my present? Dare I hope you might allow me to call again in the near future?''

''You might hope,'' she teased. ''We shall see how I feel when the time comes.''

He grinned. ''You are a fascinating woman, Mrs. Daniels. Might I call you Felicity?''

''You may not,'' she chuckled. ''Will you have another sliver of Esme's cake? I'm told it's the best in Natchez, if you like your sweets with a little tartness.''

''I do,'' he said quickly, ''and I've no doubt it is.''

She deftly turned the conversation once more to less perilous places, and as she recovered her breath and her poise, she found herself thinking that, indeed, this man Duncan was going to be a bit of fun.

* * *

It had rained in Natchez for what seemed like weeks that
September. There were storms, they said, all up and down
the Atlantic seacoast, and the winds were pushing the rain
farther inland than usual. The streets were full of mud and
downed branches, and the air itself seemed thick with moisture.

Of course, they were used to water in Natchez, for streams
were always coming up and running to whatever larger
water they could find in the wet seasons. There were rivers,
tens of them, men said, running underwater, not to mention
the Saint Catherine and the Mississippi themselves. Some
added that the good dirt that made the cotton was just a thin
veneer over a vast sea, and that's why the soil was so rich
and red.

Felicity didn't know about such things, but she knew for
sure that it was the wettest September she could recall. And
to add to the general frivolity of muddy streets and leaking
basements and sagging gutters, her horse got a ringworm
thick as her thumb, and no amounts of swabbings with gen-
tian violet had cleared it up. It was the damp, Joe the sta-
bleboy told her. And so, if she wanted to get out, rain or no,
she had to walk.

Felicity hated to go out in it, but she found if she stayed
inside for more than a day or so, her spirits sank again to
levels which almost frightened her. Determined to keep
busy, she drove herself to go out, even if it were for the most
minor of errands. As she left the protection of the porch,
however, she glared up at the dark clouds in silent protest.
Another day of rain, no doubt, like so many before it. She
opened her umbrella defiantly and took off for Market
Street, wondering if she would ever be wearing anything but
her worst boots again.

No sooner did she reach Silver Street than it opened up in
a cloudburst. The drops came hard and huge, big as nickels,
warm as the Mississippi water, hissing on the hot planks of

the sidewalks, followed by a thousand more. She ran for the shelter of an overhanging awning, closed up her umbrella with an irritated snap, and stood and watched the rain pelt down again for the tenth time in as many days. People scurried by, some with umbrellas, others resigned to a good soaking. Buggies hurried home, more open carriages than not, for Natchez wasn't used to this sort of weather. No one believed it could possibly storm yet another day. She peered up at the dark, roiling clouds. They looked as if they might be a good while clearing.

The longer she stood, the more exasperated she became. After all, it's just rain, she told herself, and my hair needs a good washing anyway. She opened her umbrella and strode off toward home, silently cursing the rain and the mud and her own determination to go out on yet another fool errand.

Felicity walked one block before she began to regret her decision. Now the rain was hard, slanting into her body with a good deal of force. The wind was whipping the trees along the road, and the mud was no longer mud but raging torrents which she must cross to get home. She bent her body into the wind, pulled her umbrella down so low that she could scarcely see, and kept walking, thinking surely this would be lesson enough to keep her home the next few days.

As she rounded the corner with still four more blocks to go to Commerce, she realized that her skirts were so sodden and muddy that she was tiring quickly. Now there were no more protective awnings under which she might stop and rest. And the thunder and lightning was louder and moving closer by the moment.

Perhaps she should stop and take refuge at a house, she told herself. In the next block she knew folks at two homes, and they would surely understand—

But she pushed that thought away. She wanted to see no one in this state, wanted to make no apologies or explanations, and impose on no one but herself. Serves me right for coming out, she told herself angrily, just keep on walking and weed this field, now you've plowed it. But oh, she was tired! And the rain was drenching her back and neck now, pulling down her hair. Her ankles felt rubbery, and her hands were clenched so tightly to her umbrella and her package that she felt she was nothing but a frown and two fists pushing on.

From behind her, a carriage came rushing, and she moved aside on the sidewalk to avoid being splashed, thinking perhaps she should hail the driver and risk embarrassment rather than be drowned within sight of her own door. A voice called out, and she turned swiftly, but the carriage was covered; she could not make out the driver. The voice called out again, her name this time, and she stopped with great relief.

"Mr. Duncan!" she gasped. "What are you doing out in this deluge?"

"Rescuing damsels," he said, grinning. "Get in here immediately," he added, hopping down to help her inside the carriage. "What in the world are you doing out in this mess? And on foot, no less."

"My mare's got the ringworm," she said, glancing down at the floor of the carriage with dismay. Between her umbrella, her skirts, and her filthy shoes, she had made a mess of it.

"And there's no one else to go out for you?"

"Oh, I didn't think it would rain yet again," she said, still trying to settle herself and pull her sodden clothing to some sort of order. "Surely it has to stop sometime."

"Perhaps by October," he said wryly, clicking to his horse. "I doubt you'll wait it out. But I'm very glad I happened along. No woman should be out in this mess today, least of all you."

At that, she looked up, amused and rankled all at once. "Why not me, least of all?"

But he ignored her question completely. "I was just coming back from the docks to see to a delivery, and I saw you from a half-block back. I thought, that can't possibly be she, but then I said, my Lord, it is, and I hurried up lest some other gallant take my opportunity.''

Felicity had noticed, meanwhile, that the carriage was stylish, new, and likely expensive enough. The seats were leather, the handles brass, and the privacy shades of heavy, watered silk. LeeAnn would love this fabric, she thought.

"Are they all right out at Graced Ground?" he was asking.

She pulled herself back to attention. "Yes, so far as I know."

"We're up to our ankles at Whitewood," he said. "The ground can't take it in as fast as heaven's putting it out. I've got cows stuck in mud up to their udders, and canyons carved out in my cotton fields that could break a mule's leg. We'll take a month of sun to dry out enough to plow."

"I guess I would have heard if Owen was having fits. I usually do," she said. "We're farther from the river, though, so I expect he's not so bad."

They were pulling up now to her front steps, and she felt almost giddy with relief, so happy she was to have been whisked up out of peril. And peril it did truly seem to her now that she was out of it. Why, she might have fallen in the road, might have wrenched an ankle in the mud, certainly would have ruined a perfectly good frock, might still catch her death if she didn't get out of these wet clothes. She said breathlessly, "Oh, I'm *so* grateful you came along, Mr. Duncan! I can't thank you enough."

"Sure you can," he said, turning to gaze at her in the shadows of the carriage. "You can return the favor by granting me one."

This seemed familiar territory. She forgot her immediate discomfort and even the nasty stickiness of her skin and hair and smiled at him appraisingly. "And what might that be?"

"You can call me Jack. Most of my friends do, and I would like to number you in that category."

"Jack?"

"Yes, I'm only John to those who don't know better."

She thought for a moment. It seemed a decade ago that she had fussed at LeeAnn for calling Edward by his first name. Even her own mother had thought her stuffy at the time. It was a small enough thing, considering the man had practically saved her life. "Jack, then," she said softly. "I think I can manage that."

To her surprise, his whole face softened when she said his name. "Thank you," he said gently. "That's quite the nicest thing that's happened to me all week."

"Well, goodness!" She laughed happily. "You must have had a hideous week, indeed."

He took her hand and kissed it gently. "Not at all. But this is definitely the high point."

Now it suddenly seemed imperative that she get out of this carriage and inside her own door immediately. She shifted nervously on the seat, instantly aware of her frock, her muddy shoes, her wretched hair—

He sensed her restlessness and turned quickly, opening the door and helping her out, holding her umbrella over her head until she could take it from him. It was only after she rushed off, scampered inside the door, shed herself of wet cloak, package, and umbrella, and shook out her hair when she realized that it must have seemed to him the height of rudeness not to ask him in for a drink of something warm and a dry place by the fire.

"What a little fool you are," she told herself as she struggled with her boots. "Why he'd want to be friends with such a country bumpkin is beyond understanding. And was it absolutely necessary to say ringworm in that sleek carriage? Oh!" She was mortified. "Esme, draw me a hot bath immediately!" she shouted now, furious with herself. "I don't want to speak to another soul before bedtime!"

The rains continued unabated, and the Saint Catherine was in high crest by the end of September. The creatures of the river had sensed the coming storms, many of them, and had done what their instincts commanded and what they could to secure their homes. Some of them left the low-lying areas, moving east from the river toward the higher ground. Others simply hunkered down and waited, for they knew that, eventually, the rains must cease.

The beaver which had moved into the vacant muskrat pond had done his best to dam the swollen river, finally realizing that he must let more water escape or he would threaten his own lodge and the best feeding areas up the banks. As the rains continued, he worked more feverishly, lest he lose an entire summer's work. His dams were holding for now, but if the river went higher still, he might be washed away along with his lodge. He was a young beaver, a hard worker, and he had a firm determination to make this place on the Saint Catherine his own. The older beaver upstream had driven him south, and he had missed his first season of mating, unable to secure a place to build his lodge. But now, he was ready. He would not lose this pond to a rival or the river.

Near the beaver lodge, a great blue heron had made his feeding platform in a high gum tree. He was also a young bird, and so he recognized the fever of the beaver who shared his part of the river, though he could not know his history. Indeed, the heron sensed in the beaver a comrade of sorts. The beaver created excellent hunting ponds for the minnows and frogs the heron craved. He, in turn, often brought sticks and twigs from farther away from the river than the beaver might travel. Neither consciously helped the other; both took some comfort from the presence of another permanent resident who did not eat what he ate.

The great blue heron had flown south from a large colony in New England to winter over in the warmer Mississippi water region. And now that he had followed his instincts and come so far, he felt quite alone, away from his own kind. He stood more than four feet tall, a large blue-gray bird with a yellow bill, and was called *Ardea herodias*.

Hero was hunting this early evening along the upper shore

of the beaver pond, doing his best to ignore the pelting rain. The fishing was not improved by the silt, and his vision was hampered by the rushing of the water, yet he had to catch something before dusk or go hungry again this day. The hunting had been quite poor for a week, ever since the river had risen so high and muddy. For some reason he did not understand, the frogs had disappeared from this part of the river. But he was strong and young and unafraid of change, for he knew little else. Driven by his shrinking stomach, he waded carefully along the high water line now, never taking his bright yellow eyes off the drowning foliage and the moving current.

A sudden movement near his foot caught his attention, and he froze. His neck was bent at an odd angle, not his usual ''S'' shape, for he must be ready to strike at any sign of life. His neck was poised and curved and strong, and his sharp bill pointed directly down at the water. There, he saw a small minnow struggling to escape from the twisted roots of a pine tree. Earlier in the month, the pine would have been ten feet from the water; now it sat in shallows, dying.

Hero struck swiftly at the minnow, spearing it instantly and flipping it up in the air. He tossed it high with an easy whipping motion of his neck, caught it again in his bill so that it went down his gullet headfirst, and then stretched his neck to ease the swallowing. It was small, but encouraging. Not enough to assuage his hunger but enough to make him glad. He gave a hoarse, guttural croak of satisfaction, flapped his wings once, and settled back again into his hunting stance.

Two large ravens flew over, cawing raucously, warning of danger, but Hero scarcely glanced up. The ravens always warned of danger these days, it seemed to him, and so it was often more trouble to listen than not. Angry at being ignored, the ravens circled him, croaking and screeching, and then flew off in the direction of the larger pines. Hero settled back down to hunting attention.

He strode through the water carefully, feeling with his

long, dark green claws for purchase in the muddy water. The footing was precarious here, for so many plants were submerged that the usual sandbank was now in much deeper water. The current was stronger than he liked, but there was nothing to do but keep hunting. He searched and searched, peering into every crevice and root. No frogs; no salamanders. Not even the scurrying water beetles ran before his wading legs.

It was getting close to dusk now, and Hero was hungrier still. The small mouthful of minnow seemed two days old. He stopped and listened. Usually this was the time when the frogs began to sing, but he heard none. He kept wading, glancing now over to the beaver lodge. The beaver's bubbles were coming up from the bottom. No doubt, he was readying himself for the night. But Hero would not retire to his nest site in the old gum without something else in his gullet.

Suddenly, his sharp eyes caught a movement among an outcropping of stones at the river's edge. A small slither of energy, a slicker of color—he froze and riveted his attention on the movement. A narrow snake had shifted suddenly and then coiled on the rocks. Dusky in color, only about ten inches long, it was now circled on the flat plane of boulder, staring back at the great blue heron with its flat, lidless eyes.

Hero hesitated an instant. In that moment, the snake raised his head and shook his tail, making an ominous buzzing noise. It was a rattlesnake, perfect and complete though youthful. Capable of delivering a dangerous strike, if pressed.

Hero had no experience with poisonous snakes, for few of them inhabited his summer quarters in New England. Indeed, he had often eaten snakes larger than this one, but something in his head stopped him from striking quickly. The shape of the snake's head, severe and angled, the loose coil, suggesting an absence of fear, and the annoying buzz all should have warned him off. But Hero was more hungry than cautious. He suddenly stabbed at the snake, caught it deftly behind the head, and shook it violently from side to

side as he might shake a larger snake to stun it. He then
slammed it onto the dry bank and stepped on its small body,
staring at it curiously. The buzzing had stopped. The snake
still writhed slightly, twisting in obvious distress, its jaw
gaping wide. Once, it tried to bite, but Hero merely moved
his clawed toe slightly aside, watching the snake closely. Its
small fangs were curved and glistening, its flat black eyes
hooded and without life, even as it moved.

Hero's stomach reminded him now that there were still
moments of daylight left, enough to find yet more to fill him
up. He snatched the snake up with his bill, tossed it in the air,
and caught it by the head, swiveling it down his throat. It
was better than the minnow. Better than a frog. He croaked
again, flapped his wings to settle himself, and began the hunt
in earnest once more.

Three nights after Jack Duncan had rescued her from the
deluge, Owen came by to go over the plantation books with
Felicity. Every month they met in this way, but to her surprise, Edward walked in right behind him, both of them
shedding their capes and umbrellas, leaving puddles in the
foyer.

"Do you think this will ever stop?" she asked, ushering
them into the study, where she and Owen generally spread
out the books and went over the accounts. "Are the roads
impossible?"

"Just about," Edward said. "The docks are about to float
away, and that juncture of Market and Bay streets? Completely under water. LeeAnn wanted to come along tonight
just to see you, but I told her it was ridiculous to come out in
this weather."

Felicity nodded, disappointed. "Well, of course, if we're
going to wait for decent weather again, it might be a month
before I get to see her. Are you able to get anything at all into
the fields, Owen?"

"Not for two weeks or more," he said glumly, pulling up

a chair and pouring himself a cup of the hot coffee Esme brought in. "I'm glad we don't sit further north; if that levee gives, the whole county will go below Natchez. If it weren't for the bluffs, we might already be swept away."

They compared notes for a few moments on the weather and the plight of various neighbors, and Felicity settled back to wait. She guessed that Edward had not come by strictly for courtesy's sake. Sooner or later, he would get to the reason for his visit. If he wants to discuss Graced Ground again, she told herself, and that eighty acres to the west we've not put to cotton yet. I hope he's prepared for another disappointment. I'm simply not ready to give that to him yet. Let them be married a few years more, perhaps after a grandchild or two—

"Filly, I wanted Edward to come along this evening," Owen was saying suddenly, "because I wanted to speak to you about a rather—difficult subject. And he knows more about it, really, than I do."

She was instantly wary. Not about Graced Ground, then. "Oh?" she said slowly, taking her time with her coffee.

"I understand you have been seeing John Duncan," Owen said carefully.

Felicity felt the breath go out of her abdomen as though she had been struck. "Why—what do you mean?" she asked.

Owen smiled charmingly. "Oh, this is such a small town, Filly, you know how people talk. I was at Bob's office two days ago, and he mentioned seeing John's carriage out front, and you know, it doesn't take but a moment for news like that to spread like wildfire round six city blocks."

Bob Follett was factor for Graced Ground cotton, a man who made it his business to know most everyone else's business in and out of Natchez. "Oh, for heaven's sakes," she said lightly, letting the annoyance show in her voice. "He's been here to tea a time or two and drove me home from market the other day when I got caught out in the storm. I hardly think that's news, even to such a busybody as Bob Follett."

"Is that the extent of your friendship with him, then?" Owen asked casually, reaching for more coffee. He did not meet her eyes.

"So far," she said stiffly. "However, I am curious why this might concern you, Owen." She was furious that he would bring such a thing up before Edward, who was only barely part of the family, as far as she was concerned.

Owen glanced at Edward.

Edward cleared his throat and said, very gently, "Perhaps I might be of some assistance here, Mrs. Daniels."

"By all means," she said archly. He had never called her anything but Missus, and now she was glad he had not.

"Filly, I asked Edward to come here with me tonight," Owen said patiently, "because I felt you might be able to hear someone else tell you a bit about John Duncan rather than me. After all, I invited him to LeeAnn's wedding, trying to be a good neighbor and all, and so in a way, I feel responsible. But he's not"—and here, Owen reached for a word—"he's not a proper escort for you, my dear."

She felt herself go cold inside and deeply sad. So this was the way it was to be, then. "I see," she said, lowering her eyes and folding her hands before her. Lest they see them tremble. "Pray tell me then, Edward. How big a monster is this John Duncan?"

Edward chuckled disarmingly. "Hardly a monster, Mrs. Daniels. But the man does have a reputation. I knew him before, when I was traveling to and from Vicksburg. He was married then." He lowered his voice confidentially. "Not that it made much difference to him, I must say."

"Go on," she said, the tremble now audible in her voice.

"He was quite a gambler, rather successful at it too, I might add," Edward said, laughing ruefully to Owen. "Did a heap better than *I* ever did, that's for sure."

"There's hardly a man I know who didn't do something he was likely denounced for in his youth," Felicity said lightly. "Is that all you have on the man?"

"I should think that's enough," Owen said, his voice suddenly grave. "Edward says he was quite a rake, to put it baldly. Frankly, Filly, I expected you to react a little differently than you have."

"You expected me to be grateful, I suppose," she replied tightly. "Well, of course I am. It's always good to be warned away from a precipice, especially if one is thinking of jumping. But I wasn't thinking of jumping, you see. In fact, I scarcely cared for the view at all."

"I see," Owen said, with some relief. "Well, then, we needn't say any more about it. It's just that it wouldn't look well to see the man's carriage here alone, not unless his was one of several invited. After all, he's a neighbor and seems to be nice enough, as far as that goes. But he's hardly the man I'd choose for your . . . confidant."

Edward said quietly, "I do hope you're not angry with me, Mrs. Daniels. I hate to be the bearer of bad news."

"If this *were* bad news, I would hardly be angry, Edward. I would of course be grateful for your concern," Felicity said coolly. "But since it's only bad gossip, I hardly think we need discuss it further. I shall simply be unavailable next time Mr. Duncan calls. And the time after that and the time after that, should he be so foolish as to continue to plague me." She laughed mirthlessly. "After all, the man is scarcely worth all this conversation and trouble. And I'm getting too old to be bothered with such intrigue."

"I'm glad you're not upset, Filly," Owen said gently. "For you know, I'd like nothing better than for you to find a suitable companion. Some gentleman who's worth your good name. But this John Duncan appears not to be—"

"Let's say no more on it," Felicity said briskly. "Now, besides an earful of silly gossip, what else did Bob have to say? How are the prices for long-staple in New Orleans this month?" And she led them off in an involved conversation about the crops, the rain, and the potential for profits in the next quarter.

After they left that night, Felicity sat down at her secretary and penned a brief note to John Duncan. It was eloquent, formal, and quite to the point. In it, she said simply that she had learned enough about his background to be discomforted with his attentions to her, and she asked him please not to call again unless invited. She begged to remain his friend and good neighbor and signed it, "With all best wishes, Mrs. F. Daniels."

The next morning, she woke to see the sealed note on her secretary, ready to send. She stood for a moment, holding it pensively. What had happened to her in all these years? Once, she had been a gay and flirtatious young girl. Once, she had reveled in her beginning beauty, in the power she felt when she noticed people looking at her. Once, she had wanted to be like her grandmother. And then she met James. He made her feel at once sanctified and loved, even at a distance. When she lost him, she lost who she believed herself to be: she was no longer a wife. No longer a woman. She was only a mother and a widow. How did a heart stretch to encompass such loss and still be capable of love?

She didn't know the answer to such things. She only knew that she had felt so numb for so long. And then Jack Duncan strenuously intruded into her life, and she was alive again. But only for a moment. A great silent sadness was on her heart, a feeling of being disconnected from even her own body. Her throat felt thick and full of tears, but she could not weep. All of nature was weeping, she sighed, but she could not. After so many days of steady wet, it was hard to care about much of anything. She glanced listlessly up at the sky. Likely it was going to rain again today; it was gray and heavy as it had been for weeks. "Esme!" she called out, suddenly angry at herself for no reason she could name.

Esme came to the door, startled into a swift response. "Yes'm?"

She handed the note to the girl. "Send Joe round to Whitewood with this." She looked out at the dark clouds. "Tell him to hurry, it's going to pour again by noon."

* * *

That night, the skies thundered again as though they were only just discovering their ability to do so. Felicity could not believe there could possibly be any more rain left in the entire world, so much had fallen on Natchez. Even though it was warm, she lit a fire in the study and put on her coziest slippers. Anything to comfort the clamminess of her skin and the cold ache in her heart.

"You be needin' anything mo' tonight, Miz Dan'els?" Esme asked her, as she set down the teapot and the ginger cookies.

"Perhaps an ark," Felicity said ruefully to the servant. "Like Jonah, we may well need to take to the high ground soon."

"You don' think de levee goin' to go?" gasped Esme.

"No, no," she soothed her. "I was only joking, child. We'll be fine. The Mississippi's got bigger fish to fry up north, it won't be bothering with us. You go on to bed now."

Esme nodded and withdrew, leaving Felicity alone with the flickering fire and her open book on her lap. It was early, too early to go to bed, and yet she was tired as though she had not slept in a week. She picked up the book again, read a page, and then set it back down. Somehow, she could not bring herself to care about the doleful world of Tess of the D'Urbervilles, though it seemed, bleak as it was, preferable to her own. She sat and thought for long moments over her life. Her marriage to James and their too-brief spate of happiness. The birth of LeeAnn. James's death. Micah's death. The passing of her grandmother, her mother, her father. The war years, when a whole way of life passed as quickly as the seasons. And now, the marriage of her daughter, leaving her alone, oh most assuredly alone, for the last years of her life.

How had she come to this place of fallow ground? She had once been pretty, she knew it. Her grandmother told her, the eyes of men told her the same thing. Once, she knew how to laugh, how to flirt disarmingly, how to dance and be gay. But that young girl had been lost so long ago! What had happened to her heart? To her life?

A knock came to the front door. She froze, listening. All the servants were in bed, no doubt, taking their cue from Esme. Who could it be so far past the supper hour? She rose reluctantly, fearing that any visitor at such a time could hardly be good news. But there was no way she could avoid an answer. She tightened her wrapper and buttoned the top button, smoothing back her hair as she went. The closer she got to the front door, the more she hurried, for the knocks came louder and more insistent.

Felicity opened the door to see John Duncan standing on her veranda, his hat in his hand, the rain still streaming off his cape. "Oh Lord," she moaned quietly. "What are you doing here?"

He pulled her note from his pocket. "Surely you didn't think I'd accept this without a fight, did you?" he said. "Please let me come in, Felicity. I need to speak with you at once."

Her ears heard all at once the pleading and pain in his voice, the determination, and also his use of her first name, the first time she had heard it from his lips. "I don't think that's a good idea," she said faintly, still standing between him and the open foyer beyond. She put her hand to her collar. "It's very late . . ."

"It's not even nine," he said. "I have come all this way in the rain, across roads which haven't been roads in a week, and I must see you. Please."

She stared at him, appalled. Owen would have a fit if he found out, of course, but she could not turn away a dog in this weather. Not without at least a chance to dry off and have something hot. "Come in," she said, as calmly as she could manage. "I'm so sorry you've come all this way."

"I'm not," he said as he came in and shed his umbrella and cloak. "Not if I can see you, even if it's only for a moment."

She blushed and led him into the study, gesturing for him to take the chair closest to the fire. Without preamble, he held up the note once more. "What does this mean, Felicity?"

"I have not given you leave to address me with such familiarity," she said, trying for some lucid place from which to begin.

"No, I know you haven't," he said firmly, "but I don't have the patience for this sort of foolishness, nor do I have the time. I don't have many years left to find happiness, my dear, far fewer than you, I suspect. And when I know what I want, I go after it. Felicity, I want you to explain to me what this note means."

She looked down at her hands. "Just what it said. I think it best that we not continue our friendship."

"Because of my past."

She nodded, suddenly unable to speak for the ache in her throat.

"I told you I was divorced."

"Yes," she murmured. "You told me."

He stared at her for a long moment. "So, then. What has someone else told you?"

She looked up at him beseechingly. "Why did you come, Jack? Why didn't you just leave me alone?"

He was by her side so quickly that she almost flinched. "I can't leave you alone," he said, "not unless you tell me that you don't give a damn for me. If you tell me that, I'll go, and I swear, I'll never trouble you again. Tell me that, and I'm gone, Felicity." He took her hand and pinned her eyes with his.

"I can't say that," she whispered.

"Then you do care for me?"

"I can't say that either."

"Well, I can and I will." He put his two hands on her shoulders. "I love you," he said urgently. "I know I've had a rather—checkered past. But that's been behind me for years. Can't a man have one last chance at happiness? I want you to marry me, Felicity. I love you. I think I loved you the first moment I saw you."

"Why?" she moaned.

He laughed aloud at that, amazed. "Why? Because you're beautiful and graceful and warm and intelligent and for a hundred other reasons besides! Don't you know that, my dear?" He pulled her up and took her over to the glass mounted over the fireplace. "Look at yourself," he said gently. "You are a beautiful woman. Has it been that long since a man's told you so?"

The tears came to her eyes then and rolled slowly down her cheeks as she gazed into the mirror. "I haven't thought of how I look for a long, long time. It just hasn't seemed . . . important."

"Then you haven't been a woman for too long," he said, taking her in his arms. "Please, Felicity. Whatever you've heard about my past, forgive it. I was a rake, I admit it. My wife was a witch, and my heart was hardened to her early on. I thought I'd never feel this way again in my life. But then I met you, and now I won't let you go."

She moaned and dropped her head to his chest. His arms around her felt so strong and sure. "I don't know what to do," she said. "Owen and Edward tell me that you're not—not appropriate."

She felt him stiffen, but his voice remained gentle. "I wasn't, I'll admit that much. Long ago, your father likely would have driven me away with a shotgun. But I've done my best to get on with my life, and I want you in it now." He took her chin in his hand and pulled it up so that he could look into her face. "After all, I didn't murder anyone. I didn't loot or steal or ravage helpless women. I would think that a man's reputation in his youth might be forgiven him in his old age. Do you want me to go?"

She shook her head mutely.

"Then I'll speak to your brother and young Edward," he said. "I believe I can convince them that I'm not General Sherman incarnate."

She smiled, despite her pain. "Oh, Jack, you're braver than I am. But I don't know if that's a good idea."

"Please just let me worry about that."

She sighed. "I really don't want to worry about much of anything anymore."

"Good," he said, "that's as it should be. Now, let's get back to the main point of this conversation, Felicity." He drew her back down to the chaise next to him, keeping her hands in his own. "I want to marry you. I love you. Will you allow me to woo you properly so that you might consider my suit?"

She laughed low in her throat, surprised at the pleasure which bubbled up out of her belly. There was something about this man which made her want to smile, to laugh, to dance, and whoop aloud with joy. "Yes," she said, "If you can convince my brother to stop pestering me about you."

"Felicity, if you wanted me to, I'd try to convince God Himself to stop pestering you." He leaned forward and kissed her cheek then, softly. "For you deserve a little peace in your life."

"And happiness," she murmured.

"Most certainly, happiness. Isn't that what your name means, after all?"

"So they tell me. But you know, I've never really cared for it."

"Your name?"

She shook her head. "It always sounds like a heroine in an English novel to me. I never liked it."

"Well, what shall I call you, then?"

She smiled. "Call me Lacey. That's what my grandmama used to call me. I like that." She added ruefully, "though I haven't heard it in a passel of years."

"Lacey." He grinned and pulled her closer to him. "That suits you better, you're right. Lacey. A fine lady."

They sat thus by the fire for a moment in silence. "I'm glad you came tonight," she finally murmured.

"I'd have been here even if the levee went," he said. "Unless you beat me off with a stick, I'm going to dog your front door like a sorry ol' hound, my dear. You'll get so sick of looking at my wistful expression, you'll finally marry me just to put me out of my misery."

She laughed and pushed him lightly away. "You *are* a rake, Jack Duncan. My brother was right."

"Yes," he murmured, and he leaned down to kiss her. "The rake and the lady."

Felicity felt his kiss slide through her like a warm knife, down to her belly, down her legs, surging through her heart with a power that made her shudder. She felt her lips tremble under his, and she could not control them. He kissed her softly at first, and then more deeply. This was a man who had kissed many women, she told herself, and kissed them well. He was good at it, unlike James, who kissed her chastely, softly, tenderly. Jack kissed her as though he wanted to taste something secret within her, something she had never given up before. When he finally pulled away, his lips still so close to hers that she could feel their heat, she was panting slightly, as though she had run from far far away to get to this place.

"My God, Lacey," he whispered, "you are such a full woman. So ripe for love."

"Yes," she murmured, almost unaware of what she said.

"You are beautiful," he said.

"No. Not anymore."

"You are beautiful," he repeated firmly. "And I am the luckiest man in the world, if you'll have me."

They sat together then by the fire, talking over their lives quietly. He kissed her twice more, but he did not press her, did not attempt to make love to her any more than she welcomed him. When he left her finally with a heartfelt hug, she felt so full of pride and joy that she thought she would likely never get to sleep. But she fell deeply, peacefully asleep the moment her head hit the pillow, and she wondered, briefly, just before she stopped thinking, how long had it been since she felt such powerful happiness. Since James? Since before James? Had she ever felt it before? Too long, too long, she told herself silently, and slid into sleep triumphant.

* * *

She waited all week, wondering when she might hear from Owen. She had no doubt that Jack would have wasted little time approaching him. With each day that passed, she was sure that he would have spoken with Owen and that any hour Owen would show up at her door. When he finally did come, she was ready. He would not tell her how to think or whom to care for again.

On the morning that Owen came, however, he had not only Edward but LeeAnn with him as well. The two carriages pulled up in the muddy street as it was raining lightly, and both of them rushed in, LeeAnn quickly embracing her and shaking the rain off her umbrella.

"The levee is going to go at any time," Owen said worriedly. "Natchez will likely be safe, but there may be so many refugees from up north, it could be dangerous for you to be here alone. They're saying more rain is coming, a big storm by tonight sometime. I think we should all go out to Graced Ground until this damned rain lets up. The farther all of us are from the Mississippi, the better I'll feel."

"I think he's right," Edward said.

"And I can't hardly look at that river without worrying!" she said. "Mama, hurry and let's go before the rains start again hard this afternoon."

No mention at all of Jack! She did not feel she could bring it up with Edward and LeeAnn right there, so she hurriedly packed what she might need for a week's stay, put Esme into Owen's carriage, and they drove out of town.

Once they were on the road with Edward driving behind them, she said, "Did John Duncan come to see you this week?"

Owen grimaced. "Yes, of course he did. I suppose I might have expected the man would not decamp and go away quietly."

She smiled to herself.

"Look, Filly, I'm not going to get into a frenzy over

this,'' he said with some annoyance. "You're a grown woman, and you're quite obviously going to do whatever you want. If you wish to throw yourself away on this man, then I can scarcely stop you."

"I hardly think that's what I'm doing," she began worriedly. "What did he say?"

"Nothing that I didn't expect. He cares for you and he wishes to continue to care for you. Nothing so terrible in that, I suppose. After all, I'm not your father or your husband, I'm only your big brother."

"Well, I don't want to do anything which would upset anyone," she said uncertainly.

"The man likely will propose to you, Filly, I guess you know as much. And it will be up to you to decide if that's the sort of man you want to marry. Personally, I can't say that I think he's suitable, but you're a mature woman, a widow with a grown, married daughter. If you think that's your best course of action, then by all means—"

"I didn't say I was going to marry the man," she said quietly. She wondered why this was not going as she'd expected. She thought Owen would forbid him the house; she would defiantly proclaim herself perfectly capable of selecting her own companions, and they would have a glorious, wonderful battle from which she would emerge victorious. Instead, she felt small and confused again. Almost as though she should apologize for caring for anyone at all.

The triumphant voice of defiance was muted in her, but not completely silenced. Something told her that this was still a battle, even if it did not appear to be so in the moment. "What did he say?"

"He said that he was in love with you," Owen said shortly. "Though how he could be in such a short time, I can scarcely fathom."

"You mean, it should take quite a bit of time to be able to love me," she murmured.

"No," he said impatiently. "I mean it takes a bit of time to love *anyone*. It's not something that happens overnight.

Before you love someone, you discover who they are. Who their family is. Whether or not they will fit into your life. Whether they are a good *choice* for you, or not. And if they are, you get to know them first. And then, perhaps, you grow to love them.''

"I sometimes wonder,'' she said.

"Well, I don't doubt you do,'' he said shortly. "You've had a lot on your mind lately, what with LeeAnn getting married and you moving to Commerce Street, and the rain and all. No wonder you feel a bit confused.''

"I'm not confused,'' she said.

"Well, lonely then. The change of scene will do you good. And if this damn rain keeps up, perhaps we'll all take a holiday someplace dry! Get up there!'' he shouted to the mare, yanking on the reins. The roads were full of mud and rushing water, and she was balking at fording a deep rut.

"Just give her her head,'' Felicity said, "let her find her own footing. Else she'll buck—''

Owen snapped, "If she doesn't get up, we'll spend the night here in the mud,'' and he yanked on the reins again, pulling the mare to one side and then urging her forward. She finally struggled to pull the carriage up and out of the rushing water, away from the worst places in the road, and they continued again. Felicity looked back to see that Edward was following Owen's example.

"What don't you like about him?'' she asked then.

"John Duncan?'' Owen asked, as though he had thought the conversation finished. "I already told you, Filly. The man's not our sort. He's a cheap gambler and a scalawag with women.''

She flushed angrily, as though she herself had been insulted.

"I'm sorry,'' he said, seeing her face. "You asked me, and I've told you.''

"And yet, you invited him to our home.''

"And I wish I hadn't, believe me. That's why I feel responsible for you now, I suppose.'' He sighed and turned to look at her with a rueful smile. "Look, Filly, I don't mean to sound harsh, really I don't. But Jack Duncan's not your kind. He can buy a big plantation, but that doesn't make him one of us. He might own Whitewood, but he's still poor white trash. He's got all the trappings, but he's not a gentleman. He's got new money and new horses and new clothes, but he's not—suitable. If Father were alive, he'd say the same thing. He's a carpetbagger, plain and simple. He might not be a Yankee, but he's an outsider, even so. Mother wouldn't like him, I can tell you that."

"I wonder," Felicity said. After a long pause she added, "So. You're taking me away so that he can't find me."

"No. I'm taking you to Graced Ground where the river can't find you, and I hope, in the process, it cools him off a little, too. If it doesn't, and you still receive him, well, it's your funeral."

With that, they drove for most of the rest of the trip in silence.

Felicity was appalled at the state of things at Graced Ground. The water was high in the fields, the trees looked so heavy with rain, they drooped almost to the ground. Several larger trees were actually uprooted and lying across one another, defeated by the soggy ground and the low-lying water. The flowers were gone, blasted by winds and mildewed to mush in the rose garden. The cotton looked bedraggled, but at least it was still standing. The horses stood in mud up to their hocks, and the chickens were so wet and muddy, they looked like guinea fowl.

Even the Big House looked melted, as though the sheer weight of the water on the roof had somehow made it sink deeper in the mud. The porch steamed, and the wisteria round the columns was so deep and wild, she could scarcely see the door.

"Lord, Owen," she said, shaking her head. "What a

mess. It'll take a month of dry weather to put things right again.''

"I know," he said glumly. "And if we get much more, the cotton'll rot in the fields. The only consolation is that every other farmer in the county has the same problem. So at least, if we can bring in a crop, we'll get a good price for it.''

They pulled the carriages up right ahead of the rain, which began to fall more heavily just as they reached the house. Felicity, Esme, and LeeAnn ran for the porch, leaving Owen and Edward to bring the bags and put up the horses. Alva met them at the door with warm embraces.

"I'm so glad you came," she said to Felicity, kissing her on the cheek. "I've been sick with worry, with you in Natchez all alone. That river could go at any time.''

"The bluffs will keep Natchez safe," Felicity said, "but Vidalia across the river is already under a foot of water, and God only knows what will happen upstream. Owen says the levee's going to go anytime.''

"Edward says it'll go someplace south of Vicksburg," LeeAnn said, embracing Alva. "I've never seen rain like this in my life!''

"Well, it's better we're together under one roof," Alva said. "Will, come kiss your grandmama and your auntie," she added as he loped into the room. Will had grown a foot, it seemed, this last summer. From a young boy of ten, he was suddenly a young man of fourteen, and he threatened to top Owen any day. He hugged the two women and then began to help Owen and Edward with the bags as they came through the door.

"My goodness," LeeAnn said admiringly as she watched them go up the stairs, "Willy's going to be one long drink of water, isn't he?''

"Yes, indeed." Alva smiled. "And he's just as cocky as my ol' banty rooster these days. If the rain ever stops, I'm going to put him out to plow, just to take some of the spark out of him. That boy drives me crazy, cooped up like this!''

The women retired to their rooms to unpack and rest, and

Felicity sat and watched the rain come down. She played
Owen's words over and over in her head. Cheap gambler.
White trash. Scalawag. Not our kind. Not like us.

A memory came back to her then, of visiting the hostler
with her father when she was just a girl. The man was so
good with horses and mules, it didn't pay to train a slave to
shoe, when a white man did it faster and better.

Ol' Tom, her father called him, and he looked as though
he'd been shoeing mules since dirt. The mules calmed
around him like sleepy spoiled cats, and he could shoe a
mule faster than most men could saddle one horse. She came
into his stable with her father that day, and Ol' Tom had a
mule leaning hard on him, one hoof in his hand, a few shoe
nails in his mouth, trimming that big hoof so he could fit the
shoe. Sweat poured down Ol' Tom's face and into his eyes.
"Get off, Captain," Ol' Tom was saying to the mule, and
trying to shove him off his shoulder. But that big mule
leaned all the more. "Push on this mule," Ol' Tom said to
her father. "The sonofabitch's like to squash me flat."

Her father had cleared his throat hard at Ol' Tom then, as
he slapped the mule on the hindquarters to let him know he
was there and gave him a hard shove off Ol' Tom. The mule
swiveled his eye sideways at Felicity and moaned a bit,
wheezing and sliding slightly off Ol' Tom. Tom glanced up
and saw her there and said, "Sorry, young miss. Don' pay
me no mind."

White trash, that's what Ol' Tom was; she knew it before
her father told her. A good man, for what he was, but not our
kind.

Jack loved her, Owen said. He'd said it to her own
brother, even though she wasn't there to hear it. That took
some courage. She bowed her head and looked at her hands.
It seemed to her that they were getting drier this year, even
though everything else around her was replete with moisture. She took a small pinch of skin from the back of her
hand, squeezed it gently, and then let it go. It took a while for
the skin to settle back down onto her bones. My very skin is

losing life, she realized then, watching her hands slowly roll and clench and move in the dim light. The spots were coming out on them, just like Mama had. What did Grandmama say she did to keep hers young? Slept with them in lemon and buttermilk? Yes, and never did a lick of work either. But those days were gone.

Regret is the bitterest medicine of all, she thought. How could I have come so far in my life and have so little to show for it?

The rain was coming hard now, and she sighed heavily, looking out the window. It was difficult to imagine that it would ever stop, so many weeks of wet had they endured. Well, there was no use in sitting here brooding, she told herself impatiently. There must be something Alva needs doing, some way I can be useful at least. And a whispering voice in her heart added, if I can't be loved.

That afternoon, the water rose higher than it had to date, and they kept gathering on the veranda to watch where it was coming from the Saint Catherine. "My guess is the levee north went," Owen said "And it's flooded the rivers all over. This one's over its banks now."

"If the levee had gone, it'd be over our heads," Edward said. "That levee holds back a mighty big part of the Mississippi, and there's no place for it to go but south."

"You mean, what we're seeing here is just from the rain?" LeeAnn asked him fearfully.

"I think so," Edward said, shaking his head. "But we're still better off here, farther from the river, than we would be in town."

All during the rest of the day, they kept coming out to the porch to see where the water had risen. First, it was up the brick path, then up the steps. As it got within inches of the porch, Owen said, "I think we best move some of the furniture to the second floor, Will."

"Oh no, do you really think so?" Alva cried.

"Those oriental carpets of Mama's!" Felicity gasped. "She'd have a fit if we ruined those."

"She's likely getting her own feet wet right now," Owen said grimly.

They all stopped and looked at him. Felicity hadn't even thought of the chapel and the graves beyond it. They sat in lower ground than the Big House. No doubt, they'd been flooded since morning. With that, they all set to work feverishly, moving lamps, carpets, pulling down drapes, shouldering the furniture up the stairs to the rooms where they could just squeeze it all in, humble-jumble, until the waters went down.

As she came down the stairs for the dozenth time, Felicity heard a halloo outside and the sound of a horse struggling through water. She peered outside the wet windowpane and saw Jack Duncan dismounting, up to his knees in the muddy current. He pulled his horse up the steps to the veranda, looped the reins over the railing, and even then, his horse stood in six inches of moving mud. Felicity raced down the stairs and opened the door before Owen or Edward could do it first.

"What in the world!" she called to him as he reached the door. "How did you get here!"

"That's the best mare in the county," he said. "I can't believe she made it, but we stuck to high ground until we got to the river. It's over the bank in at least three places."

"I know, Edward and Owen insisted I come out here, but I don't know that I'm any better off than in town."

"Oh you are," he said, "Commerce Street is up more than three feet. I was ready to rescue you there, if I had to." Then he took her in his arms. "But here will do just as well."

"I can't believe you came all this way," she said, pulling away from him and glancing over his shoulder nervously. "Owen said he spoke with you."

"Yes, and I told him how I feel," Jack said firmly. "I'm not going to sit over at Whitewood and wonder if you're floating down to New Orleans on a spar, Lacey."

"Don't call me that around my brother," she pleaded.

"Why not? That's your name, isn't it?" He grinned and brushed past her into the foyer. "Looks like we're getting ready for the worst," he said as he saw Owen and Edward coming down the stairs. "The river's breached, boys," he said. "I think we better think hard and fast about higher ground."

Edward glanced at Owen, his jaw stiff. "We've already given that some thought, Mr. Duncan. How did you get here?"

"On my mare," he said, going to the window to glance out. "I swear, she's part fish."

"More importantly," Owen said quietly, "*Why* did you come?"

Jack turned back to face the two men, his face suddenly dark with anger. "Because I thought it the neighborly thing to do," he said shortly. "Now, suppose we discuss my vulgarities at some other time. We've got two women in a house that's fixing to float downriver at any moment."

"Nonsense," Owen said, descending the stairs. "This house will stand against more than a flood."

As he spoke, the front door pushed open, and a wave of water more than two feet high rushed into the downstairs, two windows broke, and Felicity screamed, struggling for the stairs. Jack grabbed her arm and pulled her forward bodily, half-lifting, half-pushing her up the staircase before him. They stopped and looked down when they were halfway up. The entire first floor was awash now with moving mud, water, branches, and floating debris. Two walls seemed to bulge inward against the pressure. As they watched in horror, they could see the level rising visibly.

"My God, the levee must have gone!" Owen said in horror.

LeeAnn and Alva came to the top of the stairs and screamed when they saw the water. "Mama, how will we get out?" LeeAnn called anxiously.

"We won't," Edward said to her staunchly, rushing up the stairs. "The water will never rise as high as the second story, I don't care how many levees go. We'll be safer here than anyplace else." He embraced her, but she looked over her shoulder down at the rising water in fear.

Will came to the landing and called, "It's up over the fenceposts! Your horse swam away, Mister Duncan!"

"Good for her," Jack said calmly. He turned to Felicity, his voice lower. "I fear he's wrong. We won't be safer here once the water weakens the bottom floor. The whole house could go in a flash."

"What should we do?" she turned to him.

"Get out before it falls down on our ears," he said. "We'd be better off in small boats or a raft."

"That's crazy," Owen said angrily. "To leave the shelter of a house for a raft—even if we had such a thing." He took his sister's arm and began to lead her up to the second floor. "Come on, Felicity. We better get some blankets together and make ourselves as comfortable as we can."

"We can make rafts of these doors," Jack said, smacking his hand on one which led into a bedroom. "Solid cypress, knowing your grandfather, and they'll float good as any canoe."

"I'm not risking my wife's life on some makeshift raft," Edward said shortly. "I imagine if you had a wife, Mr. Duncan, you'd feel the same."

Jack swore then, under his breath, and turned to Felicity, ignoring the rest of them. "Look, do you trust me? I tell you, this house won't stand against the river, and the river's coming for us now. Now, Lacey! We've got to get out while we still can. Once the water rises too high, we won't be able to make a raft, we won't be able to get to the doors, we'll be neck deep by nightfall." He put his hands on her shoulders. "Do you trust me?"

She nodded, mesmerized by his intensity.

He turned and went back to the landing where he could see the water below. He called back to the others. "It's up at least two feet higher than ten minutes ago! We don't have

time to argue about this. Let's build the rafts at least, and if
we don't have to use them, then I'll eat them, one by one.''

"That would be a relatively useless gesture," Owen said
coldly. "But if you're so sure, Jack, perhaps you'd like to
make a more sporting wager." He glanced at Edward, who
grinned wryly. "You are a sporting man, are you not?"

Jack only glared at him.

"Let's say, we build the rafts, just as you insist. And if the
water rises so that we must use them, you will have earned
our undying gratitude and respect. But if they don't, you will
be shown up for the reckless fool some say you are. And of
course, you will no longer be welcomed in any home which
houses a member of this family. Agreed?''

"Jack, don't . . " Felicity moaned, taking his arm.

He smiled down at her, patting her hand. "Don't worry,
my lady, if there's one thing I know, it's the river." He
bowed cordially to Owen. "Agreed. With one priviso. If I
save your hide, Mr. Howard, you'll deed the house on Commerce Street to your sister, and you'll be best man at our
wedding." His grin was wide and charming, as though they
stood in a ballroom with champagne instead of huddled on a
landing watching waters rise at an alarming pace.

To Felicity's surprise, Owen laughed aloud, shaking his
head. "You are impossible, sir. I can see that you've earned
your reputation."

"You may insult me all you like, Mr. Daniels, so long as
you keep your word. May I have it, then?"

Owen matched his bow. "You may."

"For God's sake," Alva said, "we don't have time for
this! Do something, Owen!"

Jack immediately turned to the nearest door and called
Will to him. "We're going to take this thing off its hinges,
boy, and we're going to do it quick. And then we're going to
tie it to another one and lift it off the second-story balcony."

"We have no rope," Owen said calmly.

Jack ignored him. "We'll use the linens to tie the thing

together, and we'll make it big enough to float all of us to safety.''

"I don't know if I can do this, Edward," LeeAnn moaned, leaning against him.

"Don't worry, you won't have to," he said to her staunchly. "I'll not allow it. Not in your condition."

Felicity whirled around from watching Jack and Will at work and said, "Oh, LeeAnn, no! Not yet!"

LeeAnn nodded miserably. "We were so happy, I was waiting to tell you."

"We're still happy," Edward said firmly. "And you and my child will be safe and sound right here at Graced Ground, you'll see. Now go into that bedroom and rest, dear. I'll not have you getting all excited for nothing."

Will and Jack had removed two doors and wrestled them into a room and laid them on the floor. Felicity left them long enough to look down the staircase again. The water was two feet higher than it had been before. Another few feet, and she would be unable to see any of the downstairs walls at all. The staircase felt wobbly under her feet, and she kept close to the wall of the landing. She went then into her bedroom and stared out at the vast sea which stretched as far as she could see all around the house. Treetops were all that protruded up from the waters. The tops of the stable and barn were still showing, but she saw no animals, no plants, nothing but uprooted roots and trees and debris floating by in the murky current.

"The horses!" she called to Owen in despair.

"They were loose in the field," he called back to her. "I'm certain they swam to safety." He was bending over the doors now with Will and Jack as they struggled to position them and tie them together. "This will never hold more than two people," she heard him mutter to Jack.

"We'll add more doors," Jack said.

"We'll never get it out the window."

Jack grimaced. "You're right. We'll make three of them."

It struck Felicity, in that moment, that they were going to lose everything in the house. All the furnishings, all the paintings, all the clothing, the linens, everything would be ruined. Her throat closed tightly, and she felt unable to catch her breath. And then she remembered: LeeAnn was with child. If they were not very brave and clever and fortunate, they might lose far more than her grandmother's furnishings.

An odd groaning began from the bowels of the house, a creaking, shifting complaint which was more frightening than the sight of so much water around it. LeeAnn began to weep quietly in the other room, and Felicity went to her.

"Mama, I'm afraid," she said miserably. "I try not to be, but I am." She was keeping her voice down lest Edward hear her. Felicity glanced out at the hall where the men were now enlarging the raft with two more doors, moving it to the double doors of the largest bedroom so that they might get it out on the second-story balcony. She put her body between LeeAnn and them. This is the way it's always been, she thought swiftly. You give up your self, your soul, your life to become your child's guide to her own life. I wouldn't have missed this for anything, she realized. It humbled me and stretched me and awakened me to love in a way I'd allow no man to do. This child gave me whatever small spans of wisdom I possess. But she's no longer a child; she's a woman carrying a child of her own.

Felicity hugged LeeAnn hard. "I know, sweetheart," she murmured, "but I think we're going to be all right. The water will go down as fast as it came up, and we'll just paddle a few miles east, and I'm sure we'll find dry ground."

"All my things—all your things, too—everything's going to be ruined," she wept. "Edward wouldn't let me take a thing with me!"

"He was right, dear. Everything can be replaced, and we're better off than most."

As she spoke, a wretched, muffled screech came from the bottom floor of the house, from the very walls, and they felt the house lurch slightly to one side slowly, like a melting wedding cake built too tall and set in the sun.

"Oh, Mama!" LeeAnn screamed, clutching her arm.

"Shush now," Felicity soothed her, pulling her up off the bed. "Any upset at this stage is bad for the baby, LeeAnn. Try to stay calm."

"Lacey!" she heard Jack call, and she looked up to see him beckoning from the hall. "You've got to come now and bring LeeAnn with you."

"No, you stay right there," Edward said angrily. "We're not leaving this house." He came to the door and blocked it with his body, as if to keep the two women captive.

"Don't be a fool, man," Jack said swiftly. "This house is going to be nothing but floating spars in moments."

"You're the fool here," Edward said. "I can't keep Mrs. Daniels here, if she's crazy enough to listen to you, but I damn well sure can keep LeeAnn safe, and I mean to do exactly that."

Felicity left LeeAnn's side and went to Jack, brushing Edward aside. Jack put his arm around her. "I don't want to alarm you, honey," he said calmly, "but we really don't have time to discuss this anymore. The rafts are ready, and we must get to high ground while we still can."

Felicity turned in fear. One raft lay on the floor, ready to be lowered away. It was only three doors tied together, scarcely large enough, it seemed to her, to hold Jack alone, much less anyone with him. Behind him, she could see that Owen was already helping Will out the window. He was holding to a rope made of bed linens and lowering himself down to the second waiting raft below. Alva stood by Owen's side, pale but silent. Her eyes never left Will as he descended.

"Oh God," Felicity moaned, leaning suddenly into Jack's body. "Do you really think we must do this?"

"We have no choice," he said quietly. "Make your daughter listen to me, Lacey. You can convince her."

She looked back to see Owen now, helping Alva to climb

out onto the window sill and take the linen rope in her hands. He was murmuring words of comfort to her, and as she descended, he looked up at his sister and grimaced. She could read the fear in his face, but he said nothing. Then he leaned far out of the window to call to Will on the raft below. Felicity could not hear the boy's response, but when Owen pulled his head back in, he shouted to Jack, "He says it's a foot higher than when he went down!"

Felicity did not wait to hear another word. She turned and pushed Edward's arm aside, ignoring him completely. She went to LeeAnn and knelt beside her on the bed. Already, she could feel the perilous tilt to the floor under her feet, and it seemed to her that the whole house was listing alarmingly, more each moment. "LeeAnn, you must come now," she said. "They've got two rafts, and they're big enough to hold us all. Alva and Will are already out there, and Owen's right behind them. They say the water's higher by a foot than it was a few minutes ago."

Edward said stiffly, "Mrs. Daniels, I must protest this decision. My wife and I are staying here at Graced Ground. I implore you to reconsider and stay with us."

Felicity turned and smiled sadly at him. "Edward, I know you're trying to do what you think best, but you're the only one here who seems to think we should stay. Owen's already loaded his family, and I'm going with Jack. Now please, don't risk LeeAnn's life by making her stay here with you alone. If we're going to drown, let's do it together at least."

He scoffed angrily. "No one's going to drown, Mrs. Daniels, not if we keep our heads. Of course, if we run off like half-cocked fools, I can't make any promises as to our safety. But I still maintain this house is the safest place for a dozen miles."

"And I say, you're taking a hell of a chance with the woman you love," Jack said shortly. "A chance I won't take. Lacey, we've got to go."

"Mama!" LeeAnn cried out, clutching to her mother's arm. "Don't leave me here!"

"Come with us," Felicity said softly. "Come on, sweet-heart. Get up this minute, and come along. We don't have time to argue about it anymore."

As she spoke, the house jerked a second time, shuddering and settling even more to the low side, and the bed LeeAnn was on shifted and slid sharply across the floor several feet, accompanied by a low rumble from the timbers of the house and a scream from LeeAnn. She leaped to her feet and into her mother's arms. Felicity pulled her quickly to the window before Edward could react, and Jack began to wrestle the raft out the window.

"LeeAnn!" Edward shouted. "Don't do this! I forbid it!"

"Come and help me, man!" Jack shouted. "I can't do this alone!"

The house was settling away from the window, and now it was more difficult to get the raft up and outside.

LeeAnn turned then and cried out to her husband, "Edward, come and help us! I won't stay in this house another minute!"

"LeeAnn! I told you—"

"I don't care, I don't care!" she screamed. "I'm not staying here without my mother! Now come on this minute!"

Cursing, he came forward and yanked one end of the raft up, shoving it out the window. "Damn you, Duncan," he hissed. "If anything happens to her, I'll kill you, I swear it."

"If anything happens to her, I'll likely be sleeping with the catfish anyhow," Jack answered calmly. "So have at it."

They shoved the raft out the window and let it drop to the water below. "Come on, Lacey," Jack called, "you come right after me." Before she could speak, he had jumped down from the sill into space.

She rushed to the window and looked out. Jack was on the raft below, hanging on to a rope. Owen held the other end fast. His own raft, with Alva and Will aboard, was tied to the top of the cypress tree which had always shaded the bedroom side of Graced Ground. Now, only the topmost branches were standing out of the water. They were only about ten feet below her, drifting slowly in a swirling lake of muddy, moving water.

She turned back to Edward and LeeAnn, amazed. "Why, there's nothing but water and treetops far as you can see," she said.

"Come on, Lacey," Jack called. "Can you jump?" There was almost an excited challenge in his voice.

"Of course I can," she said firmly. And she climbed out on the sill. Grabbing the rope, she lowered herself gingerly to the raft and his helping hands below. Then she called up to LeeAnn, "Come on, sweetheart! It's easy!"

A flash of skirts and petticoats, and then LeeAnn was backing slowly down the wall of the house, which was tilting away from the water. She held firm to the rope and did not look down. When she got close, Jack handed Felicity the tie rope and eased LeeAnn down to the raft. "Just sit there and get comfortable," he said to her amiably. "We won't be on this thing longer than we have to be."

Edward came right behind her, glowering fiercely. "The whole staircase just went," he said. "Whole damn thing. Just slid away like matchsticks."

Jack didn't say a word, just took the rope from Felicity's hands and called to Owen, "I think we should get away from the house!"

He knelt on the raft and began to paddle with one of the boards from another door, gesturing to Edward to do the same on his side. Owen and Will paddled the other raft, and the two tiny arks moved out away from the leaning house, away from the cypress tree, and out into the wide water.

They tried to keep as close to each other as they could, calling back and forth, maneuvering around branches, tangles of drowned treetops, and floating debris. Both rafts were tipsy with the movements of the passengers, and after warning the women several times, it was clear they could do

nothing but sit very quietly in the center of each raft and do
their best not to move at all, else they'd all be in the water.

Owen said immediately, "We've got to row away from
the house and follow that line of trees to the east. There'll be
less water the farther we go."

"Yes!" Felicity cried, pointing to the dark line of what
looked to be shrubs on an open plain. "That's the line of
trees on the road to the Trace. Follow that, Jack!"

"And how far do we paddle this thing?" Edward asked,
pushing away a floating, drowned dog with his board and a
hard grimace. "We don't have a stick of food or water or
even a blanket between us."

"We won't have to go far," Jack said. "Maybe only a
few miles before we reach high enough ground to wait this
out. The first house we see on dry land, we stop."

"But there aren't any houses out this way," LeeAnn said
quietly. "Nothing between us and the Trace, except a few
little ol' croppers' cabins."

"There're the mounds," Felicity said, suddenly sitting up
and calling to Owen across the moving water. "Owen! The
mound! We can make for the mound!"

Jack laughed, shaking his head. "I forgot about that old
pile of dirt. What a head you've got on those beautiful shoulders, Lacey."

Owen shouted over, "That's three miles or more!"

"We can make it!" Jack shouted back. "We've got more
than six hours of daylight left!" He turned the raft in the
water so that it angled down the row of trees and put his
shoulder to the paddle with a will.

Felicity pulled LeeAnn closer to her and nestled her head
down on her shoulder. "Try to rest now," she murmured.
"The men will get us there safely. You don't have to do a
thing but hold on."

"I'm wet clear through to the bone," her daughter whispered. "Are you?"

Felicity nodded. "Maybe you should take off those skirts

and use them as blankets. They'll dry faster, away from your body.''

"Edward wouldn't like that," LeeAnn murmured. "When we reach dry land, perhaps we can have a fire, and then I'll do it.''

Felicity wondered if the men even had a match between them, but she kept her doubts to herself, pulling LeeAnn closer and gazing out over the waters as the girl closed her eyes.

The water around them was as vast as a sea, and the tallest trees looked, from a distance, like small ships on the horizon with masts jutting into the sky. Somehow, she could not believe that they were in any real danger, even though the water was deep, churned, and full of a thousand things of peril. With Jack and Edward and Owen, how could anything too dreadful happen, after all, she asked herself. But then she recalled that the most dreadful things could happen, had happened, no matter who held the paddle, no matter who gave commands.

The water looked as though it had no end, as if it intended to stay on for the rest of time. For all of her life, she had lived near the great river, watched the Mississippi in flood and drought, admired its shimmering path as it swept past Natchez and down south to more exotic, strange, and wondrous places. Always she had felt its presence, but never its peril.

She could recall so clearly when James was courting her, how they liked to walk along the Mississippi, watching as the moonlight changed the water to pale silver, against which the trees at Vidalia were black and distinct. River lights, set to mark each mile and bend and point, twinkled like fireflies, and frogs' eyes on the shore edge caught the lights and glinted green. Usually, there was a low-lying fog on the opposite bank which rose above the trees and hung, mysterious and ethereal, wavering over the water.

Always at the water, life seemed to beat with a faster pulse. Dragonflies darted and hovered over the cattails and rushes, and bird song was thicker and more varied. The heavy, damp scent of the river, the smell of wet mud and swampy grasses and cypress, of sycamores and sedges and willows and wild blossoms, all of it was the river, and all of it was life.

When it rained, she had walked along the river when it was at crest. She saw how it ate away at the land, gnawing steadily with slashing teeth into a caving bank and toppling trees into its waters. Then it tossed great chunks of brown foam like floating filthy bread on the current, to show that another bank had gone into its belly, to be built up somewhere else, farther downstream.

So many gray days recently, so much rain. The clouds were heavy still, though the downpour had stopped for the moment. She sent a silent prayer to the clouds to go elsewhere. It seemed to Felicity that it had been months of rain, years of rain, with the rain vanishing in the gray river, a dim world of moisture, a world of water, and she could scarcely imagine the sun anymore at all.

It came to her then, as it had before, and this time with an ache so deep that she all but cried aloud, how long she had been without love. How little of love she knew, really. Even though her mother had gently encouraged her to allow love again in her life, had tried to show her what she was missing, still she had glumly refused to admit that such a possibility could be. But as the Chinese said, "A frog in a well can't be talked to about the sea." Like that frog, she had to leave the well, to step out into the sun and set out for the sea. But choosing to leave the well was so frightening!

"That's a whole lot of water," Edward said suddenly in the silence, gazing out over the horizon as he paddled.

Felicity glanced at him, almost surprised at his nearness, her thoughts had wandered so. All of them had fallen into a sort of reverie, and the world had slipped away.

"Yes, and you're only seeing the top of it," Jack said ruefully.

"How much farther, do you figure?" Edward asked.

Felicity was surprised to hear Edward address Jack with

anything but animosity. She smiled to herself, despite the ache in her shoulder, holding up LeeAnn's dozing head.

"Probably another two miles. Maybe less. We can go as the crow flies, at any rate," Jack said.

"I wish," Edward replied.

They rowed for what seemed like hours, as the sun came and went. The rain had stopped, and Felicity dozed off and on, leaning against LeeAnn. A shout then came up from Owen, whose raft had pulled ahead of them by several hundred yards. They had spotted the mound. As they pulled closer, Felicity could see it dimly in the distance, through the haze and the clouds. The sun was actually trying to break past the gray cover in small, scattered places. And there, off to the right, she could barely make out the rise of the great earthen edifice which had been their gathering place for as long as she could remember. It was above water.

The men pulled hard on their paddles then, and the rafts moved closer. Felicity saw, swimming close to them for a moment or two, a long black snake. A moccasin. She shivered and looked away. No sense in saying anything. When she looked back at Jack, she saw that he was steadfastedly focused on the mound ahead, and she willed herself to think of nothing else but deliverance.

The raft only barely kept them out of the water, and they were largely wet clear through from the sloshings and the water bubbling up between the doors. She was frankly surprised it held them as well as it did, and as they neared the mound, she saw that it was beginning to edge apart in places. The current was swifter, too, as they got closer to the mound, as though the water was angry at having to go around something, was determined to try to take it down along with all the rest of the world it had overwhelmed.

"We'll need to watch for whirlpools as we get closer," Jack said suddenly, as though he had read her thoughts. "The current is deceptive here."

"You seem to know a lot about these waters, Mr. Duncan," Edward said.

Jack glanced at him, decided it was an innocent-enough comment, and said, "I've seen whirlpools on the Mississippi which were more than three hundred feet across and thirty feet deep. Scared hell out of the pilots, I can tell you. Boiling demons, some of them, and they could suck in a steamboat down to the pipes."

"But this isn't the Mississippi," Felicity said faintly, anxiously.

Jack turned and smiled. "No, my dear, it's not. Or if it is, it bears no resemblance to the river you knew. We won't see anything so fearsome as all that today, but still, it's good to watch for snags and eddies, for we're short on deckchairs and lifeboats."

LeeAnn woke then and glanced about for Edward immediately. "Are we there yet?" she asked him.

"Soon," he said, straining even harder on the oars.

They could see that Owen had made it to the mound, and even though the waters were moving by it swiftly, he was able to leap onto the land and pull the raft close enough so that Will was able to follow him. As Felicity watched, they struggled and maneuvered the little ark until Alva was able to jump off it, into Owen's arms. Owen then stood up and shouted to them, "Be careful of the current! It's more treacherous here than it looks!"

Emerald Mound loomed close to them now, and Jack and Edward paddled even more strenuously. LeeAnn huddled so near to Felicity that she could feel the tremor of her body when her heart beat. "Thank God," her daughter murmured as they pulled close enough for Edward to jump off the raft and pull by a loose linen cording toward the mud of the rising earth.

Owen was ushering Will and Alva to the highest part of the plateau; Felicity could see him go over the hill and then disappear up on top. Jack was holding tightly to the frayed linen connecting them to Edward, and he reached with his other hand to her. "Come on, Lacey, and watch the mud, it's slick as pig grease."

"Take off your shoes!" Edward called out. "I near sank to my knees!"

Felicity rose to her knees and struggled with her shoes, and LeeAnn did the same. She yanked them off and threw them desperately toward the hill, but one fell into the moving water. "Oh!" Felicity wailed. "Jack, my shoe!"

"Let it go," he said firmly, "and hurry now, this raft won't hold forever." He pulled her forward with one hand while he tried to keep the loosely tied boards level. With each step she made toward him, it tilted crazily in the rushing current. He half-pulled, half-pushed her onto land, and she stumbled, slipping in the mud and almost falling to her knees.

Right behind her, he jumped, his feet disappearing into the deep muck half up his calves. His weight caused the side of the mound to begin to slide inexorably downward, caving into the water. He leaped back, pushing Felicity behind him and upward toward Edward. "Come on, LeeAnn!" he shouted. "Hurry up!"

Edward was struggling now to get to the raft, having dropped his cord since Jack was holding the other one fast. But the rise was slick and precarious, and he called out, "LeeAnn! Keep low on your knees!"

LeeAnn was crawling to the edge of the raft toward Jack's hand, but he had to move back from the edge of the water as the earth was giving way. In an instant, the imbalance of her weight tilted the raft, and she tumbled into the water, her skirts rolling over her head.

Felicity screamed and darted toward the raft, but Jack shouted, "Keep back! It's caving in!," and he dropped to his knees to get closer to the raft. Owen was hurrying down the rise, and Edward was shouting LeeAnn's name, trying to get to the edge of the water through the mud. LeeAnn surfaced once, grabbing at the raft, covered with muddy, rushing water, screamed out, "Mother!," and then went under again. Jack desperately yanked himself from the grip of the mud and leaped into the water before Felicity could answer her daughter's call. When she saw Jack disappear into the current, she screamed his name, and Owen pushed her back, trying to find solid purchase on the caving bank.

LeeAnn was being carried round the side of the mound, pulled under by the current which hugged the rise as though it wanted to wipe it clean. Her hands and head came up, went down, came up again, and Jack was struggling furiously to get to her, pushing aside the water and debris with one arm as he swam with the other. Frantically, Felicity called to them both, unable to move to keep them in sight, and Edward was stumbling to higher ground so that he might hurry along the rise to keep up with their pace.

They rounded the mound, and Felicity could see them no more. She screamed, "LeeAnn! My God, Owen, do something!" and struggled to wrest herself from the unsolid, shifting ground to follow Edward up and around. Owen yanked her arm hard, pushed her forward, and they hurried up to drier ground, Felicity weeping in fear. When they ran down the rise to the other side, Alva and Will hurrying to join them, they saw Edward and Jack on their knees on the sodden bank, bending over LeeAnn.

"Thank God, thank God!" Felicity cried as she saw they were at least out of the water and on solid ground. Edward's face was contorted with fear and anguish, Jack was working over LeeAnn, struggling to roll her over. He was covered with mud, his face nearly unrecognizable, but she saw the flash of his teeth when he said, "Help me get her over, man! She's not breathing."

Felicity moaned in anguish and dropped to her knees next to her daughter's body, her hands to her mouth in horror. LeeAnn was white as her bodice, her eyes were closed, her face smeared with mud and lashed by some branch as though the river itself had clawed her. "LeeAnn!" she cried. "Oh, Jack! Jack! Save her!"

He rolled her over and pulled her arms over her head, leaning on her back with his elbows, grunting as he shoved her hard into the wet grass. Then he rolled her again on her side, calling her name and pushing at her back again, thumping her between her shoulders and shaking her. Felicity covered her eyes, weeping, for she could not bear to see her daughter's face another second. So white and still, not a flicker of answering resistance as Jack yanked her and pushed at her body.

"Oh, Christ, no!" Edward moaned, trying to clutch at her face and hands, but Jack ignored him, still thumping on LeeAnn's back and pushing at her belly. He rolled her violently on her back again and slapped her face firmly twice, calling her name loudly, and suddenly, she opened her mouth and spewed forth water, gasping and coughing and weeping all at once.

"LeeAnn!" Felicity wept, falling on her and trying to pull her into her lap.

"Honey, give her space to breathe," Jack murmured, encircling Felicity with his embrace.

Edward was holding his wife in an instant, pulling her close and comforting her as she continued to cough and gag. In a moment, LeeAnn opened her eyes and gazed up at him. She smiled when she saw his face.

And in that instant, Felicity realized that her daughter was truly a woman now and her child no more. When she was in peril, she may have called out for her mother, but when she was in need of comfort, it was to her husband that she turned.

It was fitting, Felicity told herself with great relief, settling into Jack's embrace. For she is part of a larger family now.

The sun was out. Felicity looked up at it in wonder, but then had to look away, blinded by its brilliance, unable even to make out its edges against the sky. It might go away again at any moment, but at least it was bright and warm for now. Only a fool, she told herself, refuses to walk in the sunlight because she can't see the shape of the sun. The streams of time, the current of life, had come together once more.

As LeeAnn began to rouse, Edward turned to Jack and

gruffly embraced him as well. "Thank you," he said, his voice graveled with emotion. When Jack smiled and nodded, Edward said, "I'd have killed you if anything happened to her."

Jack laughed. "I know that. I thought I'd better take my chances with the river."

Later that night, the men managed to gather enough wood and debris to start a small fire, with the matches Owen had tucked into his jacket pocket. Once they were almost dry and warm, it was easier to suppose they might actually see home again.

Felicity sat with Jack at the edge of the fire, leaning into his arms. "How long do you think we'll be here?" she asked. She kept her voice low, for the others were dozing, LeeAnn and Edward were wrapped together, Will sprawled with his head on Alva's lap, while she leaned on Owen's shoulder.

"I think the water'll be down by tomorrow. Maybe by to-morrow night, we can get back to Graced Ground," he murmured.

"How do you know so much about the river?" she asked.

He grinned. "That's one thing a gambler learns early, my dear. How to swim."

"That's one thing I never learned," she said, wonderingly. "Isn't that odd? All my life, I lived near the water, and I never thought of it as a dangerous thing. It was just always there. But I never learned to swim."

"Well, it's never too late," he said, holding her closer. "I can teach you, easy enough."

She looked up at him and smiled. In the firelight, he looked strong, appealing, and infinitely . . . appropriate. It occurred to her that just as life was a gift that came and went in its own time, so, too, the coming of love must be taken as an unfathomable gift that could not be questioned in its ways.

"I'd like that," she murmured. "You're right. It's not too late."

Epilogue

In the spring of 1983, a team of archeologists from the Mississippi Department of Archives and History began a two-year dig of the Fatherland Site to explore the mounds more thoroughly than earlier digs had accomplished. They were able to demonstrate convincingly that the Indian village site on Fatherland Plantation near Natchez did, indeed, mark the locality of the Grand Village of the Natchez Indians.

Previous excavations had proven that, between 1682 and 1729, this native village was the center of all tribal activities during the period of the establishment of the French settlement at their Natchez post. All best guesses put the population of the French at about 500 souls, the population of the Indian village at about 3500. To the great delight of researchers on site, particularly Dr. Barnard Swanton, they were able to pinpoint the location of the chief's house, the temple, their respective mounds, the burial of the Tattooed Serpent and the retainers sacrificed at his funeral in 1725, and the burial place of the Great Sun, who died in 1728.

But what still puzzled those who combed the site was the singular question: Why had the Indians built the mounds in the first place? They were not merely vast tombs, like those structures of the Egyptians, for burials often took place outside the mounds. They were not only vaults for valuables, although the Indians did bury there many objects of ritual significance, including an old Spanish sword and helmet, a steel hatchet bearing the fleur-de-lys of France, and curiously enough, some nineteenth-century ornaments with encrusted emeralds and antebellum silver pieces.

No, Dr. Swanton insisted, when his fellow archeologists confirmed the mounds as religious relics, the mounds had a more practical use, he was certain. He had studied carefully the writings of the old French explorers, the priests, and local officials, as well as the more famous visitors to the locality, including La Salle, Dumont de Montigny and Davion, Iberville, Bienville, and Hubert. Only after he traipsed the site again and again, however, did he discover that the present-day path of Saint Catherine Creek had altered dramatically from what it had been in the time of the Natchez village. Upon digging, it was obvious that the creek had, at least twice, flooded the village to such an extent that it had carried away part of the bottomland, half of the main mound of the village, likely all of the crops, and probably many of the huts of the natives.

Indeed, more recent floodings, like those of 1885 and again in 1929, when the Mississippi covered everything for miles, were dramatic examples of what the power of water had done to the land and its peoples.

Dr. Swanton took a chance and pinned his reputation on his belief that in the times of the Natchez people, Saint Catherine Creek had emptied into the Mississippi at Ellis Cliffs, or more than eight miles below its present outlet.

"In my considered opinion," Dr. Swanton wrote to the curators in charge, "the Natchez built the mounds as much for protection against high waters as for religious purposes. The Fatherland Site is less a tomb than an ark *in situ* for those surrounding natives who could reach it in time of flood."

Dr. Swanton's statement earned him the dismissive scorn of his peers, but he maintained for the rest of his professional career that the Indians of the Fatherland had at least as much respect for the water as they did for the sun.

Bibliography

The following texts were extremely helpful to me, some for only a single anecdote or fact, others for whole chapters of information about Natchez and her history. In addition to these sources, I should like to acknowledge the folks at the Historic Natchez Foundation on Commerce Street, who made me welcome and gave me enormous support for this effort.

Baldwin, Joseph G., *The Flush Times of Alabama and Mississippi,* Louisiana State University Press, Baton Rouge, LA, 1987.

Berlin, Ira, *Slaves Without Masters,* Vintage Books, Random House, NY, 1976.

Bettersworth, John Knox, *Confederate Mississippi, The People and Politics of a Cotton State in Wartime,* Louisiana State University Press, Baton Rouge, LA, 1943.

Bode, Carl, *Antebellum Culture,* Southern Illinois University Press, Carbondale, IL, 1959.

Brandfon, Robert L., *Cotton Kingdom of the New South, A History of the Yazoo Mississippi Delta from Reconstruction to the Twentieth Century,* Harvard University Press, Cambridge, MA, 1967.

Bunkers, Suzanne L. (editor), *Diary of Caroline Seabury,* University of Wisconsin Press, Madison, WI, 1991.

594 Bibliography

Catton, Bruce, *Reflections on the Civil War,* edited by John Leekley, Doubleday, New York, 1981.

Coates, Robert M., *The Outlaw Years: The History of the Land Pirates of the Natchez Trace,* Literary Guild, New York, 1930.

Collier, Louise Wilbourn, *Pilgrimage: A Tale of Old Natchez,* St. Luke's Press, Memphis, TN, 1982. (Ms. Collier's novel was an excellent source of inspiration and place names, adding to the texture of my work.)

Cooke, Grace (MacGowan), *Mistress Joy: A Tale of Natchez in 1798,* The Century Co., New York, 1901.

Cushman, Horatio Bardwell, *History of the Choctaw, Chickasaw and Natchez Indians,* 1962.

Davis, Edwin Adams, *The Barber of Natchez,* Kennikat Press, Port Washington, NY, 1972.

De Ville, Winston, *The Saint Catherine Colonists, 1719–1720,* Smith Books, Ville Platte, LA, 1991.

Dickson, Harris, *The Story of King Cotton,* Funk & Wagnalls Co., New York, 1937.

Dimond, E. Grey, and Herman Hattaway (editors), *Letters from Forest Place: A Plantation Family's Correspondence, 1846–1881,* University Press of Mississippi, Jackson, MS, 1993.

Dodge, Bertha S., *Cotton: The Plant That Would Be King,* University of Texas Press, Austin, TX, 1984.

Foote, Shelby, *The Civil War: A Narrative in Three Volumes,* Vintage Books, Random House, New York, 1986. (Mr. Foote's superb study of the Civil War was my primary source for anecdotal material, original letters, diary excerpts, and descriptions of battles, from a writer whose eyes seemed to have been everywhere at once, even within the hearts of those men who lived this history. Many of Owen's and Micah's letters are excerpted from Mr. Foote's collected material.)

Gandy, Joan W. and Thomas H., *The Mississippi Steamboat Era: 1870–1920,* Dover Books, Mineola, NY, 1987.

Garner, James W., *Reconstruction in Mississippi,* Peter Smith Publishers, Gloucester, MA, 1964.

Gutman, Herbert G., *The Black Family: Slavery and Freedom, 1750–1925,* Pantheon Books, New York, 1976.

Hooker, Charles Edward, *Mississippi,* Confederate Publishing Co., Atlanta, GA, 1899.

James, D. Clayton, *Antebellum Natchez,* Louisiana State University Press, Baton Rouge, LA, 1968.

Kalman, Bobbie, *Early Health and Medicine,* The Early Settlers Life Series, Crabtree Publishing Co., New York, 1983, 1991.

Kane, Harnett T., *Natchez on the Mississippi,* Bonanza Books, New York, 1956.

Marshall, Theodora Britton, and Gladys Crail Evans, *They Found It in Natchez,* Pelican Press, New Orleans, LA, 1939.

Murray, Elizabeth Dunbar, *My Mother Used to Say,* Christopher Publishing House, Boston, MA, 1959.

Neitzel, Robert S., *Archeology of the Fatherland Site: The Grand Village of the Natchez,* Vol. 51, Part I, Anthropological Papers of the American Museum of Natural History, New York, 1965.

Oubre, Claude F., *Forty Acres and a Mule,* Louisiana State University Press, Baton Rouge, LA, 1978.

Owens, Harry P., *Steamboats and the Cotton Economy,* University Press of Mississippi, Jackson, MS, 1990.

Register, James, *Fort Rosalie, The French at Old Natchez, 1682–1762,* Mid-South Press, Shreveport, LA, 1969.

———, (compiler), *Views of Old Natchez, Early 1800's,* views sketched by Charles A. Lesueur, Mid-South Press, Shreveport, LA, 1969.

Roland, Dunbar, *History of Mississippi, The Heart of the South,* Reprint Co., Spartanburg, SC, 1978.

Scarborough, William K., *The Overseer: Plantation Management in the Old South,* Louisiana State University Press, Baton Rouge, LA, 1966.

Shields, Joseph D., *Natchez, Its Early History,* John P. Morton & Co., Louisville, KY, 1930.

Skates, John Ray, *Mississippi, A History,* Norton, New York, 1979.

Stampp, Kenneth M., *The Peculiar Institution: Slavery in the Antebellum South,* Knopf, New York, 1978.

Taylor, William Banks, *King Cotton and Old Glory: Natchez, Mississippi in the Age of Sectional Controversy and the Civil War,* Hattiesburg, MS, 1977.

Ward, Geoffrey, C., with Ric Burns and Ken Burns, *The Civil War,* Borzoi Books, Knopf, New York, 1990.

Wayne, Michael, *The Reshaping of Plantation Society: The Natchez District, 1860–1890,* Louisiana State University Press, Baton Rouge, LA, 1983.

Webber, Thomas L., *Deep Like the Rivers: Education in the Slave Quarters Community, 1831–1865,* Norton, New York, 1978.

Wiley, Bell Irvin, *The Life of Johnny Reb: The Common Soldier of the Confederacy,* Louisiana State University Press, Baton Rouge, LA, 1978.

Woods, Patricia Dillon, *French-Indian Relations on the Southern Frontier, 1699–1762,* UMI Research Press, 1980.

Wyatt-Brown, Bertram, *The American People and the Antebellum South,* Pendulum Press, West Haven, CT, 1973.

Young, Stark, *So Red the Rose,* Scribner, New York, 1953. (A fine novel of the Civil War, set in Natchez, and a great source of background material and examples of early dialect.)

In addition, the excellent PBS series film by Ken Burns, based on his book, *The Civil War,* was invaluable for details and photographs and music to help me understand this American tragedy.

Author's Note

Besides these sources of inspiration and information, I am infinitely blessed to have in my life many people who care about my work and the well-being of my heart. Without them, I could not have written this or any of my other eight previous books. The angels sent me a wonderful agent a dozen years ago, and we've had a "marriage" which has lasted longer than many. Thanks to Roslyn Targ, who has managed my career from the first. Ann LaFarge, best editor in the business, has shepherded this as well as *Deepwater, Bayou,* and *The Last of the California Girls,* and to her I owe a debt of friendship and gratitude. My family is always applauding me from the footlights, and most particularly, this book is for Rick, my brother, to whom it is dedicated. My grandmother, Leona Roth, to whom I dedicated my first saga, *Columbia,* is gone now, and I will miss her always. But I have a host of friends and relations who enrich my life and my work, and some were especially close to me during these past two years of *Natchez*'s gestation: Chris and Judy and Sandy, Steve and Jo, Kelley and Suzi, Irv and Arlene, Vicky and Dee, Laural and Carl, Sharon and Amanda, Gail and Terra, Paul and Jackie, Jim, my dear Bill, of course, and also Leigh, Lynn and Don, Steve and Mary Ryan, my beautiful daughter, Leah, and most wonderfully of all, my beloved Jack. Thank you, each and every one, for the miracle you make of my life.